OPERATION BLACKLIGHT

BOOK TWO OF THE OBSENNETH SERIES

BY

HULTA GERTRUDE

Copyright © HULTA GERTRUDE 2017
This book is sold subject to the condition that it shall not, by way of trade or otherwise, be lent, resold, hired out, or otherwise circulated without the publisher's prior consent in any form of binding or cover other than that in which it is published and without a similar condition including this condition being imposed on the subsequent publisher.
The moral right of HULTA GERTRUDE has been asserted.
ISBN-13: 978-1973825944
ISBN-10: 1973825945

This book is dedicated to the memory of story-teller Esme. Rest in peace.

CONTENTS

PART ONE *Initial Intelligence* 1
PART TWO *Malign Influence* 111
PART THREE *Escalation* 215
PART FOUR *The Cult of Deimos* 340
PART FIVE *Justified Means* 453

ACKNOWLEDGMENTS

A number of people helped in the process of writing this story. It would be unfair of me to name any names. So instead, I will acknowledge the Atlantic Ocean itself, as without it and a Seraph or two, I may never have had the ideas I did.

This is a work of fiction. Names, characters, businesses, organizations, places, events and incidents either are the product of the author's imagination or are used fictitiously. Any resemblance to actual persons, living or dead, events, or locales is entirely coincidental.

PART ONE

Initial Intelligence

The blood stained the snow in its own unique way. Even in the diminishing white haze of the dying blizzard, it was unmistakable. It formed a red-brown frozen pool across the arctic avenue that wove through the thick, bare trees. There were indentations in the snow, indicating that something *or someone* had been dragged off the road and into the dead forest. Whether they were alive could not be determined for sure but… there was a lot of blood. The patrol, made up of three troops, paused as they regarded the blood-spattered smear on the ground directly in their path. An icy perfriction made complete silence impossible. It was, however, sufficiently noiseless to hear the dull thump of something as it landed heavily in the snow nearby.

"*Grenade!*" screamed a woman. The reaction was immediate and predictable as each soldier dived to find cover in random directions. As they moved, so did someone else. Satiah scrambled out from her hiding place, a cluster of dead trees, pistol in hand.

"Now *don't move!*" she barked at the floored people. Then she smiled as she got closer, her hot breath leaving her in clouds of whitish haze. "You're in luck, *apparently* it was a dud." It had been a ruse of course; there had never been a grenade. Two other figures joined her.

"Get their weapons and tie them up," she ordered, never taking her eyes away from the downed troops. They were all dressed in the same uniform, including her. How better to replace the patrol without arousing suspicion? One of the men, still on his front, gave a forlorn sigh, grasping how they'd been outsmarted.

Satiah and the other two who accompanied her were Phantom agents. They were part of something called Phantom Squad, an organisation set up to defend the Coalition against any threat by any means. A team made up of only the truly exceptional. They were quick and professional when trussing up the patrol. Satiah crouched and picked up the stone she had used as an improvised grenade and looked all around. The snowy wilderness looked endless and bleak. She knew, though, that less than a kilometre away a camp existed. It had been well hidden but, in this cold, its heat signature had given it away. Every pirate band needed a base, it was true. This group, however, had tried something different. Instead of choosing the interior of an asteroid or stealing an abandoned space station, they had chosen to operate planetside. The reason for this was twofold. Firstly, they had done it to avoid the ever-vigilant eye of the Colonial Federation who, under their Admiral Wester, had made pirates their main target. Secondly, they were planning on tapping into the ores to be found in the crust of this giant snowflake some called a planet.

"It's done," said the man, reaching her.

"Good," she acknowledged. She turned to face the three bound men. "*Oi!*" she exclaimed, and kicked one to be sure she had their attention. The yobbish term was at odds with her highborn accent. "There's going to be a big explosion over there in a while." She pointed. They looked. "My advice to you is: when you eventually untie yourselves… *don't go there.*" Begrudgingly the men nodded and mumbled a reluctant agreement. Satiah returned her gaze to her patient accomplices.

"Now, in single file like them… *let's go.*" Carrying the troops' guns, wearing clever imitation uniforms, they continued on the patrol's path. The whole switch had taken them about fifty seconds, hopefully not long enough for anyone to get jumpy. The three of them trudged through the snow slowly to emulate the bored and lax gait of the soldiers they had just replaced. Keeping an average of three metres between each of them, they maintained the pace with ease as, from out of the white ahead, the dark visage of an icy wall appeared.

They had found the camp perimeter faster than she had expected but it didn't matter. They had watched this camp for days and knew their routines. The instant she and her two followers entered the camp, enacting the completion of one patrol, another would begin on the same path. This would commence their forty-minute window, of which they would probably need only a quarter. These pirates were sloppy and no password or even discussion was needed for them to enter. Typical pirate incompetence! Had this been a military base, such hasty strategies would never have worked. The camp itself was made up of several fires and stacks of equipment. Satiah gave a subtle nod and the three of them split up. Each would attack from a different position at the same moment to prevent a clear enemy being shown. She closed her hand around the very real detonator in her pocket. They would have to be quick. Kelvin, through her earpiece, began the countdown.

Ten seconds. She casually deactivated the safety on the rifle she was carrying. She'd already checked it was loaded and safe to use... twice. She didn't easily trust weapons that weren't her own. Eight seconds.

"Target acquired," growled a voice, in her ear. It was one of the other Phantoms.

"Where?" she asked, her heartbeat quickening. Five seconds.

"Yellow crate, fluorescent green straps to your *right*," he replied, efficiently. She glanced around. There it was, right where he'd said, about forty metres or so from her. Now came the tricky part. Three seconds.

"I see," she said, tensing up. One second.

Satiah hurled the grenade right at the centre of the encampment. It went off, igniting a group of fuel cells with it, causing a chain reaction of fires and flashes. Everyone, except the three of them, hit the floor instinctively, trying to shield themselves from the unexpected explosions. The fire spread almost as fast as the anarchy. Satiah opened fire, concentrating on those few who were still on their feet. Screams, secondary explosions and rapid gunfire defeated the icy wind for dominance of the sound waves, as she and the other two began their work.

Satiah, while continuing to gun down anyone who got in her way, sprinted towards the crate. A ship, flown by Kelvin, roared down from the thermosphere, taking out the two gunner positions in a speedy and systematic strike. Smoke and fire tumbled upwards after him in blossoming clouds of ash and flame. Satiah had covered maybe half the distance when she saw that she was not the only one who was going for the crate. A woman, dressed entirely in white, had apparently kept her head and got there first. Having seen her coming, she aimed a pistol at Satiah and tried to shoot her. Satiah was fast enough to get behind a stand of barrels, and the laser shots slammed into them but were not powerful enough to penetrate them. Satiah peered out from her cover, ready to put down this obstruction quickly and permanently.

She was just in time to see the crate being driven away, at speed, on the back of a transporter. "*Bring it down!*" she barked into her earpiece. A few shots were fired. They glanced off; in any case they were not accurate enough to stop the thing. The transporter rammed the wall at high velocity, breaking out of the camp and on into the trees beyond. Satiah didn't hesitate. Ignoring the chaos around her, she leapt onto the nearest vehicle and accelerated wildly after the fugitive. The engine roared into life as if this was what it had waited for, for its entire existence. The front tip rose high as the surge of speed catapulted her out of the encampment and into the chase. She could see the transporter ahead as it weaved between the trees, sending up mists of snow in its wake. Satiah was gaining already. She gritted her teeth and clung on as she cut between trees and ducked low-hanging branches, trying to shave off more and more of her target's lead.

The woman driving the transporter had seen her coming, and was doing everything she could to go faster. Her efforts were hampered, however, by the weight of her cargo and the fact that the transporter itself was not built for this kind of thing in the first place. She opened the passenger viewport and lobbed an explosive out in Satiah's direction. It went off less than five metres in front of Satiah but quick reflexes enabled her to swerve successfully and avoid damage. The woman threw another, and another. Adapting to the new threat quickly, Satiah adopted a more evasive approach, using the trees as best as she could. Next, the woman tried shooting at her again but it was hopeless. She couldn't drive and aim effectively at the same time.

Closer than ever now, Satiah guessed her opponent was out of bombs and took a chance. Breaking cover, she swung in immediately behind the transporter and butted it hard.

The woman glowered as she was jolted and turned the autopilot on as she watched Satiah leap from her vehicle onto the back of the transporter. She pushed open the top hatch and began to climb out to confront Satiah directly. Satiah scrambled to cling on and hauled herself into the storage area on the back. The vehicle she had used skidded away to the side, now driverless, and out of sight. A blast from above shook the transporter violently, forcing both women to drop their guns and hold on for dear life. It was Kelvin, following the chase in the ship. The woman rolled towards Satiah and arrived in a fighting crouch. Satiah was able to get a good look at her. She was about the same height and of a similar build to Satiah herself. She had golden hair as opposed to Satiah's red. This woman's hair was longer and held down by a black band that went around her head. And her face... Satiah had seen a lot of angry looks in her time, but this woman looked angrier than anyone she could remember. Pale blue eyes that spoke of cruel death met Satiah's stern brown ones.

It was difficult to say which one of them took action first and which reacted to that action as it happened so quickly. As the transporter rocked and juddered beneath them, Satiah and the woman went head to head. Adept blows were exchanged; each quickly learnt that they were facing a clever and skilled opponent. They paused, re-evaluating each other breathlessly. Satiah came forward this time, feigning clumsiness in an effort to trick the woman into committing to something. The woman backed off all the way back to the cabin wall before flicking snow into Satiah's face with her boot. Satiah only looked away for a split second but that was all her enemy needed. The woman slammed into her and the pair rolled onto the floor painfully. Gritting her teeth, Satiah managed to grab an arm and twisted.

The woman yelled and rolled with the arm lock, wrenching herself free of Satiah's gloved grip. She looked around, right into Satiah's fist. The punch knocked her down onto her hands and knees. Satiah landed on her back, wrapping her arms around her neck from behind in an effort to strangle her. The woman kicked off from the floor and slammed her head back into Satiah's face as they landed. Satiah had turned her head to protect her nose from the foreseen blow. Then, with a shriek, every one of her muscles tensed as Satiah found herself being electrocuted. The gloved hand of the woman was on her right wrist, pumping current into her viciously. At that moment, the transporter's cabin hit a low-hanging branch, the collision ripping the roof of the cabin clean off. The roof raked across the back of the transporter, breaking the woman's hold on Satiah as she ducked out of the way. Flinching and shuddering, Satiah tore herself free, and rolled to create distance, her wrist burning, her skin tingling and her muscles still pulsing erratically. They regarded one another once more as the icy wind howled past them. The woman grinned evilly, and waved a few fingers of her gloved hand at Satiah in a mocking invitation to attack again.

Then, from her belt, using her other hand, the woman produced a long knife. Satiah instantly slid her dagger out from her boot and held it pointing down at the floor of the transporter. Another jarring knock from a tree made both of them lose balance and they struggled for better positions; however, a new blast from the sky ended it right there. The transporter flipped, throwing all its contents, including both women, out into the snow. They hit the ground hard, rolling over and over. Satiah relaxed as best as she could to prevent injury and eventually came to a stop on her back, mildly dazed. She sat up, cautious of her own potential balance problems. She was fine, incredibly. The snow had cushioned her somewhat and her reflexive acrobatics had done the rest. Nonetheless she was covered in bruises, grazes and cuts.

She ducked instinctively as the transporter exploded someway further down the incline. Half of it continued on into the trees, rolling out of sight and crashing as it went, while the rear part burned where it had landed. There was the crate, not that far away, maybe thirty paces, half buried in the snow. She'd been worried that it would land on her. She was quick to look all around, expecting the woman to be on her again. There was no sign of her assailant, besides a set of tracks somewhere behind her that vanished into the trees nearby. Satiah was debating the wisdom of following her when the roaring of a spaceship broke into her thoughts.

Kelvin was bringing it in to land close by, and it sent the wind and snow whipping frenziedly around her. She crouched next to the crate

OPERATION BLACKLIGHT

to be sure they didn't somehow lose it in the brief whiteout that the ship created. The ramp lowered and the large metallic bulk of Kelvin appeared, hurrying across the snow towards her.

"Thank you, Kelvin," she said, simply. His robotic might was always useful, especially when she was not as up for it as she could be. "Get this thing on board, I'll send the rendezvous signal."

"Yes," he said. He didn't move however, just scanned the surround. His red eyes burned out at the trees seemingly in apparent anger. Satiah followed his computer gaze for a moment. There was nothing to see, only the snow and the dead trees. The frosty cold nibbled at her.

"Forget her, we *have* what we came for," she instructed, sighing. Answering signals from the other two Phantoms were received immediately.

Satiah followed Kelvin up the ramp of the ship. The crate was too heavy for her to manage alone but Kelvin had no such limitations. He dragged it aboard with his usual efficiency. While waiting for the others to arrive, she took the time to evaluate the crate. She scanned it for any surprises, just in case. Many had been caught out by the old-fashioned concealed charge. After that, cautiously, she prised the lid off with a crate opener. The golden ingots, each about the size of Satiah's arm, gleamed in the silver lighting from the ship. Next, she checked that the gold was real and not just very convincing replicas. It had been tried before, after all. Finally, she made sure that it was *all* there...

"Twenty, *spot on*," she counted, rapidly. A few minutes later, having procured vehicles of their own, the two other Phantoms reached the ship. She slammed the crate shut again almost defensively.

"You got them, excellent," said one, nodding to her. She sealed it, trying not to look too possessive.

"Thanks. Get us back," she replied, going over the results. A throbbing sensation from her wrist made her roll back her sleeve to regard the red burn mark around her wrist where she had been electrocuted. She had been lucky to get free when she had. That woman's fingers were clearly visible in the form of red marks on her pale flesh. She held onto the railing calmly as the ship rose from the ground, leaving the snow and the blood behind. Kelvin reached her and also regarded the injury.

"Second degree burn, it will require attention," he stated. She nodded.

"I wonder how many Essps have been wasted chasing this gold," she muttered, with disdain.

***

Ten years ago, in a place called the Hellion.

A titanic ruined structure, that had stood for over a thousand years, held within it a secret entrance to long-deserted catacombs. Three robed figures, hooded and cloaked, marched through the remains with purpose. The one slightly ahead of the other two wore a white shiny plate mask to conceal his face still further and carried an elegant walking stick of the same hue. A strong wind cut through the air, sending dust clouds shifting. Upon reaching the entrance to the catacombs, the silent company halted. The door rose slowly and another cloaked figure came out from the catacombs to join them.

"Identify yourselves," he stated, grit in his tone. The masked man raised a gloved hand slowly to display a silver and green seal, held in his palm. The other two followed his example.

"You may pass."

***

Present day.

"This is Captain Benedict of the Coalition destroyer *Monolith*, respond please *Elven Star*," he repeated. The bridge was quiet and dimly lit. The personnel were at their archetypal positions, waiting for a response from the craft. Captain Benedict, veteran Coalition naval officer of eighty years' service, stroked his short pointy beard thoughtfully. They all watched on the screen as the ship drifted on silently through space without a word or a sign of activity. Scans had revealed life support systems were still in operation, but the engines were inactive. There was no response from the ship's computer either. Had he not known to whom the *Elven Star* belonged, he would simply have boarded her already or towed her back to the shipyards. But this ship belonged to a prominent ambassador and... well, it required more thought than normal.

His deputy, Lieutenant Williams, had received a reply from Naval Command almost immediately after their report of the discovery was submitted. The message was clear and broke no argument…

Do not board, wait with the ship until further notice and continue to try and contact the occupant. Do not allow anything else near it without confirmation from us. Report on any developments, expect company soon.

Williams stepped over to him quietly.

"Sir, we have continued to scan the surround, no trace of anyone or anything in the vicinity," he summarised. Benedict concurred.

"Orders, sir?" Benedict sighed; he wanted to get home too. His daughter had a birthday celebration coming up soon and he didn't want to miss yet another family occasion in peacetime. He was old enough to remember the Common Protectorate War and, as a cadet, he remembered the long tours with regret.

"Continue to scan the surround, Lieutenant," he commanded, weariness in his voice. Williams nodded, only his eyes betraying his reluctance. Benedict could understand. Who cared *who* owned the ship? As far as they were concerned they were doing little more than retrieving lost property! Evidently *someone* very high up cared… assuming, of course, that he had envisaged the right reason as to *why* such an instruction was given.

***

Change was rarely good in Satiah's opinion, certainly not when it came to security arrangements or, explicitly, Phantom business. Satiah had been heading for Phantom Headquarters on Earth where she was to deliver the gold, but there had been a change of plan. She'd left the remainder of that little task to the two Phantoms she had been working with. This had happened because, for an undisclosed reason, Phantom Leader Dyss had requested that they meet somewhere else. Normally, she almost always worked for Phantom Leader Randal, who was reluctantly sympathetic to her methods. A month had passed since Operation Orion had concluded.

She'd taken a few well-deserved weeks off to see Carl. Then, immediately after getting back, she'd been dragged into this confusion. Dyss was an unknown quantity as far as Satiah was concerned. So *that* was the first change, a change in the command chain. What *was* Randal *thinking*? The second change was the location. Phantoms almost exclusively met at their Headquarters except when extreme circumstances dictated otherwise. And those circumstances were few. This was why Satiah found herself and Kelvin docking at a space station and feeling very suspicious about it. She doubted this would lead to another gold hunt – or anything good.

***

Station Aurora was a small and entirely neutral society. It was not a part of any of the three superpowers – the Coalition, the Colonial Federation or the Nebular Union. Made up chiefly of traders and merchants, the station was a popular shopping destination... not the sort of place where one would hold a high-security meeting. It attracted criminals, amongst other things. There was no docking process; they were not even spoken to. Satiah pulled into the hangar area and set her ship down with a practised ease. She sighed, rubbed her face with her hands and then glanced over at Kelvin who was watching her silently.

"...I know," she mumbled at him. "It's probably got nothing to do with Vourne and I should stop thinking about it." Kelvin said nothing, which annoyed her as much as it would have if he answered her. Indeed, he'd not spoken to her since he'd healed her injured wrist.

"You stay here and make sure no one tries to sell the ship while I'm gone," she joked, half-heartedly. Pulling her cloak around her out of habit, she disembarked into the station. After paying the docking fee, she was free to enter without even so much as a safety scan. She could be *anyone*! And, most of the time, she was indeed acting like no one in particular...

It was busy in the station. People of many species and robots wandering around everywhere. No one gave her a second glance. The smell was... interesting. She couldn't make up her mind whether she liked it or not, or even what it was. At last, after a nearly half an hour of searching, she identified the Bulk Bar. It was a shady-looking dive with what looked like mould growing up its main wall. Delightful! She greatly respected anyone who *cared* about the environment. Also, a plant that was known for feasting on decay can only act as an invitation to *any* passing trade! Lack of investment... how commonplace. She entered, and discovered the interior to be half full but quiet. Dyss was sat in the corner, where he could watch the entrance. It would be where she would wait in a similar scenario. He removed his hood and nodded at her, just in case she had failed to notice him.

As she approached, she gave him the once over with her eyes. Tall and lean, Dyss didn't exude *confidence* so much as *menace*. Not an unusual quality in a Phantom. The hard pose of someone ready for anything and capable of delivering it too. Some people had said that Satiah herself subconsciously adopted such a posture. He smiled and indicated her to sit opposite him. She did, maintaining eye contact with him as she moved. His eyes seemed an intense amber colour and his face much more wooden than it had looked at a distance. For a few seconds neither of them said anything. Finally, he pulled a device from his pocket, activated it and then pushed it across the table to her. Satiah had typically already lost patience. She didn't want to be there!

"*What is this?*" she demanded, letting her anger flare. "I have a mission to finish."

"You have now," he answered finally, with a faint grin. She returned her gaze to the screen of the device.

"*Operation Blacklight*, classified LR..." she read, as she handled the computer carefully. "That's *locate* and *retrieve*."

"What do you know about Ambassador Drass?" he asked, his tone conversational. There was a moment of silence as their drinks arrived. The moment the waiter went away, the discussion resumed.

"To my knowledge, he is one of the richest men in the Coalition, he works alongside the Commandment Benefactor in economic matters, and has managed to steer clear of any serious scandals for the majority of his career so far," she answered, shrugging. "I only know what *any* member of the public could discover."

"His son is missing and the ship he was last seen on was found drifting in sector eighty-four," Dyss told her, calm and still.

"...*That's a shame*," she replied, sarcastically. "It's also *very close* to the area the VC war is affecting." He smiled, as if in glee.

"It is, isn't it?" he said, rhetorically. "Not a place anyone with any *sense* would stray off the neutral path, surely...?" He trailed off. Unsure if he expected her to answer or not, Satiah remained quiet. She sipped the water distrustfully instead.

"Randal tells me you're one of his best agents," Dyss went on, seeming to make his mind up about something.

"He says a lot of things," she sighed, not liking the attention.

"He said you helped in the capture of Ro Tammer," he said, as if reading from a list.

"You don't have to believe that," she pointed out. He took his turn to sigh.

"He also said you could be *difficult*," he said, allowing a wider smile to appear on his face. It betrayed the wrinkles which had otherwise remained anonymous on his face. Laughter lines at apparent odds with his occupation and history.

"You want me to find Drass's son?"

"Milo," he nodded, giving the man's name.

"Is this *really* work for a *Phantom*?" she demanded, a little tersely. They did have *better* things to focus on.

"No, it's work for *two* which is why you will be joined by Phantom Darius on this assignment," Dyss stated, still irritatingly polite. She'd heard of Darius but had never met him. Nevertheless, she didn't like working with others, something she'd made abundantly clear on numerous occasions. And in this case, she really didn't think finding a politician's son was a worthy use of the resources of Phantom Squad. Instead of exploding with rage, she chose to adopt a different strategy.

She leaned back and crossed her arms slowly, considering everything.

"There is more to this than *just* a missing boy," she stated, her voice soft and deliberate. "The war?" He raised an impressed eyebrow. She had guessed right.

"Recently one of our nearby territories has been a part of the *collateral* and has been damaged during the fighting despite being neutral. They have..." he began.

"I know, I saw the news, the CNC reported that several people have been killed and the government on Collgort-Elipsa, such as it is, have requested help from the Coalition," she interjected. Collgort-Elipsa was the Coalition territory in that area. A very wealthy planet by all accounts, although Satiah had never been there before.

"We have an ambassador there now and he has requested help from *us*," Dyss continued, taking her interruption in his stride. "Us *personally*." Satiah's eyes narrowed imperceptibly as she stared over the rim of her glass at him before answering.

"Which is part two of this *mission*," she stated, a little harshly. "You wish me to find a way of defending the world."

"No," he stated, with great finality in his tone. "I want you to *end the war*." Satiah took another sip of the water to give herself time to think of a way out of it. Maybe there was something wrong with her hearing…

"So you want me to *find* Milo whilst *putting an end* to an extended conflict that every diplomat has run screaming from?" she summarised, allowing her incredulity to show.

"You *and* Darius, yes," he replied, without missing a beat. She frowned and leaned forward again.

"I ask again if this is *really* the sort of thing that Phantom Squad should be dealing with?" she asked, seriously.

"What? Stopping wars? Ending suffering? Returning lost family members?" he rattled off, chuckling. "The heart *warms* at the prospect, does it not?" The sarcasm in his voice was not lost on her.

"I have no heart," Satiah countered, levelly. "Such a way of thinking would have got me killed long ago." A wince of doubt was his immediate reaction to her statement. That unsettled her. Why should he doubt her ruthlessness and her lack of compassion?

"Think of the advantages though, of having someone *that rich* owing *you a favour*," he tried again, swiftly.

"Someone of my training is rarely short of cash or favours," she answered, cynically. He sighed again, this time as if in defeat before he faced her again.

"I didn't want to have to do this but… you've left me *no option*," he told her, almost apologetically. She couldn't tell if he was sincere or not and, before she had time to decide, he dropped his bombshell. He activated something on the device on the table and a picture of *Carl* materialised. Being confronted with an image of the man she was starting to have very strong feelings for, in this place and context, was disturbing. Satiah fought hard to keep her face dispassionate but her shock was palpable. *How* had they found out? She had been *so careful!* Before she could ask who it was that she was looking at, her momentary hush betrayed the fact that *she knew exactly who it was*.

"Phantoms are prohibited from having *intimate liaisons*, least of all with *known criminals*," he stated, his voice suddenly becoming very cold and very hard. "And I *know* that you know that."

Denying it would be pointless. He had her, there was no way out. Her heart had betrayed her as she'd feared it would.

"If I take on *this mission...?*" she asked, her tone one of negotiation. It was her only realistic option.

"Then you *keep* your job, *no one finds out* about your little *indiscretion* and that will be the end of it," he said, firmly. "I'm sorry but *I need someone other than Darius* in charge on this mission." That answer actually intrigued her.

"*Why?*" she asked, more curious now than angry. "What did *he* do?" Dyss did not respond directly to that enquiry.

"If you refuse then I will *expose* you, wreck your career and have you both *imprisoned indefinitely*," he said. One look in his eyes left her in no doubt that he would do just that. The fact that he hadn't acted already and just arrested her, told her that she could probably trust him to stick to the agreement. At least for now. He had *tried* to persuade her to take on the mission in a few ways, including *flattery* and *appealing to her moral obligation, before* he had resorted to blackmail.

"...When do I start?" she asked, her voice even. He smiled. That would be *now*, apparently.

They walked back to her ship together, mostly in silence. Satiah was thinking fast, and not just about Carl and her problems. What about Darius? Why didn't Dyss trust *him*? Outside, in the hangar area, they stopped and turned to one another.

"Find him," he instructed, seriously. He was talking about Milo, the ambassador's son. "You will see *where to start looking* in the file."

"What if I cannot find him after legitimately trying? *He could be dead,*" she responded, casually. "If he's missing in a warzone then it's highly likely that he *is* dead."

"Then bring back the body," he replied, coldly. He handed her a communicator. "If you need *anything*, anything at all, clearance or whatever, *just call me*. Day or night I will answer, if I am alive." Satiah retreated onto her ship morosely. Dyss didn't wait around to see if she had left or not; he went back into the space city area and vanished among the crowd.

She let out a deep breath. She felt exposed... vulnerable. *Carl?* What about Carl, was he safe? She did not like feeling vulnerable... it made her *angry*. She stomped into the control room where Kelvin was still waiting for her. She slid the data cube into the computer to bring up the full mission file that Dyss had given her. Kelvin waited silently, his appendage poised on the flight controls. Satiah read quickly.

(LR) OPERATION BLACKLIGHT (LR) REPORT: Dated at end. Designation (TS). Top Secret. Status Active. Satiah reports...

Dyss had obviously written that for her already; clearly he'd been confident that he could persuade her into working on this. He was a persuasive man. There was also an important note from Dyss in another document. It gave her coordinates and informed her that Darius was waiting for her on board a Coalition destroyer called *Monolith*... along with Milo's ship the *Elven Star*. It also told her that Milo had apparently left with ten billion Essps in hard cash on him. A sum that seemed almost *ridiculously* high. Especially when you could get a power pack for a gun for less than five Essps. It was worth more than the gold she'd recently acquired for Randal. What had he needed that money for?

"Let's go," she said, to Kelvin. "Get us to coordinates 8433-1118."

"You are sweating," he pointed out, as the ship took off.

"One second," she said, pulling out her own communicator. She attached it to the main console and began adjusting the frequency.

"Rainbow, are you there?" she asked, knowing he would be.

"*Satiah?*" came his response a few seconds later. "This is *not* a good time! I just..."

"Phantom Leader Dyss, what do you know about him?" she cut across him. There was a pause.

"Same as you, most likely," he replied, being prudent. "He is one of the three Leaders of Phantom Squad. He was appointed at approximately the same time as the other two. He's untainted by the Vourne Conspiracy. Distinguished career, experienced... *ruthless.*" He paused again. "Kind of like *you,*" he added, as an afterthought.

"Can you think of *any* link between him and me?" she asked, trying to be more specific.

"*What happened?*" he asked, sighing grumpily. She almost laughed, picturing his face in her mind.

"We had a meeting recently and it turns out he knew quite a bit more about me than I did about him," she answered, cryptically. Even Rainbow didn't know about her and Carl.

"Well, he *is* a Phantom Leader, they are *supposed* to be like that," he replied, realising she was not being entirely frank with him.

"Can I see his file?" she asked, smiling as she spoke. She knew that such a question itself was a crime.

"*No!*" he cried, in apparent alarm. He followed that up with a hushed and predictably insistent statement. "You *know* that is against the law!" Satiah couldn't accept that answer and went in for the kill.

"Does *she* know that you have images of her on your computer? *I can't remember,*" Satiah asked, grit in her tone. There was a stunned and perhaps even hurt silence.

"*...Satiah!* Come on!" he hissed, suddenly desperate. "That's not fair! *I thought we were friends...!*"

"We are, that's *why* I've not told her yet. It's just *one* file," she said, unable to stop herself from grinning mischievously.

"*...Fine, but only* if you promise to say nothing to her!" he instructed, seriously. She needed to know everything there was to know about Dyss and this file might be her only chance.

"Not a word shall pass my lips to her or to anyone else," Satiah assured him. She didn't actually know *who* it was they were talking about but she didn't have to. Some time ago she'd fathomed that he had a startlingly active love life and often dated more than one female at a time. She'd had the postulation that his wife and children knew nothing about this state of affairs and had accordingly taken advantage of that. A message arrived on the communicator in front of her. Dyss's personnel file.

"Thank you Rainbow, you're *very* efficient, a pleasure as always."

"...*Thanks*," he grumbled, as he disconnected. Well, if he didn't like it, maybe he should be more respectful to the poor women he was involving himself with!

"Insurance?" Kelvin asked, from next to her.

"Dyss knew about *me and Carl*," she explained, anger returning to her voice. "That's how he forced me into going on this crazy mission! If I can't find out *how* he found out... then at the very least I want to know something about him that I can use as a backup." She knew the file was a long shot, as surely anyone with any sense would have anything dangerous erased. But... it might be her *only* shot. And when Satiah had a chance at a shot, she almost always took it.

"These coordinates take us close to a warzone," Kelvin informed her.

"*I know*," she said, grim. She didn't know much about the war, other than it had been going on for a while and it was escalating. She'd get hold of that ambassador who had called for help and try to get more information out of them. She wasn't even entirely sure who it was that was actually fighting, never mind why. Never a good start. More than ever, she was convinced that change was almost always bad.

***

Administrator Bavon swallowed nervously as he adjusted his collar. It was feeling rather tight suddenly. It often did that when he felt nervous, which was all too often these days. His subconscious cogitation on the hypothetical noose around his neck, perhaps. This nervousness also tended to turn his normal laugh into more of a shriek that made heads turn in his direction. Dressed in the brown uniform of a palace administrator, Bavon looked nothing special. He *was* nothing special but he himself felt that he could be. Being overlooked, passed by or just ignored throughout his life, Bavon had grown bitter. He concealed it well though, maintaining his pleasant demeanour of enforced jollity in the face of virtually everything around him. This act further enabled him to escape the notice of those around him, dismissing him out of hand, never believing he could be a threat. And, until the war started... he hadn't been a threat.

The VS war, or Vinu-Shintu War, had started as many conflicts did – a dispute over a border line. Two planets, Vinupisha and Shintumpa, claiming ownership of a single satellite. This then led to cargo seizures both legal and otherwise, each planet claiming that the other had invaded their territory. Then, about three years ago, it had turned nasty. A final warning was issued, not by the government but by a high-ranking military officer, whose name Bavon couldn't recall, and then swiftly acted on. A ship, with its cargo and crew still aboard, was destroyed. Within the hour, full-scale war was declared on both sides and an endless back and forth fleet battle began. Naturally they were not fighting for the entire time, mostly they just acted as deterrents for the opposing battleships. A few all-out battles had taken place but there was never an *all-out* winner. As a result of this: the war continued.

It was in a new era now though. Blockades had become the order of the day, along with hit and run bombing attacks and intensive spying operations. Having failed to batter each other, they were now trying to slowly strangle one another into submission. A war of attrition. A terrible, awful thing for everyone involved... except Bavon and one or two pirate gangs of his acquaintance. Instead of seeing doom or disaster, they saw *profit*. A thriving black market was created almost overnight, leading to weapons, technology and information becoming simply *merchandise*. To the cynical, this included Bavon and his *friends*; it seemed ludicrous to allow the war to end as it would mean an end to their business.

It was at that point, nearly a year ago now, that Bavon had encountered a man called Quint. Pirates were one thing but Quint terrified Bavon. The pirates were not too keen on him either. He had become involved after finding out about a shipment of gold.

Somehow, Quint had learned of Bavon's dealings and identity. Increasingly bizarre instructions were being given to Bavon by Quint, the obvious goal being to extend the war. Quint then set out to use Bavon in order to make the pirates hijack the ship and steal the gold. It had been crazy! Unlike their *usual* targets – civilian freighters or the odd lone cruiser – this one was special. This ship was well defended, having its own escort and *Coalition* forces providing security. The theory being that, as they were *neutral*, neither side would attack them. Quint though had acquired a device – illegal, of course – that would effectively paralyse the ships and allow the pirates to infiltrate with little resistance.

At first, everything had gone well. The device worked, the pirates got aboard, and the gold was located and retrieved. The crew had been dealt with and the computer destroyed accordingly. *That* was when the pirates had got greedy and decided to keep the gold for themselves. Bavon had had to tell Quint what they had done, but Quint seemed to have expected nothing less. He'd recommended a freelance bounty hunter, a woman called Purella, also known as *the hourglass*, for Bavon to hire. She would take the gold from the pirates on their behalf and return it to them. Or at least, that had been the plan. He'd just had a call from Purella explaining that she'd failed to escape with the gold due to the untimely intervention of a group of well organised operatives. Identity unknown, employers unknown, although Purella stated that she suspected they may have been hired by the *original owners* of the gold. Now... Bavon had the job of informing Quint of the outcome *again*. He swallowed and tried to loosen his collar still further.

***

Phantom Darius watched as the ship, the *Elven Star*, slowly drifted through space. He was standing in a corridor near the command deck of the Coalition destroyer *Monolith*. He was tall and well built, had piercing grey eyes and a well-kept brown moustache. His head was completely bald and his arms were crossed. He watched his target like a hawk would watch a potential meal. A pistol rested in the folds of his grey Phantom cloak. A young flight officer approached him and half saluted before talking.

"Are you sure you don't want anything?" she offered, politely. Slowly he dragged his gaze from the ship outside to her face. She went pale but held her ground.

"No, thank you," he growled at her, before slowly returning his gaze back to the ship. She nodded and then hastily marched away.

This was intolerable! Normally he would have boarded and searched the ship already but he couldn't as he had to wait for someone called Satiah to *turn up*. He chaffed at the unforeseen deferral! Dyss had made it clear he was to do nothing without *her* permission or instruction. So he'd spent virtually twenty-four hours *waiting* on board the destroyer *within sight* of his target. He debated if he should start pacing again. Anything to pass the time. A siren sounded and he reeled, excited that something had broken the monotony.

"Amber alert, Captain report to the bridge, incoming vessel!" called the automated computer voice. Darius ran to the bridge himself, wanting answers. Crew were running around too, following their standard procedures. Darius reached the command deck and nodded to Williams, who nodded back.

"Who is it?" he asked, impassively.

"Not sure," Williams answered, "could be your friend." Okay, Satiah was not his friend but if it *was* her at least he could start work soon! He looked hopefully out of the viewport. A distant speck was growing there. It seemed agonisingly slow to him. Benedict, the Captain, reached the bridge.

"Hail them, Williams," he ordered, gruffly. Clearly, he had been napping. Williams touched his hat to Benedict before sending out the call.

"This is Lieutenant Williams of the Coalition destroyer *Monolith*, identify yourself," he said.

"*Monolith*, this is Phantom Agent Satiah," she replied, quickly. "Request permission to join you."

"Confirmed," Benedict allowed, yawning. The ship accelerated. Darius was pleased as this indicated to him that Satiah was not someone who liked to waste time.

He headed down to the hangar area so that he could greet her when she arrived. He arrived just in time to see her ship sweep through into the hangar and slide into an easy landing. The ramp began descending before the engines deactivated. Satiah and the bulk of metal that was Kelvin marched out resolutely into the hangar area. Darius raised a hand and moved to intercept them.

"Phantom Satiah, I am Phantom Darius," he stated, calmly. Phantoms had no salutation or greeting signal, formal or otherwise, they would just start talking. Such things were considered a waste of time by the trainers.

"Good," she said, glad she didn't have to delay things further while tracking him down. "How long has the ship been here?" She gave him the once over with her eyes and noted his golden belt buckle and its odd design.

"At least two days," he replied, quickly.

"Has anything been touched?" she asked, as he expected she would.

"No, it's been left alone as per the instructions." He shook his head. He couldn't resist pointing out the obvious though: "But much could have been done in the time that has already elapsed."

"Okay..." She paused, considering their options. "Come aboard, we'll head over there now and have a gander." Darius nodded, pleased. At last, someone who wanted to get something done! As they went up the ramp into her ship Satiah regarded her new associate sceptically.

"How much do you know about the mission?" she asked, clearly. "The objectives, I mean?"

"We are to track down the son of an ambassador, a young man by the name of Milo, son of Ambassador Drass. A politician with the ear of the Commandment Benefactor herself, no doubt he pulled a few strings," Darius answered, as if reading out a weather report. "That's his ship there." He nodded out at the drifting freighter.

Satiah was confused. Okay, he knew they were there to find Milo but he didn't know about the other half of the mission. The bit about stopping the war, arguably the most important part. Certainly it was the most *challenging*, to put it moderately. Instantly, she theorised that he'd been kept in the dark deliberately and she had no idea *why*. Nothing about him screamed at her about anything, and maybe that was the problem.

"Good," she acknowledged, sagely. "Would you mind conducting a scan of the craft yourself using *my own* scanners? It's not that I don't *trust* the navy *but...*" She left it at that, knowing he would understand. He nodded, this time at her. People missed things all the time and a fresh eye was always valuable. Darius began the process with practised ease and awaited the results nonchalantly. Satiah watched him warily out of the corner of her eye. If he was any good he would pick up on her scrutiny quickly enough, question was: what would he do about it? She was in command and had done nothing that would cause him to doubt her competence. That didn't mean, however, that he would do nothing. The results came through, providing a mere echo of the hundreds of scans performed by the officers aboard the *Monolith*. Darius turned slowly to look at her.

"Life support operative, no engine operation or communication traces..." she mused, studying it herself. "Kelvin, when we board, check for toxins or gases... the usual."

"Yes," he buzzed, dependably. Darius regarded Kelvin peripherally, wondering if Satiah usually worked like this. She was, by all appearances, trustworthy. But then were not *all* appearances deceptive in one way or another?

"Off the record?" Darius asked, chancing his luck. Satiah nodded. "What did Dyss say to you? About *me*, I mean." Satiah was surprised by the direct question but actually a little relieved. At least she wouldn't have to pretend that she trusted him.

"It's what he *didn't say* that's my concern," she stated, without accusation in her tone. She of all people knew Phantom agents had their secrets. She herself had some of the darkest. She had knowingly aided Vourne to gain power for herself and she had helped him avoid capture... only to murder him herself when he had refused to let dead dogs lie.

"He basically told me he didn't want you working on this assignment *alone* but didn't clarify why." Darius had expected nothing less.

"Very well," he nodded, smiling. "I appreciate that." She certainly hadn't had to tell him that, nor did he have to let it drop so quickly. She was angry with Dyss for extorting her to take this on in the first place, angry enough to give Darius all the leeway she could. She naturally wanted to ask him *why* Dyss would have said *or not said* these things but decided to wait a while. They did have a job to do, after all.

There was the familiar jolt as the craft docked with the *Elven Star*. The tell-tale *fuumm* noise. Satiah and Darius drew their pistols in almost complete equilibrium. Heading along the corridor side by side behind Kelvin, to the hatchway, they didn't say a word. They slipped breathing devices into their mouths as a precaution. Kelvin was good but nothing was perfect, there were new contaminants being invented every day. The hatch slid open, revealing a dimly lit corridor beyond. Kelvin entered first, running the customary checks. Satiah and Darius hung back and awaited his prognosis patiently.

"It's clear," Kelvin stated. Satiah passed an earpiece to Darius who quickly inserted and activated it. Now they could all talk to each other.

"You go left, I'll go right, Kelvin will act as backup and guard the hatchway," Satiah stated, firmly. Darius nodded. In his mind it was the optimal strategy, although he personally would have used the navy as additional backup too.

Satiah, pistol raised, began to venture cautiously toward the living quarters and control area. It was quiet. Only the low hum of the power core could be heard. Always reassuring... The air was stale *but breathable*, as Kelvin had told them. She judged that the filters had been non-functional for at least four days.

"It goes without saying that you don't touch anything," she stated, more as a check on whether he could hear her than anything.

"It does," he confirmed, taking no umbrage. A door swished open to her left and she swung instinctively to cover it. Inside was a standard kitchen by the look of it. She entered cautiously, even though she was almost certain the ship was unoccupied. There could be booby-traps. A laser beam here or a rigged explosive there could have lethal consequences to the unwary.

She sniffed the air and thought she could detect the acrid odour of smoke. It was faint and didn't seem to be coming from anywhere inside the kitchen. She eased open a cooling unit with her pistol carefully. There was still plenty of food in there, purchased a few weeks previously, due to expire in another week. She growled softly to herself as she realised that there was nothing more to be learned from it. She turned back to the corridor again and continued on. She could already see the door to the control room dead ahead. It was closed. A door to her right swished open and again she covered it reflexively. Inside was the comfort area, living quarters or sleeping area, and she entered with the same circumspection as before.

Two single beds, one was ruffled and had clearly been slept in and made up again afterwards. On the table next to the bed was a picture of a woman, framed and set there next to the head of the would-be sleeper. Satiah picked it up and examined it more closely. The woman seemed to be in a hospital bed, or at least *so the background suggested*, but she looked *happy*. Who was she? She'd already seen pictures of Milo's mother and sister and this was clearly neither of them. Friend? Lover? A mark on the glass drew Satiah's keen eye. A sort of smudge over the woman's lips. Satiah closed her eyes, envisioning Milo kissing the picture before he went to sleep. Lover. The files didn't mention a lover. It just went to show that the files often missed the most important things. Satiah would keep the picture and get Rainbow to do a sweep for her. She slipped the picture into the large pocket inside her cloak and then regarded the rest of the room, seeking more veiled treasures in the vicinity.

She noticed an open safe in the wall and peered into the empty space inside, curious. What had been in there? Nothing big, that was for sure. Documents? Money? That *ten billion Essps*, perhaps? No sign of any damage inflicted... She briefly pulled a disappointed face to herself in the mirrored reflection before slowly turning back to the bed. There were clothes, folded and ready for use at the end. No boots though... *Where* were the boots? She crouched and checked under the beds. Nothing, just a few empty storage containers. She rose again, noting something else that was missing. No personal computers. No data cubes. And... no signs of a fight. No blood, no burns and no damaged property *as of yet*. She frowned, deep in thought. Anything could have happened.

Darius reached the storage area first, and, maintaining a steely vigilance, he entered. It was small, as was to be expected from a craft of that size. Power units, standard emergency repair kits. Basic medical equipment and provisions. Darius halted as he observed an apparently used hypodermic syringe on the floor. He crouched, and stared down without touching it. Something *green* had been inside. Possible drug use? A light green, the remnant glowing phosphorescently.

"Satiah, I have a used syringe here on the floor, in the storage area," he reported, calmly. "Requesting permission to bag it?" He hoped there would be enough left for a sample to be studied.

"Granted, well found." He was testing to see how closely she would stand by the instructions she had regarding him. How much room would she give him to work his own way? When would he need her permission? When wouldn't he? In his estimation, she was fair enough so far.

"Got anything yourself yet?" he enquired, interested.

"Too early to know, I'm about to enter the control room. When you're done you can join me there," she replied, her voice low. Darius retrieved the needle with care and bagged it quickly before turning his search onto the engine area.

Satiah slid into the control room, careful to take everything in. Again, no serious damage but... she frowned as she noticed the flight computer had been smashed. She checked it more closely. It was trashed but whoever had done it had taken the time to remove it from the console first. *They* – she kept thinking 'they' out of habit – had removed it with care and then placed it on a chair before disabling it. She noticed a flight jacket still hanging on the back of the pilot's chair. She went through the pockets, careful to check for secret ones. She found a communicator, battery exhausted but it could be recharged and might be useful. She pocketed that. A set of identity cards, all belonging to Milo, were also contained within. She took those too. Next, she found a holographic map display unit. She activated it, and it revealed the area of all sector eighty's zones.

"So..." she whispered, to herself. "You were planning to come here all along? Or has this been planted here by your putative captor to make me *think* that you were?" With the flight computer gone, there was no easy way for her to find out.

She made a mental note to check that it was *a fact* that he'd actually *been* on the ship in the first place. That way she could at least rule out the possibility that this ship was a decoy. She slid her pistol back into its holster and stared out of the viewport into space. Her gut was telling her that he *had* been on this ship and that someone had taken him out of it. Who, how and why, however, were not so easy. Judging by the fact that there were no signs of combat, whoever had got him had apparently been friendly enough at first. Darius and Kelvin reached her.

"Kelvin, document everything about this ship," Satiah sighed. "When he's finished, Darius, tell the Captain of the *Monolith* to impound this ship and return it to Phantom Headquarters. I want standing instructions that only you and I can go inside it."

"As you say." He nodded, and handed her the bagged syringe.

***

Hours later, Satiah was once more aboard her own ship, testing a theory. All her life, she'd had a passion and a talent for chemistry. And the moment she'd seen that syringe, she'd had a theory about which chemical it had contained. Darius had informed her that he thought that it was probably an intoxicant of some type. Plausible, indeed probable, but she knew better. There was a polite knock at the door, Darius himself of course. Kelvin wouldn't knock.

"Yes," she called, quietly. She didn't look up from what she was doing. Darius entered and stood by the door.

"Ship's been impounded, they're taking it back to base now," he told her. "What's our next move?"

"Well, it's clear that Milo, if he is still alive…" she paused, as the result arrived, and smiled triumphantly, "…would have slept well." Darius wasn't stupid.

"It was a sedative," he stated, referring to the chemical.

"A powerful one, a dose this size would have knocked him out for a couple of days," she explained, motioning to the syringe. "A little more and he'd be dead. And as a doctor himself, or a *doctor to be*, he'd know that."

"So… whoever took him drugged him first?" Darius confirmed.

"I can't think of a reason why he would dose himself," she shrugged. It was only logic, not flippancy, which made her say that.

"Do you want me to check on recent purchases of that chemical?" he asked, seriously. She'd already thought about that and gave him the answer she gave herself.

"No, too vague and it would take too long," she said. "I know we're already out of the ninety-minute window." The *ninety-minute window* was the window of time that it remained *likely* to find someone who had disappeared *alive*. "But, given the lack of damage to the ship, I'd say it's unlikely their goal, *whoever they were*, was to kill him. I'm thinking *ransom*."

"That was my first thought too. It would have been *easy* to destroy that ship, very little firepower required. The only issue with *that* theory – ransom – is that *no one* has tried to contact either the family *or* the authorities regarding this," Darius reminded her. This was true and unsettling. It hinted, if they were right about extortion being the intention, that something had prevented them from carrying it out. At least carrying out the final part of their plan. Something fatal. Perhaps they had accidentally killed him. To the inexperienced, sedatives were dangerous things. On the other hand... he may have escaped by himself.

"Yes..." She trailed off, reconsidering everything. "You've already done substantial research into his life?"

"I know him as well as it's possible to know anyone so... not well," Darius joked, cynically. She smiled, understanding.

"Any... *fractious factors*?" she asked, using official terminology. "Depression? Family arguments? *Drugs*?"

"He and his dad *did* have a protracted disagreement regarding his career choice," Darius stated, thoughtfully. "That *was* two years ago though." *Protracted disagreement*? What was *that* supposed to mean?

"Milo is a *medical* doctor?" she asked, trying to remember the file she'd breezed through before she had arrived. She thought he was but he could have been a doctor in any field.

"Well, he's training to be one," Darius corrected, nodding.

"I don't understand... Why would *that* cause an argument?" Satiah asked, casually. Then she smiled, equally sceptical. "Sorry, I meant *protracted disagreement*."

"His father wanted him to follow in his footsteps in politics, and also it had to do with his work with refugees," Darius elaborated. "Milo worked in a relief centre for war victims..." Satiah's heart jumped in that way it did when it was trying to tell her something. "*Which war?*" she cut in, intensity in her voice. She feared she already knew the answer. Catching onto the fact that she knew something he didn't, Darius fell silent for a moment.

"The VS war," he answered, at last. They made eye contact. "Is there something wrong, Satiah?"

"*Very probably,*" she growled, her mind chewing on this latest development with distaste. "Keep talking." Professional as ever, Darius continued.

"While he was there he developed this *tendency* to give them money, the patients I mean, and sometimes even the other facility staff. As rich as he is *or was*, a few thousand Essps here or there were *nothing* to him. This *charity* really didn't go down well with his father, his father being of the opinion that these people were taking advantage of him and that he needed to stop," Darius explained. "Milo refused, saying it was his moral duty, even asking his father to do the same... basically the issue was never *really* resolved. However, like I said, it *was* two years ago."

Satiah could see how it could look. The son of a prominent politician *illegally financing* soldiers in a war. A war that until recently had had nothing to do with the Coalition. Perhaps those he had been paying had decided to do something to him. Milo might even have refused to keep financing them because of his father and they hadn't liked that... It was all starting to make sense. He was a well-known figure; his ship was easy to track. No guard, not even a distress call. It was just too easy. Yet the money they could make from having Milo alive vastly outweighed what they could get if he was dead. *Ten billion Essps!* That would be one almighty windfall for just one abduction.

Had they known he had that money on him? Was he trying to pay someone off? Maybe they had taken someone he cared about... and he had tried to pay their ransom only to be held captive himself? That meant that even if he was dead, these hypothetical abductors would *have* to pretend that he was still alive to further extort the family. Whichever way you looked at it: they *had* to make contact with *someone* to get the money... *unless*...

"Have we been monitoring Milo's finances?" she asked, curious. They might already *have* the money! Ten billion Essps had already gone, what else was there?

"*I* have, no change from a week previously," he confirmed. "The money in his accounts is still there. No one has done anything with it either."

Satiah went quiet again. Something was nagging at her, some clue or answer just beyond her sight. Darius sighed and sat down opposite her.

"I think it's unlikely we'll ever find him. I know what Dyss said but… it's a *big* universe and it's clear that the trail leads into the local war next door. You might want to think about reporting back and getting some kind of sanction *before* we walk into that," he suggested, not unreasonably. He had a point and, considering the political implications, it would be a smart move, but then he was unaware of the second half of the mission. Had Dyss guessed, or worse, had he *known* the two matters were linked? He'd certainly known other stuff he shouldn't. *Her stuff!* She had to go through his file as soon as she could and *return the favour*.

"I'm waiting for one of my team to call me back regarding another angle," she admitted, referring to the picture of the woman. The one Milo could have been trying to *rescue?* "And that communicator should have recharged by now."

"It has, but it's password protected," Darius replied, casually. He'd already tried to access it. "An attempt to wipe it *was* made but was unsuccessful." That hinted at sloppiness… although someone like Satiah might fake incompetence to throw off investigators.

"Kelvin can help with that," she said, smiling. "You check these out." She passed him the identity cards she'd recovered. "Contact anyone or anything on there you feel might help."

"Will do," he nodded, and then he paused. "What will you be doing, if that's not an unfair question?"

"*Getting that sanction*," she lied, easily. "I'll join you soon." Unsure if he believed her or not, Darius returned to the control room where Kelvin waited. Satiah made the call she knew she shouldn't, but her heart compelled her to check.

Carl answered immediately, the speed of his reaction made her smile despite the circumstances.

"*Satiah?*" he said, sounding pleased. "What's up?"

"I just wanted to ask if you had tried to contact me yet?" she asked, forcing herself to sound playful.

"*No*, certainly not, I remember what you said about… *I don't want you to do that to me*," he replied, flustered.

"*No…*" she trailed off, believing him. "Just thought I'd better ask." She would have cut the call there once without a second thought but much to her own annoyance she realised she missed him.

"What are you doing?" he asked, interested.

"You *know* I can't talk to you about that," she replied, grinning.

"No, of course not, *sorry*. When are you coming *back*?" he asked, pining for her.

"…Have you been missing me?" she asked, flirtatiously.

"I dream about you every night," he replied, levelly. "It's inhuman."

"I *hope* you behave yourself," she admonished him, with false severity. "In the dreams, I mean."

"Always," he answered, far too quickly. She wanted to giggle. She suddenly realised she had this overwhelming desire to tell him she loved him. She shook herself inwardly, telling herself it was merely hormones and she should guard against it. None of that now, bury it, *concentrate*.

"Well, I have to go now, Carl, so *sweet dreams*," she purred, before she disconnected.

So Carl seemed normal. Dyss *seemed* to be keeping his word, although there was no easy way to confirm that. Satiah had originally thought about telling Carl to go on the run. She had two locations she kept prepped for such an eventuality. He could lay low at one of those until she could collect him. She'd decided against that, however, figuring that if Dyss knew about *him* the odds were that he was already under scrutiny. Better to keep him in the dark and pretend everything was normal. At least until she decided to change her game…

She slid back into the seat and opened the file Rainbow had sent her. Phantom Leader Dyss… Seventy-four years' operational Phantom career. Most Phantoms that died were killed within the first two years in the field. Satiah herself was somewhere over the thirty-year marker; oddly it had never mattered enough to her to bother to remember exactly how long she had served. She continued reading about Dyss – four months as Phantom Leader: understandable, given the fallout from the Vourne conspiracy. Assignments completed: 493. That seemed *a lot*, especially when you considered that some operations could last years. Satiah herself had probably clocked less than half of that. Assignments taken: 494. She paused... was that last one significant in some way? While it was not unheard of for a Phantom leader to take on an assignment themselves, it wasn't common practice. Whenever he had started it, for whatever reason, it wasn't completed. Satiah wondered why.

She read through a few of the debriefings, notably one written by Vourne himself about ten years ago. *Operation Jackdaw*. The surveillance of a neo-remnantist money laundering scheme. Dyss had been ordered to intercept a payoff and it had gone badly wrong... resulting in the deaths of six Phantom agents. The way Dyss told it, it implied that *someone* on the team of Phantoms involved had let the enemy know about the interception. She cross-referenced it with the standard database she had, seeking other members of the operation. She sighed as the name she had expected to see came up. *Darius*. He and Dyss had been working together on *that* operation. Ten years ago! There were six other names too. Jook, Pingrey, Alarris, Narm, Gacka and Vallin. Six deceased, two survivors. She didn't take those in because she only saw the one she had been expecting to find.

So... Dyss believed that Darius had betrayed him and the rest of the team to the terrorists, but had clearly been unable to prove it at the time. Darius' continued employment was proof of that. That also gave her a theory as to why Dyss had apparently *failed* to complete one mission. Perhaps he saw it as his last mission. The one remaining objective outstanding. To bring Darius to *perceived* justice? Either *get the proof he needed* or see to it that Darius didn't survive...? None of this told her how Dyss had known all about *her* though. Satiah thought about Darius a little longer. Could she trust him? Only as much as any operative, she reasoned. He seemed to be completely by the book about everything so far. While *that* strategy rarely fitted in with how she worked, she did respect it when it stayed out of her way. Maybe she could casually bring up Operation Jackdaw in conversation with Darius and watch him closely. See if it rattled his cage or anything. That would be fun, she thought sarcastically.

She continued reading, trying to find a link between Dyss and herself. Nothing. It was like the only thing they had in common was the fact they worked in the same place. She even went into associates, trying to find someone who knew them both, someone they had in common. *Vourne* had known them both... but the trouble with that notion was that she had murdered him before she had even *met* Carl. Next she went through his history, trying to find out if maybe he was somehow involved in her sister's trial or her own recruitment or... *anything*. No, their careers had been entirely separate *until now*.

Her communicator went off abruptly, snapping her out of her reverie, and her pistol found itself in her hand in a split second. She smirked, exasperated by her own jitteriness, and replaced it in its holster. She'd been reading for nearly an hour and it only seemed like a moment ago she'd started.

"Yes," she answered, trying not to sound as irate as she felt. It was Darius.

"Kelvin has hacked into the communicator you recovered and we've been listening. There's something on here that you should hear," he told her, cryptically.

"On my way," she replied, quickly turning everything off. She didn't want Darius to know she had been prying into his past too. He most likely already suspected she had, but there was little she could do about other people's suspicions. She disconnected before hurrying back to the control room. She entered her customarily dimly lit cockpit cautiously. Darius and Kelvin were sitting there in silence awaiting her.

"What's up?" she grunted.

"There are a lot of tearful messages from his mother, a few angry ones from his father and several from the authorities asking him to contact someone. You know, standard stuff. The day before he went missing officially is where I decided to start and if I found nothing I was going to go back further. That may not be necessary though..." He paused. Not for dramatic effect but to find words to say that would offer better context. Satiah waited, a little excited.

"It's Milo talking, certainly, I know because I doubled checked with the voice sync computer. My question is... *who* is he talking to?" He nodded to Kelvin who obligingly activated.

Crackles could be heard as the sounds began.

"I think it's encrypted." It was Milo talking. The next voice, however, didn't sound quite human. It was dull sounding, like it was being intentionally altered. Perhaps a computer being used to hide someone's identity, perhaps not.

"You *think*? You had better be sure. If anyone nearby picks you up, I can't promise I will get there in time to protect you."

Satiah frowned, listening hard. Darius just watched her.

"I'm still close to the neutral section," the voice answered, almost scoffing. Clearly he didn't think what he was doing was particularly dangerous. No one listening to the recording shared his optimism, and neither did whoever it was he was talking to.

"Okay. I won't have long; patrols are like clockwork along the border. There *are* gaps but they are not around for long. I'll be at 8433-1116 in two hours, see you there." That was where it ended.

"Coordinates 8433-1116 are *very* close to where the ship was found drifting," Darius told her.

"8433-1118," murmured Satiah, from memory. "Kelvin, take us there, to 1116 I mean, we will do a sweep. It's probably a waste of time but it might give us something."

"Disguising their voice like that tells me that they *knew* there was a high chance someone else was listening," Darius stated, thinking hard. "Trouble with this scenario is, *it could have been anyone*."

"Especially seeing as *we* cannot tell who it is we are listening to," Satiah concurred. "Anything interesting about the frequencies?"

"First thing I checked. The encryption package was a basic one. Anyone with a half-decent computer could have de-coded that conversation," Darius reported. "The frequency itself was *standard*. They couldn't have been any easier to hear if they were in the next room." Satiah almost laughed. If only everyone was so easy to spy on.

"What about the *incoming* messages?" she asked, casually. Darius, who hadn't got that far, reran the test but not on Milo's signal.

Essentially, this process involved trying to reconnect with the signal, should it be transmitting. While they didn't know the code for it, the computer might and therefore should supply it automatically. The only problem with this method was that it would most likely alert whoever it was that someone was onto them. Darius already had the computer recording and, luckily, the computer did remember and did reconnect. The call was diverted though; clearly whoever it was either wouldn't or couldn't answer. A computer service answered.

"Please enter your command code or wait for an officer to become available," it said. Satiah and Darius exchanged looks. It was a military line.

"*Wait, leave the talking to me*," Satiah ordered, calmly. Darius nodded, compliant.

It was nearly four minutes before an officer finally answered.

"Yes?" came the man's voice.

"This is Flight Officer Kim of the transporter *Galileo*," Satiah lied, casually. "I have a shipment of medical supplies here awaiting delivery and I was told to contact the CO when I arrived, on *this line*. Who does this line belong to?"

"The base colonel," he answered, unhelpfully. Satiah had been hoping for a name or, even better, a direct transfer. "Where are you? You're not showing up on any of these scanners. What is your number?"

"I may have drifted slightly off course," she said, drawing out the conversation while Darius followed the signal. "Sorry, can you repeat the question? I have distortion, repeat I have distortion." Obligingly the man repeated himself twice.

Darius gave her a nod, they had the location.

"Call you back later," she stated, disconnecting. She focussed on Darius.

"Permyon," he told her, quickly. "It's one of three moons orbiting the planet Poro 8."

"Means nothing to me," Satiah admitted. Her astronomy was poor, at least when it came to remembering planet names and locations. Kelvin activated the cosmos overview and stabbed at a highlighted area with his appendage.

"Right in the middle of the war zone," growled Darius, inadvertently voicing Satiah's thoughts. "Now what?" He was looking at her and Satiah hadn't made up her mind. Tempting as it was to go charging in: Satiah decided to take her time.

"Call Dyss, ask him if he can find out from the family which side in that war Milo was volunteering for, and when you've done that and let me know, begin collecting data on that moon. I want to know everything there is to know about it," she instructed. "*Kelvin*, take us to Collgort-Elipsa after we've completed the sweep."

***

It was not as bad as it could have been. Purella had to acknowledge that she was lucky to be alive, luckier still to have avoided a potentially crippling injury. She still wasn't exactly sure what had caused the six-inch laceration along her forearm. It had been deep enough to rip muscle but with the help of a medical kit, it had healed quickly. She stared at herself in the mirror, her pale blue eyes steely and evaluative. She pushed her long golden hair behind her ears before replacing the black band around her head that held it in place. She'd heard nothing from Bavon since she'd reported the aborted operation. He'd taken it well enough but he was worried about what his boss would think. She'd promptly and rather stereotypically told him that *that* was his problem.

She had two mercenaries working with her, one a medic and the other a communications expert. She'd needed the expert to *find* the pirates, and the medic had been for emergencies. She hadn't expected to have to use both. That would certainly add to the ever-growing list of expenses. She pulled on her dark green elbow-length evening gloves. She thought of the tan-line on her left middle finger, created by the ring that was no longer there. That was why she'd taken to wearing gloves in the first place… she couldn't look at the mark. To her, it meant failure. She shook herself and tried not to think about it. She had other concerns now. After one last glance in the mirror, she vacated the room.

She padded down the corridor and then went downstairs into the hold. On the way, she passed a dark room. She halted on the threshold of the doorway and then entered. Blue and red lights illuminated the small room, activated by her own motion. There were four shelves but only two were occupied. The skulls stared back at her as she regarded them. Seven of them. Three were human and four were not, yet they all had two things in common. They had all once been alive… and they had all once been an enemy of hers. An enemy that still remained... These skulls were now her trophies. Their empty eye sockets devoid of life and energy still seemed able to see. She sighed restlessly and then returned to the corridor, the room plunging back into darkness behind her.

She hadn't checked her prisoner in hours. While escape was impossible, self-harm was always a risk. She approached the metal cage; the one she was currently using as a makeshift cell, and slapped the side of it to get a reaction. No reply. She grinned to herself before she started talking.

"Still not speaking to me, huh?" she enquired, checking the computer. Still there and, more importantly, still alive. She'd been astonished at the lack of conversation. Normally there was the *whos*, *whys*, and the pleading. She'd had nothing at all from this one. Well, a few grunts when she'd taken him down but that was all. Saying that, she didn't really mind, as she had nothing to *specifically* ask him yet, the lack of screaming suited her fine.

"Don't go anywhere," she smirked, as a parting shot. It was time to return home.

***

On a planet that was almost entirely ocean covered, it was fathomable for there to be such huge clouds spreading across the sky. Clouds that seemed to encase you in a bleak, some would say almost chilling, whiteness. Somewhere in these skies of Collgort-Elipsa, there were gigantic cities, floating through the clouds. Satiah, who was piloting the ship herself (something she liked to do), broke them out of the clouds and into the void between the clouds and the water. Deep blue, pocked with the foam of waves, thousands of feet below them.

Darius, sitting in the co-pilot's seat but doing nothing, just stared out. She *knew* he must be wondering: what exactly did she think she was doing? Instead of chasing Milo and going straight to Permyon, she'd detoured to a Coalition territory that, even *she* felt pretty sure, had no link whatsoever to Milo. He kept silent though, never questioning her. It was starting to unnerve her a bit. She already knew he was not a trusting man, understandably. She even had good reason to suspect his loyalty to Phantom Squad. Yet her gut was telling her, this man was no traitor.

"We're here to meet the Coalition Ambassador," she announced, breaking the silence. "I want to know as much about this war as possible *before* we get involved." Of course she'd already reviewed most of the information Darius had provided her with regarding the conflict.

"...Who says we're going to get involved?" he asked, not sharply but with a subtle intensity.

"If Milo's in it, I can't see how we can avoid it," she shrugged, nonchalant.

"How long has there been a CA stationed *out here*?" he asked, levelly. She hid the smile she knew she had on her lips. He knew she was hiding something but he was being sneaky. He was a good actor. What he was really asking was this: how did *you* know there was an ambassador here?

"I wouldn't know, but I imagine that one would have been nearby since the start of this war," she answered, evasively. She caught a twinkle of amusement in his eyes in the glance she stole. He didn't say anything else.

The craft jolted, buffeted by an unexpected blast of the gales that breathed across the surface of the ocean below. The communications unit blinked into life.

"This is Central City arrivals," stated a brisk sounding woman. "You have entered the cityscape air zone seven: please transmit your identity codes." Satiah did and then opened a channel.

"Morning," she smiled, pleasantly. "As you can now see who we are, I have to tell you that we have business with the Coalition Ambassador. Where can we find... *them*?"

"*He* is expecting you, and gave us standing instructions to pass on to you when you got here," explained the woman, a little excited now. Darius noted the word *expecting*. There was a clicking noise as she checked on her computer. "I'm going to send you some coordinates to a private landing area on the south side of Central City. The current Embassy Office is being refurbished so they are using the old *Forest Plaza* facility as an alternative."

Satiah hoped there was nothing sinister in that. Refurbishment was a popular euphemism for sundry nefarious activities. Clandestine removal of bodies, illegal demolition and large-scale theft being obvious examples that Satiah could list off the top of her head. On the other hand, it could genuinely be legitimate building works.

"*How long* has it been out of commission?" Satiah asked, curious. If it had only been *temporarily out of action*, that would look *very* dubious.

"Nearly eighteen months now, they had a funding issue that delayed the start of the works apparently," chatted the woman. Satiah relaxed somewhat. Darius was searching the database for a layout of Forest Plaza. Such information was restricted, as it was a security establishment; however, Phantom records would have the latest blueprints and schematics. He found them quickly and began familiarising himself with them.

Satiah adjusted the path of the ship onto the new course without thinking about it.

"I don't suppose you know who the ambassador is, do you?" Satiah asked, unable to resist the query.

"I've never met him, I'm afraid," she answered, informally. Satiah decided she probably wasn't lying. There was no coherent reason why a traffic controller would have had cause to meet an ambassador in person. She may not even have been the one that directed the ambassador's ship upon its arrival.

"No problem, just curious," Satiah laughed, simulating indifference. "Thank you for your assistance, may your day remain positive."

"Yours too." She cut off. Satiah glanced across at Darius, who was still immersed in the designs. The glance was enough to get him to look at her though.

"Anything?" she asked, wondering if there were any inconsistencies. He shrugged.

"I've not had enough time to check everything, but the layout seems standard enough for the most part. There is *mention* of a set of infrastructural tunnels *somewhere inside* the building that lead into a large disused maintenance area. They're not identified on the maps but there *are* references to them in the margins. Something relating to fire evacuation procedures before the last modernisation of the building," he explained casually. Satiah restrained herself from telling him to go into the history, as he already seemed to be doing it. "According to these files, the project concluded about forty-eight years ago."

"Probably due for another one soon," she joked, nonchalantly.

The city itself looked like many millions of metal boxes of all shapes and sizes, massed or collected together, making up a titanic-sized megastructure. If it could be seen through the clouds from the ground there would be no question in it dominating the skyline. According to the file, there were nearly seventy of these floating settlements planetside. They had apparently all been parts of some superstructure that, upon deciding to stay on the planet, had fractured apart in order to form a network of habitats. The idea behind this was to maximise the water vapour consumption for the giant hydroponic factories that fed the populations and provided fresh air. Also, it prevented any harm to the planet through prolonged gravitational strain. The cities were completely automated and self-sustaining, allowing the already rich population to concentrate on growing still wealthier. For a thousand years, despite the odd bad business deal or pirate attack, everything seemed to have gone well here. They had even avoided the Common Protectorate War. Now though, it seemed trouble had finally found them…

Landing on a long but thin pad, Satiah brought them down. She leaned back in her chair briefly, considering what to do next. Darius followed her example. He was not surprised that no one was there to meet them on their arrival. Phantom agents, when invited anywhere, seldom were welcomed like anyone else. The back or side doors were usually open to them but rarely the front. He glanced across at her.

"Is there something wrong?" he asked, matter-of-factly. He'd asked her that before and both of them knew it. There was an elephant somewhere in that room, or some such lame metaphorical idiom. So what was new?

"No," she said, sitting up again energetically. "I was actually thinking about food," she lied, adeptly. "Let's go and announce ourselves." Darius rose to his feet with an accepting nod.

They reached the ramp as it was lowering. Kelvin followed them out onto the landing pad as a strong, howling wind battered them with an unrelenting force that demanded respect. Bracing themselves against it, cloaks thrashing wildly out behind them, they walked towards the building. Even up at that altitude, swathed in the never-ending clouds, it was still possible to hear the roar of the oceans below. The seas must be heavy indeed to make that much noise. Satiah imagined some people would be spiritually touched by this experience, those with poetic sensibilities anyway. *Her* first thoughts were: that they needed more railings, and what would happen if a tidal wave hit the city?

There were glass doors and beyond, behind a desk, sat a neatly dressed woman. A receptionist, no doubt. Two guards, dressed in green uniforms, appeared and began to approach the doors. They were openly armed. Satiah could not help but identify their weaponry and calculate how dangerous they would be in a fight. Standard 77D rifles. Two hundred shots a pack, three a second if you held the trigger down. Not very accurate and prone to overheating. The men themselves were clearly overweight, unfit and not very disciplined. They reached the doors and entered. Instantly, over the threshold, the wind and noise all but ceased.

"Morning," smiled one of the guards. "Passes?" Darius handed them over. "What about that thing?" asked the other, pointing at Kelvin.

"He's our domestic help," Satiah deadpanned.

A flame thrower, repeating machine laser and explosive charges were just a few of the weapons that Kelvin was always equipped with. She supposed he could clean too if she ever needed him to. He stood there, taller than any of them at seven feet two inches, lean and dark, his red eyes taking in everything... He did look a little *intimidating* for a cleaner. Maybe she should do something about that one day. The woman, upon noticing them, scuttled over. She was young, not even twenty, and had clearly just been eating her breakfast.

"Excuse me, are you the ones meeting the Coalition Ambassador?" she asked, breathless. She straightened her uniform as she spoke and fished a computer from her pocket. Immediately it became clear she had something like chronic hiccups.

"That's us," Darius answered, still facing the guard.

"It's okay, they are extra security," she explained, to the guards.

"Your quarters are prepared; I will take you up now?"

She extended her hand for Satiah to shake and beamed. Satiah shook her hand firmly and nodded curtly.

"Where is the ambassador?" she asked, casually. "I was told to expect him on arrival." She hadn't been told that, she was fishing again. The woman let out a snort of giggly laughter and Satiah almost recoiled.

"I imagine they must have been referring to *his* arrival, not yours," she corrected, politely. "Please follow me." She stopped, her eyes wide, when she finally noticed Kelvin.

"I'm Satiah; this is Darius and Kelvin," Satiah told her, trying to hurry this up. "What's your name?" She'd already spied the woman's name tag but since when could you trust those? Some companies, in order to save money, refused to create new ones and instead recycled older badges that had previous employees' details on them. Gabriela, it *said*.

"Gabriela," she smiled, starting to lead the way to a lift door. She handed out identity badges to them as they went.

"Welcome to the Forest Plaza, as you can see we do our best to keep the aesthetics as bland and pleasing as possible. Recently we've been catering to several functions and..." she was saying. Satiah concentrated on the layout, tuning the girl out, going through the blueprints in her mind that she and Darius had looked at fleetingly. It was all greens and blues but with many square lights adorning the places where wall, floor and ceiling met. The lights were tinged purple but were easily bright enough to read by. The lift interior was identically festooned too... finding their way around would be tricky if everywhere looked the same. Apparently, it did.

"... They will be serving..." She was *still* talking! Satiah sighed and made a note of the floors... two were missing. Missing, as in: they were not on the selection pad. Perhaps they could only be accessed by *particular* lifts. She caught sight of Darius's exasperated expression behind her and tried not to laugh. They were soon in another corridor and walking along again. Now though, they were passing many people. Personnel and locals alike. Half glances were exchanged, curious looks were taken, and the sensation of being constantly watched hung over them. Gabriela kept talking, oblivious to Satiah's change in mood. Maybe she was part of it, maybe not. Darius too seemed to have detected that something had changed. He kept looking over his shoulder, an unconscious gesture of discomfort. Somewhere in *this* crowd was a threat... Satiah was certain of it. She could sense danger sometimes and though she wasn't sure *how*, she knew the feeling was never wrong. Her ever-present sixth sense.

The more time they wasted, the less likely they'd ever find Milo alive.

"Do you know the ambassador's *present* location?" Satiah asked, rephrasing her previous question.

"I know he is with Lady Hollellster but where they are I cannot say. She's the Royal Advisor," came the answer. Satiah didn't know how the hierarchy worked on this world, but that *sounded* like someone very high up in the ranking system.

"And roughly *when* will he be returning? I apologise if I seem impatient but I've come a long way and I do have one or two other pressing matters that I could be dealing with," Satiah said, starting to get very edgy.

"I was told *just before lunch,* so maybe *four hours*...?" Gabriela said, sounding awkward for the first time.

"*All right,*" Satiah sighed, deciding not to give Darius an excuse to think she wasn't being proactive. "Darius, I want you to return to the ship and investigate the location we discussed earlier. Keep me updated please."

Darius hid his enthusiasm well. *Finally,* a possible gesture of trust... or desperation. Either way he could work with that.

"You will be staying here?" he asked, nodding as he spoke.

"Yes," she said, leaving it at that.

"I've just heard back from Headquarters, apparently Milo volunteered to help for *both sides* of the conflict but the last stint was with the *Vinu* military," Darius reported, quietly.

"Good to know, good luck," she smiled, filing that in her memory.

Darius nodded again, smiled respectfully at Gabriela and then turned to go back. Satiah then faced the woman herself.

"Do you know *where* he will arrive when he returns?" she asked, talking about the ambassador again.

"Well, I *think* so..." she began, a little flustered.

"Perfect," Satiah smiled, acting amicable. "Why don't you show me *there* first?" She used one of her most compelling tones that made her sound just a little harder. Gabriela complied, a bit nervous now, acutely aware of Kelvin following them along.

"I thought you guys were just additional security?" she asked, confused. She tittered nervously.

"We *are* but we also have *other duties*," Satiah smiled, slickly. "Have *you* met the ambassador?"

"Yes, he's a *lovely* man," she answered, smiling. "*Very* charming, err... and *very* innocuous. In fact he's completely unlike any other ambassador I've ever met. Normally they are *so* formal and *clipped* in manner. He seems *very* friendly and personable by comparison." Well... that was a huge help!

"What is his *name*?" Satiah asked, frustrated.

"...I didn't catch his name, sorry," she blushed, nervous. Satiah, for a moment, wondered if Gabriella had liked him a bit too much. Was *everyone* on this miserable planet useless? She felt that they might be... it was what too much apathy did.

"Well, what did he look like then?" Satiah enquired, allowing a little more of her irritation to become apparent.

"Quite short, *you're* taller than him actually, very strong eyes, but I couldn't say what colour they were..." she described.

Satiah suddenly realised, much to her shame, that she should have realised *a long time ago* who it was. It was all starting to fit into place. Reed. That would explain *how* he knew who she was, where she was and by what method to compel her to help him. *He knew about Carl* and he had told Dyss, despite promising her never to tell anyone anything about anything! He *was* an ambassador too, after all. After the rage and shock departed her mind, a slight relief entered. Why hadn't he just asked her to help him? *Because* she would have refused and he would have known that. If he hadn't told Dyss about Carl... but then she would *still* have declined to get involved. Trying to avoid tricky assignments was what she always did and Reed would have known *that* too.

She allowed the tension to leave her shoulders, reasoning that Reed obviously trusted Dyss to keep her secret. How many more times would he jerk her chain, she wondered? She was going to have to say something. He *knew* one of her deepest secrets... which, for anyone else, would have been as good as a warrant for their own execution. Yet she liked Reed... that only left her with one option. She must find out his secrets. So, a secret for Dyss and a secret for Reed... she had a lot of work to do. She hated people knowing her business at the best of times and this, as ever, was not the best of times.

Gabriela escorted her to a waiting area with a bar and a viewing zone. Satiah told her to escort Kelvin to her room to ensure everything was in order there. While wandering around, Kelvin would have had ample opportunity to make his own diagram of the structure. She made a mental note to compare it to the maps she had already seen. She ordered an Amber Fall, a strong golden alcoholic beverage she'd developed a taste for. She slid an earpiece in, took the drink and then strolled over to the viewing area. She could, while there, sit in comfort and look out across the landing pad with ease. The entrance too was in full view so there would be no easy way for him to slip past her. She'd done that kind of thing so many times and she knew her own positioning was the key to the success of finding her target. The earpiece had a thin line that went all around it and it was glowing deep blue in colour. Someone had tried to call her. She reconnected with a few discreet, light taps.

Rainbow answered.

"Sorry, must have caught you in transit," he apologised, seriously.

"Must have," she agreed, taking a big gulp of the drink. It refreshed her, made her feel calmer and energetic at the same time. She didn't even mind the frothy moustache it momentarily gifted her with. She looked out across the clouds and thought, just for moment: maybe the universe wasn't so bad.

"Well, I'm sorry I'm going to have to disappoint you but we have *no idea who* this woman is," Rainbow stated. He sounded genuinely upset about it. This was unusual as normally they could find anyone. "I checked all the data twice myself."

"Surgery?" asked Satiah, closing her eyes and enjoying the warmth.

Sometimes people who had extensive surgery – facial adjustments, DNA substitutions and skin regenerations et cetera – were hard to identify because they no longer appeared anything like themselves. Such treatments were commonplace, if expensive, but what criminal would be worried about that?

"There are none of the obvious signs, and the eyes are certainly alive and human," he stated.

"What about the lips?" she enquired, trying not to sound too smug. There was a pause.

"…What about them?" he asked, puzzled.

"Not *her* lips. You should see smudges on the glass *around her lips*… I think these lip marks are *Milo's*, can you confirm if they are or not?" she asked, staring into her bubbly beer pensively.

"…Oh, ah, *sorry Satiah, we missed that*," he admitted, almost amused.

"I should have left a note," she apologised, shrugging slightly.

"Listen, um, we will check that out and everything… About *that file?*" he asked. He was talking about Dyss's file that she'd illegally asked for and he, just as illegally, had sent her.

"Yes, thanks, it was informative. I was going to give it back actually, but… is there *any chance* I could hang onto it for a *bit* longer?" she asked, seriously.

"What for?" he asked, perplexed.

"My gut tells me not to give it away yet," she said, being deliberately mysterious. Knowing that Reed was the one behind it didn't necessarily mean that Dyss wasn't a problem now or wouldn't, at some future stage, become one. There was an irate sigh. There was nothing he could do to make her give it up. The clicking and bleeping began as he hurriedly checked on the database for the lips.

"Wow, yes, they *are* his, ninety-seven percent match. The last three percent that are missing must be mainly because of overlaying smudges," he said, considering.

"He must have kissed it more than once," she guessed, her eyebrows rising a fraction. She *was* his lover, had to be.

"…This isn't a *personal question*, Satiah, but how did you *know* it was him?" he asked, amused. She hadn't known for sure of course, but she was good at making assumptions that were correct.

"I spend most of my free time snogging the sons of rich men, I call it *investment planning*," she jested, keeping a look out for any approaching vessels. "Or *kiss of death, depending on whether I like them or not.*"

"Just out of interest, could *you* tell me who is the current Coalition Ambassador for Collgort-Elipsa?" she queried. She knew they were often switched around for leave, illness or by request from time to time. It was worth bearing in mind that the ambitious rarely lingered for too long in one place. The fear of missing out… something more and more common in people that didn't even care about careers. And she still hadn't had it *confirmed* that it was Reed yet, she was only deducing.

"Let me check that for you…" he said. More clicking and bleeping. "*Oh*… It's been restricted by *Dyss*," he stated, unnerved. She murmured, not in the least surprised. Reed must have told him to do that in case she checked.

"…You okay?" he asked, sensitively. "I can give Randal a call if you need help…"

"Goodbye Rainbow," she grinned. "Be in touch soon." She disconnected. She tapped her ear again, adjusting the levels of encryption to maximum. She made the call and Carl answered very quickly. She took a quick and sneaky glance around but no one was paying her any attention.

"Satiah?" he asked, confused but happy. "This is twice in as many days."

"It is," she breathed, enjoying the sound of his voice. It was better live but she took what she could get. "What's happening?" Pleased she was interested, or maybe just happy to talk to *anyone*, he launched into a typically rambling explanation of his day so far. She closed her eyes, fantasising about being with him. She'd forgotten what it was like *actually having someone*, and the amount of thinking-time they demanded from her. Not that she minded. Indeed the distraction was… *pleasant*. Easier to deal with than murderous nightmares in any case. Nevertheless, no matter how pleasant, it had to be the last time for a while.

"I sense that soon I will be in the shadows but never forget I'm going to come back," she told him, softly. "And I *will* know if you have even *looked* at another woman in the time I'm away. *So don't get any ideas.*"

"Good, because I want you to come back and if I should happen to come across another woman while you're away I'll most certainly look the other way," he promised.

"Love you," she whispered, so quietly she scarcely heard herself. She disconnected, suddenly aware of tears in her eyes.

She blinked them away hurriedly, and eyed her drink in a shifty manner. These new emotions were potential hazards and she made up her mind to guard against them. Then she noticed something that made her freeze completely. There was a mirrored bar, part of the décor, not far from her and it reflected part of the walkway above. There, standing in plain view, arms resting leisurely on the railing, was the woman from the pirate base. The golden hair and black band holding it in place could have been dismissed as happenstance but *that face...* Besides, it was too much of a coincidence that in all the places in the cosmos... Satiah remained where she was as evidently the woman hadn't observed her. Or if she had, she'd taken no action yet. Satiah sipped her drink again, behaving naturally. The woman was waiting, much like Satiah herself. It seemed impossible for her to have followed Satiah, so that meant she had to have some other purpose in being there.

She was dressed in a dark green and black long-sleeved dress that was subtly designed to minimise restrictions. A dress for a warrior. Satiah could even make out the disguised padding of flexi-armour. She was also wearing her long gloves. The same gloves as before, perhaps? *Who was she?* Her posture was alert but relaxed. She was confident of her own safety... confident enough, anyway. Satiah couldn't see a gun but it seemed sensible to postulate that she was armed. The woman didn't move much, and was apparently more interested in the doors at the end of the walkway than what was below her. Satiah continued to play the role of a disinterested onlooker as she wondered if there were *others* she needed to be wary of too. Strangers nearby who might be more.

Her drink was almost empty. Which was more likely to attract attention? Someone sitting there with no drink or someone casually getting up to get another? Funnily enough, Satiah was no longer in the mood for drinking anything. Nevertheless, she chose the second option. She slipped on a pair of glasses that looked more like safety googles of the kind you saw people wearing who deal with hazardous materials. She set them to record as she stood and moved back towards the bar. As she moved, she glanced up in a way that oozed indifference at the woman. In the left lens, pictures were being taken at the rate of one hundred a second. In the right lens, a body scan occurred. It was skin level stuff so Satiah wasn't sure what she would get. This device was new and, up until this point, Satiah hadn't had cause to use it. Her glance was only two seconds, any longer and she risked giving herself away. She reached the bar and removed the specs as if to study the drink selection more closely.

"Same again?" asked the serving robot.

"Why not? Thank you," she replied, sending herself the results. She handed over the money, while consciously resisting the urge to look over her shoulder. There was no mirrored panelling at the bar so there was no way she could see behind her. A movement in the corner of her eye made her look back out of the viewport, into the clouds. A ship was approaching. Hoping that the sight of it would distract the woman enough for her to take another look, Satiah took a chance and looked up at the walkway again. She had gone. Returning to her seat, maintaining the act, Satiah's mind ran wild. Was it reasonable to think that this woman, probably some kind of hired hand, was there to harm Reed? She called Kelvin.

"Yes," he answered dependably, in her ear.

"Room okay?" she asked, seriously.

"Checks complete, no bugs, no dangerous life forms and no lethal chemicals," he stated. "Rooms on this floor are currently vacant. I have installed listening devices inside all of them as a precaution."

"...Good thinking," she smiled, relieved. "I've just seen that woman who tried to stop us retrieving the gold from the pirates."

"Where?" he asked, immediately.

"She was just in the waiting area – or rather, the walkway above it. I don't *think* she saw me," she told him, uncertain on that last point. "I'm sending you the info from the specs."

"I will create the profile then run analysis," he acknowledged.

"Let me know," she ordered, pointlessly. She knew he would. "Will Darius have reached the moon yet?"

"No."

***

"Quint won't pay for undelivered goods and *neither will I*," Bavon declared, all bravado. Purella sighed. She had expected this to be a long and tedious meeting. Part of her wondered why she was even bothering to negotiate with this *shallow buffoon*. He was beneath her! Quint was the real player here – why he insisted on using this lowlife as a go-between, she couldn't imagine. He could trust it all to her! She pushed those thoughts away and concentrated on winning the exchange.

"If you don't pay me, I will kill him," she stated, calmly. Bavon froze for a moment, her blunt tactics leaving him no room to dance around the dispute. Her cold blue eyes told him that she would have no difficulty delivering on the threat. She went on, taking the opportunity his silence provided.

"He is costing me money by the hour. Food, drink, oxygen... none these things are *free* and if you *don't pay me* for that pirate job then I'm sorry but I will *have* to bleed him," she shrugged, sounding regretful. She was bluffing of course. She knew what Quint would do to her if she killed the man, or *allowed him to die*. Question was... did Bavon? His flustered face told her that he didn't.

Bavon was terrified of Purella and was doing his best to hide it which, unbeknownst to him, was not a very good best. He couldn't believe she was serious about this! He had half a mind to tell her that her money was with the pirates, just to get her off of his back. And where the hell was Quint? He was supposed to be there! He was afraid of Quint too, but Quint could keep Purella in order.

"All right," he sighed, trying to act as if he'd intended to give in all along. He would remember this and one day he'd make her *pay* for this embarrassment! He hated being belittled by anyone, even if they were completely in the right. It made him want to lash out... though he rarely dared to.

In the meantime, he would have to pay her out of his own money just to make her go away for a while.

"How much is it?" he asked, knowing she would exaggerate. Purella did a quick mental recalculation and deliberately rounded up. Who wouldn't?

"Seventeen hundred for my time, another six thousand for housing of the prisoner..." she listed, casually.

"*Six thousand!*" he blustered, fuming. "That's not even *close* to what we agreed!"

"That's because *what happened* was not what we agreed either," she smiled, making it clear she was forcing herself to remain civil. "I did make Quint aware that I do not *do* refunds, plus in *high-risk operations like that* the chances of success are slim at best."

"Five thousand total, *no higher*," he stated, seriously.

"Who is he, by the way?" she asked, changing the subject.

"The prisoner?" She nodded. "*None* of your business, that's who," he snarled, doing his best to act tough.

"I suppose not," she shrugged, unruffled. All she had been told to do was keep him alive and keep him locked up. There was nothing else to it so it didn't matter who he was. She was curious though. Quint rarely did things for profit alone. That meant, *whoever this man was*, he was important. Important to Quint, in any case. She should have known better than to have expected Quint to share anything that important with Bavon. Who would?

"If you don't give me what I'm asking for, he won't be *anyone's* business," she grinned back, all poised to strike. "Why don't we call it *eight?*"

Eight thousand Essps! Bavon had the money but he resented having to pay her himself when it had been *Quint* who had made him hire her.

"I don't have a sum that large on me," he lied, incredulous. She could smell the fearful lie almost as strongly as the money itself. She played along though.

"I'm not going anywhere," she shrugged, apparently amicable. "So it's a deal?"

"Of course," he answered, pleased at being able to deceive her.

She smiled, extending her gloved hand across for him to shake.

He took it and convulsed to the current as she clung tightly to his hand. Her smile became vicious, her eyes wide, almost animal like in their look. A condescending snarl. He yelped as he shuddered and tried ineffectively to free himself from her grasp.

"You lie to me like that again... *I dare you*," she hissed, in his ear. She abruptly let go and pushed him back into his seat with her other hand.

All the acting was over now; he looked how he was. Petrified. His face was red and sweaty and his body still shaking – only now, out of fear alone. With Purella, the normal smile was back. It has been said many times before, but because of her good looks, she could have been a renowned actress or model. Looks could kill and she was an expert at both. It was almost like the last part of the exchange had never happened, if you were looking at her. Not a single lock of golden hair was out of place. That evil little smile was still on her lips... Bavon gave it away with his trembling. He stared at her, eyes brimming with fear and pain.

She made a rotating gesture with her hand. "In your own time," she encouraged, courteously. Clutching his burning hand in the other, he shuffled out to get the money. Had he been remotely dangerous, she would have followed him, but she'd scared him so utterly that he would only do as she said now. At least for now. As much as she enjoyed the power this afforded her, she still had a distain for dealing with someone like him. Quint though, he was different. She wouldn't have tried anything like that on him. She was still amazed that he wasn't there... and a little suspicious.

She began to search Bavon's office, more out of inquisitiveness than anything. As she had expected there was nothing out of the ordinary. Who would be stupid enough to leave anything incriminating lying around? In her experience, quite a few people. If she'd had time she would have had a go at the computer too. As it was, she left it well alone and was careful to leave everything as she had found it. She returned to her seat and awaited Bavon's return. He came back after having recovered some of what he had in place of dignity.

"It's all there," he stated, putting the case down on the table. It was small, like a satchel but squared off and neat in design. She just took it, not even bothering to count it.

"Quint will be in touch about the prisoner," Bavon said, his voice hard to read.

"Be as well that someone is."

**

Cutterboats were the main form of travel on Collgort-Elipsa. As the planet was oceanic, the machines had to be able to traverse the waves at great speed without falling prey to their colossal power. Of course, as all the cities were airborne, the cutterboats had to be able to fly too. This requirement was fulfilled by caged rotating blades located on either side of the torpedo-shaped vehicle. These, each supported on omnidirectional arms, offered great manoeuvrability as well as additional speed. Most of the cutterboats Satiah had seen so far were standardised open-deck designs, where the driver and passengers were exposed to the elements. They were all bright orange; presumably to aid people, who were looking for them, in finding them. This one arriving, though, was different in three main ways.

Firstly, its size. It was almost four times as large as anything she'd seen so far. Secondly, it was painted white, blue and grey in a pattern of wavy lines. Thirdly, it was not open-top like the others, but sealed. Satiah decided that this particular cutterboat was probably meant for someone very special, who might need to leave the planet on it, hence the sealed hull. It also had an additional propeller, this one smaller, located at the rear. It landed on the arrival zone outside the waiting area Satiah was sitting in. Guards had arrived to protect the new arrivals and Satiah stood with the intention of being there too. The guards saw her coming but for whatever reason didn't attempt to prevent her. The ramp of the ship lowered as the occupants disembarked. Satiah crossed her arms as she saw a familiar little man emerge. Reed.

Onto his arm clung a woman, taller than him. She was probably a little taller than Satiah too. They were both laughing and shouting at one another in the wind about something. Satiah glared as she waited there. She wanted him to be in no doubt about how she felt about all of this! They had a small entourage of guards that followed them from the ship to the doors. The doors opened and they entered.

"...Have to agree!" Reed was jabbering. "Most excellent, quite possibly one of the best I've had the pleasure to dine on. I appreciate that tip about the sauce, very thoughtful." The pair of them together looked a little merry.

"Not a problem, but *remember*, I wouldn't just tell *anyone* that. Normally I like to see people wince the first time around," the woman responded, her tone similar. Reed chuckled out an infectious laugh. His eyes found Satiah and he just carried on like he'd not noticed her at all.

So, their *ambassadorial morning* had been filled with an elaborate meal? Satiah wasn't surprised to find Reed doing that sort of thing but in this case, it irked her. In other words, she had been waiting for *four hours* for him to finish his food. Now he was as good as ignoring her! She stepped out to block their path and stood there, arms crossed and eyes blazing.

"*Reed?*" the woman enquired, noticing Satiah for the first time. "Is she one of yours? Her uniform, if it *is* a uniform, is unfamiliar to me but I'm terrible when it comes to that kind of thing."

"Why *yes* Lady, this is my *special associate* Satiah," he answered, acknowledging her finally. He gave a discreet pleading expression. He wanted her to play along. Satiah relented somewhat and decided that she would.

"You are late," he pointed out, much to her infuriation. "Can I help you?"

"We have a *baggage* problem," Satiah stated, crisply. "I'm sorry to interrupt your *meeting* but it's rather urgent."

"Sounds serious Reed, you had better see to it, she doesn't look *at all happy* you know," stated the woman, sounding far more concerned than she probably was.

He pulled a slightly insincere smile.

"I will *see* you later," she stated, in a way that had Satiah wondering exactly what he was up to. She and her guards moved away, in the direction of the lifts. That left her and Reed alone. The urge to punch or slap him was almost overpowering.

"Well, I'm glad you made it," he began, acting like all this was perfectly acceptable. "Drink?"

"Did *you* tell Dyss about Carl?" she asked, through her teeth. He cringed as if ducking an imaginary blow, but didn't answer. "*Did you?*" she growled, knowing the answer.

"You look divine?" he offered, feebly.

"Do you want me to shoot you where you stand because if you do you're doing all the right things?" she spat, furious.

"*Come on Satiah*, I had no choice!" he protested, at last talking to her properly. Leaving aside the argument about there *always* being a choice, an argument *he himself had used many a time*, she simply switched accusation.

"You must understand what pressure *you* have put me under?" she asked, rhetorically. Of course he knew! "I'm guessing you are trying to force me into helping you end the war?"

"Dyss will *not* have you arrested, *I promise*," Reed stated, suddenly serious. "*Even if he did I could get you out of it*! I just needed someone *I could trust* on short notice and *you* were ideal." If *that* was his idea of a compliment...

"Because you *knew* you could *blackmail* me into helping you?" she demanded, remembering to keep her voice down. People were already looking, expecting further drama.

"*Coax*," he corrected, pulling a hurt face. He looked around, expecting Kelvin to be there. "Where is your big friend?"

"If you ever do that again Reed, I *will* kill you," she told him, waving her finger at his face in time with her words.

He closed his eyes, seeming to go paler with fear. Then he slowly opened them and a smile crossed his lips.

"...So *you'll help*?" he asked, almost childlike in his eagerness. She looked into his eyes and the last of her anger crumbled. How could he do that? Look so... *pathetic*. She hated herself for it but she was starting to feel sorry for him. He'd somehow made *her* feel like the wrongdoer here. Like he was some clumsy puppy or something... like Carl. Even despite all that, she wasn't going to let him get away with it unchallenged.

"...Well, I'm here now," she grumbled, sullenly. He tentatively put his hand on her back and patted softly.

"Why don't I buy you a drink and tell you what all this is *really* about?" he offered, grinning almost wickedly at her. Her shoulders slumped.

"Fine."

***

Poro 8 was like a ball of fire, burning light in the dark, endless silence of space. Darius had arrived some way off from the planet itself to get a better look. There was some debris, skeletal remains of ships that formed a loose orbit. It seemed likely they had been caught up in recent battle. Soon scavenging ships would arrive in an attempt to salvage anything that could be sold. A quick scan revealed no immediate threats, the planet and only *two* moons. The database had stated that there were *three*. He double-checked quickly. Yes... unquestionably three. So where had the other one gone? He scanned again on the off chance it was a blip. Same result. Sighing and shaking his head, he began a cautious approach.

As he got closer it became clear that Poro 8 was in the midst of a planet-wide volcanic winter. The scanners picked up an immense amount of seismic activity and counted over two billion individual volcanos within the northern hemisphere alone. Darius decided it would be best not to pay the surface a visit. Which one of the moons was Permyon? The second moon... Both, according to the standard scan, seemed to be little more than balls of bare rock, pockmarked with impact craters and wrecked battleships. He remembered he was in the middle of a battlefield now; which was why he was amazed to see no military activity. He knew they couldn't know *he* was there as he was cloaked, and he continued his slow journey around Poro 8 towards the moons.

To determine which moon was Permyon he ran yet another scan and was rather annoyed to discover that neither of them were. He leaned back and stroked the sides of his moustache thoughtfully. It *could* have been destroyed in the time it took him to get there but if *that* was the case: *where* was the wreckage? It might have crashed into the planet but there would still be something. Some mark of its destruction for him to find. He had one last notion and deactivated all engines to just drift. He was interested in what gravity could tell him. The computer began instantly calculating compensatory routes to prevent him crashing into anything. Using mathematics and checking against the pulling and pushing, he found what he was looking for. A suspiciously *constant* region. Everything should be being pulled towards the planet, the moons included. There would be some reverse pull around the moons themselves and there should be no constant region in that area.

Activating the drive system again, he began to edge the ship towards the constant region. A constant region was an area of space where there was no gravitational pull. It was... well, constant. Maintained by gravity pulling against itself exactly equally in every direction around it. It took a lot of energy to create such a large region but it was not outside of mankind's capacity. A scan revealed nothing inside the region but then Darius didn't expect it to. He kept up the gradual approach, once again ensuring nothing else was happening nearby. Darkness. A sort of artificial darkness... *blacklight?* Darius smiled to himself, he was right. *The moon was still there.* Permyon was there... cloaked just like he was. There was a tiniest flash of energy as the cloaks passed through one another and suddenly... there it was.

Permyon was bigger than the other two. It had an atmosphere and a large forest. There was what looked like planetary shipyards down there too. Darius took the time to perform a detailed scan which he then sent back to Kelvin so Satiah could review it herself. He still was not wholly sure why she'd not gone with him and it bothered him. He knew she didn't entirely trust him. Dyss would have seen to that, but Satiah had not made up her mind about him yet. Darius could tell she had not as she'd sent him all the way out there to chase their mutual objective *without* her direct supervision. At first he'd felt it was either a red herring, or a test of some kind, but now he felt it was more like a diversion. Like there was *something else* that she considered more important and this, to her, was merely a sideshow. He wondered what it could be.

An alarm bell broke off this reverie and he shook himself inwardly: *never* was the *best time* for reflection. A squadron of fighters were coming closer. They were not coming directly towards him and their formation pattern suggested a standard patrol but it could be a bluff. While they ought not to be able to see him he nevertheless powered up the drive so he could make a quick getaway. *Should all else fail,* in any case. These frantic preparations proved unnecessary, however, as the patrol zoomed right past him without a second thought. He began to follow, curious as to where they had come from. Obviously the moon, but where *specifically*? They hadn't come from the shipyards, unless it had been some time ago, he was certain of that.

Darius took the opportunity to run a check on one of the fighters in order to get a better idea of just who it was he was following and what their potential strength was. According to the file it was a C88 or Speck-Fighter. Fast but lightly armed, ideal for fighter-to-fighter combat but not the sort of thing one would use against a capital ship… not if one intended to win. The yellow trapezoid it sported on its wings betrayed its allegiance too. They were Vinu forces, fighting for Vinupisha. Or at least that was what they looked like. Darius theorised that it could have been stolen by the opposite side and used for some complicated scheme. If he took these fighters at face value, however, this indicated that the moon, hidden and cloaked from sight as it was, was under Vinu command. At least currently. According to the data, the moon had been lost and regained twice during the conflict so far. There was precious little detail as to the circumstances of any battle scenarios though.

Some references to sudden and overwhelming assaults one way, and a clever blockade or some kind of slow strangulation method on the other, was not much to work with. There was no sign of recent fighting on the moon's surface. He suspected this was thanks largely to being cloaked. They may even have convinced the opposition that the moon had indeed been completely destroyed. At less than an hour away from Shintumpa, the moon plainly made an ideal outpost for either side. They were cruising close to the surface now, as they would if they were flying a hit-and-run raid. The fighters performed simple dodging moves while retaining their formation. This was probably for practice against either ground defence batteries or pursuit from enemy fighters.

Looming up close was a substantial facility, maybe seven or eight miles long. The command post, Darius presumed. This was the place he and Satiah must have got through to when they made the call. Or at least, he hoped it was. The fighters circled it once and then flew into a hangar area. Darius obviously couldn't follow them in there. He selected a suitably small clearing in the forest and made his own secret landing, away from the outskirts of the facility. He remained in his seat thinking deeply on what to do next and how to do it. Infiltration was the clear strategy here. First, he would check out the detention area; if they were holding Milo here he was likely to be there. Getting him out could be tricky, especially if Milo wasn't up to it physically. Darius was also curious about the capacity of the base. How many personnel were stationed there? Why and how was the moon cloaked? There were a lot of unanswered questions.

He ran an atmosphere check. Oxygen was low... too low for him, anyway. He pulled the breathing device from his belt casually and checked his pistol. All ready as always. The atmosphere was thin, but enough for a forest to grow. He exited the ship cautiously. No sign of anyone. Insects seemed to be the main form of life and the air, such as it was, teemed with them. They hummed and buzzed constantly. He made his way through the undergrowth in the direction of the facility. There didn't seem to be much in the way of other animals, even birds. This explained how insects had become so dominant. They might not even have *any* natural predators... That thought ended when he caught sight of a plant that seemed to be catching them in its sticky foliage. Through the next group of trees he spied what had to be the perimeter fence. At five metres high, topped with needle-like metal protrusions, it was pretty standard. Darius noted a drone hovering nearby, acting as a sentry. There would of course be others.

There was no way he could climb over, dig under or cut through *that* without setting off every alarm in the base. He followed the fence along, still using the cover of the forest. His best chance would be to find the entrance and slip inside when the opportunity presented itself. It didn't take him long to find it, he'd chosen his landing area with access to the entrance in mind. It was highly likely he would have to make a quick escape and so it made sense that he was near the way in. The gap in the fence had three drones guarding it and a mobile barrier across it. He had three days and twenty-three hours of air left before he'd need to get a new supply. It was logical to presume that inside the base he wouldn't need to rely on that supply. He resigned himself to a long wait.

***

"Operation *Blacklight*?" scoffed Reed, eyeing the file with some incredulity. "*That* was Dyss's doing! I would have played no part in such a badly chosen name! And *who* exactly is *Milo*?" He had insisted on scrutinising it the moment she had decided that no one would easily be able to overhear them. She trusted him to see it as there really wasn't all that much to see at that point. Besides... he had proven his discretion before. Even if he had just blackmailed her. Saying no to Reed was very difficult and she intended to save her strength for when she really needed it. Satiah sipped her new drink, which she had made him buy for her. She found herself unable to stop glancing back up at the walkway from time to time though. Reed noticed and stared obviously up at the empty spot.

"Is something wrong?" he asked. Why did people keep asking her that? Of course there was! Wasn't there always?

"Milo is the son of *Ambassador Drass*, an incredibly rich..." she began, sighing. This was *not* what she wanted to talk about. Dawning comprehension was Reed's instant reaction.

"No, he's *not*," he interrupted, erratically. "He's the *adopted* son of Ambassador Drass's *wife*." Satiah paused... the file had neglected to mention that. As had Dyss. Was it a *significant* oversight? That was the question.

"Be that as it may," she went on, making a mental note to double check that later. "It is *secondary* to this madcap idea of ending the VS war."

"*Madcap idea!*" spluttered Reed, in objection. "..." His fruit beer nearly went all over the table.

"I'm guessing *your* idea," she cut across him, coolly.

"Too many people have *died* for it to be allowed to continue and it has the potential to create a full-on galactic conflict," Reed stated, levelly. "It should be the duty of all civilised beings to try to stop it."

"Whatever," she dismissed, her tone mocking. "Let's say I agree, which *I don't!* How do you propose we *do* stop it?"

"Isn't it *obvious?*" he blustered. Once again, she found herself questioning his sanity.

"*No*," she answered, sagely. A call came through into her ear and she held up her hand to get him to be quiet for a moment. She expected it to be Darius or Kelvin but was unpleasantly surprised to find it was Randal. *Phantom Leader* Randal.

"*Satiah*! Where the hell are you?" he demanded, without preamble. She glowered; this wasn't going to be much fun.

"On a mission," she replied, trying not to sound too patronising.

"Yes, you are, *my* mission!" he argued, as if vindicated. "Where is the gold?" She frowned. This conversation didn't make any sense. She had believed that Dyss would confer with Randal to explain *where* she was and *what* she was doing. That had apparently not happened. That was one problem. His question, however, pointed to another slightly more dangerous problem…

"The gold we took from the pirates?" she asked, trying to buy time to think.

"You know of *another stockpile?*" he enquired, sarcastically. "I *repeat*: *where the hell are you?*" He sounded livid. His anger didn't so much frighten her as it confused her.

"Randal, I'm on a mission for *Dyss*, right now I'm on Collgort-Elipsa talking with the ambassador," she spelt out, coldly. "The gold should have been delivered to Phantom Headquarters about two days ago." A silence. "*Randal?*"

"Well, it's not here," he replied, the anger gone. "Who did you send to deliver it?" She gave the names of those who'd assisted her in that operation. Another silence. Reed was watching her and she had a sneaking feeling he was going to ask her if anything was wrong *again*.

"They've not reported in, they never returned, I assumed you three were still together. *It's a good thing I never told the people who own it that we had retrieved it for them*. When did you last see them?" he asked, urgent.

"Maybe forty hours ago," she replied, rapidly working it out. "I left them on a straight course to Earth and home. I don't see *how* they could have ended up anywhere else." Her eyes looked once again at the walkway where the woman had been and Reed turned in his chair to look properly himself.

Had the pirates somehow pulled off the impossible and stolen it back?

"I'm not in a position to really do much this end that you can't do yourself," she admitted, shrugging. "It's conceivable that they had an engine problem and haven't been able to report back."

"How would an engine fault...?" he stopped himself. She knew what he was going to argue. How could a problem with a drive affect communications too? It was no use, something bad had happened.

"The gold was the real thing, there was nothing dangerous about the container it was in," Satiah stated, remembering. "I can *only speculate*, Randal."

"*What gold?*" mouthed Reed, perplexed. She waved at him again to keep quiet.

"...I'll call you back," he told her, disconnecting.

Satiah frowned, deep in thought.

"Can I help?" Reed offered, seriously. She decided that for now she might as well forget the gold, either they still had it or they didn't. She couldn't *help or hinder* in either case.

"You can help by telling me how to stop this war," she stated, a little frosty. He smiled.

"Well... I did have *one idea*," he replied, the hint of smugness in his voice. She rolled her eyes. She'd heard some of his *ideas* before and she was not going to bite on this. She swigged her drink and began to fiddle with her communicator as if no longer paying attention. Reed chuckled, seeing through the act.

"What is the *one thing* that both sides want?" he asked.

"Money?" she joked. He chuckled again. "A good kicking?" she offered, enthusiastic.

"Besides those *recognisable* things?"

"From what I've been told, it seems that this began with a border dispute, so I'm guessing they both want territory. In this case, *the same territory*," she answered, at last giving him the answer he sought.

"Correct, and I thought to myself: how can this be obtained?" he went on.

"It can't, *not by both sides*, that's *why* they are fighting," she sighed, again knowing he already knew that. His way of talking was thought provoking at the same time as plainly provocative.

"Let's look at this from another angle… is there a way to put both sides off wanting said territory?" he asked. She raised her eyebrows to show that she had not considered that.

"…What are you thinking?" she asked, leaning forward. "Contamination? Mines?" He laughed loudly.

"Good lord, no," he guffawed. "We get *someone else* to take over the territory and form a demilitarisation zone between them, thus ending the war. Neither side has shown *any* inclination to start a fight with anyone else."

"Except for just recently when they attacked this place," she pointed out.

"*Well…*" He paused for effect. What now? He had that shifty look about him again, the look that said he knew something.

"I'm *not* a patient woman, Reed, you should know that by now!" she growled, unwilling to reward his ego anymore. "What are you thinking?"

"I think the attack was done by *someone else*," he stated, conspiratorially. "I think a *third party* is interfering anonymously in the struggle." It was plausible.

"*Who?*" she enquired, curious. If he'd got this far by himself he may even have a suspect.

"That *I don't know*. Personally, right now, I'm more interested in *why* than who. Profit? Something personal? No way to know… until *you* find out *who they are*," he said, with significance. She crossed her arms and thought about it. She would have to go over the circumstances of the attack in every detail, which had most likely been done several times by several people.

"I'll look into it but as you know I do have *another* objective," she told him, standing. She downed the last of the drink and then paced away. Reed watched her go without a word. Well, he'd done it again. He'd got her interested… and she hated him for that too!

***

"Did you hear that?" Satiah asked, to Kelvin.

"Every word," he said, in his trademark monotone. "The man you need to speak to is Administrator Bavon. He should have footage and access to records of the actual incident." She entered the lift, making way for two other people as she did.

"Are you going to do anything about the missing gold?"

"No, not yet. Where can I find him?" she asked, casually.

"Sending you details now. If he's not in his office, check the staff area," he suggested.

"Will do. Anything from Darius yet?" she asked.

"Nothing." This did not worry *her*. Darius was an experienced Phantom with many years under his belt. He would report when *he* was ready. It might bother *Dyss* though...

"If Reed is right and, for whatever reason, someone is interfering in the war... wasn't it a bit reckless to draw attention to themselves by hitting a neutral?" she asked, thinking it through.

"Yes, but their hand could have been forced. With their motives unknown, even such contingencies as mistakes and coincidences remain on the table," he said. He was correct, too. Reed was just theorising, as usual.

"True," she said, as she exited the lift. As she moved out, someone else moved in and they brushed shoulders as they passed one another. Purella turned to see who she'd bumped into, just as Satiah glanced over her shoulder, and eye contact was established. They both froze, pinned to the spot with a blast of recognition. The lift doors, however, prevented anyone taking further action as they closed, separating them.

"Guess who I just bumped into?" Satiah asked, recovering herself quickly. Her hand was on her pistol now and she did a circle in the corridor, checking for any threats. "She knows I'm here now."

"Where is she?" Kelvin asked. Satiah took note of the direction of the lift.

"Going *down* in the elevator, any news on her identity yet?" she asked.

"Still checking, are you in danger?" he asked, levelly.

"...Not sure," she murmured, continuing on. Even if she did come back up, Satiah would be long gone. Arguably, now there was no gold, they didn't *need* to fight one another. That didn't mean they wouldn't though. No gold... *She* couldn't have stolen it back and been able to get here... Why was she here?

Purella couldn't believe it! The woman from the pirate base? *Here?* No ambush so... that *had* to mean she'd not expected Purella to be there. But she'd got the gold so *why* would she...? This made no sense! She called Bavon.

"I'm clearing your fuel allowance now, *I swear*," was his guarded response.

"*It's not about that.* Have you spoken to *anyone* about our little deal *other than Quint?*" she asked, deadly serious. She knew that even if he *had* he'd most likely deny it, but she still had to warn him. Purella didn't know what the woman was doing on the planet or even who she was, but it seemed likely she'd be paying Bavon a visit. Perhaps in an official capacity.

"No, *of course not.* Why?" he retorted, predictably.

"You're about to have a guest," she told him. "*Record* the encounter and send it to me."

"*What? Why?*" he asked, baffled.

"*Just do it*," she snarled, and disconnected. She then smiled disarmingly at the person in the lift with her.

***

Bavon had only just set up the camera when the door bleeped. He sat down hurriedly.

"Yes?" he asked, pretending to be occupied. Satiah entered, her eyes flashing circumspectly.

"Administrator Bavon?" she enquired, almost robotically.

"That's me," he beamed, wondering if *this* was who Purella had warned him about or not. She seemed so... then he noticed the laser pistol on her hip and realised that maybe she was not so harmless. She smiled politely as they shook hands. Her slender physique betrayed a honed strength and suppleness that seemed only to solidify her warrior's gait.

"My name is Kim; I'm working for the Coalition ambassador. I was wondering if I could take a look at all your records regarding the incident that took place recently involving the war," she stated, giving her habitual alias. "Terrible weather out there."

She handed her identity badge to him nonchalantly. He smiled politely, trying to hide the fear he felt within as well as he could. Why did *she* want to see *that* stuff? Everyone else already had. Things had passed beyond that stage or, at least, they should have! Perhaps, there was some overlooked technicality?

He knew Purella was listening in. He had to act normal and do what he would normally do with such a request.

"I'll just check with the supervisor," he said, picking up his communicator.

"Thank you," she replied, without smiling. She proceeded to look all around his office while he waited to be connected. Satiah could tell that Bavon was organised by the state of the room. Everything in its place, nothing odd… except those injuries on his hand. She didn't remark on it though because she also spotted a still steaming beverage on the table. Burns and scalds were common injuries in places where hot beverages were readily available.

"Yes, I've got Kim here from…" he began. "*Ah*… right, I see." He disconnected and smiled at her. She did not return the expression. "It seems I'm to give you all the help I can."

"I hope I've not caught you… at an awkward moment," she said, scrutinising his eyes and face.

"No, no," he chortled, very convincingly. There was a stillness as they both stared at each other; finally Bavon squirmed under the scrutiny.

"It's through here," he went on, taking her through to the archive area. "I *thought* all of you had gone over this already?" he chanced, interesting in what she was doing.

"Something was missed," she remarked, giving nothing away. He pulled out the relevant file from the stack and handed it to her.

"The access codes are on the back," he prompted, as he would normally.

"Good," she said, taking from him and heading for the door. "Thank you for all your help, Administrator Bavon."

"*Do* let me know if you need anything else!" he called, after her.

Satiah didn't reply and the door closed. Bavon scrambled over to his communicator again.

"*Well?*" he asked, breathlessly.

"Nothing yet... I'll check with Quint," Purella answered. "In the meantime, keep me informed as to *everything* she's doing."

"Do you think...?" he left the question unfinished.

"Of *course* she suspects, she's clearly a well-trained operative working for *someone*. Most likely the Coalition or the Union. I thought at first she might have *followed me* here somehow..." she mused.

"*Followed you? She's* the one who...?" he began, in dawning comprehension.

"Yes, *she* got the gold!" Purella growled, reluctant to revisit her failure. Bavon swore as he ran a hand stressfully through his hair.

"*They're onto us!*" Bavon hissed, starting to panic. "We'll have to..."

"Stay *calm*, Bavon," she purred, soothingly. "No one is onto anything *yet*." Then she added something else in a whisper. "If I thought they *were* I'd be killing *you* to cover my own tracks. Tell Quint what's going on and sit tight. *I'll be in touch*."

He shifted in his seat as he remembered the electrical effects of her last touch. She disconnected without another word and he hoped that this was all just some massive misunderstanding. How had he got himself into this? Maybe this woman was someone who just *looked* a lot like someone else? That happened *all the time*, cases of mistaken identity. But Purella didn't make mistakes like that... He put in a call to Quint again but he was still not answering. *Where was he?* This was important!

***

Darius had set a small explosive charge close to where he was watching the road. After nearly six hours of watching, Darius was drifting in and out of a catnap when some activity *finally* occurred. A transporter was growling its way slowly towards the gate, and the gate was starting to open. Darius took off running and emerged from the woods to jump up onto the side of the long grey transporter. He slid into an alcove full of what felt like sleeping gear. The transporter stopped and did a sensor sweep having detected his movement. He held his breath. The sweep, he hoped, would not include the transporter itself, only the surrounding woodland. He put his ear to the metal and thought he could hear the murmur of voices but the engine was making it difficult to be sure. A minute or so later, the engine revved up again and the transporter slid in through the gates.

Darius did his best to take in everything he could about *where* they were going. It was a large complex, so getting lost was something he had to plan for. There was another gate they passed through, the secondary gate he presumed. In some ways it reminded him of the fortresses of old. Gates, walls and keeps were a lot like gates, perimeter fences and inner fences. This all made sense certainly, because leaving aside this being a military base, they had prisoners to keep. One in particular… His only real worry had been that one of the drones might have detected his body heat, and luckily that hadn't happened.

He'd deployed another of his small explosives on the ground as they had sped past. It was not clear whether he'd need them or not but there was no harm in being prepared. He stayed where he was as the transporter made its way toward the vehicle area where it was stationed. Once there it disgorged a patrol of troops. They were wearing the uniform of Vinu with the yellow symbol on their armbands. Still he didn't move, waiting to be alone. Once he was certain that he was the last one in there, he slipped out into the silent depot area.

The place had become eerily quiet and echoic since the departure of the soldiers. Darius crept along, keeping in the shadows as much as possible. There *were* cameras but not too many. He was able to stay out of the focus zones of them until he reached a door. The last camera was focussed right on it. Darius checked carefully. No obvious wires to cut, no useful things to hide behind. He returned to the transporter and found what he was looking for. Someone's discarded hat. He sneaked back to the place just out of range of the camera, and then crept up underneath it. He shoved the hat over the lens, effectively blinding it. He slipped over to the door and attached a device to the code input area. The device, a codebreaker that a dying man had given him years ago, took less than three seconds to display the required digits. Darius was in.

***

Lady Patricia Hollellster slowly sipped her Kinpo from the crystal glass. Sparkly purple in colour and icy to the touch, as Kinpo served properly should be. It hummed audibly. Just one note that went on until it was consumed. Heated to ninety degrees and then stored for thirty hours ensured the fruity taste was perfectly exploited. Expensive and civilised, it was a drink she felt suited her, though at that moment she wasn't sure she felt all that civilised. She watched Reed as he sat there, his eyes seemingly watching everything, but she could never pin their focus down.

"I *can't* stall the Viscount much longer, Reed," she told him, honestly. "He doesn't want to do anything but he feels he's being trapped into taking action, and I can understand why."

"Lady…"

"It's *Pat, please*," she reminded him. In the company of others, it was only proper that he addressed her by her title, but in private…

"My agent has arrived," he smiled reassuringly. "I promise you, she's highly competent and if anyone can solve this it's her." He sounded *so confident*, but in his mind he knew he was gambling.

"*Satiah*," she recalled, thinking about it. He nodded before elegantly sipping his drink. "I'm no expert, you understand, and correct me if I'm wrong by all means, *but*… she did not look pleased to see you." Reed shrugged enigmatically.

"Appearances are rarely a sound ground for an *accurate* prediction," he evaded, deftly. "Just look at me and you have your proof on that point." Her eyes narrowed and she pushed her long black wavy hair away from her face.

"Is she your lover?" she asked, a little too bluntly. She almost winced both at her own forwardness, and his reaction. Reed guffawed and spluttered out his drink slightly, apparently completely taken aback by the question. He knew what he had said and done, that might have given her the impression that he and Satiah were more than acquainted, but he'd not expected her to ask him so directly about it. Also, the idea of that happening felt to him like an anomaly within an impossibility.

"No, *certainly not*, no," he stated, chuckling. "She's a wonderful woman, *don't get me wrong… kind, gentle, loving*." This was where being a pathological liar helped Reed greatly. He respected Satiah and would never slur her, assuredly not to her face, but he was *definitely not* romantically attracted to her. And the qualities he was now fraudulently imbuing her with were contemptibly preposterous. He could just imagine her expression if she heard him! A kind of charmed indignation. The kind of look she would reserve for someone who had placed a wager on two asteroids, on opposite sides of the galaxy, colliding with each other. And that would be the look he would get if she was having a good day…

"My only reproach, *if it could be called such*, would be that she is headstrong in a way that leaves endearing behind and approaches…" He paused, deliberately allowing her to see himself struggling for the right word. "*Doctrinaire.*"

Pat cursed herself inwardly for betraying her own interest in him. She found herself almost breathless as a muteness closed in around them. Reed sensed it too. Perhaps if he changed the subject tactfully…

"When he does act, what do you think will he do?" Reed asked, softness in his tone. Pat thought about it.

"I… He will reach out for intervention and I think he will ask you first, seeing as you are already nearby," she said.

Reed gave a noncommittal growl.

"And if he is unable to secure it from you he will ask the Union instead," she established, logically.

"I understand *they* have *many interests* here…" Reed mused, indifferently. Then his eyes found hers again. "Only *financial* ones, of course?" She paused.

"You *know* I don't believe this and it's just rumour, but…" Pat sighed. She didn't need to explain further, he'd already guessed her concern.

"You think they may try to use this war to their advantage, to get the Viscount to break off with the Coalition and instead join the Union?" Reed surmised.

"The Union have been interested in this place for a very long time," she told him. It was true; they had, for hundreds of years.

"What is the Viscount's opinion regarding their interest?" Reed queried, seeming to re-evaluate his drink with his eyes.

"He fears change, not just with this, but change in general – and I get the impression he's thinking of relocating," she admitted. Reed's brows shot up.

"Abandon Collgort-Elipsa? Recombine the cities into the ship they once were *and run*?" Reed asked, to be sure.

"Well… *yes*. No one would want to go, but he *does have* the authority and the reason to force the issue," she elaborated. "He doesn't *trust* the Union enough to stay, but he *would* ask them for military assistance."

"If he does *that*, they will move in and may never leave…" Reed muttered. She went quiet. "You do know that, don't you?"

"And the Coalition *would* leave?" she asked, pointedly. They shared another glance.

"I cannot answer that. Not at present, anyway. You are *already* a part of the Coalition though, I know you're concerned about some of your clients but *this war* is more dangerous than *any* potential political ramifications, surely?" Reed countered. "It may not come to *that* anyway: *if we can solve this ourselves*."

"I hope it doesn't," she allowed, fretfully.

"We must continue to delay him, to *defer* the final decision by any means possible," Reed advised, as he had before.

"All his other advisors are pushing him for his verdict already…" she sighed, standing and moving over to the window. A gap in the clouds beneath them revealed the restless oceans below. Reed joined her there and followed her gaze.

"Tell him you're conducting your own investigation and he should base his ultimate judgement on it," Reed advised, strongly, "and that if he values you at all, *he should wait*." They made meaningful eye contact.

***

There is only so much a human mind can take in effectively. Satiah had reached that point. After three hours of going over the attack, she decided to have a bath. Kelvin stood by the door, his bright eyes adding a reddish hue to the candles. The bath was two metres across and three deep, designed for up to four occupants. She left her earpiece in and after adjusting the buoyancy settings, she slid into the water. The gentle bubbles ensured she could stay in an upright position, her head above the surface, with no additional effort on her part. Her long red hair extended out in all directions behind her. She concentrated on her heartbeat, slowing it down more and more as she had been trained to do many years ago. Her pulses in turn decelerated. After the last of the tension had left her body and every muscle was suitably relaxed, she allowed her mind to refocus on the problems. She let out a sigh, for a moment wishing Carl was there with her.

The attack could be split into *three* main events. The arrival, the hit and the departure. Collgort-Elipsa didn't have much in the way of defences; arguably it hadn't needed them... until now. No shields, no sentry drones and no battle ships. Satiah couldn't believe they were still alive. So... Out of, for want of a better phrase, *nowhere*, twenty fighters and four cruisers had appeared. They had arrived together, without warning, as you would expect for a standard hit-and-run operation. The first thing that Collgort-Elipsa did, within seconds, was transmit the details of their neutrality. Again, standard procedure, nothing unusual. The traditional warning message, known *affectionately* although not *formally*, as *the desister*.

Desist, this is a neutral power, code 776244/2213, desist all hostile action immediately. Desist.

That was when everything *stopped* being the usual in that they didn't *stop* at all. Firstly, there was no response from the attackers. While there was nothing uncommon in that, this time it proved to be a sinister sign. *The hit*. The fighters moved in, targeting the closest floating city. It was nearly thirty seconds before the bombing run was completed. Much damage was done and several people were killed. The most interesting thing about it, in Satiah's mind at least, was that the fighters, despite being on a bombing run, did not assume any *recognisable* formation. They were all clearly Shintu fighters, the design and the emblems were beyond dispute. The dark blue cross was there on all craft for anyone to see. Some efforts to conceal the designs had been made, but nowhere near enough, which in itself was strange.

Almost like they were *supposed* to be seen… *supposed* to be identified.

Lastly, once the crime had been committed, they all retreated into space and vanished. A clear act of aggression, one would say. Yet it was *too small*, Satiah realised. Had that *really* been the navy of that planet attacking, they could and most likely would have done much more damage. There would have been nothing to stop them, certainly. In what circumstances would you commence a bombing run on a defenceless target out of formation? To confuse the opposition? Possibly. But in this case there was no opposition. Granted, they may not have known that before they started, but Satiah had another theory. They didn't bother with a formation simply because they knew they didn't need one. Or maybe, if Reed was *right*, because they didn't know which formation to form as they were not actually Shintu forces at all. Someone pretending to be the Shintu navy had conducted the raid.

Reed had provided the correspondence between him and Shintu command. The diplomatic response Shintu gave, after being accused of the aggressive act, was a very long winded and drawn out way of saying basically: *huh?* The trouble was, it was a denial and a denial that sounded like a million other denials issued throughout history. As a consequence, everyone had been reluctant to believe it. Then the counter accusations began where Shintu accused the Vinu forces of staging the attack and so on and so forth. Satiah yawned. All of this was as stupid as the reason for the outbreak of the war. Wars like this shouldn't be *her* business. They were started by idiots about things that really shouldn't matter and guess who suffered? She sighed, realising she was starting to sound, in her own mind, like a student protester. The cynicism returned. What are a few innocent lives when you're making so much money? Costly was her immediate answer to that.

So… onto the next problem. Now that she'd decided to adopt the mind-set that there was a third party interfering, how was she supposed to figure out who they were? Who would gain from a prolonged war? What were the gains? Money? Non-existent border control? Too vague. Her mind wandered back to the gold issue and… her gut tensed. Gold. Gold was significant in this matter in some way. Collgort-Elipsa was a rich world and they had great gold reserves. She gave Randal a call and smiled as she visualised his enraged countenance. He answered.

"*Yes!*" he snapped, clearly preoccupied.

"Found the gold yet?" she asked, grinning.

"No," he retorted. "I have *five* ships out looking for it. Did you have a reason for calling, apart from annoying me?"

"As you would expect, I *have* a mission-related matter to discuss with you, I know how valuable your time is," she mewed, sarcastically.

"Spit it out then," he muttered.

"The gold that we stole from the pirates, whose was it?" she asked, curious. "*Originally*, I mean."

"Didn't I tell you?" he asked.

"Probably," she admitted, careless.

"*Polvine Limited*, a legitimate business..." he began.

"I wonder... where are they based?" she cut in, a theory in her mind.

"...*Collgort-Elipsa*," he said, also seeing the link. "*Well spotted, Satiah.*"

"*And* the gold was initially stolen by pirates at coordinates 8433-1098," she went on, thinking about it. "That's not a million light years from 8433-1116... *where Milo's ship was found.*"

"*Who?*" he asked, baffled. "I still need to read your case file."

She disconnected. All this was starting to hint at pirate involvement. If pirates *had* faked the attack, it would explain why they didn't adopt a formation. One question still remained though: why? The gold seemed to be intrinsic to this for some reason. And Randal still hadn't retrieved it. And what if pirates *had* got Milo? If *that* was true, Darius was nowhere near him. It all seemed to be a bit confused. There was too much going on, abduction, theft *and* military imitation? She slid out of the water and began to towel herself dry. She favoured that over the air blaster units which she felt made far too much noise. She eyed Kelvin.

"Have you finalised your map yet?" she asked, expectantly.

"Yes." She smiled.

"I'm going on an excursion tonight. You know? To see some

more of the city?" she explained, grinning smugly. She knew no one could overhear her but she still couldn't help using euphemisms. "If Reed, Darius or Rainbow call me, patch them through. Anyone else can get lost. It's time to find this woman again. I *know* she's connected to the pirates but I don't know exactly *how*. She was going to run with that gold, I'm certain of *that*. She came equipped, she had a plan. The only thing that stopped her was a contingency she could never have expected. *Me*."

"I have her profile but I'm awaiting access codes," he said. She thought about that. They, as in Phantom command, *knew* who she was but she wasn't for open operative viewing. That did *not* bode well.

"Okay well... when you get in, let me know. I think I'm going to need everything I can get on her," Satiah mused, pulling on some fresh clothes.

"There is a chance she may have already departed," he stated.

"Agreed, then I will find whoever it was she came to see... assuming they are still alive."

***

The detention area, as convention dictated, was in one of the deepest and most central parts of the base. Darius had procured himself a uniform but still did his best to avoid the cameras. He passed by some troops on patrol, doing his best to seem completely normal – 'normal' being immensely disinterested in everything going on around him. His subterfuge was to arrive in the security area with a set of newly tested replacement lights. He would proceed to replace the lights in the corridor outside the cells. Whilst there, he would take the opportunity to learn the identities of all prisoners. The lift took him down to the deepest level and the doors opened. It was exactly how Darius expected a prison block to be. Grey, cold and quiet.

He held the box under his arm, and took surreptitious glances at the doors he went past. Cell numbers, no names, as predicted. He entered the main security cabin where two men lounged in the seats.

"Morning," Darius grunted, nonchalant. "Light replacements are here. Where do you want me to start?" The two men glanced at one another, clearly perplexed. They would be, seeing as no one had ordered anything of the sort.

"Sure…" answered one, sitting up. He was going for the communicator on the desk in front of him. Presumably he was going to check up on this, as he rightly should. Darius dumped the box heavily on the table with one hand, partly to distract them – then, with the other, drew his pistol and stunned them both. They collapsed to the floor. Darius checked all the screens, camera eye views of corridors, to see if anyone had been alerted. Ironically, the main surveillance area was not itself under artificial scrutiny. To be fair, this was not unusual.

Darius moved quickly. There would be no need to install *any* lights at all if he could get a list of inmates from the computer. Fortunately all the logs were open already, as the two men probably always kept them so for ease of access. Sloppy, but Darius could understand that such a mistake was made by human nature. There were over three hundred cells: three hundred and twenty, to be exact. Darius scanned through the names of the inmates. Annoyingly, there were *seven* individuals that were listed as *unnamed*. And another possibility occurred to him: they might be using a false name to hide the fact that they were illegally holding a Coalition citizen! He then called up images of the prisoners themselves, mugshots, and compared them to the image of Milo that he had on his computer. Most of these men and women seemed to be captured Shintu soldiers. There were two deserters of the Vinu forces awaiting court martial too, a few reporters who'd probably wandered into classified areas.

The prisoners with no names were suspected spies but their identities couldn't be established, and… none of them looked anything like Milo. Disappointed, Darius tried to think of somewhere else to look. The transmission *had* come from that moon, that was beyond doubt. That didn't mean it had been them who'd captured Milo though. Someone might have beaten them to it. The messages had been laughably easy to hear, after all. He tied up the two men capably as he thought about his next move. He knew he couldn't stay there, not for long. Was it not possible that Milo was somehow special to the command here? They *had* contacted him individually so they certainly knew he existed. Special enough not to be held with the other detainees? Then: where and why? No time, he had to get out.

He debated whether or not to take the lights with him. Deciding that he should, he exited the cabin, and headed back towards the lift.

The doors opened as he arrived and an officer stepped out. Darius, without missing a beat, saluted as he went past. The officer nodded to him in response to the typical greeting. The doors closed and Darius vanished as the officer reached the cabin. He glanced in the glass window but could see no one on duty. Scowling at the apparent breach of regulations, he tried to access the cabin, only to find his code was rejected. Even the override code failed to get the door to move. Fishing out his communicator with one hand, he thumped on the door with the other.

"*Henry!*" he bayed, irritated. "What the *hell* do you think you're doing? What if I had been the Captain?" He listened hard and thought he could hear something but wasn't sure what. A muffled cry or something. That wasn't right! Taking a chance, he pulled out his pistol and blasted the door open, setting off several alarms. He entered cautiously, gun first. The room was apparently empty, but when he rounded the control desk, he found the operators tied up and trying to wriggle free. Swearing under his breath he made a call.

"Put me through..." he began. He was interrupted, however, by the woman he was trying to reach.

"Lieutenant, you'd better have a damn good reason for shooting open that door," she stated, coolly.

"Base Colonel," he breathed, in relief. "*We have an intruder.* Maybe more than one!" He explained the situation.

A new klaxon sounded and red lights began flashing. An automatic computer began speaking.

"This base is now in lockdown stage one, all non-essential personnel report to your assembly points," it said.

"Untie them and report to your station," the base colonel ordered, her voice serious now. "What did he look like?"

"He was a private – at least, he was wearing a private's uniform and his hat was down over his eyes, he was carrying a..." he went on, trying to remember, "... a box full of replacement lights or something. He'd locked the door and..." He pressed for the lift but the controls didn't respond.

"He's also apparently jammed the lift somehow," he stated, guessing.

"All right, I'm sending an engineer," she stated, calm still. "I'll want to see your statement and those of the men assaulted as soon as possible."

Darius had still been in the elevator on his way up when the alarm had gone off. He'd known since he'd entered the cabin that it had only been a matter of time. At that moment he was more irritated by his failure to locate Milo than he was in his own discovery. As the lift reached the floor that he'd originally entered it on, he took the time to ensure it didn't move from where it now was. The door to the cabin had given him a few seconds' head start; the lift might also contribute to this lead. Then, still playacting, he walked along, a bemused expression on his face as a few people started appearing from office doorways. Then the lockdown was declared and bulkhead doors began sealing the entrances. He rubbed his moustache thoughtfully as he placed the box of lights on the floor. He was effectively trapped in the corridor.

His stolen uniform would no longer help him, he felt sure, and he decided he had maybe thirty seconds before someone monitoring the cameras spotted him. He couldn't chance opening the bulkhead door. He probably could get it open but it would only attract attention faster. Pulling a silver tube from his belt, he activated it. The explosives he had left outside went off together. The first was some distance from the main gate, where he had lain in wait. The second was the one inside the inner fence, the one he'd tossed away on his approach to the vehicle area. These two he hoped would be a big enough distraction for him to get away without being noticed. The computer promptly declared lockdown stage two and, much to his delight, all the doors began to open as the computer now thought that either he had already made it outside, or the base was under attack.

In either case, sealed doors were not much help to the defence efforts. This being the case, protocol had demanded they be unlocked again, and the computer had obliged. Everyone was dashing around now and he joined the organised chaos that had been mobilised. He managed to return to the vehicle area, only to find his trojan horse had already gone. It was going to be another long wait. He slid into a maintenance hatch on the wall and sat there in the darkness. He would wait for them all to calm down, which could take days. Then he would escape the same way he'd entered... he hoped.

In the meantime, he would report his failure to Satiah.

***

The security guard crushed the stub end of her smokie under her boot as she blew out the last lungful of rehydrated carboxide, the healthy alternative to the regular variety. The lime scented smoke rose, vanishing through the metal grid walkway above her. Gloved fingers slid through the gaps and silently eased the grid up and out of its aperture. Satiah peered down from the darkness above, her face expressionless.

"*Cat!*" yelled someone, from somewhere nearby. "We're done!"

"*About time,*" grumbled the guard, as she marched off. Satiah landed softly behind her and then hurried down the corridor. She had intended to enter the security room via the ceiling but the ventilation was not wide enough for her to get through. As a result she'd been forced to await the hallway to be clear of guards. Luckily they changed shifts regularly and were far from diligent. On a world where the last crime occurred outside of living memory, their complacency was hardly unexpected.

The door was *unlocked!* She entered the office. There were chairs but it was unoccupied. Completely automated, machines left in charge, she shook her head. Apathy at its most subtle, Satiah thought of it as the slippery slope of defeat. She sat before the main terminal, wondering how far she could get before anyone noticed her. She began to review the footage from that day. She wasn't even asked for an access code! Never before had she known such a compliant security system. She found the woman on the walkway quickly and then tracked her progress through the complex until she identified the ship she had arrived in. She had arrived a while *after* Satiah had, nearly two hours. Satiah then returned to the initial footage she had reviewed of the woman when she was back on the walkway, and endeavoured to see where she went.

The records ended there and she was unable to trace the woman's next movements. It seemed a number of footage data cubes were blank. Just empty. Satiah wondered at that. A technical fault? Most unlikely. Sabotage? Possible. The woman herself could have done it, though it seemed more plausible that someone else already working there had instead. Perhaps the person she came to see? It could be a simple case of bribery or intimidation but Satiah felt it went deeper than that. The missing gold surely implied she had an established contact on the planet somewhere. Probably someone working for the company. It was clear though that she could learn nothing more from the footage. Disconnecting and disappointed, Satiah crept back out again just before the next guard arrived. At last, once back in a place where she was allowed to be, she made her way to the commercial landing area. Bay seven.

Upon reaching the bay, instead of going straight towards her target ship, she took a circuitous route via a walkway overlooking the hulls of the craft. It was highly likely that her target, now she knew she was there, was on the lookout for her. Maintenance teams were at work, but no one paid her any attention as she paced by casually. There it was... The ship was advanced, although the bodywork showed signs of damage. Recent damage. As she passed by, Satiah casually dropped a homing device over the railing. It fastened itself onto the hull silently and discreetly. Once out of sight, she checked she was receiving its signal. She was. Now she could track that ship anywhere it went so long as the device wasn't discovered and removed. As she was watching, a supply cart, driven by an android arrived and the ramp of the ship began to slide down.

And there she was again... Purella strolled down the ramp, now dressed in a purple version of the same dress she'd worn before. Still gloved and now sporting a pistol on her hip. Satiah slid on the glasses again, this time to get intel on anyone *with* the woman. She would have associates, possibly even more dangerous than herself, to be considered.

"Well?" Purella addressed the android.

"As requested," it replied. Satiah strained her ears. Supplies, food by the look of it, were unloaded by the metal hands of the android. Purella, and two men who came out to assist her, began carrying them aboard.

Purella checked everything, both the items and the cost. Bavon had at least provided the extra food she had needed for Quint's prisoner. Her main worry was the fuel, not only was it the most expensive thing, but Bavon could make things difficult for her if he messed up the amount. A movement at the corner of her eye made her look up at the walkway. No one. She felt she was starting to get twitchy and decided she'd stayed in one place for too long.

"Get us ready," she ordered, to the nearest of her two assistants. "Twenty minutes." He nodded as he vanished up the ramp.

A clunk from the shadows made Purella spin around instinctively. Nothing. While Purella was looking the other way, Satiah slipped inside an unwatched storage crate. Shaking her head at her own anxiety, Purella marched back on board the ship. They would be ready to go in minutes. How long was she going to have to look after this guy for Quint? And why wasn't he talking either to her or, apparently, to Bavon? Satiah, standing next to a large replacement fuel cell, gritted her teeth in the constricted space she'd lodged herself. There was a jolt as the android moved the container up the ramp. Satiah let out a groan as, without padding, she was sandwiched painfully against the fuel cell. Then she got a call from Kelvin.

"Not a wonderful moment," she growled.

"It's Darius," he said.

"Patch him through," she gasped, in relief. The fuel cell was leaning against the wall now instead of her, always a relief.

"Satiah, I'm on the moon. There's a *Vinu* military base here that I have *infiltrated*. I'm still inside *now* and will have to wait a while before I can get out. I checked all the *prisoners* they have here and guess what?" he asked, sounding grim.

"No Milo?" she grumbled, seriously.

"Spot on," he said. "It may be as long as a day before I can leave here."

"Shame," she replied, without meaning it. There was a pause.

"How are things going for you?" he asked, as she knew he would.

"I'm starting to think pirates are involved," she said, honestly.

"If pirates took him, wouldn't there be more damage?" he asked, reasonably. He still didn't know about the second half of the mission yet and she still hadn't made up her mind whether she should tell him or not. And while they couldn't rule out pirate involvement in Milo's disappearance, it was at the unlikely end of the spectrum of explanations. Plus, Darius was right about his ship being almost completely undamaged.

"You *said* he wasn't on the base," she replied, levelly.

"Not *now* no, he may have been brought here *originally* though," he stated, the hint of impatience creeping into his voice.

"What do you want to do?" she asked, unsure what else to say. She had no idea where else to turn now. Her own clue, the picture of the woman, had been no help at all and now Darius had apparently drawn a blank too.

"...I want you to tell me what you're really doing?" he asked, brazenly. Of course, the inevitable challenge, Satiah would have done the same.

"Well, if you *really* must know, I'm hiding in a crate next to a fuel cell," she quipped.

"*Satiah*... If we work *together*, we might actually get somewhere," he said, shortly. It was clear that he did not believe her (ironically enough!) truthful account.

"We *are* working together," she whispered back, more harshly than she intended. "Things are just a little inconvenient right now."

"Then why even bother to answer me?" he asked, astutely. "Is it about *the ambassador*?" He was seeking the truth and, in a roundabout way, he wasn't that far off.

"*Sort of.* Look, if it's all the same to you, I will get back to you soon," she replied, vaguely. The fact that Reed was behind Dyss *didn't mean* that Dyss wasn't justified in his suspicion of Darius.

"You do that," he responded curtly, and cut off. She gritted her teeth, frustrated.

"You're planning on sneaking aboard her ship?" Kelvin asked, in her ear. His voice made her jump marginally.

"Yes... I want to know *who* she's working for and I doubt a tracking device will be enough this time," Satiah answered. "I don't know if she's involved in the attack on this planet but I *know* she was involved with Randal's missing gold. So I'm sure I'll get *something* out of this." There was a jolt as her crate was lifted up and conveyed into the storage area. She could hear the clacking sound of the machine doing the lifting. She tensed as the cell nearly crashed into her when the crate stopped moving.

"Reed will wonder where you are," Kelvin reminded.

"Tell him I'm checking out security at border control," she remarked. "Get me the intel on those guys I sent you, they are most likely aboard too and I want to know who I'm dealing with." She cut him off before he could answer.

She could hear the sound of a drive roaring into life. They would be moving soon. Satiah wondered about why Purella was going. Was she leaving because of Satiah? It wasn't inconceivable. Satiah knew there was a good chance that the answer may lie in among the cargo. She knew they had already completed their inventory and so would be unlikely to revisit the cargo until shortly before or even after arrival. She didn't know how long the journey would take as she didn't know the destination, but Satiah hoped it would be long enough for her to get a good look. She forced the lid open as quietly as possible to peer out. Darkness. She half crawled, half climbed out and stood there, her stance wide. The craft was moving now and could jolt unexpectedly.

She pulled out the glasses again and adjusted to night vision mode. A light was always a good thing to have but she didn't want anything tipping off Purella that someone was rooting around amongst her cargo. A torch flash, no matter how carefully deployed, might be picked up on the cameras. She was standing in an aisle, for want of a better phrase, between rows and rows of crates. The craft shuddered a little but now that she could see, Satiah was not so worried about balance. She approached the first crate and opened it carefully. Bottles, three rows of five. She picked the closest one out and read the label. A fine wine. There was no way she could determine if it really was wine or not without tasting it, but she was prepared to assume that it was. This belief was reinforced by the food that she came across in the next crate. Supplies. Good quality supplies, but nonetheless, nothing incriminating.

Data cubes, energy packs, power packs, laser pistols... She paused and examined one. Standard in quality and prone to sight realignment issues if she remembered correctly. New clothing, military in style. Again nothing illegal, *per se*... assuming all licences and permits were there. She didn't think they would be, but a little gunrunning didn't bother her. She was seeking something far more insidious. She checked the garb more closely, wondering if it might belong to the forces of the current war. No... all blank. Of course, the moment they were altered it may reduce their usefulness. Say, if operations against both sides had been planned, it made sense to avoid the detail of the uniforms and rely on more obvious signs. It would then cost much less to switch sides and maybe even help to conceal your own identity, should you be suspected of not being the usual enemy.

That last crate contained the strangest thing of all. Satiah, with practised expertise, prised it open in such a way that it could be closed again with little evidence that it had been tampered with. Inside was... a gemstone. A type unfamiliar to her. It was almost as clear as a straightforward crystal, except for the faintest of orange tints. She strained her eyes, trying to make out more detail. What was *that* all about? A crate full of them would be what she would expect, not just one on its own. There were no others, and there was nothing about the crate that indicated what was inside or what its properties were. No warning signs, nothing. Unwilling, but too curious to stop herself, Satiah reached in and poked it gingerly. It was smooth, cold and ... well, exactly what she expected it would be.

She picked it up and inspected it more carefully. It was lighter than she anticipated, about the size of her palm, rhombus shaped. As she ran her finger down the edge, endeavouring to see how sharp it was, the orange tinge seemed to get brighter in time with her movement. She stopped; concerned the light might give her away. It faded away again instantly, looking the same as it had before. She waited a few seconds and then repeated the action. If she ran her finger down the edge from tip to tip, the orange light grew brighter and brighter. It resembled a ball of light, somewhere in its core, suspended there by forces unseen. She stared into its depths, trying to understand what it was she was looking at. To begin with, she thought it was her own imagination or a trick of the light, but gradually the light evened out and formed a shape. That shape then became a pale orange translucent image... of her own face.

That was when Satiah naturally presumed, as most people would, that it was simply her reflection. Until it started smiling. She wasn't smiling. She realised she was feeling very calm suddenly. The image stopped smiling and stared back. Satiah wasn't sure how long this went on for, several minutes at last. A faint noise came to her ears and she froze instinctively. It sounded like a faraway voice calling...

many voices all talking in complete synchronicity. The mouth of the image was opening in time with it, like it was trying to talk to her.

"Satiah? *Satiah?*" it called, invitingly. A shiver of primal terror went right up her spine and all the tiny hairs on the back of her neck stood on end. She replaced the stone back in its crate and slammed the lid shut, breathing hard. Mercifully... the voice was silenced. She made herself calm down, taking stock of her environment; she was in no immediate danger. Everything was exactly how it had been before she set eyes on that... that *stone*. *What was it?*

She sent everything she had recorded with the glasses to Kelvin. Someone surely would be able to explain it... she was at a loss. Regardless... what was it doing on this ship? And again, why just one?

"Talk?" Kelvin asked, in her ear.

"Yes..." she murmured, and then cleared her throat. "*Yes*, now is good," she stated, more clearly. "What have you got?"

"The woman, the one from the walkway. Her name is Purella; the delay was because for the last three years she was presumed dead and her record had been archived accordingly. She was presumed dead because she was a member of the Varn-Utto." Satiah let out a breath and ran a hand through her hair, stressed.

The Varn-Utto had been one of the most powerful criminal organisations in recent history. Named after two of its founding members, it had been operating for nearly twenty years. They became so powerful that they had been the force behind several governments and planets throughout the cosmos. That was until about three years ago... Satiah had not been involved, but she had heard all about it. A Phantom operation had brought the organisation down in a brutal and almost unprecedented way. Of all the history of Phantoms Squad jobs, this operation ranked third on the highest enemy death count tables. The Phantoms had infiltrated the organisation and, although it took nearly a year, managed to get all its leaders and major players in one place. By the time it was over, more than twenty-four thousand people had been assassinated by Phantom agents. Apparently, however, they had missed one...

It had not been completely one way; about seven Phantoms had died in the fight too. Most were killed by a prearranged explosion. Purella was obviously missed somehow... maybe she wasn't important enough to have been there. It didn't matter! She was indeed an *extremely* dangerous woman.

"You there?" Kelvin enquired.

"Yes," she replied, steeling herself. "What about her associates?"

"They are known mercenaries, but there is nothing special about either of them," Kelvin answered. "It is not known if they have worked together before."

"Best to assume they have," she muttered, as much to herself as to him. "Anything else?"

"This footage you have just entered…" He paused, he actually paused! It happened so rarely that Satiah realised he was going through literally everything he had, to understand what he was looking at.

"How did you feel while it was happening? What was your *emotional* state?" he asked, at last. To be honest, she had started to expect that.

"Curious, perplexed… *and then frightened*," she admitted. She wasn't generally ashamed to admit being scared, especially to him. "It was the voice that did it for me, I was anxious and then that pushed me over the edge."

"What voice?"

She frowned, concerned. "You didn't hear the voice calling my name?" she queried, starting to worry. Had she hallucinated it?

"There was a sound detected but it's not easy to identify. A high-pitched moan that was quiet. My initial readings suggest *an infant* or possibly a *feline animal* noise," Kelvin told her. "A primal distress call or attention-seeking plea to acquire the support of another. *Specifically, a parent.*"

"Are you saying it was *asking for its mummy?*" Satiah growled, very uncomfortable suddenly. She did not like the sound of this.

"Or its father," Kelvin answered, dispassionately. Being a robot, he didn't have her unsettling subconscious evocations. Lucky for him. "It's clear whatever you did caused it to interact with your mind. Also, it started when you began touching it. So we can logically assume that proximity may not factor in this, only direct touch."

"*What is it?*" she asked, sourly.

"It's not matching anything in my database, as far as my records are concerned *this is a new substance.*" She sighed in defeat.

"Brilliant."

***

Ten years ago, in a place called the Hellion.

The catacombs were completely black, impossible even to see a hand before your eyes. Every sound seemed changed. Unnatural.

"Fifty paces," grunted someone. The man in the white mask led the way, despite having never been there before. The mask was flat and seamless. It was face shaped but, aside from the nose, there was nothing obvious there for the mouth or the eyes. In the sand, under their feet, things cracked and crunched. Broken bones of those long dead littered the floors, to be crushed or shattered underfoot. Unburied, unremembered and now almost unnoticed. Ahead, a faint flicker of light was detected by eyes both organic and mechanical. As the light got closer a sound began. A sound of chanting. The path, marked by a few flaming torches, led downwards for a considerable distance.

***

Present day.

The alarms had fallen silent nearly two hours ago but Darius remained where he was. He intended to give them as long as was comfortable to calm down. Satiah was clearly up to something, the question was only if Dyss was behind it or not. Darius had realised his obsessive focus on Dyss may have blinded him to Satiah having her own agenda. Regardless of the explanation, she had not wanted to tell him exactly what she was doing. For now he'd go on as he had already. Play it by the book. Satiah was considering pirates as a viable option in this investigation. Pirate activity was indeed rife. It was a war zone, after all! Yet Darius remained convinced the answer lay in the military. They *knew* Milo existed, hell, one of them had spoken with him personally and was intending to rendezvous with him. From the start it had been their strongest lead and most probable explanation. Annoyingly this did not rule out pirates. Neither did the fact that there were no signs of a fight on the ship. That sedative he had found, however, did hint that someone had been drugged.

His communicator went off and he stared down in astonishment as it was Dyss calling him. The last time they had spoken had been months ago and it had been a conversation made up of yes's, no's and maybes. Wary but inquisitive, Darius answered.

"Yes?" he said, remembering to keep his voice down.

"*Darius…* I'm trying to get through to Satiah but having no luck. I want an update on the operation and have heard nothing since I sent her to find you," he stated, staying professional. The short-lived silence told Darius all he needed to know… but was it supposed to do that? Had that pause been premeditated? Created only to give an impression of a non-existent emotional state to mislead.

"We have examined the ship and are chasing a few leads," Darius rattled off, keeping it nebulous. In reality, he recognised he knew very little more than that himself. Satiah was ostensibly keeping everyone in the dark, not just him. "I know she's going to have talks with the Coalition Ambassador of Collgort-Elipsa. Maybe *that's why* she's not answering."

"I see…" Dyss answered, deep in thought. "Is he still alive, do you think?" He was asking about Milo. That was a question Darius could answer and had no reason to hide.

"No idea." That was the short answer. Darius went on. "We're miles outside the ninety-minute window now but that is no fault of Satiah's."

Darius couldn't resist throwing that one in. It had been *because of Dyss* that they had both been delayed twenty-four hours before they could even start investigating the abandoned ship.

"I take it you're being pressurised by Milo's family?" Darius asked, unable to stop himself smirking.

"…No," Dyss admitted, coldly. "Thankfully dealing directly with them is not down to me. I was just curious."

"We are doing everything we can," Darius offered, convincingly. It was the kind of line any authority figure could throw out that would cover most scenarios.

Darius was secretly concerned now and not about Milo or even himself. Satiah had answered *him* when he had called. She'd answered *personally*. If she and Dyss were in cahoots why would she refuse to speak to Dyss? This was of course assuming that Dyss wasn't lying. Bearing in mind that he loathed Darius and would do anything to avoid interacting with him, this seemed doubtful. This indicated to Darius that something might have happened to Satiah.

"Very well, carry on," Dyss said, and terminated the call. Darius decided it was time he got out of there. He peered out from his hiding place into the vehicle area. They were back and once again in inactive mode. He slipped out, cautious of anyone standing around. There was no one. He slipped back onto the same area he'd been on before and sighed. It would be sometime before it was used again but when it was he'd ride it out of the camp and slip away into the jungle.

***

The *Dreadnaught* was an old ship. Its paint faded, its hull dented and scratched, it spoke of better days. Purella eyed it as they got closer. She had never known it to look new, as it had been old when she had first found it almost a decade ago. It must have had a name at some point, most ships did. She had called it 'the *Dreadnaught*'. She was not a particularly creative or nostalgic person, nor was she prone to anthropomorphise *things*. Sentimentality was for the weak. And Purella did not see herself as weak. Nevertheless that ship, the *Dreadnaught*, belonged to her and her alone. It was her home. Even her crew were left in no uncertain terms in regard to that reality. A coded message reached her and she replied in kind. It was always good to know who was who.

Most of the people who acted as her crew she had known for years and had proven their loyalty to her. Even when it had all ended... that black day nearly three years ago. For Purella it might as well have been yesterday. And there would be a reckoning, she had no doubt of that. She landed her personalised shuttle in the main hangar area and stood.

"Begin unloading the cargo," she ordered, to the man behind her. "I want to move on in less than an hour." He nodded and went out ahead of her. She went down the ramp into the hangar area beyond.

Another man was waiting for her there. He was tall, obviously muscular in a way that his clothes did not hide, and dressed in a standard military bodysuit. His hair was thick, neat and white in colour despite his apparent youth. He stood there, hands clasped behind his back, rigid, as if he genuinely was a military man.

"Major Clyde," Purella smiled, agreeably. "Any updates?" They shook hands formally and then she passed him the money Bavon had given her.

"Nothing to report," he replied nonchalantly. "Bavon will be contacting the pirates soon. They *may* reveal where they have the taken the gold, *assuming it was them who have taken it*. It's all set up if you wish to listen in."

"We both will," she said, after briefly thinking about it. It was always good to keep one eye on someone like Bavon. Someone who might cut and run at any time.

"Did you get in contact with Quint?" Clyde asked, walking alongside her.

"...No," she admitted, a little cross. "I don't understand *why* he has fallen silent. Bavon paid me though, so it's not my problem."

"And the prisoner?" Clyde asked, interested.

"Strangely clueless on that front," she replied, thinking about it. "I know Bavon is only a middleman but I'm undecided as to why Quint didn't even tell *him* who it is. How is he?"

"Still eating," Clyde smirked, remembering something. "He's not said a word."

"*Makes a change*," she muttered, sarcastically. He'd not uttered a word to *anyone* since they'd captured him. They walked along the badly maintained corridors together.

The walls were dusty, dirty, and damaged here and there. The floor panelling was dented, and in some places corroded. Purella was saving up the Essps for a renovation team. Despite its looks though, all the technology on board was the latest and most reliable. They reached what used to be the command deck. Early on in her ownership, because of her lifestyle, Purella had reengineered the ship so that it required only one person to pilot it, as opposed to the sixteen it would have needed before. There was a room to the side that they both entered. The room was empty apart from two seats, which were placed before a vast screen – a screen on which she could do practically anything.

"Drink?" offered Clyde. She nodded as she began setting up the channels. Bavon, being the fool he was, only ever used one of two frequencies. This meant that no matter how much encryption he used, she could easily find the correct signal. She set up the system and waited. Clyde sat next to her and handed her the drink he had prepared, while sipping his own. They sat there for nearly half an hour.

"I don't remember him being *this late* before," Clyde noted, concerned. Purella was thinking about the woman, perhaps she was responsible for the delay somehow. She might be quizzing him on the staged attack. Purella informed Clyde about the woman.

"Have you told Quint?" he asked, levelly. He was starting to count the money carefully.

"Not yet," she replied, shrugging. "I'm not sure where he is, he's not responding. Allegedly Bavon can't get hold of him either." It was all starting to look rather worrying.

Their tête-à-tête ended abruptly when, at last, Bavon contacted the pirates. Clyde adjusted the sound, ensuring white noise and feedback was cut to the minimum.

"Do not use this frequency *again*," warned a gravelly voice. Purella frowned, this was a stranger to her and that meant it was a stranger to Bavon too. She'd listened in on tens of these interchanges before.

"Who are you? Where's Visvenvar?" demanded Bavon, pompously. Purella winced, knowing what would come next. Visvenvar was the name of the leading pirate. *The boss* essentially.

"*Do not use names!*" hissed the voice, in reprimand. Purella had expected that. Bavon was an idiot.

"It's *encrypted!*" protested Bavon, irritated. "No one can hear us." Purella and Clyde exchanged glances. "I want to speak to your boss."

"He's not here, you can speak to me," retorted the man, standing no nonsense. Purella was impressed; this man seemed unusually efficient for a pirate.

"I'm not going to do that until I know who you are?" Bavon objected, petulantly. Clyde shook his head, not at all impressed.

"I'm Kyle," he responded, quickly. Too quickly: it was a lie, though codenames were normally a given. How they'd made it this far without anyone else working out who was who was a miracle. "I'm his deputy."

"It's about the gold..." Bavon began.

"We don't have the gold anymore, it was stolen," Kyle stated, without preamble. There was a stunned silence on the other end. Well, there was a silence that was supposed to be stunned. Bavon was pretending he hadn't known they no longer had it. Purella sighed, maybe he wasn't *completely* useless.

"Then I shall expect compensation," Bavon responded, as anyone would.

"Yes, you can expect what you like," Kyle replied, levelly. "You won't get anything back though. And you won't try to force us either. Not unless you want us to expose all the other things we have been doing for you and whoever you work for." Another silence. Again, Purella and Clyde looked at one another. Things were going exactly as Purella had anticipated so far.

"This is *not over*," Bavon said, trying to sound tough. "We will overlook it for now. *We have something else to discuss.*"

"Another attack?" guessed Kyle, astutely.

"Correct," Bavon answered.

"Where and who this time?" Kyle enquired.

"This time we want the attack to come from *Vinupisha*, not from Shintumpa. Collgort-Elipsa is once again the target – pick another city this time. Same as before," Bavon instructed. Purella leaned forward in her chair. Bavon didn't call those kinds of shots, *Quint* did. Therefore, either Quint *had* been in touch with Bavon recently, or else Bavon had been lying.

"Have *any* additional defences been installed?" Kyle asked, sensibly. As they had been attacked, it made sense that next time they would not just be able to waltz in and start shooting like last time. For one thing, they may even be expected.

Since the first attack there had been a lot of heated debates about what kinds of defence to employ. It reignited a lot of past disputes between the pros and cons of a shield-based defence versus laser batteries. With *their* funds, they could easily afford the best of both and make them work, but as usual their tightfistedness had delayed the process. Despite the fact that some of their *own citizens* had been killed, *money* still did the talking, at least at that level. It was a sad fact that governments seldom distanced themselves from financial concerns, even when their own people were suffering.

"Not yet, they're trying but they have had *administrative* difficulties," Bavon told him, pride in his voice. Purella knew that it had all been out of his hands and he was just trying to make himself look more important. Like he was playing the role of a Machiavellian maverick and he was *so good no one else knew*. In reality, it had had very little to do with him.

"If *that* changes you need to let us know," Kyle said, in a tone that broke no argument. "It's my understanding that there were no casualties last time. *Despite* the errors."

"*Errors?*" Bavon probed, instantly alert.

"Not enough time was taken to ensure that the insignias were well hidden enough to look *convincing*. Also, when deployed, the fighters spent nearly ten seconds floating there *like a bunch of crippled escape pods*! It was shoddy and poorly organised. A military operation would *not* have looked like that," Kyle complained, seriously. Purella had to agree, it could have been done a lot better.

"*That* is down to *you*," Bavon dismissed, recovering himself.

"I'm going to need to know what a *normal attack* would look like in order to replicate it *exactly*," Kyle argued. "*You* must supply me with that intel."

"How exactly would you like me to do that?" Bavon scoffed, genuinely scornful.

"Contact the other side, I'm sure *they* would tell you," Kyle chuckled, grimly. Clyde smirked. Another silence descended. Purella wondered how Bavon would acquire that information and whether he would ask *her* to help. She would charge him double, of course. Knowing Bavon, though, he might do something stupid, like make something up himself and pretend it was real. He'd done similar things before when he'd been out of his depth… which was pretty much always.

"I'll do that," Bavon said, disconnecting. Purella ended the recording there.

"I wonder *why* this Kyle has stepped into the game," Clyde muttered. "Not that I'm complaining, but he's not the fool his boss is." Kyle's appearance pointed to a potential change in command. Or at least a role switch. Visvenvar, the pirate leader, was a short-sighted bully. And, just like most bullies, he was a complete coward. He was also stupid and prone to not thinking things through properly on a regular basis. The security around the gold had been laughable. So poor, in fact, that it allowed *two* rival groups to break in successfully to get at it.

"No, he's not," she concurred. Then she smiled sardonically. "Maybe they're going through a little *political upheaval*."

"*Pirates*? Going through a political upheaval? *Not a chance*!" he declared, as if outraged. They glanced at one another and then started to laugh.

***

"There is *still* the chance that it was a genuine mistake which they are too scared to own up to," Reed argued, unwilling to give in. This debate had been going on for hours, but so long as he could keep them all disagreeing with one another, Satiah would have time to find out what was really going on. "And if that *is* the case, it will not be repeated." The Viscount nodded slowly in agreement. Reed was pleased to see he had an open mind. His council however… were not so easy-going.

"Mistakes like that are not *made*! They are planned!" objected one, a particularly belligerent individual who seemed to have something to say about *everything*, and it was never positive. They reminded Reed of a lot of politicians he'd crossed paths with before.

"Not intentionally, no, that's what makes them mistakes," joked someone. Reed chuckled.

Lady Patricia Hollellster remained silent, next to her Viscount, as she observed the ongoing debate. The Viscount had given her four days to investigate. If he waited any longer it would make him look weak, and may even trigger a fight over the throne. For a monarch, he seemed ridiculously young at only nineteen, yet since the age of seven he had been sitting in on business dealings with his father and had a sturdy grasp of the basics of all things political. He was not naïve, not at all. He was, however, rather indecisive, as normally he had plenty of time to make his decisions. Months and even years were the norm… days and hours were hard for him to adjust to.

He paced back and forth, perhaps out of agitation and perhaps out of habit, his long golden-platinum coloured robes swirling around as he moved. His perfectly manicured face was framed by a mane of curly dark brown hair that was held back from over his blue eyes by a shiny white diadem. His eyes spoke of the pressure he was under. He really believed that his planet was under threat, and that he was in political peril too. That would be enough to set most people on edge. His bare feet tapped lightly on the mirror like silver heated plaglell tiles. Plaglell was one of the rarest and consequently most expensive metals. It could only be found in two places in the cosmos. He liked heated tiles, not just his own but in general; he thought they were a true symbol of peace and wealth. Also, they were a comfort as woes besieged him.

Reed had not been shocked, despite pretending to be. Even in the most placid of democracies, the hunger for power always lurked somewhere. No matter the risks or the situation, there always seemed to be *someone* who wanted to take over. Someone who wanted power! Someone who felt they could solve everything! Reed tried not to laugh at the manifold ironies queuing up in his mind. Lady Hollellster had told Reed that she couldn't *publicly* side with him and that it would work better if they appeared to be *against* one another. It was a shrewd play but predictable. Reed knew that not everyone in their government would be stupid enough to fall for such an act, no matter how well played. But so long as the Viscount fell for it…

The Viscount stopped abruptly and everyone else fell silent, as protocol dictated.

"I have much to consider," he said, in a tone that inferred he really didn't. "Leave me." Obediently, the councillors filed out, squabbling quietly among themselves. Reed was glad to see that opinion was still divided. They would be much harder to dismiss were they all under one banner. Once they were gone the Viscount put his head in his hands and sighed heavily.

"Do you have anything for me?" he asked, at last. Pat shrugged and nodded at Reed. The Viscount faced him. Reed smiled a helpless smile.

"It's circumstantial, but we have reason to believe that the attackers were *not* who they looked like," he stated, carefully.

The Viscount did not seem particularly amazed by this revelation.

"I myself theorised that no attacker of this world would be so open, therefore it had to be a trick," he responded, a little tetchy. "This does not help me identify the real culprits. Neither does it help me defend my people."

"Then, there is one thing I can do..." Reed began, as if he was reluctant.

"I do not *want* Coalition naval forces in orbit around this planet," the Viscount objected, tersely. "Our relationship with the Union would be pressurised."

"One moment, Your Majesty," Pat pleaded, reverently. "I believe that Reed was alluding to something else." The Viscount sighed again and waved a hand in an approximation of an apology.

"You must excuse my lack of patience and my bad manners, Reed," he muttered, sadly. "It's been increasingly spiky recently." Reed acknowledged the excuse with a politely raised hand.

"The situation is *most* disagreeable, Your Majesty," Reed smiled, cordially. "I was going to suggest something a little... *risky*."

"*Suggest* what you like," Pat giggled, playing to the role of the Viscount's woman well. The giggle was mocking but within the appropriate boundaries. "Suggestions are *free*, orders and investments are not." It was a cliché... one from *that planet*. Reed was familiar with it.

"You cannot have a ship from the Coalition guarding you, as it might provoke the Union into action," Reed proposed, always so calm and cool. "You cannot have a Union ship there either, same problem in reverse. I'm a friend of President Raykur of the Federation and I'm sure I can persuade him to loan us a ship."

"*The Colonial Federation*," the Viscount mulled, softly.

"Are you sure?" Pat confirmed, seriously this time. "You *know* President Raykur?"

"A little, I have even spoken with the illustrious Admiral Wester too," Reed went on, completely honestly. He *had* spoken with him, although they were hardly friends. Indeed, Wester probably wouldn't even remember him.

"How is President Raykur?" Pat asked, rather pointlessly. It was pointless as everyone knew very well that Raykur had been having medical troubles for a prolonged duration.

"Clinging on to everything *most tenaciously*," smiled Reed, the very soul of understatement. "Despite recent politics however, *thanks to Wester*, he's stronger than he has been in years."

"What would they want in exchange for assisting us?" The Viscount asked, thinking of costs. Reed shrugged.

"I only suggested *them* because the only other option would be to hire your own mercenaries to act as defenders, and I know you would not like that *type* around your society," he responded, dextrously. "Better to rely on someone with a reputation to protect than someone with no reputation at all." Pat winced discreetly and Reed almost chuckled. It was a ridiculous thing to say. Nevertheless, the Viscount didn't really notice. Weighing up options, consequences and potential expenditures: it was rare for any decision of a ruler to be easy.

"There is also that added risk that, *should you hire mercenaries*, they may somehow be involved in the war already and would exploit their position of trust."

"We can at least *talk* to them," prodded Pat, earnestly. "If they refuse, then we know where we are and if they are interested… we can take it from there." Reed winked discreetly at her, in thanks, and silently congratulating her.

"I will take some time to think about this," he said, shuffling towards the door.

"We await your command, Your Majesty," Pat smiled, placidly. The door closed after him. Reed had the profound impression that the Viscount would prefer to discard the room and its remaining occupants he had just left, like the snake discards the skin of a former life. Since the attack, his authority was under threat. No names yet, no easily discernible rivals – it would happen, it was inevitable. But being a young man, there were other things he'd much prefer to do than discuss these matters, regardless of his responsibilities.

"We are pushing him," Pat warned, awkwardly. "He will find little comfort in the arms of his mistress tonight." Reed eyed her enviously: how did women always seem to know?

"I have not yet seen her, what is she *politically*?" Reed asked, concerned. Pat shrugged.

"No idea, I've never seen her either but I *know* she exists," she answered, with certainty. Reed paused, still anxious. It was highly likely of course that nothing political would be discussed at all; indeed Reed hoped it would not. However, the Viscount was in a frame of mind where bringing up his troubles to anyone he could trust was entirely natural. Only in a *'to be listened to'* context, of course, but he might ask for advice… Or she could venture an opinion… Either way, it could affect the outcome.

***

Satiah crouched at the top of the ramp to peer out from Purella's empty ship. The *Dreadnaught*'s hangar bay was now empty – empty of people, anyway. It had been nearly an hour since they had arrived. She had waited, concealed, whilst all the checks and unloading took place. Refuelling had been next and once that was over… the ship was left alone. Silent and still. Keeping to the shadowy side areas, Satiah crept towards the nearest corridor. Two people chatting noisily came out into the hangar and she slipped out of sight quickly. Her sharp brown eyes took in their weapons and direction. Nothing to write home about, they went straight through into another area of the ship. Satiah had determined that she was on a dreadnaught and was familiar with the layout. She had no idea where the dreadnaught *itself* was yet, or who owned it.

She padded softly down the corridor, vigilant and wary. She noted the absence of any cameras with a mixture of elation and mistrust. The sockets were still there but the cameras themselves had been removed. Removed some time ago, judging by the dust. This made moving around *undetected* much easier… in theory. She clattered down a set of aged steps almost casually and peered around at the bottom. No one in sight. Even were the dreadnaught fully manned, it was large enough to lose yourself in. In the night shift particularly, you could walk around all night and not meet a single being. *Nothing* but the low hum of the drive system for company. There was even a two-hour period when more than two thirds of the crew would all be asleep at once. It was informally known as the blinking time. This was because of an old saying known as: *in the blink of an eye*. The idea was that it would only be for the very shortest of durations that their guard was theoretically down. That would be the blinking time.

Going through the outlines of a dreadnaught in her head, she made her way to where the crew should be billeted. The sound of several people breathing heavily whilst sound asleep was the only real noise. Satiah crept past their bunks and entered the changing area. Quietly, she washed, relieved herself, changed into clothes that the crew had in reserve and slipped back outside again. She also took the opportunity to snack on some supplies and rehydrate herself. She didn't know when she would next get the chance. The grey uniform was more casual than she had expected. This indicated that the vessel was no longer in military hands, which made sense given who it was that she was following. This probably meant all the ideas she had had about coordinated shift patterns could be launched from the window.

She paced more confidently in the open, now she was disguised. This would aid the impression that she was hoping to give. The impression of belonging. Nevertheless, she ensured her gun remained as readily available as usual. She'd already attached the silencer when she'd been on board Purella's ship. She would most likely be seen at a distance, if at all, unless she chose otherwise. A uniform was all well and good, but being female, it would be more likely that people would notice that she was new. She pulled the hat a little further down over her eyes.

After a long walk, nearly ten minutes, she got to the end of the main corridor without event. The air was fresh and actually scented, giving the place an almost laid-back vibe. Odd for a battleship. She entered an area she hoped would be the backup computer zone. Whoever was in charge of the ship, however, had regrettably altered the arrangement. It was instead the solar energy bank. Satiah considered her options. She could capture someone and force them into helping her but then that would make her discovery only a matter of time. Wandering aimlessly around, endeavouring to happen on what she wanted wasn't a good idea either. There was only one place she could go that could not be moved. Control. Granted it would be the most guarded and busy place on board, but she had no choice if she wanted to get her answers quickly.

She went back the way she had come, resolute, and this time at pace. Again, she did not meet anyone along the way and she went back up the flight of steps. The control was easy to find, even if you didn't know the layout. Just keep going up and forward, towards the bow of the ship. She passed a pair of crew members in a corridor and, as she had predicted, they ignored her completely. Perfect! At last she found the bridge. Well, she found what had once *been* the bridge. Now, only a few control panels remained. Satiah frowned deeply, rethinking her plan. Someone had effectively hotwired, bypassed and *relocated* the control room. Not an easy task but they must have had their reasons. Clearly because of the electrical and mechanical limitations of the ship, the control room could not be that far from the original. That was, unless someone had *literally* taken the ship apart and re-engineered it so that all the main systems had different paths.

Engines, communications, security, housekeeping, life support... all those things had to feed up to the main computer in the bridge *at some point*. Not to mention all the extras. A movement caught her eye and she backed instinctively into the shadows. Purella and Major Clyde came out of a room to the side and left via the opposing exit. They seemed casual enough. It could always be an act, of course, but then, why bother? Before the door closed, Satiah caught a glimpse of a promising sight. Essential flight controls! So... *there it was*! With all the nonchalance she could muster, Satiah ambled across the room and towards the door. She glanced over her shoulder as she went, just in case. No one was there, as you would expect in a room that no longer had any real function. The door to the control room was locked and required a code for entry. Satiah pulled her communicator out and, after selecting a function, ran it over the small console.

On the tiny screen, numbers began running down in tiny lines and ten were quickly identified. Lastly, their order was established. Satiah inputted the code carefully. How many people had died because of wrong codes? Too many. The door slid open. She slipped inside and smiled to herself, thankful. She sat down slowly as the door closed behind her and eyed the flight settings. They were going nowhere, just drifting in open space. Coordinates currently 8387-7741. Okay so... a fair distance from Collgort-Elipsa. She thought about that for a few moments... so Purella was staying *nearby*.

What were her interests on Collgort-Elipsa? Who had she been talking to? What was she waiting for? She'd taken supplies, fuel and presumably information of some sort. That indicated to Satiah a familiarity with the world – the ability to come and go at will with no interference. Granted, the planet wasn't exactly security conscious but still... the advanced communications gear came to Satiah's attention. She checked the manufacturer, confirming that these were indeed the best of the best. The very latest in communication and surveillance apparatus. Her eyes narrowed, what did Purella need that for? She glanced through the logs but they had all been erased... only minutes ago. *Very systematic.*

Next she noticed that there were indeed cameras on board... but only one that could have seen her. They were monitoring specific rooms at angles just as specific. Satiah leaned in close to make things out better. There were four of them, each displayed in a quadrant of the same screen. The first was keeping an electric eye on the interior of an unoccupied elevator. The second was watching over what looked like the main entrance to the ship. A place where, should they ever land, things could be loaded or unloaded directly into the cargo area. The third was in the hangar area, keeping all the smaller ships under scrutiny. Satiah studied that one more closely, wondering if she could have been spotted earlier. *Possibly* but with that low lighting... *unlikely*. The last was most interesting of all... a metallic looking crate. It was big, a few metres in area. Just the one crate by itself...

Why would she want to keep eye on that one crate? Logical answer was that it was important and would likely contain something of great value. The gold? Trying to get a better understanding of what it was she was looking at she started flicking through different modes on the screen. Infrared, enhanced, *thermal*... She froze as a very human-shaped heat signature appeared before her eyes. A *person* was inside the crate! A prisoner! *Milo Drass.* So it had been *Purella* that had captured him. She was an attractive woman and may have been able to get close to Milo without him suspecting her true intent. It didn't explain why she'd not demanded a ransom but, as she was clearly monitoring him, it showed she had some other purpose for keeping him there. She could have been listening in on the discussion he had had with the military and chosen to snatch him before they arrived. It might not even have been Purella herself but *the pirates* who then sold him to her after taking him?

Self-conscious suddenly and aware she'd probably stayed in one place too long, Satiah left the room. Lingering anywhere was dangerous enough, but the control area was surely the most risky. She did this *after* disabling that camera and noting its location. The brig. Of course, where else would you keep a prisoner? First, she had to at least let Darius know about her progress. There was no sense in making him waste further time on that moon. She found herself an empty side room, dark and quiet, and put a call through to Kelvin. She stared out of the glass slit in the door to keep an eye on the corridor outside.

Kelvin answered.

"I need to speak to Darius," she said, quickly. Kelvin was efficient and hardly a second later it was done.

"Here," said Darius, tense. "You okay?" She made a conscious effort to keep her voice low.

"*I've found Milo*," she stated, grimly. "He's on a dreadnaught, being watched over by pirates. I'm going to get him out and then run." There was a suspension in the conversation after that disclosure. She'd not exactly been expecting a cheer of happiness but silence seemed overkill of the opposite kind.

"Oh..." he said, sounding somewhat less than jubilant. "Well found." Satiah didn't particularly want to, but she knew she had to ask.

"What is it?" she asked, trying to stay patient.

"Dyss called, wanting an update, said he hadn't been able to get hold of you," Darius explained, sourly. This was no surprise as Satiah had not included Dyss in the names of those Kelvin would allow to be connected to her.

"What did you tell him?" she asked, seriously.

"I kept it ambiguous," he stated. Then he seemed to decide that *now* was the time to confront her. "I know you don't trust me, I know why and that's fine. I understand. You *didn't* have to send me out on a wild chase you *knew* was pointless though!" She hadn't *known* actually, at the time it had been their best idea. He wasn't finished; as if now he'd started he was unable to stop himself giving full vent to his disapproval.

"Also, *why* are you not talking to *Dyss*? *You're* the one in charge, not me! *You're* the one who has all the information, not me." She waited, eyeing her nails sagely, for him to stop. She knew from experience that interrupting an angry person was seldom smart. Let them overstretch and make the first mistake. "If nothing else, you have to tell me what you're doing so the least I can do is not look like a *total idiot* when Dyss calls *next time!*" Still she waited. He seemed to realise she was not responding.

"*Satiah?*"

Satiah had been expecting this confrontation for some time and had already planned how she would deal with it. Sometimes attack *was* the best form of defence.

"Care to tell me what happened with *Operation Jackdaw?*" she asked, her tone razor sharp. "*Off the record, Darius.*" A pause.

"You ran me through?" he asked, figuring that she'd illegally read his file.

"No," she replied, honestly. It was Dyss's file she'd stolen, not his. "I just like to know everything about who I'm working with. And, *for your information*, when I sent you to that moon *I genuinely believed* it was our best lead." Another break in the dialogue occurred while he re-evaluated and she waited. Her hand rested on the handle of her pistol, as if seeking reassurance. She could hear him breathing, deep, slow and controlled as he collected his thoughts.

"Operation Jackdaw was botched," he sighed, sounding regretful.

"Indeed, *badly* botched, perhaps even sabotaged," she agreed, keenly. "Question was – *and still is, by the way* – who botched it?"

"You think it was *me?*" he asked, as she knew he would. The mere fact that she was directly questioning him about it was enough to hint at an accusation and she knew it. She was not there yet, however, not in *her* mind. Not ready to commit to an opinion about who had done what.

"*I wasn't there*," she spelt out, levelly. It was a bit of a cop out after the heat of the discussion so far but they had other priorities. The past was the past, it wasn't going anywhere. Besides they had a job to do *now*, specifically.

"We will talk more about this later, give you more time to get your story straight, *now* is not the time for this! When I have Milo I will return to Collgort-Elipsa. I will meet you there where we can discuss this and… the second part of our mission." Another unexpected exposé would keep him on his toes, she reasoned.

"The *second* part?" he enquired, bitter. He'd suspected of course, anyone with half a brain would.

"That's right," she confirmed, grinning victoriously. "See you soon." She then disconnected.

***

Darius had expected a dispute with Satiah. Since day one it had been incoming. He had not been at all shocked to learn she had delved into his past, illegally or not. He knew that, had their positions been reversed, he would most likely have done the same. As she had said: you had to know who you were working with! The fact that she went right for Operation Jackdaw though, had thrown him. The memory of that still haunted him from time to time. What had gone wrong and then what he had done to counter it. To say it had ended in calamity would have been callously dry. And, to this day, Darius still didn't know…

He dragged himself back to reality, reflexively checking his belt buckle as he moved. *That* was ancient history! Certainly, as far as *this* operation was concerned. And what was all that about a *second part* to the mission? He knew she'd been keeping him in the dark but he'd assumed that was just her dealings with Dyss and that matter with the ambassador. Apparently, he'd been wrong. However, the fact that she wanted to meet and talk was a little reassuring. She obviously wanted to know more. And, if there was a second part, how many other *parts* would there be after that?

He adjusted his pistol. He'd been there too long; he had to get out of there. He still had a few unanswered questions about the base, but if Milo was not there it no longer mattered. He had been planning on breaking out sooner or later but he'd not decided on how yet. He glanced at the means of transportation he was using as a hiding place. It would have to do. Unfamiliar with the specifications, Darius could only hope that it would be enough. Sure, it would be thick enough to take a laser hammering, but if they brought out the heavy-duty stuff he'd have to rely on his speed to save him. And this thing was not as fast as he would like. Coming out from his hiding place watchfully, he entered the vehicle and sat at the controls. It had been a while since he'd driven anything like it but he had more than enough experience to get him through. He strapped himself in and began powering up the drive.

Talking as they went, the two guards on patrol plodded along the side of the closed-off vehicle area. It had been hours now since the alert had been declared and after nothing else had happened, the whole place had begun to calm down. There seemed to be no explanation as to the somewhat bizarre set of circumstances that had left two personnel unconscious and a lift out of commission. An intruder? *Where?* Frankly, if they wanted to start spontaneous drills again, you'd think they could come up with more convincing scenarios than that!

Without warning, the armoured vehicle reversed, full pelt, straight through the containment bulkhead right behind them. Fragments of metal were flung in all directions and there was a screech as purchase of the ground was fought for. Darius gritted his teeth as he swung the thing around, running over the remnants of the door as he went. It had a wider turning circle than he had anticipated. Alarms went off and drones were on him instantly. The men, having recovered themselves, got to their feet and opened fire. Driving frantically and hearing the lasers bouncing off the plate armour, Darius sped madly forwards. Normally he wouldn't bother but as he was angry, he activated the missile system. It began targeting the pursuing drones. Missiles flew out from their tubes and made fireworks out of them. Patrols, which had no hope of stopping him, dived aside. A few detonators were thrown but not with any great accuracy.

He followed the road around the complex, trying to get to the entrance. He knew he wouldn't have long before someone made use of the other armoured vehicles. A voice erupted from the speakers.

"Surrender now!" ordered an official voice. "You cannot get away!"

"They never think positive," he muttered, under his breath. He punched the controls to try and shut it up whilst hoping that that was all they could do to him from their control room. He'd checked for remote units and found nothing but he'd not searched inside the engine housing. At last he reached the entrance. The vehicle rocked after a blast from anti-spacecraft guns almost hit it and tore up the ground directly behind it. More drones swung into his field of vision. No more missiles left! He activated the automatic lasers. The guns emerged from the bodywork and danced left to right and back again as they targeted the drones proficiently.

Strong as it was, the armoured shell was starting to fall apart. Hot spots were building into cracks. Close enough, he reasoned. He couldn't get any nearer to the main entrance without falling foul of the anti-spacecraft guns a second time. And a second time, he felt certain, would be fatal. Steering violently to the left, he recklessly charged the perimeter fence, guns still blazing. A small explosion occurred as the electrical charge went off on contact, and the fence was savagely ripped up from the soil. Hardly able to remain seated, despite being strapped down, Darius didn't even see the second fence as he slammed through that too. On into the trees he drove, struggling to remain in control. Weaving, bucking and scraping its way through, the vehicle ploughed on.

He knew he had to be close to his ship now. An alarm wailed, silencing all others. *Missile lock on!* Unstrapping himself, Darius wrenched open the door and threw himself out. He rolled with the impact and heard the screaming howl of an incoming missile, followed by the concussive blast as it destroyed the vehicle utterly. Remembering the lack of oxygen, what with it being tough to ignore, he replaced the breathing device in his mouth. He struggled to his feet and did his best to sprint and find his way at the same time. Shouts, shots and drones could be heard now. They would be converging on him quickly.

His lungs bursting and his legs burning, he ducked in and out between the trees. He was happy that he was wearing breathing apparatus now; all the insects would have made running highly unpleasant otherwise. As it was, he had to keep waving his hand before his eyes to prevent any of them flying into them. Buzzing was all he could hear now as the swarm enveloped him. They were not attacking him; he'd just disturbed them from their ground area and they were trying to get out of his way. About ten desperate seconds later he emerged from the insect cloud and reached the cloaked ship he'd left behind. Entering swiftly, he raced to the control room, the door sealing closed behind him. In a moment, he was airborne.

Before he'd left the ship, he had prepared the controls for just this sort of situation. Gradually the ship rose into the air, invisible as far as the radar would be concerned. He nearly lost control when the ship shook violently under the blast from some sort of mortar unit from the ground fired into him. A warning flashed. Cloaking system disabled. They could see him again! He began a rapid ascent to the stars, not even giving the standard approach a second thought, to get out of range. He ran a systems check: everything was in order… exactly how he had left it.

Detectors picked up a group of fighters chasing after him. Eight, the standard intercept pattern, they had been scrambled as a precaution, most likely. There was no way they could have known that he had a ship of his own. Then again, how else was he supposed to have got there? Darius knew that it was doubtful he could take all of them and emerge unscathed. He adjusted his course to go directly away from them. They were slowly gaining on him and would be on him in less than a minute. Setting his coordinates for Collgort-Elipsa, he only vacillated briefly… He still didn't know how the moon was cloaked. He did have some idea as to the amount of troops stationed there, but after his departure that would surely be out of date. Finally, he reminded himself that it was no longer his concern. He had other things to worry about. Just before the fighters caught up with him, he initiated the main drive and vanished.

***

As she made her way down, Satiah was thinking about two things. Firstly, what she would do if the brig wasn't where it was supposed to be? It seemed ridiculous to move it anywhere else, but she'd thought that about the control room. And the brig would be easier to move than the control room. The second thing was, *once she extracted Milo*, how best to get away. Naturally she'd prefer not to have to fight her way out. Yet that crate was likely to be the least of her problems if someone realised what she was doing. She hoped he was in good enough condition to move. If he had been tortured… She'd deal with any of that when she had to. Without Kelvin nearby, or even Darius to back her up, she would have to play this very carefully.

She hurriedly descended the same corroded steps again, and this time continued all the way to the lowest level. Again, she met no one. She realised she'd been on board nearly four hours. She wished she'd brought some mines with her! An explosive distraction was always a good thing. She rounded a corner, and arrived at a sealed bulkhead door. The brig was beyond it. She once again employed her communicator to prove the entry code and the door swung open. She stepped through and smiled when she realised that the brig was indeed where it should be. The smile faded however when a guard confronted her.

"Hey, *you*, what are you doing down here?" he demanded, exasperated. Satiah kept cool.

"Purella sent me to check on the prisoner," she replied, shrugging. "Apparently that is my job now."

He chuckled.

"Don't let her hear you say that," he warned, in a friendly manner. "*You're new*, aren't you?" She ignored his query, instead asking her own.

"How is he?" she asked, curious. She looked past him to indicate she was talking about his detainee.

"Not a word from him so no change as far as I know," he answered, careless.

"Even during the torture?" she quizzed.

"*Torture?*" he asked, confused. Satiah was almost dumbfounded. It was almost unheard of for a captive of pirates to be found *completely* unmolested.

"No one has tried their luck on him yet?" she enquired, letting him know that she was surprised. He shrugged.

"Not that I know of."

She'd clearly convinced this guard that she was supposed to be there. He probably believed that as she'd got past the bulkhead she was who she appeared to be. Unfortunately, that was *not* the be all and end all. If anyone *called him* whilst she was around, he would no doubt say something that would give the game away. He seemed like a perfectly nice pirate who maybe hadn't even done anything more than guard doors his entire career. Somehow, though, she doubted it. She'd make it painless for him, she decided.

"Want to show me in?" she smiled up at him. He smiled back, happy to help, unsuspecting.

"Of course," he nodded, turning to the door. She brought her pistol down *hard* on the back of his head. He went down instantly, almost too fast for her to slow his fall. She felt for a pulse and smiled when she found it. She dragged him along and propped him on his chair by the door. Then, using a drug from her small collection, she sedated him. He'd wake up in about a day... maybe he'd have a headache.

She faced the door, hands on her hips, relaxed. It didn't look anything special but it was rare for well-chosen security to give itself away. She slid the entry key she'd procured from the guard into its slot. The door buzzed open slowly. So slowly in fact, that Satiah grew impatient and ducked past it. Inside it was dimly lit and silent. Keeping her pistol in hand she began a guarded advance. There was the crate at the end, partly in shadow. She glanced over her shoulder, back out of the open door reflexively, before continuing her approach.

***

Ten years ago, in a place called the Hellion.

The chanting was becoming louder, as was to be expected. The silent, sombre threesome passed by another in the long descending line of flaming torches on the wall, the fire gleaming orange on the white facemask of the lead cloaked figure. A wide chamber opened up before them, packed with cloaked figures. There were tables full of refreshments. A parting occurred as the crowd made way for the newcomers. Ahead was a stage. The chanting had ended now and someone was addressing the crowd. A red-robed figure began speaking. It was a speech that had been given before: such was the style of delivery used that this was easily determined by anyone.

"As at all times my brethren, we *honour* the occasion with the *Ritual of Distance*... Where we distance ourselves from *all* worldly concerns with this gesture... We draw *our line of fire* to set us apart from that *accepted yet malign corruption*..."

It was memorised rhetoric. It was delivered with a theatrical passion to stir and to move. The utter silence was evidence of this strained attention... an obsessive, fanatical devotion. It wasn't meant to be taken literally of course, and there was always room for *interpretation*... almost as though it had been *specifically written* that way on purpose, so that years later, it would start a war based on two different viewpoints of the same text... sound familiar? It sounded *very* familiar to the man in the white mask. Behind that mask burned invisible eyes that had seen the consequences of it all.

The masked figure climbed slowly and formally onto the stage, and faced the crowd as they listened in rapt silence to the speaker. He gave the handle of his walking stick a sharp twist and it retracted section by section into a hand sized shape. He then covertly slid it into his robe. The speaker continued. As he spoke, clearly a talented orator, he built himself up into a crescendo of volume.

"No serpent that still slithers may enter... *We* embody *the only* alternative path, the path where the light and the dark are one... And so with these sacred words *the ancient one stirs...* He hears us my brethren, *he hears our call!*"

Behind the stage where the masked man and the orator stood, a wall of fire began to burn. Some flames reached the roof of the cavern, some thirty feet. The man in red raised his arms, hands upturned to his audience.

"With the shedding of our false selves *we cross that distance!*" he bellowed, dramatically. As he shouted, a shrieking began from the flames, one voice screaming in agony as they were burned alive. A cheer sounded from the sinister, shrouded spectators. The shrieking continued for several seconds before falling silent. The man in the white mask made no move but seemed to stare at the man in red to the exclusion of all else. About a minute passed and the people calmed and the flames ebbed away almost to nothing. The man dressed in red made a gesture to the crowd and they all began talking and engaging in the types of frivolities any crowd might.

Finally, he approached the man in the mask who still made no move.

"You are now initiated, brother," he told him. When the masked man eventually spoke, his voice sounded deep but artificial. Like that of a computer doing a poor imitation of a human vocalising.

"Good," was the unreadable response.

"We all *in some way* mirror what goes on around us," the man in red went on. Clearly he believed that talking in riddles made him look clever. He was wrong. "I am the Bishop, although you probably already know that."

"I do."

"We all have much to discuss about the future, do we not?" the Bishop said, smiling thinly. "Let us begin."

***

Present day.

Major Clyde entered the control room. He glanced at the screen briefly and then regarded them again more intensely. One of the cameras was inactive. Instinctively he reactivated it. The crate was still there. He frowned, puzzled but satisfied, about to turn away, when he noticed movement elsewhere on the screen. Beyond the crate, someone was walking towards it. A woman. For a moment he thought it was Purella herself until she got closer. That was when he recognised her to be the woman that Purella had been describing earlier. He snatched up his communicator.

"Purella, we have an intruder," he growled, quickly. He elaborated further.

"*Don't hit any alarms...* We don't want her to know we know she is there," Purella instructed, thinking hard. "*She's* the woman I told you about. She must have stowed aboard *my* ship to get here. Get a team together... I'll join you directly."

***

Satiah reached the crate. She tapped the side with her pistol to let Milo know she was there.

"Don't say anything, I'm here to get you out," she stated, firmly. She'd always found reassurance hard to manufacture, her voice was naturally cold sounding. Silence was her answer. She worked quickly on the latches and made short work of all six of them. She then eased the panel down onto the floor. She stared inside and froze in astonishment. Peering out at her, from under bushy grey eyebrows, was an elderly man of solemn demeanour. Not Milo Drass by any stretch of the imagination. She covered him with her pistol, perplexed.

"*Who are you?*" Satiah demanded, grimly.

PART TWO

Malign Influence

The gargantuan planetoid rolled unstoppably along among its many brothers in seemingly blissful silence. Tiny specks of distant suns were visible on every imaginable bearing. To wander the endless void without a concept of noise, governed only by gravity, would seem a terrible fate to any sentient being. Dust particles, travelling at fantastic speeds pinpricking, scratching and sticking to you constantly. Life as a barren space boulder would be bleak enough without the prospect of being caught in the crossfire of someone else's war!

A flash of light occurred as the stray torpedo slammed into its rocky surface, cracking and fracturing it into smaller flying hazards. Laser fire intermittently began to pelt in its direction as the dogfights intensified and sped between the newly made rocks. There, the fighter craft could use them as cover and test their flying skills to the limit as they fought tooth and nail to the death. The nearest destroyer, a large battleship dwarfed by many of the heavenly bodies that surrounded it, was turning to face the enemy destroyer approaching it. Head to head, with no room to move, the two ships began a blitzkrieg of devastating volleys. They pounded down each other's shields and then began to slowly destroy one another. Still the fighters dodged and darted around, chasing one another and trying to damage the capital ships.

The Vinu forces were losing, outnumbered and outgunned; they found themselves in the unenvious position of being unable to retreat. Capitulation was not a possibility. A spectacular detonation occurred as the Vinu destroyer received a crippling blast to its main power core. Wreckage exploded out in every direction, like a wave rippling out in a four-dimensional lake. The remaining Vinu fighters scattered, some fled further into the asteroid field and some made for the stars with everything they had. Despite having won the battle, the Shintu destroyer was too badly damaged to move. Going into the asteroid field in pursuit of the enemy had been reckless to say the least and now, those giant rocks relentlessly tested the badly depleted shields. Scuttling seemed the only option…

Before anything else could happen, however, a fleet of eight destroyers, all Vinu, showed up, too concerned themselves only with retrieving such escape pods that had survived the attack. The other six concentrated on the beleaguered Shintu destroyer. It was dragged by gravity projectors out from the field and surrounded. It could offer no serious resistance. Captain Arnos orchestrated the affair; his face bore the red line of a scar that ran from midway down his forehead to the lower half of his cheek. The decades old slash had missed his eye… just. His bare scalp was well tanned and if blue eyes could smoulder… his certainly did.

"I want the officers *alive*, if anyone else can be saved do so – *if not*…" he said, not needing to finish the instruction. The other captains and two lieutenants saluted and nodded. They then departed back to their own ships.

"Contact our destination outpost!" he barked, at a flight officer. She nodded.

"Colonel Celestine here," came a woman's voice.

"This is Wolf Fleet flagship, the *Master*, *Captain Arnos* here," Arnos said, clearly. "We have been dispatched to defend Permyon at your request. I'm calling to inform you that our arrival will be delayed and we will have both prisoners and wounded."

"Thank you, Captain, I will prepare our facilities," she replied, pleased. "*What happened?*" her voice softer but desolate.

"Two destroyers down, one of ours *and* one of theirs, we arrived too late to affect the outcome, but in time to save lives," he answered, all too aware of the mixed blessing.

"I see. Thank you for the update and I hope your journey remains harmless to you," was her answer.

"I see from your report that your outpost is *cloaked*… what is the *nature* of your emergency exactly? Was the cloak compromised?" he asked, curious.

"The system remains online but we were infiltrated by *at least one* intruder," she explained, sounding baffled. "He penetrated our facility and even made it down to the detention area. However, despite incapacitating some of the personnel and damaging some of the assets of the base… I'm at a loss to explain his purpose here."

"…*Interesting*," he murmured, deep in thought. Espionage seemed most likely, especially as nothing had been sabotaged or taken. How had the Shintu rediscovered the moon?

"*Embarrassing* is the word. Three months of radio silence *ruined*… Shintu agents will already have our position and an assault will be incoming," she went on.

"If it is, we will deal with it," Arnos promised, grimly. "The Shintu forces are weakening. Their economy is in chaos, our victory is inevitable…!" He stopped himself mid-rant and then smiled. *Easy*, he was not on parade now. "We should be there in six hours."

***

Dyss looked up as Randal entered his office with resolve in his stance. The two Phantom leaders regarded each other in silence until Dyss offered Randal the chair facing his desk. Randal took it and smiled cordially.

"Is this about Satiah?" Dyss enquired, without preamble. Neither of them were men with time to waste and it was an educated prediction. Why else would he be here?

"It is *not* standard procedure to *borrow* each other's agents," Randal stated, not rudely but firmly. "I was using her for something and while I'll admit that that something *was* almost over *at the time*… Her absence might have been the very thing that started it off again. I *need* her back." Dyss motioned at the drinks on the cabinet but Randal shook his head.

"I needed someone... *distanced* from my other agent," Dyss explained, eyeing Randal. Randal paused and maintained the eye contact, his mind obviously calculating.

"Is this about Operation Jackdaw *again?*" Randal asked, impatience getting the better of him. "*When are you going to let go of that?*" Dyss looked troubled. Randal was aware of a *history*, and even though he didn't know all the details, a lot of the remaining older Phantoms did.

"...I *can't*," he stated, with finality. "You know what it's like to have unanswered questions?"

"And you *know* what they say about picking at old wounds...?" Randal began, persuasively.

"I *cannot* leave this to Darius alone, it's too much for one agent, he needs help... even *if I did trust him*," Dyss replied, irritably. "I *promise*, I will return Satiah to you once Blacklight is concluded."

"I'm *astounded* you managed to convince her to help you *in the first place*," Randal uttered. Dyss shrugged artfully, revealing nothing. Randal watched him, not sure about it. "How did you do it?"

"It's amazing where compliments can get you," Dyss answered, mysteriously.

"*Never worked for me*," he mumbled under his breath. "Top secret, is it?" he queried, sarcastically. Dyss didn't answer but didn't look away as he was used to such exchanges. Randal leaned forward.

"I want my agent back *as soon as possible*, Dyss," Randal growled, allowing his displeasure to show fully now. "And I will keep talking to her in the meantime... when she bothers to answer, that is."

"*You'll get her* and that's fine," Dyss assured, and meant it. Dyss wasn't exactly over the moon with Satiah's management of the mission so far... This was because she didn't seem to be keeping anyone in the loop at all. Also, she was proving just as hard to predict and control as he'd feared she would be. If Reed hadn't suggested it, he'd never have picked her.

He'd wanted her to keep Darius in the dark but not *him* as well! As he was the one who'd forced her into it, however, he could hardly carp too much about it. If he put any more pressure on her she might cut and run… just vanish the way some operatives did. Never to be seen or heard from again. Ever. Randal stood up slowly and turned to leave but halted on the threshold.

"She's one of my best and should anything happen… I would be obliged to take action," he stated, grim.

"Acknowledged and respected," Dyss told him.

***

Darius's craft roared through the clouds of Collgort-Elipsa. Now their ship was on record he didn't even need to announce himself. Despite the recent attack security was still shockingly lax. Why was there no patrol fleet out there? Or at least a squadron of fighters? He plunged down from space at an unnecessary velocity. He was still angry after his chat with Satiah, even though the escape from the moon had allowed him to use most of that pent-up rage. The computer alerted him to 'atypical movement' below him, in the ocean. Not knowing what to expect, he ran a scan. Currents were churning around and around, all following various patterns. Then he noticed the… *speck*… for want of a better term. It was tiny. He tried to zoom in but, with something so grainy, it was impossible to make out what it was supposed to be. He broke out of the clouds and landed in the same spot he'd taken off from nearly two days ago.

He'd slept for the majority of the way back from the moon and so was relatively well rested, considering. The blustery wind was still a shock to him after the still warmth of the control room. He wrapped his cloak around his shoulders more tightly and didn't hang about as he made his way back into the Plaza. He decided to pause and look over the guard railings. The restless ocean, loud as ever, thrashed endlessly below. There was no sign of the speck that he could perceive from that vantage point. He didn't expect there to be but he'd not got where he had without being methodical. He pondered on how much money Milo would have lost. Still no one had contacted anyone for a payoff. This was looking more and more like he was dead.

Satiah would probably arrive tomorrow, if things went according to whatever plan she had, so he would hear about it all then. He shivered in the howling winds and finally retreated indoors. He was surprised to meet Kelvin, standing in the entrance way. It was like the big robot had been awaiting him. Darius had just assumed Kelvin would be *with* Satiah.

"I thought you were with her," Darius stated, by way of greeting.

"One is easier to hide than two," came the monotone response. Darius nodded.

"Did she leave any instructions?" he asked, doubting she had.

"No."

"Would she have any objections if I were to meet the Coalition Ambassador?" Darius asked, curious.

"No," Kelvin said.

"*Anything of interest* happened here during our absence?" he asked, the hope dying in his tone.

"No."

Darius sighed and waved a dismissive hand at Kelvin before marching away down the corridor. He would have to try and prise some answers out of the ambassador because, as far as Darius could gather, he seemed to have something to do with this second part of the mission. Satiah had seemed very interested in this man upon their arrival and hadn't he been *expecting* their arrival? He quickly tracked the ma – Reed was his name – to an area outside of the main palace. A *bar* of all places... a bar that would normally be the last kind of place an ambassador would be found in. It was quite fancy, in a tourist attraction kind of way. Plenty of reflective, shiny blues and greens. Darius entered casually, taking the liberty to give the place a good look before he did anything else.

"Ah, Darius!" called Reed, toasting him with his own drink. "*You're here at last, excellent*! Drink?" Darius stopped in his tracks, a little taken aback at being recognised so easily. He took another quick look around, everything seemed normal.

"Mine's a Gadrim," Darius growled out, in habit.

"*Man after my own heart,* join me!" Reed invited, summoning a serving robot with a wave of his hand. "A Gadrim please, large or small?"

"Large," Darius smiled, thinking that this man was by far the most laid-back ambassador he'd ever met. The beverage arrived in its traditional silver jug with a marble handle. Darius fished in his cloak for some Essps.

"No, no," implored Reed, chuckling. "What are expenses for?"

Darius grinned in a comradely way. This could be fun. They clinked the drinks in mid-air, an age-old custom that no one could truly claim as theirs. Some believed it was to do with ancient religious customs while others felt it was more likely to have developed from flavoured drinks and certain female names... and still others felt it may be something to do with testing the quality or indeed the safety of the fluid itself. Poisonous drinks had been in legend after legend since time immemorial. Basically *no one knew* but no authority ever liked to admit that.

"Your health," Reed beamed, seeming to be in the highest of spirits. Darius glanced out of the window, across the square, at the main Forest Plaza building. The Viscount himself was *somewhere* in there... Darius made a mental note of the few guards that there were out of habit. There didn't seem to be enough of them considering the person inside they were responsible for. It was quite lamentable – in Darius's opinion, at least. He gulped a mouthful of his drink as he glanced, to hide the look he took. Then he focussed fully on Reed. The little man seemed both congenial and welcoming. A rather disconcerting deportment for an ambassador...

"What's Satiah doing?" Darius asked, going straight for the heart of the matter.

"Didn't she say?" Reed dodged, artfully.

"*Come on*, that's not how this works. Answering questions with questions is tantamount to being uncooperative," Darius said, remaining pleasant.

"Is it?" Reed gasped, as if Darius had just told him the world was flat. Then his face spread into another disarming smile. "I suppose it is," he allowed, modestly. Darius waited for more but he seemed to have finished.

"Well?"

"Satiah is your superior and is currently following a lead as to the whereabouts of some chap named *Milo Drass* whom I've never heard of," Reed lied, adeptly. "Had *I* been in *her* position I would have told you *that much* at least."

"She seemed very anxious to see you when we first arrived," Darius nodded, letting it go for a while.

"She was indeed," he chuckled, having prepared beforehand for the question. "*We are old friends*! Didn't she tell you about the time when we were at a social gathering, she'd developed the idea that the wine was poisoned, yet it was *I* who had to fish *her* out of the fountain later as she was too drunk to manage it herself?"

Darius let out an involuntary laugh at the idea of that ever happening. Satiah floundering haplessly in a fountain while Reed struggled to drag her out. Yes... that really happened.

"Don't get me wrong though," Reed continued, amiably. "Ninety-nine point nine, nine, nine recurring percent of the time: she *is* the perfect professional." Darius wasn't so sure about *that* but he was hardly going to say so. Especially not to someone purporting to be a close friend.

"*Certainly seems to be*," agreed Darius, quickly. "How are things going here?"

"Well, *after the attack*, things have been a little tense as you can imagine," Reed muttered, sweeping the bar with a glance of his own. "*Terror tactics have never been popular.*"

"The attack?" Darius confirmed, trying to conceal his confusion. He failed and Reed eyed him in dawning comprehension.

"Satiah didn't tell you about *that*, did she?" Reed asked, seriously. "*Why not?*" Darius hadn't yet seen the mission report or discussed anything with Satiah.

"We had a bit of a falling out," Darius shrugged, recovering quickly. "I am supposed to wait here for her to return and update me on the latest developments. She *said* she'd got the man."

"*Ah*," Reed smiled, his brows rising. Darius thought he seemed pleased. "*Great! Fan-dabby-dozy!* That means she'll be able to devote her famous skills *exclusively* to solving *my* problems."

"*I wouldn't bet on that*," Darius mumbled, inaudibly. "I'm sure she'll want to help out. What problems are those?"

"Highly complicated ones."

**

Bavon answered the call.

"Have you given the pirates the information on the military formations?" asked that voice. The voice that Bavon feared the most. Purella was terrifying but Quint was something else entirely.

"I... yes... what I mean to say is that I have forwarded the information you gave me," Bavon answered, his voice quavering. He cleared his throat.

"Good," came the computerised voice. It wasn't exactly a monotone; it was more like a computer's primitive approximation of a human's voice. That, in its way, made it even creepier. "Did Kyle tell you *when* the attack would take place?" How did *Quint* know about *Kyle?* Bavon had only recently found out about him himself.

"No, no, he will want to go over the information *first* but he knows what we want," Bavon answered.

"Has the Viscount made his decision yet?" Quint asked, still the same voice.

"If he *has* he's not made it public," Bavon replied. "I will let you know what the outcome is."

"If he's not already said then the odds are it will be a long wait," Quint stated. It was difficult to say if he was surprised, smug or just nonchalant but Bavon thought he could detect a knowing vibe from Quint.

"Are you saying...?" Bavon began.

"Various elements of the government are putting pressure on him to *delay* his verdict and they have temporarily triumphed. There was even talk of employing the Colonial Federation to protect your planet," Quint told him. Bavon was thunderstruck; those bugs he placed must really have got lucky this time.

"*Admiral Wester*," he breathed, simultaneously in awe and fear.

"The Federation does not worry me, Bavon, it will not matter soon enough, you will see." Quint disconnected.

***

It is an unwritten rule, when it comes to prediction and probability, that certain possibilities are discounted because the percentage of their occurrence is too small to make them likely. Correct location – the prisoner *was* where he was supposed to be. Right circumstances – he *was* a prisoner of Purella's who Satiah was so sure *had* abducted Milo Drass. He was… Satiah could feel the anger building.

"Who are you?" she demanded, aiming her pistol at him threateningly. Had Purella somehow predicted Satiah finding Milo and substituted him with this old man to trick or trap her? That didn't seem probable as Purella surely couldn't guess that she was *after* Milo and even if she *had*, she couldn't know that Satiah was even *there*! The alarms were still silent and no one was shooting at her! The man, after looking right at her, looked away again, seemingly ignoring her completely. This further puzzled Satiah.

"*Where* is Milo Drass?" she asked next. It was her only move left.

The old man faced her again, confusion on his face.

"*Who?*" he asked, his voice deep and strong sounding. Satiah scowled, convinced now that this was some sort of trap that she just didn't understand totally yet.

"Forget it," she growled, moving to shut him in again.

"No, *wait!*" he cried, suddenly standing. "*Sorry,* I thought Purella sent you here to trick me. *I thought* this was some sort of unorthodox interrogation technique." Satiah raised her gun at him again because of his abrupt movement, but she did not fire. He was not armed, and did *really* appear to be what he was. A prisoner.

"I don't have a lot of time," she stated, her voice menacing. "I am here for a *very specific purpose*. To retrieve a man called Milo Drass. Are you this man?"

"…No," he admitted sadly.

"Then *I'm sorry* but…" Satiah began, harshly. A movement in the corner of her eye triggered her sixth sense and she ducked. A laser bolt scorched the wall near where her head had been.

"Down!" she screamed, to the man.

She spun, firing back at the gang of figures by the door. The pirates dispersed, taking up positions behind crates or outside in the corridor. Satiah slipped behind a crate and held out a hand to ensure the man stayed where he was. He did. They made eye contact, at last reaching the mutual conclusion that they were both on the same side. That side being: those *not* with the pirates. He looked panicky and also seemed to be seeking an escape route.

"You're trapped and outnumbered! The *only way* out of there is by this door!" Major Clyde shouted, from somewhere near the doorway. "Might as well be smart and give in *now* before anyone tries anything irresponsibly heroic!" Satiah, swearing furiously under her breath, fired a few shots in his general direction in defiance of that instruction. Anxiously seeking another way out, she looked all around her. She wondered if there might be anything in the crates that might help her. They *were* gunrunning after all and she might get lucky and stumble over the illegal arsenal! Then she noticed the doors *above* the crate! They would lead straight to the hangar, no doubt where the crate had originally been lowered down from. And in the hangar was where the ship she had arrived on would hopefully still be…

Decision time. Take the old man… or not? If she left him behind, what was the fallout? They would most likely either kill him or simply confine him again. He was not Milo Drass so his fate was irrelevant to her. He knew nothing that could compromise her. If she took him with her, he would slow her down and potentially work against her. She still didn't know *anything* about him. While it was now clear he was not *with* the pirates, that didn't mean he wouldn't present a danger to her further down the road. If she took him with her he *may* have vital information or useful resources. And taking him would no doubt really anger Purella.

Satiah aimed and fired at the cable housing around the loading doors. There were sparks and small explosions as the doors swung down and open with great reluctance. She broke from cover, skidding over to the old man.

"Hold onto me!" she instructed, producing her grapple gun. She fired at the ceiling of the hangar and they were both speedily eased out of the storage area, out into the hangar area. She deactivated the link as they had floor under them and they fell a metre to the floor. She rolled. He landed with a crunch and a cry of pain. She turned, pistol at the ready, covering the hangar area.

"Get into that ship!" she ordered, seriously. Groaning, the old man limped up the ramp and into the ship. She rushed after him as the sound of running feet reached her ears. After sealing the door, she overtook him in a mad sprint for the control room.

"*Come on!*" she barked at him, unsympathetically. She began powering up the shields and engines just as several pirates ran into the hangar area. They instantly began firing on the ship. Wincing in pain, he slumped into the co-pilot's chair.

"My leg…" he hissed, through his teeth.

"I'll take a look at it when we're out of this mess!" she growled, activating the lasers. She began blasting at the pirates. The lasers were more powerful than any of the small arms they possessed and after an initial rush, they were retreating fully.

Looking around, there were several other craft in the hangar. It would be tricky enough getting away from the *Dreadnaught* itself without additional ships in pursuit. Inflicting further structural damage might also aid the escape attempt too. So, she also took the time to cripple any other ships in immediate range, turning the place into an inferno as engines and power cores ignited. Emergency fire control systems sprayed the area with gas and coolant, trying to contain the fires. Seeing that she could do no more there, she spun them around, so they were facing open space and triggered the main thrusters.

They rocketed out of the hangar area, followed by a jet of fire as something else exploded. She swung to the left immediately, dodging a laser battery that opened fire on them. She adjusted the shield coverage, flicked on the flight computer and basically did ten other things at once. The old man wrestled to stay in the chair as Satiah barrel-rolled them this way and that, trying to avoid getting hit. The controls were customised for Purella but they were still mostly laid out in the usual places.

First Satiah stuck close to the hull of the *Dreadnaught* itself to prevent being overly exposed to the batteries which could only dip *so far* no matter how good the gunners were. They both jolted as a direct hit enveloped the cockpit with smoke and the man shouted in pain. Straining to see, Satiah tried to read the damage report while holding them on course. Three engines, engine two was now leaking. Rate of depletion was in excess of automatic repair works, even after she tried to computer compensate.

She swore vehemently and hit the controls harder, probably not a good idea but she was getting desperate. Another blast rocked them hard.

"*Don't let us die!*" screamed the man, unhelpfully. If he kept distracting her like that she'd shoot him herself! This was not working. If she didn't make her move soon she wouldn't be able to move at all. She tried to set coordinates but the computer too was now damaged. This was getting better and better! So much for those shields! More sparks flew, and showered them. The old man was shouting something else now but there was so much noise she couldn't make out the words.

Every light on the console seemed to be lit; every alert imaginable was going off. They had to get out of there! Fraught, Satiah just set a random course, punched the button and hoped. They burst forward, leaving the *Dreadnaught* behind. The shuddering stopped but the alarms continued. She glanced across at the old man, who was staring at her, slack jawed.

"Two minutes!" she said, holding up a finger. She darted back into the engine area to assess the damage herself. It wasn't over, this was Purella's ship and Purella was smart. Smart enough to be able to track her own craft at least!

Satiah reached the room, opened the door and smell *alone* told her that things were not good. Smoke was one thing but there was the unmistakeable odour of fuel mixed with it. And, worryingly, melted metal... That told her instantly that the damage was likely even more extensive than she had feared. As she stepped fully inside the room there was a splash, as her boot landed in spilt coolant. Coughing, she eyed the few remaining functional readouts. One tank wasn't registering at all! Just a connection problem, she hoped. The other two seemed only half full and one was only operating a reduced capacity. And they were going down too quickly.

She did everything she could to make it as safe as possible for as long as possible. She even took the precaution of reactivating the blast shielding so that if anything *did* go up, they might stand a chance of surviving. She went back to the control room, where the old man was still waiting, silently. He might be in shock but she didn't care enough to worry about that right then. She sat down again and began to go through the alerts on the computer... such as they were. According to the computer, basically, *everything* was badly damaged. She turned all the alerts off, if for nothing else than to conserve power and get something approaching quiet. She rechecked the atmosphere settings. At least the life support systems seemed to be doing okay *for now at least*. At last she relaxed, slumping back in the chair with a heavy sigh. They had been lucky... Then it hit her!

She'd told Darius that *she had Milo* and would be returning with him. That was clearly not going to happen now and she'd made him come back from Permyon! *Essentially for no good reason*! She ran her hands through her hair, stressed. One problem at a time! She had to get back to Collgort-Elipsa but, given her situation, she would need a new ship before anything else. She didn't even know where they were going! *And*... She turned to face her passenger.

"You okay?" she asked, rather pointlessly. He was still staring at her, maybe mesmerised.

"Who are you?" he managed, at last.

"I'm the one who asks the questions," she cautioned, crouching before him to check out his wounds. "Where does it hurt?"

"*Everywhere!*" he grumbled, mock seriously. "*My right ankle...* I think it might be broken."

She quickly examined him herself and, to her dismay, she discovered that he was indeed correct. It was a bad break and had to be treated as soon as possible. She searched the ship again, this time for medical facilities. There *were* painkillers and a few other drugs but nothing else. Nothing that would help a broken ankle anyway. She injected him with her own painkillers as they were better quality and she knew she could trust them.

"Where are we going?" he asked, wearily. She couldn't bring herself to tell him that she had no idea.

"Away from Purella, *where do you think*?" she stated, rather rudely. "Who are you?"

"I'm Doctor Bertram Blake Clark," he told her, his grey eyes half closed. They were *strong* painkillers. "My friends call me *Doc Bert*."

"I see. In what field?" she asked, next.

"PBC, specifically microbiology," he replied. PBC, in that case, he probably meant physics, biology and chemistry. The big three. Satiah herself had become quite an authority on chemistry but she decided not to mention that. So, Bert was an all-rounder.

"How long have you been a prisoner of Purella?" Satiah enquired, seriously.

"Purella being that woman with the black band around her head?" he clarified. Interesting... he had to make sure he knew who she was talking about. They couldn't have interacted much then unless she'd never identified herself to him.

"Yes."

"I can't say for sure, had no way to measure the time, not even a sun... maybe a week, *certainly not a month*," he answered, considering.

"Why was she keeping you prisoner?" Satiah asked, more than a little baffled.

"*I don't know!*" he insisted, thinking hard about it. "She *never* questioned me, not even once, never showed me to anyone that I can think of and no one else even spoke to me." This was not helpful.

"You *must* have some idea," Satiah asserted. "Do you have enemies? Are you involved in anything *off the record* or illegal?"

"What are you suggesting?" he demanded, offended. What did he think?

"I thought I was making it pretty clear," she sighed, starting to lose patience. She poked his ankle hard, getting a cry in response. "That is some further motivation for you to think again." He glared at her but she just stared back, like nothing had happened.

"I... no! *I swear!*" he stated, angry.

"People don't lock people up *without reason!*" she hissed, at him. Saying that, they didn't have to be *good* reasons.

"Agreed," he nodded, trying to stay calm.

"Yet you seem *incapable* of coming up with one," she summarised, sharply.

"Obviously *they* thought they had one!" he argued, irritated.

"*Obviously!*" she concurred, also starting to get frustrated. She gave it one last try. "And you maintain that you don't know who Milo Drass is?"

"…Yes, I'd never heard of them until I met *you*," he stated, honestly. Satiah could tell he was not lying about *that*. She checked the computer again, time to arrival kept changing. It had said three hours and eighteen minutes before and now it was saying four hours and fifty-one minutes! They *needed* another ship! Bert was watching as she paced up and down, like a caged beast, getting increasingly uncomfortable. He felt like maybe being rescued was not such a great thing after all. As if detecting his ingratitude, she whirled on him again.

"You *said* no one had spoken to you when you were incarcerated, so why did you then claim that you thought *I* was trying to trick you somehow?" she demanded, trying to get at a potential lie. "When I first met you, you refused to answer me. Why would you do *that* if no one had ever asked you anything?"

"*I don't know!* I never knew when and if they were going to *start* asking me questions! I thought that *might* have been it!" he cried, fearfully. She let out a huff and continued to pace again. It was unlike her to conduct an interview in such an uncontrolled way but she was floundering slightly. She was off balance after so many unexpected things happening at once.

"I *wish* I could tell you what you wanted to know and I wish *none of this had happened* but I'm *sorry* that my explanation upsets you," Bert apologised, trying to calm her down. She was armed and he was in fear of his life, arguing with her seemed rather a mad idea.

Satiah reasserted her self-control and returned to the pilot's seat. There were always more reasons to lie than there were to tell the truth! If she took how she had found him at face value then he had no reason to lie. She slipped her specs on and regarded him through them. She would get Kelvin to identify him, and if he was telling the truth about who he was then… she'd have to accept the rest of it. *Whatever…* Milo Drass was her target and Bert was just a mistake. A costly one that had given her away to Purella and almost got her killed. This led her to the next problem: if Purella didn't have Milo then who did?

The ship jolted, ending the silence, and Satiah rushed to see what was wrong. Her first thought was the engines. She was correct. Engine two was down and now engine one was having difficulties. Dragging a tool bag, she raced back to the smoke-filled engine room. Red lights were flashing now, never a good sign, as she wrenched open the plate coverings. More smoke billowed out and she stuffed a cloth in her mouth to breathe through. A component had overheated, probably because too much energy was going through. Pulling on protective gloves, she tried to see what else was wrong. An idea came to her... they were most likely being tracked by Purella. They would have to land soon somewhere! But what if they apparently *crashed and died on impact*? It was their only chance... They couldn't go on for much longer as things were and it might just throw Purella off their trail!

She rigged up a charge on a nearby fuel canister and then sprinted back to the control room, leaving the tools behind.

"Strap yourself in," she advised. "I'm going to take us down."

"*What? Why?*" he asked, scared.

"Purella will be after us; this ship is wasted and will get us nowhere fast. If we crash it badly enough they *may* conclude that we did not survive," she elaborated, still coughing. She still didn't even know *where* they were but, according to the highly unreliable scans, a hospitable planet *was* nearby. She deactivated the engines, which resulted in a crunching, rending, crashing noise from the engine room. The dark planet loomed up so fast, Satiah's eyes went wide and she slammed all deceleration systems on.

Molten metal detached from the ship as they tore through the atmosphere. Bert was transfixed by the main viewport. Satiah gritted her teeth as she tried to pull up. Bert wrenched his eyes away from the approaching treetops to look at Satiah as she fought with the controls. Sweat was almost pouring down her face now but she never stopped. A hammering began as treetops began to joust with the hull of the ship. Satiah tied herself into her chair too and braced herself. A long low moan occurred as the front dipped towards the ground, battered by trees. Alarms wailed again until she kicked the console to silence them. They hit the ground, bounced and continued on flattening trees until they finally lost momentum and skidded to a halt. Bert shouted when his ankle hit the chair from the momentum of the rapid stop.

"*Come on!*" she uttered, unclipping her safety harnesses swiftly. "We have about sixty seconds to clear the ship!"

***

The pilot turned to get the attention of the figure in the seat behind him.

"We're here, sir," he said, flatly. The man in the white mask may be looking right at him or he may not be able to see at all, it was impossible to know. When he spoke, his voice sounded like that of a computer trying to imitate a human voice.

"Where is the *Dreadnaught*?" he asked, a softness belying the angry undercurrent. The pilot shrugged. "Get me Purella," he ordered. Purella answered quickly as usual. Something was clearly preoccupying her though.

"Quint?" Purella shouted, both alarm and rage in her voice.

"Why have you moved from the coordinates you sent me?" he inquired, a serenely patient air about him. It was a few seconds longer than normal before she replied.

"We have a situation, I can't go into details but we were attacked," she explained, breathlessly.

"By whom?" he enquired, interested.

"We don't know, the *same woman* who prevented me recovering *your gold*," Purella expounded. "She *somehow* got aboard the *Dreadnaught*, rescued *your* prisoner and escaped in my personal ship. We are tracking her and hope to regain her when she…"

"Very well, while you're doing that, do you have any evidence I could review? Perhaps I could shed some light on your mysterious problem," he suggested, knowing not to interfere. He could order her to return at once but such an action would not be necessary.

"We recorded some from when she took my ship," Purella said. "She sabotaged the camera in the storage area but not the one in the hangar area."

"Good… Remember I want the doctor *alive*, Purella. I would hate to have to refuse to pay you if you presented me with a corpse," he threatened. *Refuse to pay* might well have been a euphemism for something far more fatal.

The footage arrived and he raised a hand to the pilot who began to set things up on a big screen behind then. Communicator still in one hand, walking stick in the other, Quint rose and stood before the screen. As he moved it was clear he required no stick at all. The footage began. The doors opened, smoke rose, Quint assumed correctly that they had been shot open from the other side. Then the grapple line appeared and the doctor and the woman shot out onto the floor of the hangar. The doctor seemed to sustain an injury in the landing. The woman rolled and spun around, gun raised. Quint paused and zoomed in. He stared for several seconds at the image of Satiah's face and a long, slow exhalation came from him. He lifted the communicator again.

"Purella, are you still there?" he asked, casually.

"Yes, did you get it?" she asked, clearly busy.

"You're following a Phantom agent from the Coalition called *Satiah*; she is one of their best field agents. My advice to you is: back down," he stated, simply. "We should concentrate on damage control."

"...*What?*" she exclaimed, astonished. "*She's got your man!*"

"Who won't be able to tell her anything," Quint replied, levelly. "If you fight her: she *will* beat you."

"*She stole my ship!*" screeched Purella, enraged. "I don't *care* who she works for, she will pay for that! I've tangled with her before, she's not so tough and we outnumber her over one hundred to one!"

"The doctor can tell her nothing, eventually she will let go of him and when she does *you* can reacquire him for me, in the meantime... I strongly recommend that you let her go," Quint persisted, still unemotional.

***

Purella couldn't believe how sanguine Quint was being about all this! She was beside herself with fury. The worst part of it was that, as Satiah had sneaked in on *her own ship*, she had no one to blame but herself. Things had been quiet after Bavon and Kyle had had their little chinwag. Purella had retired to her quarters for some sleep. A few hours later, she was awakened from a deep dreamless half-coma otherwise known as the sleep of the exhausted. It had been Clyde. He informed her that they had an intruder. Then, when it had transpired who the intruder was, she and Clyde had moved quickly. Clyde had assembled a team and tried to capture her *before* she freed the prisoner. Somehow she'd got lucky and seen them coming. Next thing that happened was, she'd created a war zone in the hangar bay and escaped with the prisoner on Purella's personal ship!

They had been pursuing them for over two hours when…

"She's stopped!" Clyde announced, puzzled. "We must have hit the engines after all."

"*Where?*" Purella asked, immediately.

"Planet called Bishna. Know it?" he asked, interested. Purella *did* and the news did not please her. The last time she'd been there she'd had to leave in rather a hurry. Bad memories resurfaced.

"Okay, we're going to have to play this *very carefully*," she said, her voice low. "Get all the females we have working here into a team." Clyde frowned at her but obeyed anyway. It was unlikely that Satiah would go to that planet out of choice but if she *had*… Purella would need help. One woman would have to stay behind and operate the communications instead of Clyde.

"You will need me with you," Clyde stated, as she assembled a laser rifle. She then slung it over her shoulder.

"You're probably right but I might be killing you if I take you down *there*," she stated. "Check out the database, it's all explained."

"Right," he replied, in reluctant agreement. "I'll let you know when I have the landing location."

"Good. If Quint calls back, you'll have to deal with him," she advised.

"Not a problem. And if he's right about Satiah being a Phantom agent… will you be bringing back her head?" he enquired. Purella smiled.

"Of course… I swore on the blood of Varn-Utto that I would not rest until I had my revenge on those *Phantoms*… Satiah will be just another skull on my wall," she replied, through her teeth.

**

The forest was not the best place for anyone to run for their lives, least of all for someone with a broken ankle. Satiah was supporting him as best as she could. They'd made it out of the ship and were struggling through the trees when it exploded. Satiah glanced back, checking for any large chunks of wreckage that might come flying their way. Just the mushroom cloud was visible. Bert collapsed onto his backside with an aggrieved cry. Satiah pulled her blade from her boot and sliced a suitable stick for him to lean on from a nearby tree. Out of habit she began to sharpen the tip so that it could double as a makeshift spear but then she stopped and eyed him. Again, take or leave him? If he didn't before, now he really would slow her down for sure. Purella could not be far behind and for her to believe that they had died in the crash, they would both have to be nowhere in sight.

Satiah didn't know why but her thoughts led to Reed. What would he do? She knew what he would ask her: would you want someone to try to save you? Of course, in most circumstances. Grimly she continued cutting, while checking out the surroundings. She still didn't know where they were and she was hoping that this world was not an uninhabited one. Bert was watching her as she cut down more branches and began to improvise a primitive splint for his ankle. She was fast, having done it many times before.

"We have to move," she said, by way of explanation. "I don't know how far we will have to go before we can get you help."

"Where are we?" he asked, wincing as she saw to his leg. She still refused to allow herself to admit that she didn't know.

"In trouble?" she remarked, raising an ironic eyebrow.

She got him to his feet and then handed him the spear for him to lean on.

"We need to get away from *that* before anything else," she told him, pointing a thumb over her shoulder at the wreck. She began to assail the steep incline, using the tree roots as handholds.

"You seriously expect me to follow you up there?" he uttered, in disbelief. There was a stilted silence.

"You seriously expect food to magically appear before you down there?" she called, over her shoulder. "Just keep moving, follow me. If you can't see me, don't worry I will come back." She reached the top and quickly ducked down, out of sight. She peered through the trees. Lush forest, good cover, recent rainfall drying fast and lots and lots of thorn bushes. She sniffed the air. Smoke.

She checked her pistol while she thought about what to do next. If this world was uninhabited... then wandering anywhere would be pointless. And worlds were hardly left uninhabited *without good reason*... She pulled out her earpiece and tried to make a call but the signal was being blocked. It was nearly ten minutes before Bert reached her, sweating and groaning. She next led him, more slowly now, through the trees. Her gut was screaming at her that they were in grave peril. She could see nothing other than forest though and put it down to Purella. They had been walking and stumbling along for nearly an hour when the sound of a ship passing by overhead was heard. Satiah pulled out her specs and tried to get a fix on it but couldn't see it through the cloud cover.

"That will be her," Bert grumbled, his morale sinking still further.

"Could be *anyone*," she muttered back, unwilling to surrender the point. She had to admit that it *was* likely. "We carry on."

"For how much further?" he objected, starting to lose patience. "I'm in pain, I'm hungry and I'm tired."

"*Enough!*" she snapped, irritated. "We keep moving or we die, that's our *only* choice." She was starting to seriously regret choosing to save him. This was exactly how compassion could be a weakness. She'd justified it to herself at the time by choosing to believe that he may be of more help than he first seemed. That looked like hollow thinking now! They struggled on for a nearly an hour until he tripped on something and went down with a shout.

Satiah scrambled back to him dismally, not even bothering to admonish him for shouting. He stared up at her as she looked down at him.

"...I can't..." he uttered, softly. "*I'm sorry.*" She crouched next to him, pulled off her top and shoved it under his head as a pillow. She made him as comfortable as she could then handed him the spear. There was no way she'd leave her pistol with him.

"I'll have to leave you," she stated, emotionlessly. "Don't light a fire or shout or drawn attention to yourself, okay?"

"Good luck," he smiled, breathlessly. "Thank you for saving me by the way... I'm not sure I thanked you before." She shrugged.

"I didn't do it for you," she admitted, coldly. "And frankly the longer you lie there the more chance that you'll die anyway. I'll do my best for you. If anyone asks you anything, claim loss of memory." He nodded.

Able to move at pace now, Satiah took off at a light jog, careful not to injure herself as she went. That really would add insult to injury. For two hours, as the daylight slowly waned, she went on. Jumping streams, leaping over fallen trees and forcing her way through the thicker vegetation as best as she could. As she was moving, she heard something that made her stop dead. A distant booming sound. An explosion. Another! Then distant gunfire sounded. Well... at least it *was* inhabited. She started again, into the twilight, heading directly towards the noise. While this was doubtless not the smartest of tactics, she was out of options. A ship was needed above everything else.

Shouting could be heard now, along with small arms fire. Screams of death were the kind Satiah was intimately acquainted with. Satiah abandoned speed for stealth and began a slow commando crawl forward through the foliage. She reached the edge of a ridge overlooking a plain. A few bodies lay around and fires burned: a scene of war. Satiah put on her specs and ran a scan. She trusted her own eyesight but computers were so much better for analysis. They just lacked imagination...

A group of twelve women, all armed, were moving in skirmish order slowly across the plain. Someone opened fire from the treeline they were approaching. No one was hit and they returned fire. Satiah was able to make note of the interesting mix of firearms they carried. One, presumably the one in charge, had a reasonably well-kept rifle. The others were all older models. One even carried just a pistol. While some were clearly wearing a uniform of some kind, the others wore basic bodysuits or even rags in one case. More gunfire. It was sporadic, inaccurate and ineffective. Again, no one was hit.

Satiah wondered if they would shoot her if they saw *her*. Probably.

Making contact would be foolish but she made up her mind that she would follow them. After collecting the two bodies, also women, the group, under the direction of one who was obviously an officer, made their way back the way they had come. Satiah followed. The officer had long black hair, tied back and wore the best-looking uniform of all of them, seeing as it matched completely with itself everywhere and wasn't dotted with dirt, stains or blood. Keeping low and quiet, Satiah didn't have to try too hard to keep up. The burden of their dead slowed them sufficiently. She didn't recognise the uniform, such as it was, but there was nothing unusual in that. There were literally *billions* of military uniforms in the cosmos and that was leaving out all the outdated versions that had gone before.

As they moved along, another group of women joined them, clearly fighting for the same side. An exchange took place and there was some mild cheering. Still following, Satiah began to realise… there were *no men*. A horrible suspicion began to build inside her mind. She tried her earpiece again, it was still jammed. Then she saw two women carrying a stretcher between them. Using her specs, she zoomed in and to her shock she realised they were carrying *Bert*. He wasn't moving but it seemed unlikely they would bother with a stretcher if he was dead. Satiah debated what to do. Arguably this actually made her task easier… *in a way*. She would certainly continue following them for the time being anyway. There was no point in trying to rescue him now, not with his ankle. She was edging closer and could actually hear some of the discussions taking place.

"Was he the lone survivor of that crash we saw?" demanded one, probably the officer.

"Most likely, his ankle was broken but there might have been someone else with him. At least at first," was the reply.

"Another *male?*" asked someone, a woman with hatred in her tone.

"Can't say but he was using *this* as a pillow," she said, handing them Satiah's top. The officer examined it closely then had a long slow look around. Satiah continued to watch, lying on her front among the bushes in silence.

"So do we kill him?" asked the first, nonchalantly.

"I will check with command, they may wish to interrogate him," the officer stated.

"*Come on!*" barked the second, enraged. "You don't need to ask her permission for *everything*! Just waste him and let's go!"

"*Who is in command?*" screamed the officer, suddenly getting in her face.

No answer came. The officer seemed to take that as backing down and made a call. Satiah waited breathlessly, wondering what she should do if they chose to kill him. She'd be able to kill most of them she decided, so long as she had surprise on her side.

"We take him back with us," the officer concluded, before a few sighs of irritation. The company, such as it was, began to move along again. Satiah went after them cautiously. They moved more quickly now and Satiah could see what looked like an encampment on the top of a hill nearby. Using her specs, she could make out snipers concealed in the trees nearby... they were coming up to where the patrol would be challenged by the guard. Satiah knew she'd be able to get in but it would take some time. She only hoped Bert would stay unconscious, as the second he awoke the interrogation would commence.

***

Purella stared at the wreck of her ship in dismay. No one inside could have survived *that* explosion! How was she going to tell Quint that his prisoner was dead? Her team were picking around amongst the debris. She did the same, searching for any sign of a living being. That was when she noticed a footprint in the mud. She recognised the sole of the boot, as she had purchased them. It was on its own, going towards the trees. There were no others as they were keeping to the grass and the roots. Yet it was there... So... it was a trick! They were alive and hiding somewhere out there. She sent a message to Clyde telling him to let her know if any ship left the planet.

"This way!" she shouted, getting the others to follow.

A shot was fired from somewhere and one of Purella's team went down with a scream. Purella and the others reeled and opened fire at the forest. Several women melted away from a treeline overlooking them. Purella ran a scan and was pleased to see that they were retreating. They had probably been interested in the remains of the ship.

"Do we give chase?" shouted someone.

"No!" Purella hissed, not wanting to get distracted. If Satiah was nearby, and didn't already know they were there, she would now. She turned back in the direction they had originally been going in.

"Let's go, quietly now!" she ordered, in a lower voice.

***

After a while thinking about it, Satiah decided that playing the role of *potential employee* had the best chance of working. She would approach the entrance and pretend she had come to the planet specifically to join the forces on it. It was a flimsy argument but hard to prove wrong. She didn't call it a potential recruit, because she never saw soldiers of any sort as recruits, only employees. Her main concern was that they might not bother with things like *evidence* and kill her out of hand. Yet in *any* war, workforces were *always* needed. And she was on her own... as far as they would know. She would have to surrender her pistol, certainly, but she hoped they wouldn't notice her blade or her specs. Satiah took a deep breath, held her hands up in the air and then strolled casually out from cover. She hated gambling at the best of times, most of all with her own life, but this was her best chance at getting access to a ship.

"Freeze!" yelled someone. "*Don't move!*" Satiah obeyed, trying not to smile. How many times had she heard those words? It was going well so far, in that she was still alive. A young woman, most likely a teenager, scampered out from cover and stopped about six paces from Satiah. She was holding a rifle.

"Who are you?" she demanded, more curious than angry. Satiah's calm confidence was unexpected to the girl who was used to either confronting the aggressive or the fearful.

"A *friend*," Satiah lied, easy going. "I have made the life changing decision to leave behind my old life and join you in your cause here." The girl looked awkward. Clearly she'd not expected that answer. "*Maybe you should call for your officer,*" suggested Satiah, in an undertone. "*Always a good idea to let the higher ranks do the thinking.*" A woman stumbled out from cover, also armed.

"You have got three barrels on you and that's *not* counting ours," she stated, in a snarl. Satiah raised an eyebrow of displeasure.

"Are *you* supposed to be the officer?" Satiah asked, condescendingly. She expected to have to duck a blow but none came.

"...Who are you?" was the guarded reply.

"A friend," Satiah persisted. "I want to join." The *officer* and the girl exchanged looks and in that moment, gave away that they were mother and daughter. The girl ran off, presumably to fetch someone else.

"Can I lower my hands now?" Satiah asked, quizzically. The woman didn't answer, just watched her warily. Like someone would watch a dangerous animal that was being unusually docile. The girl returned after about six minutes' agonised silence, another woman following.

She was taller than the other two, taller than Satiah as well. She had short, spiky brown hair and a long sword at her side. *Swords as well as guns?* What was Satiah about to blunder into? She made up her mind that it would *not* be the blade.

"I'm Captain Vann," she stated, simply. "I fight for Asgardame Unit Seven of the Firestones." It was all Satiah could do to keep a straight face to that. Asgardame was a word that had many complicated meanings but in this sense it meant all-female fighting force. This usually meant between eight and twenty women in a team. *That word was fine*; it was the Firestones that nearly had Satiah in hysterics.

"Satiah," Satiah said, deciding against using her code-name here. They, in all probability, didn't even know what Phantom Squad was. Her actual name wasn't common *per se* but neither was it unheard of. In any case, she wasn't exactly planning on a long stay. If she could get Bert out of this she would but her *first priority* was to get a ship.

They made a move somewhere between a nod and a bow towards one another.

"We don't just take *anyone*," Vann stated, eyeing the pistol resting against Satiah's hip. "Do you know how to use that?" Satiah glanced down as if noticing it for the first time.

"I'm familiar with it," she shrugged, casually. That was certainly one way of putting it.

"When *and if* you join us, your past life doesn't exist anymore, ok? Where you come from and even who you are shouldn't matter to the sorority. All that being said... *it might matter to me*," she stated, assertively. Ah, at last, someone with a brain. "Why would you come all the way out here to join us?"

Satiah made herself start to look uncomfortable, like she was trying to hide something.

"I didn't think you would care?" she offered, as if caught out.

"This *is* war and I'm not an idiot. I want to know who is guarding my back," Vann stated, not unreasonably.

"Some would say it's not the greatest reason..." Satiah sighed, as if she was giving in. She trailed off, feigning light emotional trauma.

"If it works for you," shrugged Vann, then she glanced at the other two. "Let's go somewhere private, shall we?" And, just like that, they entered the camp. "*Well?*"

"...It was a man," Satiah said, becoming tearful.

They sat down by a campfire and Vann listened intently. She'd probably heard loads of these stories and Satiah knew it was best to keep it plausible.

"I thought he loved me," sobbed Satiah, convincingly. Vann looked up and waved a hand at someone. A boy ran over to them.

"Get us some food," she growled, at him. The boy ran away again. A slave.

"I... Is that *a boy?*" Satiah asked, in slight confusion.

"We do not agree that *all* men should be killed," Vann stated, seriously. "They are useful as slaves and we do need them to ensure the race survives. That is where *we* differ from most of the other sororities on this world. Go on."

"His name was Carl," she went on. She mentally apologised to him for throwing him under the loading transporter. "He *said* he loved me and I... I believed him." She could have won awards for her acting but she was careful not to overplay it.

"*Ah*," Vann nodded, seeming to see where this was meant to be going.

"He was cheating on me and I was so angry I just..." Satiah trailed off again. She raised her hand to indicate she'd struck something.

"You murdered him?" Vann guessed, as anyone logically would.

"I killed them both," Satiah told her, embellishing just a tad. "And I found myself wondering *how* we could ever let men do this to us? How could we keep *letting it happen?* That is when I decided to come here."

"That and the fact you would most likely be *arrested* if you remained," Vann added, smoothly.

"I worked *in security* and I could have got away with it *if I had wanted to*," Satiah stated, pretending to be a little insulted. "I didn't have to come *here* in any case."

"That's true," Vann noted, holding up a hand. She hadn't intended to affront her.

"That's my story," Satiah shrugged, wiping the last tear away. She sniffed melodramatically and then eyed Vann directly. "*What's yours?*" Vann gave her an evil grin as the boy returned with two bowls of something hot. Vann shooed him away and then turned back to hand Satiah what was most likely some kind of field stew. No army should be without it.

"How did you know I wasn't born here?" Vann asked, interested. Satiah hadn't known that but she acted as if she had.

"*Just a feeling*," she mumbled, as if she was reluctant.

"Well you seem to be good at reading people," Vann said, blowing into her bowl to cool it down. "I *was* just a normal girl until I was sixteen when I was abducted. For years I was moved around and... *used.*" Vann glanced at Satiah expecting the usual reaction, either a squirm or a look of horror. She found neither. Satiah didn't believe her and even if she did, she'd heard too many stories like that. Too many to warm the icy core of her heart with either sympathy or rage. Another day, another crime. Everything was relative.

"I had given up; I really was becoming just a piece of meat. Then this man found me... decided to try to help me for whatever reason. It went wrong and he was killed but I managed to get away. I heard about this place and have stayed here ever since," she concluded. "That was... maybe fourteen years ago." Satiah was inwardly hoping the stew wasn't poisoned as she sniffed it carefully.

"You lose track of time on this world. Your senses become dulled but only because you know that here is the only pace that you are truly free." If that was her idea of a selling point, it didn't appeal to Satiah. She nodded, in apparent understanding. It smelt nice, if a little sweet for her tastes. The boy sat opposite them with a musical instrument across his lap. He eyed them, eagerly. Satiah nudged Vann who hadn't noticed. Vann eyed him and then nodded. The boy though was staring at Satiah. She winked and smiled encouragingly at him.

The boy plucked the strings of the instrument, finding a tune easily, his dextrous fingers working adeptly. The campfire was pleasant to look at and Satiah fought against the temptation to relax. He began to sing. This song he knew he would get into trouble for, but he liked it and if possible he liked to get on his captors' nerves. It had been two years or thereabouts since they had killed his father. He had been a slave too, but he'd been free once and had taught his son this song in secret.

"You can walk until your boots are worn. You can scream until your lungs are gone. You can curse the day you were born. But you can't keep doing all that for long," he began, softly. A few of the other women, while eating, glanced up to listen and watch him. Satiah had the distinct idea he was trying to impress *her*. Perhaps, as she was new, he was hoping that she might treat him better than the others did.

"You can love them with all your heart. You can hold on with all your strength. You can only ever find the smallest part. But you can't just measure a journey by its length." He glanced up at the sky as if seeking what made it, to some, look so sublime. Satiah saw it as him endeavouring to add some depth or mysticism to the words that might not otherwise have been there. Artists were forever doing that... particularly when they lacked talent.

"For the answer the equation gives you two halves. You cannot have one without the other. One is a woman and the other... *is a man!*" he sang, knowing what was coming. Of all the things to sing to a bunch of fanatical feminists! Satiah almost laughed. Almost. What happened next though was no one's idea of a joke.

She had expected some kind of reaction but even she was taken aback by the ferocity of the response. One of the women nearest to him threw her bowl of the scalding stew over him; others hurled verbal abuse at him, while Vann ripped the instrument out of his grasp and broke it across her knee. He winced in pain but did not cry out. Clearly he had expected nothing less and had been mentally prepared for the punishment. He maintained eye contact as best as he could with Satiah. Satiah just watched, the beginnings of pity stirring inside her. She knew she could do nothing to help him, especially at that moment as she had her own cover to think about. Yet she made a mental note of the incident to avenge, if she had the chance, his needless, endless, heartless suffering.

"*Get out of my sight!*" screamed one, kicking at him on the floor. Two others came over and started to pick him up.

Vann sat down again, next to Satiah, in a huff.

"That boy will die if he carries on," she muttered, furious. Who doesn't? Satiah was still watching as he was dragged away. She wasn't disturbed at all by this scene, as she had encountered far worse so often that she'd become numbed to the brutality of it all. She'd liked the song and the fact that he'd dared sing it. She knew a fellow rogue when she saw one.

"Where are they taking him?" she asked, disinterestedly. Perhaps the same place they kept *all* their prisoners?

"The cells, where all the other slaves are," she replied, sourly. "Some were born here, some we captured from other sororities in raids and *some...* some apparently just crash landed here." She glanced right at Satiah as she said those words. Satiah noticed and gave no visible reaction.

"*Lovely*," Satiah mused, without meaning it.

***

Darius, slightly drunk, was sitting in the room he was staying in. He was playing back the recording of Milo's last conversation over and over. As if he could somehow gain further inspiration from the exchange.

"I think it's encrypted," Milo's voice was saying. He was followed by the oddly computer-like voice.

"You *think*? You had better be sure. If anyone nearby picks you up, I can't promise I will get there in time to protect you."

"I'm still close to the neutral section." Milo again.

"Okay. I won't have long; patrols are like clockwork along the border. There *are* gaps but they are not around for long. I'll be at 8433-1116 in two hours, see you there." The final words from the mysterious other.

Darius had once again tried playing it *very loudly* to see if anything in the background could be heard but there was nothing. He was still convinced everything led back to that moon! All right, so he'd found no trace of Milo in the detention area! So what? That just meant he wasn't there *while he was searching it*! He smashed the empty glass against the wall, fury building inside him. Dyss was going to love this! Satiah had set him up to fail! And now she'd just swanned off whilst keeping him off balance! Ten years! Ten *bitter* years after Operation Jackdaw and now *this*! Again, as he had been many times before, he was tempted to call Dyss and finish what they had started back then once and for all. He didn't though, knowing that that was the drink talking. He would play it the way he always did: say nothing unless asked directly.

To take his mind away from the darkness of the subjects, he decided to indulge in something he rarely had time to do these days. Cohesion Motion exercises. Stripping to his waist he clasped his hands behind his back, lowered his chin to his chest and closed his eyes. Breathe. The routine came back to him easily. Still with closed eyes, he stretched his hands towards the ceiling and began to arch his back. Slowly he went through a therapeutic sequence of stances and moves designed to test every muscle and yet relieve stress and help the subject to relax. Next, he went through the equilibrium routine, adopting various poses that required complete concentration to achieve perfect balance and stillness. At last he felt the rage start to distance itself from his mind. Lastly, he simply did some more standard core body exercises.

This enabled him to pass an hour more peacefully than he might have done otherwise. He settled into a chair, pulling a black and gold silk robe about his shoulders. He activated the computer. The central news corporation, or CNC, was on.

"And today tensions mounted over the ongoing conflict in the eighty-fourth sector as yet again the Shintu ambassadors failed to attend the negotiations, I have here…" Darius turned it off, smirking. Typical scaremongering! He tried to call Satiah again but he couldn't get a response. If she was in trouble, without knowing where she was, he couldn't help her. He had to trust that she would eventually return... hopefully with Milo alive. At last, he allowed himself to settle into sleep.

***

Purella and her team made their way quickly through the forest in the dark. Satiah had left no tracks but the man she'd taken *had*. Every so often there were crushed plants and signs of someone forcing their way through. Then, abruptly, the tracks ended. Purella glanced up, wondering if they had hidden up in the trees. Nothing other than the gentle whispers of leaves in the night breeze.

"*Tracks here!*" whispered someone. "What do we do now?" Purella came to see. A group of people had gone this way... and recently. One had even discarded an empty water container. Purella knew that had to mean troops had found them. But troops from which side? Purella wanted to follow but she knew they would run into someone else if they did. This was pointless!

Pulling out her computer, she checked the map. They were close to the constantly moving border between the Firestone and Pale Brigade sororities. When Purella had last been there, nearly three years ago, a warrior queen had been leading the brigade, and had managed to win more than a few victories. While they had not exactly parted on friendly terms... Purella was confident that, should that queen still be in charge, she could get help from her. It was likely that the Firestones had Quint's prisoner and Satiah ... So if *she* could get the Brigade to attack the Firestones, in the confusion, she could acquire them. It was a bit of a risky strategy but she had precious few options. She led her followers in the opposite direction of the tracks.

***

Satiah had catnapped the night away, remaining aware of her surroundings while her body rested. The fire had slowly died to embers and the night sentries were replaced by the day ones. She had been warm enough, if slightly clammy, wrapped in thick woollen blankets, which were stitched together with thick string. Kicking away the covers, she found the communal showering areas and cleaned herself up. As she was alone she checked her earpiece, blade and gun were still there and untampered with. They were. She tried again to call Kelvin but the signal was still being blocked. She knew why now too. Because of the never-ending tribal warfare on the planet, all signals were blocked to prevent radio communication on and off world.

That was when she made a discovery, one she couldn't believe she'd failed to make before. In her pocket she'd found that weird orangey gemstone from Purella's ship! She could have sworn that she'd thrown it back in its crate! Had it been with her *this whole time*? Unsure what to do, she just put it back in her pocket. It gave her the creeps but... she had other concerns. She concealed her earpiece and then headed outside again, putting the gemstone out of her mind.

She needed to find a ship, Bert and... She stopped when she saw that the boy who'd been punished the previous night for playing music 'harmful to the state' was chopping fire wood up with a small hatchet. She leaned against the wall, arms crossed, and a plan formed in her mind. He stopped and turned, seeming to sense her watching him. She moved out to address him.

"Where is Captain Vann?" she asked, casually.

"I don't know," he answered, tensely.

"Do you need more wood to chop?" she enquired, motioning to the dwindling pile next to him. He stared down at it, confused by the question. He managed a feeble shrug. She guessed what he was imagining and crouched in front of him to face him eye to eye.

"You don't need to be afraid of me," she told him, seriously. "I'm not like the others. We can be friends. Secret friends. What's your name?" He shrugged again, looking chagrined. Then she realised, they had never bothered to name him.

"My name is Satiah and I will think of a name that you can have," she assured him, putting her hand on his shoulder. She squeezed reassuringly. "From now on, I will do what I can to protect you," she promised him. "For you are useful to me." A confused look came over him.

"How?" he asked, levelly. "Are you a spy?"

"No, I'm just compassionate," she lied, smoothly. "What if I was a spy though? Now that we are friends, would you tell anyone?"

He looked around cautiously then shook his head.

"Do they have spaceships here?" she asked, interested. Before he answered, a shout interrupted him.

"Satiah!" It was Captain Vann. Satiah looked up, affecting a nonchalant air. Vann was stood about twenty paces away with some other women. They were all armed but not hostile. "Come on! We're on patrol!" Satiah nodded, winked at the boy and hurried off to catch up with them. The boy winked back and watched her go, trying to hide the smile he had on his face. Satiah caught up with them as they reached the main gates leading out into the forest.

"What were you talking to that boy about?" Vann asked, irritated.

"The way he was chopping up that wood he was going to *hack off his own hand*," Satiah muttered, waving dismissively. "Someone had to tell him to be more careful or he would face punishment."

Vann gave her a look but didn't pursuit the matter further.

"Scouts spotted movement to the south; we're going to check it out. Are you ready for some action?" Vann asked, grinning.

"I'll do my best," Satiah assured her, mordantly. Vann caught her arm.

"I *know* you've killed once before but you've got a long way to go before you see things as we do. The couple you killed, it was *personal*. The people you will end up fighting have done nothing to you personally and you might find dispatching them difficult because of this," Vann lectured. If only Vann knew who she was really talking to.

"*I see*," Satiah concurred, as if she'd never considered that. "What do you suggest?"

"You will be tested later... a test of your *ruthlessness*. I felt I had to give you fair warning... If you do not take life... yours might be taken instead," Vann said. Satiah had expected this. It was a common if flawed way of testing both fidelity and brutality.

It was flawed because ultimately it proved nothing. People like her, Phantoms, had no qualms about killing anyone in any way. They were not alone in that ability either. Loyalty was always going to come down to a leap of faith. And there were such things as *genuine mistakes* that could muddy the waters when it came to judging someone's commitment. She would put on a show of course, make it look like she was struggling with her conscience when it came down to it. Vann had implied that if she failed to kill *for them* then they would try to kill her. If it came to that she was sure she would not make it easy for them.

The forest was soundless, as if in expectation. No birdsong. Not even the sounds of small mammals foraging for food. They were hardly twenty minutes away from the camp. Satiah had already spotted the enemy before anyone else. She kept silent about it though, interested to see how good these women really were. There were forty or so of them, travelling in two groups. Vann and her troops seemed to be spending more time watching Satiah than they did the surround. Pity, she mused, as there was not much to see – they would be much smarter to watch out for their regular enemy. She looked around at their faces, trying to imagine what worlds they had seen and what had driven them to this madness. They all wanted a world where men didn't rule them and had created a living hell where they battled each other for dominance instead. They failed to comprehend the very nature of being human.

How many had tried to tell them? Even tried to help them? And how many of those had they murdered as heretics? A scream of alarm broke her out of that depressing cynical reverie. Her pistol was in her hand, in the usual kneejerk style she'd made her own over the years. She clamped down on herself though, trying to look fearful, inexperienced and confused at once. For her, this was not easy. Rapid laser fire was exchanged. As someone who was afraid would, Satiah half covered her ears with her hands and dived for cover behind the nearest tree. She was sure Vann had seen her; she'd made it as obvious as she could. A detonator went off and Satiah caught sight of someone, burning as they went, flying through the air.

Shouts, screams, smoke and destruction sounded from behind the tree and Satiah just sat there almost like she didn't have a care in the world. A grenade rolled over to her and she casually lobbed it away heedless of where it went. Let those idiots fight it out amongst themselves... Then she stopped... she couldn't allow the other side to win, if she did then... Growling in irritation, she peeped out from cover. A sandy-haired woman staggered out from the smoke. She was one of Vann's so Satiah didn't shoot her. She was hit in the arm by a stray bolt from somewhere and went down with a scream. Satiah darted out from cover, grabbed the woman's collar and dragged her backwards to where she had been. The woman was wincing, tears in her eyes, with pain. She was young, less than twenty. Satiah eyed the wound.

"Flesh only, *you'll be fine*, stay down," she ordered, coldly.

After leaving her with a rifle, Satiah charged into the smoke. She quickly found Vann and the others clustered around the remains of a building.

"Finally decided to join us then!" barked one of them. Vann eyed her irately.

"Sorry," Satiah apologised, quickly. "I panicked. One of us is back there with an upper arm injury. She's got a gun so she should be okay. How many of them are there?" There were about forty, as Satiah had already counted but she wanted to know how good Vann was. Vann's expression changed from one of anger to one of bewilderment. How could someone change from panic to complete calm so quickly? A survivor?

"At least twenty," Vann growled, straining to see. Satiah had to stop herself from telling her to split everyone up as together they presented a very easy target.

An explosion occurred very close and the screaming started. Satiah saw that at least four of them were down now.

"Do you think we should spread out?" she shouted, over the din. Vann seemed to be floundering a bit. Satiah grabbed her arm and forced her to look at her.

"*We need to split up!*" Satiah screamed, in her face. Vann, recovering herself, wrenched her arm free from Satiah's grip.

"*I know!*" she barked back. "Swamp pattern!" Reluctant but obedient, they began to drift apart but not that far away. Satiah, starting to think this was still going to end badly, decided to help them properly. She aimed, and began picking off enemies that got too close.

Vann and her *warriors* seemed to favour sending hundreds of shots in the general direction of the enemy and then advancing only when no answering fire came back. Satiah only took shots that killed. Cleverly though, she did it without being observed. A whistle was blown from somewhere and the enemy retreated. Satiah had fired eight shots and killed eight people. She had no idea how many shots Vann and her troops had fired but they had managed to kill three. They did, however, succeed in capturing an unconscious woman they found in among the bodies. They returned to the wounded woman that Satiah had saved. After they had rested for a few minutes the accusations started.

"Next time, how about actually *fighting?*" snarled one, pushing Satiah aggressively. Satiah did her best to look intimidated and didn't look up from the floor.

"You can't just hide *sweetie*, they'll dig you out and eat you," said another mockingly.

"She saved my life!" bellowed the one Satiah had dragged free of the firefight. "She did more for me than *any of you!*"

"*Enough!*" barked Vann, getting silence. "Normally, when we meet the enemy and win, *like today*, we kill five maybe six of them. Today we got eleven, *twelve if you include the prisoner*. I'm not saying it was *all* because of her because I *know* it can't have been. Yet I ask you all to give her another chance, it *was* her first day, don't forget." There were more dubious glances at Satiah, evidently opinion was divided.

***

It was not clear exactly *what* they had interrupted. Some kind of party? Purella and the remainder of those she'd chosen to bring with her had made contact with an officer of the Brigade. Some of the people with her had succumbed, first to a brief friendly fire incident when they had mistaken a mannequin for an enemy, and then to two traps set by no one could guess who. A team of thirty down to twelve in as many hours. The officer of the Brigade had then, with almost one hundred troops, escorted Purella into the city. A city! This hadn't been here three years ago, Purella thought. The Queen must really be doing well. It was mostly wooden but some effort had been put in to rebuilding a ruined structure using stone. It was an odd mix and vaguely disorientating to see. Laser rifle but log fires. Stone walls but modern motion-activated flash-lighting.

There was shooting, cheering and all kinds of insanity going on. Purella enjoyed it. It was like an anarchist's vacation resort. A place where literally anything could happen. *Anything*. And anything *without* any real consequence. It reminded her of the good old days… the days of the Varn-Utto before… She remembered Satiah and the pleasure of the moment left her. Somewhere out there, on that planet, under that sun, a Phantom agent lurked. *A Phantom agent.* The inconsolable wrath that built up inside her actually distracted her from the fact that someone was approaching her.

"This is the Prince," hissed a woman, in her ear. She snapped back to reality and faced the man in confusion.

"*Prince?*" she mouthed, to herself. Since when were *men* allowed into positions of power on *this planet*? She had no private objection, of course, but this world was known for its extreme outlooks.

"Your Majesty," she smiled, amiably.

"Purella," he smiled, courteously. He was tall, broad but not very muscular. Instantly she could tell this was no man of action. He was a man of leisure. Someone who should in theory stand no chance of survival in such a place. "My mother spoke very highly of you." She wasn't sure which word to question: *spoke* or *highly*. She'd not left this planet on good terms with anyone, least of all the Queen, three years ago. Granted, things may have changed, but the people of this world never forgot a grudge. Neither did Purella.

"*Spoke?*" she queried, curiously.

"She passed away last year… *We still deeply mourn her loss*," he said, with a strange twinkle in his eyes. Like he was trying not to laugh or something.

"…Understandable," Purella limited herself to replying.

"*Please…* join me in the palace," he invited, waving a hand in its direction. "There is much we need to discuss." There was? Purella sighed, unsure what to expect but ready to unleash chaos if she had to. He led her away from the carousing, violent streets and into a quieter, more heavily guarded area. Finally, they reached a room filled with comfortable chairs and other items of comparative luxury.

"Make yourself comfortable. Wine?" he offered, pleasantly. She only took some water, not wanting anything to affect her judgement.

"You're being *very* friendly," she noted, allowing her suspicion to show. "That in itself is not in keeping with the traditions of this world."

He let out a laugh at that while easing himself onto a padded sofa.

"I'm a *progressive*, so I'm told," he elaborated, with artificial flourish.

"You want something from me," she stated, seriously. "What is it?" His smile faded and a darker look edged forwards throughout his countenance.

"I know that you and my mother parted ways on less than good terms," he said, sagely. "Understandable, she like many here, was a difficult person. I was able to secure my power here with the help of certain individuals when I poisoned her…" Ah, now she understood.

"You usurped her and now you're worried about kickback," she spelt out. "*Understandable*." She chose the word deliberately.

"*You* want something too, from me, *otherwise you would not be here*," he went on. "I *think* we can help each other."

"I'm not here for recruits," she told him. "Not this time."

"I see you have not brought us any either," he commented. For some reason that remark made her even more mistrustful.

"I'm tracking a woman called Satiah who has stolen some valuable property of mine," she lied, "its value lies not in terms of finance, but of *sentiment*."

"And you want *me* to help you find her?" he guessed, easily.

"I think she has fallen into the hands of your rivals *the Firestones*," she elaborated, hoping that just their mention would encourage him to help. "I need a force strong enough to challenge them in order to retrieve her." He nodded in comprehension.

"We have a loose truce with them *currently*, but that can be made to fade away," he mused. "We possess the military advantage."

"And what can I do for you in return?" she enquired, grimly.

"Like I said, I secured my power with the help of *certain individuals*. These individuals *were* useful but I fear they have become somewhat difficult to control. And I cannot use my own people, *not any one of them*, to deal with them. They *could* betray me," he elucidated. "I've already suspect some of colluding and making plans to remove me."

"And you can trust *me* to kill them for you. You can trust that I won't join them because I'm not from here and so cannot be trusted *by them*," Purella concluded, knowingly. He nodded and toasted her with his drink. She fell silent, weighing options.

"Well?"

Purella downed the last of her water and stretched casually. This was too easy... *too convenient.*

"Give me their names and I'll deal with them tonight."

***

Darius sat up abruptly. A scream had awoken him. Alarms were blaring.

"Stay in your homes!" announced a voice. "The city is under attack, stay in your homes!"

Darius raced out, pistol at the ready. Civilians were running here and there along with the guards. He glanced out of a viewport and could see the distant dots of approaching spacecraft. *Another attack*! It had to be! Where were the defences...? *Oh yeah, there weren't any!* Taking the stairs three at a time, as security had deactivated all lifts in accordance with emergency procedure, Darius sprinted for Satiah's ship. There was no way he could take on their whole force single handed, but he figured he might be able to take one of them down or draw them off – or *something*! Something had to be done! A guard tried to stop him as he ran out onto the landing pad but Darius shoved him aside.

He made it on board, not bothering to try and see what was going on; he'd use the ship's computer for that and it would be much more accurate than using his own eyes. He launched off the landing pad and plunged straight down to avoid laser fire. On the way towards the swirling oceans, he ran a scan and prepared the ship for combat. Fully fuelled, fast and agile, he was sure he'd be able to achieve something other than his own death or escape. Scan was complete and to his surprise Kelvin sat next to him in the co-pilot seat.

"How did...?" he began, preoccupied.

"Satiah wouldn't appreciate you stealing her ship," Kelvin stated, his red eyes focussed on Darius.

"I'm not stealing *anything*!" he retorted. "The city needs something to at least take the heat off!" Kelvin said nothing to that.

Turning the craft around with a nifty front flip, Darius propelled them back upwards at four times the speed of sound. The scan was complete – one capital ship and twenty fighters, all seeming to be of Vinu manufacture. Darius decided to chase the nearest fighter: it was obvious that it was not expecting resistance of any sort. Its shields were not even up and Darius cleaved it in two with a vicious laser attack. Instantly there was a change as the fighters abandoned their attack on the city and began to do one of two things. Some came at him, on the attack. Others, more puzzlingly still, headed back towards their mothership. Darius, a skilled pilot, dodged this way and that to avoid the retaliatory laser attacks with ease. Kelvin launched a locked-on missile that homed in after its target.

To avoid being hit, that ship disengaged and began an erratic course to try to lose the projectile. That left twelve others. They didn't attack as one though, but as individuals. This helped a lot as they got in each other's way and actually made things easier for Darius.

"These guys must be newbies," he growled, barrel-rolling them to the right.

"They are not following military guidelines," Kelvin noted. A blast from behind them occurred as Kelvin's missile finally found its target. Darius blasted another craft stupid enough to fly by right in front of him. Their luck then ran out as a blast shook them. Darius winced as another narrowly missed them, flashing dangerously as it went past.

"Check the damage reports please," Darius ordered, to Kelvin. "*Now* I think is the time to get out of this!"

He swung out of the open and into the clouds, still being chased by five other fighters. Within moments the fighters abandoned their chase and promptly retreated. Darius stared at Kelvin in astonishment. They ran another scan. Since the fight began a new arrival seemed to have settled the matter. A *colonial* destroyer hovered there as if it were the most normal thing in the cosmos. The cruiser, wisely, had chosen to abandon the attack there and then. It was no match for a destroyer. A light flashed on the console and Darius raised an eyebrow.

"I'm popular today," he muttered, answering the call. "Yes?"

"This is Captain Ogun of the Colonial Federation destroyer *Froissement* to unidentified ship, do you require assistance?" came a strong, Colonial, male voice. Darius eyed Kelvin casually. Froissement was a fencing term, as far as Darius knew, meaning an attack that shifts the opponent's blade by a robust grazing stroke.

"Captain, this is Darius, negative, we're okay now," he answered, guardedly. "Thanks for being there." A third voice joined the exchange.

"Captain, this is Reed, *I'm the Coalition Ambassador*, welcome, it seems your timekeeping is impeccable," Reed said.

"My transit was uneventful," Ogun responded, flatly.

"Please, come down in one of your shuttles and join us for our evening meal, the Viscount will be there," Reed invited.

"...Very well," Ogun said, not sounding particularly enthusiastic. "Send me the time and location, I will be there."

"Congratulations Darius, I thank you *as do the people you just protected*. I hereby extend the same invitation to you," Reed went on. Darius grimaced. He, like Ogun apparently, was not in favour of socialising like this.

"*Okay*," he confined himself to saying.

"Any word from you know who yet?" Reed enquired, his tone conspiratorial.

"No," he answered, sourly. He eyed Kelvin who had nothing to add.

"See you soon. *By the way*, a crowd has gathered to welcome you back... *Try to be normal*," Reed ordered, grinning.

"It's a stretch," Darius deadpanned. Kelvin showed him the damage report and he rolled his eyes. Hopefully they could get it fixed *before* Satiah came back.

***

It didn't matter who you were or who you knew in life: a thorn bush was a blasted thorn bush! And of course, thorn bushes being typically thorny and difficult at the best of times, were rarely alone. Satiah, Vann and the others trampled through a never-ending plantation of them on the way back from the skirmish. Satiah couldn't bring herself to call it *a battle* but *fight* didn't seem to do it justice either. No one made it through that shrubbery untouched, not even Satiah.

"Are they venomous?" Satiah asked, concerned.

"No, just painful," Vann grumbled, picking one out of her own shoulder.

"Here," said Cherry, handing Satiah a small bottle. It was a remedy to prevent infection. Cherry was the woman Satiah had earlier saved and now was doing everything she could to repay the favour. It was actually starting to get on Satiah's nerves. Like a child who kept quietly asking you to play, they were doing nothing wrong *per se*, but it was still irritating.

"I just wanted to say *thank you*, you know, for saving me," Cherry said, rather feebly.

"*You have already said that*," Satiah grunted, at her. Cherry was the baby of the group, Satiah had discovered. She'd been born on the planet too, about nineteen years ago, and so she knew no other life. She knew that Satiah *did* know other lives though and kept asking all sorts of questions about anything and everything imaginable. It was only natural curiosity... not a suspicion of Satiah herself that was her motivation.

"Is it true that some planets have no *flowers*?" she asked, eyes wide.

"Yup," Satiah nodded, seeking an escape. Cherry gawped at her.

"Then how do people *breathe*?" she asked, incredulous.

"They don't," Satiah answered, flatly.

Cherry seemed to pick up on Satiah's mood and flushed red in discomfiture.

"I'm *sorry* if I'm bothering you but *I think you're interesting*," she apologised. "Just so you know: if you need a favour, and I mean *anything*..." She touched herself in a suggestive way, running one hand across her thigh and pulling down her collar with the other. "*I mean anything at all*. Just ask and I *will* do whatever you want."

"*Thanks*," Satiah smiled tightly, taking it all in stride. This was not the first time another woman had made a pass at her. A *favour* was always useful, however... particularly the kind that Cherry *didn't* mean. On a planet where men were rare it was quite understandable that Cherry would behave like this.

Satiah could just imagine Carl, *what a waste* he would say. That thought made her snigger. Cherry noticed and coloured up even more, shyly.

"There is something you can do," Satiah said, putting her hand on her shoulder. Cherry tensed, expecting to be told to shut up or something. Satiah leaned in close to whisper in her ear.

"Tonight, you can join me for a *polite conversation* about other worlds if you're *really* that interested." Cherry brightened.

"*Really?*" she asked, awestruck. *No, I made it all up,* Satiah alleged to herself sarcastically!

"*Yes, really,*" smiled Satiah, letting her go.

Much to Satiah's relief, this seemed to satisfy Cherry and she backed off gradually. Satiah had no problem with that category of women who were not into men, but she knew that she was undoubtedly not one of them. The prisoner had woken up now, tied down and gagged – there was nothing she could do to prevent her fate. Satiah never tried to convince herself that they would interrogate and incarcerate the woman. Unless she escaped somehow, she was as dead as her comrades that Satiah had gunned down. Satiah didn't feel any pity for her; such madness was to be expected if you chose to live in this hell.

At last they made it back to camp about mid-afternoon. Vann wasted no time in preparing the execution by ordering some of them to build a pyre. She didn't tell Satiah that it was for the prisoner but Satiah had seen these kinds of things before. Remote tribes, desperate criminals, religious ceremonies… the list went on and on. Satiah pretended not to know why they were building it. The prisoner was crying as *she* clearly knew exactly why and Satiah decided that this lunacy had gone far enough.

"Why are we building *this* when we already have campfires?" she asked, to Vann. Vann eyed her and just shrugged as if she didn't know. The more Satiah got to know Vann, the less she liked her. The prisoner, still tied up, was deposited on top of the pyre like the carcass of an animal.

Satiah glanced around, a plan forming in her mind. She gauged the other women and their attitudes towards what was about to happen. Vann and two or three others looked happy, almost eager at the prospect of someone else's pain. Most of the others looked a little gloomy. Perhaps they were considering the roles being reversed and that one day it could be their turn. Cherry was keeping her eyes on the ground. She unmistakably wanted no part of what was happening but lacked the bravery to either walk away or challenge it. As Satiah had guessed, Vann handed the flaming torch to *her*. This was another test of her ruthlessness.

"Kill her," Vann ordered, pointing at the prisoner. Satiah grinned manically back at her, as if she would like nothing better. She took the torch and approached the pyre, under the expectant eyes of the whole Asgardame. As she got close, the prisoner's tearfully pleading eyes greeted her determined ones.

She stopped at the base of the pyre and turned to face Vann and the others, still grinning. Vann nodded in encouraging approval. Satiah drew her pistol and shot the prisoner in the head, killing her instantly. A mercy kill. As close to a painless death as Satiah could offer the poor woman whose only reason for dying was that she wore a different uniform to these other women. Satiah doubted that the woman would have been *that grateful* but it was all she could do *without* starting a fight. There was an astonished silence. Vann was livid. Cherry gaped.

"You were supposed to burn her!" she raged, furious. Indulging sadists was a lot like allowing plagues to spread, counter-productive.

"That's not what you said. You told me to kill her. *I killed her*," Satiah replied, completely calm. This was true.

"What did you think I gave you the torch *for*?" she demanded, still angry.

"To be sure I had enough light to see to shoot with?" offered Satiah, playing incredibly dumb. Vann knew she'd done it purposely and that there was nothing remotely stupid about Satiah. An uncomfortable silence began.

All of a sudden, Cherry found her tongue.

"Let it go, Vann, *dead is dead*," she interjected, beseechingly. A few of the others also stepped up as if this act had snapped them out of the trances.

"She did do what you said *technically*," said another, trying to excuse it.

"It's her first day; *she'll get it right next time*," allowed a third, shrugging.

"You can *still* burn the body if you *want*; it's not the end of the world," Cherry offered, earnestly.

"*You're all cowardly sycophants!* I wanted to see her *burn*," hissed Vann, unhappily. Her bloodlust was plain for all to see but what interested Satiah was everyone else's reaction to it. Mixed would be the best word to describe it, yet those who disapproved were more vocal.

Vann finally looked away from Satiah at the other soldiers, also trying to see who wanted what. Basically no one was ready for a fight, as Satiah had predicted. She'd also, in theory, done as she was told, meaning that any punishment would be deemed hugely unfair. Most importantly of all, however, was that not one of the troops *wanted* a fight, certainly not about *this*. Vann was on her own in wanting to prolong this. She had to surrender and she did after considering all her alternatives.

"Fine. *Dismissed!*" she barked, waving her hand at everyone. She stared again at Satiah and Satiah stared back. Now they were in a new battle. A battle over the *leadership* of these soldiers. Satiah hadn't *wanted* this fight and she'd prefer *not* to make an enemy of Vann, but she wasn't into torturing people without good reason. And, secretly, she'd sometimes had a problem with doing what she was told.

Satiah knew to watch her back, like always. The sooner she got out of this the better. She went back to the area she called her own. A place where her back was against the wall and she had good visibility of the camp. The boy scampered over to her the second he saw she was back.

"Food?" he offered. She nodded. He hurried away obediently. Okay... maybe this lifestyle did have *some* rewards. As long as you *weren't* a slave, that is. Cherry shuffled over timidly and sat nearby.

"*You shouldn't have done that*," she warned, in a low voice. She was talking about the execution.

"Who says?" Satiah glowered, abrasive. "I did what I was told...

just like you do every day until you die." Cherry glanced up fearfully. Satiah made eye contact.

"Relax, I mean *you* no ill will but... Remember, *here* you are as much a slave as *that boy*," Satiah told her, levelly. Cherry deduced that that was true and nodded in reluctant agreement. She obeyed all orders, that was in fact all she did and lived in mild poverty despite obeying everything. The only difference was that she carried a rifle.

The boy returned with a steaming bowl of *something*.

"Did anyone other than *you* touch this?" Satiah asked, grimly. He shook his head. She sniffed, trying to detect anything recognisable. There was nothing, just normal food. Satiah didn't *know* if Vann would have access to poison, or even if she had the wit to use it correctly, but she was taking no chances.

"May I ask him to get me something?" Cherry asked, pointing to the boy.

"I don't know, *ask him*," Satiah chuckled.

"But *he's a slave*, I'm not *allowed* to..." she stopped herself, her forehead furrowing. "*You're right!*"

"You're learning," Satiah congratulated, nodding to her.

"So on other worlds is *everyone* equal?" she asked, trying the other extreme for size.

"Not so that you'd notice," Satiah sniggered.

"Even... *men?*" she queried, almost choking on the word. Satiah couldn't resist teasing her.

"Men rule mostly everything out there," Satiah lied, casually. Cherry looked horrified. Satiah grinned at her. "Only because we let them think so."

"*Stop it! You're confusing me!*" she hissed, laughing quietly. She turned to the boy. "Would you mind, *if you're not too busy*, getting me some soup *please?*" The boy looked muddled and stared at Satiah for guidance.

"Go get the blasted soup!" she commanded, briskly. That was the trouble with freedom and equality... they led to a lot of confusion. But she'd take confusion over tyranny any day.

"What did you do before you came here?" Cherry asked, curious. "You don't have to answer that if you don't want to," she added, quickly.

"General administration and refuse removal," Satiah answered, unable to stop herself sounding a little sinister. "Basically, I was a kind of problem solver."

"Vann said you were in security," Cherry noted. So, Vann had been gossiping about her. She was not surprised. Satiah could have given her an explanation that a lot of so-called managers offered. Dressing up their roles in such costumes of ostentatious verbal drivel that what they actually did was impossible to work out. Instead it was time for a bit of honesty, just to keep things interesting.

"Cherry, can I trust you?" she asked, watching the younger woman closely.

"Of course," she answered, sitting up. "I owe you my life so… I'll pretty much do anything you tell me. So long as it's not crazy."

"What about Vann?" Satiah enquired, curious.

"I follow her orders but you are my friend," she said, compellingly. "Friends are worth more to me than anything on this planet."

"If you ever had the chance, would you want to leave this planet?" Satiah quizzed, smoothly.

"I…" she paused, really thinking about it.

"If your answer is *yes* and I really can trust you…?" Satiah tested deliberately.

"Yes, you can, *I swear*!" she insisted, understandingly. Satiah left out the line about people who lie usually said that they swore it was true.

"Then we can do a deal," Satiah said, keeping her voice low. Cherry edged closer to hear better.

"A *deal*?"

"In the time I've spent here I've already decided I have no interest in staying here any longer than I have to. I know there must be *some* ships here. I plan to steal one and leave. Want to come with me?" she offered. Her reasoning behind this offer was not as generous as it might appear. Cherry might have information about the ships, but even if she didn't, it would be easier to steal one if she had someone with her who was capable of running. She would need help to get Bert out and the boy might not be enough. Cherry's smile spread into a grin.

"And see other worlds?" she asked, spellbound.

"Only if you promise not to tell anyone else – *no matter what happens*, your mouth *stays shut*," Satiah said, grit in her tone. Cherry swallowed nervously but nodded, purposely not saying a word to indicate that she really agreed.

"Okay," Satiah said. "Now I don't know how long this will take, less than three days I'm hoping. We will not be going alone. The boy is coming with us and… one of the prisoners." Cherry seemed to take this very well. She nodded again.

"What do you want me to do?" she asked, her own voice excited but low.

"There's a new prisoner, *caught sometime yesterday*, I don't know *when* exactly. He is an old man, with a broken ankle on his right leg and he claims he has no memory of anything. I want you to find out where he is. If you are unsure, say my name to him when no one else can hear you. Then you come back and *tell me where he is*," Satiah instructed, slowly. Cherry nodded.

"I *won't* let you down," she assured, her eyes betraying her enjoyment. Satiah then realised… secretly Cherry had never really wanted to be here at all. Another thing they had in common.

***

Purella emerged from the doorway, slipping her pistol back into its holster. It had been a long day. There had been thirty-six people she'd had to murder. Now there was only one left. She had done it professionally without making any scenes or even bothering to dispose of the bodies. She'd had to work with a guide, seeing as she had no clue who any of these people were or even what they looked like.

"Dead," she stated, to the guide. The woman nodded and motioned for Purella to follow. Purella and two members of her crew did. Marching through the streets at twilight was a surreal experience on this planet. The madness and the *mess* were unspeakable. Even

Purella had lost patience with it. It was interesting to see this place again and that it hadn't changed.

Some saw it as utopia, a place free of the supposed male influence. In reality it was more like a kind of dystopia, only with women ruling their own dictatorships. The more powerful still victimised the less powerful, as always. The failure of this society was no different than that of all the others and, as usual, those in it were usually too blind to see it. They had achieved nothing and changed very little in the process. As far as Purella was concerned, it was just another war. Why would they live like *this* when, if they joined together, they could make a lot of money? They had a huge army and could cause a lot of trouble if only they weren't so busy battling each other for supremacy over a bit of mud! They turned a corner and the guide stopped.

"Up there," she said, nodding at a ramshackle building. "Your last target awaits you."

"Name?" Purella grunted, impatiently.

"Yellow," smiled the guide, in a knowing way.

"*Yellow?*" Purella repeated. Strange name but it wasn't unheard of for people to be named after colours. "What does she look like?" The guide shrugged unhelpfully. Purella sighed and advanced towards the building. She shouldered the door open and listened. Silence. She advanced up the wooden steps, her boots making no noise. Her gloved fingers slowly moved close to her gun handle. There was only one door at the top. She took a deep breath and kicked it in.

As she took in what was beyond, she saw a brief countdown begin on the bomb she'd just activated. With a shriek she hurled herself down the stairs as it went off, bringing down the whole edifice in a concussive wave. Purella landed on her back in mid roll at the bottom of the steps and just managed to get clear from the collapsing structure. She got to her feet and froze. There was a silence and a crowd that watched her, guns trained on her.

"*Yellow* is the colour of *betrayal*," said a voice from behind her. She spun around and her eyes gleamed in knowing anger.

"So, you're not dead after all, *Queen Linkarni?*" Purella stated, trying to stay calm. "Who was the Prince? One of your slaves dressed up for the occasion?"

Queen Linkarni was old; Purella wasn't sure how old, and small. The harmless appearance belied a truly evil person. She was by all appearances frail, spotted and wrinkled with age. Her long hair was white and pulled back. She was sitting on a throne, supported by about ten men and surrounded by armed female guards.

"*Precisely*," Linkarni smiled, almost lasciviously. "The moment I heard you were back I concocted this little scheme."

"Who have I *really* been killing?" Purella asked, grimly.

"Oh, they really were dissidents and traitors and I could have done it myself but why bother when you can make your enemies fight one another?" she asked and let loose a cackle of triumphant laughter. Purella looked all around for an escape but she was completely surrounded. She'd have to talk her way out of this.

"What do you want?" Purella asked, sourly.

"*Me?*" Linkarni questioned, all innocence.

"I assume you want something from me or else I'd already be dead?" Purella enquired, sagely. "Or perhaps you had forgotten, *can't be easy at your age.*" Linkarni acknowledged the taunt with a twitch of the eyebrows.

"I see your wits have not *completely* deserted you," Linkarni noted, irately.

"I knew something was wrong the moment a man seemed to be in charge of the *so-called* planet of womankind," Purella told her. She *had* suspected something but she'd not anticipated *this*. "The removal of rivals was always plausible and, if these really were rivals as you say, then very little of what you told me was lies. There was one flaw in your plan, however."

"Go on," Linkarni mused.

"I only *just* escaped that explosion. What would have happened had it killed me?" Purella asked, gaining confidence with every word.

"Then I would have lost my chance at a new regular food delivery system," she stated, crisply. "But you *did* survive, as I had faith you would."

"So you need someone to keep your troops well fed?" Purella asked, rhetorically. "Suppose I agree but then never come back?"

"I have your entire team as prisoners," Linkarni shrugged. "If you do not return in a certain amount of time, I would, shall we say, make things very *unpleasant* for them."

Purella pretended to care about this. Only to allow the Queen to think she had something on her. Frankly her *team* were mercenaries at the end of the day. *No one she actually cared about.* Purella had no feelings one way or the other for any of them. She had seen this coming which was part of the reason why she'd forbade Clyde from joining her.

"What about the Firestones?" she asked, changing the subject. "I have some property I need to recover from them! It's why I came back."

"*What could be important enough?*" the Queen pondered, rhetorically. "You *knew* that you would hardly be welcomed if you ever returned here. Our last exchange would have left you in no doubt of *that*. You came anyway... is it money?"

"...*Indirectly*," concurred Purella, considering. Linkarni smiled knowingly.

"It's *more* than money! What is it?"

"You wouldn't believe me if I told you," Purella stated, firmly. That was actually probably true, especially now that she'd said that.

The old woman laughed but not out of amusement. A mirthless cackle that reminded Purella of smashing glass.

"I can't have someone as dangerous as *you* hanging around my city. *Not even for a few days*," she said, dryly. "You would bring the place down with your destructive stimulus."

Would anyone be able to tell? Purella wondered cynically. "I take that as a compliment, coming from *you*," she shrugged, darkly.

"If you *agree* to bring whatever supplies I order when I order them, nothing will happen to your team and we help you attack the Firestones?" she offered.

"Suits me."

***

"*We never agreed to that!*" Pat shouted, angrily. "The Viscount has not made a decision on it!" Reed sat there, blinking slowly as she continued. "Do you have any idea what you've started?"

"I'm sorry," Reed smiled. "I took action because I expected that attack and *your* Viscount is taking too long to do anything." Pat let out an irate sigh, ran her hands through her hair stressfully and began to pace up and down.

"A Federation ship *in Coalition territory*?" she went on. "That is not going to look good, especially for the Union!"

"I see. You'd *rather* I'd done *nothing* and simply allowed many more of your citizens to die?" Reed enquired, still annoyingly calm.

"*No!*" That really was the only sensible answer to that question she could offer.

"If that destroyer *hadn't* shown up when it did, half the city could have been destroyed. Even Darius was there *trying* to defend your people and he could have been killed too."

"A local fighter is *one thing*, that's not the issue! *Darius did nothing wrong!* You are the *one* who called President Raykur!" she yelled, groaning. "You're the one who involved the Federation, and now they are here, who knows what they will do!"

"The Coalition will do nothing because of the Federation destroyer in your space zone, especially as it is here *defending* Coalition territory. The Union will do nothing because of the same thing. The only people directly affected by this are those attacking you," Reed explained calmly. A squadron of Federation fighters swung by the city, passing a viewport she was standing by. She waved a hand at them as if they somehow proved her point.

"And what the hell did you think you were doing inviting them down here for have dinner with us and the Viscount?" she hissed.

"Being friendly, it is important we get to know the officer in charge, build a rapport with him, gauge his character," Reed listed. "Learn if we can *trust him or not*."

"The Viscount won't trust *either of us* now!" she moaned, shaking her head.

"The way I see it, he has *no choice* but to trust us now," Reed shrugged, trying not to laugh. "We are the only way he can control that destroyer. He'll probably even try to make it look like it was what he wanted even if it wasn't."

"*Is this all some joke to you?*" she muttered, knowing it wasn't.

"Even *you* must admit its intervention was a godsend! You're just angry that I didn't tell you what I did before I did it," Reed said, softly.

"Don't you trust me?" she asked, hurt.

"There wasn't much time to trust *anyone*," he replied, dodging the question. "Look, I've worked with the Federation navy before and while I can't speak for everyone, Admiral Wester is a man of honour."

"Admiral Wester isn't here," she argued, quietly.

"Which is exactly why I wish to meet this Captain Ogun and get to know him as soon as possible," Reed smiled, as if she'd somehow proved his point.

"This had better work," she glowered, watching the distant fighters start another circuit.

"*Trust me*," he chuckled. She closed her eyes, and let out a breath as she shook her head.

"Relax, we have more time now. And if the Viscount isn't pleased you can blame it all on me."

"*Why* are they attacking *us*, Reed?" she asked, bleakly. It was a question asked many times by millions of people.

"To get what they want... *whatever that is*," he responded, unhelpfully.

"Is this a private conversation?" Darius growled, from the door. Pat jumped and spun around but Reed was unmoved.

"It *was*," Reed chuckled, smugly.

"Still no word from Satiah and I'm officially *concerned* now," Darius went on, moving to the window. "Last time we spoke she was just about to rescue Milo Drass. Something must have gone wrong."

"And Kelvin says?" Reed shrugged.

"Nothing at all," Darius muttered. "Nothing useful anyway."

"I think he would be aware of it if she was dead," Reed said. "Something may well have gone wrong but if we don't know where she is, there's not much we can do to help."

"I can go to her last known location *and start looking*," he suggested.

"That's up to you but I fear you would only be wasting your time," Reed sighed, standing up casually. "In any case we need you here for dinner."

"You're planning on eating *me?*" he quipped.

"No, you look too tough to chew," Reed replied, dryly. "*Besides*, the table would not be the same without *your witty banter*. As Coalition Ambassador, I *formally* request your presence." It was only because Darius knew that Reed was right about not finding Satiah that he accepted. He raised a dubious eyebrow.

"After your help today it would be rude of us to not invite you," Pat said, joining in.

"Ah, is the front *reunited?*" Reed chanced.

"*...For now*, yes," she replied, begrudgingly. "Do you have any more for me on our attackers?"

"Not yet," Reed answered. "I'm waiting for Satiah." Darius cleared his throat meaningfully.

***

Bert lay on the battered bunk that acted as his bed. His ankle was no better but at least they had bothered to give him a real splint for it. As Satiah had told him, he'd pretended to have no memory of anything, even his own name. At first, they hadn't believed him, until an officer arrived. She told them all to leave him alone for some reason. While a few meals had been missed, they had been keeping him fairly well, considering. This officer had eventually visited him and questioned him herself and he'd claimed the same thing. He had no memory of what had happened or who he was but his ankle hurt. She didn't seem to care about whether he was telling the truth or not and had been most concerned about how much he was worth. Clearly she had plans to sell him back to whomever he was part of. As he couldn't remember, she'd taken the decision to keep him until he did remember.

At night, he could hear the bestial howls of the other prisoners.

They sounded like animals of the jungle and it made sleep very difficult. He expected to find that some dreadful act of abhorrent violence had taken place in the night when he awoke but nothing had. He had not been told who was keeping him there, or even what planet he was on. He wondered how long it would be before he got out of there. He hardly knew Satiah, but he knew how determined she was and she had said she would come back for him. He was starting to lose faith by the second day, however. Perhaps she had been lying. He tentatively tried to move his leg and then thought better of it. Shouting came from outside and he sighed, wondering if it was time for his breakfast yet.

Cherry came in, package of food under one arm and rifle ready in her other. Bert didn't know she was Cherry, to him she was just another guard. Cherry looked hard at him. She noticed the splint on his leg, but it took her a moment to work out exactly which leg was injured. Right leg, right. Yes, definitely right leg, and he was old. She handed him the food with all the nonchalance she could muster then she muttered Satiah's name to see what happened. He stared right at her.

"*What did you just say?*" he whispered, uneasily.

"Satiah is the name of your *friend*, she sent me to find out where you were. I have to go back after my shift here and I will tell her," Cherry elaborated, discreetly.

***

Satiah was on laundry duty, something she felt sure had been picked by Vann to humiliate her. She was amazed to find that there were no androids that did it automatically. While her task was menial, it gave her mind a chance to once again gnaw on her real problems. If Purella didn't have Milo... then who the hell did? Would Dyss lose patience and punish her? She knew what Reed had said, but she wasn't sure herself what Dyss would or wouldn't do. *Why* were the pirates attacking Collgort-Elipsa in the first place? That gold, so far as she knew, was still MIA. She *still* had to talk to Darius to work out if she could trust him or not. Operation Jackdaw may even be the key to getting on Dyss's good side. *And* what was the deal with that weird orange rock in her pocket?

She'd noticed another strange thing about it last night. It could change temperature. In her pocket it was close to her body and so became a similar temperature. Then it apparently froze and felt like a block of ice. At the time, she'd not wanted to look at it in case it did anything. So she'd quickly switched it to her jacket pocket, where she couldn't feel it at all. About ten minutes later, she'd become aware of heat radiating from her jacket pocket and had cautiously prodded the gem with her finger. It had been really hot, almost hot enough to burn her. Again, at the time she chose to ignore it and catnap. Cherry had been sleeping beside her. Satiah only tolerated that because, if for whatever reason something happened, someone else would be nearby that might actually help her.

That led her onto her more immediate problems. If she was to steal a ship, could she be sure there were no ground defences? It was likely that they wouldn't get away cleanly. Purella might have been fooled by their fake crash, but what if she hadn't been? What if she was in orbit of the planet right now, waiting for Satiah to make a run for it? Bert, Cherry and the boy, she would have to take them all with her. Bert was mandatory, because he was important, even though she wasn't sure why. She didn't want to give Darius the satisfaction of her turning up empty handed. Cherry should go too. She'd asked to come and she *was* useful. The boy also because... because he deserved a life beyond brainwashed servitude. The notion of being a slave or allowing others to remain trapped didn't sit well with Satiah. A year ago she'd not have troubled herself with such thoughts, a year ago... Where was all this empathy coming from? It would be the death of her if she wasn't careful!

Speaking of death... It had suddenly all become rather quiet around her. Satiah knew what was coming so she didn't bother to look up. She had been expected Vann to retaliate in some form since their clash the previous day. It had been inevitable. Their own shadows on the floor gave them away. Three of them. They were approaching her back as a group. There was no question of simply taking the beating; they would be there to kill her. Therefore she would have to give a beating to them. She clasped the fabric she was holding and began to twist it with her hands as if wringing the water out of it. Her well-honed instincts took over and she spun, wielding the fabric as if it were a lashing weapon. It struck a hand holding the knife hard enough to make the woman let go of it. All three women were bigger than Satiah but they had not expected her to be ready for them.

Everyone else in the room had backed off to the sides and were watching.

Satiah send her chair flying at one as she took on the other two. A punch came at her but she ducked underneath it and thrust her own fist into the other woman's gut. She was down and out for a moment, heaving pained breaths on the floor. The second woman, the one who'd originally been holding the knife, was trying to grab Satiah. Satiah slapped her hands away, redirecting them. The third woman, who'd by now returned after fending off Satiah's chair, came charging in. Satiah couldn't go anywhere and took the other woman's shoulder in her belly. She landed hard on her shoulder with a groan as both of them tried to pin her. That was when Satiah turned nasty.

She rammed her fingers into the left eye of the first woman. She shrieked and fell back. Satiah then grabbed the other woman's arm and twisted. The woman was presented with this ultimatum: let go now or I break your arm in two places. She let go. Satiah rolled onto her feet to confront the one she'd downed first. This woman did not look at all confident now. Satiah pulled her in close and head-butted her nose. Satiah felt the bone crack under the blow. She went down, howling. Two were down now and would not be getting up any time soon. The last one had reclaimed the blade and was coming at her again. She slashed at Satiah who sidestepped nimbly. She snatched two pots off a table as she moved away and then brandished them as weapons.

The woman thrusted at her, going for the face, all speed but little accuracy. Satiah bashed the knife away with one pot and slammed the other into the woman's face. She went down, stunned, but this time Satiah continued battering her head repeatedly. She would write a message in these women's blood! *Don't try that again*! Again and again she brought the pot down, turning her features into a bloody pulp. A gunshot went off and everyone froze. There was a clatter as Satiah dropped the bloodstained pots onto the floor. Two women, whom Satiah had never seen before, were standing there, rifles ready. They both wore actual uniforms... *Officers*. Satiah thought she was dead for a moment.

"It was self-defence," Satiah stated, breathing hard. Several others nodded in assent.

"*We saw what happened*," said one, grimly. "*You*!" She barked this at one of the onlookers. "Get these three to the medical area."

Satiah watched as two women and a corpse were hauled away by several other women. The officer approached Satiah and looked her up and down.

"That was impressive how you handled them alone," she noted, in admiration. "What is your name?"

"...Satiah," she answered, tentative. She did not need this; she really did not need this! Okay, at least they hadn't *shot her* but this attention would only make things worse.

"I *need* fighters like you in my commando squad," she told her, seriously. "Interested?" Satiah got the impression that saying no was not an option.

"My CO is Captain Vann; if you want *me* shouldn't you be asking *her*?" Satiah asked, playing dumb. "I've only been here two days and I've not been trained by anyone here yet."

"You could have fooled me," she shrugged. "And you're *right*, I *should* be asking her, *but I'm asking you first*." She leaned in close to Satiah, to whisper in her ear. "*Captain Vann is not the greatest officer in this army. She is...*" she paused looking for the right word.

"Overly enthusiastic?" offered Satiah, diplomatically.

"*A bully*," smiled the woman. She patted Satiah's arm. "People like you, *good people*, make her jealous. I suspect these *girls only* attacked you at all because *Vann* ordered them to do it."

"But *you* can't *prove* that?" Satiah guessed, seeing the difficulty.

"No, no, she's not stupid," the woman shook her head in concurrence.

"Who are you?" Satiah asked, starting to like this rather different woman.

"Captain Rebec," she smiled, more softly. They shook hands. "Honoured to meet you."

"I would love to join your unit, Captain," Satiah said, part of her even meaning it. "But I have *a friend* in the unit I'm in and she might get into trouble, especially without me there to protect her."

"*Loyal too*," Rebec noted, understandingly. "Well, if you change your mind, come and find me. And remember, we are not *all* like Vann." She started to march out and then turned on the women that had done nothing.

"*What hell did you lot think you were doing?*" she bellowed, making them all stiffen into stillness. "If *you* hadn't chosen not to get involved, *that* could have been avoided!" Their heads went down as the harangue continued. "Call yourself *soldiers*! You are not fit to clean my boots with your tongues! *You might as well be men*!"

She then turned, winked at Satiah, smiled and left. Yes, Satiah was loyal… *to a point*. Satiah almost laughed, but she had that familiar feeling that *someone* was watching her. Her sixth sense was tipping her off once again. She slowly turned and spotted Vann, leaning against the side of the building, her arms crossed and her expression sour. Satiah smiled benevolently at her and waved before retaking her seat. Her shoulder hurt after that landing on the floor, but other than that she was unscathed. As if nothing had happened she began to wash the clothing again. A woman sat down next to her and eyed her.

"I think you're really brave," she whispered, quietly. "Those three had it coming and I *really* enjoyed seeing them get it." Satiah raised an eyebrow, unsure how to take that comment. The woman though didn't seem to be expecting a reply.

Later that day, just before twilight, Satiah returned to her usual spot near the campfire. The boy was waiting for her.

"The spaceships are over there," he murmured, nodding in their direction.

"How far?" Satiah asked, bluntly. She'd wanted model numbers, capacities and all sorts of technical data to know which one to steal. The trouble was: he only *knew* what a spaceship *was* because she'd told him the previous day.

"A few miles up the hill," he told her. She faced the hill, thinking of Bert's broken ankle. This was less than ideal. "Food?"

"The usual, and be sure *no one other than you touches it*," she replied, repeating her instruction from the previous mealtime. Next to arrive was Cherry and she was flushed from running there.

"I heard what happened, *are you okay?*" she asked, sympathetically.

"*I'm* fine; you should have seen the other three," she replied, shrugging. She winced as her shoulder let its discomfort be known to her once again. Cherry saw the look and gasped.

"Sit down, *you need to stay strong*, eat…" she began, concerned.

"*All right, all right*, I *have* been in a fight once or twice before, you know?" Satiah interrupted, unwilling to be nursed.

"It's not over yet," Cherry hissed, in her ear. "I know you think you've *won* but…"

"Do you not remember our *deal* yesterday?" Satiah cut in. "We won't *be here* to have to worry about further reprisals."

"That's *if* it all works out," she stated, reasonably. Satiah felt Cherry's hands on her shoulders squeeze softly. "And you said I wasn't supposed to *talk* about that."

"*It will*," growled Satiah, stubborn.

"Listen, I've found Bert, I know *exactly* where he is," Cherry whispered, rubbing Satiah's shoulders. Satiah would have asked her to stop if she wasn't so good at it.

"Where?"

"Cell E14," she answered. Satiah already knew where the prisoners were housed.

"Good work," she stated, thinking hard. Get Bert to the ship or bring the ship to him? That was the question. There were obvious snags whichever way she chose. In his condition, even *with* Cherry under his other arm, it would be a struggle to get him to the ship *quickly*. But if she stole the ship and came down for him, then he may be moved as part of some prearranged evacuation procedure or something. Plus, by that time, the guards would have been alerted. It was a pity there were so few ground vehicles!

"Hey," breathed Cherry, in her ear again. "*Vann isn't done with you yet.* You took out about half her gang but that *doesn't mean* you're safe." Her hands seemed to become a little more firm. Cherry clearly still had eyes for her; Satiah knew she had to get her off that track straight away.

"It's so sweet of you to assume that I'm done with her," Satiah grinned, evilly. Cherry stopped for a moment, and then continued, less insistently. Message received.

"You're scary," she stated, seriously. Satiah's hands landed on hers suddenly and she jumped.

"We *need* to get off of this planet soon," Satiah smirked, moving away.

"Okay, but won't we need a ship to do that?" Cherry asked, in all innocence. Satiah spat out the water she'd just been in the process of gulping down *as if she'd never thought of that*. The boy returned with her soup. Cherry smiled at him and ruffled his hair.

"May I have some soup too *please?*" she asked, smiling as she said it. The boy nodded and went away again.

"Did Captain Rebec offer to let you in her group?" Cherry enquired, awestruck.

"She did, but I refused tactfully, couldn't leave you behind so soon, could I?" she replied, guardedly.

"I wouldn't have minded, *Rebec* is brilliant," Cherry said, understandingly. "Vann would hate *that* if she knew."

"She already does," Satiah said, carefully sniffing her soup. "With any luck, tomorrow should be our last day here."

"Okay," Cherry nodded, suddenly serious.

"We will get the ship first and bring it down here, and *then* get Bert," Satiah told her. "We will do it at *about* this time of day, while mostly everyone is either on patrol or eating." Cherry nodded. "There's *something else* I don't understand about this place. *How do you survive?*"

Cherry frowned. "How do you mean?"

"This situation, *this planet*, how does it keep going? This is a planet where there is an overwhelmingly female population which is *at war* with, I presume, all sororities?" Satiah guessed.

"Not *all*, some are neutral and try to mediate but they are minorities," Cherry corrected.

"Right, but *where* does your food come from? I've not seen any *farms* here or even any *deliveries*. Why are you not dying out?" Satiah went on. "At war, a population *like yours* can *only* decline without fresh recruits or... *a new generation.*"

"Mostly, all the new fighters we have come from other worlds now," Cherry shrugged. "I was born here and I'm in a minority. I know that there *were* insemination programmes years ago but *no one ever talks about it.*" Cherry's body language had changed. She now looked... ashamed. Satiah noticed but wasn't sure why. "They are *very* secretive about new technology."

"*They* being *the leaders?*" Satiah nodded, understanding.

"I... *Please don't tell anyone this*. I know I said I was born here and while that's technically true, it's not very *accurate...*" she confessed, looking upset. Satiah put on a jokey smile and let out a nervous laugh.

"What are you trying to tell me, Cherry?" she asked, uneasy.

"...I'm... *a clone*," she admitted, sadly. "I'm *sorry*, I should have said earlier... I guess you won't want me with you now, will you?"

"Why would *that* matter?" Satiah asked, curious. Clones, while not exactly commonplace, were treated no differently from non-clones. Mainly because it was almost impossible to tell them apart from non-clones. "Makes no difference to me."

Cherry's face lit up immediately. "*Here*, clones are not treated *nicely*, we are seen as *imitations of women*... an invention of *men*," she explained, intently. "That's *why* I don't want anyone else to know."

"I'm hardly going to go around telling everyone, am I?" Satiah smirked. "So, *returning to my earlier question*: you are sustained by new recruits from other worlds, cloning and insemination?"

"As far as I know," she shrugged. "Some sororities *have* died out... or at least *haven't been seen for so long*, it's *assumed* they have died out."

"...This place is terrible," Satiah growled, seriously. "Breeding people, indoctrinating them *just* to make them fight in a never-ending and ultimately pointless war." She'd seen it before in other ideological clashes but not in such an *automated* arrangement. Run out of troops? No problem, we can either grow our own or buy them from other planets. Human trafficking and experimental weaponry corporations most likely had their hands in this too! They would be doing everything they could to perpetuate this. And Satiah was *sure* that it was all *most profitable*. One day, those people would *pay* for this and not just financially! But, sadly, that day was not today. Was it ever?

"It *is*," Cherry agreed, looking incredulous. She couldn't believe how long it had taken her realise the truth. In the event that you were *inside* something, it was much harder to look at it from the outside.

"The sooner we get out of it the better," Satiah muttered, decisively.

***

Captain Rebec peered over her shoulder to be sure the corridor was clear before closing the door of her office. The officer block was quiet, as always at this time. The secret room hidden directly behind the false wooden panelling at the back of her office was where her computer was concealed. She wasn't sure but it was likely to be one of the most advanced computer terminals planetside. Removing her hat casually, she sat down and began activating various things. The usual security protocols to ensure no one had discovered it. A microphone inched out to her, it was time to report.

"This is Agent 5," she said. "Field report, urgent, have encountered Phantom agent Satiah. Request orders from Division Sixteen high command."

"Please hold," said a monotone, in response.

***

Purella watched, arms crossed, from the shadows as the Queen gathered her forces for the attack. There were thousands of troops. Quantity had never impressed Purella though, she preferred quality. The *soldiers*, such as they were, were poorly equipped, poorly disciplined... the list went on. They were a mass of sheep, shepherded by their queen. The individual was a threat to everything. Organised religion, government... the lot. Why? Because they knew who they were and they saw everything else for what it really was... or at least they had the capacity to. Purella and the Queen, and even Satiah, although Purella hated to admit it, were *individuals*. This planet, despite its methods, was arguably no different from anywhere else. And, just like everywhere else, Purella did not trust anyone to do her job for her. As the numbers of women arriving grew, so did her contempt. Using a special frequency, normally reserved only for the Queen herself, Purella called the *Dreadnaught*.

"It's *me*. Get Major Clyde, *there's been a change of plan*," she murmured, subtly.

***

Bavon adjusted his collar and patted the sweat on his forehead away. He'd seen it all from his office and he knew what he would be accused of. *He* hadn't known though! *Really*! The Viscount had never finished deliberating and no one else had said a word! Yet *someone* must have called that destroyer in. Visages of Kyle and Quint appeared before him. They were not together *physically* but they both wanted to be a part of this discussion.

"Thanks for the warning, *Bavon*," Kyle snarled, sarcastically. "We lost fighters this time! We didn't have time to do any real damage either."

"I didn't *know* it would be there," Bavon stated, flushing. "It shouldn't have been there!"

"Who will pay for those fighters, Bavon? *Who?*" Kyle demanded, furious. "We want out! This is too much for us! We want our money too!" Bavon tried to talk and stop him as Quint would not like this, but he couldn't think of a good argument to counter with.

"This is not a matter for concern. The solution is easy: destroy the Federation ship," Quint suggested, his voice computerised and slow. Kyle almost immediately calmed down and Bavon, for once, felt relieved at Quint's intervention.

"How?" Kyle asked, more respectfully.

"*That* will not be down to you," Quint dismissed, curtly. "A Federation ship in Coalition space has political ramifications, even with a legitimate purpose. If that ship is destroyed, the Federation will accuse the Coalition or the Union of a set-up. More ships will move in and there will be a standoff as no one will risk all-out war, least of all the Federation. The Coalition will probably look at replacing the Viscount, *only temporarily*, with their own ambassador. Eventually a scapegoat will be chosen, and the only real mystery will be which one, Vinu or Shintu? I imagine that they may even punish both as the evidence of incrimination has been well spread."

"How will *that* help *us*?" Bavon asked, his throat dry. "Even if all that comes to pass it will mean an end to the war and I thought…?"

"The advantage is, *we* will know the end is coming and will sell off *all assets* before it becomes apparent to everyone else," Quint elaborated further.

"Assuming that the Federation destroyer *can* be destroyed," Kyle pointed out. "So long as it stays there, we are in limbo."

"Agreed," Quint said. "I will see to your funding, Kyle. I can also suggest a place to get replacements. I will be in touch later today." Kyle, realising that he had been dismissed, vanished from before Bavon. Bavon swallowed, he was alone now with Quint. For a long moment Quint just seemed to stare at him... through his white mask.

"I *will* investigate..." Bavon began to assure him.

"*Find out who* requested that destroyer to be there. *Find out who* is in charge of that ship. *Find out* if any more are on the way," Quint commanded, his tone almost buzzing it was so sharp. Bavon gasped, he hadn't considered *that*. They had one, what was to stop them asking for another?

"It may be necessary to end this business for the time being," Quint went on. Bavon didn't know how, but he instinctively knew that Quint was livid. Unlike Kyle or Purella though, Quint remained disturbingly calm. Bavon wondered if he was bluffing, trying to get out of paying *him*. His greed and fear battled it out and, as usual, his greed won.

"No, no, that's a last resort, *if you don't mind me reminding you*. I'm *sure* things will change for our benefit," Bavon said, although he was making it up as he went now.

Again, as before, Quint went silent as if considering this for the first time. Bavon wondered if he was crazy. Maybe he was listening to voices in his head or something equally insane.

"How, *if you pardon me asking*, do you intend to remove the Federation ship?" Bavon enquired, nosily.

"*That* is up to me, *not you*. I have a few options and will weigh each carefully before I choose to act," Quint answered, firmly. That reminded Bavon of his place. The last one to know and the least important part of this machine they called profit.

"In the meantime, get me the information I require," he instructed tersely, and disconnected. Bavon let out a breath and rested his head in his hands for a short time. This was too much for him, but he had to hang on in there.

***

Reed had been expecting a shouting match over dinner, despite their *guest*. Captain Ogun was a nondescript fellow. Back straight, eyes forward as he sat: most likely a military trait. He wore his uniform well, it was neat and made to measure. He had greying brown hair and beady brown eyes. His eyes hinted at a *certain level of calculation* to Reed. A man with an agile mind. He was a Captain, after all! The Viscount, who was the one Reed thought would be yelling at him, was at the head of the table, being very cordial and quiet. Pat too hid her temper well.

"You made record time, Captain," Reed said to him. "It's a *long way* from the Federation here."

"Must have had the solar winds behind us," he replied, smoothly avoiding an explanation. "That was your *second* attack, I understand?"

Darius was sitting next to Reed, apparently more interested in his own cutlery than he was in the conversation. However, Reed could tell he was paying close attention, despite appearances.

"It *was!*" Pat concurred, earnestly.

Don't overdo it, please, Reed silently pleaded.

"What were the casualties?" Ogun asked, his manner and tone not changing.

"Seven dead, twelve injured," she answered, honestly. "You interrupted them before they could do any more harm."

"I wasn't the only one," Ogun reminded her, nodding in Darius's direction. "How long are you asking me to remain on station here?" Everyone looked at the Viscount, who had been listening.

"We negotiate this through you directly?" he queried.

"You don't have to but you can," Ogun stated, respectfully.

The Viscount looked at Reed and Pat did the same.

"The current situation, being by definition a complicated and uncertain matter as it is, would make any sort of forecast a bit ambiguous..." Reed prattled, a little caught out.

"*We don't know,*" Darius interrupted, speaking for the first time. "We're playing this by ear. Can you work with that?"

"I can do that," Ogun said, a comradely smile paying on his lips. Darius answered it with one of his own.

"At the moment we're still looking for answers," Darius went on. "We'll keep you updated. I understand you have other duties you want to get back to and we'll let you go as soon as we can."

"Protection of civilians comes first," Ogun noted, appraisingly.

"How are things in the Federation these days?" Reed asked, interested.

"Turbulent. The Ro Tammer hearing has started and the first trimester is nearly concluded. Raykur keeps having health scares. On the positive side, we've been knocking the hell out of the pirates in our sectors," he replied, sipping some wine.

"That's *the prosecution stage*, right? I heard she is pleading innocent, is that true?" Pat ventured, unsure how to proceed with the subject. It was impossible to know if he supported her or not.

"Actually, the first trimester is basically administration. They discuss the category of crimes, past records, relevant politics and then decide which topics will be ruled inadmissible. It usually only takes a day at most. I regret to say that I have no idea what she's pleaded, I have not been following the proceedings," he said, prudently. "My *guess* would be that she does plead innocent as she thinks she's done nothing wrong. What manner of enemy do you have here?" Ogun asked, changing the subject abruptly. He turned to face Darius again. "I understand there is a war going on between the Vinupisha and the Shintumpa realms, and I've looked into their military capacity. Ships, troops, areas and so on. I hardly had much time to observe when I arrived as they scarpered very quickly. They had one capital ship, a cruiser. Cruisers are quick, only gunships are faster, and there was only one of them. I'm curious as to what they were trying to accomplish with such action."

"Aren't we all," Reed murmured, pouring some sauce over his steak.

"Unpredictable, in a word," Darius said. "I've only seen one attack but they both seem to follow a similar pattern. That of a hit and run. They move in fast, without warning, attack and then flee."

"Is there anything in particular they are targeting?" Ogun wanted to know. It was a reasonable question. Again though, the answer was not known by anyone at that table.

"*My people*," the Viscount grumbled, unhelpfully.

"There are *no* military targets on this planet. We are at a loss when trying to explain these attacks," Reed replied. "We do have an agent working on this and she should be reporting back soon."

"There is now: my ship," Ogun pointed out, seriously. "My attendance here changes everything as far as they will be concerned. *I'm* troubled about what they will try next." No one bothered to ask if he really thought that there would *be* another attack: it seemed depressingly likely.

"There was seven days between the first attack and today's," Darius noted. "I'm not one for patterns, but maybe we'll find out next week."

Ogun smiled grimly. "As I am stationed here for the foreseeable future," he said, softly, "I wanted to talk to you about *facilities*."

"Your crew are welcome to walk the cities, Captain," the Viscount said. "We do have strict firearm protocols here and I'd prefer that they respect them." Ogun thought about it. It was always good to honour the host's wishes in any circumstances, but in the event of an attack...

"Many worlds have such protocols, in my opinion they should be *universal*, it would be discourteous of me to violate *any of them* without your permission," he prevaricated, smoothly. Reed smiled, this man was a decent diplomat. He'd countered the worry without actually saying what he would do. Wester had chosen well.

"Fuel goes without saying," Darius stated, shrugging. "Right now, you are our only defence and we would be irresponsible if we didn't give you every assistance we can." Again, the military kinship between Darius and Ogun seemed to be aiding the metaphysical bridge building.

Darius was deep in thought at that moment. He was thinking about back when he and Satiah had first arrived. Something was wrong. After they had attacked first: it was logical *for them to assume* that the defences would have built up or changed *before* their next attack. Yet they had done the exact same thing again and were completely unprepared for any resistance at all. Why had they not changed tactics? The reason was obvious. They didn't think they had to. That meant somehow they were aware that nothing had changed. Did that mean that someone on the planet was working with them? Updating them on developments there? As he reached this minor epiphany, his communicator went off.

"I have to take this," he said, excusing himself with a wave of his hand. He hurried outside.

"This is Phantom Leader Randal," Randal said, as Darius answered. "Is that you, Darius?"

"It is," Darius replied.

"I'm trying to get hold of Satiah," he elaborated. Darius rolled his eyes. *Where was she?* He went on talking about the missing gold and *Polvine Limited*. Darius's eyes widened. So, gold had been stolen by pirates *from* Polvine Limited, a company *based on Collgort-Elipsa*. Satiah believed pirates had got Milo but... If pirates had stolen the gold from the company that had to mean someone had tipped them off. Could it be that the Vinu and the Shintu really hadn't attacked Collgort-Elipsa at all and that it was simply pirates pretending to be them? If that was true it would be plausible to believe that whoever had tipped them off about the gold had done the same in regard to the planetary defences before the attacks. And... was it not logical to presume that that person would *be working for,* or at least *be associated with,* Polvine Limited?

"Darius! Are you there?" Randal was asking.

"Sorry sir," he grunted, coming back to reality. "I haven't spoken with her for nearly three days. I'm awaiting her return on Collgort-Elipsa."

"And you have no idea where she is?" Randal repeated, exasperation evident.

"Last I heard she was about to acquire the man we are looking for on a pirate ship, then silence," he told him, honestly. "I don't want to presume anything yet but..." He left it hanging there. The possibility of her death or capture.

"I see," sighed Randal. "Let me know if you hear anything."

"Will do," Darius concurred. Randal disconnected. Darius returned *in mind* to his last thought trail and *in body* to the dinner table.

How could they know about the defences so intimately if they were just associated with Polvine Limited? They might have bugged certain rooms or frequencies. They might not be working alone! Darius's eyes rose slowly, for the first time in suspicion, from his food to watch the people around him. Captain Ogun obviously couldn't be involved. Reed, probably not, seeing as he was the one who had called the Federation. That just left Lady Patricia Hollellster and... *the Viscount himself.* Darius knew it could even be both of them working in concert but his mind told him that their involvement was unlikely. Nevertheless, they might be unwittingly revealing things to whoever was *the real traitor.* Traitor, he'd used the word. Without Satiah there to give him orders, technically he could proceed no further. Darius, however, was a seasoned Phantom and knew when it was time to be independent.

He would wait until the Captain and Reed were alone and then he'd give them the plan he was now creating. They would fake a disappearance. *The vanishing warship trick*! They would let it be known *to certain individuals* that the destroyer would be off station for a certain period of time. In reality, it would be cloaked in the clouds, out of sight but still very much there. If an attack occurred *during that timeframe* he would have proof that there *was* an insider at work. Most likely somewhere on the planet. The destroyer would come out of hiding and defend as it was meant to and no one would be hurt. Only Reed and Ogun would know the truth, even the Viscount would be kept in the dark. It was just easier that way. He patted Reed's shoulder to get his attention and leaned in.

"*I want to talk to you after this,*" he growled, in Reed's ear. Reed twitched in apparent displeasure.

"If you *wanted* the last prawn you should have said something," Reed whispered back, unforgivingly.

***

Satiah opened her eyes. She had taken the decision to try and get all the sleep she could and had not paid for that. Catnapping was only good for a couple of days. Cherry had been the one catnapping and Satiah had trusted the younger woman to at least raise the alarm should anything happen. She looked fairly energetic and smiled as she saw that Satiah was awake.

"Morning," she smiled, quietly. The boy too was sleeping nearby. She yawned. "I watched the sunrise. Knowing it was the last time made it seem somehow more beautiful. Nothing happened... I'll just grab a few minutes..." She slumped and was asleep herself in moments. Satiah looked around. They were not the first awake but they were one of the first.

Satiah stood and stretched. This was it! Last day! She smirked to herself, she'd better be careful or it really would be her last day. She flexed her arms, testing her shoulder. It ached but seemed better. She made a mental note to tell Cherry that if she ever needed a job, *when they got out of there*, she could become a physical therapist.

Knife, pistol and specs. She was ready. She looked up at the hill where somewhere the ships would be. If they were not flyable, this would end very badly.

"You all right?" Vann asked, wandering over. "Heard what happened yesterday. Can't have been the most pleasant experience."

"I enjoyed it," Satiah replied, shrugging. That was partly true. There was very little that was more satisfying than giving someone a well-deserved kicking. Vann was the very soul of innocence, not giving away that fact that she had orchestrated the whole thing.

"I heard Rebec approached you with an offer of recruitment?" Vann probed. Ah, so that's what she wants. She wants to know why Satiah had decided to stay. Mostly everyone, very understandably, would have jumped ship immediately.

"She did but I like it here," Satiah smiled, deviously. "How are they, by the way? *The two who are still alive?*" Vann paused, and gave her a look as if she was starting to realise Satiah was not what she appeared to be.

"Recovering," she limited herself to saying. She turned to leave.

"Vann?" called Satiah politely, over her shoulder. Vann turned back and Satiah decked her with a punch that would have killed a smaller mammal. Vann hit the ground with a cry and Cherry sprang to her feet, rudely awoken by the sound of the blow. Satiah drove a knee into Vann's back, pinning her to the floor. Vann, trying to say or do something, froze as she found Satiah's knife at shaving-distance from her throat.

"Now I *know* what I said that night when I first got here," Satiah said, calmly. "There are a couple more things you should know. *I don't like it when prisoners are killed for no reason. And I hate it when someone tries to kill me, whatever the reason.*" She put more weight on the knee pinning Vann, who groaned in pain. "Try it again and I'll kill you."

She stood, letting Vann roll onto her side, panting. A few of the other women had come over now, unsure whether to step in and even more uncertain about whom they would back up if they did step in. Cherry had her gun on Vann now too.

"I'll have you executed for this!" Vann blustered, angrily.

"Yeah? Shame no one saw it to back you up," Satiah replied, smoothly. She faced the onlookers. "*Did you see anything?*" The women looked at one another again unsure what to do: this had never happened before. Vann always beat anyone who challenged her, it had been that way for so long no one could remember a time when she wasn't there.

"Must have been asleep," Cherry growled, meaningfully. "Sorry." A few of the other women nodded.

"Didn't see what?" asked one, displaying something akin to wit.

"Right answer!" Satiah announced, grimly.

"You're all cowards!" Vann roared, at the crowd. Satiah turned and booted her in the stomach. She shrieked and breathed in loud agonised breaths. A little cheer rippled through the people watching. The boy, who was also looking on, smiled.

"You know how the old saying goes?" Satiah said. "No body, no crime." She turned to the onlookers. "Burn this deserter!" Delighted at the prospect of getting revenge, mostly all of them surged forward to drag the screaming Captain off to a fiery demise. Satiah didn't stay to watch and her thoughts weren't with Vann or the soldiers killing her. They were with the prisoner. The one she had killed to save from being burned alive. Was it an even score now? Satiah knew that the score was hardly ever even.

"Is that your way of saying it's time to go?" Cherry asked, a bit shaken.

"She started it," Satiah stated. "But yes, we might as well go now that everyone is distracted." With the boy in tow, Satiah and Cherry began the long, slow journey up the hill. They followed the road, passing checkpoints and guards without incident. When they reached the top, Satiah put her specs on and zoomed in to get a better view. There were nearly thirty ships of various sizes and types, parked haphazardly in a large meadow. There was a freighter that looked promising.

"Those are space ships?" the boy asked, pointing. Satiah nodded and gave him a grin.

"They are, well done," she congratulated him.

"Which one are you thinking about?" Cherry asked.

"White freighter, third from left towards the back," Satiah replied, not pointing. She didn't want anyone whom might be watching them to guess their purpose.

"How do we get past the guards? We would need an officer to get us through," Cherry asked, glancing behind them. She kept doing that and Satiah stopped her.

"Behave naturally, don't get twitchy, it will attract attention," she cautioned.

"Sorry but I've never done this before," Cherry quavered, nervously.

"Pretend you're showing me around if anyone asks," Satiah suggested.

**

Queen Linkarni turned as Purella arrived at the doorway to her throne room. Her way was barred by the guards.

"Let her in," she instructed. Purella entered fully and strolled forward to face the Queen head on. There was a silence as each challenged the other to speak first.

"Your army is pathetic," Purella stated, in disgust. "I have doubts you *can* defeat the Firestones."

"Their army is much the same as mine, but we have superior numbers," the Queen shrugged.

"The deal is off," Purella said, shaking her head.

"You know what will happen to your followers if..." Linkarni began, unsure why Purella was doing this. Surely the time to change her mind would be after the battle, not before it.

In the corridor outside Major Clyde and two other men appeared, literally materialising out of thin air. They shot the two guards before either woman snapped out of their shock. The Queen moved to rise but Purella levelled her pistol at her.

"No, no, old hag, you stay right where you are," she ordered, smiling cruelly. Clyde entered and moved to stand beside Purella. The other two men took up the guards' positions at the door.

"How dare you defile my palace with your creatures!" Linkarni spat, furiously. Purella giggled.

"I never saw you as my creature before, but then you do make me feel like a wild animal sometimes," she said to Clyde, flirtatiously.

"The feeling is mutual," he smiled, grimly. Neither looked at one another though, they both stared right at the queen.

"Shall I kill her?" Clyde asked, softly. Her eyes went wide.

"No, she has one more task to perform," Purella stated, crisply. "If she does it well then I might let her live. If she fails... she's all yours."

"Not much of a prize," he muttered, in mock disappointment.

"Agreed," Purella smirked.

"What do you want?" Linkarni growled, sensing the only way through this was to talk.

"*You used me!*" Purella screamed, suddenly. "You used me to kill your enemies and you never even paid me! However... If you tell your subjects that *I* am now their ruler, I'll be prepared to overlook this. *If you don't...*" She trailed off and Clyde made a shooting gesture at her.

"What happens to me if I agree?" she asked, as anyone would.

"Not sure yet," Purella shrugged. "This rat hole of a realm *might* mean something to you but I doubt its citizens do. Future historians, *should any of them find out about this*, would condemn me for leaving *you* in charge to perpetuate your carnage until you finally lose your frail grip on life. Perhaps I should let your people decide your fate; they will have earned that right, if nothing else."

"No, no, don't do that! *They'll kill me*!" she protested, fearful. "If I die either way, I swear I will not help you."

"There is the manner of your death to consider," Clyde pointed out, like ice wouldn't melt in his mouth. "If you help us, we won't drag our feet about it." Purella nodded. "Should we decide to do it at all."

"That's fair," Purella agreed, sadistically.

Seeing that there was no way out, Linkarni decided she'd have to play along and hope that a chance of escape might present itself. She pulled out her communicator and began a global transmission. This would ensure that every single person in her kingdom, that had a radio, would hear her. Both Purella and Clyde moved in closer, each standing a little behind and to either side of her throne.

"This is an address to the people of Brigade from your Queen. Today, in a secret ceremony, a new dynasty began for you. I hand over the crown to another…" she began. Purella whispered something quickly into her ear. Linkarni looked up at her in confusion. Purella nodded.

"Lady Protector of the Brigade is your sovereign now," the Queen concluded, sadly.

Clyde snatched the crown off the old woman's head and shoved it at Purella. Purella eyed it as she held it and then held out her gloved hand for the communicator. Linkarni handed it over lamely.

"My first order to you is to continue your preparations for war. *We move in one hour*," she said. She didn't put the crown on; she just held it at her side. Like she would hold a crate of pressure pads or used clothing. It meant nothing to her. She had never been in favour of becoming part of a hegemony, least of all for somewhere like this! She preferred to be close to the top but not actually there. A place where, should she need to, she could slip back into the shadows and escape the fallout. In this case, however, it was a necessary step on the path of revenge. She disconnected and just stood there, a thoughtful expression on her face.

"Release the prisoners," Clyde prompted. She nodded.

"Who do I call to get my crew back?" she demanded, sharply.

"Channel four, detention," Linkarni murmured, bleakly. She was wondering if she would end up there herself. People recently removed from power were often, soon enough, removed from life. Purella gave the orders and then turned back to Clyde.

"Did you get a fix on the Firestone habitation area?" she wanted to know.

"Yes, but if we hit it from the *Dreadnaught* we might take out Quint's prisoner," he replied, guessing her plan. She swore.

"That means we're going to have to do it the hard way," she replied. "My concern is that these troops might make a mess of this."

"You're probably right," he agreed. "They might kill him too."

"We are going to have to go in ourselves," Purella hissed, irritated. "Ahead of the main force... that way, even if we don't get Satiah, we might be able to prevent the prisoner's death." Clyde nodded indifferently. To him it hardly mattered as he wasn't taking a role in this.

"Quint wants to talk to you," he stated, in her ear. "Something about blowing up a ship."

"He'll have to wait," she retorted, uninterested. "He still hasn't even told me why this guy is so important."

"Bet he hasn't paid you yet either," Clyde stirred, a mischievous glint in his eyes.

***

"I don't care *what* you're doing, *you shouldn't be here*," the woman stated, obstinately. Satiah, Cherry and the boy were trying to persuade her to let them into the ship area. Satiah had already clocked the cameras... someone else was watching. The main entrance was not worth the effort. The changeability of levels regarding the technology of this world was bewildering. Swords and laser rifles? Security cameras and camp fires? Synthetic combat clothing... and rags! Wars of attrition often went that way where, despite beginning with the best, people eventually had to make do with what they could get. This guard, for example, was toting a weapon that, though resembling a rifle, clearly was two rifles welded together. It had the bodywork of a WW50, a typical rifle that had been in use for about seventy years. Yet the sights were from what to Satiah looked like an emerald-seeker. That was a highly expensive sniper rifle. The two things together seemed wrongheaded to Satiah as, in combat, it might mean she could see things that she hadn't the range to hit.

"It's okay, I'm sure it's nothing special," Satiah said, grabbing Cherry's arm. "You can show me another time." She led Cherry and the boy away casually.

"What are you doing? *That's the only way in,*" Cherry protested, mildly.

"That guard is not the only set of eyes devoted to it. There were at least two lenses as well. If that's the *only* entrance then we will have to make our own," she replied, glancing over her shoulder. Her gut was telling her that she was running out of time.

"Up there!" She gave a discreet nod in their new direction. Cherry slowly turned to look.

"If we don't want anyone to see, it could take us a while to get there."

"Better start now then."

They eventually returned to the fence from the cover of the woodland. Using her knife, Satiah began to efficiently cut a hole in the mesh. Cherry watched the woods nearby for anyone else sneaking around. Satiah cut a square hole but left it attached in the centre at the top. This would help conceal the hole and make the mesh act as a flap. The boy went first and held it open as first Cherry and then Satiah scrambled through. Satiah put her specs on and had a good look. There were no cameras inside the landing area which was good. There *were* several women wandering around though. A few were in pairs but most were on their own. Mechanics? Fourteen of them, to be exact. There *were* two gun turrets but that seemed to be all they had in terms of ground defences. They were well placed and could cover most approaches with ease… but they were facing away from the craft on the ground.

Satiah toyed with the idea of sabotaging them somehow before they made their escape attempt. It would give them a better chance of reaching space, but the longer they stayed on the planet the more time everyone else had to realise what was going on. Next, she used her specs to analyse the craft more closely. Eighteen fighters, *probably* the local garrison's air defence squadron. Since she'd been there, she'd not heard a single flyby but they may be grounded for a reason. Judging by the signs of wear and tear, maintenance might be that reason. In any case, they only could only accommodate a single pilot and would not be suitable for her purposes. She made note of their type: Lance 70s. About fifty years old... fast, deadly and agile in the air. They didn't have a specific weakness... but they all looked rundown. As they would be the craft most likely chasing her she *had* to look into putting them out of action. Turrets were one thing but fighters would always be a problem.

Next were four transporter ships, six freighters and... a cruiser. Satiah zoomed in on it. A cruiser, if it was in working order, would be ideal to escape in. Fast, armed and roomy enough for twenty or so. It was newish too... certainly by the look of it.

"Know anything about the cruiser?" she asked, her voice hushed. Cherry and the boy looked blank. "Sorry," Satiah apologised. She kept forgetting that they knew nothing about off-world travel. She wanted to know its purpose in being there and, preferably, who it belonged to. A twenty-strong crew might not be easy to oust.

"The cruiser is the big one, correct?" Cherry whispered, peering over the top of Satiah's head.

"*Yeah*..." mused Satiah, slowly. Why did she feel that it shouldn't be there? By *there* she was thinking the planet, not the settlement.

It was too... new. Too impressive. Too *fortunate*? Fortunate that such a vehicle *happened* to be there at the exact time she needed it to be. Was this a set-up, a coincidence, *or* was someone trying to help her? She ruled out the last one as no one knew who she was or that she was there. She automatically distrusted happenstance. That left a set-up... then who? Someone who knew she was there and who she was and that she wanted a ship. Satiah *slowly* turned to regard Cherry and the boy, suspecting one of *them* of betraying her. Perhaps even both of them working together? They were not even looking at her, however. They were spellbound by the ships, eager eyes wide and excited. No, it wasn't them, they didn't know enough. Vann never knew she was seeking to leave or even that she *wanted to know* about the ships. It *had* to be Purella. Purella must have seen through the fake crash and arranged this to trap Satiah and recapture her prisoner. Perhaps she should use one of the other ships, just to avoid this potential trap. One of the freighters, perhaps?

No... That didn't feel right either. If Purella was behind this she wouldn't be so subtle. Besides, as a plan, it had a lot of pitfalls. It required Satiah to *stay in the area*, required her to be *looking for a ship* and *not* calling her own in, plus it needed Satiah to actually see it to go for it. There was too greater probability of her not taking the bait. Speculating further seemed pointless... there was only one way to find out.

"Follow me," she whispered, and edged forward on her belly. Sticking to the thicker vegetation, the three of them crawled, in single file, towards the ships. If Purella *was there* she was keeping a very low profile.

***

"Really, is she?" Reed asked, into his communicator.

"It's definitely her," replied the distorted voice. "The ship is in position like you ordered, she'd be mad not to take it."

"*Well...*" he mused, his eyebrows rising. "*I seldom mention other people's mental capacity.* Thank you very much; as I said before, Lord knows *what* she's doing there. If I were you I think I'd distance myself now, just in case things turn nasty."

"Sir." They disconnected just as Darius came out.

"What's this about?" Reed asked, tetchy. "I promised Lady..."

"I had an idea about these attacks," Darius began, prudently. "I wanted to talk to you and Captain Ogun alone."

"I see," Reed mused, with a heavy nod. A moment later Ogun joined them.

"I got your message," he said, to Darius.

"I have a scheme I want to discuss with you and only you, it concerns the recent attacks. It will depend on what *you*..." he gesticulated to the Captain. "...are willing to do. Or rather *not do*, depending on which way you look at it."

"Go on," Ogun encouraged, interested.

"Unless they think they can take a destroyer, a highly unlikely contingency, they won't attack because you're sitting there like a trained canine or feline on guard duty. If you were to schedule in some *routine maintenance* there would be a window of opportunity for them to attack while you are away. I suggest we fabricate your departure and while you wait, cloaked, they may choose to attack," Darius explained, calmly.

"How exactly will *they* know it is time to attack?" Reed asked, frowning.

"That's the question," Darius shrugged, grimly.

"You think there is an informant," Ogun mused, catching on.

"Someone here must be in contact with them, it would make sense," Darius answered, leaving it at that.

"Well, it's an interesting test," Reed said, shrugging lightly. "I have no objections. If they come in again, provided you get them, you might be able to destroy all of them this time."

"That would be my intention," Ogun nodded. "Yes, I am as you say… game. When?"

"I'm assuming, due to the fact that you have met with us alone, you have no wish to involve the leaders of the planet in this?" Reed presumed.

"One of them could be the insider," Darius stated, inflexibly.

"This is true, but *suppose* something goes wrong and the attackers return and do great damage? Who will the leadership here blame, do you think?" Reed asked, calmly.

"The biggest danger will be that whoever is helping them *realises* that this is a trap," Darius responded.

"Yes, but how will the attackers *know* to attack if no one tips them off because *no one knows?*" Reed elucidated. "See, if you keep this a total secret, when the ship vanishes *no one will say anything* as they will naturally assume it is patrolling *elsewhere*. No one will betray its absence as they will not realise that it *is* absent. You will need to leak the information out somehow…"

"*Who to?*" Ogun asked, curious. "I'm assuming you will tell them to *keep it to themselves* and not to tell anyone to make it more credible?

How long am I supposed to be gone?"

"Twelve hours, that *should be* a long enough period of time to organise…" Darius began.

"*Twelve hours!*" hissed Reed. "Since when did routine maintenance take *that* long? No, no, we should think of something else *more plausible* if *that* is the duration you want. Perhaps you have been sent to investigate something and you *estimate* that you will be gone for twelve hours or something."

"Investigate suspicious ships in a nearby zone," Darius concurred, nodding. "*That's what we say you're doing*. In reality, however, you're just sitting there… invisibly waiting."

"*For twelve hours*," Reed repeated, chuckling. Ogun rolled his eyes. Part of being a military man was learning how to wait. Most of the career was literally waiting. Waiting to move, waiting for orders, waiting for the enemy… waiting. This was interspersed with brief but deadly periods of intense action, however, so people cherished the waiting more than some might think.

"*Who* are we going to tell?" Ogun asked again, seriously.

"…Someone with connections to *Polvine Limited*, a company on this planet," Darius stated, seriously. Reed eyed him in comprehension.

"Do you have *an individual* in mind?" he asked, softly.

"Three people are easily connected to the attacks and the company," Darius said. He had researched it while eating. "I suggest we try one at a time."

"Do it *carefully*," Reed warned, gravely. "The *last thing* we want is to get the wrong person *because* the right person overheard."

"That is a calculated risk, in either case it would certainly confirm that we have a traitor here," Darius stated.

"We should at least *try*," Ogun nodded. "There should be little real danger for the people of the city."

"Let's hope not, *otherwise*…" Reed trailed off, remembering the Viscount's options.

***

Satiah emerged from cover slowly, staring intently at the back of the woman who was spinning a refuelling cable back into place, now that it was no longer needed. The woman was daydreaming as she probably did a lot – until Satiah knocked her out. Carefully she was dragged backwards into the shrubbery. Satiah then switched her own worn military jacket with the woman's pale green one and stole her cap. Cherry and the boy bound and gagged the unconscious woman promptly.

"Right," Satiah said, while crouched before them. "I'll go on board, have a gander. When it's clear I'll tell you." They both nodded silently. Satiah wandered back out from the vegetation and began to finish the woman's job. She glanced up to check that the shutter was closed on the refuelling line. It was. That had to mean it was ready to go, fuel wise. A good start, but she would double check that when inside.

She edged out into the open from the gap between ships, and looked left and right casually. There were still about ten other women around doing various tasks. Satiah slipped around to the entrance ramp that was conveniently lowered. The floor was polished, the walls clean and even the low hum of the power core seemed to welcome her inside. She produced her pistol and began to edge forwards. She could hear nothing other than the hum of the energy and the pumping of her own heart. It would take her a while to search the whole ship on her own so she planned to go to the control room and run a scan from there. Plus, if anyone *was* anywhere on board, the likelihood was that they would be the control room.

She reached the first junction in the corridor and observed a slight discolouring on the wall. Plainly something had been removed; judging by its large size and location Satiah presumed it had been a symbol of some diversity. An emblem announcing the ship's owner to any who might see it had certainly been there. Satiah even knew who had once owned the ship now. The Coalition. *Her own side...* technically. *Interesting.* A ship of this quality, in this condition, was unlikely to have been stolen. That inferred that it was bought or willingly given in some other way... She reached the control room and paused. There was someone in there, in one of the console chairs, facing the viewports and the forest outside.

The door swished open and Satiah went inside, just the way anyone would, like she was meant to be there. The woman didn't move or even seem to notice that she had company. Satiah seized and swivelled the chair around to disorientate and… the corpse lolled forward before slumping limply to the floor. Stone dead. Satiah spun, expecting an attack from behind but none came. The corridor was empty. She crouched and felt for a pulse, just to be sure. Nothing. The body was cold but not stiff… dead for two or three hours. The cockpit was fairly warm so that might factor in the condition of the body. There were no external injuries she could identify without a more thorough check. It was when she noticed the pills on the console near the flight control that a possible explanation appeared. There was also an empty bottle of something strong, on its side… empty. A suicide. Satiah wasn't that astounded by this revelation: this was hardly a vacation world after all.

She ran a scan using the computer while checking the fuel levels. As she had hoped, she was the only one there and all tanks were full. She also initiated an immediate area scan before hastening back outside. She'd deal with the body later; it wasn't like it was going anywhere. Outside, everything seemed the same in that her presence hadn't been noticed yet. She whistled an agreeable tune noisily. The song the boy had tried to play that first night had seemed a pleasantly pertinent choice. Cherry and the boy came running from cover quietly and vanished up the ramp into the ship without a word. Satiah took the time to ensure that all cables had been removed and there was nothing to delay a swift take-off. There wasn't. She had already seen the fuel line removed and there was nothing else visible. She returned inside, closing the ramp behind her.

***

Purella led the group she had chosen, in some cases handpicked, through the trees quietly. The jamming units were in operation. No heat sensors, vibration sensors or motion detectors were working. Radio was also not an option but that was nothing new on this world. She paused and held up her hand flat. Everyone stopped. She pointed at the floor and everyone crouched. She peered down the scope of the sniper rifle she had acquired. She could see a patrol and a lookout presumably exchanging a password. She waited until the patrol had moved on, then she dispatched the lookout from her tree with a shot to the head. This was the third lookout they had taken out. This effectively created a large blind spot in their defence. It was at this point that Purella and her team would infiltrate and, after ensuring that the rest of the army had a reasonable foothold, began a search for the prisoner.

If it wasn't for that old man, she would have commenced a planetary bombardment and had done with it! However, if Quint said he was important, then he was important – but important in a way that his capture was of minimal concern… Purella didn't get it and she didn't like things she couldn't explain. When she finally got that man back, she would interrogate him. Find out who he was and *why* he was *so* significant. It was middle morning now and it would be time for the patrols to swap. Purella passed the rifle back down the line and drew her pistol. She stood and everyone followed her example. Under her instruction they fanned out and began their attack approach.

***

Satiah sealed the ship as best as she could. The main problem now, assuming they were not shot down, was that when they landed again, other people were certain to try to board. She and Bert had to be able to get back and Cherry couldn't fly the ship. Satiah herself would struggle, the computer could manage mostly everything but she would *need* to keep the flight controls on manual. She reached the control room and they were both waiting for her, nervously regarding the woman's body on the floor.

"Cherry, take her away and leave her in the room to the left, we will deal with her later. When we get out to space I'll see to it she is let loose out there… maybe there is some solace available in the next world for her should she be aware that her body also escaped this place eventually," Satiah said, trying to think of everything.

"Right," Cherry nodded, glad to have something useful to do.

As she dragged the body away, Satiah crouched before the boy. This was insane but she only had poor alternatives. He looked worried and she smiled reassuringly, perhaps he thought she was about to tell him that he couldn't join them after all.

"I came up with a name for you last night," she whispered, softly. "*Riff*. I don't know exactly *how* but it's something to do with music. I know you like music so… anyway; let me know if you like that and we'll stick to it, ok?"

"*Riff,*" he repeated casually, trying it out.

"*We'll talk about it later.* I need you to do something *very* important. I need you to watch me as I fly this ship, ok? Watch what I do. When Cherry and I go in to get the prisoner… I'm going to programme the ship to keep circling the area. It will do this on its own. I need you to watch and the moment you see *me* on the roof of the building, press to activate route two," she instructed. He looked blank. She fought to control her impatience.

She tried again while reminding herself that until recently he didn't even know what a ship was! Cherry came back in and listened.

"You watch the *roof*. You see *me*. You press *this*," she smiled, indicating the button. Slowly he began to nod. She nodded, making her mind up to go over it again once she'd programmed the flight computer. If she couldn't get that to work then she'd have to just risk everything and land the thing on the roof! By the look of the building she couldn't be sure if the structure was up to supporting the additional weight of cruiser… or even a person. Cherry dutifully repeated the instructions to Riff.

"His name is Riff," Satiah said, preoccupied.

"Oh… you named him," she noted, in surprise. Riff repeated what Satiah had told him about the meaning behind his name.

"What does *Cherry* mean?" Cherry asked, inquisitive. Satiah glanced at Riff from under her lashes and winked.

"Oh, err, servant of man I think," she murmured, as if not really listening. Cherry gaped.

"*What?*" she asked, horrified. Riff chuckled and Satiah realised that this was the first time she'd ever seen him laugh. "*That can't be right!* They would *never* have called me *that!*" Cherry protested, still outraged.

"Cherry, *it doesn't,* I was *only joking,*" Satiah explained, ruefully. Cherry flushed red.

"I see," she said, a bit snippy. "Is *this* what passes for humour out there among the other worlds? *Lying to people?*" Satiah started to laugh as well. "And what does *Satiah* mean then? *Mighty warrior* or something."

"Would you believe *I never asked?*" Satiah replied, deadpan.

"Maybe we should talk about this when we're out of this place," she said, huffily. Satiah grinned before refocussing on the controls.

She pre-set the flight computer to have three stages. She would pilot to the building herself and set in the first phase which was a circle low enough for her to jump onto the roof. The second phase would then automatically begin there, the cruiser would move to a higher altitude, and circle the area while keeping the building in full view the whole time. When Riff saw her on the roof he was to activate the third phase. A repeat of the first phase, in essence. Another circle close enough for them to jump back on board. It would continue this flight path until manual control was reasserted. In other words, it would keep coming around at that exact level until she stopped it. Broken ankle or not, it was the safest way of doing it without risking losing the ship.

She glanced over her shoulder at them, a question in her eyes. Riff nodded determined and Cherry tightened her grip on her rifle.

"This is it, wait for me by the entrance ramp," Satiah commanded. Cherry nodded and hurried away. There was a soft droning noise as the drive came to life. With a jolt that made Riff's tummy feel funny, they rose into the air sleekly. Almost immediately the communicator activated.

"You have no authorisation to move that vehicle, *what are you doing?*" barked an angry voice.

"This is an unscheduled test of the craft and of security," Satiah answered, completely calm. "Talk to Captain Vann about it, she will explain and provide all codes required. I'm just a pilot following orders."

A distant explosion made Satiah glance up. Riff too saw it.

"An attack," he said, warningly.

"Don't worry, this *may* actually help us," she stated, nonchalantly.

"This is a priority command, you are to provide air support to defence area three," the woman said. Alarms began blaring everywhere below them on the grounds and the scanners revealed that the fighter craft were starting to move. Swinging up from the ground like birds of prey, soaring upwards to confront their intruding rivals. More explosions, some closer than before.

"Understood," Satiah replied, in answer. She stood, got Riff's attention and pointed to the viewport. "You know what to look for, just ignore the voices on the communicator."

She sprinted towards the entrance ramp where Cherry was waiting. She activated the ramp, causing alarms to flash as; it was considered emergency action to open the ramp while in flight.

"You ready?" she screamed, over the wind.

"I think so!" Cherry shouted back. There was much movement on the ground below them as soldiers ran towards their defensive positions.

"Who's attacking you?" Satiah yelled.

"From that direction, it's probably the Brigade!"

"What are they like?"

"You wouldn't like them!" Satiah felt like saying she hadn't liked any of it yet. Cherry gave her a grin. "Nor they you, I suspect!"

Passing over the roofs of what Satiah knew were the storage areas, they got their first glimpse of the prison or 'slave barracks' as it was referred to by the sorority command. Like most of the structures of this decadent, degraded excuse of a society, it wasn't easy on the eyes. While some tried to romanticise the jejunity and meditative calm of prison life, Satiah knew it for the terror that it was. On this world, she was expecting all the old favourites to have been rediscovered. From bronze bulls to Judas cradles; she was sure they would all be there. She had been concerned from the beginning about Bert's safety but Cherry had informed her that, for whatever reason, he was being left alone. Satiah had wondered at the reasoning behind that but had got nowhere fast. There *was* a reason Bert was important *to Purella*, could it be that *that same reason* was what was protecting him inside those walls? There was no way to know yet.

The pass the cruiser made was as close as Satiah could get: about a metre from the roof. One at a time they jumped. Rolling to a halt, Satiah paused, pistol ready. Cherry, not used to this sort of thing, had been unable to manage so gracefully. She scrambled onto all fours, snatching up her rifle. There was a square aperture that led down into the prison; only three rusty metal bars blocked their way. So badly corroded, a few determined kicks were all that was needed to remove them. The smells and the noises of suffering greeted them. Satiah glanced around just to be sure the cruiser *was* following the course she had set. If not, there would be little point in continuing. It was. They descended a set of steps and walked out onto a metal walkway overlooking the cells. From there, as they hurried by, it was possible to see inside every room.

Gruesome and sickening weren't really enough to describe the conditions: suffice to say, it was distinctly unpleasant. The alarm was already hammering constantly and distant rumbles of explosions could be heard over it. Such was the din that a lone guard didn't hear them coming. Satiah shot her and then searched her body for door cards, keys or whatever they used to open the cells doors. If they only worked with face, retina or palm scans… well there was an answer to that too. The woman had nothing of use on her.

"We should try the warden's office, *it's this way*," Cherry suggested, quickly. Satiah followed as they clattered down the steps into the main isle that had cells on each side. A few of the prisoners stared out at them from their tiny rectangular windows.

"Should we get bottled up in here, it might be a good idea to open all the cells and release everyone," Satiah said, seriously. "They would be useful distractions."

"…*Okay*," she replied, uneasily.

The door to the office was open and someone was already coming out. Satiah and Cherry both opened fire this time, bringing down the warden herself. Bursting into the office, Cherry snatched at the cards that allowed entry into the cells. Satiah, however, didn't bother and simply took the master card.

"Cell E14," Satiah remembered. They darted along the next aisle, Aisle A. Unfortunately, the few personnel that had remained in the building clearly now knew that something was wrong. A different alarm was sounding too. It was when they reached Aisle D that they all but collided with a patrol. Fire was exchanged as Satiah and Cherry leapt to opposite sides of the corridor and the patrol did the same.

"They are calling for backup!" Cherry hissed, through her teeth. Satiah shrugged.

"Too much going on outside for anything to come *immediately*," she replied, levelly. "Did you see how many...?"

Her sentence was cut off by an explosion. A rocket or a missile or *something* slammed into the side of the prison at that moment. Screams! Fire! Dust! Satiah crouched and covered her eyes as shrapnel ricocheted around wildly. The patrol recovered more quickly and began firing on them again. Satiah couldn't see anything for the smoke and filth in the air. A gaping hole in the side of the building had been created. Satiah caught sight of the cruiser; still circling, only now it was not alone. Two fighters were following it. It was only to be expected and the shields should be able to take two of them but if any more piled on there would be trouble. This momentary view was cut off by another wave of smoke. Cherry began shooting again even though she was just as blind. Satiah, with renewed urgency, rolled out from cover and began shooting too. She aimed low, as she guessed that the women they were fighting would be at floor level.

"Is there another way around?" Satiah asked, breathing hard.

"Well, there *is* but we would have to go all the way around *the whole building*," Cherry responded, not wanting to give up but starting to worry that this wasn't going to work.

"Okay, stop firing," Satiah ordered, pushing Cherry's rifle to the side firmly. "Leave this to me!" She slowly rose to her feet as some fire still kept coming.

"Stop!" she bellowed, at them. "Cease fire! They are dead! We got them! Cease fire!" Through the smoke they couldn't see who they were talking to and that was what she was gambling on. The shooting stopped.

"What's happening? Were they infiltrators?" called someone.

"Don't know," Satiah replied, as she began to inch forward into the smoke.

"What are we going to do? The whole place is under attack! Are you an officer?" A barrage of questions assailed her as she crept through the smoke, slowly getting closer to the person asking them. A shape loomed ahead of her in the smoke but Satiah didn't shoot, she needed to get all of them.

"Don't know that either, keep talking so I can find you!" Satiah instructed, smiling to herself.

"We are over here...!" said another shape. Two of them, the rest must have either died in the explosion or been killed during the exchange.

"Got you," Satiah stated, almost robotically. She shot them both adeptly. "Come on Cherry! It should be the next Aisle along."

***

Captain Rebec watched the unsanctioned departure of the cruiser through her binoculars. She was standing on a wooden walkway suspended high among the trees. Two other women flanked her on either side, watching grimly.

"I told you she'd find it," she said, as if vindicated.

"No one doubted you for a second," remarked one of the others.

"So... what about *our* escape craft?" asked the other, a little bitter. Rebec smiled, amused.

"I have sent for another, in the meantime we are to observe and remain unobserved."

***

Purella threw herself down into the trench as more rapid laser fire cut into their attack. It had begun well enough and they were well and truly inside the defence perimeter, but a sudden counter attack that was unexpectedly resolute had halted their progress. The main bulk of the army was similarly caught up further back and the sky was strewn with dogfights. Purella was basically cut off and would struggle whether she chose to press on or go back. She knew if the worst came to the worst she could call Clyde down to rescue her. Had she managed to get further in, things would have been easier. How was she going to find Bert and Satiah in this chaos? She had an idea, and began to crawl along the trench, over the bodies of those already dead and those still dying. Dirt showered her briefly as a charge went off nearby.

She shrugged a large wooden splinter off her back and as she did, she noticed a cruiser flying overhead. It was circling. It wasn't even firing at anything! She scowled up at it and spotted that it was being chased by two fighters but they were, all three of them, fighting for the same side... *Satiah*! It had to be. She was using the battle as a chance to run. So why was she running in circles? Purella lobbed a grenade and ducked down into the mud. It went off and she peeped over the edge. It seemed for a moment that the area she was in was now silent. There were buildings close by and she could see the cruiser was circling with one of them in the middle. Slowly, with more caution than she normally employed, Purella began to crawl towards the nearest building. Her hands, gloved as usual, were invulnerable to the slithers of glass on the ground that threatened to slice into the nearest blood vessel.

She reached the door and barged in. No one there. Just an empty hall area. She darted across it towards the next door. She had suddenly realised what that building was. A prison. That was where Bert *would have been held* if he had been taken, as he was male. Satiah was trying to get him out... it was the only logical explanation. So long as that cruiser stayed there, Satiah was still in the area. Picking up her pace, Purella raced up a set of steps onto the next floor where she encountered and killed a guard. She crossed from that building into the prison along a sheltered walkway overlooking the ginnel. Another explosion shook the whole place and she steadied herself against the wall. She glanced across at the prisoner watching her. The woman started hammering on the door, begging for escape. She probably believed the building wouldn't be around for much longer and she was most likely correct. Purella just grinned and waved mordantly back.

She was about to leave her there and go on when the sound of gunfire came to her. Close by... inside the building. Somewhere above and to the right. She tried to call Clyde to order him to get a fix on that cruiser but the airwaves were still jammed. Cursing under her breath, she rounded the next corner and bumped straight into another soldier. Purella didn't attack though.

"What's going on upstairs?" asked the soldier, searchingly. "I heard gunfire." Preoccupied by that topic, the trooper didn't even consider the fact that Purella was a stranger.

"Don't know but it's getting closer. I think *they* are getting closer," Purella answered, clearly not happy about it. "Stay there, guard my retreat." She hurried off towards the next set of stairs. They *had* to be close! As she was halfway up and gunfire was still raging, something hit the building.

A concussive wave of debris narrowly missed her as she dived onto the floor to avoid it. For a moment a thick layer of smoke and dust obscured everything. Coughing, Purella crouched low and peered out of the new hole in the wall. As she leaned forward she felt the floor start to give under her. She backed off towards the wall and tried to skirt around the dangerous edge. Two more shots were fired, very close by. She scowled, still unable to see where she was actually going. If the layout of the building remained the same, she should be nearing the next aisle any moment now. That shooting, still above her, she was sure, was on the next floor. She cleared the jagged chasm that now occupied most of the floor, still being extra careful with every step. To be injured in something as mundane as a fall would not look good. Satiah was one of the best, so Quint had *said*, so Purella would take care, but she was certain that she could win. If it hadn't been for that blast from the ship chasing them before, Purella imagined she would have killed her there and then.

***

Bert lay on the filthy floor under the bed he had been unable to get used to. His ankle throbbed constantly but, if the building came down on him, the bed might be the only thing to save him. The alarms, the screams and the sounds of battle were not in any way reassuring. What if Satiah was dead? What would happen to him then? No one even knew he was *on* this planet! Another explosion, this time from inside the prison itself, shook everything. He closed his eyes, willing his own survival. Shooting! Another explosion! Ships shooting past overhead! Survival seemed like a dying flame to him. Another bang sounded, this time seeming to come from inside the room. He tensed, thinking that these were his last precious seconds of life. The bed was thrown off suddenly and he looked up at Satiah and Cherry.

Cherry went back to the door to check that the corridor was still safe.

"How's your ankle?" Satiah asked, breathless.

"Thank you for coming back!" he managed, after a few seconds. She scowled.

"Get up!" she hissed, grabbing his arm and dragging him onto his feet. He cried out as he put weight on the injury. Satiah slipped under his arm.

"Lean on me!" she growled. "There should be a ship we can use to get off this planet but I'm going to need you to…"

"I'll do whatever you need!" he shouted, getting the gist.

"Come on! Corridor's empty!" Cherry implored, grabbing at Bert's other arm. Bert just concentrated on large hops as, half running; Satiah and Cherry conveyed him down the corridor with unforeseen speed.

The building shuddered again and they halted as things began to fall from the ceiling onto them.

"Eyes!" warned Satiah, conscious of splinters. Something flew by outside so fast that it broke the sound barrier. Glass flew everywhere as the remaining windows shattered. A beam came down next, landing right in front of them. Cherry shrieked in shock but didn't panic. They had to climb over it one at a time. It seemed to take Bert an agonising amount of time to get over the beam but in reality, was less than thirty seconds. They rounded a corner and stopped in fury. The stairs were gone!

"We can't go back! That way is blocked too!" Cherry cried, over the noise. Satiah's sharp brown eyes noticed a thick heavy-duty power cable suspended from the ceiling. One of the support brackets had come loose and was causing the heavy cable to dip down towards the floor. She glanced across, picking out the next bracket from the shadows.

"Stand back!" she warned, slipping ahead of them. She aimed carefully, not at the bracket but at the cable further on. She didn't know how much power it could take but if she could cut through it with concentrated laser fire, then take out the bracket… when it fell they could use it as a rope to climb up onto the next floor. Three at a time she poured rounds into it. Sparks flew and the trademark blue lightening effect of naked power discharge licked the ceiling around the cable. She winced, and tried to stay motionless as she continued. At last the red glow of molten metal could be seen. She shifted aim onto the bracket and fired. As she had hoped, the cable swung downwards, sparks still flying and crashed into the wall. She'd taken out the bracket last as it had been useful to ensure the cable didn't start to move under her shooting and thus make it harder to hit.

"Oh no!" Bert growled, guessing what he had to do next.

"Cherry, up you go and secure the top. How much do you weigh?" she addressed that last question to Bert.

"Why?" he asked.

"If I'm going to carry you up there…" she began, thumbing up at the next level. Cherry was already halfway up the cable.

"I don't know, maybe seventy kilos or so," he estimated. It had been some time since he'd weighed himself, and he was certain he had lost some recently – after all, he'd not been getting much in the way of food. Satiah called to Cherry.

"It's clear!" Cherry called.

"Catch these!" Satiah ordered, throwing her pistol up at her. Cherry did.

"Wrap your arms around my shoulders… I'll let you know if you're strangling me!" she instructed. She grasped the cable firmly. She winced as she took not only her weight but his too. Where was Kelvin when she needed him? Tears in her eyes, red with the effort, she gradually began to move up the cable. Each move was slow and laborious. Her arms were burning from the exertions and her legs too from gripping the cable. Bert gasped as he almost lost his grip on her. His forearm slipped back over his other arm, pushing against her throat. She fought for air and reached up to grab the next bit of cable. Reach, grip, drag, wrap and reach again. Satiah was in agony now but she forced herself to keep going with iron willpower. Finally, she reached up and found Cherry's hand. They made eye contact. She couldn't speak so she tried to convey her intention through a desperate, wide-eyed nod. Cherry got it.

"Bert, give me your hand," Cherry ordered. Carefully, Bert grabbed Cherry's hand. "I'm going to drag you up and over Satiah's head!" she shouted, to him. She gripped his hand in both of her and began to pull with all her might. Satiah growled as Cherry pulled him along her back, over her head and onto the floor. So exhausted was Satiah that even after his weight had gone, she was struggling to hold herself there. Panting, Cherry, now also red faced, returned and helped Satiah of off the cable. The three of them just sat there for a few moments, breathing and trying to recover.

"Thank you both," Bert said, earnestly. "That was incredible."

"It wasn't a pleasure," Satiah moaned, rubbing her arms to try to mitigate the pain. She stood, a little wobbly on her feet and gave another short nod.

Cherry rose too and between them they got Bert moving again. Progress was easier now and no one saw as Purella reached the area they had just vacated. Purella just saw their backs as they vanished from view. She rushed to the cable and began to climb up after them. Satiah, now drenched in sweat, recognised that they were now close to the steps that would lead out onto the roof.

"Not much further now," Cherry encouraged. "We are doing fantastic."

"I hope this ship isn't like the last one," Bert was saying, grimacing with restrained pain.

"It's not!" Satiah uttered, with difficulty. They reached the steps and fought their way up them onto the roof. Satiah turned, leaving Bert to Cherry, and waved to get attention. The cruiser was still circling but now it was being fired upon. The shields were shimmering as they absorbed most of the hits.

Cherry had secured the hatch on the roof and Bert too started to wave. The ship changed course after what seemed like an eternity. Riff had seen them. "One arm each!" Satiah ordered, as they grabbed Bert.

"Oh no!" he mumbled.

"All three of us will jump together!" Satiah stated, loudly. A loud thump sounded on the other side of the hatch. The cruiser swooped in low, mirroring its original path it had taken when they had jumped from it before. They began to run along as if to jump off of the building. The cruiser came between them and the edge, ramp extended. They jumped. The cruiser remained steady and they judged it correctly. Bert fell back and wouldn't have made it had Satiah not snatched his flailing arm. Cherry grabbed them both in a sort of bear hug and used her body weight to cause them all to fall inside the ship. They landed with a crash onto the floor, wind howling around them along with the sounds of lasers shooting past.

Purella finally burst the hatch open and charged out on the roof just in time to see her prizes flying off. She pulled out her communicator.

"Clyde, can you hear me?" she asked, hopefully. A crackly but understandable voice answered.

"Right here," he said.

"Cruiser, Coalition manufacture, get a fix on it and send a shuttle to pick me up," she ordered, clearly.

"Done."

***

Satiah hit the controls, making the ramp close, and then sprinted to the control room. Riff was there waiting for her, looking frightened.

"Are you okay?" he asked, noticing her beleaguered look.

"Yes, having a whale of a time," she said, quickly. She slumped in the pilot's seat and deactivated the autopilot completely. "Go and help Cherry get Bert into one of the rooms, please." Riff fled. She ran a scan, there were nearly ten fighters chasing them. The shields were badly depleted at less than ten percent power levels. She began heading up towards space. The communications unit sounded like it was listening in to every channel, there were so many voices on it. That must have been partly why Riff looked so scared. She turned it off and concentrated on flying. A familiar designation symbol came to her attention on the scanner... the *Dreadnaught*.

The fighters, after apparently driving off the theorised threat that the stray cruiser posed, quickly returned to the battle. Satiah just kept going, eager to leave everything about that place behind her. She kept one eye on the *Dreadnaught*, which was keeping pace with her and not engaging. *Fine, good enough for me,* she thought. She set the coordinates for Collgort-Elipsa and then activated the main drive. Done. Gone. End. She leaned back into the chair, eyes closed, ragged breathing and aching body. That climb had really taken it out of her. She sat there for a few minutes without moving, slowly regaining her composure. Cherry crept in and Satiah jumped but stopped short of going for her gun.

"Everything all right?" she asked, weary.

"Bert is fine, Riff is getting some of the water out of the packaging," she nodded, awkwardly. "Are you okay?"

"Yeah," she smiled, standing. "I'm going to collapse in one of the rooms. It will take us a while to get to our destination."

"Where's that?" Cherry asked, inevitably. Satiah could understand why she wanted to know but was too tired to go into anything with anyone no matter how fleetingly.

"Tell you later, goodnight," she replied, dismissively. She paced out, leaving behind a rather puzzled Cherry. She found what was probably the Captain's room and decided to stay in there. It was like luxury compared with what she had been forced to live with planetside. She began to strip off and noticed her earpiece was blue again. She rolled her eyes. Apparently everyone was trying to get hold of her. Knowing they had all most likely been deferred long enough it was a tricky choice to decide who to talk to first. Kelvin would wait for orders like always. Dyss and Randal would be awkward conversations but they would have to happen.

She put in her call to Randal. He answered immediately.

"Satiah, I'm here," he said, simply. He was composed, ready for anything and for once *wasn't* bombarding her with questions. He knew what it was like and wanted not to put her under any additional pressure.

"Sorry I've not been available much lately," she said. It was a sign of how tired she was, normally she'd never bother to apologise about anything. "I was following a lead on the Milo Drass search. It's… well, I have some *more* things to look into."

"I see… I wanted to let you know that I've spoken to Dyss about you, let him know that I'm not *just fine* with him borrowing you," he stated, sourly.

"*Thanks*," she smirked, glad that Dyss wasn't having an easy time. "No gold yet?"

"No…" he trailed off. "I was going to ask you about Darius."

Satiah sighed. Now what? She didn't need this.

"As far as I can tell he's on the level," she replied, honestly. Okay, they'd had a bit of an argument but only about the correct course of action. The trust issues stemmed only from what she had been *told*, not from anything he had actually *done*.

"That's *something* I suppose, it did concern me. I *know* Dyss suspects him, *has done for years*, but there was never any proof," Randal stated.

"Proof of *what?*" Satiah asked, interested.

"Proof of guilt," he replied, unhelpfully. "I know you're busy, I was just checking in. If you need anything do let me know."

"...Thanks," she said, as he cut off. She rarely liked it when people behaved differently than usual, even if it made her life easier. He must really think she needed to stay focussed, so much so that he'd stopped berating her about things.

One down. Reed was next.

"Ah, *there you are*," he answered, promptly. "How have you been? I thought for a moment you had forgotten us."

"*Us?*" she echoed, wary.

"What happened?" he asked, ignoring the question.

"I got delayed, that's all. I'm on my way back now, maybe twelve hours," she explained. She stepped into a washing unit and gasped as steamy water pounded her skin.

"Well, we've been attacked again, probably by the same people as before. However, I had the foresight to order in some help. Plus *your friend* was on hand at the right moment too," Reed went on. "He's even come up with a scheme to root out the traitor *or traitors*."

"You mean Darius? *Does he have a lead?*" she enquired, intrigued.

"He *says* he does," Reed replied, cryptically. "We have a Federation destroyer on loan, currently acting as our *politically dangerous* protectors. They will likely confront you first on arrival, *just so you know*. We will catch up, probably when you get back here." He was gone before she even had a chance to respond to that. This was weird! It was like he couldn't get away quickly enough. She remembered the lady he had been with when she had first encountered him. She had *thought* there might be something going on there at the time. Well, two down, no casualties yet. She put in a call to Dyss next. He too answered very quickly.

"*At last*, where have you *been?*" he demanded, grimly. Finally! Someone behaving as she had expected them too. Feeling a little better now, she couldn't resist being difficult.

"Doing my job, *like you told me to*," she responded, drawing on memories of difficult teenagers. Their belligerent stubbornness was just the sort of thing that would really annoy someone like Dyss.

"Did you find him?" he demanded, tensely.

"Who?" she asked, being deliberately stupid. He sighed, starting to realise he might do better to adopt a less abrupt style.

"I spoke with Darius and he told me that you were getting close."

"I thought I was, turned out that I was wrong. Right now, I'm returning to Darius and when I meet him we will talk about all this and try to come up with something else. Reed, however, will be throwing things for me to catch." Reed was a useful buffer, someone to use as a shield against Dyss.

"I understand," he said, sounding disappointed.

"The family been onto you again?" She asked, curious.

"*No...* just the father and just the once. That was before I even met you, *I have heard nothing*," Dyss remarked. "I had assumed they were searching for him themselves." He paused.

"But *now* you *don't* think so?" she replied.

"*...I don't know...* there is something not right about this," he replied. "Ambassador Drass is still on this planet, he's not left to search at all. The mother has gone to look."

"*Adopted* mother," corrected Satiah, testing him. Did he already know?

"Adopted?" he queried, immediately. Perhaps not, but then she already knew he was good enough not to be caught out like that. "If *that's* true... *it's not on the file.*"

"I know."

"*Why wouldn't it be there?*" he mused, rhetorically. She didn't answer. "Thank you for sharing that with me. I will talk to the father about that. And... *The fact that we haven't found him yet*. If he gets funny with me I can drop that adoption business on him. If he had been holding that back, then it's possible he might be holding other things back."

"Fine, let me know his reaction if it's relevant," she asked. It was even possible that the father didn't know, assuming he and his wife got together after she squired Milo as a child.

"Of course," he said. "Thank you for getting back to me, I'll be in touch soon." He disconnected. She thought for a while, enjoying the shower. It really was a great place to think. So Reed and Darius were dealing with the attacks directly. Darius thought someone on Collgort-Elipsa was working *with* them. He was most likely right about that. Security *was* appalling on that world.

No gold. No Milo. Darius better have something for her... She called him next. He didn't answer at all. She rolled her eyes. He was making a gesture. *Yes, I know you're in charge but you're making my life difficult. I can do the same to you.* She had made *many* such gestures in her long career and so didn't hold it against him. She tried again and this time he answered.

"What?" He sounded no less pleased to hear from her than he had the last time they had spoken. Now was the hard part... she had to get him to agree to do her a favour. This was not going to be easy.

"We will talk when I get back, obviously, but I wanted to let you know that I didn't find Milo. The man I have rescued is someone else entirely... I would be *grateful* if you didn't tell Dyss about this," she stated, carefully. There was a silence.

"Whom did you rescue?" he asked, without committing.

"Doctor Bertram Blake Clark, *a scientist*, I was going to ask *you* to look into his background please," she ordered.

"I will," he replied, coolly. "The moon is still our best lead on finding Milo but security will have been tightened *considerably* since my departure." That was her fault, he was telling her. She shrugged it off.

"Understood," she said, casually. Dyss already knew about her failure to find Milo but Darius didn't know that Dyss knew. She hoped to use this as a way of making him *think* he had something on her. She wasn't going to bring it up again though; it might make him suspicious if she *kept* referring to her own failure. He might start to wonder why she was so willing to remind him of it.

"Have you spoken to Reed?" he asked, quizzically.

"I *have* and I'm aware of the *new defensive measures*. He also told me that *you have a theory*?" she queried. Darius explained his conversation with Randal and the link with the company, the pirates and the gold.

Satiah had to concede that he was onto something. Purella's presence on the planet meant it was highly probable that she *too* was connected to these attacks. She then told him about Purella and how she'd identified that the pirates were responsible for the attacks, the research into the previous attack, and the subsequent missing security records which *also* pointed to insider involvement. It was, without doubt, their most successful interaction to date. A healthy exchange of information, ideas and *compliments*. Each took the time to thank the other. Each bothering to display that they were impressed with the other too. She still had to remember to keep an eye on him though. Just in case. She was more certain than ever that Dyss was wrong about him. Nevertheless, he could still cause her problems of another kind if he chose.

"Are you prepared to wait for me to get there?" she asked, casually. "Before you do your missing warship show?"

"Plan is already in motion; you should arrive maybe two hours into it. So you won't be intercepted, I'll let the Captain know to expect you," Darius assured her.

"I'm travelling in a stolen Coalition *cruiser, military grade six*," she admitted, recognising that that alone could cause complications.

"*Ah*," he said, the hint of amusement in his voice. "I'll update him so he won't think you're them."

"Your biggest worry would be *another* Coalition force or Union force arriving in your timeframe," she cautioned. "That could cause trouble."

"*And* it would also scare our attackers away," he added, sincerely. "Ok, is there anything else?"

"No, I'll be there soon," she said, cutting off. She exited the shower and froze in shock. That stone was on the floor, in the doorway. That stone that had somehow managed to stay with her all the way from Purella's cargo area. She stared down at it, wary. It looked the same as always... innocently stony.

"*What?*" she asked, out loud. No answer. She scowled and stepped over it as she returned to the sleeping area. Part of her wanted to lock it up somewhere out of sight where it *couldn't* watch her. That's what she felt it was doing. Watching. Watching *her*. She didn't know how or why but it was *not* her imagination. She knew that much at least. Its weird shifts in temperature, and ability to stay with her, was unnerving – to say nothing of those voices she'd experienced when she'd first found it. Locking it away, however, would likely not make a difference. Besides ... she didn't want to touch it when she didn't have to.

She slipped between the sheets of the bed, pistol and earpiece under the pillow. She was asleep in moments, exhaustion from the last couple of days at last taking its inevitable toll on her. Her mind, never truly restful, continued to go over the questions again and again, seeking answers as always. Since the resolution of her sister's trial and being with Carl she had not been troubled by the nightmares. Away by the doorway in the dark, there was movement. The stone, little by little, silently inched its way towards the bed.

PART THREE

Escalation

Twelve hours! A whole twelve-hour shift and the city would be totally unguarded... Bavon couldn't believe such an opportunity could arrive so soon. But then, maybe they thought the threat of a destroyer was just as impressive as the destroyer itself? There had been a high-level security message, something so rare that *everyone* noticed and it had been disseminated to just a few individuals. Due to the system working a certain way, however, *all* the administrators saw it too. Privacy was a meaningless word in the age of the artificial intelligences. If something existed, it could be copied, stolen, amended and reconstituted. It could never be deleted. Everything you do, everything you say will remain recorded in the minds of the computers. And whose thoughts do those computers think? The price of progress was often higher than it first appeared.

That being said, with such a vast, perhaps limitless amount of information there... it was easier to hide than one might think. Obscurity was the best defence. Bavon, without considering any of that, only knew it was an opening for another attack. Immediately, knowing they would need time to mobilise, Bavon called Kyle. Quint would pick up the signal and join in halfway through the discussion to listen in. He usually did that. Bavon wasn't sure why but, after a lengthy absence, Quint was very much *hands on* all of a sudden. So far, Bavon's task to find out all about who had ordered the ship, had met with mixed results. Bavon had enough guile not to draw attention to himself while seeking answers but he'd been pushed to his limitations. There seemed to be a respectful discreetness that wasn't there before. A suspicious reluctance to share details.

Quint had been very clear about what he had wanted to know. *Find out who* requested that destroyer to be there. *Find out who* is in charge of said destroyer. *Find out* if *any more* are on the way! While he'd speedily established that the Federation destroyer was commanded by a *Captain Ogun*, the other two matters gave the impressions of being permanently shrouded in silence. One thing he *had* discovered though was that it had had *nothing to do with the Viscount*. Were there more ships on the way? That was the biggest question, to Bavon's way of thinking in any case. He had also brought up a few other questions that Quint *hadn't* asked. How long would they be staying? How would the Union and Coalition react? These also had no answers yet. Everyone was playing this very close to their chests.

Kyle and Quint answered together. It was good to feel important.

"I have good news," Bavon told them, keeping his voice confidential in tone. He explained about the twelve-hour gap in protection over Collgort-Elipsa. And that the ship itself was under the command of Captain Ogun.

"That's fantastic…" Kyle began, positively.

"Where is it going?" Quint asked, softly.

"Something about investigating ships in a nearby area," Bavon dismissed, as if it was irrelevant.

"We can get there in that time," Kyle said, seeming to make the effort to be calmer. Perhaps he and Quint had been talking in private. He didn't mention *money*, which was rare. "It *may* even be possible to use this to create further distrust between the Federation and the Coalition."

"That's what I was thinking," Bavon agreed, too quickly to be believed.

"*No*," Quint said, his strange computerised voice giving nothing away. "It's a trick. The mere fact that you *could* find out about it gives it away." Both Kyle and Bavon were stunned into silence. It had never even occurred to Bavon that it might have been *planted* for him to find.

"Not *just* me, it went out to quite a few…" Bavon reminded.

"They must have realised that they have a leak," Quint went on, interrupting him. "There will be *no attack* during this twelve-hour window, *is that understood?*" Another silence.

"…Sure, you're the boss," Kyle replied, shrugging.

"*How* could they know?" Bavon asked, almost to himself. Were the eyes of officialdom already seeking him?

"Double your precautions," Quint advised, dispassionately.

"How do we counter this?" Kyle asked, curious.

"Leave it with me," Quint said, vanishing from the exchange.

"In the meantime, Bavon… I suggest you keep your head down," Kyle said, cutting off too. Bavon just sat there, unsure what to do next. A trap? Was that true or was Quint just overreacting? No, Quint didn't do that. So… Bavon had been right, they really were onto him? He adjusted his collar again, agitated. It seemed to be getting a little too snug. He had to behave normally, not do anything suspicious. Who were they? The government? Or the Coalition agents? Were they working in concert? Did any of that matter? He returned his attention to something else he'd been working on. Something that he hoped he'd never have to use.

***

Permyon wasn't there. Just like how things were meant to be. The cloaking *hadn't* been compromised. That was the first thing for Captain Arnos to report when Wolf Fleet arrived nearby. The Vinu base should have remained undisturbed. He waved lazily to the nearest flight officer.

"Transmit the consent code to Colonel Celestine," he instructed, calmly. "Let her know it really is us." The man saluted and obeyed. It was quiet. A long-range scan revealed no threats. If the Shintu forces really did know about the base then they should make their move any day now. There was the possibility that they might not have the forces available but Arnos didn't like leaving things to chance. A woman held up a hand at him, informing him there was an incoming message. He nodded, telling her that he was ready.

From the speaker in front of him Colonel Celestine's voice sounded.

"Good to see you, Captain," she said, formally.

"Good to be here," he grunted, in acknowledgment. "I'm not seeing any incoming attacks on my long-range scanners. Have there been any more developments?"

"We think this man, *whoever he was*, was an operative working for someone else. He was able to trick us into thinking he'd escaped the complex when he *hadn't*, and then when he did finally make his actual escape, he had a ship concealed in the jungle. It's not a breathable atmosphere so he would *have* to have had some kind of breathing apparatus with him. He managed to get all the way into the detention area but *didn't* break anyone out," she elaborated. "Conclusion: we know he was an operative, but have no idea who he was working for and therefore no clue why he was here."

He grunted again, as if unimpressed.

The fact that he'd infiltrated the detention area, the hardest area to infiltrate, meant he must have had a very specific aim.

"You have checked for any planted charges?" he enquired, considering.

"Four times," she answered.

"If he wasn't there to put something in, he had to have been there to take something out or learn what *was* inside," Arnos reasoned, plausibly.

"Nothing's been added and nothing's missing," she murmured, eliminating two contingencies.

"So... to learn... what could he have learned?" Arnos asked. "And who would it benefit?"

"*Just being here*, he learned that *we* are here," she muttered, irritated. "That points to someone giving us away, either accidentally or deliberately." Signal or noise? Always the question.

"I recommend you do one more sweep, just to be sure there really is nothing left behind, and my fleet will maintain vigilance should an attack come," Arnos suggested.

"Very well," she agreed, and disconnected. Arnos frowned, deep in thought. Permyon had remained secret for a while but if it *had* been discovered it may become mandatory to evacuate everyone. The moon had fallen before, after all. He requested a complete list of all personnel and assets to work out if he would require additional ships to perform this, should it prove necessary. In the meantime... he would drill the fighters.

"Lieutenant!" he called. "Run tests three, five and nine in that order. Let's see if we can beat our record."

***

Purella had lost patience. After Satiah had slipped away, presumably taking Quint's prisoner with her, Purella had called in Clyde. The *Dreadnaught* had abandoned its chase of the cruiser and had returned to pick up its owner.

"Are you tracking her?" Clyde had asked, upon her arrival. Letting her escape a second time could well prove fatal.

"There's no need to track her because I know exactly where she is going," she had told him. "Collgort-Elipsa." The logic was sound. That was where she'd slipped onto Purella's ship, was where she had been going over the analysis of the attack, and that was also where both of the pirate attacks had taken place. Running or walking, she would head for the conflict. Purella and Clyde were in Purella's quarters back on the *Dreadnaught*. She was sat on the edge of her bed, crown of the Brigade in her hands, and he was standing nearby, arms crossed.

"I shouldn't have wasted all that time playing that *old witch's* games," Purella admitted, with scorn. This was after several minutes of silence. Clyde regarded her solemnly. He knew her impulsive, aggressive nature well and respected it. Also, he was aware that sometimes it got her into situations where she would flounder.

"Quint seems in no hurry to recover his prisoner," Clyde noted, with significance.

"If we knew *who he was* that might mean something," Purella argued, irately. Clyde grinned and she simpered as she shook her head. "Did you mention that precious stone?"

"I said nothing to him about that and he didn't ask," Clyde replied, shrugging.

"And you're sure *she's* got it?" Purella confirmed.

"Must have, it's not on *this* ship," he reported, with cast-iron certainty. Purella closed her eyes, uttered some filthy term in another language and then removed her black headband. Her golden locks, so unused to freedom, took their time as they slowly dispersed.

"It's not over yet. Satiah may have both the rock and the man but she doesn't know what they are," Clyde stated, hopeful.

"She *will* find out," Purella grumbled. "Then I can kiss goodbye to my membership potential."

"You know how it is with *female members*…?" he asked, as he had before. "There have never been any."

"First time for everything," she murmured, her eyes closed. "Besides, with *that rock*, they would have had no choice."

"Quint will still support you," Clyde stated. "He values you and is not a staunch traditionalist *like the rest of them*." There was something about the way he said *rest of them* that got her attention. She opened her eyes and focussed on him.

"You don't like them, do you?" she asked, a cynical edge in her tone.

"It's what they stand for, rather than anything *personal*," he replied, maintaining eye contact. "Like children taking all the toys and refusing to let anyone else play. *It's childish*." Purella scoffed and grinned flirtatiously at him.

"Are you calling *me* childish?" she purred. He moved closer until he was stood before her.

"You know I'm not," he replied, putting his left hand on the crown she was still holding. "These guys are nothing like anything either of us has dealt with before. I would rather steer clear of them than join them."

She looked disappointed.

"They have the ultimate power," she said, her eyes wide. "With *that* kind of power, *nothing could stop us.* We could rule everyone." Clyde almost rolled his eyes, he'd heard this kind of thing before and it enamoured him about as much as a broken ankle would. And he had other concerns too…

"*You* could," he allowed, softly.

"You think I would *betray* you?" she asked, sourly.

"No, I think you would leave me behind. You might not mean to but you would," he replied, seriously. "And you *would* be contended, you're forgetting the *rest of them.*"

"It's *a risk!*" she smiled, excited. "We *all* started taking those a long time ago."

"You know what your problem is?" he growled, abruptly. "You're *too* ambitious." He grabbed her shoulders, pulled her to her feet and kissed her savagely on the mouth. The crown hit the floor and rolled away as she wrapped her arms around his shoulders. While the clinch continued to escalate with passion, Clyde ran his hand along one of her arms and began to tease her glove off. A bleeping sound stopped them and they stared into each other's eyes for a few seconds. Purella looked away first and took a step away as she answered her communicator.

"*What?*" she demanded, tetchy.

"I have a job for you," a familiar computerised voice answered.

***

Satiah had had a quiet morning. She liked those. Having finally healed Bert's ankle using the advanced medical facilities on the stolen cruiser, she was sitting at the controls alone. Riff was still asleep and Cherry and Bert were eating in the kitchens somewhere. Satiah hoped Cherry wouldn't react badly to the new food. It would be very different from what she had been used to. They were less than an hour away from Collgort-Elipsa now and Satiah felt like she was ready to face anything. She had the stone in her pocket again after finding it on the pillow next to her. It was eerie and she couldn't tell if it was harmful or not, but no one had died yet so she was becoming more optimistic. She'd frequently scanned to see if anyone was still chasing her, but there was no sign of that. They had given up too easily as far as she could see.

All night she had been dreaming about the answers to her questions. Pirates, Purella and Polvine Limited. Where was the money? Pirates only ever did anything because of money... that and rivalry. The gold clearly had been a part of this too... but where did it fit in? Who wanted it and who was it for? Assuming they weren't the same person. Perhaps the person who was leaking the information had those answers. She'd even considered the possibility that the two Phantom agents she'd left with the gold had gone rogue and decided to take it themselves. It was risky but they would have the training to pull it off. Yet she knew those two well enough to know they wouldn't do that. They had to have been hijacked, or maybe destroyed in some freak accident.

The door swished open behind her, disturbing her thoughts, and the other three of her new crew joined her.

"How far out are we?" Bert asked, curious. Satiah rechecked... a little closer than when she'd last looked.

"Not far," she replied, being vague.

"What is Collgort-Elipsa like?" Cherry asked, throwing herself into the chair next to her.

"Right now? *Tense*," she answered, mysteriously. She caught sight of Cherry's pleading expression in the corner of her eye. There was no harm in telling her about the world.

"It's an *oceanic* world so... there's a lot of water. The cities are in the sky, hidden among the clouds," she explained. She left out the bit about there being other things hiding up there.

"It's one of the richest planets in the cosmos," Bert added, casually.

"*Yet they didn't bother buying themselves anything that might actually protect them*," muttered Satiah, sarcastically. Her hand ran along the handle of her pistol out of habit.

"I have *heard of* Essps..." Cherry stated, rather uncertainly. "They are the currency?"

"Yes," Satiah said, emotionlessly.

"I see," she mused, nodding slowly. Satiah leaned forward,

concentrating, her hands running over the controls. Piloting the cruiser singlehanded was no easy task.

"Here we are," she said, cutting the engines.

The blue ball that was Collgort-Elipsa loomed up and continued to grow as they got closer. Cherry and Riff watched, spellbound.

"Is there any chance I would be allowed to go home?" Bert asked, seriously. Satiah glanced over her shoulder at him, incredulous.

"*No!* You'd be dead in a day," she stated, flatly.

"*Thought not,*" he grumbled. Satiah could understand him wanting all this to be over, but until they worked out what his role in it was, she couldn't let him leave. They came in quickly, Satiah transmitting the codes as required. A scanner started bleeping and instantly she thought they were being followed but the reading wasn't coming from space... it was coming from the ocean below them. She tried to zoom in as, whatever it was, was so small it scarcely registered. Nothing. She frowned, shaking her head.

"What's wrong?" Riff asked, concerned.

"Apparently nothing," she said.

She began transmitting her codes and was allocated a landing area. She could see her own ship there, parked neatly to one side. As she got closer still she could make out the figure of Darius, standing by the guard railing, his cloak rippling in the constant strong breeze. She sighed, here we go.

"I need you three to go inside when we land, I have to talk to him," she stated, in a tone that broke no argument.

"Who is he?" Cherry whispered.

"An associate," she replied, mysteriously. She brought them in to a reasonable landing. The cruiser was very large and it only just fitted on that landing area. Perhaps they would have been better going to a shipyard or something. She began powering everything down, making it safe for anyone who might come on board.

When she reached the ramp the others were gathered nervously there, awaiting her instructions. Cherry and Riff looked quite pale. For them this was a huge step. Their first alien world. She felt she had better point out to them that here, *they* were the aliens. Bert just looked tentative, as if he didn't know what was going to happen to him. She gave them all a smile she hoped was encouraging and activated the ramp.

"Off you go," she said, motioning for them to walk. The wind greeted them first, making Satiah start to wish that she too wore a headband. Her gingery red hair, swept everywhere by the wind, almost stung her face. Bert, Cherry and Riff went straight for the reception area. Satiah marched over to the railings where Darius stood. He would want to speak with her first to clear up their... inconsistencies *before* anything else was discussed. He wanted a united front if he could get it, and so did she.

She stood next to him and followed his gaze over the edge into the clouds.

"Operation Jackdaw," he said, loudly to overcome the wind.

"Yes?" she prompted, in a similar voice.

"How much do you already know?" he asked, facing her properly.

"Not enough," she answered, wisely. He nodded once and leaned on the railing, getting ready to tell her.

"It started about ten years ago. Intelligence reported a neo-remnantist money laundering scheme. It was big, involving everyone from pirates to the Union. It was an eight-strong team. Dyss, Jook, Pingrey, Alarris, Narm, Gacka, Vallin... and me. Dyss was in charge, second only to Vourne himself. After a few months we had the names, the locations, the accounts... *all of it*. Everything *seemed* to be going fine."

"Never a good sign," she smiled, cynically. He gave a sort of crooked half-smile in response to that. Up until now, everything he had said tallied with the official report that Dyss had filed.

"There was a special job, some sort of pay off had been arranged and the pirates were told to deliver it. We were ordered to intercept them and recover the Essps. We didn't know *who* they were paying at the time but it became apparent later that it had been terrorists. *The Sons of Venelka* if I remember rightly, but that didn't matter as things went wrong long before they arrived on the scene." Satiah listened intently, trying to work out if any of this was lies or guesswork. Again, this was where Dyss stopped in the official report, but still so far everything they had said was pretty much the same. An interception that had gone badly wrong and resulted in the deaths of six operatives.

"The freighter was stationary when we arrived which was weird to start with. I at least had expected it to be moving and I expressed doubts at the time."

"To Dyss?" she guessed.

"Dyss wasn't there at that point, he was already on the freighter," he answered. She rolled her eyes, complications were on their way, she could feel it.

"Okay... *hold it there*. When Vourne and Dyss *weren't around*, who was in charge?" she asked, wanting clarity.

"*Vallin*, and that's who I expressed my concerns to. She agreed with me but as she'd heard *nothing* from Dyss, she said we *had* to continue. I agreed, as pulling out *then* would have effectively meant abandoning Dyss. Had I *known* what he was really doing I would have insisted that we pull out."

"What was he really doing?" she asked, levelly.

"Telling the pirates all about our little ambush. He was the only one *on* the freighter and that freighter had stopped. Maybe they captured him and he talked, or he decided to betray us all by himself. I don't know which but one of those *must* have happened."

"Go on, what happened next?" she queried, anxious not to get bogged down in denunciations.

"We *knew* the money would be in the hold. The fact that the freighter wasn't moving made our jobs a little easier. We scanned the ship, picked up one life sign, and then took out the engines as planned, to be sure that it couldn't move. We boarded but didn't encounter *any* resistance," he continued. Her eyes narrowed and he raised his eyebrows, acknowledging her suspicions, and indicated that they were the same as his had been at the time.

"Was it Dyss?" Satiah asked, seriously. "*The life sign, I mean.*"

"I can't answer that. I presumed it was *at the time* and it makes sense to continue to assume that it was, but I cannot prove that. Anyway, we got into the hold and some of us began to search for the money. We're just uncovering the main crates when Dyss, using the ship's announcement system, warns us of an impending attack. That was when it happened. Sentry robots, tens of them, came at us from every direction."

"If Dyss is the one who betrayed you, *why* would he warn you about the attack?" Satiah asked. Darius, who had expected that question, held up a finger.

"Because he wasn't *sure* that the ambush would get *all of us*. Some of us were in the corridor outside and could conceivably have fought our way out," he answered. "He wanted to be sure that, even if there were any survivors, he could avoid the charge of treachery being pointed at him."

"But *by warning you*, he made the chances of your survival *higher*," Satiah pointed out. She backtracked a little. "I'm not taking his side, I'm *just* trying to make sense of what happened."

"*Perhaps*," he allowed, raising his hand again. "Next thing I knew, after a few minutes, maybe longer, it was just me and Vallin left. Everyone else was dead. We were cornered in the hold, using the crates as cover to hide behind. I was holding them off while she mined the wall to create another way out for us. We'd studied that ship inside out over the days before the operation and we knew that taking out that wall would get us into the engines. From *there* we could circle around and get back to our ship."

"What about the money?" Satiah asked, before she could stop herself. He smirked down at her.

"It wasn't there. In any case we couldn't exactly carry it with us, even if it had been," he said. She nodded, seeing that they had clearly been in an untenable position. It seemed the whole thing had been set up specifically to kill them.

"The wall was blown and we got out. The robots were still after us and we were running to stay ahead of them. That was when we found Dyss. He was in the corridor, by the self-destruct system. It was activated. He told us that he'd found it that way and was trying to stop it. *I* maintain that he had literally just set it in motion *before* he departed for our ship. An argument broke out between him and Vallin. Vallin had reached the same conclusion I had and was trying to arrest him. He was resisting, saying *she didn't have the authority, it wasn't true* and… well, to be honest I didn't catch everything but at that moment something exploded. Not the self-destruct obviously, or else none of us would have made it out. *I think it was something else in the cargo area, although it may not have been.*"

"Engines?" suggested Satiah, shrugging.

"Could have been," he acknowledged, casually. "Next thing I knew, Vallin was down. Dead or not I still don't know. Dyss told me she was but I didn't take the time to check myself. I didn't hear a gun, but if you're a trained Phantom you hardly need one. Dyss was also on the floor but still alive, having also been hit. There was some debris near them, a pipeline I think. He *could* have killed her during the blast but I can't prove that either. The robots caught up at that point and we retreated towards the ship."

"You left her behind?" Satiah asked, grim. He looked pained for a moment but nodded.

"I had to, in order to stand any chance of survival myself," he replied, without shame. The number one rule among Phantoms was: you survive. "That was what I had to do and… *what I regret the most about the whole thing.*"

There was a moment of silence before he carried on.

"Because Vallin had accused *him* of betrayal *and* tried to arrest him, Dyss then used *that* as evidence of a plot between her and me to ruin the operation, whereas in reality, he was trying to kill us and escape but had to change his plan when we caught up with him. He had to make it *look like* he was trying to *save us*, not destroy us."

"Why didn't he just kill *you*?" Satiah asked, astutely. "If you're right and he *murdered Vallin* to prevent her from *exposing* him, why not finish you off too? There was no one else left to *witness* your death. He could have said anything he liked and no one would be able to substantiate otherwise."

"We were under attack from the robots at that time. He *needed me* to help him get out *alive*," Darius answered, plausibly. Satiah stopped herself from asking the obvious. If Dyss had set it up, *he would have control of the robots* and therefore they would be no threat to *him*. Darius could easily counter this by saying that Dyss hadn't been running from *them*, he had been running from the self-destruct system. She knew that as she would say it herself.

"We made it back to the ship and while I held them off, he took off. I only just saved myself from being dragged out into space," he stated, sourly.

"He didn't close the airlock while you were in there?" she asked, starting to think he might be right.

"It was starting to close when he disconnected with the freighter," he explained. "By this stage I had pretty much come to the conclusion that I had better get back to Earth before *he* did and get my side of the story straight." Satiah realised, that from Dyss's point of view, assuming that he *wasn't* guilty himself, this would look *very* suspicious. She could guess the rest too. They had submitted conflicting accounts of the mission to Vourne and he'd only put the parts that both of them concurred with on the record.

Dyss couldn't demonstrate that Darius had betrayed them, but suspected him because he'd run and survived. Darius suspected Dyss because of Vallin's death and the fact that the ambush had occurred; however, he had no evidence of anything either. So, no resolution, no conclusion, just years of distrust and dislike between them. No proof either way!

"Now... *I don't know*. Perhaps I should have just locked myself on board the ship and tried to do something..." he trailed off, desolately. Satiah let out a breath and patted his shoulder.

"Thank you for telling me all that," she said, hoping he'd leave it at that. He didn't though, of course.

"*Who do you believe?*" he asked, directly. If she told him that she believed *him* she wasn't sure he'd believe *that*. She *could* say that she believed that they were *both* mistaken and it had just been a terrible mess made worse by bad decisions and wrong conclusions, but that somehow rang hollow. She knew one thing; she certainly did not believe Dyss about Darius being a traitor.

"I don't know," she managed, at last. "It's... I don't know. I would *like* to believe you." Millions of missions were conducted and often there were *disagreements*. The magnitude of this one though, was worse than any she'd encountered before. Normally the differences occurred over timings, locations or occasionally equipment that was needed. There were even missions where the operatives had flatly refused to carry out their orders for one reason or another. She'd never once read an account where the agents themselves were at odds against each other. Darius nodded, as if he had expected her to say that.

"What did Vourne do?" she asked, interested. "When you both returned and reported in."

"The usual, took statements, went over the scenario, and *retook* the statements and then... I'm guessing he gave up," Darius finished. "I know the mission was never closed out, it's still technically active." That would explain the number difference in Dyss's file, Satiah remembered. Assignments completed: 493 and assignments taken: 494.

All of this aside, Darius had done nothing to warrant *her* distrust. After hearing him out: she decided that her gut was probably right about him. They could work together.

"Okay," she said, seriously. "I'm sincerely sorry about pulling you out of Permyon and..."

"No one's perfect," he growled, seeming to soften. "Dyss will hear nothing from me about it." She smiled, grateful. "It's not like he trusts me so even if I did, I doubt he'd take my word over yours." He chuckled and she laughed quietly.

"I also should thank you for stepping in with Reed so well. I should never have kept the second half of this from you..."

"No worries. If I had to work with someone that my boss had told me *not to trust* I'd have done nothing different," Darius waved away her apology.

"In your case I doubt you would have trusted your boss's word in the first place," she grinned, trying to be funny.

"Exactly," he said, still smiling.

Satiah looked over at the building and spotted Reed staring out at her. He mimed a meaningful yawn and she rolled her eyes. Time was getting on. *Wasn't it always?*

***

"*What?*" Reed blurted. "You mean to tell me that you've been missing *all this time* and you've discovered *nothing?*"

"Something like that," Satiah quipped, sarcastically. She rolled her eyes. "*Of course not!* After seeing Purella's cargo I'm now more convinced than ever that pirates are behind the attacks and it slinks in nicely with Darius's theory regarding the missing gold and the mole."

"The *mole?*" Lady Hollellster frowned.

"*The traitor,*" Reed substituted. Pat nodded and rolled her eyes too.

"So, let me just recap. You want me to tell the Viscount that neither the Vinu or the Shintu have ever attacked *us* and the people who have are *pirates* who have agents here," Pat ranted, unhappy. "You expect me to go to him without a shred of proof or even a suggestion of motive for this?"

"Greed is usually enough," Darius muttered.

"A *specific* motive!" she argued, pleadingly. "Why here, why now and why like this?"

"Because they can," Satiah replied, unable to stop herself trying to be funny. Reed winced.

"Look, we need *more* than hasty hearsay," Reed stated, apologetically. "Lady Hollellster is the one who has to explain all this to the Viscount, and I know what it's like to go to the being in charge and try to convince them of something when you have no evidence."

"I'll get you some," Satiah hissed, sourly. Everyone looked at her.

"*How?*"

"You're better off not knowing," she stated, standing up and marching off. Darius, Kelvin and Cherry filed out after her.

"Is she with us?" Darius whispered, poking his thumb over his shoulder at Cherry.

"Yes," Satiah replied, deciding that she might as well be. She was young and utterly guileless, but still useful.

"What are we doing?" Darius asked, hoping that the walkout wasn't just a walkout.

"We're going to have to attack this again," she stated, thoughtfully. "You and Cherry… You will have to return to Permyon. You can focus on collecting Milo *if* he is still alive. If Dyss comes back to me with anything more on his father I will update you."

"*Me?*" Cherry asked, shocked. "But…" She motioned to Darius meaningfully. Satiah grinned impishly.

"What? You scared of *him*?" she provoked, amused. Cherry's eyes narrowed and she shook her head fervently.

"And you?" Darius asked, talking to Satiah while eyeing Cherry thoughtfully.

"Kelvin and I..." Satiah trailed off. She was going to have to be creative on this one. "Let's just say we're going to fall victim to a bit of piracy. I will try to keep an eye on what goes on here too... should the traitor reveal themselves."

"*What?*" Cherry asked, bewildered. She still hadn't been told anything of substance and was duly bewildered.

"I'm going to take the cruiser, pretend to abandon it and then... *when the pirates come to steal it*... we will jump ship," she said. "It may not be the same pirates, of course, but basically I'm going to get Reed his proof."

"So long as the warship remains on guard here, we don't have to keep an eye out for further attacks," Darius mused, nodding. "Won't *Purella* recognise the cruiser?"

"It's possible but I'm gambling on her greed, assuming she is the one who finds it first."

"Now, what have you got on this doctor character?" Satiah asked, curious. "I would have asked earlier but it's sort of tacky to do it in earshot of him." He grinned.

"Doctor Bertram Blake Clark, a microbiologist from Nimmbar 7," Darius said. Satiah looked blank. "*Nebular Union territory*. Until recently that's where he was living..."

"How recently?" she asked, quickly.

"Two weeks and six days," Darius answered, taking the interruption in stride. "Works as a teacher, semi-permanent status, after a long but average career in research. He's mentioned in a few notable papers concerning vaccination, genetically modified plant life and tranquillisers. No living family. I've not had time to look into them yet..."

"Political background?" she queried, looking at it another way.

"Nothing out of the ordinary but he *is* a scientist so... *who knows?*" Darius joked. She nodded in agreement.

"Anything unusual whatsoever?" she asked, disappointed. Darius eyed her, for the first time realising that she had no idea what this man had to do with the mission. He could have been part of anything but he *was* evidently significant to Purella. She'd never questioned him though and, so far as anyone could tell, she'd not even attempted to make money from his capture. It was like she had no interest in him whatsoever and was merely keeping him for... Satiah realised that that might be *why* Purella had never interacted with him. He wasn't *her* prisoner at all; she was holding him for someone else. *Someone behind her...* It was only a theory but it felt right. Someone had to be paying Purella, for a start. The same someone who was paying the pirates to attack the planet? What was to be gained? Who would benefit?

"Nothing, nothing at all," he said, amused. "It does happen *occasionally*. Not *everyone* is a criminal or a lunatic or a conspirator. No wonder they keep trying to get me to watch those paranoia management manuals. Seeing shadows stalking shadows."

"I know what you mean," she agreed, her mind elsewhere.

"Naturally, as this time infiltration will be harder, I'm going to have to warn you that I may have to start damaging things to get answers," Darius warned.

"I would expect nothing less," she replied. Satiah and Kelvin peeled off their corridor, heading back towards the cruiser. Reed slipped out from behind a wall and trotted along to catch up.

"I see there are plans afoot?" he grinned, casually.

"Where did *you* come from?" she demanded, a little caught out.

"Here and there," he evaded. "Are you going to tell me what you're up to or do you want me to guess?"

"...No," she stated, being deliberately obstinate. "Kindly go away and *bother* someone else." She turned up her nose at him with finality.

"You're going back to the landing pads which means you're planning on going somewhere... this means you have decided where to go," pondered Reed, aloud. "You're taking Kelvin, not Darius so...?" He trailed off, wanting her to jump in and correct him or say something. She didn't and she just smiled annoyingly at him.

"Are you even going to answer me when I call you *later*?" he sighed, apparently giving up. She knew him too well in that she knew he never gave up on anything.

"No, but I might if you call me by my name," she jested, shrugging. Reed smiled and stopped following. He merely watched her until she was out of sight.

"If Darius returns to the moon *while* you and I are elsewhere...?" Kelvin indicated, in his usual monotone. Satiah understood what he meant. Even *with* the warship there to guard the planet, the traitor could work or escape more easily in their absence.

"Whoever it is has most likely been here a while. I doubt they will make a move unless they have to," she reasoned. "Besides, *if we can get the right pirates*, listen to the *right* conversations, then *we* can find out who it is." Instead of going outside and walking across to the cruiser, where she could be seen, Satiah chose another option. They would enter the ship from under it, using the refuelling system as a way in. The spy would most likely be monitoring arrivals and departures, whilst looking out for the destroyer. They would see the cruiser leave but have no idea who was inside it. They may suspect, of course, but they wouldn't know.

Back in the control room, Satiah began to do a systems check. Kelvin took the co-pilot's seat. It would be much easier to fly now he was there. The refuelling was done, all supplies delivered, they could go. Taking off, Satiah decided on a craftier tactic. As strategies went, their current one had a few flaws. These flaws being: what if no pirates found them, what if the pirates did find them but didn't want the ship, and what if they were somehow previously informed that Satiah might be aboard? She would activate a distress call on an endless loop. She would use her Colonial accent to deceive anyone listening into thinking the ship was abandoned because of unstable engines and that a repair ship was incoming. They rose into the clouds swiftly and were back in space in moments.

She would head for an area near 8433-1116, close to where Milo's ship was found drifting. She recorded the message in her best Colonial accent, and then distorted the sound too. Then she began to dress in a survival suit. To make things look more realistic she intended to deactivate life support systems. She and Kelvin would remain concealed aboard, protected from scanners by Kelvin's distortion capacities. The pirates would conclude that no one could be aboard as no one would survive. Then, when they came aboard to check it out, she would slip aboard their ship. There was a chance that they would not bother searching the ship and just drag it back to their base, but even pirates had some brains. Their base would be a secret location and it would be unwise to bring back an unchecked ship. The cruiser itself was a good ship so the pirates would be unlikely to pass up the opportunity. They would be distrustful of course, but gluttony often overcame doubt.

She sealed her suit, checking that it was working properly. It was. She'd have heat and air for forty-eight hours. She hoped that that would be long enough. The distress call should attract the pirates faster than that, but they might wait to see if a repair ship did show up. Kelvin left to adjust the engines. He would create a few faults. Nothing that a basic technician couldn't overcome. Too much damage might create a problem for them should they have to use the cruiser to escape. Satiah attached her suppressor to her pistol efficiently and then replaced it in its holster. A few hours and they would be ready.

***

All the damage had been repaired on Satiah's ship, for which Darius was grateful. They were on better terms now than they had ever been but he wanted to keep it that way. Trashing her ship, even in the pursuit of mission objectives, wasn't likely to go down well. Cherry sat next to him, watching as he operated the controls. The ship shot off the landing ramp and banked sharply upwards. Cherry reflexively grabbed the armrest and Darius grinned subtly.

"You're new to all this, aren't you?" he asked, as an icebreaker. She glanced across at him, trying to decide how to answer that.

"Is Satiah your CO?" she asked, stilted.

"*For now*, yes," he remarked, as they entered space. Out of habit he checked the scopes. No approaching ships and no odd oceanic blips either. All good.

"What are we supposed to be doing?" she asked, still very tense.

"Right now, we're supposed to be getting to know one another," he replied, easy-going. "Who do you work for, by the way?" She glanced at him sharply and then made a conscious effort to try to relax. She couldn't believe Satiah had made her go anywhere with some *man*.

"Satiah, same as you," she responded, honestly.

"Yes, I know that, but who did you work for *before* that?" Darius enquired, starting to regret this already.

"Just people," she remarked, vaguely. She gave a sigh that sounded unduly emotional. Darius rolled his eyes and pulled his hood over his head. This was going to be a long journey. Why had Satiah chosen to dump this girl on *him?*! It was tough enough already without having to supervise her too.

He was just closing his eyes, his intention being, as he had done so many times, to cap nap the trip away, when she started talking again.

"So... what are we doing?" she asked, seriously.

"How much did Satiah tell you?" he asked, his hope fading.

"Nothing," she shrugged. He let out a frustrated growl.

"We are trying to find a man by the name of Milo Drass. Listen, from now on, it would be best if you followed my lead and instructions..."

"Who put *you* in charge?" she demanded, affronted. Another smaller growl. He decided she would serve best by guarding the ship in his absence and *do nothing else...* while he did the rest.

"Satiah," he lied, easily. "Problem?"

She shook her head but looked disappointed.

"We're going to a very dangerous place and it's important that no one works out we are there. I need you to guard the ship to ensure I have an easy escape should I need one," he said, sternly. "I cannot emphasis the seriousness of this enough." She pulled a disrespectful face without meaning to.

"*Guard the ship?*" she qualified, crestfallen. She opened her mouth to argue but then decided against it. "Okay."

"Now I suggest you get some rest," he stated, willing her to stay quiet. He needed to plan how he was going to get back inside that compound and her prickly questions were not helping.

***

It had been about five hours, long enough for the ship to have lost all heat and air, and more than long enough for Satiah to be getting impatient. Satiah and Kelvin were standing in a maintenance tunnel, right beside the airlock. She presumed they would use the airlock as anyone would. There was a chance they might use other means such as transmat technology, or even cutting their way in. Those possibilities were doubtful.

"Look at this," she said, producing the gemstone. She handed it to him.

"I thought you left this behind on Purella's ship," Kelvin stated.

"*So did I*," she murmured, softly. Kelvin stared at the crystal for a long time then he ran one of his metal fingers along it, trying to get it to do what it had done before. It remained inert. He offered it back to her.

"Repeat what you did back when you first touched it," he recommended.

She ran her gloved hand along its edge. This time nothing happened though. She scowled, dissatisfied.

"Maybe it has run out of power," she suggested, guessing. She had no idea how something like that worked but it seemed feasible that some sort of energy played a role.

"I can only advise that you ask a more advanced computer. Perhaps Mensa could help," he proposed.

"*I don't know*," she answered, frowning. "Why do I get the feeling that this gemstone is *much* more important than it looks?"

"Human instinct?" he offered, unhelpfully. "I can only give you a twenty-seven percent probability that it is important."

"*That's low*," she said, smirking. Then she gasped.

Kelvin was a robot and his hands were metal. Her hands were encased in synthetic fibres. Maybe *that* was why they were getting nowhere. It would recognise her flesh, maybe her skin print or her DNA or something.

"I think we're not getting anywhere because it can't sense us. You're artificial, and I can't think of a physical direct link between me and it," she explained. She held up her gloved hand to demonstrate.

"It's possible," he agreed. She told him about its strange behaviour from before. The temperature swings, the ability to move on its own... interestingly enough, only when unobserved. Behaviour was a crucial word as now she was thinking of it more as a living being, perhaps even a sentient being, rather than just an odd lump of rock.

"You're certain it presents no danger?" he asked.

"*Of course not!* Although I have no idea *what* it can do. I'm just telling you that it's done nothing to make me think it's dangerous... *yet*," she added, as an afterthought. "*Apart from stalking me.*"

"When it spoke to you, did it ask you any questions?" he asked. He already knew but memory was an interesting thing.

"It just called my name a couple of times... At the *time* that was all I could take," she said, flashing an uneasy grin. Kelvin fell silent. Satiah replaced the gemstone in her pocket. Something told her that leaving it behind would not be the smartest thing to do. Leaving aside the odds that it might somehow find her again: she was growing more and more convinced that it was significant.

"You trust Darius?" Kelvin asked, out of the blue.

"Yes," she replied, honestly. "*Dyss, on the other hand...*" She trailed off, not needing to explain further. She'd already told Kelvin everything about Jackdaw.

"I'm going to ask Dyss what happened *too*... see if his version tallies with Darius's," she told him. Kelvin held up an appendage.

"Ship incoming," he warned, levelly. She fell silent and listened. "Two freighters, one standing off, the other coming in. Both ships appear to have been extensively modified. Latest standard scope laser cannons, strong shields and engines. Expanded storage areas..." "I get the picture," she said, wanting him to be quiet.

It was a few more minutes before the clamping noises began. The ship lurched and a few alarms automatically came on.

"They took that a bit too fast," she murmured, wondering if there had been any damage.

Sparks began flying as cutting equipment was brought to bear on the airlock. Satiah sniggered... it wasn't even locked. They were quick, clearly having done this many times before, and were inside in less than a minute.

"Let's see what's what!" shouted someone. "Usual teams and *this time*... report *everything* you find!" Satiah couldn't see what was going on but she didn't have to. The pirates were splitting up to search their latest prize as quickly as possible. They would probably already have a good idea as to the layout of the ship and so had planned their incursion well.

"Anyone nearby?" Satiah growled.

"There is a group of four on the other side in their ship. A backup force," he replied. She wondered if, should they be called in, they would be replaced by another group.

"Let's go," she said, easing open the panel. The airlock area was empty and Satiah crept over to the hatch. She crouched and peered around the corner. Four men were standing around, chatting among themselves. Satiah edged back slowly. She hadn't seen any cameras and that encouraged her. She couldn't kill anyone; she had to get in undetected. She leaned forward again, checking out the lighting system. Her specs quickly identified the controls on the wall, just in sight. She didn't have to tell Kelvin what she had in mind. She lowered the power level on her pistol and aimed. She took the shot, her bolt making no noise thanks to the suppressor. The room plunged into darkness. In the confusion of noise, and the flashing of torchlight, Satiah and Kelvin darted through the room and out into the darkness of the corridor, narrowly skirting around the blundering pirates. The lights were on again quickly enough and they examined the damage.

Satiah, always a good shot, had hit it just the right way. Just enough damage to make it look like a circuit blast and nothing more sinister. They quickly found a side room, also in darkness. Satiah entered, made room for Kelvin to get past her and then sealed them inside.

"Scan this ship," she instructed, removing her helmet. "I want to know everything about what kind of force they have. Also, if you can, see if you can keep track of their movements."

"Scanning," he said. Satiah yanked open an equipment box and began planting a mine inside, just in case she needed a distraction later.

"Crew size, fifty-nine," Kelvin told her. She nodded, noting it was about the amount she had expected. There was nothing on the cruiser, no cargo, no passengers… absolutely nothing. It should take the pirates about half an hour to figure that out. When they did, they would tow the cruiser back to their base… wherever that was.

"You find somewhere else for us to hide; I'm going for a wander. Should anyone find you, kill them," she ordered, coldly.

"Yes," he said, as always. Satiah returned to the corridor and took a moment to just listen. She could hear the distant chatter of the men still waiting near the airlock. She padded softly away from them further into the ship. The first thing, which would have been obvious to *anyone*, was that maintenance was visibly not of primacy on this ship. The bare minimum had been done, *as cheaply as possible*; to ensure nothing *actually* broke down. Rust and other forms of corrosion were endemic. Every other light was flickering, dim or, in some cases, non-functional.

The air filtration system was apparently clogged up with dust if that intermittent whistling noise was anything to go by. More voices: she paused in mid-step, trying to determine their direction. An open door on the left where brighter light streamed from. Nonchalantly, Satiah walked over to the side of the door and slipped into the shadows there, listening in.

"These have gone up, you know? Last year these were *half the price*," a man was complaining. Someone grunted in response. Satiah stole a quick glance inside. Four men, in various stages of undress were sat around a table enjoying, well *playing*, a game of Gairrun. Smoke rose from smokies placed at the corners of the table. Satiah slipped past the open threshold and continued on with her exploration.

The next section of the craft was in a slightly better state. The engines were nearby. She sneaked inside and examined the engine system. The engine was a good quality brand. Jockhue, one of the most expensive and reliable products in circulation. However, they had been on the CNC news recently, and not for a good thing. Apparently some new engine they had brought onto the market had to be recalled due to a defect that caused *inconvenient discharge*. Thousands of models had been caught up in the confusion and a lot of money, not to mention kudos, had been lost. Satiah toyed with the idea of sabotaging them in some minor way but decided against it.

The immediate objective was to get to the pirate base, which could not be done on a crippled ship. She passed through some deserted workshop areas and lastly she reached the central corridor.

This corridor, if she followed it all the way, would take her straight to the command deck. Well, freighters didn't have command decks. They had either control rooms or, possibly, bridges. Technically only warships had command decks but all these terms were casually employed to a degree where it largely didn't matter. Why did she always end up thinking about those kinds of semantics? More voices. She casually entered a room to the right and stopped in the darkness there. A large group of people went by, maybe ten or twelve strong.

"The sluggishness of those repair companies beggars belief! Why anyone pays those giant insurance pigs I can't imagine!" ranted a woman. "Think what could have happened had it been an emergency or something!"

"Is that why you joined?" laughed someone.

"*Seriously*! They must have one hell of an advertising campaign!"

"It's all about subliminal messages and corporations spying on people. They create a picture that you're watching but what you don't see are the words hidden in the background that only your subconscious picks up on and *that* is the reason why people get conned into doing what they want. Have you ever noticed how when you buy something, the computer suggests *similar things* to you to buy as well? They're recording everything all the time so they can figure you out and then…"

They moved out of earshot.

Satiah walked back out into the corridor and continued on towards the control room. It would not be long now before they began the voyage back to their base. She needed to know where that was. She reached the control room and peered in cautiously through the filthy window in the door. A lone woman was sitting at the console, eating what looked like a fish of some sort. Satiah paused, knowing she'd not be able to get through the door without alerting the woman to her being there. She backed off quickly, anxious not to become cornered should anyone else happen to come along. She found another maintenance tunnel outlet and got inside. She closed the hatch behind her and activated her specs so that she could see.

Dust and darkness greeted her. She edged along, knowing the tunnel had to encircle the control room. If she could find a gap or something somewhere she could listen in without them knowing she was there.

She found one and arrived just in time to hear one of the pirates berating the woman for having eaten his food.

"The life of a pirate," she grinned, to herself. "*Robbing others only to get robbed yourself.*" A screaming match erupted briefly. Something to do with him having stolen something of hers in the past. He flatly denied the accusation and blamed someone else for it. And so it went on, back and forth for a few minutes.

"*Come on*, talk about your *actual* job," Satiah hissed, irritated. Someone else entered the conversation. A computerised voice, coming from the speakers.

"Kyle, why are you not where you should be?" it asked. There was a silence and then the man, Kyle, answered.

"Sorry, had to check out a new acquisition," he explained, evidently talking about the cruiser.

"That area of space is dangerous, *do not linger*," replied the voice. There was something strange about that voice to Satiah's ears. At first, she thought it was the same sort of distortion she'd heard from the voice that spoke with Milo Drass. Then, after hearing more, she discounted that. It was not *quite* the same. *This voice* was deeper, less fake sounding and grittier.

"Have you changed your mind about the attack?" Kyle asked, interested. "I can still…"

"No. Those plans *remain* unchanged. I will update you when I hear more," Quint answered. Satiah strained her ears, knowing what she was listening to was crucial.

"That ship still not back?" Kyle asked, curious.

"We have been over this," the voice answered, still unnervingly emotionless. "It's an obvious trap. The ship will be cloaked from view somewhere nearby. *They are waiting for you.* This was why I ordered you all to stand down."

"…Point taken, you're the boss," Kyle sighed, uneasy. He had started to say that more and more lately.

"I will be in touch again later, in the meantime remain alert and mobilised. You may have to move in a hurry," Quint instructed, signing off. Kyle heaved a sigh of relief. The woman shuddered visibly.

"...That Quint guy... is *weird*," the woman stated, after a silence. Satiah hoped her specs were getting all this. The pirates were working for *Quint*, whoever that was, *not* Purella.

"Everyone says that," Kyle dismissed, faintly. "Did they find anything?"

There was a clicking noise as the woman used the console.

"Ship's completely empty. Engines look *a bit dodgy* but nothing the boys can't handle, so they say," she said, sounding bored now. Despite the size and price of their haul, cargo was usually the most profitable part.

"Disappointing," Kyle smirked. "Still, the ship itself is the real trophy here. Tell them to make sure it's snagged then we can get the hell out of here."

"No sign of any repair vessels..." she said, clearly unsure as to what the hurry was.

"There shouldn't be, I had the team deactivate that beacon," he replied. "I just don't want to get on the wrong side of Quint. He's got some scheme going and he's very good at problem solving... I don't think that Colonial destroyer will be there much longer."

"Quint will get them to move it?" she asked, doubtful.

"I'm not sure that *moving it* is the plan," remarked Kyle, darkly. Satiah listened harder but that unfortunately seemed to be the end of it. She could draw the evident conclusion that Quint intended to destroy the Federation ship guarding Collgort-Elipsa and, even though she had no idea *how* he was going to try, she *could* warn them. At least she now had a scrimption of what was going on. A tiny segment of the plans of her enemy confirmed. A potential purpose of theirs gave her a potential answer to it. A quick counter with a view to deterrence. Also, she was starting to see their command structure. What was the motivation? What was the real goal? And who was really in charge? She felt the rumbling vibration under her feet as the engines began to power up. They were getting ready to leave, taking their prize with them.

"Did you get all that?" she whispered, to Kelvin.

"Yes," he replied. "All storage. Running a query…"

"No, don't bother," she replied, quickly. "Did you find us a good place to hide?"

"Yes, a spares area, the dust levels indicate that no one has been inside here for months," he explained.

"I'll join you there," she replied, pleased. She glanced over her shoulder out of habit. "Remember to keep track of where we are going." Astronomy was not her strongest talent.

"Yes," he said, as she cut off. Next, she placed a call in to Rainbow.

"What do you want *now?*" he asked, sounding frustrated.

"You can revoke my access to Dyss's file now, I'm finished with it," she said.

"Thank you," he stated, relieved.

"Anyone ask about it?" she enquired, with a grin.

"Maybe," he mumbled, grumpily. That would be a no then.

"Any more news on the picture of the woman?" she asked, interested.

"Still coming up with nothing… Is it possible that she's an android or something?" he asked. "Maybe some kind of shapeshifter?"

"*Possible,*" she concurred, considering that for the first time.

"Right, well if that is *all…*"

"No, it is *not* all!" she interrupted, annoyed. "I'm sending you some audio data in a moment. The voice you will hear is the voice of a man called Quint. I know nothing else. I need you to tell me who it is."

"*Oh come on!*" he complained, seriously. "Pictures, places, faces and samples I can *do* but…"

"It's *important*, Rainbow," she said, levelly.

"…I was going to have steak tonight," he muttered, sadly.

"You will be rewarded for your diligence, Rainbow," she smiled, softly.

"*Yeah!*" he laughed, sarcastically. "I'll call you if I get anything. Goodnight." He cut off and she sniggered. After a few more minutes of spying on the occupants of the control room, Satiah decided that nothing more was going to be worth watching. She crept away, back down the tunnel to reunite with Kelvin, silent as a Phantom should be.

***

Purella sat down casually. The detonator on the table was almost as big as she was. It had to be if she intended to eradicate a destroyer in one blast. It all depended on location; she'd have to plant it at exactly the right point. The power core. If that went up, the chain reaction would destroy the whole ship in minutes. Anywhere else and it wouldn't work. Even the ammunition stores wouldn't work, they were too well enclosed. How to get it aboard, set it, and get out again? There were a number of possible strategies to adopt for such a task but Quint had his own scheme. She was going over the conversation she had had with Quint a few hours previously in her mind.

"I have a job for you," Quint had said, his voice the customary artificial sound. "There is a Federation Destroyer protecting Collgort-Elipsa from pirate attack. I have put pressure on a few of the Nebula Union politicians to get it removed. They are too slow, as politicians often are and allegedly they are having trouble contacting the Viscount in person. A destroyer *is* being sent to Collgort-Elipsa *from* the Nebula Union to counter this apparent threat to their territory posed by the Federation destroyer. A destroyer named *Fearsome*... it was dispatched a few hours ago. It's more of a *political gesture* than an actual attempt to force the Federation away. I'm asking you to destroy *that* warship."

"*Which?*" Purella had enquired, a little baffled.

"The destroyer *Fearsome*," Quint had clarified, without any forthcoming explanation. Purella had been befuddled by this. Surely, if either had to be destroyed, it should be the one preventing *their* attacks.

"Quint, I don't understand, why not take out the Federation ship?" she had asked, sensibly.

"That serves no purpose," he had told her, confusing her still more. "If the Union ship is destroyed on arrival in the Collgort-

Elipsa area, it will immediately implicate the Federation, no matter what they say. Its destruction will provide grounds for a whole fleet of the Union to be sent to Collgort-Elipsa to destroy the Federation ship for us. When and if they perform this task, the Union will take the control of Collgort-Elipsa completely away from the Coalition." This response stunned her into silence. Finally she understood what Quint was trying to do. He was trying to remove Coalition control of Collgort-Elipsa permanently. Clyde was by her side and he leaned in to whisper in her ear.

"*And the Federation will do nothing about that?*" he had asked, mordantly. Quint was not meant to have heard that but he did and... he answered.

"They have no claims in this sector and that ship being there was a risk from the start," Quint told them. "They should never have been involved but I have taken advantage of their intrusion."

Clyde had raised an eyebrow, astounded by Quint's hearing. It made them both wonder what else he was capable of. Learning his lesson, Clyde had remained silent from then on.

"How am I going to blow it up right *on arrival?*" Purella then demanded, not unreasonably. Time would be needed for infiltration, planting *and* escape, time not readily available if the moment they arrived they would be standing off against another warship.

"*Fearsome* will be stopping on the way to Collgort-Elipsa to pick up supplies. *That* is where you will sneak in and plant the bomb," Quint told her. "I have already worked out the correct countdown you will need to set." She and Clyde had exchanged glances again.

"...Fine, let me know where and when," Purella had sighed. It was pointless arguing with Quint, his mind was clearly made up. Clyde had then gone to procure the explosive for the hold.

It seemed Quint was pulling many, *many* strings to say the least. Purella began to appreciate *why* Clyde didn't like working with him. Clyde was... *difficult*. She couldn't say that he was unambitious, cowardly, superstitious or stupid but he was... unpredictable. He refused to comply with anyone's order, even her own sometimes. He was very good at what he chose to do, which was why she tolerated his unknowable loyalties. Plus, right from the start, she had liked him. She sometimes imagined him as a man still struggling to decide whose side he wanted to be on.

He embraced most crime, mainly for profit, but was rarely excessive. If he could let someone live, he'd invariably let them live… unlike her. If he felt a venture would lose more than he gained he'd not go through with it. He was also popular with the mercenaries and he could get them to do things much more easily than Purella could. She would threaten and cajole them into doing her bidding. He would persuade, play on their greed or bribe them. He was the buffer between her and them and she mostly left them to him to manage. It was a much less volatile working environment on the whole. And all this didn't mean he couldn't turn *nasty*… He had shown just how ruthless he could be before, yet she'd never seen him lose his cool. He was not someone you'd willingly tangle with. Even she had a healthy respect for him.

When he got back with the device, he placed it on the table in front of her and regarded her. She hadn't moved since he'd gone. She was certain *this job* was Quint's ultimate test of her and, if she succeeded, it would get her to where she wanted to be.

"You have it?" Quint asked, probably already hearing Clyde returning.

"Yes." Purella nodded. "What about the prisoner and the gemstone?"

"I'm going to have to rethink it. No one *other than the three of us* knows what that stone is. Its loss therefore means nothing to anyone else as they never knew we had it. You *must* reacquire the man, however. As you know, his role in your future is essential," Quint stated. Purella looked up, suddenly guessing *why* this man was so important.

"…*I see*," she managed. Clyde watched her closely, his eyes asking the questions his voice wouldn't.

"I'm sending you the location where you will infiltrate the destroyer, the precise coordinates. It will be docked in a shipyard. I leave the details up to you," Quint commanded.

Quint was gone, vanishing into the white noise of static. Purella still didn't move as she eyed the explosive. Clyde slowly switched off the communicator and faced her, arms crossed over his broad muscular chest.

"I'm not into going somewhere I can't get back from," Clyde said, with significance.

"It's my path," Purella said, rare softness in her voice. "*I want what I had before* and this will give me that. I just want to *belong* again, Clyde. Surely you can understand that?" He shrugged lightly.

"Sounds like a done deal anyway," he growled, dismissively. He almost sounded sulky. "Are you going to tell me what you guys were talking about, or is *discretion* part of the oaths too?" Now that *was* a loaded question.

"*I'm sorry*," she allowed, stiltedly. "I wish… I wish you would change your mind."

"*I* would never join the Cult of Deimos," he almost spat, walking briskly out again. She didn't go after him… it would be pointless. She slowly replaced the black band around her head again, her eyes sad but resolute.

***

"Memory? *What about his memory?*" Satiah and Kelvin were slouched in the semi darkness while the pirates unknowingly conveyed them straight to their secret base.

"I performed a scan of Bert the moment you returned with him, as I scanned both Riff and Cherry. His memory is inhibited by an implant," Kelvin explained.

"And you only thought to tell me this *now?*" she demanded, in a harsh whisper.

"The implant wasn't instantly identifiable, I had to go through all data, the manufacturer cannot be identified," he responded. Satiah sighed heavily. "It may even have been cannibalised." This was what happened when she had too much to think about! She missed things!

"…So, after all that, he could very well *know* exactly why they were holding him prisoner, but thinks he doesn't because that part of his memory has been hidden from him," Satiah summarised, bitterly.

She had to tell Reed, the man might be dangerous and he was still on Collgort-Elipsa with the boy and… *the Viscount!* Alarms bells ringing in her mind, Satiah began to fear he might be some kind of sleeper-assassin. An assassin who didn't even known they were an assassin until the invisible implant kicked in or did whatever it was supposed to do.

"Ah, change of heart?" Reed answered, jovially.

"Are you alone?" she began, seriously.

"*Yes*," he answered, all jollity gone. She could imagine his face changing from pleased smile to daunted frown.

"*Where's Bert?*" she asked, quickly.

"In his cabin, as far as I know, *why?*" Reed asked, obviously concerned now. She swiftly explained the scenario.

"*Ah*," was his stunned response. "Are you coming back?"

"Not *really* in the position to do that," she said, torn. Part of her wanted to get the implant out of this man to free up the memory and to see what else it did. It might also house a transmitter that Purella or Quint might know about – or whoever else was after him.

"No, *I thought not*," he said, the jolliness starting to return to his tone. "Any suggestions to what I do about this development?"

"Besides watching him like a hungry bird of prey?" she asked, scoffing. "Lock him up, tie him down, cut him open and *grab* the…"

"Steady on, Satiah, I'm not exactly in the correct location to commence brain surgery here!" he objected, stoutly. "…That's just outside in the corridor."

"*Reed!* I'm *serious!* He could pose a threat to *that entire city*," she argued. "He could *literally be* a walking, talking time bomb. Speaking of threats… I think there will be an attempt on the destroyer. I don't know exactly how but they intend to remove it."

"*All right! All right!*" he silenced her. "Surely if he *was* dangerous he'd have been activated by now, most probably when *you* rescued him?" He wasn't even listening properly! This was typical Reed!

"I agree there *have been* plenty of good times to activate something that have been either missed or disregarded. That doesn't take anything away from his potential danger *now*, does it?" she pointed out, influentially. "And don't forget the destroyer!"

"…Very well," he replied, making it sound like a chore. "I'll invent some sort of decontamination procedure or something…"

"*What?*" she asked, baffled.

"Catch you later," he called, disconnecting. Satiah ran her hands through her hair, stressed.

Reed could be so annoying sometimes – and that was nothing when she thought about her next conversation! Now seemed just about as reasonable as any time to have it out with Dyss about operation Jackdaw. She had Darius's story... now she needed *his*. Between the pair of them they should reveal the truth... eventually. A detail would be changed in the end, only the truth would remain the same as that couldn't change... *in theory*.

"I haven't got hold of the family yet..." Dyss began, as he answered.

"It's not about that," she cut in, levelly. "It's time you explained *Jackdaw* to me." Muteness. "Darius wants to talk to me about it and I wanted to hear your version first." It was a lie but one she felt sure he'd believe.

"*Version?!*" he almost exploded. "..."

"You *know* what I mean," she interjected, not wanting to waste time. "I'm not *accusing* you of anything. I need to understand what happened and why you distrust one another so badly but... *if you refuse to tell me...*" She let the threat speak for itself in the next silence.

"...I don't have to tell you anything as I outrank you, but if it will help you see *who Darius really is* then I will explain," he responded, in a hard tone. She quirked a smile at his bluster. This was part of her revenge for his blackmail of her and he knew it. Plus, she had always enjoyed winding up her superiors.

"Please," she encouraged, her tone neutral.

"The events I'm now telling you about took place about a decade ago. Operation Jackdaw was a TE mission, assigned by Phantom Leader Vourne. All this was long before the Vourne conspiracy or even Balan Orion's term in office," he told her. TE stood for targeted espionage which was a fairly rare category to use. The rest she knew. So far, so good.

"Vallin and I were in charge of six Phantom agents. Darius was one of them, as you should already know. Narm, Jook, Pingrey, Alarris, Gacka and Darius. If you're wondering *how* I recall all of this *so easily*, I'll just say it's been on my mind for a while. The operation had been proceeding according to plan, within about fourteen weeks we had pretty much everything we needed. That was when we found out about an illegal payoff. The gang we were investigating had just done a deal with a terrorist group called the Sons of Venelka. There was no actual proof it was them but that was who we suspected. In any case their relations were... *tenuous*. One sign of distrust, *one breach of contract* and they would be enemies *for a long time*. Vourne's instruction, *upon learning this through us*, was the one *I* would have given were I in his position at the time: intercept the money with a view to fracturing any chance of a future alliance."

"It's what anyone would do," Satiah stated.

"The plan was: I would stow aboard the gang's ship and place a homing beacon aboard so that Vallin and the others could track us. When the ship got to a certain area, the ambush would take place. Vallin would come out from hiding and paralyse the ship. When that happened I would take the bridge and force a surrender while the others boarded, stole the money and then we would leave. The gang would fail to pay the terrorists and everything would collapse back into deadly rivalry. Only Vallin and I knew *exactly* where the ambush would take place, or at least that's what I *thought*. She and Darius had worked together *a lot* before, so I'm assuming she confided in him... and it cost her her life. I *suspected* that they were lovers but that I admit is unfounded information."

Satiah's eyes narrowed, remembering the wince of regret on Darius's face when he had been remembering Vallin's death... or rather the fact that he left her without *confirming* that she was dead. She had up until now presumed they were just friends but after what Dyss had just told her about them *working together in the past*... maybe she had been much more to Darius than just a friend. Relationships among Phantom agents were against the rules but she knew they happened.

"So that was the plan," she said, softly. "*What happened?*"

"Things went differently to how I expected they would go, right from the start. When I first got on the ship while it was still parked, I couldn't *find* a crew. There was no one aboard, *everything* was done by the computer," Dyss elaborated. "At the time I didn't see it as a problem: I saw it as a good thing. It meant I didn't have to hide from anyone along the way, and it also meant I didn't have to hold anyone up at the end."

"But *now* you see it differently?" she queried, understanding.

"It was the first indication that this was a set-up and that *someone* had betrayed our mission," Dyss replied, harshly. "Like I said, *at the time* I merely thought that the gang didn't trust the Sons of Venelka enough to endanger their own people. I thought it was a simple precaution." Darius had been correct about Dyss being the only life sign on that freighter then. Again, at *this* stage, their testimonies would be in full agreement with one another. Dyss was considering betrayal *after the fact*, not during, and *that* was a critical thing. At the time he had not suspected Darius, *or anyone else*, of betraying him. Therefore, something must have happened to change his mind…

"*Now* you *don't* think so?" she asked, rather needlessly.

"They weren't there because they knew *we would be*," he stated, grimly. "I didn't report this development at the time because we were operating in radio silence." Again, nothing unusual there.

"I got to the control room and my qualms about the ship being under computer control were confirmed. Everything was password protected, as you would expect. At *that* stage I presumed the only people who would *have the codes* would be whoever was being sent to retrieve the money. I spent the next few hours *unsuccessfully* trying to hack into the flight computer. I was interrupted when the engines began to power down, clearly because the flight computer had been pre-programmed to do that. Even at the time I *knew* something was not right. Why would it be programmed to stop *in the exact place* where we were planning to intercept it?" It was a good question, even if it was rhetorical. "I was still in the control room when Vallin and the others took out the engines as planned. I knew they would be inside the ship in moments to get the money from the cargo area. We had all studied a diagram of the ship before so they all knew where to go."

"That was when the next stage occurred. I'm calling it *the next stage* as the computer was clearly working through *someone's* plan. A plan that had *stages*. Sentry robots, I'm not sure of the *exact* number but *too many of them to handle*, were activating and converging on Vallin's team…" he was saying.

"Why didn't Darius have you killed while you were *alone* on the freighter?" Satiah had to ask. "He *knew* you would be there, the computer could have been programmed to…"

"If Vallin *couldn't* detect me on the freighter, she might pull out and prevent the rest of the team falling into the trap," Dyss replied, as if he had answered that question many times before. Conceivable, she supposed.

"I managed to notify them about the sentry robots, using the ship's speaker system, and was about to help them when I noticed something," he continued, sounding miffed. Satiah could see it coming… the self-destruct system was automatically activated.

"A countdown had started on a screen and I realised that somehow, probably another built in *stage* of the plan, the self-destruct system was in operation. In ten minutes that ship would no longer exist."

"Ten minutes is *a long time*," she noted, ponderously. If the robots had, for whatever reason, not attacked or had been unable to contain the team, they would have had time to get clear.

"Not when you're under siege it isn't! Luckily, even though I couldn't hack the computers, I *knew* where the manual override for the self-destruct was. I'd seen it earlier. So, *instead of helping my team*, I *had* to stop the countdown first… or there wouldn't be a team to help." Still all very plausible, she had to admit.

"After fighting my way to it, I got to the self-destruct and went about trying to stop it. I had to prevent it from exploding or at least, by some means, delay it. *That* was when Vallin and Darius suddenly appeared and *Vallin* pulled her gun on me. She *thought* I was activating the self-destruct system. Why she would imagine such a thing I'm not *certain* but it seems feasible that *Darius* might have somehow convinced her that I had betrayed her. On the other hand, they *may* have been working together from the start…"

"Then why bother to confront you at all? If they were *working together*, why not simply ensure you never saw them approach and either kill you or slip past you?" Satiah butted in. "And why allow themselves to be attacked by the sentry robots?"

"They *or* he had to make it *look real* in case anyone else, *namely me*, made it out alive," Dyss argued, with an angry sigh. She sighed too; annoyed that he kept coming up with good answers.

"Vallin basically accused *me* of activating the self-destruct system. Right there, to my face. I thought, while it was happening, that as she didn't *know* that I had never *had* any control over the craft, it was understandable. The freighter *had* stopped by itself but they might have assumed that *I* had stopped it, seeing as I *was* the only one aboard at the time. I didn't have time to explain any of that though, so I just pulled rank and told her and Darius to obey orders..." In retrospect that might not have been the best move, Satiah reasoned: hindsight always made the eyes water.

"Which were?" she cut in again. What had he told them to do?

"Hold off the robots while I stopped the ship blowing itself and us apart, *what do you think*?" he countered, smoothly.

"Okay, then what?" she asked, letting that go.

"She wasn't listening, maybe she couldn't hear, and she tried to *arrest* me. Next thing I knew there was an explosion and we were on the floor," he replied.

"What was it?" Satiah grilled, interested. Darius didn't seem to know and it could be important.

"I don't know but it came from Darius's direction. As I tried to get up I realised that Vallin had been knocked out or killed by a pipeline that had fallen on her. I couldn't find a pulse but before I had time to really do anything else the robots were on us again. I ordered an immediate withdrawal. There wasn't anything else we could do other than save ourselves. We were outgunned, pretty much surrounded *and* we were almost out of time. I told Darius to act as rear guard to stop them boarding *our ship* to give me time to get us away. We had to clear the area or we might be caught up in the blast. I got us away. At the time I still hadn't worked out what Vallin and Darius, *assuming she was in on it*, had been doing."

"Seeing as she tried to arrest you I doubt that she was involved," Satiah muttered. "So... *when did you work it out*?"

"Well, for a start *Darius just left*, took an escape pod without a word and sped off into space. I thought at first some of the robots might have made it inside but a scan revealed nothing. He didn't answer my hails and ran straight back to Earth. I set course for Earth too and started to wonder about the whole thing. What clinched it was when Vourne called me to explain that Darius had accused *me* of setting the whole thing up," Dyss said, starting to sound sad. "*That was when I knew.*"

"Where was the money?" Satiah asked, switching topics to catch him out.

"What money?" he asked, momentarily bewildered. "You mean for the payment to the terrorists?"

"I do," she said, wondering if his confusion meant anything.

"I never checked the cargo area but Darius said the money wasn't there and I have to admit I believe *that much*. He wasn't going to torch his own reward, was he?" Dyss concluded. "He also implied that while I was on the ship alone before the ambush, I must have squirrelled it away somehow."

"How did *Vourne* resolve this conflict, exactly?" she quizzed, starting to feel forlorn.

"*It's never been resolved.* He just took statements and then left it active," Dyss answered, still sounding gloomy. "Darius covered his tracks well. I didn't even realise what he was up to until he ran for Earth. I've been watching him ever since, trying to catch him out. The money never resurfaced so far as I could see." Satiah groaned inwardly. Until just now she'd felt it would be possible to sort it out provided she could get the information out of both men. Trouble was... their stories were the same. In each account both men did what seemed in order. Indeed, the events were identical in both stories. The only things that were different were what they *thought* was going on. The testimonies themselves seemed consistent both in timescale and in action. The rest was all opinion, which naturally was different and, just as naturally, were the opposites of each other. Maybe that was why Vourne had decided to drop it.

"When you were still in the control room and you noticed the robots attacking the others: why did no robots attack you?" Satiah tried again.

"Probably because I wasn't *meant* to be in the control room, I was supposed to be in the cargo area. Conceivably it might even have been to lure me away from elsewhere to stop me *noticing* the countdown," he responded. "If I hadn't seen *that*, we might all be dead." They *had* been set up; there was no doubt of that in Satiah's mind. This wasn't all one big misunderstanding born from an unlucky happenstance. Too many things lacked sufficient explanation. Darius blamed Dyss and Dyss blamed Darius. Neither could win as no one could prove anything. It was ludicrous!

"When you ask him about it, do tell me what he said," Dyss instructed, sagely.

"No problem," she grunted.

"Will that be all?" he asked, a little sardonic. "Am I dismissed, *Phantom* Satiah?" She disconnected, not even bothering to answer. Now what? She stared over at Kelvin in the darkness.

"What do you think?"

"Both accounts begin with fact and become conjecture. Each explains the gaps in the other perfectly. If there was no accusation of betrayal, these would look little different from normal reports. For every question you thought of, each was answered quickly and credibly. My suggestion is you find another account to compare them both with," Kelvin stated, unhelpfully.

"That's *impossible*," she retorted, irritated. "Even any video footage from the ship would have been lost when it exploded. These two men *are* the only sources of information left."

"Do you *need* to resolve this in order to complete *your* mission?" Kelvin asked, flatly.

"...I don't know," she mused, frustrated. "It's an unanswered question, an unsolved mystery. Darius or Dyss? I'm not sure I can just forget about it."

"There is no pressure for you in this," he pointed out. "You had decided to trust Darius and Randal can defend you from Dyss."

"I know I only dug this up in the first place to get at Dyss and to cover *myself*, but *now I know this much*..." She didn't need to finish her sentence. She wouldn't rest until she knew exactly what had happened.

***

Darius had been expecting change, not an armada. Their ship cloaked, he and Cherry had just arrived at Permyon and had been greeted by the sight of four Vinu destroyers lurking there.

"*That's a bit of an overreaction*," he murmured, softly. He stroked his moustache thoughtfully. Cherry opened her eyes and yawned. She'd mercifully dozed off a few hours ago. In order to get silence, he'd secretly considered administering a light tranquilliser into her food. He'd established where she was from and why she knew so little about anything and frankly, that was all he cared to know.

"What are those?" she asked, pointing at the nearest destroyer.

"Bad news," he replied, quietly. "*And… they were not here before.* I knew they'd ramp up their security after my last little adventure here but this seems a bit overkill, what do you think?" She shrugged. For the tenth time, he found himself irritated that Satiah had sent her with him.

Cherry was both enthralled by, and afraid of Darius. She wished, if Satiah had had to leave her with anyone, she would have left her with Reed. He was much smaller and far less intimidating. She got the impression that Darius didn't think much of her and she wasn't sure *how* that made her feel. She decided that she had to show him that he couldn't bully her and that she was in no way inferior to him. Trouble was, every time she tried, it just made her look worse. She decided to try something else. If they got into trouble, she had to be sure that she was on good enough terms with him for him to be obliged to help her.

"I'm *sorry* about what I said earlier," she began, watching his profile closely. No reaction. Was he even listening? "It's just you are very new to me and I don't think I deal with change very well." Still nothing. "If I've done anything to offend you, I'm *really* sorry, *I didn't mean to.*"

Was it her eyes playing games or did his ears seem to prick-up minutely then? He *was* listening! He was just pretending not to! It was so hard going against her nature but she tried, bearing her heart in the earnest request for forgiveness.

"I shouldn't have called you a sexist, jingoist bigot. *That was wrong of me.* I understand now that you were just being *kind* when you offered to get my supplies for me and you were not inferring that I was incapable of getting them myself. I'm not used to being around males, *okay*?" she apologised, honestly. Slowly Darius turned to face her, an intense look on his face. She held her breath, bracing herself mentally for an ear bashing.

"...Could you hold this for a second, please?" he requested, holding up a communicator. He'd heard but he just didn't care! She scowled and snatched it from him.

"*Fine*," she snapped, flushing red with anger.

She stared ahead, ignoring him for a few moments before turning to find him grinning at her.

"First rule about living in the big bad universe," he said, still grinning. "Learn how to take a joke." He was teasing her. She blushed this time and didn't know where to look other than away. Laugh or cry? Indifference was impossible for her now. Why did she feel obscurely chastened? Like he was beating her in some game that she didn't understand?

"Satiah told me about you," he went on, impassively. "She said you were insecure, oversensitive and *easily manipulated*." Cherry gaped, stung by the words. How could she...?

"But you're going to prove her wrong, aren't you? There's a *very* easy way to do that. She told me that you were so neurotic that you wouldn't even hold hands with me if I asked you to," he said, shrugging. "I wasn't sure what to believe but I bet her three Essps that you would." Satiah would never have...

A knowing look came over Cherry's face and Darius grinned again. She crossed her arms, a self-righteous expression on her face now.

"Easily manipulated," she repeated, her tone mocking. "*I am not.*"

"Almost had you," he chuckled, facing front again. Cherry didn't know why but she wanted to keep playing this strange new game called teasing.

"You didn't," she argued, smiling.

"Really? Your face said I did," he replied, running a scan.

"It did not," she said, trying not to giggle.

"I think it did," he answered, casually. She didn't know why but she had this impulsive urge to hit him or something. She backhanded his forearm good-humouredly.

"*Didn't!*"

***

Reed peered cautiously around the corner. Bert and Riff were there on some padded chairs, talking casually. Reed thought for a few moments and then turned. He bumped into Pat and shrieked in apparent terror. She screamed too because he had frightened her. For a few seconds they just stood there panting and staring at one another.

"Why are you sneaking around everywhere suddenly, Reed?" she asked, calming down.

"Me? *Sneak?*" he gasped, as if offended. "I was just stretching my legs, cogitating about how nice a change of scenery would be, you know? The usual?" Her eyes narrowed disbelievingly.

"Why does that not ring true?" she pondered, aloud.

"*What?*" he demanded, blustery. "How can you *possibly* doubt *me?*"

"Because you have this apparently compulsive tendency of lying to people," she argued, keeping her voice down.

He grinned suddenly, in that disarming way that he could. He leaned in close to whisper in her ear.

"Isn't the weather lovely today?" he inquired, waywardly. "The way that the gravitational strain of all these cities in the sky turns that ocean into a tempestuous beast. Sublime but deadly. Intriguing but baffling. Have you ever given any thought into reverse-causation before? Specifically, *why doesn't* correlation equal causation?" What if she had? It was a bit of a gamble, he knew *he* hadn't.

"…You drink too much of that beer, Reed," she stated, shaking her head and walking off in minor aversion.

"*That got rid of her,*" he muttered, rubbing his hands together and returning his attention to Bert. He'd gone! Exasperated, Reed began to scurry along the corridor in the hope that Bert *had gone that way* when his communicator went off.

"*What now?*" he glowered, as he answered.

"Bad time?" came Captain Ogun, sounding amused.

"There never seems to be a good time these days. What can I do for you?" Reed asked, trying to pick Bert out from the crowd.

"The twelve hours has expired and no attack has taken place. I'm about to deactivate the cloaking device and return to my regular patrol pattern. Unless *you* have anything better for me to do?" Ogun wanted to know. Reed groaned. Someone must had realised it was a trap unless they were wrong about there being an informer; this was assuming they had had enough time. This wasn't the sort of thing one could repeat too often though without it giving the plan away.

"*Twelve hours gone already, miraculous how time flies when you're not paying attention,*" Reed grunted. "Return to your regular patrol… I'll talk to the Viscount."

***

In elliptical orbit, Comet Sunkiss sailed out of the blue giant's outer corona, trailing trillions of ice fragments in its wake. Its orbit took four hundred and seven years to complete but, just like all comets, this was subject to the limitations of natural degradation. Sunkiss itself had been in existence since the formation of the solar system, some fourteen billion years. Its size and mass had been dwindling since its creation. Now it was a mere one hundred and eighty miles, two hundred and ninety kilometres, in diameter and it left a tail stretching over one billion kilometres. A stumpy sixty-two million miles or so. Made up of hundreds of millions of tonnes of ice, rock and other debris, Sunkiss weighed nothing in space. Its glacial rotation was not enough to generate its own gravitational field, much like that of a poorly propelled ball.

Corkscrew Base was buried deep under the icy surface of Sunkiss. Made up a series of interconnecting bunker-like structures, the base was a small network of shared compounds. Building it had been a challenge, but maintaining it was an objective of Herculean proportions. The only parts of the base that could be seen from anywhere was an opening for ships to enter, and huge booster engines used to alter the tumbling motion of the comet to aid the landings of said spaceships. They fired. The comet, still moving along its orbital path, began to rotate more slowly until eventually it stopped spinning altogether.

"What's the password?" Kyle sighed at the ludicrousness of the question. Why would anyone attempt an approach, never mind land on a comet, unless they were part of the gang? He hoped those dimwits had not changed it recently, otherwise there was going to be yet another altercation.

"My communicator has grown wings," Kyle stated, in all seriousness. There was a pause.

"That was yesterday's password," the voice replied, exasperated. "And *you* were the one who insisted we upped our security…" Kyle rolled his eyes and flicked through some notes on his lap. He did not need this! Those bickering brainless oafs seemed to love it when he was made to look stupid. How they'd ever made it so far without him guiding them was a constant source of mystery to him.

"Your dinosaur is my dinosaur but it *has* no wings!" Kyle muttered, dismissively.

The comet was now no longer spinning at all – Kyle nodded to the pilot, and she began their approach. They would fly past the comet, swing in on its path and gradually decelerate in line with the opening. Kyle began packing his things away and pulling on his jacket. Those jokers on checkpoint would get a piece of his mind later, but they could wait. The hangar area wasn't clear like it was supposed to be. Instead of gliding down smoothly in the centre, like normal, the pilot had to squeeze them in beside a burning freighter that someone had left on station. Kyle had seen enough and stormed down the ramp.

"*What the hell is going on here?*" he demanded, lividly. Two men, both so drunk they could hardly stand, were ineffectively attempting to put out the fire. One staggered over with a groan and the other stopped, slack jawed.

"What?"

"*Right!*" Kyle spat, yanking out his communicator. "Activate the emergency dampers in the hangar area."

"Sir," said a woman on the other end. White gas poured up from the floor and engulfed the freighter, dousing the flames effectively. Someone was on the ball, he mused. Other pirates were starting to arrive now, to aid with the constant loading and unloading that had to be done as a matter of routine.

"Someone get rid of those two!" he ordered, pointing at the drunks. "I'll deal with them later. I need this thing shifted in *one hour*!" Continuing to bark out orders, Kyle marched away from the ships towards the corridor. In relatively good order, the cargos were dealt with respectively and the freighter was dragged away from the other ships. It was almost an hour later when Satiah finally came out of hiding.

"*So* Comet Sunkiss is a pirate stronghold," she muttered, slipping her specs on. Kelvin was running a scan as always, but she did her own out of habit anyway. No cameras, always a good sign. Crates littered the hangar area but otherwise it was astonishingly bright and clean. Unlike the interior of the freighter she'd been hiding in for hours.

"There is a gargantuan quantity of data," Kelvin explained. "Reprioritising."

"I wonder how long this has been here," she pondered aloud.

"Serial number on that floor panel ran up a product registration nine years, seven months and two days old," Kelvin told her. "It's reasonable to assume this facility was established at least ten years ago."

"This also means they had to build this place themselves and that would not have been cheap," she replied, thinking about it. "They must have some very powerful people behind them."

"Quint," Kelvin said. She nodded slowly.

They walked casually over to the corridor and began to wander down it.

"Nine thousand seven hundred and thirty-seven life readings," Kelvin told her. She nodded, having expected something like that. This wasn't a gang, it was a small army. She took the time to mine the hangar door. It could be a useful distraction or a vital delaying tactic if they had to escape in a hurry. Having now found the base, even though she couldn't know if it was their only one, Satiah put a call in to Randal. Phantom Command had to be made aware of it.

"Yes," he answered.

"Comet Sunkiss is a massive pirate installation and needs to be taken out at some stage," she told him, nonchalantly. "If you *could* wait until I've safely departed I would be grateful." She cut off before he could say anything else.

She didn't know exactly what form of action Randal would take but she could guess what was likely. The decision might simply be taken to destroy the comet. She suspected that he might want to acquire the facility for the Coalition. If they knew they had been discovered the pirates would likely abandon it, although in this case there may be other factors involved. Whoever was behind them would certainly not be pleased, should they lose it. She had been a witness to the shocking display of incompetence displayed by the pirates in the hangar. While it was nothing new in pirate gangs for them to be a little lax, she had been a bit surprised by Kyle's reaction. He was having discipline problems; this might be why, throughout their attacks, they had failed to convince her that they were military. Indiscipline.

"How is the layout coming?" she asked, quietly.

"Eighty-seven percent," Kelvin answered.

"I'm going to want to see *everything*, figure out how they are coordinating things and who is at the top. I might even contact Dyss and update him on how we're progressing," she told him. She knew that Darius wouldn't.

"The ships they used in the attack are located near here," Kelvin stated.

"Makes sense they would be close to the hangar area, one of those walls must be a partition," she reasoned. "It might be worth tampering with those ships to prevent further attacks." If they succeeded in removing that Federation destroyer then nothing would stop them from attacking unless... their ships couldn't fly.

***

"So what you're saying is, is that something very important must be happening down there as one intruder wouldn't normally make them bring a whole fleet in to protect one facility?" Cherry asked, thinking about it.

"Precisely," Darius said, still staring out at the destroyers. "I knew sneaking in again would be challenging, but assuming we get in undetected, getting out might not be possible." Cherry stared hopefully at him.

"So we're not going to bother?" she asked, expectantly. He glanced at her in surprise. "Satiah doesn't have to know, we could just say..."

"I'm not lying to my boss," he stated, inflexibly. "Besides, aren't you curious?"

"Yes, but not so much that I want to get my brains blown out in process of searching for..." she replied, honestly, "... this guy, what was his name again?"

"Milo Drass," he reminded.

"You said yourself: the odds are that he is dead already. You've been and checked down there before..."

"I know, but I was interrupted before I was done. Do you *normally* disobey your orders or is this a new thing?" he asked, grinning.

"To be honest, if I can get away with something I usually try to. It's often safer that way, but I owe Satiah my life so... I'm still new to all this and if this place is as heavily guarded as it looks, then I'm scared we might die," she admitted. He started to laugh.

"You've seen nothing yet," he told her, almost smug.

"What are you going to do?" she asked, a little uncomfortable as he went for the controls.

"Find a new place to land in," he replied, seriously. "I'm not going to land in the same place, you can see why, obviously." She nodded, understanding.

Unable to see the cloaked craft, the destroyers continued their never-ending patrol paths. Darius took the time to run scans of everything. As they edged forward he checked to see what else had changed since he'd last been there. Very little, apparently! Cherry gasped in surprise as the moon suddenly appeared in front of them.

"Can you hide anything with a cloak?" she asked, interested. He shrugged. Potentially, but he couldn't say for sure.

"Breathing mask," he said, passing her one. "The oxygen is too low for us. You don't mind insects, do you?"

"To eat?" she asked, confused.

"You'll be fine," he replied, guessing that if she was fine with eating them she'd most likely be okay wading through a swarm or two. She stood, hefting her rifle. Darius eyed the firearm dubiously.

"What *now*?" she demanded, trying to be polite. Darius took in a breath as if he was going to say something but then turned away.

"Nothing," he replied, over his shoulder. Cherry glanced down at her gun, puzzled. Had he messed with it or something?

"*What?*" she repeated, starting to follow him.

"Nothing, I just wondered if you'd ever had trouble with distances," he mused, as if deep in thought. "Remind me of that thing's range again?" Again? She'd never told him… *ah*, this was *another* test. He was trying to work out if she knew how to use her weapon correctly.

"I *have* used it before, if that's what you're asking," she stated, riled.

"I know," he said, suddenly turning and presenting her with a sleek looking black rifle. "Fancy using this instead?" All pretence and one-up*woman*ship went out of her mind almost instantly.

"What is *that?*" she asked, spellbound.

"Yes, I thought you'd like it, it's a bit different from what you're used to but I'm sure you'll conquer it swiftly, it's an ML92," he said, a knowing grin on his face. "Try it." They switched rifles, whilst making playfully distrustful eye contact. The first thing she noticed was how light it was in comparison to her old one.

"It's *completely* composite, no remaining heavy stuff at all," she stated, peering down the sights. She smiled up at him. "Thank you, this is a fantastic gun."

"Accurate at two kilometres, it can let them go at five a second so don't forget the light trigger," he advised.

"Does this mean you trust me to go with you?" she asked, seriously. She wasn't going to beg, her pride wouldn't let her, but she hated the idea of just sitting there waiting for him. She was scared, but she did not wait easily.

"Does this mean you will follow *my* orders?" he smirked, crossing his arms. "*Without* taking it like an insult to you or one against all woman kind?"

"Yes, of course," she grinned back. "I may change my mind later though," she winked. "I'm allowed to do that."

"If you do, I'd appreciate a warning first," he said, checking his pistol.

"That's fair," she agreed, pulling on the breathing mask he'd loaned her. Darius put his on and returned to the controls. She leaned against the wall, watching him as she breathed in the filtered air. It tasted funny but it was better than suffocating.

"We're going in," he told her. The craft began a stealthy descent.

**

"There it is," Clyde said, nodding to the destroyer. As Quint had said, it was still docked at the shipyard, preparing to depart. Purella came over to look.

"*Fearsome*," she murmured, eyeing it. Clyde hadn't told her that this plan was, at best, complete madness. Instead he'd opted for stony silence that whole journey. Clyde was not afraid when things got rough, but he knew his limits. He was certain they were going beyond those limits now. Purella had checked the device, literally stripping it down and examining each component. There could be no mistakes, not this time. This time, Satiah would not be there to stop her, nor would any other Phantom. However, that did not mean this would in any way be easy.

"Dock nearby but not directly next to it," she instructed, crisply.

She didn't know *exactly* what was bothering Clyde but she had her ideas. Right now though, he was the only one she judged competent enough to help her. Normally she wouldn't have hesitated in finding out exactly what the problem was but she couldn't risk him flying off in a temper. He'd never done that before but there was a first time for most things. She stood, pulled the mechanics hat on, and stuffed her golden curls up inside it. Clyde donned his too. If Quint had done everything correctly, no one would challenge them – not until they were near the destroyer, anyway. She grabbed one end of the device, and Clyde the other. Together they carried it down the ramp and onto the floor of the landing area.

"I'll get a loading transporter," Clyde said, quietly. She nodded and took a quick look around. No one was looking their way.

The unit hovered next to them, under Clyde's control. They carefully lowered the bomb onto it and then walked beside it as it glided along rapidly. Soon they were in among a throng of beings. Mechanics like them, loading robots of many sizes, navy personnel and numerous others. They joined a line of people going into the hold of the destroyer and waited for their turn. A guard was sat on a chair by the ramp but he wasn't stopping anyone to check anything. He looked bored out of his mind. Purella and Clyde were sure to look just as bored as they passed him by.

Once inside, they quickly split away from the bustle and made their way out of the cargo area. The corridors were long and empty as mostly everyone was outside. They were either helping with the processes ongoing out there, or trying to grab a last few minutes away from the warship before it departed.

"Floor seven," Clyde whispered, as they got to the elevator. They went into the lift, careful not to look up in case the cameras were recording. When the ship blew there would have to be an investigation and it might be possible that the footage could survive the blast. There was also the chance that, for whatever reason, routine or otherwise, the footage might be transmitted to the fleet controllers. They would realise a bomb had been used but they would never be able to work out who had done it. The Federation would be blamed purely for *that* instead of the attack on the warship.

They reached floor seven and exited the lift there. The power core was nearby, and that would be guarded no matter where the ship was or what it was doing. But Purella didn't plan on entering through the door. They passed by the entrance, ignoring the two guards stationed there, and rounded the next turn. There, they stopped. There was the room to the side, as she'd predicted there would be. Its back wall would be right against the wall of the power core area. Clyde noted that they had been inside over twenty minutes already. They began to remove the panels quickly, using the tools they had brought with them. A trickle of sweat inched its way down Purella's face. At the pace they were working, this simple but lengthy task became hot work.

They pulled the first panel away, revealing the piping and wiring concealed behind it. Beyond those cables and pipes, they could see the wall to the power core. She inserted a support joist under the cables, supporting them on its bracket. Gradually it rose, lifting the cables and pipes out of the way by a few inches. Clyde was already there, unsealing the screws and pushing them around and back to release them. Purella started on the other side.

"We need to be out of here within the hour," Clyde prompted. She nodded, breathing slightly harder now. At last they were through and Clyde crawled in ahead of her. The odds were that it was unoccupied, but taking chances was for the amateur.

"Clear," he whispered, to her.

She heaved the bomb across the floor, over the wall joints and into the room. Clyde got hold of it from the other side and pulled as well. Purella scrambled in after it. There was the power ball, glowing bright green and humming like a reactor.

"In there," she hissed, pointing to a gap between support beams. They pushed and shoved it into position where it couldn't easily be seen, should anyone bother to check. Sweat was now giving both of them a sheen. Purella pulled her communicator out – it was counting down. They had less than a minute before it was time to activate the pre-arranged countdown of the device.

"*Countdowns for countdowns,*" murmured Clyde, amused. Twenty seconds. He had insisted on checking the bomb and making sure that Quint didn't betray them somehow, and blow them up when they planted it.

"Isn't everything a matter of timing?" she countered periphrastically, poised over the controls. They watched the red digits as they descended from two to one. Purella activated. As pre-set, the new countdown began. Now all they had to do was put everything back and get out undetected before the ship took off. They scrambled back through the gap they had made in the wall and began replacing it. Purella was already thinking about the next stage. She had to get that man back next. Satiah was most probably already pointlessly interrogating him. It was almost funny. Quint had told her that the man could reveal nothing and she believed him, but he'd not told her why he was so sure of this. At last, after a fifteen-minute slog, the wall was replaced. She grabbed the loading transporter's controls and they returned to the corridor.

They had decided to leave via a different route, just in case anyone who'd seen them before confronted them. Despite encountering several people on their return journey, no one asked them anything about who they were or why they were there. The hustle and bustle had only intensified in their absence and the cargo area was now almost full. They left the ship as part of a large group of departing workers. Within minutes they had returned to their shuttle and had closed the door on the world. Purella went immediately to report to Quint, despite Clyde saying she didn't have to. Clyde watched her go, disappointed. He paced into the washing area and stood under a very cold shower.

Purella entered the control room and sealed herself inside. She put a call through and sat on the pilot's chair.

"Well?" Quint's artificial voice, answered.

"It's done," she said, serenely. "Device is planted, countdown started... all of it."

"Good," Quint replied. "You need only reacquire the prisoner and bring him to a set of coordinates I shall provide you with."

"Satiah will not give him up without a fight," she stated, wondering what reaction that might get.

"Phantoms are the very best kind of operative. By defeating her, you will be demonstrating your suitability most distinctly," he answered, mysteriously. "But you do not have to do it at all."

"Quint... You never told me *how* you found out who she was," Purella noted, uneasily.

"I didn't," he concurred, without any noticeable aggression.

"Do they know *everything*?" she asked, awestruck.

"They can *find out* everything," he qualified. "Mainly through strategically placed people. People like you." Purella smiled to herself. It would be just like how it was before... before those Phantoms had ruined everything! That thought reminded her of Satiah. It was time to add another skull to her collection of Phantoms she'd killed before.

"Glad to be of service," she said, starting to activate the engines. Quint cut off. She set the coordinates for Collgort-Elipsa.

***

Satiah sat in front of the screens and began looking through everything. Kelvin was busy bundling away the body of the pirate she'd just killed.

"Yes, I was right, this is their central database," she murmured, reading quickly. Lists of equipment, supplies in general, money transfers... The records went back eight years. She ran a search on

Quint as she called Rainbow again. She'd not given him very long at all. When he answered he sounded groggy.

"No, I've got nothing," he responded, dejected. "Maybe I've lost my touch." Satiah was busy reading the agonisingly short description of Quint that the pirates had on their client list. Middle-aged human male, which could mean anything from fifty to one hundred and fifty, main liaison of the Organisation. Organisation had a *capital* O and was clearly meant to mean something specific.

"I've got some more for you. I think he's male, human and middle-aged..." she said, softly.

"You *think?*" Rainbow sighed. His lack of enthusiasm was understandable; it was hardly a nailing-factor.

"In connection with some kind of *Organisation*..."

"Satiah, you *know* how I work, right? You give me *half of something* I find you *the other half.* It doesn't work at five percent," he protested. A woman's voice could be heard in the background.

"Are you at home?" she asked, grinning.

"I'm *in a* home," he muttered.

"You know, you disgust me," she stated, mockingly. She grinned. "Your poor wife and children have my sympathies."

"That *was* my wife!" he hissed, annoyed. "We're staying with her family tonight – not that it's *any* business of yours."

"I know where you are, I can see you through the window," she purred, amused.

There was a hesitation.

"No, you can't," he said, uncertainly.

"Stop swearing, it's rude," she mused, trying to guess what he might be doing.

"*Ha!* You're not there," he replied, in triumph. "I was waving."

"You know what else *isn't there?*" she asked, getting serious again. Another sigh.

"*I know, I know* but I still need *more*. A description...?" he tried hopeful.

"I've never seen him, only *heard* him, and that information I've just got is second hand, to say the least," she explained. Then she noticed something tiny on the page. A symbol, perhaps a logo in the corner, underneath the text. She tried to enlarge it.

"Well, I *need* more, and *yes*, I appreciate the irony of that!" he spat, thinking she would make some smart comment.

"I might have something here you can play with," she said.

"Yes?" he asked, interested. "What is it?"

"An image. Not of the man but I *think* it might be *who he represents*," she told him.

"Ah, *nice*, now *that* I can do something with," he said, yawning. She adjusted her specs, focussing on the image. It took over her vision for a moment as it was made clearer and bigger. Gothic in attitude, it was the sort of thing that might have been designed to scare children. Mostly golds and blacks. The face of *something*, maybe a dragon, maybe a gargoyle, with dark slit like eyes and long teeth. It seemed to be surrounded by a red circle.

"It's weird," she murmured, unhelpfully. She continued to tweak the picture, trying to improve the quality.

"Sounds promising, the more outlandish then the easier it should be to find... *in theory*," he encouraged.

"I've sent it to you, see what you think," she said, not sure what to make of it herself. "Could be a commercial entity or some kind of gang marking." Rainbow went quiet. "Do you have it?"

"...*I swear I've seen this before*," he stated, sounding enthralled. "Not recently. This or something *very* like it." She felt the hairs on her neck rise a little in apprehension. It could be a bad idea to rush this though.

"Sleep on it," she suggested, trying to be reasonable.

"Are you kidding? I'm not going to be able to rest *now I've seen this*!" he laughed, sounding oddly grateful. "I'll get back to you as soon as I know what you've found." He cut off and Satiah leaned back in the chair, concerned. If this was something Rainbow had seen before, that meant it was likely to be bad news.

No news on Quint, still nothing from the picture of that

woman... She continued sifting through the data. Quint was their *highest* capital provider. He'd invested *millions of Essps* in these pirates. Why? To get them to prolong or exacerbate the war. *Why*? And *whom or what* did he represent? Quint was the key to unravelling most of this, she felt sure. She closed down the console, certain there was no more she could learn from it. There was one man there who might know more, though. Kyle. Getting at him would be tricky, and making it out afterwards would be harder still. She glanced over at Kelvin.

"Still clear," he reported. No one was onto them yet.

She put in another call, this time to Reed. She didn't want to ask for advice but she was not sure what to do for the best now. Dyss would order her to grab Kyle, and Randal would probably advise she did that too, but Reed had a different way of looking at things.

"Ah *Satiah*!" he answered, quickly. "I'm keeping an eye on Bert as you instructed. He seems to be behaving himself..."

"Reed, *listen*. I'm inside the pirate headquarters on Comet Sunkiss. They are most definitely behind the attacks on Collgort-Elipsa as we discussed before. I'm going to send you some evidence. It's nothing particularly concrete, but it should be hard enough to make a dent in the Viscount's mind," she stated.

"That's *great*!" he chuckled. "Marvellous, I knew my trust in you was not misplaced..."

"Hold it, *cancel the party*," she hissed, levelly. "Reed, there's next-level stuff I can't get to yet, I don't know exactly who is behind the pirates but they are not doing this off their own backs."

"All right, I wasn't expecting a miracle, what you have given me might be enough to at least make both sides of the war aware they are being used," Reed explained, forgivingly.

"I have a name and I wondered if you might have any ideas. The name is Quint," she told him. "Quint seems to be the mastermind behind the pirates but I don't know who he is working for or even who he is."

"*Quint*..." he repeated slowly, as he thought about it. "No bells ringing, I'm afraid. What does he look like?"

"I don't know, that's the trouble. I've only heard his voice," she explained. "I overheard him when he was talking to the pirates. In the conversation they were smart enough not to use names, but afterwards, when the discussion was over, someone gave their opinion about Quint and used his name then."

"I see," he murmured, pondering.

She waited for a few minutes but he seemed to be done.

"*I see?*" she echoed, irately. "That's *all* you've got?"

"Sorry, have I missed something or are *you asking me* to tell you what you should do next?" Reed asked. She could tell he was smiling. That urge to slap him was back.

"I wanted *your opinion*, that is all," she growled, mulishly.

"Just keep digging," he said, sounding unruffled. "Or is your position untenable?"

"Not yet…" she muttered, wondering how long she would remain undetected.

"No worries then. Again, *thank you for your latest update*, and *good luck*," he replied, cutting off.

Kelvin turned to look at her. "All data sent," he confirmed. She nodded silently as she deliberated her next move very carefully.

"Thank you, Kelvin."

"Objective?" he queried. She sat there for a few moments longer, deep in thought. She reached a decision and stood with intent gleaming in her brown eyes.

"*We get Kyle.*"

***

"This *isn't* proof it's… it's…" Pat objected, uneasily.

"*Difficult to ignore*, isn't it?" Reed jumped in, persuasively. "After all, *didn't we all agree* there was something about those attacks that was off from the start? I mean, *you* certainly had your suspicions from the word go. Even if you cannot prove they used them, it proves that the pirates have vehicles *that match* those which attacked you. It proves they were paid to use them. It certainly indicates they were buying materials used for altering the bodywork of fighter and capital ships alike. It also shows *how long* they had been in their possession…"

They were in the Viscount's palace, pacing the corridors together. Pat was trying to work out what to make of this information and if it was trustworthy. Reed was just trying to get her to do something about it.

"*I know! I know!* I believe you Reed, I always have, and you know *that*! But it doesn't tell us *why*, and that's what the Viscount will be interested in..." Pat protested, urgently. "I mean, if we are *wrong* about *this*..." Her concern was that if this information was incorrect, the Viscount might not trust her again. She was pushing things as they were, constantly spinning out time to get him some further information. And Reed's stunt with the Federation ship made her feel even more like things were on a knife-edge. The ball was firmly in her court, as the phrase had it, so she had to *do something soon* but she never liked rushing anything. Reed, however, was relentless.

"If *everyone* always begins with the presumption *that they are wrong* then *nothing* is achieved!" he argued, softly.

"I know, but..."

"I'm sure you have *already* realised what this gives the Viscount the chance of doing?" Reed interrupted, smoothly. She looked a bit blank. "Armed with *this information*, he can *not only* clear the names of both the Shintu and Vinu forces, but he can use this as a way of getting *them* to cease hostilities. *At least for a while*. Giving time for the pirates to be investigated *more* closely. Imagine that, if the pirates are attacking you disguised as them, *what else might they be doing?* You can tell him that his name *could be* known for one of the noblest causes: *peace-making*. And later, *regardless of whether he succeeds or not*, he will remember that *you* provided him with the opportunity, and so may reward you."

"Reed, I... you make it sound *so easy*," she managed, faltering.

"I paraphrased a smidgeon but you get the idea?" he remarked, influentially. "At the very least you must show him what you have before he decides to do anything else without you saying your piece." She looked indecisive but at last began to agree.

"*You're right*," she breathed, nodding. "He undoubtedly *should* see this *before* he decides anything..." She didn't move though.

"Let's go," he said, taking her arm. He unsuccessfully tried to lead her down the corridor.

"What *now?*" she almost yelped. She was still reluctant to risk her reputation on this, Reed could tell. He had to get her to move now. If he delayed, she had more time to change her mind.

"There is only today, as tomorrow's circumstance can only ever have been decided yesterday," he said, pulling gently. "*Trust me,* the Viscount will understand why you're telling him this." She began to give in and allow him to drag her along.

"This *Satiah,* you trust her?" she asked, still justifiably hesitant.

"*With my life,*" he smiled, believably. "She *did* in fact save my life once, *not so long ago either.* She's an avid advocate of peace and serenity with a *deep* dedication to the sanctity of life." He cleared his own throat abruptly after saying that and uncrossed his fingers.

They reached the reception area and could see the Viscount staring out into the clouds in the room beyond through the glass. The strain was evident in his pose and expression. A pensive wistfulness… thinking back to a day when this wasn't his problem. Eyes, half sunken from lack of sleep, staring off into the middle-distance. Bleak.

"Lady Hollellster to see the Viscount, it's urgent," Pat said, to the guards. They entered and the Viscount turned to face them. It was difficult to say what he was expecting as his face gave nothing away.

"You have something for me?" he asked, very interested.

"Yes, you must look at this," she said, handing him a device. He began to review the data in front of him keenly. "You can see there is a *substantial indication* that pirates *are* behind the attacks on us." She had already picked out the relevant information and broken it down into three simple chunks for him to digest.

Firstly: the pirates *owned* the exact same craft used in both attacks. Secondly: they also possessed *the right equipment* to disguise said means of transportation. And lastly: they were *still* being paid to keep and use them.

"And you agree?" the Viscount asked, to Reed. Reed appeared careless, still acting as if he was reluctant to side with her lest the Viscount become aware of their collusion.

"I certainly can't discredit it," he countered, shrugging.

"Viscount," Pat pleaded, sincerely. "You can use this to *end the war*. You could say that the pirates are being paid to prolong the conflict, disguising…"

"No," he said, cutting her off. Reed frowned and Pat looked completely bewildered. The Viscount returned to the window for a moment as if forgetting they were there.

"But… *I don't understand*. This could stop *all* the madness…" she tried again.

"There's not enough known for me to try that," he answered, a little sadness creeping into this voice.

"What do you mean?" she asked, disappointed.

"What you have is good, *don't get me wrong*, and I *believe* you about the pirates attacking *us*. Trouble is… we don't know *why* they are doing it. We don't know that one or other of the *sides in the war* didn't originally hire them to incriminate the other side. This doesn't prove *anyone's* innocence, only another party's guilt," he argued. Reed was prepared for this but hadn't told Pat what to do. She just sat there, realising that the Viscount was quite correct.

"Of course, both sides will just accuse one another of *this* and the fighting will continue," Reed said, casually. "The only way you could convince them of the truth would be if you gave them details about whoever is behind the pirates."

"Assuming it *isn't* one of them?" he said, seriously.

"Neither side have that kind of money *to waste on pirates*," Reed said, softly. "They're both fighting an all-out war. Now, that's very expensive even for the richest of worlds! You know this to be correct. Pirates are unreliable *and* expensive. We even know *exactly* how much they cost. If you look at all of it, the money required for this venture far exceeds anything that either side would have to spare…"

"I agree with your reasoning but supposition is *not* proof. *They may have rich friends*."

"You don't *need* proof, you just need to tell them *your theory*," Reed suggested, cleverly. "You could offer to help them resolve this? Perhaps *organise* a small armistice?"

"It... *is* plausible," the Viscount allowed, attentively. There was a silence and when it seemed that nothing more was forthcoming Reed chose to back off.

"We will leave you to mull it over," Reed smiled, nodding to Pat. She moved over to him. They headed for the door, padding softly over the expensive carpet, leaving the information with the Viscount. After the build-up it felt like somewhat of an anti-climax. The Viscount was in a very precarious position. This was evident in all ways. He probably felt trapped between his trusted aids, Pat, a few others, and the council beneath him that was desperate for him to make a decision... or a mistake. If he did genuinely care for his people, a rare quality in a ruler, then that would place even more pressure on him. Reed felt that they had pushed him far enough. Certainly for one day.

"This is worse than I thought. I mean, *he's* worse than I've ever seen him; this is really getting to him now. *It's like he's trying to shut everything out*," Pat voiced, in a nervous whisper. "Maybe he's losing it..."

"He didn't jump to a decision because he wants to retain *the impression* that he is capable of weighing the options up correctly," Reed explained, patiently. "Leadership is as much about image as it is about proficiency – perhaps *even more so*. You can be as capable as the best, but if you don't *look it*, no one will follow you. On the other hand, if you look perfect but are in fact useless, you're still able to draw people along, at least for a while." He didn't add that the fallout either way was often fatal.

"I wish we could help him more," she hissed, feeling like her hands were tied.

"We are already virtually standing on his toes, I doubt he'd *tolerate* any more," Reed insisted, gently. "We have done all we can do today, short of cajoling him. My advice is: we think about something else."

"That's easy for you to say, this isn't even *your* world," she scoffed, without genuine anger.

"True, but it *is* important to me," he deftly responded. "And *you never know*, Satiah might turn up with something else for us to take to him."

"*I hope so*," she murmured, miserably.

"While I have you, you don't happen to have any resident brain surgeons here, do you?" he asked, as if he were discussing the weather.

"*What?*" she demanded, bamboozled. "You're *mad*, aren't you? I mean *actually* certified *and* registered…"

"I never said they were for *me*," he dismissed, suddenly serious. "*Do you have any?*"

***

It had been a two-hour hike from the ship to the base perimeter. Darius had decided to approach from the opposite direction, away from the area where he had broken through the fence last time. As before, he was wearing a breathing mask. Cherry, on her front next to him, was peering through the sights of her new rifle at the base. The sentinel drones were in fully active mode and Darius had even spotted some going out to check the neighbouring woodland. Cherry was doing well; not only was she not at all bothered by the insects, but she was fit enough to keep up on the journey there. Finding a way in though would be a challenge for anyone if they didn't want anyone else to know about it.

"How do we get in?" Cherry asked, annoyingly.

It was annoying because that was not only what he was asking himself, but it was also precisely what he couldn't answer.

"We will do a circuit," he said, quickly. Maybe there was something he'd missed when he had last been there. This time though he would keep his distance more. There were too many drones, and it would only take one of them to spot him or Cherry to ruin things. After several minutes of very slow, very careful exploration, they came to a river. A river that seemed to be going directly towards the base, and went underground not far from the fence. It was a risky longshot for Darius to hope that it might lead to a way in, but he had reached the conclusion that there wouldn't be any other easy options.

"Okay, can you swim?" he asked, casually. She didn't answer and looked into the water dismally. "Cherry?"

"*I can swim*," she answered, a little too angrily. He winced and she seemed to realise she was doing it again. "Sorry… I *can*, I just don't like it."

"Just follow me," he smiled, trying to be reassuring. "You'll be fine." He waded in, ignoring the bitter chill of the water. Cherry gasped and restrained herself from exclaiming, especially as she got deeper than her knees. Darius reached the tunnel where the water flowed under the rocks. He dived after activating his torch. Cherry looked a little panic stricken when she realised where he was going but, unwilling to be outdone, least of all by a *man*, she dived too.

The tunnel was dark, cold and claustrophobic, not dissimilar to what a submerged fogou might look like, and led downward. Darius was concerned immediately as the current was strong enough to make going back difficult. It wasn't fast but it was insistent. Cherry was now seriously scared. She didn't like being underwater at the best of times and she was shaking so hard with the cold, she feared she'd die. She refused to give up, telling herself that it was too important... even though she didn't know why. Darius reached the bottom of the tunnel, determining that they were about under the perimeter fence and turned to look for Cherry.

The torch momentarily blinded her but she kept coming. He adjusted something on his mask.

"You okay?" came his bubbly voice. She tried to answer but nearly lost her mask in the attempt. He activated her talking system.

"Fine," she managed, at last.

"I think we're under the boundary fence... we will soon be directly underneath the base," he said, between breaths. She nodded.

"Are you sure that coming down here was a good idea?" she asked, too frightened to hang on to that question.

"Not even close," he said, and reached out to squeeze her arm to show that he was making light of it. "If I'm wrong you can blame me."

"If you're wrong... I don't think I... will be able to blame... you about... anything ever," she said, amid inhaling and exhaling.

As Darius had predicted, they soon found the wall of the base. He knew it went down a long way and he hoped it would not be too far. He felt his ears popping as the pressure increased. A noise sounded. A rumbling, clanking noise, and Darius realised that they were in luck. He had no idea how long it would be before fresh water would be required… an hour tops, he'd hoped. The darkness ahead seemed to be opening up and the force of water propelled them forward uncontrollably. Wisely, Cherry placed her hands on her mask to ensure it did not get ripped from her face. She couldn't see anything suddenly, as Darius's torch was off. They were pulled forward at some speed. Darius could make out a dim blue light ahead. If there was a point in this plan that was most dangerous, this was it.

The base reactor, its power supply, would need regular cooling. He had a theory that, as they were cloaked and hidden, supplies would be rare. That being so, they would need to be as self-sufficient as possible. *Coolant* for the reactor would need to be supplied, but if you had a natural alternative, say… an underground river… then, every so often, fresh cool water would need to be pumped in. A possible way in if you timed it right. He was jarred out of his thoughts when, as he spun, his leg struck against something. Something hard. It might have been a stalagmite, a rock, or something else entirely. Whatever it was, it hurt. He shouted but managed to keep control. Cherry, only a few metres behind, felt something skim her belly as she shot past but, probably due to her smaller size, she missed it.

Darius shot out of the end of the tunnel, into the light, flushed out into a vast tank. Cherry was out almost directly behind him. Blood ran from Darius's leg and he tried to see how bad it was. Nothing was broken but as flesh wounds went, it was deep. Cherry stared at the huge machine they were floating around. The water was not very warm and bubbles were everywhere. It was going to get warmer though… as the reactor burned never-endingly. If they couldn't get out they would boil away.

"What's this?" she asked, over the noise.

"The base reactor," he replied, distracted by his injury.

"Are you okay?" she asked, noticing the wound.

"This is the tricky bit… how to get out of the tank," he said, ignoring the question. He rose, trying to reach the surface, and Cherry followed.

Erupting from the foam, Darius realised they were in one of probably many support tanks for water storage. Above them, within a few meters, were metal walkways. They crisscrossed the tanks and the reactor itself. Apparently, no one was around. Cherry looked around for a way out, but there was none. As you would expect, there wouldn't be, as no one should be swimming around inside the cooling tanks in the first place. On the walkways though, at various places, metal ladders were there. Extendable ones that were folded up. Darius tried to tread water, a painful task for him now, and aimed his pistol at the holding clips. On lower power, the shot was enough to unclip the ladder. The ladder, section by section, folded down towards them.

"After you," he said, indicating to Cherry. She struggled up and he followed, ignoring the pain in his leg. They reached the walkway and Cherry took a good look around... and then took another at his leg.

"That looks bad," she stated, biting her lip.

"It's nothing," he remarked, still looking around. Now they had finally made it in, the real trouble started. If Milo Drass *wasn't* in the detention area, where was he? As he was thinking about where else to look, he made use of the time by injecting himself with various chemicals to protect and heal the wound.

"I'm going to find a list of all employees here," he stated, thinking about it. Maybe if he *wasn't* a prisoner there, perhaps he was working there in some capacity. There was also the remote possibility that, for whatever reason, he was a high priority prisoner and thus might not be held with the others. This all was, of course, assuming that he was still alive.

"Right," she nodded, eyeing him doubtfully.

Darius took a few lunging steps forward, testing his injured leg. He limped at first but gradually the medication took effect and the bleeding stopped. They were able to dry efficiently as their combat suits were designed to maximise evaporation. These things were fortunate as there were many hundreds of steps to climb. They had got in right at the nethermost part of the reactor. It was probably fifteen storeys in distance to the highest part.

"Is there *any* chance you can find us an *easier* way out?" Cherry panted, seriously.

"I'll do my best," he assured her, still irritatingly fresh. Steam rose constantly around them as the reactor cooled off. They eventually reached a walkway that led into the complex.

"From now on, stay behind me, there were a lot of cameras," he warned.

"*Fine by me*," she grumbled, her legs heavy from the stairs. So heavy that they were almost shaking now! Darius reached the door, pistol drawn. The door opened automatically. There was no one beyond. Darius was counting on there not being that many personnel hanging around on the lower levels. The low lighting and soft hums of the machines allowed him to live in hope of less activity. Cherry was dying for a rest but too afraid of looking soft to ask. Darius found a computer and sat in front of it. She almost grinned with joy.

"I'll keep watch," she managed, struggling to stay upright. He grunted, without looking at her. She returned to the corridor, looked both ways and then slumped to the floor, exhausted.

Darius quickly gained access to the network. There was no list of personnel, but there was an organisational chart that listed them in order of the command. There was Base Colonel Celestine at the top, and everyone else all the way down to second portfolio corporals. Darius was *fairly* sure that Milo Drass would not be working there as a soldier. He checked medical personnel, remembering the young man's volunteering work. Thirty-seven staff were registered. All of them were *apparently* different people. He called up a base layout schematic. He was unable to get authorisation to any but the most basic of maps. He was looking for the medical centre. *Typical*! Right underneath the main command area! Maybe the staff here had captured him and brought him here because of his medical skills. He was only recently qualified and… the motive for this was still hard to see.

There were billions of more qualified people than Milo Drass and probably half that amount willing to work here for an actual job. What was so special about him? What did Milo Drass have that no other doctors, or *few* other doctors, had? Specialist knowledge? Specialist skills? Was he involved in some strange military medical experiment? Had he seen something he shouldn't have? People that knew too much rarely had a long lifespan. Victims of the many and varied secret systems. Careful not to be on the network for too long, Darius deactivated and pondered for a moment. How best to proceed from here? He stood and slipped outside.

Cherry stood unsteadily as he joined her outside.

"No luck yet," he stated, simply. "We're going to have to gain access to the medical area. I know where it is."

"Okay," she said, weary. He eyed her bedraggled condition and handed her a long bar of something that looked like liquorish.

"Eat that," he ordered, turning to go on. She was doing her best but he couldn't have her too sleepy to move suddenly. She bit into the bar and chewed hard. It was tough and sweet to the taste. Not unlike dried meat. Instantly she felt a rush of energy. He stopped suddenly and peered around the corner before slipping back again.

"Camera," he hissed, irritated.

***

It was hard to concentrate on grilled fish, especially when the man sitting across from you might have a bomb in his head. Pat smiled and offered to pour more wine. Reed's eyes widened at her in concealed warning. Getting someone drunk was not the best precursor for emergency brain surgery. Pat gave him a look, trying to tell him that if she *didn't* behave naturally then Bert might get suspicious. Reed pulled a face, which implied she *regularly* tried to get her guests as intoxicated as possible *on principle*! She was on the verge of throwing the bottle at him when Bert let out a groan and slumped back in his seat, unconscious. Bottling Reed was still on the table as an option for her though: it wasn't like help was far away. She rang her service bell.

"I do hope he's not going to have complications because of *that*," Reed stated, pointing at the wine.

"Reed, since you got here we have left complications *far behind* and are now stuck somewhere in the darkened woods, fending off bats with sticks whilst arguing about *if we are due to see a specialist tomorrow!*" she ranted, her tone savage. "*Not to mention the wine!*"

"You've noticed that *as well*, have you?" he nodded, looking very guilty. She knew he wasn't *really* feeling guilty, but trying to soften her up by looking so.

"How can she possibly *know* that he has a chip in his head? *She's not even here*," argued Pat, unwilling to let it rest.

"If Satiah thinks he's got a chip in his head then *he's got a chip in his head*. Makes a change from having one on your shoulder, don't you think?" he stated, wittily.

"*Oh, why don't you just have a union with her?*" barked Pat, irritated. Reed glanced at her, eyebrows raised, intrigued by the heat in her response. Poked a nerve there.

"I'm not into dying before my time," he muttered, with a grin. "I *know* it's frustrating, placing all this trust in someone you don't even *know*, but believe me: *she's very good.*" Instead of servants answering the bell, a team of doctors arrived.

"I hope you're not proposing to do it in *here?*" Pat asked, raising an eyebrow.

"Good lord no, it's not even sterile. Besides, I just want to look at it first," Reed replied, erratically. "And I *really* don't think it's a bomb. *Please* don't worry."

"*Don't worry, he says,*" she muttered to herself, shaking her head as he followed the doctors out.

***

The woman, clad in a silky dress, waited patiently on the bed, a few chocolates in front of her. She watched the lift remain five floors down. She had been waiting for him for a while, long enough to dim the lights and get ready. A noise! A shuffle from a darkened room to her side made her look across in its direction. Nothing to be seen. She returned her attention to the lift door. Another noise, this time louder, sounded. It sounded like something had fallen over. The woman frowned and got up to investigate. She entered the room and waited for the light to automatically come on. It didn't. She took another step further into the darkness. Something hard slammed into the back of her head and she was down and out in less than a second.

"Tie her up and get ready," Satiah ordered, slipping into the bed and effectively taking the woman's place.

The indicator was flickering as the lift approached. Satiah lay on her side, with her back to the lift. The doors swished open and Kyle entered, muttering under his breath.

"*Sorry I'm late, honey.* You would not *believe* what those lunatics have gone and done now!" he stated, stressed. Satiah let out a non-committal but sleepy moan. Kyle began to strip off.

"One of them decided it would be a smart idea to replace the engines on three of our freighters with the new type we got in last week. So him and his team spend *sixteen hours* refitting them only to realise what I told them *before I left*... we don't have the right kind of *fuel*!" Satiah rolled her eyes and mumbled something incoherently.

"*I know!*" he yelled, nodding, as if she had agreed with him. "That's what I said to them! They have got *no idea*, they really haven't! Utterly clueless!"

He smirked as he eyed her in the bed.

"How tired are you?" he asked, grinning.

He leaned in to kiss her when she rolled fully into view, pistol aimed at his chest. He froze in dread.

"*Hello, Kyle*," she said, coldly. "It looks like they're not the only ones." Kyle didn't move or say a word, still stunned. Kelvin grabbed his arms and pulled him away from Satiah as she stood. They forced him into a chair and tied him down.

"What do you want?" Kyle managed, at last starting to recover himself. "Where's...?"

"No, no, let's *not* waste time expecting me to answer *your* questions. *You should already know how these things work. I'm* going to ask *you* some questions and if you don't answer *or* I suspect your answer to be untrue, you will suffer," she explained, lightly. "If you answer every question honestly, then the odds are I *won't* kill you. Are we all clear?"

He stared ahead, steeling himself. Satiah exhaled sharply with impatience and lit two smokes. Kelvin, knowing what to do, held Kyle's mouth closed and his head straight. Satiah inserted one smoke up each of his nostrils. The idea was that every time he breathed in, it would burn the inside of his nose. And as he could only breath in through his nose... He started to squirm around and talk immediately. She wanted to show him that she meant business and so waited for a little longer. When they were about half down, she gave a nod. Kelvin released Kyle and then hit him on the back of the head sending both smokes out onto the floor. Satiah crushed them under her boot.

"More?" she offered, displaying the rest of the pack to him.

He shook his head, coughing and spluttering.

"Good, they're not great for your health," she smiled, crisply. "Who's Quint?" Kyle's breathing slowed to normal and he met her eyes but did not answer. "Who's Quint?" she repeated, knowing he was going to be difficult. Still no reply. "Okay," she snapped, pulling a leather bag out from somewhere. "We tried *fire…*" Kelvin pulled the chair backwards powerfully, leaving Kyle facing the ceiling. Satiah roughly pulled the bag over Kyle's head. Kelvin passed her the first box. She poured the water over the bag, careful to get most of it around his mouth and nose. He thrashed as well as he could, trying to breathe. Kelvin again moved in to hold him as still as possible.

"It's not worth it," Satiah insisted, calmly. "I will rip you apart to get what I want but it doesn't have to go that way."

More gargling, spluttering and gagging came from inside the bag as she administered a second box of water. Sweat was all over him now. It was halfway through the third box when he stopped moving. Satiah nodded to Kelvin and he replaced the chair, Kyle lolled forward. Satiah ripped off the bag and grabbed him by his chin.

"Well?" she asked, expectantly. He spat a mouthful of water out at her, still stubborn. Clearly Quint was clever enough to use people that could be trusted. "*Oh, dear me,*" she said, the first signs of anger now in her voice. "I should warn you, I don't deal well with disappointment." Kyle unleashed a torrent of insults, threats and expletives at her. The usual. She grunted, as if she agreed and nodded sarcastically at him. Her smile turned spiteful. She grabbed his ear and started twisting.

He winced and tried to pull away, exposing his neck in the process. In a well-practised move she slammed the needle in and injected him. He started screaming. The chemical simulated the feeling of a septic wound… only *everywhere at once*. That kind of pain would drive the average person mad in less than four minutes and would kill them in less than six. He howled and screamed and wept while she looked on, apparently unmoved. She took no pleasure in making others suffer but she got satisfaction when she got what she wanted. She just had to wait… everyone broke eventually. After three minutes she countered the effects of the drug with another chemical injection. In moments he was moaning in relief that the almost inconceivable pain had faded. Satiah pointed to the timekeeper.

"I've been on you for nearly fifteen minutes and I estimate it will be at least four hours before anyone thinks to wonder *where you are*," she said, in his ear. "Who's Quint?"

"If I tell you…" he breathed, a little hoarse from all the screaming. "He'll kill me."

"Yeah, they *all* say that," she smiled, unimpressed. "Besides… *If you don't, I'm sure to kill you*. So… here we are. The advantage in telling me is that *maybe* you can escape before he finds out. And you never know… maybe I will kill him *before* he gets the chance to kill you."

"You don't know him," Kyle muttered.

"No, that's the trouble, I *so want* to get to know him," Satiah persisted, trying to encourage him.

"He's not into redheads," Kyle joked, in a disgusted tone.

Satiah laughed and went for another needle.

"*Wait!*" he hissed, guessing what was coming. He didn't think he could go through that again. "Quint is our main financial backer in this sector. He tells us what to do."

"Good, where is he?" she asked.

"I don't know and *that's the truth*. He always calls *us*," Kyle insisted, sweat pouring down his face.

"Who does *he* work for?" she asked, next. Inwardly she was starting to get excited as she could sense she was nearing some of the answers she needed. Her face, though, remained a facade of unreadability.

"I don't know exactly, all I know is that he represents the interests of *the Cult of Deimos*," Kyle said, going paler by the moment.

"…The what?" she asked, disbelieving. She'd never heard of them. Kyle was tough and smart. He could be inventing a cock-and-bull story to put her off.

She grabbed his hair in her fist and yanked hard.

"Are you making stuff up now, because *if* you are…" she began, sneering down at him.

"*It's true, it's true!*" he shouted back, fervently. She let go and then wiped her hand on the back of the chair as if in revulsion.

"All right. What does he use scum like you for?" she asked, seriously.

"They want us to attack Collgort-Elipsa..." he began, sweat stinging his eyes.

"*Why?*" she spat, commandingly. She already knew they were disguising themselves as one side or other of the warring factions, and the reason they had done that was obvious. To hide the fact it was really them. She wanted to know specifically: why was Collgort-Elipsa their target? She began to walk slowly around him, dauntingly.

"He never told me *why*!" Kyle cried, plausibly. "And I never asked!" That was probable, she had to agree.

"Where's the gold?" she snarled in his ear, changing subjects to try and fox him. He looked blank for a moment.

"What gold?"

"*Wrong answer*!" she barked, cuffing him over the back of the head punitively. "I asked *where* it was!"

"I don't know what gold you're talking about, *I swear*!" he replied, shaking his head pleadingly. She backed off, crossed her arms and regarded him coolly. She exerted her formidable self-control and lowered her voice down to nearly a whisper. It was very easy to get carried away by the aggression during interrogations.

"So you're telling me that Quint works for the Cult of Deimos, the Cult of Deimos has paid you to harass Collgort-Elipsa but they haven't told you why, and that you have *no idea* about any missing gold?" she asked, her voice deceptively soft and menacing. Breathing hard, he just nodded quickly. She smiled knowingly into his eyes. "And you *really* expect *me* to believe all that?" she asked, still very quiet. She slid her hand along one of her needles and his eyes went wide.

"It's *true*!" he said, starting to tear up all over again. "I *swear*, it's all I know. *I don't ask questions*! I just do what they say because if I don't *I die. Please*!" She picked up the needle nonchalantly and smiled at him more sadistically. "No, no, no more, please, no more." He was crying now, tears slipping down his face. He was either a brilliant actor or she'd nearly broken him. She tilted her head to the side, the smile still there.

"I'd *love* to believe you, *I really would,*" she lied, as if talking to a small child. "*Unfortunately...*" She leaned in close to his ear, letting the tension continue to build.

"Would *you* trust *your* answers?" she whispered, only just audible over his pathetic whimpers. "*Would you?*" she asked, in a soft rhetorical tone. Her lips were scarcely an inch from his ear lobe now.

"*Would you?*" she screamed, as piercingly as she could. He shrieked in fright at the noise. He'd not expected her to do that.

"I don't know..." he managed, miserably. "*I don't know.*"

"You don't know?" she repeated, shaking her head as if disappointed. "You're no use to me, are you?" He let out a noise somewhere between a sob and a blubber. "No use at all," she went on, false sadness in her voice. "What do you do with *things* that are of no use to you, Kyle? What do *you* do?" Sensing that this might be his only chance of survival he had to just tell her everything or...

"The gold was stolen from us," he said, his voice thin and reedy. She leaned in again, listening intently. "Visvevar got greedy and stole it from the Polvine Limited freighter. He conveyed it back to camp but then the camp was attacked and it was stolen. I don't know what happened to it after that. Is... is *that* the gold you're talking about?"

"Yes," she said, clearly. "But don't stop *there*, I can *tell* you have more for me."

"I don't know much about the Cult of Deimos but they are one of the most dangerous organisations around," he warned, ominously. "They're planning something big to take care of the Federation destroyer guarding the planet, I don't know what though. They have a man in the *inside*. His name is Administrator Bavon. He won't know more than me but he's the one who tells us and Quint when it's a good time to attack." She waited until he was finished, rapt. She knew to treat this information sceptically but things were at last starting to materialise. It would explain all that business about the empty data cubes neatly though... and Darius too had believed there to be an infiltrator.

"Recently there was a period when the destroyer was not on station. Why didn't you attack then?" she asked, curious.

"We were going to but Quint stood us down, he thought it was a trap," Kyle admitted, glad Satiah had seemed to have calmed down.

"*Did he?*" she murmured, thoughtfully. So... Quint had a brain... never a good sign.

"Yes, he did," he answered, unsure if that was rhetorical or not. It was.

"So if *Quint* is in charge of you all, where do Purella and her mercenaries fit in?" Satiah asked. "Is she *also* a member of this cult of yours?"

"*It's not mine* and I'm sorry but I have no idea who Purella is." Quint may be dealing with her separately. "*Curious*," she muttered, letting that go. "What is the ultimate goal here?"

"I don't know, I'm sorry," he said, starting to get worried again.

"Do you have any interest in Doctor Bertram Blake Clark?" she asked. He looked blank and shook his head.

"I've never heard of them," he said, hoping she would believe that.

"What about *this*? Can you tell me anything about this?" she asked, producing the gemstone and showing it to him.

"What is it?" he asked, giving away that he knew nothing about that either. It began to glow orange and suddenly she realised what she had done. She was touching it without gloves. It was glowing, brighter and dimmer again and again. She frowned at it. Kelvin too watched it, his red eyes recording everything as always. Satiah then noticed that Kyle was starting to shake all over. He was staring at the stone too and seemed unable to look away.

"I... I have... *I can't...!*" he began and then started to scream. Satiah looked from the gemstone in her hand to Kyle's face and then back again. It was doing something to him. It *had* to be. He started shaking more violently, like he was having some sort of seizure. Satiah looked at Kelvin, a question in her eyes. *Do we try to stop this or don't we?* Kyle let out a wail and every muscle in his body tensed with a massive cramp attack then... he went limp and continued to stare, his eyes half open, at the crystal. Then Satiah felt it... or heard it. All the tiny hairs on the back of her neck rose like before and she stared into the stone again.

"*Satiah...*" whispered that voice. She still couldn't tell if it was out loud or only in her mind. This time though, Kelvin was there with her so she was not *as* scared.

"*What?*" she growled back.

"He doesn't know any more," said the voice.

Unlike before, there was no image of her own face talking to her. And this time, the voice was definitely that of a man. Deep, rich and powerful sounding as it spoke again. It was no longer just a whisper.

"Kyle's mind does not have any more for you," it told her.

"What are you?" she asked, her voice wavering.

"I am Obsenneth," he said, and the light faded to nothing.

"Obsenneth?" Nothing, no response. It was just like a normal gemstone now. What the hell? She slowly turned to look at Kelvin.

"*What was that?*" she asked, feeling a little lightheaded suddenly.

"Explain what happened to me while it is still fresh..." Kelvin began, not wanting to spoil her account by telling her what he had recorded.

"*He's dead*," Satiah stated, pointing down at Kyle. She dropped the stone onto the floor and recoiled as if it were alive. She went pale as she stared down at it, anxiety in her eyes. Her mind seemed foggy and she couldn't think straight. Her balance too now seemed impaired.

"*Satiah...*" Kelvin began again. He moved towards her as she seemed unsteady. She staggered forward, staring blankly ahead.

"We must... We have to..." she interrupted, trying to talk. Her eyes rolled back and she fainted.

***

Clyde listened hard to that last part again. Satiah, trying to say *something* and then collapsing into unconsciousness *or death*. He had bugged Kyle's room a long time ago, before Kyle himself had even been employed by Quint. *He had heard everything.* Every word. Most of it had been as expected. *Worrying*, but as expected. Satiah was always going to track down Kyle and his gang; it had only ever been a matter of time. That last couple of minutes though... Clyde didn't know what to make of it. He wished he could have *seen* what had happened rather than just heard. Who was Satiah talking to at the end? Clyde had turned it up to maximum but couldn't hear an answering voice. He deactivated the device and remained seated for a few minutes. A few days ago he'd have told Purella straight away about this… now, though, things had changed. He chose not to.

***

Darius edged around the corner cautiously. Cherry followed, just as careful. They had managed to get inside the main security area. Base personnel were a common problem now, as well as the cameras. At last they reached the main billet area for the medical staff and entered.

"We need to borrow some clothes," he said. She nodded. They rummaged through the room, and quickly found suitable uniforms to disguise themselves with. They wouldn't fool anyone *up close* as you would expect, but they'd be enough to get past the cameras and people *at a distance*.

"Won't our guns give us away?" Cherry asked, seriously.

"Maybe, but I'm not leaving without mine," he mused. He eyed her rifle. "You?"

She gripped it possessively. He noticed her indecision.

"I have loads of them," Darius prompted. He hadn't, but he was sure he could get her another one if he had to.

"Okay," she said, slipping it inside the container she'd stolen her clothes from. He had his pistol concealed inside the white jacket he was now wearing. A rifle, on the other hand, couldn't easily be concealed anywhere.

"What makes you *so sure* he's still here?" Cherry asked, a little puzzled. "I know you explained to me about that transmission you and Satiah heard, but that was ages ago now. He could have been and gone."

"Nah, if he's alive he's *here*… a pirate abduction was the only other possibility, and not only has Satiah already been down that road but, *as I said at the time*, there was not enough damage on his ship for that to seem credible," Darius explained.

"Fine," she sighed, giving up. "Let's get this over with." They returned to the corridor and began to pad along, in full view of everyone, towards the hospital area. Cherry was trying very hard not to keep looking over her shoulder. Darius could tell, just from her body language, how tense she was. He decided against telling her to do anything about it, on the principle that bringing it to her attention would most likely exacerbate it. The doors required an access code but, fortuitously, someone else was just leaving. Darius prevented the door from closing again and ushered Cherry ahead of him. If Milo Drass was anywhere, it *had* to be around here.

***

Satiah opened her eyes. She was lying on her back, in the dark. She remembered it all instantly and sat up abruptly, almost smacking her head on the low ceiling. Kelvin's red eyes swung to face her, detecting her movement. She felt the familiar weight of the gemstone in her pocket.

"*What happened?*" she asked, very concerned. Whatever it was, it had caused her to black out, which was never a good thing.

"Kyle is dead. I administered a memory drug on the woman so she will recall nothing. The room has been returned to the condition we found it in. I have placed Kyle's body on the chair. She will awake to discover him like that. This should preserve our secrecy. We are hiding inside a disused air duct. You have been unconscious for one hour and fifty-seven point three minutes," Kelvin summarised.

"...Two hours," she hissed, shocked. "*What happened to me?*"

"Physically I can detect nothing wrong with you," Kelvin replied. "What is Obsenneth, Satiah?"

"*Obsenneth*," she uttered, the memory becoming more real somehow. "*I asked* what it was..." she began, thinking back. That voice, the sensations, and then that wave of... *dizziness?*

"If you did, you didn't use your vocal cords," he stated. She touched her neck pensively.

"I'm *not* telepathic," she frowned, confused. "Anyway, I asked what it was and it said, like a man would say, *I am Obsenneth.*"

"So it has a man's voice?" Kelvin confirmed. Last time it had been different.

"*I don't know,*" she sighed, rubbing her face with her hands. It was all a bit difficult for her to describe.

"If you try…" he began.

"I'm *not* touching that thing again," she hissed, guessing what he was going to suggest. "Not until we're done with this."

"Does it have a hold over you?" he asked. "I have calculated that it has the capacity to affect people's minds."

"How *did* Kyle die, by the way?" she asked, grimly. She could see why he thought that, it was logical.

"Inconclusive," he replied, unhelpfully.

"*It was Obsenneth*, Obsenneth killed him," she stated, with conviction.

"You don't know that," Kelvin pointed out.

"My human instinct tells me that *I do*," she replied, shrugging.

"Let's assume you are right – then, *why?*" Kelvin asked, in his usual monotone.

"And *how?*" she added, taking her turn to be unhelpful. There was a long silence. "*What is Obsenneth?*" she echoed Kelvin's question. "Or whom?" Had Kyle known something it didn't want her to know? Something about *it?*

Her earpiece went off and she jumped, her pistol somehow making it into her hand before she could stop herself. It was Rainbow. She answered while forcing herself to calm down.

"You're not going to like this," he stated, without any preamble. She sighed, realising she hadn't liked much of this at all so far.

"Well, it least it will be *consistent*," she grumbled. "What have you got?"

"That symbol you sent me… Now, I *know* you're not into conspiracy theories, so just wait before you shoot me down, but this one is at the centre of tens of them. Apparently it's an emblem of something called *the Cult of Deimos*." Satiah recalled the look of the image. A creature's face, with long, sharp teeth and black slit-like eyes. Encircled in a red line. Why did that make her think about blood?

"That *would* make sense," she allowed, her tone ponderous.

"Why's that?" he asked, interested.

"No reason," she mused, deciding to leave Kyle's interrogation out of it. "*Go on.*"

"Well, firstly – these guys, *if they do exist*, are *ancient*," he stated, clearly excited. It would be so rare that he'd get to investigate something like this, she supposed. "They have been around maybe four or five thousand years. At least, that's how far I've been easily able to find them."

"What are they? Do they have some kind of creed?" she asked, curious.

"I'm not sure; the way it looks is that they originally were sort of a secret social elite group. Made up of prominent individuals. And they would go and indulge in, some would say, *reckless revelry* together *in secret*," he explained.

"*Like a club*," she murmured. "You said *were*."

"Well, that was how they *started*, or are *rumoured* to have started. *There's nothing official here at all, let's put it that way.* They've moved on and off the network ever since, basically. *Implicated in conspiracy theories.* Disappearances, economic fluctuations, secret governments… you name it, they're all there. Anyway, this goes on, all low-key stuff, until about ten years ago…" What did he just say?

"Oh please *no!*" she moaned, out loud. "Not ten years *again.*"

"*What?*" he asked, baffled.

"Forget it, keep going," she said, stressed.

"Well… there was an investigation, err, two seconds… I thought I had it…" he said, scrabbling to find something. Silent agony was in Satiah's mind. *Find it! Come on, find it! Don't leave me hanging on here, not after all that.*

"I *had* it; I know I did… Ah! Got it! *Operation Gnomon,* yes this is the one. Unlisted espionage, status closed…" he listed.

Satiah had been convinced that he would be talking about Jackdaw. Now she didn't know whether to feel relieved or disappointed. Relieved that not *everything* was to do with that contentious assignment, but disappointed that she now had to remember yet *more* information.

"The VS war hadn't yet started, but two Phantoms were looking into missing cargos from Vinu ships," he told her. "They identified several groups of pirates in the region, but nothing out of the ordinary."

"Then what's it got to do with the cult?" Satiah asked, hoping she'd not missed something.

"Not a lot, but it seemed that the pirates – *not all, but some* – were being backed financially by someone claiming to represent the cult. Back then we, *as in Phantom Squad*, seemed to think it was either a cover for something else, or a joke, because *at the time* they thought the cult didn't exist. *Just another municipal legend, I guess.* But now, *looking at what you're doing*, it's clear that someone is either part of or *pretending to be* part of the cult."

"Does it exist or not?" she asked, directly. There was a long and exhilarated sigh from Rainbow.

"I can't tell you but I *think* it does," he replied, honestly. "*It certainly existed once* and there's no light without power."

"True," she said, an uneasy feeling in her gut. "My source seemed adamant on the point, and quite terrified too. I think Quint is a member of the Cult of Deimos."

"*I thought you'd say that*," Rainbow murmured, obviously deep in thought himself. "I've still got nothing on him, by the way, but at least I can search for stuff with that. Nothing new on the picture yet either, before you ask."

"And how much do you get paid to keep coming up with nothing *so diligently*?" she mocked, grinning.

"Not enough," he complained.

Her smiled faded as she wanted to ask him about Obsenneth, but couldn't bring herself to. She wasn't sure why, but she felt it was better not to mention anything about him... or it. Was it her own mind or *its influence* making her feel that way? She did not like this.

"Keep digging," she encouraged, casually.

"You too, and be careful, Satiah, this one could turn nasty," he said, cutting off.

"*Bit late for that,*" she said, sourly. She already felt like she had dodged a few laser bolts.

"You didn't tell him about Obsenneth," Kelvin pointed out.

"*That* stays *between us,*" she insisted, pointing at him. "At least until we know a bit more about it."

"Is that wise?"

"Possibly not, but in this case I think it's right," she shrugged. Then she remembered Bavon and knew she had to warn Reed.

***

"Well," said the neurologist. "It's *certainly* a memory inhibitor. Not been there long, maybe a month, certainly less than three months." Reed nodded. That was two *certainlys*... going well so far. The man demonstrated by drawing Reed's attention to some faint scarring, recently exposed after Bert's hair had been shaved off.

"Is there any way you can tell...?" he began. He hoped to learn exactly what this man was trying to forget.

"Not without removing it, and that would cause him to remember," the specialist said, shaking his head.

"And it doesn't do anything else, does it?" Reed wanted to know. "It's not *dangerous* at all?"

"No way to know for sure, but it *looks* normal if that helps." It didn't. Reed stared down at the sleeping face of Bert, a pensive look in his eyes. The only way to know was to remove it, and in doing so it would mean Bert would remember whatever it was.

The other two doctors eyed one another. They wanted to know if they were going to be allowed to continue or not. Bert's chest rose and fell as he breathed normally and he looked deceptively peaceful in the way that most do when benumbed to the world. What had he been trying to forget exactly? Had his captors done this to him for some reason? Reed began to pace up and down, trying to make his mind up. They didn't have to wake him immediately after removing it. They could keep him on ice for a while... giving Reed a longer chance to decide what to do.

"Go ahead, doctors, remove it," Reed instructed, waving his hands at them. "When you're done, *could I ask a favour?*" The lead surgeon paused, machines poised.

"*What?*" he asked, interested.

"Keep him under. At least for a day or so," Reed requested. They looked at one another, shrugged and then nodded. That was an unusual request; most people wanted the patient up and about as quickly as possible.

"Great, thank you so much." As Reed looked on, they began the extraction operation. They didn't seem in the least put off by him being there. It would only take about forty minutes, provided nothing went wrong.

He stared out of the viewport into the clouds, uncertain. *If only* the Viscount had tried to stop the war. There was no guarantee that he could, of course, but this conflict was getting nowhere. Reed strongly suspected that it had gone nowhere by intention. Not the intention of those fighting, no – the intention of whoever was behind the pirates. They'd seen to it that the fighting continued no matter what. Now that he had Satiah out there causing chaos, things were bound to change soon. This change would no doubt take the form of escalation. Satiah was the human equivalent of a catalyst; whatever reactions were going on, she would inevitably speed them up. And as for this Milo Drass business… He sighed, knowing it was selfish of him, but he'd rather Satiah and Darius concentrate on the same thing at the same time rather than dividing their efforts. Still, Satiah always asserted that she worked better alone. This was a bit of a lie, Reed thought. How anyone could work with that thing, *the mountain of metal otherwise known as Kelvin*, and claim to be working *alone*, he wasn't at all sure.

He glanced around, morbid curiosity getting the better of him. The room, already completely sterile, was almost completely white and had bright white lights in each corner in order to give the surgeons the best light cover. Most surgery was carried out by computers and robots but occasionally, when no records were to be taken, actual beings performed the task. Some maintained that it was a science that no machine could ever truly replicate, or at least not achieve in the same way that a living being could. It was part of that age-old battle between living beings and artificial intelligences. They were working quickly and had already gained access to the brain. Reed chanced a peek and could easily make out the dull grey of the implant against the pulp of the organ. A muttered conversation occurred between the surgeons. Reed didn't interrupt, knowing it was best to stay out of it. Once they had finished conferring, the lead surgeon produced a very slender form of pliers and gently gripped the implant.

Reed didn't need to be a doctor to know this was the dangerous bit among dangerous bits. With practised ease, the man slid it out in a slow move, careful to disturb nothing. As he moved away, the second man was quick to move in, ready to begin damage control work on the socket should any be needed. None was. They were a competent team who'd worked together enough to maximise their efficiencies and compensate for their weaknesses. The wound was cleaned and, with some encouragement in the form of *Barnicular-Sealant*, the skull sealed itself up. The implant was placed in a tray and the surgeon turned to Reed.

"Hold this a moment," he said, handing it to him. Reed took it and eyed the remarkably clean and innocent-looking device. It was rectangular, similar to a component from a circuit board. Not unlike a primitive resistor. It was dark grey with silver connectors at one end and the neural emitters in the other. They were often referred to as NEs and were very expensive. They could convert computer programming into brainwaves and broadcast the brainwaves at a level so low that they would be undetectable to anything but the most advanced scanning equipment. The bit in the middle was simply storage.

Each implant would only ever work for one person, as everyone's mind was different, so there was no chance it could be used on anyone else. It could be reprogrammed, of course, but all that would take days. Reed waited until the skull was reassembled and the flesh sealed over it before he asked anything.

"No issues?" he asked, with a heavy sigh.

"No, that was one of the fastest extractions I've ever done… just two minutes behind the record," he replied. Reed hadn't known that they were trying to break anything and was duly thankful to learn that it was only a record.

"You'll need to take that through to the technicians now," he told Reed. Reed gave him a mock salute, bowed his head slightly in thanks and then wandered off in the direction the man had pointed him in. All the while he was wondering what he would see in the implant.

Mostly everyone has an element of interest when it comes to the microcosms of other people's memories. Some more than others obviously, and by that Reed meant that some people were more interesting than others, and also some people were more interested than others. Reed was now intensely interested in what Bert had apparently been so eager to forget that he'd gone to the trouble of using an implant. A highly expensive way around the problem. Reed himself would simply have had a few drinks and the memory would lose itself easily enough. Bert was apparently not an advocate of that method. Each to their own! He entered the laboratory, hoping to find someone unoccupied. On most worlds that would have been a near impossible dream, but not on Collgort-Elispa.

"Can I help?" asked an eager man, almost immediately.

"Yes," smiled Reed, holding the implant up. "I need to see what's on this, is there a way I could do that?"

"Of course, follow me," he said, setting off at a jaunty pace. Reed was led down another corridor and into a room that reminded him of some kind of flight simulator. This would make sense as Reed was essentially going to be immersed in the past, watching from Bert's vantage point as events took place. He would hear, see, smell, taste and feel things exactly as Bert had. It was an interesting way of putting on someone else's shoes. The technician was setting up a few other computers to monitor Reed and record what he was experiencing into a separate database where it could be analysed more closely. There would also be the potential to pick out certain events for later review and mark them accordingly. Memory in itself isn't linear, it jumps around, neither is it always the same *type* of memory.

You can remember something happening. That would be an event. You can also remember recalling something before. This would also be an event. Then you could imagine something entirely fictional. This would be called a dream. Trouble is, you can *remember* dreams *too*. You can remember *recalling* a dream and so on... Memory also subtly changes over time, which is why most specialists state that it is never completely reliable as a form of testimony. They also cautioned people from confusing fantasy with reality, although Reed couldn't remember why. In any case, it was going to be tricky for Reed to truly know which was dream and which had actually happened. The sensations would be real every time. The clock might give clues, for example it may be possible to work out when the subject was asleep and therefore that would tell you if what you were looking at was real or not. And then there was daydreaming… Confident that the specialist at least would have some idea of what was going on, Reed prepared himself mentally for the next challenge.

***

As before, Darius would have much preferred a list of names he could effortlessly look through to find out if he was there or not. Failing that, a selection of mugshots next to the applicable data. No luck here though. There were only a few beds taken in the hospital area, it was mostly empty. As a secret base, aside from the odd illness here and there, there would not be a lot going on and thus fewer injuries received. That was a logical reason to suppose that a young and enthusiastic doctor wouldn't want to stay *here* to work. He would want to be working closer to the main battle or perhaps working with injured refugees. Why would he stay here? Yet Darius knew, somehow he just *knew*, Milo Drass had been on that moon at some point. Even if he wasn't there now, there would be a clue to find. But where else was there to look if it was not to be found in the hospital?

Cherry looked how she felt: like this might all be one huge waste of time.

"Do you think he might be a consultant for something?" she asked, pointing to a screen. "It lists a few consultants up here."

"Are any of them called Milo Drass?" he asked, trying not to sound too irritated.

"…No," she replied, sadly. "But he could be using an alias."

"*Yes*," he hissed, through his teeth. "But without knowing what that *is*…" A door opening and a group of people coming in interrupted him. Darius and Cherry slipped to one side and did a good job of pretending to be studying the screens as the group approached. They were talking about the possibility of an attack on the base. Darius earwigged them and then looked around. As he did, he spotted a woman who, judging by her uniform, had to be the base commander. Her face… it was the face from the picture Satiah had found on Milo's ship. The one that no one could identify. *It was her*! The hair was a different style now and she looked healthier, not being in a hospital bed, but that face and those eyes were exactly the same.

Darius quickly dropped his gaze, careful not to attract attention by staring so openly at her. This changed everything! If Satiah was right about this woman being romantically involved with Milo then it meant he'd never been abducted at all. He'd purposely set things like that to make it *appear* as if someone had snatched him to cover his own tracks. But why would *she* be a secret? She was clearly a Base Commander, roughly equivalent to colonel or even Brigadier General in some forces. Tantamount to Captain in the Coalition navy. Maybe she wasn't *his secret*; it could be the other way around. On the other hand, there was clearly something clandestine going on here, militarily speaking. Why else send eight destroyers to guard one outpost? Perhaps Milo had got involved in some kind of secret operation.

All of this was very helpful and it gave Darius another possible move to make. If he could get hold of her and trick her into talking somehow... No, that would never work. He sighed, steeling himself. This could backfire but if it worked it would save a lot of time. He eyed Cherry.

"Stay here," he said, softly. She scowled, put out.

"Why? *Where are you going*?" she asked, immediately.

"Not sure yet," he replied, grimly. "If it fails, I'm trusting you to help me escape."

"*What?*" she demanded, very frightened suddenly. "*Wait*! Just let's talk about it..." She was talking but he wasn't listening, he was watching, as his target got further away from him. He grabbed her shoulders and shook her.

"Just trust me," he hissed, seriously. Cherry, wide eyed, went quiet. She gave a reluctant half nod and Darius hurried after the group that had just gone out and into another corridor.

Cherry stood there, feeling distinctly unhappy. No wonder no one trusted men, they could hardly communicate! It wasn't even as if she could continue without him, she had no idea what to do. Help him escape? Well... she would try of course, but he would owe her! She didn't have to be here, she could leave anytime she wanted. She had no obligations to him. Okay, Satiah wouldn't like it, but Cherry was sure that if she explained how she had been treated... No, no that wasn't true. She liked Darius. She liked him more than she'd ever admit to anyone, even Satiah. He had been respectful, even good company. Considering all of this, Cherry decided that she had to do something. She began to follow and wished she'd not had to leave her new rifle behind.

Darius turned a corner and could clearly see the huddle moving along ahead of him. He began to follow, his pace just a little faster than theirs. He needed to get her on her own, or at least some distance from the others. He overheard a part of their conversation and someone addressed her as Colonel Celestine. She was talking, her voice slightly too quiet for him to hear.

"Colonel!" he called, loudly. The group all stopped and turned to face him. "I apologise for the interruption but I must speak with you urgently." Celestine seemed to roll her eyes and then look at him more closely. She was starting to realise she didn't recognise him. While it was not impossible that she had staff here she didn't know well, it was improbable she'd missed someone completely.

"What is it?" she asked, curious.

"Confidential, it shouldn't take long," Darius replied, mindful of the others listening in.

"Excuse me a moment, I'll join you in the conference room," she said, to the others.

They moved on as she approached Darius, her expression impassive.

"What is so urgent *Doctor*...?" she demanded, a little impatiently. She wanted him to remind her who he was. It was not good, in her opinion, to be unaware of the names of important personnel. Darius waited until she was close enough for him to grapple with before he answered.

"Where's Milo?" he asked, his tone hard and grave. A flash of alarm in her eyes told him that she knew exactly what he was talking about, but she wasn't going to give up easily.

"What?" she asked, her hand sliding closer to her pistol. "What are you talking about...?" He grabbed her wrist, swung her around and clamped his hand across her mouth. She struggled.

"Listen, it would be better if we didn't have to jump through too many hoops regarding this," Darius growled, in her ear. "I'll be very up front with you. I'm the intruder from last time who broke into your detention area. I'm the man who assaulted your men and smashed through the fence to get out. I'm an operative who is here to find a man called Milo Drass, and I have seen a picture of *you* on his ship. Now, I'm going to let you go if you agree to be sensible. If not, I'll take you to a site where we can continue this conversation in a far less favourable style." Celestine stopped struggling, and nodded. Carefully he released her. She turned to face him, rubbing her wrist.

"I know Milo," she admitted, carefully. "What do you want with him?"

"I'm not here to kill him, if that's what you're thinking. I've been ordered to take him back to his family. He apparently left without telling them where he was going," Darius answered.

She looked relieved for a moment. That surprised him. Just because she wouldn't fight now, didn't mean she'd given up.

"Whom do you work for?" she asked, curious.

"Does it matter? I'm Darius, by the way," he said, trying to give her *something*.

"How did you find this place?" she asked, softly. He guessed it had been *her* that had called Milo to tell him she was on her way.

"It's my job," he shrugged, playing it cool. "Did you ever call Milo on his ship to warn him about *clockwork border patrols*?"

"I think it's encrypted." Milo's voice was saying. He was followed by the oddly computer-like voice.

"You *think*? You had better be sure. If anyone nearby picks you up, I can't promise I will get there in time to protect you."

"I'm still close to the neutral section." Milo again.

"Okay. I won't have long; patrols are like clockwork along the border. There *are* gaps but they are not around for long. I'll be at 8433-1116 in two hours, see you there," *promised Celestine.*

She looked dumbfounded.

"...*It was encrypted,*" she whispered, incredulous. She was remembering the encryption process... seeking a mistake.

"Nothing is ever encrypted well enough," Darius smiled, grimly. She still looked stunned for a moment, then seemed to suddenly realise they were still standing there. In the corridor, in full view of anyone who happened along.

"We should have this conversation somewhere more private," she stated, suddenly looking all around. "*No one else knows he's here and if they found out: I'll be shot.*"

They paced together along the corridor, back the way they had come. They passed by Cherry on the way. Cherry looked bewildered to see them walking together. She fell into step behind them.

"She's with me," Darius stated, when he realised Celestine had noticed they were being followed.

"How many of you are there?" she asked, irritated. It was a bit embarrassing for her to discover that not only was her security not as good as she thought, but also that *she* was the one who'd betrayed the base's location. There was no spy, no careless personnel... only her own actions.

"Just us two, but my superior knows where I am," Darius was quick to add. Celestine wanted to scream at him suddenly. She was furious! She knew she could only blame herself, she had known at the time she had to be careful. She thought she had! Clearly not careful enough.

She couldn't do anything though. Not only might Darius decide to do what he threatened to do, but she knew it was her own fault and that making a fuss was *not* in her interests.

"I'm going to make a call, I need to *explain* my absence or *someone might come looking for me,*" she explained, slowly pulling out her communicator.

"Sure," he said, nodding. Darius planned to be as reasonable to her as she was to him, like always. That was the way he had been taught to treat those he encountered in this fashion. If they did what you told them, they were treated well. If they resisted... well, there was an answer for that too.

"This is Celestine, yes, I'm going to have to try your patience sir," she said, sounding apologetic. "Something has come up and I'll let you know when I'm free again. In the meantime just continue the conference and if I don't make it, send me a recording."

Whoever it was agreed, and she replaced it after showing Darius that she *had* turned it off. Eventually they reached her office. Cherry caught up and joined them inside. Cherry was very relieved; she'd actually been considering stealing a guard's gun or something. It was a cosy office space, dimly lit and neat. Celestine locked them in and deliberately sat on a chair by the wall rather than her own chair which was behind her desk. She had alarm buttons there and she didn't want Darius to think she was just playing along to lull him into a false sense of security.

"I appreciate your cooperation," Darius stated, seeing why she had done that. "I'm sorry for having to do..."

"No, no," she sighed, looking sad. "It's all *our* fault really. You can't help who you fall in love with, can you?"

"*I wouldn't know*," he growled, shrugging. "Where is he?" Something about the way he said *he wouldn't know* made Cherry look at him for a moment. What had *that* meant?

Pensive now in mood, Celestine looked into the middle distance and let out a long slow breath.

"I was dying when we met last year. I didn't know straightaway who he was, *I just remembered...* his hand. His hand on mine. Being connected to someone when you think it's the end... It made a lasting impression on *me*," she began, a little self-deprecatingly. Darius didn't let his exasperation show. He didn't think she was playing for time or anything; she was just working through her shock at being caught by reliving a good memory. Maybe she thought he would take pity on her if she gave him a bit of a story.

"I decided that whoever this man was, I loved him more than *anyone I'd ever known* before," she went on. "I'm a soldier and I've done well in my career *so far...*" She shot them a rueful smile as she said that, meaning that her continued success was now hanging by a thread. "...Anyway, I never knew he was rich or clever or so *irresponsibly caring* so... when I told him about my feelings, he was just as love struck. I was the first woman to say they loved him without knowing who his father was."

Cherry, also listening, had no idea what to make of what she was hearing. Falling in love with a man still made her feel very uncomfortable. She knew it was just residual though, and that the more she heard the more she'd learn. Darius was much more cynical, as expected. Some kind of Nightingale effect or Transference must have occurred, Darius thought. The problem of people falling in love with their doctors or vice versa was an age-old issue. Many books and ethical guidelines had been created to deal with the matter, but none of them had ever managed to stop it completely. He didn't mention it to her obviously, not when things were going so much better than they could have.

"Why did you make his disappearance look like a kidnapping?" Darius asked, although he thought he could guess. Trying to throw potential investigators onto the wrong tracks had evidently been their strategy. It had certainly worked out that way.

"Someone as, for want of a better word, *famous* as him, couldn't just abscond or run away... So, one night, we stayed up late and planned the whole thing. I even left a tranquilliser behind to give the impression that someone had drugged him. It was a stratagem to lead anyone trying to find him down the wrong lines of enquiry." Nice touch, Darius thought to himself.

"It did throw us for a while," Darius told her.

"I'm fighting a war and... *no one else knows he is here*. Every day I was getting more and more worried that *someone* would find out I was keeping him here. It would be the end of my career if they did..." She trailed off and stared right into Darius's eyes.

"No one *here* will know if you let us take him back, you career will be saved from that," Darius stated, seriously. "And it doesn't mean you'll never see each other again. He just needs to *straighten out his own affairs properly*."

"I know... And I think I now understand something else..." she mused.

"What?" That question came from Cherry who was starting to get impatient.

"Milo told me that him and his father do not exactly gel well," she said, waggling her hand to demonstrate a problematic affiliation. "And his father is one of the richest people alive."

"So?" Cherry asked, bluntly.

"Milo gave me something," she said, pulling down her tunic's neckline. Against her skin was a chain necklace with a large red diamond surrounded in cubic zirconia. "If his father is behind you, it will be *this* he wants, not his son." Cherry had never seen anything like that before, and couldn't help but stare in fascination at the jewel. Darius was not so impressed, however, having seen many in his lifetime.

"Family heirloom?" Darius guessed, seeing it all now. Indeed he'd seen this *particular stone* before too… in his research.

"Milo said he knew exactly what it was worth but he would rather give it to me… At the time, I was so shocked I couldn't refuse it. I wanted to. Besides anything else, it's just something else for me to have to hide, but I couldn't hurt his feelings. And it is a lovely looking rock."

It was called the One-Eyed Lady but was also known as the Red Claddagh and was worth almost one billion Essps… As gifts went it was pretty formidable. And yet Celestine didn't really want it. She just wanted Milo, but all this secrecy had made her life a bit of a misery. Darius understood the implications. She had to keep it on her so that he wouldn't be offended, no one else found it and it didn't disappear. Yet she could never show it to anyone, or even tell anyone she had it.

"That may be true, but it's Milo himself I've been told to retrieve," Darius reminded her. "Where is he?" Celestine was about to answer when she was interrupted.

"He's here!" said a voice from behind them. A young man, Milo Drass, moved into the room. The wall was actually a panel leading into a secret room beyond.

"Sorry…" Celestine began, to him.

"We *knew* it might happen," he said, forgivingly. "Don't worry, this is still saveable."

"*You* have caused me a lot of trouble," Darius told him, raising an eyebrow. "…"

"I'm not going *anywhere* with you. My father has never cared about anyone other than *himself*. You can leave and tell him I'm alive if you like, but I'm not going back, and neither is Celestine's necklace," Milo stated, stubbornly.

"Milo... I have been ordered to..." Darius began, calmly. It wasn't as if they were likely to call for help, but that didn't mean other people might be alerted if it came to a fight.

"*I don't care*," he snapped, defensively. He sat next to Celestine and put his arm around her protectively. "You can't make me do anything." Darius's eyes narrowed.

∗∗∗

Reed wasn't answering. That was not a good sign, normally he answered... even if he didn't always *listen*. Satiah hoped Rainbow would find where this mysterious cult was hiding. The pirates probably didn't know themselves, and what had happened to that blasted gold? One thing was for sure, they couldn't stay where they were.

"We find out when the next departure is and, *no matter where it is going*, we sneak aboard," Satiah said, slowly. "Then we hijack it if we can, and after that, if Rainbow can figure out where to go next... we go there."

"And the gemstone?" Kelvin asked, as she knew he would.

"We will deal with that *later*," she said, briskly. She moved ahead of him, not wanting to revisit the subject. She would just have to remember not to touch it with her bare hands. A gunshot made her stop. It was distant, possibly as far as three hundred metres away. Another!

"Scanning," Kelvin informed, without her having to ask.

More laser fire, this time closer.

"They are fighting each other," Kelvin surmised. Satiah pulled a face. The saying *pirates will be pirates* didn't somehow cover this scenario well enough for her. Perhaps, as Kyle their leader was dead, a battle of succession had broken out, or an argument over what to do about it. Either way, it was the first good thing that had happened for a while.

"They're not under attack from anyone else?" she queried, seeking clarity. A rare commodity in her business.

"No, there have been no arrivals," he reported.

"...I wonder how long it will take and who will win," she muttered, unable to stop herself smiling broadly. The less of them that survived, the better, as far as she was concerned. Quint would probably not find out Kyle had been killed because of her being there, he'd most likely blame the pirates. From what she'd learned, it was apparent to anyone that Kyle was hardly popular among them.

"In light of this, a new plan! Steal a ship and escape," she shrugged, casually. "Everyone will assume we are just pirates fleeing the fight." She kicked the hatch open and they moved out into a corridor. Laser damage was plain to see on the walls and there were two bodies at the end.

"Three to right and one to left," Kelvin warned. Satiah crouched and then turned the corner. She could see three of them and dropped them instantly with precision shooting. The forth just started running, not even bothering to fight it out. Smoke was now visible in the air and a small explosion sounded. Satiah scowled. Who would be stupid enough to use grenades or explosives in this kind of place? Pirates! Who else?

"Back to the hangar," she instructed to Kelvin. He took the lead.

The door ahead of them unsealed slowly to unveil the real firefight. Apparently, everyone had had the same idea – get a ship and get out. The place they entered had once been the makeshift shipyard, a place for maintenance of ships and their components alike. Walkways crisscrossed each other at two levels of catwalks and higher viaducts. Now it was a warzone and this myriad of skyways made a haven for snipers. Satiah took cover behind a container, and Kelvin began using his repeating lasers to clear the immediate enemies. He was hit too, several times, but his armour prevented any real damage. Satiah poked her head up and sought a target of her own. A helmeted head slowly rose into view, using a support beam as cover. *Wait for a target,* she thought to herself. It lowered again and she smirked. Fire was the response from Kelvin, as he switched to his second appendage and his customary weapon.

A burning, screaming figure, still running in mid-air as it

plummeted down from the walkway, narrowly missed another lower catwalk. Satiah hauled herself on top of the container and used her grapple gun to drag herself upward and onto the highest walkway. She scissor kicked over the railing and crouched with her pistol at the ready. A masked figure slowly turned to face her but she unleashed two bolts into him before he had time to bring his rifle to bear. She sprinted forward, going for his rifle. She could hear Kelvin's repeating lasers hammering away, and then whooshes of fire below her. She snatched up the rifle and aimed at movement she saw. Two people running. She managed to take one out with a shoulder shot. The second made it to cover. A blast struck the railing she was leaning on and she hit the floor to avoid the next shot.

She began to crawl forward to the next gap in the grating. As she reached it, the second shot struck and she flinched from the blast. She backtracked, trying to return the way she had come, only for the same thing to happen. She was pinned and she couldn't even find the shooter! Besides her tiny bit of cover, the rest was open ground and she'd be picked off easily if she moved. There were a couple of things she could try, but none were exactly ideal. She noticed the metal sheet that the first man had been using as cover and grabbed it. It was thick, and while awkward to carry it, it was light enough for her. She rose, using it as a shield. As she ran for cover the metal pane she was using was hit twice and both times it nearly knocked her off of her feet. Life wasn't a noun, it was a verb, because it was always moving or basically, if you want to stay alive, then you should keep moving. She reached the safety of the final group of containers and gladly dropped the metal slab. She wrenched her pistol back out and crept towards the end of the container.

The sniper, wherever they were, should still be able to cover the entrance to the main hangar area. A place she would have to pass through and out in the open. She could still hear shooting from inside. They would be waiting for her to make her move too. And she had to get down two floors... There was the ladder, *again* in a completely exposed area. Gradually she inched around to get a look. There he was, slouched against a support column, rifle pointed right at her. She backed off quickly in case he noticed her. The gunfire in the background had died down now to virtually nothing. Kelvin might have already secured a ship. She gripped her pistol more firmly and prepared herself for a lightning fast shot. She visualised exactly where he was, in her mind, and worked from memory to decide exactly when to pull the trigger.

She moved, spinning out and unleashing four shots. As she was still moving she noticed two things. Firstly, her target was no longer there, *he'd* moved. Second, another figure was crawling across the ceiling towards her. Gritting her teeth, she retreated back behind the container just as a blast from rifle struck the walkway where she'd been. *Great!* Now there were two of them. She crouched and stared directly upward, awaiting her next visitor. To her surprise, there was a shot from the sniper and a scream as the man creeping across the ceiling plummeted down to the floor. Apparently they had not been working together. Seizing her chance, she raced out from cover and used her grapple gun. This time she swung off the catwalk and across the open area, down onto the area directly beneath the sniper.

He let off one shot but had to crouch to avoid Satiah's shots. Now she had *him* pinned, as opposed to the other way around. She fired a shot at what might have been his boot. No reaction. She could run now, before he realised she was no longer watching him. She could probably make it into the hangar area before he'd realised she'd gone. No... this man was good enough to realise she would try that. She propped up a crate with a discarded opening bar, a long pole of metal, with a serrated edge at one end, used to ease open sealed containers. Finely balanced, she judged that if that man moved at all, it would fall loudly. Very slowly she began to back away, careful not to dislodge it herself. All it would take was one careless step or even a transference of weight and it would fall. Still she backed away, pistol still trained on the column he was concealed behind.

The crate fell with a crash and she fired but he didn't appear to take a shot at her. Using a grapple gun of his own, the man swung outwards in a tight arch, away from her and landed further down the walkway. She didn't fire again; it would be a wasted shot. She instead took her chance and slid down the ladder, using her boots and her hands to squeeze the outside of the ladder. It was a short descent; nonetheless, her hands were already burning when she reached the bottom. She dived behind the nearest cover, a cleaning unit of some variety, to ensure he had the smallest amount of time to target her back. She turned when behind it, putting her back to the hangar bay door. If anyone came out she'd be completely exposed but she trusted that Kelvin had cleared that area of any wayward pirates.

A laser bolt hit something above her, showering her with shards of glass and sparks. The next bolt took the head off of the unit itself and made her duck instinctively. He was cutting down her cover, trying to hammer his way through and his rifle was powerful enough to manage that. She leapt behind the adjoining supporting buttress. The firing stopped. He'd need a rocket or missile to get through that layer of solid metal. Now, though, she was within spitting distance of the hangar door, but it was still in the open. She would *still* have to cross his sights. She strained her ears, hoping that he would take the opportunity to move closer. If he was approaching, he had to be particularly light-footed. She heard nothing. She glanced up again, trying to think of another way around this. There was always the temptation to just make a run for it, but that was rarely a smart move when snipers of this quality were around.

She slipped her specs on and switched to heat seeking mode. There he was, a patch of dotty orange and yellowy red. He wasn't moving. She flicked through various settings and found what she was looking for... *stream paint*. A coating of material used to protect metal against all forms of corrosion and... *most usefully*... it had the durability to deflect laser fire when fired at an angle of *less than* thirty degrees. She made calculations, all the while conscious of him remaining in place. It wouldn't work. He was in the wrong position. Assuming the bolt did actually ricochet in the exact way she hoped, it would hit the column to the left of him. But then her plan was never to hit him, just get him to think there was *someone else* shooting at him. She fired twice and then turned to fire directly at him.

The bolts hit the pillar and he whirled, seeking the other enemy he'd not spotted before. There was no one there to find and the next bolt, direct from Satiah's pistol, took him in the shoulder. He was rocked backward by the kinetic force of the blast on his armour. Her next shot, this time more accurate, kissed his helmet, and the third struck him right in the larynx. His last breath left his body in the guise of smoke as he collapsed onto the metal floor heavily. Intrigued by the talents of her downed opponent, using her grapple gun, she was quick to arrive by the body. She kicked the rifle aside, taking no chances. This man had been far too good to be just a pirate. She pulled off the helmet and scanned him with her specs. Nothing obvious but Rainbow could do the rest.

Flying back down again with the aid of her grapple gun, she bolted into the hangar area. Littered with bodies and burning wreckage, the place looked completely different from when she had first arrived there hours ago. Kelvin was waiting for her in the entrance to a freighter. She darted over to him.

"I think I just cut through a Federation agent," she explained, seriously. "That sniper was far too good to be a regular pirate."

"The ship is clear," was his reply. They entered the control room and she instantly started powering up the drives. As craft went this was the most average anyone could find. Spinning, the ship twisted around in the narrow gap between two other ships and shot out into space.

***

It had been a few minutes since anyone had spoken. Celestine had gone. She had appearances to maintain, and they were all safely ensconced in the secret room. That last thing any of them wanted was any other people getting curious as to what was taking her so long! It had once been a storage room that she'd surreptitiously removed from the blueprints of the structure. Gradually, over the months, people had completely forgotten it was even there. At first she'd intended to use it as a getaway area for herself. A place to go and distance herself from her stress and find some peace. More recently, though, it had become home for Milo and her. There was a bed, obviously, a table, and two chairs. Everything was all pure functionality, as there was no room for anything they didn't absolutely need.

Milo lay on the bed, staring at the ceiling. Darius and Cherry were sitting opposite one another at the table. Cherry was staring at Darius, watching him as he thought hard about his new problem. She felt a sudden desire to laugh and didn't hide it well enough to avoid him noticing.

"What's the joke?" he grumbled.

"Nothing," she said, a bit sheepishly.

"No, no, you nearly laughed just then, out with it," he said, smiling a little.

"It's just… you and Satiah… all that fighting to save this guy who may or may not have been alive… you find him, only to discover that he doesn't want to be rescued," she said, sniggering. His smile faded.

"Yes, *hysterical*," he mumbled, returning to his thoughts.

Forcing Milo wasn't an option. He had to find a way of persuading him to come voluntarily. Celestine wouldn't be a problem. Darius actually got the impression that she would prefer it if he was away for a while. Then she could hush up all this controversy about infiltrators *without* harbouring one of her own. Cherry wasn't done though.

"Come on, you must see the funny side?" she insisted, grinning. "You have all these theories about him being abducted by pirates or being employed in some kind of secret medical experiment and in reality he's…"

"Cherry, people could have died because those two decided to run off together," he growled, irritated. "And they still might. We can't have been the only ones to pick up on their encrypted conversation. The enemy *really might* pinpoint this base."

"…You're just cross because he wasted so much of your *time*," Cherry surmised, pouting.

"Is there any chance you could focus less on the comedy of the situation and more on a *solution*?" he asked, smiling tightly at her.

"You have to take him back, *that's your mission*. He doesn't want to go and you're not in a position to force him." She shrugged after thinking about it. "He came all this way for *Celestine*, right? Maybe *take her* and he will chase you?" Darius hadn't actually considered that, but the chaos it would cause would not be worth the prize. He had been thinking along the lines of bribing Milo somehow. With what? The guy hardly needed or wanted money! He'd also really started to wish this business with Milo was over and he could concentrate on what Satiah was working on. This seemed like a very tedious sideshow now that the truth of the matter had been dredged up. Cherry seemed to take his silence as a sign of disappointment.

"We could get Celestine to play along with us, not by *threatening* her, but by promising that things will work out how she wants…" Cherry went on, starting to realise that might be easier said than done. They didn't know how Celestine wanted things. Darius wondered if Milo had an ego he could use. If he could be *goaded* to work with them… There was clearly no love lost between him and his father. Perhaps he might be interested in bragging about what he had done face to face? And if Celestine had been right about the necklace being what his father actually wanted…

"I know what I'll do," Darius stated, with finality. She looked up at him expectantly. He didn't tell her though. He'd have to talk to Dyss. Once Dyss could report to the father that Milo was indeed alive but refused to come back it might change things. Trouble was that Dyss could say it made no difference, as the objective was to bring Milo back; he might even refuse to answer completely. Darius didn't think Satiah would have time to referee this one, not with everything else she was dealing with.

"*What?*" Cherry asked, progressively exasperated with the silence. "Fine… I don't care." She crossed her arms, shrugged and looked away to display her apparent disinterest.

"Call Dyss," he smiled, at her. "This is just the sort of thing that *really* winds him up." She eyed him subtly and then studied her nails as if hardly listening. She was a terrible actress. He made the call. Dyss answered.

"Milo is alive and I've found him," Darius said, getting straight to the point. There was a staggered silence. Dyss had been expecting the worst.

"…Very good," Dyss managed, at last. His voice sounded funny just for a second there, like a computer or something, it had to be interference. Dyss didn't sound *that* angry yet, but he couldn't bring himself to congratulate Darius.

"I have a problem though," Darius elaborated. He explained the scenario accurately and without an opinion. Darius was himself surprised by Dyss's lack of rage.

"… *I see*," he replied, after a thoughtful pause. "So you think this necklace is the cause of all this?"

"Has the father been behaving like someone *worried for his son's life?*" Darius asked, meaningfully.

"No," Dyss replied, sagely. "His mother though… Have you tried reminding him that he has *other* family *besides* his father and the least he could do is call them? You might be able to use that as a gateway for further gestures." Darius raised an impressed eyebrow and scratched his moustache. He hadn't thought of that. Emotional blackmail, always fun.

"I'll run through it," he said.

"Does Satiah know?" Dyss asked, curious.

"No, I've not spoken with her," Darius told him.

"*I see*," he said, again. He sounded like he was engrossed in something else or distracted in some way or other. Darius listened intently but couldn't hear anything going on in the background. Why wasn't Dyss ranting about something? He usually went into a rant or a criticism. Silence was unnerving.

"Was there anything else?" Dyss asked, at last. Again that slight change in voice… Was Darius imagining it?

"No, thanks for the input," Darius responded, and cut off. He frowned deeply. He became aware of Cherry staring at him intently. She was dying to know what they were going to try next but too obstinate to ask. Darius approached Milo and took a deep breath.

"I know you and your father don't see eye to eye and I can see *why* you've done this," Darius began, trying to sound empathic. Milo sat up. "*What about your mother?* She's been worried about you, why haven't you called her; it's free to do that?"

"We are in the middle of a secret army base that operates in *radio silence*," he pointed out, seriously. Darius handed Milo his communicator.

"Use *this*," he instructed, grimly. "It will not be detected."

Milo took it slowly.

"Are you trying to manipulate me?" he frowned, eyeing the older man. Darius shrugged.

"You're a doctor, right? I honestly thought you would have more compassion," Darius smirked, bitingly. "I suppose I was wrong, not the first time, my apologies." He began to withdraw, snatching the communicator back deftly. Milo stood as if to go after him – clearly torn, he looked at Cherry. To her credit, she just stared at him as if disappointed and shook her head slowly to indicate how shaming his behaviour was, in her opinion. Darius sat opposite her again and also stared, his eyes and face hard as metal. Milo put his hands on his hips and started to laugh shakily.

"I know what you're doing and it won't work," he said, wavering.

"I'm sure *you do* but your mother doesn't," Cherry stated, softly. "When you left… I shouldn't need to tell you how worried, *how sick* you made her."

Darius was pleased by Cherry at that moment. That was both highly manipulative and completely true. Milo took another step towards the table, eyeing the communicator.

"And that thing won't give our location away?" he clarified, seeking an easy escape.

"No," Dyss shrugged. "But that shouldn't matter, as you *didn't* want to use it?"

"What I *want* doesn't matter, *it never has until recently*," he raged suddenly. His buttons had evidently been pushed now. "My father had done his relentless best to *ruin my life!*" It took a lot of effort for Darius not to roll his eyes.

"We're not asking you to call *him*," Cherry stated, calmly.

"But when I talk to my mother *she* will then talk to *him* and he…" he began, levelly.

"What are you afraid of, Milo?" Darius enquired, interested. "If it's your father, he can't get you here. If it's losing Celestine's respect or love, I *really* don't think that's going to happen."

"This is none of your business…" he began, trying to get out of it.

"*You made this* our business," Darius argued, seriously. "If you have an ambassador for a father and then you go missing, regardless of what *he* does about it, it's going to have implications at a *very high level. You* are a security risk. Frankly you're a security risk – not only to the Coalition government but also to your girlfriend's government too."

"*Not now that they know I'm safe!*" Milo shouted.

"But you're *not* safe, Milo," Cherry stated, very laid back. "Neither you nor Celestine are safe. Just the way things are should tell you *that*." Milo, for whatever reason, seemed much less able to argue against Cherry than he could Darius. Darius wondered if she was aware that she was pulling off a very good joint questioning. Darius was in the role of bad and Cherry was in the role of good. It was time to ramp up and move onto the idiom of incentive and correction.

Incentive and correction, also known as *the carrot and stick*, is a technique used to induce good behaviours or better reactions. A system of rewards and punishments are used to help facilitate this.

"If you don't come with us, and return that property of your family, you're potentially going to ruin your girlfriend's career," Darius told him, before he could reply to Cherry. "*You* would have a criminal record as a thief. It would be down to the legal system when it came to the sentencing, but I don't think they would exercise leniency – not when their own society's security was threatened. And have you even thought about all those lives that would be wasted because you're *not there* to save them? Not there because you are imprisoned or still in hiding."

"Look, it's not *that*. I wanted this to..." Milo began, struggling now to keep pace.

"We understand how sometimes people can lose control of things *as they happen*. How things can run away with you, and before you know it you're *way* out of your depth. *It's not too late, Milo*! If you're prepared to do the right thing then we *can* resolve this."

That came from Cherry. Darius realised that she was a natural at this. *Manipulation*. She was good at understanding how to win people around to her way of thinking using social influences. Her strength seemed to lie in partial reinforcement strategy. She was constructing a climate of doubt, in this case *self-doubt*, and she was forcing him to question himself.

"...Maybe I *shouldn't* have taken the necklace, but I wanted Celestine to know *how much* I think of her," Milo was saying.

"If you love her, you should help her by taking this pressure off her," Cherry shrugged, so extraordinarily nonchalant. Darius began to suspect that she had been playing dumb this entire time. She was better than some apparent *professionals* he'd encountered. "You're hurting her by staying here with this hanging over you."

"...*I know*," he sighed, rubbing his face with his hands. Darius gave Cherry a 'why am *I* here?' look and she frowned in apparent puzzlement. Did she not know what she had just done?

Darius decided to leave her to it and just sat there looking stony and stern. It was not hard for him to look like that.

"Why don't we wait for Celestine to come back and then we will talk about it some more? Then, *if we are agreed*, with her help, we *can* get you home," Cherry stated, seriously. Darius wondered what would happen if they *didn't* agree but still said nothing. Milo nodded slowly. In truth, he was most likely just trying to find a way of getting rid of *them* as he was in a similar position. He couldn't force anything on them either. Celestine's position had effectively immobilised everyone. And it was the case that Celestine was the one who had the most to lose in all this.

"Okay, that's *reasonable*," Milo said, seeing sense at last. His former defensiveness had been born out of panic at his own discovery after a period of drawn out morbid expectancy.

Milo sat down on the bed to mull it over.

"I saw what you were doing there, *very* crafty tactics," Darius congratulated, quietly.

"*What?*" she asked, suspicious. "I was just trying to help, and *you* were too…" She stopped herself from saying *stupid*. "*Aggressive*," she finally settled on. "You were being too harsh. You were never going to win him around."

"I was *not* aggressive," he stated, playfully becoming argumentative.

"Whatever," she muttered, shrugging. "At least Milo is thinking about going along with you now."

"For *now*,' he allowed, being pessimistic.

***

"His name is Nerva and he works for the Primary Agency of Investigation," Randal said, slowly. Satiah groaned and ran a hand through her hair. He was talking about the operative she had just been forced to kill.

"Was and worked," she corrected, feeling very guilty. "I just killed him." There was a silence.

"*Ah…*" Randal said. "I was not aware of any operatives from PAI in the area."

"How could you be? We didn't even *know* there was a pirate base there! *This* is why we need to share information with each other! This constant rivalry is not helpful…" she ranted, angrily.

"It's fine, we'll sort it this end, *don't worry about it*, keep going," he replied, trying to calm her down.

"*He* shot at *me* first," she insisted, honestly. "And he didn't even have to! You need to find out what he was doing there and what we've just messed up!"

Randal sighed. Primary Agency of Investigation were a rival intelligence agency that also operated for the Coalition. Older and more established than Phantom Squad or Division Sixteen, they had many operatives working all over the cosmos. In the days of the Earth Empire they had been known as Internal Security & Intelligence or ISI. It was always something that made Satiah exasperated, how the same departments could have so many names! As their work was secret, in very much the same way as Phantom Squad's was, they did not like dealing with them. Every year there was always some incident where they got in each other's way, simply because they never shared any intelligence unless they had to. It was not a good working relationship. The operatives themselves were not all bad and some were very proficient. The problem was the leadership. They were too possessive, too pedantic and too politically tangled to be of much use to anyone.

"I'll take care of it," Randal promised. Satiah had gone to Randal with this after deciding that Rainbow had enough on his plate. Besides… Randal had offered her help if she needed it.

"Thanks," she murmured, eyeing the screens. The fuel was only at forty percent.

"How are things going with Dyss?" he asked, as she had been waiting for.

"So far it's been less than great, but there's nothing unusual about that," she replied, trying not to sound too resentful. "Any news on the gold?" This gold business was starting to become a bit of a bad joke. No one seemed to know where it had ended up.

"No, the search is continuing, I'll let you know if they find it," he replied, sounding concerned. "I've let the company know and smoothed things out with them. They were very cool about it; I suspect they have lost cargos before."

"In this place, I would *not* be surprised."

Actually, since taking the ship, a stroke of good fortune had occurred. Whoever had been piloting the ship last had failed to erase the flight computer records. Kelvin had analysed the data and, using fuel readings, astronomical zonal knowledge, and other records they had chronicled from the main base computer, he'd been able to create a map of pirate movements. They had several bases and, while some of the movement was random, most seemed to follow a pattern. Supplies, security patrols etc. The only time there was any deviation from this was when the pirates attacked Collgort-Elipsa or a warship was in the area. With this new information they were now moving to infiltrate the next pirate base along. They would be there in less than an hour.

"Thanks for finding that out, Randal," she said, and meant it. It was, in a way, a good thing. The idea that it could have been anyone didn't sit well with her. She liked to know everything about her enemies. Who doesn't?

"Not a problem... *not a problem right now, anyway*," Randal replied, as if he was preoccupied. "Let me know if you need anything else."

"Will do," she said, and disconnected. Slowly she turned to face Kelvin's red eyes. "Whoops," she said, sourly.

"You are blameless," he stated, not just because he was trying to make her feel better. Technically he was right. The other operative had shot at her first although, given the situation, he was hardly to blame for that. He had had to assume she was a pirate... Just like she had had to assume he was too. There had been no time to think anything else.

"Bunch of gobermouches," she muttered, referring to the PAI.

***

Virtual reality was one thing; someone's memories were something else. Reed had struggled with direction at first. Using a complicated filtration application, he'd gradually been able to get to what he thought were the important parts. A lot of it had turned out to be important. The implant had been *very* cleverly programmed to inhibit only certain memories. Not too many, or it might have alerted the patient. If sizeable chunks of time were noticeably passing *without* being in any way remembered, it might cause the subject to think they had some kind of neurological disorder. If a portion of memory removed was above a certain duration, the implant would instil false memories to cover itself. It really was a brilliant device, however misused one might argue it had become. Nevertheless, what Reed was witnessing would be the sort of thing a lot of people would greatly want to forget.

The Cult of Deimos was very real and *Doctor Clark had been a member*. For about three years he had attended secret gatherings in a place called the Hellion. He'd seen sacrifices, murders and acts of such stomach-wrenching debauchery that Reed had initially wondered if the man was quite sane. Unfortunately, it was beyond doubt that he was. Absorbed in Bert's memories for hours, Reed learned a great deal. Bert himself had never actually partaken in the acts themselves but he was party to them through his silence. *Silence*: a conspiracy among conspiracies. Reed watched as people came and went, some he even *recognised*. Politicians, leading scientists, beings of great prominence, they made up the ranks of this abhorrent guild. They seemed to be involved in everything from trafficking and drug smuggling to gunrunning and market manipulation.

There was too much, literally *too much there* in three years for Reed to get his head around. Despite his horror and righteous rage, he concentrated on the issue at hand. Less than two months ago, Bert seemed to have had an attack of conscience. Reed already knew that leaving the cult was not an option. Once you were in you stayed that way or you died, it had been spelt out to Bert when he had joined. It was that simple. Bert had run... He couldn't sleep – perhaps tortured by his memories – and so he ordered the construction of the implant. *They* had been after him and he had allowed himself to forget... *What an idiot!* Reed couldn't believe how stupid this man was. Leaving aside everything he had allowed to happen, *all those despicable crimes*, he'd then made himself an easy target. How could you expected to hide from an enemy that you did not remember? Maybe that was his intention: to be found and killed. Was he punishing himself?

Reed recognised Purella because of Satiah's description. There she was, finding and capturing Bert and taking him... where? *Why had she not killed him?* Then Reed worked out why. The cult would want to execute him, as they viewed him as a traitor *to them*. His attempt to flee had clearly been taken *very* personally. Why had he left? Why had he run? Guilt? There was nothing in the memories that gave Reed a definitive answer in regard to what Bert was actually thinking. The fact that he'd been forced to hide his own recollections told Reed that Bert had a bleeding heart but why had he left? He'd been a part of that vile thing for a long time... there must have been something that tipped the balance. Outweighed the benefits. Gave him a reason to want change... *perhaps change itself*. Was it because the cult had a new member? *A man in a white mask... him*. He was significant. And there was a name too... *Quint*. That also tallied with what Satiah had found out.

But what had he done? What had Quint done? Reed went back over it, going deeper, calling on all his wits to uncover the truth through this mesh of false flashbacks and the real reminiscences. Bert had had a wife... she was dead. Dead on the floor. She hadn't known he was a part of the cult... had she found out? Bert was a coward but he didn't have it in him to kill someone, so that meant someone else did it for him. Or in spite of him. Quint? No... *Purella*. She did it, she strangled her... and he came in but couldn't do anything. Quint was there. There was an argument. First it had become apparent that his wife had found out about the cult because Bert had been talking in his sleep. Another sign of a restless integrity battling to do the right thing against all the odds. Then... what about the body? What had they done with it? Reed knew already... she was *in* the wall. Immured behind the metal just like a memory that wasn't wanted. Reed went cold all over.

Bert had then decided that he couldn't forgive or forget this and could think of only one thing to do before they decided he was a liability. *He would run*. Then his conscience had *really* kicked in with the face of his dead wife, *pale and ghostly*, haunting him. Dredging up all the other faces he'd seen slain in the most terrible and wicked ways, dread had engulfed him. There was no one to confide in, no one to talk to. He was drinking, taking drugs, anything he could to block out the pain. *It was not enough*. It felt like his mind was trying to kill him. So he had the implant made. And then, when what he'd done had become apparent to the cult... Purella had been sent to get him. A tear ran down Reed's face. How could anyone condone such heartless cruelty? He knew the answer to that, of course, but for anyone who knew the difference between right and wrong this was too much to tolerate.

Reed had had to stay focussed. He had to tell *Satiah* and give her something she could use. The cult was behind the war; he needed to stop the war. Where were those snakes hiding? *The Hellion*. A bastion to all that was them. As evil as it was humanly possible to become. Systematically tainting the lives of the innocent. Where was the Hellion? Reed pushed himself again, feeling dirty and sullied, as he mentally forced his way through scenes of unspeakable remembrances. A fortress... a *ruined* fortress. Where? There was something blocking that... a blank area that he couldn't get through. Maybe he'd erased it somehow. Reed went back, thinking of another way. The journey to it, seeking the coordinates on the computer screen. The screen was blank too... but the ship was there. Bert had glanced out of the view port of the spaceship that he had been on at the time and Reed could see what he had seen. *A stellar conjunction*! That might be enough. Reed added the image to the data cube he was preparing for Satiah.

He felt drained as he turned everything off and just sat there for a moment, wishing he could unsee what he had seen. He might have to go back into it at some point, but he'd had more than enough at that moment. He leaned back in the chair, pale and shaky. It was not like watching a program on a screen, it had been like living through it. Traumatising. He sipped the warm drink that someone had brought him at some stage and eyed the data cube. He took a few minutes to compose himself and made the call. Satiah answered quickly.

"Listen, Reed," she began, immediately. "Darius was right, there *is* an insider there. It's a man called Administrator Bavon..."

"Satiah..." he interjected, bleakly. "*I know where they are.*"

"*Reed*, are you listening?" she demanded, sounding testy. "You must arrest him and interrogate him at once, he may know..."

"*Satiah*," he said again, and just started talking.

Satiah listened as Reed explained. Bert had been a member of the Cult of Deimos. They had killed his wife and he had fled but he'd been unable to live with himself without the aid of a memory inhibiting implant. The cult, clearly not fans of loose ends, had sent Purella after him to bring him back for a ceremonial execution. He was unsure as to why it had been delayed for over a week. They had a location where they met, a place called the Hellion. He didn't know which planet it was on but he had a picture of a constellation that she might be able to use to pinpoint it. Satiah updated him on what little she had learned from the pirate base again and included what she now knew about *Bavon*. Finally there was a silence. Reed felt completely exhausted and rather wretched. As if he too had stood by while those things had happened...

Satiah was aware that Reed must have suffered. There were words of comfort she could say but she opted for blunt truth instead. She needed him to be concentrating.

"There's no point in me telling you anything, Reed: you'll just have to get used to it," she said, sympathetically. "I cannot even tell you that what you saw was as bad as it gets, because it's not."

"...*I know*..." he replied, darkly. "I just didn't like seeing something that I could do nothing to stop."

"What will you do about Bavon?" she asked, changing the subject.

"Well, I don't know, I'm not even sure what to do about Bert," he replied, changing it back unhelpfully.

"He's *still* a target for Purella," she reminded him. "Keep him asleep. He will only be tortured by his memories again should you wake him up."

"*He deserves to be*," Reed stated, sounding unusually harsh.

She shrugged.

"We both know people rarely get what they deserve, they just get what they get. It's not right or even funny but that's the way it is. There's nothing you can do about it," she told him, softly.

"*I'm sorry*," he said, suddenly snapping out of it. The old Reed was back, smiles and all. "I shouldn't have... never mind. Bavon is our man then, is he?"

"Yes," she said. She couldn't help but smile, hearing the change in him, even though she knew he couldn't see her. Reed was Reed and she still didn't know if he was soft or hard inside, even after all this. But just for a moment then she felt she glimpsed a darker side to him. Not evil... just angry.

"Any thoughts on proving it?" he asked, hopefully.

"Any smart questions like: *how would I know?*" she smiled back. "*Trust me, it's him.* You want proof; *you'll* have to catch him somehow. Don't do that cloaked ship thing again though, Quint saw right through it. And don't forget to warn the Captain that he could be in trouble."

"Yes…" Reed mused, considering what to do. The Viscount had to do something soon. He knew Pat would expect him to talk with her rather than go directly to the Viscount, but Pat was becoming increasingly hesitant about everything. Cutting her out of the loop though, might have consequences. How could he draw Bavon out? Even if Bavon was stupid, *Quint* certainly wasn't. He began to wonder how they intended to destroy the Federation ship. Bavon might try to get aboard. Reed called the Captain to warn him that they now knew whom the insider was, but couldn't prove it.

***

Satiah looked at the constellation while Kelvin worked out where in the cosmos it was. If it didn't appear on the charts, if it was outside of known space, then they would have nothing. Kelvin turned to her, he'd found it.

"The Kinkarren constellation," he explained, simply. Now he said that, she could see it but it was upside-down. It had once been one of the centres of the Kinkarren Confederacy, the fourth superpower that had been destroyed at the end of the Common Protectorate War about ninety years before. Now, this part of that empire was controlled by the Nebula Union. Kelvin was able to calculate exactly where the ship was when that image was created. After the fall of the Confederacy, its territories had been broken up and redistributed among the three remaining powers in the Treaty of Dreda. Even ninety years later, the peace had been mostly maintained by that treaty.

Dreda, an immortal not of the Authority, had acted as peacemaker in the nine-year conflict. In the end, according to the story, she had died in another dimension but had taken the enemy with her: Venelka. What was true or false didn't really matter to Satiah, but that treaty was real enough. A lasting legacy to remind everyone of the pointlessness of all-out war. Astronomically, the constellation was interesting too. The stars, as they were often depicted, seemed to create the shape of a face, or a mask, depending on whom you asked. Hence the nickname: the masked constellation. Again, too many names for Satiah's liking.

"Planet Tweve," he told her. "Nebula Union world." Satiah had already looked it up.

"Uninhabited... *apparently*," she mused, cynically. The Obsenneth crystal was getting warm in her pocket again, she could feel it against her skin through the fabric. Kelvin too had detected the new heat signature. He faced her, red eyes focussed on her pocket. She sighed. She *really* did not want to do it.

"We have things to do..." she began.

"It will take us a few hours to get there," Kelvin interjected, seriously. It was rare that he did this. Almost arguing with her. He must really have thought her life was threatened for him to start making a fuss now. He was right... they did have some time.

"You win," she grunted, shrugging off her jacket. Slowly, in case it burnt her, she reached into the pocket. Her hand was still gloved but when that thing got hot, it got very hot. She placed it on the console in front of them and sat down, facing Kelvin. It was cooling already, and she slipped her glove off whilst staring down at the gemstone. Her eyes rose one last time to check Kelvin was watching. What else was he likely to be doing? She knew she was just delaying the inevitable. Slowly she extended her hand and made contact.

"Obsenneth?" she asked, unsure if she was saying or just thinking it. No answer. "*Don't get funny*," she growled, starting to think it was playing with her. "Rocks can be ground to dust, as I'm sure you already know."

"Satiah," answered that voice. "What do you want?" She looked up at Kelvin who remained motionless. Could he not hear this?

"No, that's my question to you," she spat. "What do *you* want?"

"Why do you need to know?" Obsenneth answered.

"If you don't tell me I will throw you into space," she threatened, angry. "You killed Kyle, didn't you? Why?" Silence. "I'm not going anywhere and *you* drew my attention to you, you clearly want to say something!"

Suddenly she wasn't on that spaceship anymore with Kelvin. She was standing in a forest. She was still holding Obsenneth in her hand and she was still exactly how she had been on the ship. A cold wind blew but she couldn't feel it, nor could it move her deep red hair. Leaves flicked and darted around her, one passing right through her like she wasn't there.

"I had to show you *this*," Obsenneth said. She began to walk forward although she had no control over her body now. Curiosity won out over fear in her mind. "If you promise to help me, I will promise to help you."

"Help you do what?" she asked, trying to get some control back. She was approaching what she could only describe as a temple.

It had probably once been completely white, but now it was grey and worn with age.

"What is this?" she asked, as anyone would. "What are you showing me?"

"The past," it replied. "My past, specifically. I have seen inside your mind, Satiah, it is only fair that you now see inside mine."

"Really?" she demanded, sceptically. Her immediate reaction to that was to test if it was lying. "Prove it. Tell me something about me that you could only know through reading my thoughts."

"*Vourne never saw your betrayal coming*," Obsenneth told her. Fear welled up inside her but she couldn't do anything about it. "He thought you were on his side until that last moment when you shot him in the back."

Even though it wasn't accusatory, it wasn't mocking or even chiding, its words brought out her defensiveness.

"Someone *had* to stop him," she blurted, self-justifying. "Besides, I was certain that I would not survive a second attempt…"

"Carl is a liability and he makes *you* weaker," Obsenneth said next, before she could even finish.

"*Enough!*" she hissed. It had proved its point. Okay, so Obsenneth could see inside her and read her like a book. It was going through her deepest darkest secrets like they were weather reports from a bygone age. She forced herself to think sensibly. It wanted her for something and had not threatened her directly *yet*. Obligingly it fell silent.

They were inside the temple now where it was much darker. There was a rock... a rock that looked just like Obsenneth, only much larger. Something, she didn't see what, hit it. There was a crashing noise and sparks flew. It broke apart into five pieces, energy sparking everywhere.

"I want to be whole again, Satiah, and you can help me achieve that," he said.

"And if I don't, you'll do what?" she demanded, levelly. "Expose me? Kill me?"

"You are special, Satiah. You didn't know me. You didn't want to use me or my brothers but as we work together I can help you. You are capable. You can bring me back," it said. That didn't answer her question!

"What are you talking about?" she growled. No answer.

Then... she was back in the ship, facing Kelvin. The gemstone was still there in her hand, inert. She slowly placed it on the console again and sat there silently for a moment. Help her? How could... she paused as she remembered what had happened to Kyle before he had died. Obsenneth had done something to him. Was it volunteering his services to her in exchange for her helping it find itself?

"Well?" Kelvin enquired, aware that she was no longer holding it.

"What did you hear?" she asked, interested.

"Same as before. There was auditory phenomenon but nothing that could be described as a conversation. Whatever communication took place, happened only in your mind," he said. She stared down at the gemstone again.

"Yes, *my mind*," she breathed, remembering that Obsenneth now knew everything about her.

And there were *four others* that it wanted her to help it find. Why?

"Satiah... I can't scan you," Kelvin stated, his red eyes focussing right into her brown ones. "I can see you sitting there, but I cannot scan you." This was starting to get scary again.

"My body?" she guessed, eyeing the Obsenneth crystal again. "It's the Obsenneth, it's stopping you."

"What is the Obsenneth, Satiah?" Kelvin asked, his usual monotone sounding... urgent.

She slammed her hand down onto the gemstone and screamed at it.

"*Stop!*" she shouted, hitting the console twice with it. "If we're going to work together, then you're going to have to do what I say when I say."

"You are registering again," Kelvin confirmed. "*Work together?*" She explained all that she'd seen and heard. Kelvin made a move, going for the gemstone.

"No!" she ordered, guessing he would attempt to crush it.

"It has affected your mind, Satiah," Kelvin stated, towering over her. She shoved the Obsenneth back into her jacket pocket.

"No, *I* am in control!" she assured him, seriously. She gestured to herself rapidly to emphasis. "I have control, its fine." Again Kelvin moved, this time grabbing her arm and pulling her toward him. One of his appendages went for her wrist and the third went for her pocket.

"*Code twelve!*" she screamed, throwing herself backward. Kelvin froze... all motion systems deactivated. His eyes blazed a brighter red as if angry, and his processor was still functioning. "What the hell do you think you're doing?"

"Satiah, you are not yourself and you are a danger to yourself," he warned, still able to talk.

Breathing more slowly, Satiah forced herself to calm down. This was not good, not good at all. How could she explain that she was fine? *Was he right?*

"Kelvin, how can I possibly convince you that I am completely sane and completely myself?" she asked, though she thought she knew. He was going to ask her to go through a Rosenhan-Ring test. A device placed on the head, close to the brain in other words, that would assess all mental activity over a period of several minutes. It could diagnose as well as any specialist. Even if she happened to have one on her, *which she did not*, there was no way she was going to do that! Not in the middle of a mission! Those things messed with people's minds, and not always in a good way.

"You must…" he began.

"*I command!*" she barked over him. "I made you! I still need you, but you're endangering not only the mission, but me too by physically attacking me."

"You *know* that you were not my target," he replied. "You must be tested using a Rosenhan-Ring. Once your sanity is confirmed, I will once again obey you in all things."

"Kelvin: *we don't have one!*" she almost screamed. She was starting to feel insane now! This was ridiculous! "You *know* we don't have one! Kelvin, I *need* you for this! If I can't trust you to do what you normally do… I *will have to leave you behind.*" She knew that it was virtually impossible to prove sanity or even insanity without such a test, as he did. "Trust me, I am under pressure but I'm in complete control." To demonstrate, she pulled out her pistol and put it to her own temple. She stared right into his eyes, making the point of not being suicidal last for four whole seconds before replacing it.

She sighed and sat back down, suddenly feeling very tired.

"I know it presents a danger and I know you are programmed to protect me *even from myself*. How could I not know *that* when *I'm* the one who programmed you?" Kelvin didn't answer. She slowly put Obsenneth back onto the console – carefully. "I know this thing, this Obsenneth, is listening to this and I know it is dangerous but… to harm me wouldn't serve its purpose. If it needs my help, I have to be *alive* to give it," she reasoned, softly.

"Assuming your death isn't *what it needs*," Kelvin said.

"It's not," she stated, with certainty. "*Not yet, if at all.*" She eyed Kelvin as she replaced the stone in her pocket and sealed it inside. "Code three." Kelvin moved back into his usual stance and made no further moves.

"Now then," she stated, firmly. "We will discuss this again *after* we have completed this mission. Until then it's staying *in my pocket.*"

"Yes, Satiah," he replied.

"We will *find* this Cult of Deimos and…" she stopped and realised something. She'd not heard from Darius. Not a word. She touched her earpiece, putting in the call. She had to tell someone other than Reed where she was going and what she was doing, in case something happened to her. Darius answered quickly.

Their discussion lasted the remainder of the journey. He told her that Milo had been found, but getting him to return was trickier than first imagined. Satiah felt as if a tiny weight had been removed. Celestine was the woman in the picture. She was half tempted not to tell Rainbow and let him struggle on, but that would be too nasty. She would update him on what she had been up to.

"It might be worth calling in a force to back you up. You and Kelvin are tough, I know, but you can't take on a whole cult singlehanded," Darius stated.

"They may not be there at all – this is simply reconnaissance. Reed may be the one needing help if they succeed in taking out that Federation ship," Satiah countered.

"Okay, what do you want me to do?" he asked. "I can't leave here without Milo making a move."

"I know, I… Okay, leave it with me," she said. "Good luck. Let me know what happens."

"Will do," he replied, cutting off. Next she called Dyss. He answered quickly too.

"Yes?" he said, grim. He was probably expecting another trip down memory lane in the form of another conversation about Jackdaw.

"Are you busy?" she asked, also grim.

"Why?" he asked, seriously. "Has something happened?"

"I need you to go to Collgort-Elipsa," she stated, determinedly. "*Now*. Your pal Reed needs someone there capable of defending him." She had been expecting a blazing argument over this but he didn't even refuse.

"I'll be there," he stated, after a small hesitation. "Reed knows about Bavon, doesn't he?"

"He *does,* but it's who else that *might* be there which worries me more. Bert is *still* Purella's target. They may use an attack on the warship as a diversion to try and snatch him back," she suggested. "*That's why I need you there.* Darius is tied down with Milo and I can't be in two places at once."

"I'm on my way now," he said, disconnecting. Satiah frowned. He agreed to that much more easily than she had expected and she wasn't sure she liked that.

They had been in the area Kelvin had identified nearly half an hour already and she'd done nothing. Time to move. Planet Tweve.

***

"What is the point of being an administrator if you can't find me a place to land where no one will notice?" Purella glowered.

"I have no control over that ship, *it's Federation*," Bavon objected, flustered. Clyde sat there in the co-pilot's chair, listening to the exchange with practised disinterest.

"Your target is in your city and as you are too useless to hand him over to me, I'm going to have to come in and get him…" she began, building into a rant.

"You're the one who lost him in the first place," Bavon retorted. Clyde raised an eyebrow, it was never a good idea to criticise Purella. Ever. She hissed with rage, her face becoming red and angry.

"You have my money again, Bavon," she reminded him. "Quint should have sent it to you."

"Yes," he admitted, reluctantly. "You will just have to stay where you are until Quint's attack begins, then you can slip past."

"Quint isn't going to attack anything!" she stated, rolling her eyes. "Hasn't he told you what he is planning?" What a stupid question, Quint never said anything to anyone unless he needed to.

"I was told just to keep my head down. Something about a trap," Bavon replied. "That was the last I heard." Quint hadn't told him about the bomb. Perhaps, if Quint felt that someone might be watching Bavon… he would be keeping him out of the loop intentionally. Purella decided not to fill in the gaps.

"I need to land to refuel, pick up my money and get Bert, and *you* need to make that happen," she stated, inflexibly.

"I don't know what they're doing with Bert, he seems to have vanished. I have your money but you can't land without going past the Federation destroyer," Bavon argued.

"Bavon..." she began, her tone menacing. "Just do it."

"Fine, but if you get boarded, don't blame me," he snapped, cutting off. Even if they did, there was nothing to be found. It was an empty freighter... if you didn't include the team of twenty mercenaries. She would struggle to not kill Bavon when she saw him next.

"Do you want me to take us in?" Clyde offered. "They may know your face and voice." She nodded.

"Yes, thanks," she replied, getting out of the chair. "Any news from anyone?" Clyde shook his head.

"Not a word," he lied.

Clyde began an approach and they were almost instantly hailed.

"This is the Colonial Federation destroyer *Froissement* to unidentified ship, *state your intention*," demanded a man.

"Hey there," Clyde grunted, nonchalantly. "Freighter *Moondust Three* here, refuelling and trade." There was a pause as they were scanned, most likely.

"You are cleared to approach, *Moondust Three*, your landing will be handled by the local authorities," replied the man and cut off. Clyde carried on. Purella returned, communicator in hand.

"You and the others will remain on board here, *be ready should I call*. I first need to establish if Bert hasn't been smuggled away somehow," she explained.

"Whatever you say," he replied, contributing more fumes of poison into the ever-darkening atmosphere between them.

Purella was about to say something short and harsh when the communicator went off. She answered. It was Quint.

"Where are you?" he asked, his voice as automatically inscrutable as ever.

"Collgort-Elipsa, picking up *my money* from Bavon," she replied, casually. It was hard not to get bitter about dealing with lowlife like Bavon.

"There is something going on," Quint stated, apparently not listening to anything other than her location. "I have been unable to contact Kyle. There is no return signal." Purella scowled and Clyde eyed her casually. As before, he wasn't going to say anything with Quint there listening to everything.

"Radio silence?" she offered, interested.

"I gave no instruction," he replied.

"Maybe there's a battleship nearby," she suggested.

"*No...*" came his voice again. Purella waited but he didn't elaborate. "While you are there, retrieving your payment and the doctor, find out if *Satiah* is still there." Purella's gloved hand tightened its grip on the communicator.

"Of course," she smiled tightly, anticipating a fight.

"Should you encounter her, try not to make a scene," Quint cautioned. *A scene?* Who did he think he was talking to?

"That will depend on *her*," she replied, leaving it at that. The familiar hatred welled up inside her. Hatred is more than just an emotion. It could be strengthened if played with. It remains the easiest emotion to build up, and has the capacity to reshape a person's perception. The power to corrupt *their* own reality... and create a world that does not exist. Clyde looked around, watching her, as if he sensed the crouching tiger inside her.

Clyde had seen the skulls she kept. Those Phantoms unlucky enough to cross her path since the destruction of the Varn-Utto were now her trophies. He understood revenge, and indeed advocated it, but he also recognised obsession. She was so close to achieving what she thought she wanted that she was starting to become reckless. She had been his friend once, his lover. Now, though, when he looked into the icy depths of those eyes, he wasn't sure he recognised her anymore. He loved powerful women, always had, and they seemed to like him too, but he was ever his own man. Always he had his own game to play. And what she wanted to be part of threatened him just as much as the security forces of any government. After all, what were governments other than powerful organisations which could *and would* often turn to criminal means to get what they needed? He wanted no part of that, never had.

"She is stronger than you think, Purella," warned Quint, still talking. "She is *not like* the other Phantoms you have faced before. They were younger. She has twenty years on them, she is a senior agent. People don't last that long if they don't have something special. She's one step below Phantom leader in terms of ability. If you take the decision to move against her again, *don't misjudge her.*" Clyde began to notice something: it sounded like Quint knew Satiah. *Knew her personally.* How could that be? Purella though was so worked up at the prospect, she wasn't taking this in fully.

"I won't," she stated, flatly. Quint cut off. Clyde knew that Satiah wasn't on Collgort-Elipsa and he knew precisely why Kyle was no longer answering. He was amazed that Quint didn't know. Still he kept it to himself, interested to see how this would change things.

He smiled sarcastically at Purella.

"Good luck," he stated, coldly. She whirled on him.

"*I wish you would change your mind!*" she hissed, lividly. She'd tried every argument she could think of to get Clyde to join the cult. He had remained stubbornly opposed. Her reaction to his comment, however, told him that somewhere, deep inside, the Purella he once knew still cared about him. Cared enough to get angry, anyway.

"Take a closer look at what you're aiming at before you take the shot," he advised, meaningfully. "You might not have time for a second." She scowled at him, trying to figure out exactly what he meant by that. Was he talking about the cult or Satiah? She didn't display her inner confusion though, hiding it well. Instead she raised her pistol slowly.

"I won't need two shots," she said, determinedly.

***

"That's what I want," Celestine told him, softly.

Darius and Cherry were still in the secret room while Milo and Celestine spoke to each other in the office. Some space had been given so that they could go heart to heart for a while. Darius was becoming increasingly restless. He knew Satiah needed him now, and he wanted to get into the thick of it. Normally he was okay with waiting, sometimes even enjoying it. Yet this whole assignment was not like the others. Satiah trusted him, believed him about Jackdaw.

He did not want to let her down. He paced up and down endlessly, making Cherry feel increasingly uncomfortable. Cherry knew what was going on too, and could see why he was so edgy, but his nerves were contagious. When someone so calm, even in situation of high stress, became stressed... *you noticed.*

"Please sit down," she uttered, a bit shakily. She wasn't sure how he would react to her request. "You're making me anxious." Darius reeled but seemed to calm instantly. He sat down heavily and tried not to fidget.

"I'm pretty sure they will come round to our way of thinking," Cherry assured, trying to calm him down.

"Me too," he smiled, briskly. At last, hand in hand, Milo and Celestine returned. Darius remained seated, although it took a conscious effort to do so. They looked at one another, half smiles and knowing looks.

"We have decided to give Milo back to his family *on the condition* that he is allowed to return here after everything is settled," Celestine stated, seriously.

"We accept. How do we get out of here?" Darius asked, seriously. That had been his main concern. If their leaving was to be a secret, that could be tricky with all those ships playing *I spy* out there.

"I'll make a few calls," Celestine sighed. "I can get you clearance."

"And the necklace?" Cherry enquired, curious.

"She says she doesn't need it," Milo stated, a bit rueful. "She just needs me." Darius winced, a little put off by the sickly-sweet discussion.

"Let's go," he stated, pleased to at last get things moving. Cherry smiled after him, amused at his apparent discomfort.

"Take care, I'll see you soon," Celestine said, hugging Milo.

"I won't be long," he promised.

***

It was just possible to see the city through the white clouds of Collgort-Elipsa. Captain Ogun peered out of the main viewport of his destroyer as they slowly continued their patrol. He'd just had a conversation, albeit a short one, with Vice Admiral Keane. Pressure was mounting back in the Federation. The Nebula Union were threatening all sorts of things to get them to withdraw. Keane had wanted to know Ogun's feelings. Did he see any reasons to stay and what were they? Ogun had given them. If he departed, the planet would almost certainly be attacked by a force that was potentially pirate in origin. Everyone knew the Federation fleet's stance on pirates. Wester had made it clear in public that pirates found in their space who did not surrender immediately would be destroyed. No prisoners were to be taken. They had been warned…

Also the Coalition had called them in to help, admittedly through the back door, to protect the planet. Tension between the Federation and the Coalition was another big ongoing issue, thanks mostly to Ro Tammer and her trial. Ogun put it to Keane that by helping the Coalition in this way, it could only aid the diplomatic situation between the two superpowers. Keane had accepted these two points but had rhetorically asked the question: why doesn't the Coalition use *their own* fleet to protect it? Ogun told him what Reed had implied: that they were too concerned about the Nebular Union seeing the presence of Coalition destroyers as a prelude to something else. Something against *them*. Keane had told him that he had Wester's authority to remain on station as long as he needed to, but not to take action outside of the area for any reason.

Ogun's usual reaction to politics was to shrug it off as meaningless sabre-rattling. If someone wanted to do something they did it, they didn't talk too long about it. Despite the 'Tammer propaganda' as it was called, Ogun respected the Coalition and he'd been impressed by Darius and Reed. They had included him in everything that would affect him, which he appreciated. An alarm sounded, snapping him out of his thoughts.

"Ship approaching," the lieutenant called.

"Battle alert," Ogun replied, immediately. "What are we looking at?"

"Sir… It's a Nebula Union destroyer, coming in fast," he said, his face pale. Ogun frowned. Just the one? If they were trying to force the issue they would need more than that to make him think twice.

Looming through the clouds like a giant black bird of prey, the Union destroyer approached, it was slowing as it got nearer. Ogun ordered the destroyer to confront the intruder. Okay, technically it wasn't an intruder as this *was* its space, but as guard dog he had to make the moves. Before it reached them or even tried to communicate, in a bright burst of fire, it exploded. Fortunately the shields were up and the Federation destroyer was between it and the city so neither were damaged. Several windows exploded, however, as the explosion broke the sound barrier. The wreckage plummeted down, burning as it went, to crash into the violent oceans below. Ogun stared, slack jawed. They hadn't even opened fire! This was bad...

PART FOUR

The Cult of Deimos

In a place called the Hellion. Present day.

The statue, steely blue in colour, known among the brethren as *Banshincubus* or *the ancient one*, occupied the centre of the stage. Its slit-like dark eyes, and its long, sharp, pointy teeth, presented a facade of demonic fortitude. Its entire body was wrapped in a crisscross pattern of ceremonial swords and sharpened bones. The red figure of the bishop appeared from a passageway leading further into the catacombs. Quint was standing alone, in front of a large screen. Text, figures and all kinds of other data were being displayed.

"You wished to see me?" the bishop asked, interested. Quint did not turn to face him as he answered.

"We have a problem," he said, activating something. The picture of Satiah appeared. "It seems our activities have attracted a Phantom agent. At first, this was to be expected… then contact was lost with the pirates."

"Was the warship destroyed as planned?" the bishop asked, with significance.

"It was," Quint answered, his computerised voice betraying nothing.

"Then I daresay the pirates are no longer required," the bishop surmised. Technically he was right, but that wasn't what was bothering Quint.

"She is one of their best and may learn of our involvement through the pirates," Quint warned.

"Even if she does, the situation has changed. Collgort-Elipsa will either become a Nebular Union territory, or it will become the eye of the storm. She will most likely be pulled out," the bishop told him. Quint looked right at him sharply as if he was going to challenge the point then, for whatever reason, he let it go.

"It will be difficult for the Viscount to talk his way out of this," Quint allowed. This was true, and it was dubious that the Viscount would do anything at all, but Quint was uncertain. He'd asked Purella to check if Satiah was still on Collgort-Elipsa because the pirates had fallen silent. He didn't trust Bavon to be able to find out. If she *wasn't*, then that meant they could recapture Bert, assuming he wasn't with her. But if she *was* still there…

"Collgort-Elipsa is the key to this, once they are a part of the Union we can make use of their vast funds to continue the research," the bishop said.

"We have only one part of five," Quint stated, unimpressed. "It will take decades to find the others. We should shift our focus onto the Coalition."

"What of the Federation?"

"Since their revolution they are hardly a serious threat," Quint dismissed. "*To us*," he added, as an afterthought. The *pirates*, on the other hand, had been suffering dearly at the hands of the Federation recently.

"You need to put aside your hatred for the Coalition, *for now*, my brother," the bishop advised. He moved away to talk to two other robed figures who'd entered.

Quint remained where he was, white walking stick in one hand, watching the screen. He was like a statue, completely unmoving. Two other cloaked figures entered and stopped to regard him. Slowly Quint turned in their direction and they quickly moved on. There was something different about him. Everyone in the cult was powerful or unique in some way. Qualities like that had enabled them to join in the first place. No one there was ordinary. Yet none of them wore masks, not *inside* the Hellion. Their cloaks and clothes were all dark and mysterious. His robes, pale white and spotlessly clean, stood in stark contrast against the others. There was nothing readable about him. Not in voice or tone, not in expressions... *no eyes*. It was as if he were some sort of manikin or android. A walking, talking dead man.

With a repentine conviction, he turned to follow the bishop, who halted upon seeing him coming.

"What is the status of the Nebula Union battle fleet?" Quint enquired.

"They are being prepped, although there is still some debate as to the *size* of the force to send. One destroyer should not be able to eradicate another so quickly. As a result of this obvious deduction they have drawn the conclusion, *as we theorised they would*, that there has to be a stronger force there. A mistake by the Captain doesn't seem credible. They will be forced to send at least four," the bishop answered.

"*Four*," Quint pondered, aloud. The bishop frowned.

"Not enough?"

"Eight," he replied, after considering.

"I'll pass that on," he nodded.

Quint began a purposeful walk towards the tunnel leading back out to the ruins. It was time he found out just what had happened to Kyle. If Bavon spoke to him and tried to organise another attack and Quint *couldn't* oversee them, they would get slaughtered. Along the dark tunnel and past the guard, Quint was back outside among the ruins in minutes. The breeze made his cloak flick and shudder. A small black disc awaited him. Known as a stealth bubble, it was one of the most expensive ships anyone could own. It was only about three times his size but it was what all members of the cult used to get to and from the Hellion. The signal each emitted, unique and subtle, informed the cult exactly who was approaching or departing. Quint slid into the chair, the pod-like door closing quickly after him, and activated the flight computer. The craft had no offensive capability whatsoever but it was fast and virtually invisible.

He was in space in moments, setting his coordinates for Corkscrew base when he paused... there was another ship out there. A freighter. It was still some way off yet, but it seemed to be coming closer. He scanned it. Single occupant, and the ship was *one of Kyle's*. Quint pondered that for a moment. Kyle didn't know where the cult was, nor did any of his pirate associates... as far as Quint knew. Purella knew, of course, but she was separate from Kyle's operations, and she was supposed to ask him for permission to approach. He debated hailing the freighter and trying to learn more but decided against it. The cult should be safe enough in the event that it turned out not be an ally, and if it was a friend then there was no problem. He watched the ship a few moments longer before making the jump. He would return to his cruiser first and *then* move to check on Kyle, he'd decided.

***

The explosion could best be described as: *difficult to miss*. Even in the Viscount's private chambers, the rumble had been palpable enough to rock furniture. Glass had been shattered everywhere and the people had fallen silent in shock. The first person to react had been the Captain of the Colonial destroyer. Captain Ogun had instantly contacted the Vice Admiral again, informing him of the recent development. Both officers agreed that some kind of trap had been sprung on them as this *had to be* a set up. Inside the Viscount's chamber, Amber sat up on the bed in reaction to the blast.

"What was *that*?" she asked, her eyes wide. The Viscount, sat at his desk, his back to her, was also stunned.

"I don't know," he replied, pulling on a robe. "Stay there," he called, over his shoulder. He departed and the doors swished shut after him. Amber stood slowly, wrapping the blanket around her. She went over to the desk and pushed the finial of the golden desk lamp down subtly.

"Amber here, reporting in," she qualified, seriously. "Has the Colonial destroyer just been taken down?"

"Transferring you now," replied a voice. Amber, an agent of the SRB, the Security and Research Bureau, was operating in the role of deep cover. The Nebula Union government was trying everything it could to get Collgort-Elipsa to leave the Coalition. She had been ordered to worm her way into the Viscount's affections and influence him to make him fully join the Union. The seduction had been the easy part and she'd been gaining ground over the Viscount's former favourite Patricia Hollellster. Everything had been going well until that little man had arrived from the Coalition. Reed was his name, and ever since he had started interfering, she'd been struggling to get the Viscount to do anything. She'd asked for permission to kill him, but the government had refused, stating that they did not want to risk all-out war with the Coalition. So she'd continued fighting her losing battle of words.

Now... She didn't know what to think. This whole plan was unravelling and she wasn't sure what to do for the best. She pushed her chestnut curls out of her eyes while she waited.

"What is it, Amber?" a voice asked, gruffly. She explained what had just happened.

"There was a ship sent to Collgort-Elipsa, a destroyer, perhaps a fight broke out, but we have heard nothing. Is the Federation ship still there?"

"*I don't know* and I'm not in a position to find out either," she argued levelly. "Why else do you think I am asking you?"

"Continue operating as you are. What is the situation with the Viscount?" he asked, impatiently.

"Reed is gaining more of the Viscount's respect by the day, mainly because he keeps saying the right things at the right times," she stated, bitterly.

"And you're *convinced* he's working with Patricia?"

"I'm certain of it. They tried to fool me by *pretending* to be opposed to one another. They have tricked mostly everyone in the government into believing that they are rivals and not a team. I... this guy Reed is good. *Very good*. I can't beat him and Patricia together. And these pirate attacks are not helping! They play straight into Reed's hands. You should have sent in the fleet to protect the world directly *like I originally suggested,* regardless of what the Coalition thought. As it is, your prevarication has..."

"The government is not interested in your opinions regarding their policies and, while they do amuse me sometimes, we do not have time for this," he replied, tersely. "Do you see your mission as a lost cause?" She paused, and sighed. She hated giving up but this was getting dangerous now. She was not trained in this kind of work. Political manipulation she could do, along with discreet assassinations. All out fighting? Not really her style.

"I don't know if I'm under threat or not. I will continue to try but I may have to evacuate," she stated, after considering. She had a ship on standby just in case. Who wouldn't? It had been a gift from the Viscount so she could leave quickly if she needed to.

"Find out what happened and report back," he instructed, cutting off. *Thanks for nothing*! She deactivated and returned to the bed, thinking hard. This had been an easy job just weeks ago. Good luxuries, pleasant company, but nothing lasted forever, did it? She didn't want to play the 'I'm leaving' card. The Viscount was a very sensitive and impressionable young man. A lot of work would be wasted if she left now. She grabbed her communicator and paused, thinking it though again. It was a reckless move to try but she had to know what was going on.

"Hi Gabriela, it's Amber," she said, sounding casual. "I understand Reed has *some people* working for him. There's an employee, *a woman*. I want to speak to her, can you make that happen?"

***

The Viscount was staring in utter confusion at the scene in front of him. The Federation ship was still there. What had just happened? Another pirate attack? There was a lot of debris trails in the cloud but he couldn't actually see any. Pat dashed in, her face pale and scared.

"*Viscount*," she began, about to perform the usual honorary gestures of address. "I saw everything. The Nebular Union destroyer appeared and then... just... *blew up*! We were protected from the blast..."

"Did Captain Ogun fire on it?" the Viscount asked, starting to look as scared as her.

"I don't know, I didn't *see*," she answered, honestly. This was bad.

"...Where's Reed?" he asked, quickly.

Having at last recovered from the ordeal of seeing life through Bert's eyes, Reed was awaiting the Viscount's attention. He hadn't told Pat about any of that Cult business yet. It would be interesting bringing that up. The Viscount, apparently *in session*, couldn't be disturbed. Reed heard the explosion, but he was so deep in thought it hardly registered. As he paced up and down on the balcony, overlooking the bar area, nothing registered other than his own thoughts. He was deliberating on celestial anxiety as usual when he noticed a familiar figure. He'd not seen her before *in person* but he'd seen enough images from Satiah to know who he was looking at. *Purella*. Even if the clothes and the golden hair weren't enough, that black band she always wore was unmistakable. She was walking at pace towards *him*. He continued to pace up and down as a stranger would, the very soul of the mundane. Nevertheless *she*, upon seeing him, slowed and her eyes, blue and cold, turned evaluative.

Reed continued to pace, up and down... up and down. She passed him, staring quite openly. Reed met her eyes with his, as anyone behaving normally would. He reacted quickly again, doing and being a stereotype: the most likely thing to annoy her or put her off. He put on a lascivious smile. Her eyes narrowed. She was an attractive woman and therefore would be constantly fending off advances; all suspicions were put aside and replaced instantly by lofty disdain. The safety afforded by subliminal typecasting was limited but enough in this case to avoid the danger.

"*Hello*," he leered, flirtatiously. This strategy had the desired effect. She swore at him, telling him basically he had no business trying it on with her and continued on, unknowing. Reed continued pacing until she was gone and then fell against the wall in relief. And *what* would have happened in the unlikely event that she been attracted to him, exactly? He shuddered to think.

He fumbled with his communicator. Satiah, no answer. Darius, no answer. Pat answered.

"Yes, Reed?" she answered, casually. "Surgery over? *We need to talk!* Have you seen what just happened to...?"

"Well, you never know," he replied, thinking about other things. "We have a problem in the shape of a *highly dangerous professional killer* who wants to steal back Bert. What security do you have...?" He stopped talking, remembering that their security force consisted of about fifty guards, all of whom had no experience or ability to deal with someone like Purella. "Forget it... *we need to move Bert*." Pat, still with the Viscount, couldn't think *why* Reed wasn't at all bothered about the huge detonation outside the city. She had learned, however, that it was often best to just trust him.

"*Where is he?*" she asked, urgently.

"Prepare your quarters, *I'm going to get him,*" Reed ordered, cutting off. He scuttled off in the direction of the infirmary.

***

Satiah had seen too much to be truly shocked by anything she saw in the data that Reed had sent her. It was disturbing footage in anyone's estimation: especially when you considered how long all of it had been going on. Centuries, at the least. Kelvin, she knew, despite scanning the entire planet, was still monitoring *her*. When she'd learned who Bert *really was,* she had been initially furious that she'd bothered to save such a pathetic individual. But then, if she hadn't saved him, they might never have discovered the truth. The cult was real. Quint was a part of it, and Bert had run away only to fall into Purella's clutches. He didn't know what the cult were planning *now*, but he'd witnessed enough to give Satiah a fair idea. The cult wanted to rule, but only in secret, and they could only do that through influence. They had a strong influence in the Nebula Union, but hardly any in the Coalition or the Federation. That was what they were doing: trying to force the Coalition out of Collgort-Elipsa. All of this was the culmination of many years of very careful and very deliberate manipulation.

They clearly threatened Coalition interests. That made the cult an enemy of the Coalition. Her hand slid onto the handle of her pistol as she rose from the chair.

"We're looking at maybe five or six thousand individual members," Satiah said, to Kelvin. "Two High Priests *at the to*p function as the decision makers, *Bishops* next and they are numbered *eight*. The subsequent layers of command are *the acolytes*, of which *Quint* is one and then the rest are basically *members*. Simply put, that's too many for us to handle. We will need backup but first we have to prove they exist which means..."

"Infiltration," Kelvin stated, guessing the rest. She nodded grimly.

"They don't have *any* female members but they all wear *cloaks* so... I *may* be able to get in," she went on, going through options.

Her brow furrowed as she thought about it. "This planet seems to be littered with ruins of alcazars, ships, settlements and all manner of other things. There might have been some kind of lost civilisation involved, I'm not sure. This is a shame as the data Reed sent *does show* the entrance, but as the whole place looks very much alike, this is not enough to pinpoint its location. Particularly as the inhibiter erases the images that would compromise its *exact* location."

"Scan is inconclusive. An external influence is blocking some of the readings," Kelvin told her. She nodded, having foreseen that steps would have been taken to conceal it in every way. The cult had been there for a while and, in that time, they would have had much opportunity to keep the place as under wraps as possible. In a way, this was still good news as it indicated that someone was there, or else how was he being blocked?

"They will have seen us coming," she said, still thinking. "They will most likely have detected *me* on board already. I doubt one life reading will bother them, particularly as this craft is largely useless as a weapon." She hoped that was the case anyway. She sat down and began to think of the best strategy when her communicator went off. She swore and eyed it irately.

Just for once it would be lovely if she were left alone *long enough* to actually get somewhere! But it could be urgent, in fact it most likely was.

"Yes?" she answered, her tone prickly.

"Hi," said a voice, an unknown voice. "Is that Satiah?" It was a woman's voice. The accent sounded Union-ish in origin but it was faint.

"No," she lied, immediately. She wasn't going to admit anything and the fact that someone had managed to get a way of talking to her was worrying by itself.

A sigh sounded.

"My name is *Amber* and I work for the *SRB*. I want to talk to you *agent to agent*, I think something *weird* is going on," Amber elaborated, her tone both hard and professional. Satiah made eye contact with Kelvin. There was no point in asking how she found out about whom Satiah was, there wasn't time. She knew the SRB were a government security agency employed by the Nebula Union and had operatives everywhere, just like everyone else. The fact she'd chosen to talk meant what exactly?

"Right," Satiah said, cautiously.

"Don't trust me, *just listen*. My assignment was to gradually facilitate the movement of the planet Collgort-Elipsa *into* the Union. I know that *you* would not want that, *assuming you care at all*." Satiah grinned, of course she didn't. "There has been an explosion. I don't know for sure, but it *might* have been the Federation destroyer, and I know the Union have sent a warship of their own with the purpose of forcing the Feds to withdraw. Yet they were, under no circumstances, to follow a course of action that would provoke war with the Federation *or* the Coalition. I'm talking to you to tell you that somehow something has gone badly wrong."

"Let me stop you there," Satiah said. This woman, clearly an operative, had just blown her cover. Unless this was a trick she would not have done that unless she felt it had to be done. "For me to trust what you say to not be a trick, you're going to need to prove it," she stated, clearly.

"I am working *directly under* the Viscount," she said, clearly smiling. Ah… the lover that the Viscount had been taking great cares to keep a secret. "Your man Reed has been giving me headaches for weeks but I really don't think he planned *this*."

"You think the Federation destroyer took out the Union one?" Satiah guessed, intrigued. "A pre-emptive strike?"

"I can't *see anything* from where I am hidden, but common sense tells me that unless anyone devoid of common sense was in charge of either ship… no shots *should* have been fired," she replied, smugly.

"No… Though common sense seems to be in short supply these days," Satiah reminded her. "Why are you calling *me*?" Surely Reed would be a better listener for this kind of thing.

"I don't trust Reed and my records on you, *vague as they are*, indicated that you might listen." Well, that was understandable at least.

"I think my mission is as good as over, the only thing that stops me from pulling out right now is *curiosity*," Amber admitted. "I'm great at what I do, but I know when to back down. *I want to ask you a straight question.* Are the Coalition and the Federation working together against the Union?"

"No, *and kindly delete* those records you have on me," Satiah smiled, knowing she wouldn't even if she could. "I have a question for you *too.*"

"Go ahead," Amber replied.

"Are you aware of something called the Cult of Deimos?"

"The what?" she asked, confused.

"Your mission and theirs seem to align in terms of common interest. They want the Coalition out *too.* The cult is most likely pulling strings in *your* government. Do not report this to anyone, as they could be involved with the cult too, I don't know how deep their network is. This is merely a warning to you to watch your back."

"I will, thank you," Amber answered, her tone one of appreciation. "I don't know where you are or what you're doing, but things here *are* escalating. You or one of your pals might do well to pay a visit, assuming you're not already here in secret."

"Why don't you hang around and make yourself available? I'll be coming back to talk to you," Satiah replied, nodding to Kelvin. If that Federation ship was already destroyed and Purella was on the loose, then Reed would need help *before* Dyss could get there. The cult would have to wait.

"I'll stay as long as it is safe for me to stay, but I won't promise something I can't give… *not unless I have to.*" That was her reply and she disconnected straight away.

There was a silence as Satiah stared into the middle distance. Yet another complicated development.

"You trust her?" Kelvin asked. She eyed him, hoping he would not see this as further proof of irrationality.

"Yes," Satiah replied, seeing that candour would help. "She evidently only wants peace to endure between us and has nothing to gain, that I can see, by lying. We *need* to secure Bert and make sure the instability doesn't get out of hand. If the Federation ship *is* down, *Wester will retaliate.*" They changed course. "If the Union ship is down, they might send in their whole fleet which will mean Wester will react to *that* instead. In order to get there fast enough to make a difference, we're going to have to do some serious work on those engines."

***

"No problem," Bavon smiled, indifferently. There was something *different* about him now, Purella realised, as she sat opposite him. He didn't seem scared of her anymore. He was behaving as if he could be talking to anyone about anything. Like this – tracking Bert down to ultimately kill him – wasn't in any way risky or clandestine. He never once touched his collar, an idiosyncrasy Purella had noticed about the man before. A sign of agitation born out of fear and lack of confidence that anyone would instantly identify as his weakness. His office was hushed but had an odour that was not as it was before. Purella hadn't been able to place it at first but she had eventually recognised it.

"*So where is Bert?*" she asked, coldly. Bavon had already agreed to get her funds for her and, unlike last time, there was no attempt to renegotiate *anything*. This was fortunate as she was in the sort of mood where, if anything went against her wishes, she would lash out. This *lack of resistance*, though, didn't seem to have its origins in the fear that she'd made him feel before. He seemed to be completely without emotion. He was constantly smiling but it was a bland, meaningless expression designed to trick, fode or lull people into a false sense of security. Bavon was a small time criminal, prone to paranoia, unreliability, and a complete lack of self-control. What was he playing at? It shouldn't concern her, as he'd given her what she asked for, but part of Purella couldn't let go of that question. It bothered her.

"He, *according to records recently updated*, has been enduring an intensive medical examination. It's unclear if the analysis is over or not yet, but he *should be* within the infirmary somewhere. I can direct you to the infirmary if you would like?" he offered, still annoyingly blithe. Was he intoxicated? She stood and shook her head.

"No, I know where it is," she replied, seriously. She took an extra second to stare hard at the man who, still watching her, had no change of expression or manner. Still that aroma was hanging around, almost like an unseen presence that had a sentience of its own. What was he up to? She picked up the suitcase that contained her payment, and went for the door. He said nothing, just watched her go. It was all exceedingly odd, but it was not her problem. Purella headed back to her ship, first to stow the money aboard *before* she went in search of her next target. She departed once again, this time in the direction of the infirmary.

***

Reed had somehow forgotten how hard it was to push bodies around, even on a wheeled carrier. He couldn't understand why they didn't have hover modes. *On a planet this rich…. never mind.* Pushing Bert along, still unconscious, Reed scampered down the corridor, anxiousness of discovery being his main concern. Pat was supposed to be coming down from wherever she was to help at some stage, but after the destruction of the Union ship, things had gone a little awry. Ogun had spoken with Reed, insisting that they'd not fired a single shot. Reed believed him; the explosion had been too quick.

There hadn't been time for Ogun to do much other than change direction. Trouble was that the Union government wouldn't believe the truth, as it seemed like a lie. This was most likely how *whoever it was that had set this up* had wanted it to look. The truth, unbelievable, and the lie, completely plausible. Any time now, Reed knew that the Viscount would have a heated discussion with the Union about this. Pat had already gone to him to try and help convince him of the truth. In the meantime, it was up to Reed to keep Bert *away* from Purella without leaving the city or letting her know what he was doing. Not exactly the simplest of tasks, though he infinitely preferred it to the last one he'd endured. It was an odd sensation, being haunted by *someone else's* memories.

He had already tried to call Satiah but she wasn't answering. He hoped that was not a bad sign. Darius was also apparently missing in action, so that basically left it up to him, Riff and Pat. Not an ideal scenario, but perhaps the fact that they were not the usual type of people Purella had to deal with might work in their favour.

"Let's try this way, shall we?" Reed asked the sleeping man, rhetorically. He pushed him down another corridor, passing through an entirely glass walkway. As Reed pushed Bert along it, he glanced down just in time to see Purella passing by underneath. She was already almost right outside the ward where Bert had been. That meant that, very soon, she would know that Bert had been moved, and she would start searching for him. She may even work out that someone was keeping him from her. When she did, if he was right about her, she would quickly become dangerous. That wasn't to say that she wasn't *always* dangerous, of course, but there was dangerous and then there was *actively dangerous*. He continued on, wishing that the wheels of the carrier would not keep squeaking so loudly! Turning another corner, Reed debated where he could hide the man.

He remembered Darius talking to Ogun about the city when they had planned on cloaking the ship to provoke a pirate attack. Infrastructure tunnels… a potential hiding place for the insider who, at that time, they hadn't identified. It would be *a lot of fun* pushing this thing around in a set of tunnels! Yet it was probably the best place to elude Purella long enough to figure out what to do next. This was always assuming that Reed himself could find the tunnels. No luck so far.

"I hope you appreciate this," he berated the unconscious man. "I should be conducting premeditated political intercession instead of conveying you around for free like a concerned relative. Also, my back is killing me, *not unlike what Purella will try to do*, so you will have to forgive my increasing lack of civility." The next corridor along looked the same, felt the same, and Reed began to wonder if he would ever find the entrance to the tunnels.

His communicator went off and he placed it on Bert's face before activating so that he could continue pushing.

"Reed," Satiah said. "I'm coming back, what did you want?"

"Well, *I wanted you to come back* so *I'm glad* you are already on your way. I'm currently playing hide and seek with Purella and would really love it if you were to oblige me and shoo her away."

"I'm on my way but it will take hours… Dyss should be joining you too," she said. Then she told him about Amber and the highly dubious conversation they had had.

"*Ah*,' Reed grinned. This confirmed what he had long suspected. A Union agent *inside* the Viscount's bedroom was pretty understandable. He then told her that it had been *the Union ship* which had been destroyed, and that Ogun was blameless.

"A bomb, it had to be," Satiah stated, taking all of it in her stride. Reed nodded. He had reached that conclusion too, but proving it would be difficult to say the least.

"Reed, wait for Dyss or me to take on Purella, don't try anything *clever* yourself. She is lethal, okay?" Satiah asked, troubled. She knew what Reed was like, and wouldn't put it past him to attempt something absurdly heroic.

"*Watch out, Satiah*, you're letting your *caring nature* show again," Reed joked, grinning. She glowered a bit, remembering his and Carl's use of said information.

"I'm trying to save your little life, Reed, *be nice*," she admonished. He chuckled self-deprecatingly.

"I'm going for the infrastructure tunnels that Darius mentioned. I'm worried that Purella might do something nasty if she can't find her target," he explained.

"She will, but I will be there before she runs out of patience," Satiah promised, cutting off. Reed smirked, hoping she was right.

Dyss's arrival was also unexpected. She had to have called him in and Reed wondered what *that* meant. Satiah had made it clear she did not like being blackmailed *by anyone* and she certainly was not keen on Dyss. Reed hoped this wasn't some strategy of hers to get Dyss killed.

***

Purella entered the main ward, and approached the area Bert was supposed to be – land found... an empty cubicle. She scowled. Perhaps they'd not finished the *tests* yet. *Whatever they were*. Even his mobile sleeping table was missing. She approached a nurse.

"Excuse me," she began, pretending to be confused. "My dad was here a while ago; can you tell me where he is now please?" The nurse turned to regard the cubicle serial number.

"I'm not sure... he *should* still be there. Did his doctor say anything to you about anything additional?" Purella shook her head, her golden curls swishing through the air. "I will find out for you, please wait here." Purella sat down and waited. She didn't like waiting. It looked like somehow someone had guessed Bert was being sought. It looked a lot like that. She clenched her fists, feeling her gloves tighten. Yes... She stood and tilted her head from side to side to stretch. It was a pre-combat practice, much like an athlete limbering up, that she always did when she felt a fight was heading her way.

She debated inwardly whether to continue to wait for the nurse to return or not. Her debate ended when the nurse came back, looking perplexed. Purella already knew what he was going to say.

"He *should* still be here," the nurse told her. "Perhaps…"

"It's okay, I'll return directly." Purella smiled, cynically. She began a brisk walk back out into the corridor, her boots clumping on the floor. She turned this way and that, trying to decide *where* her prey had hidden. She pulled out her communicator.

"Clyde, has *any* ship departed the city since we arrived?" she asked, without preamble.

"No, and we are still the latest arrival," he replied, instantly. "What's going on? You need backup?"

"No,' she replied, cutting off without further explanation. She thought hard; trying to imagine what Bert would do if he knew she was after him.

She began to pace along the corridor casually, keeping an eye out for anyone who might be watching her. She smiled as someone, a woman, who was walking towards her, made eye contact with her.

"Excuse me," she said, amicably. "We're trying to track down a missing patient. I was wondering if you could help." The woman had seen a prone man being pushed along a corridor several minutes ago and… they had been going in *that* direction. Purella thanked the citizen for her help and continued on, renewed amusement in her. Weren't nice people *so* helpful? *So stupid!* Anyone she met, she asked the same questions and while most were useless, *some had seen what she was after*. So… Bert had had help. Help that *wasn't* Satiah. Even better. She liked a good hunt, particularly when her prey could offer no real challenge. The path she was following was clearly meant to confound *any* would be pursuer. It crisscrossed itself, went in circles, and seemed at times to take erratic detours, only to return to ground already trodden.

Half an hour had passed as Purella walked across *the same corridor* for *a third time*, an entertained grin on her face. This man was clever, but she would catch him eventually. It was inevitable. Reed watched as Purella stalked down the corridor, about fifty meters *ahead* of him. Slowly, *he* was following *her*. He couldn't go to Pat's quarters as she was not there to let him in, and he couldn't find the infrastructure tunnels. His logic was: the one place the huntress would not look was where she had just searched. He wished more than ever that Satiah would hurry up and kindly take care of this problem.

Until she did, however, he could dance with death because first, he'd always considered himself a *brilliant* dancer and second… it made time seem to go faster. Purella kept asking people she met, and annoyingly they were being very compliant. Sooner or later, one of them would spot *him* and point him out to her. When that happened, he had a plan for that too, but it was the kind of plan even he was greatly reluctant to carry out. He glanced at Bert's countenance. Part of him actually wanting to give Bert up… just because of what he had allowed to happen in his past.

***

Darius turned in surprise as Cherry appeared, a drink in each hand. They were returning to Earth to deliver their passenger, the *infamous* Milo Drass, back to his family. Milo had gone to bed hours ago, as had Cherry. She halted close to the threshold of the door, a questioning look in her eyes. He said nothing.

"I couldn't sleep," she explained, coming in fully. "I thought you might want something." He took her offering a little distrustfully.

"Thank you," he said.

He was quick to reinforce gratitude for a selfless act in her eyes as a demonstration to aid her growing understating of the universe. Yet wasn't any act *in some way* selfish? She sat down next to him and sighed.

"I don't understand this cosmos," she said, without even waiting for him to ask a question. She gave him a sideways grin. "But I do like it. I wanted to apologise for being *anything other* than helpful."

"Apology accepted," he replied, dispassionately. He wasn't sure what to make of any of this, but his mind was on other things, notably the cult and what he'd just heard about on Collgort-Elipsa from Reed's message. The destruction of the Union ship would have ramifications, perhaps on an intergalactic scale. He needed to get back there.

"Are you sure?" she asked, interested. "Am I disturbing you?"

"Yes," he said. He said it with a smile though. After what she had done, to help persuade Milo to leave willingly, she had earned the right to get his attention if she wanted it. She saw his expression and smiled too.

"Yes, I can see how that might be looked at as a silly question," she said. There was a silence. It was not a quiet that naturally occurred between old friends remembering, or the quiet of exhausted bodies resting... it was an awkward silence. A prelude to something. Maybe another question, maybe not. Darius thought he could tell what this would be about. It wasn't hard for him to tell what she was thinking about. When you looked into what background she had, it was not a difficult conclusion to reach. She had changed her mind enough about men in order to do something about it. He waited, silently wondering how she would broach the subject.

Loyalty and respect had been proven, in her case, through experience, and yes there were inequalities. There were *differences*. Equality was an unfortunate word as it was often misused. Its concept was also misunderstood by so many. Differences *as a word*, however, was much better. Much more flexible. Why should males and females be equal when they could be different? When you take *any* idea to extremes: failure often occurs. It becomes a monster that cannot be controlled and often leaves the idea that was once the objective far behind. Fighting was counterproductive.

"We can celebrate?" she asked, raising her glass. "To the fact that we completed our objective? *I mean, your objective*. I *know* it's not over, but this stage could be seen as dealt with, yes?" Darius shrugged noncommittally. A typical male reaction that, in this situation, could be seen by some as ironic, but nothing was ever truly certain.

"We can," he allowed. She regarded him, her eyes evaluative. Studying his face to try to learn... something.

"I want to thank you for giving me this chance," she said, softly. "I know I was a burden on you and I hope I have not..." She paused, eyeing his leg and remembering the wound he sustained when they had infiltrated the base.

"You did okay," he said, calmly.

"Is your leg okay?" she asked, curious. Darius raised an eyebrow and eyed it himself. It had been healed before they had even left the planet.

"It is," he replied. She smiled a bit shakily and nodded before guzzling the drink somewhat unsteadily. Then she stood as if to leave.

"That was it, what I wanted to say," she trailed off, staring at the empty container in her hand. She hung her head a bit too.

He could tell she was still watching him, awaiting his reaction. He was a Phantom agent and, despite knowing what she wanted, he was forbidden from it. She waited a long time, nearly two minutes before backing away. She reached the door and glanced over her shoulder at him. He remained where he was, careful not to turn to look at her. He knew, if he did, she'd come back. She sighed sadly and then the door closed behind her. Darius let out a breath and chuckled to himself. He doubted he would be able to resist if she tried again. Luckily for him, she was an inexperienced seductress and hadn't realised how close she was.

Still, the mission went on. Darius returned to his train of thought that had been put on hold momentarily. Once he got Milo back, he could return to Collgort-Elipsa and then, with Satiah, they would take the fight to the cult. This madness had to end. That stunt with the Union ship, the destruction of which was certain to be by the cult's design, in his eyes, was dangerous and had the potential to start a whole new war, one far larger and more terrible... the kind that hadn't been seen since the Common Protectorate War some ninety years ago. The kind of war no one could win. He couldn't know if *that* was their goal or not, but either way it had to be stopped. He'd missed another call from Reed too and, despite trying to call him back, he'd got no answer. There could be many reasons for that but he knew he had to get back there as quickly as possible. He eyed the countdown to the time of arrival and groaned. Another hour.

***

Dyss eyed the scanner results as he began his approach to Collgort-Elipsa, his eyes narrowing as he regarded the world for a millisecond without computer aid. It had been over two years since he'd been out on a mission of any kind. Too long, in his opinion. He had missed it. A life behind a desk was rarely a life of any kind. An unusual reading, coming from the ocean itself, caught his attention but when he redid the scan, there was nothing. Dismissing it as a blip, he made contact with the Federation destroyer and quickly learned of everything that had happened. No wonder Satiah needed extra hands. Just because he hadn't been out among the stars for a while, didn't mean he'd forgotten how to be a Phantom.

He glanced at the silver rifle on the chair next to him. It was small and light for a rifle, only slightly longer than an average forearm. Illegal in all three superpowers, the Ironmack was a highly dangerous weapon. The personalised handguard, blackened and chunky, was made from enamel and was smooth to the touch. Only where his fingertips reached on the barrel did tiny rubber grips exist. The optic mount, detachable of course, was tailored to his extreme and, some would say, pedantic specifications. Each power pack, of which it took a load of six, could deliver one thousand shots. Each would be increased in power by a modulator concealed in the barrel itself. The modulator used stored solar power to boost each shot, making them up to three times more powerful than normal. A black belt or leash was fastened to it so he could carry it under his arm or over his back as he needed. It was just small enough to conceal in his cloak.

He brought his ship in to land and fought his way through the unrelenting winds across the pad and into the building. After a quick conversation, he'd found out that Reed *wasn't available* and everyone was *very scared*. Not much help at all really, but hardly unexpected. He marched purposefully down a corridor, deciding to go straight to the Viscount. As a Phantom Leader, Dyss did have a certain political weight. When instability occurred, it was part of his job to bolster it as and where he could.

Before he could get there to bring his *ponderous weight* to bear though, he spotted a familiar figure. Purella. He knew her from intelligence reports Satiah had provided and here she was, large as life. He was glad that he'd not donned his usual cloak and instead had used an older dark green one that had once been his brother's. She approached him as he advanced towards her. She asked him what she had been asking everyone and Dyss was easily able to read between the lines.

"No, unfortunately not," he smiled, casually. "If I see anything, I'll be sure to let you know." She thanked him and continued on. Then, much to his shock, he turned a corner and was almost run over by Reed who was still pushing Bert around.

"Dyss, what are *you* doing here?" Reed began, before answering himself. "No, no, don't tell me, there isn't time, besides I think I already know. You must help me hide this sedated patient."

"You mean *Bert?*" Dyss clarified, seriously. He took Reed's place and easily controlled the trolley. "Where are we going?"

"I was following my hunter actually," Reed replied, breathlessly. "She doesn't hang around much though."

"Of course you were," Dyss replied, not bothering to hide his amusement. "Why don't we just leave him in one of those cutterboats over there?"

"Good idea," Reed agreed, hastily. "What's happening on Earth?"

"That Union destroyer is a problem," Dyss answered, cryptically. "The Federation and the Union are already arguing over what happened."

That annoyed Reed. No matter what the Viscount said about that or the war now, no one would believe him. *That* opportunity to end the war had been missed. He hoped there would be others. They stowed Bert inside the cutterboat and then slipped back inside the city. Purella would know within seconds if any ship left the city, and so flying off with him wasn't an option. They quickly returned to meet the Viscount, who by now was talking with Ogun, Pat, and another member of the council.

"What is going on?" the Viscount sighed.

"It's a trick. The someone who is behind the attacks is *also* behind the destruction of the Union ship," Reed spelt out. "We have no proof but we *know* it is true." The Viscount sighed and began to prowl up and down again as he often did. Reed eyed the carpet and wondered how long it had to go.

"If it's any consolation, even if it hadn't been destroyed, it would *still* have caused you problems," Dyss stated, shrugging. "A Union ship on Coalition territory could have made the Coalition send a ship of their own, and you would be in the middle of a three-way standoff."

"What do you suggest *I do?*" the Viscount asked, at a loss. Things were so dire that he had dropped all pretence of control or even of having a plan of his own.

"Contact the Union and back up Ogun's story of *what really happened*," Reed answered, thoughtfully. "It is the truth so no one *here* will be against you doing that. Then… contact the Vinu and Shintu ambassadors. Tell them everything we have learned and then... ask them to defend *this world* from potential Nebula Union hostility." Everyone stared at him, completely bewildered.

"Even if I agreed to such a bizarre request, what makes you think *they* will?" the Viscount couldn't help but ask.

"You're risking turning this world into their latest battlefield," Dyss warned, casually.

"Not with a Federation ship present," Reed countered. "Inform Ogun they will be coming and he is to operate as a peacekeeper."

"One destroyer is not enough..." Pat objected.

"It's a start! Don't forget the Union will likely send another ship too, we need as many parties involved in this as possible," Reed insisted.

"*Why?*" the Viscount demanded.

"To create confusion," Dyss answered, guessing. Reed nodded. "No one would want to risk being attacked by everyone at once."

"The more powers that are here the less likely it will be that war will break out," he replied, as if it were obvious. Dyss wasn't convinced but did not say so. If Reed were wrong, he'd get the blame and if he were right then arguing would not help.

Finally the Viscount, shaking his head, agreed.

"Fine, I'll do it. So far I've not done much of anything and things keep getting worse," he stated, irritably. "Perhaps I was too cautious, I will try another approach."

"No one should pretend that command is easy," Dyss told him, levelly. Uneasy rests the mind in which authority is vested, so the old saying went.

Pat remained silent, unsure if she and Reed were still playing their game to manipulate the Viscount or not. Her communicator went off and she eyed the new message from Reed. This seemed incredible being as she'd never actually seen him using it. The message was simple: *from now on unity only*. She placed her communicator back onto her belt and joined the others. They didn't realise they were standing right next to a very innocent-looking energy charging unit.

Amber, listening in to the conversation from inside the Viscount's chamber, had quickly decided to report in. She would tell her superiors that the Federation had *not* destroyed the Union battleship after all. She would not be believed and neither would the Viscount, but the truth was the truth. In this case, misinformation was not required. All-out war, never on her agenda, had to be avoided at all costs. She speculated that her report may be viewed as an *early warning* in years to come. Or a bit of intelligence that prevented the worst from happening. Trouble was that history was only ever written by those who never knew the full story. Or, you know what? Maybe they did and just *chose* not to tell it, who cares? She picked up her bags, looked around in mild regret and sighed heavily. She would miss the Viscount. Time to get out.

Reed listened intently as the Viscount backed up Ogun's report to the Union diplomatic embassy office. As expected, his testimony was treated with thinly veiled condescension in the guise of a *candid chat in complete confidence*, but at least he was listened to. After that was the even trickier task of bringing about a ceasefire. To his credit *he alone* explained it all from the pirate's attacks, through the incident just witnessed by all on his world, to the end where he presented his plea for peace. Foreseeing that he would not be believed, he stated that he had no way of proving anything but he had fears that some unknown force was trying to start a war. A force *independent* of everyone. Mentioning the cult would not help: it was best kept in the dark. To Reed's grateful astonishment: the communications unit suddenly exploded into life. Calls were coming in return. Some of them *had* listened and, even better, some wanted to talk.

The truth was that the war had gone on too long. Both governments, though promising themselves and each other that they would stop only if a complete surrender was offered or complete victory was obtained, were glad that the chance to end the fighting had come. Neither side would lose face either; it was the perfect excuse, provided enough of them took advantage of it. Both were struggling financially, militarily and their people wanted peace. It was an unsaid desire that you could see in their tearful eyes. All had paid the price. Not one family had remained untouched by the fighting. The idea that *someone else started the war for another purpose just to use them as tools* was what was needed to end the conflict. Besides, some leaders insisted that they too had harboured similar suspicions about being influenced over the years. True or not, unfounded or not, they added fuel to the fire of armistice.

Fleets stopped moving, coming to uneasy halts where they were in space as their orders were cancelled and a brief silence fell. On worlds where fighting was still taking place, ceasefires were ordered on both sides and officers used the time to retrieve the wounded and secure their positions. Even though it couldn't be proved, their craving for harmony was so great they were glad of it as an off-the-cuff justification to end hostilities. All-out war was impossible to sustain for long. It had drained everyone involved and robbed many of a life it shouldn't have done. Hope rose in a lot of hearts and minds, hope of change and of peace. Well, one of those was a certainty; the trouble was no one could say *which*.

***

Quint could not believe what he was hearing. The Vinu-Shintu War was... *suspended*. The Viscount had done the one thing that no one ever thought he would do. He had directly intervened. Still in his ship, Quint knew not to make any decisions suddenly. Suspended did not mean *finished*. It did not mean that they, as in the cult, were undone. He needed to know more. Was this a ploy, perhaps? Some kind of *acute propaganda*. And even if the Vinu-Shintu war was ended... the Union would still attack the Federation ship on Collgort-Elipsa.

Nevertheless, the cult would not be pleased by this development. How had this happened? Who could have...? *Satiah* had done this, somehow she was behind it. *Where was she?* And what had happened to Kyle? He could see the cruiser he was using as a home, a tiny speck in the distance. Everyone was talking now, and that was bad for sure. He had to do something. Something big enough to plunge everything back into chaos before people worked out what had really been going on.

***

Purella was starting to realise that, against all probability, she had been eluded. This game was not fun anymore. She pulled out her communicator.

"Major Clyde. Mobilise the men; I want you to..." She stopped as Quint was trying to call her. "Hold that thought." She answered. "*What now?*"

"Have you been monitoring the communications on that planet?" he asked, his voice giving nothing away. She frowned, wondering what he thought she might have stumbled on.

"Quint, I am searching for Bert, I have not had *time* to listen to *anything*," she retorted, flatly.

"Why have you not found him yet?" Quint demanded, sincerely.

"Someone knows I'm looking for him and has hidden him. Until recently he was in the hospital facility..." she began.

"Why?" Quint asked, cutting across her.

"I'm not sure why, Bavon mentioned *scanning*," Purella told him, starting to get impatient because of all these interruptions. Quint fell silent. "Quint...?"

"The Vinu-Shintu war has stopped," he elaborated. She gaped for a moment.

"How? *Why?*" she demanded. She knew all about what the cult had been doing and had herself been aiding them in doing it. Peace seemed a highly dubious exigence. Even now, she couldn't think *how* it had been achieved.

"The Viscount did it," Quint stated, in answer to her question. He went on to explain everything that the Viscount had broadcast and the almost immediate effects it had had. She was stunned. Why had they all believed him? How had they found out that they were being manipulated? *Satiah* seemed the only plausible answer as she was the newest development. And if *she* had figured all that out: what else did she know? And if she wasn't on the planet either: where had she gone?

"What do you want me to do?" she asked, inevitably. This changed everything. "Kill Satiah?" Quint seemed to hesitate: clearly he still believed that she was not capable. She had failed last time, but only because Satiah had got away, not because Satiah had beaten her. He started talking again, emphasising that there was still a strong chance the Union *would* retaliate *against the Federation* because of the *perceived* act of aggression. It was certainly in their interests to do so.

"Can't you *make that happen?*" she asked, a little incredulous. She didn't know the exact extent of the power that the cult wielded, but she was certain that the Union was practically their pawn. She was wrong. Quint knew she was wrong but what she was suggesting was pretty much what he felt should be done too.

"Leave that with me," he replied, leaving it unresolved. "Continue to search for Bert and then bring him back to the cult as we agreed."

"...Very well," she said, cutting off.

This was typical Quint! Keeping so much back and never telling her the whole story for no reason other than his own vanity! She would soon be a member of the cult, the *first female member*, no less! She already *knew* the plans and schemes and had no objection to any of it, why keep cutting people out of the loop? No one would ever capture *her*. She turned around, considering what to do next. Someone was hiding Bert from her. Someone that was still there, as Clyde would have alerted her if anyone had left the city. She had been just about to get Clyde and the others to move in and cover more ground but, after thinking about it, she decided on trying something else. She made her way back to Bavon's office. He was still there and eerily untroubled by her return. A short while ago he'd been terrified that she was going to kill him. Now he was acting as if he hardly knew her.

"I need to access your security camera system," she stated, by way of explanation.

"Certainly," he smiled, standing. "I'll just input the access codes."

"I'm staggered that you bother on *this planet*," she muttered, casually. "This lack of simple security procedure is unrivalled *anywhere*."

"*I* have to be more careful *as you know*," he remarked, still totally at ease with her. Well, so long as he was completely compliant she could live with that. She began going through the footage. When she noticed *Reed* her scowl deepened. She'd suspected that *someone* had lied to her but... Then Dyss had joined him. Her narrow eyes spotted *something* in Dyss's cloak and despite zooming in she couldn't make out quite what it was. A weapon obviously, but the type was a problem. His poise and his impressive capacity for lying to her face, even more convincingly than Reed, told her that her enemies were gathering in strength. *And where was Satiah?* If she *was* orchestrating this, she had to be able to at least *hear about* what was going on.

Bavon stood behind her, completely silent and watchful. Purella watched as they placed the apparently torpid Bert into a cutterboat, and then headed towards the Viscount's offices. Purella couldn't know for sure what words had passed as there were no cameras in the Viscount's offices but, based on what Quint had told her, she could guess. Now that she knew where Bert was, however, she could get at him. She stood and nearly walked right into Bavon who stepped out of her way only just in time. She gave him an acid look over her shoulder but said nothing. She left and he deactivated the screen before calmly returning to his desk.

Purella made her way to the area where the cutterboats were awaiting use. She searched each one. No Bert. She didn't spot that one of the double seats was not real. It was a hologram, left there by Dyss to fool anyone who happened to glance inside. Instead of a chair, Bert's bed and Bert himself were there. Purella reached the conclusion that either Bert had awoken and left, or someone else had removed him in the time it had taken her to get from Bavon's office to the cutterboats. She crossed her arms, trying to decide what to do next. This would be so much easier if she could just... A noise came to her and she spotted a freighter coming in to land nearby. She retreated inside, correctly guessing who it would be.

***

Satiah hurried down the ramp onto the landing pad, Kelvin in tow. She'd practically destroyed the engines to get the freighter to move so fast. They were smoking now, almost on the point of collapse. She had been endeavouring to keep pace with the developing situation as much as the constant power fluctuations. The destruction of the Union destroyer had changed everything. She could see what the cult had been trying to accomplish; Reed had somehow, more by luck than judgement she suspected, made it work to their advantage.

Her first step was to talk with Reed and Dyss personally. Everyone had to be in complete understanding of what was happening and what they had to do, but that didn't mean she couldn't multitask.

"Reed, is Dyss with you?" she asked, breathlessly. She was practically running down the corridors of the city.

"Yes, are you back?" he asked, hopefully.

"Yes, join me in my room, I need to get ready. Where's Bert?" she enquired next. He was the target, he was what Purella was after.

"Hidden in a cutterboat," he replied, quickly.

"Right, our first priority is to get him off the planet," she stated. "If other fleets arrive we could end up being trapped here…"

"Hold it right there," Dyss protested, a little irked at having been told what to do *by her*. Strictly speaking, she was a subordinate, but then she wasn't supposed to be working for him in any case. "Purella is here, probably watching all departures. I'm pretty sure leaving is exactly what she wants you to do. It gives her an easy target to follow."

"True, but…" she paused, another idea coming to her. "Do you know where Purella is now?" She had just reached her room and was frantically swapping her clothes for new baggy black combat gear.

"We think she's still in the city somewhere," he replied, a little unhelpfully. "Probably still looking for Bert." A bleeping sound began at the door. She shoved her blade into her new boot in a well-practised move.

"*It's open!*" she yelled, pulling her top roughly over her head and pushing her hair out from the seal. Dyss, Reed and the Viscount himself bundled into the room a little clumsily. She replaced her belt, pistol holster and grapple gun as they regarded her.

"Sorry boys, I'm not doing all that again just for you…" she began, levelly.

"What is your plan, Satiah?" the Viscount asked, directly.

"Tell me what's happening first," she requested. Reed went into explanation *again*, telling her all about the Viscount's announcement, the ceasefire, and the state of affairs with Purella. Satiah listened, making plans and thinking ahead. She then told them about the cult and where she believed they were, and how they fitted in with everything. The Viscount looked utterly shaken but mercifully didn't interrupt. Dyss too was taken aback by *that* development. She eyed him.

"Sorry sir, it's been a bit of a day," she stated, leaving any apology in infancy.

"It's nowhere near over yet either," he allowed, letting it go.

"Right, the first thing we have to do is get Bert off this planet,"

Satiah stated, repeating what she had said before. "We need him to show us *exactly* where the cult are hiding. *He may even be able to get us inside.* I know Purella is watching and waiting and I'm going to do something about that."

"I *don't* think a strip show will work," Reed pointed out, without being serious. She ignored him.

"I will be a decoy," Satiah smirked, at him. "If she sees me running in a cutterboat she will chase me as she will jump to the conclusion that I'm trying to escape somewhere with Bert."

"Does she know that *you know* she's here?" Dyss quizzed, intently. "If she does she might see through the ploy."

"And Bert *is* actually in the cutterboat already," Reed pointed out.

"We can move him out, that's not a problem," she replied, shrugging. "If she knows that I know that she… *you know what*? Let's just get it done." And with that Satiah pushed past them to get back out into the corridor. Rushing ahead, Dyss and Kelvin following, they raced towards the cutterboat area.

***

Purella stormed out of Bavon's office. She'd seen the movement by using his security camera system again and guessed what was about to happen. Bert *was* in the cutterboats, he was just hidden somehow. Perhaps one of them had a secret panel or something.

"Major Clyde!" she called in to her communicator, still running. "I need backup! Assemble the team; make an attack on the ships on the landing bay or something! I need a distraction, there are too many for me to handle alone!"

"Moving in," came his cold reply. She leapt down a set of steps; kicking off of the wall as she got halfway and rolling dramatically back onto her feet at the bottom. Pistol in hand, she shot a guard who seemed to be considering impeding her progress and then sprinted out into the cutterboat area. She was just in time to see Satiah moving out into the sky. The others were already gone! Eager to tangle, Purella jumped nimbly into the next cutterboat along and sped after her.

***

Kelvin and Reed were dragging the still unconscious Bert between them back to the Viscount's chambers. Once there, as Satiah had instructed, they would wake him up and force him to help them. This time Reed didn't object when she had suggested torturing him if he failed to comply. The man had earned a punishment. Pat arrived and tried to help too. Seconds later, sirens were sounding and gunfire could be heard.

"Oh dear," Reed hissed, peering over his shoulder. Pat gasped in shock. *Gunfire in the city?!* After so many years without crime or war or... it was all over now. Dyss turned, rifle at the ready.

"Get him to my ship, activate all systems and wait there," Dyss growled, seriously. "We can't endanger the Viscount." Kelvin let go of Bert, leaving him to Reed and Pat to manage.

"We will cover you," Kelvin stated, in his usual monotone.

"Retreat in stages, on me," Dyss said, to Kelvin.

"Order acknowledged," he said. Dyss raised an eyebrow, spotting that Kelvin had *not actually said* if he would obey it or not, but Dyss understood that as Kelvin was Satiah's property that was most likely not a problem.

First came a few terrified locals, trying to stay ahead of an invading force. Dyss awaited his first foe, a certain gleam of relish in his eyes. This was what being a Phantom should be like! Forget the endless sea of paperwork! The first couple of mercenaries arrived and were too complacent to react in time. Dyss, using his highly illegal gun, basically shredded them. The rest of the team, seeing that they had at last hit resistance, held back and awaited reinforcements. Clyde thoughtfully eyed what remained of a nearby corpse that had been one of his men. He'd known Satiah wasn't alone, but he'd not expected to meet anything serious until he got close to the Viscount.

"Split up, we will bypass them, try the floor below," he ordered, motioning to some of the team behind him. He peered around the corner and leapt back to avoid a wave of flames that came from Kelvin.

Clyde let out a breath and couldn't help but grin.

"*These guys mean business,*' he remarked, to himself. "Use grenades, force them back." He backed off as two others, a man and a woman of equally grim countenance, flung explosives around the corner. Kelvin and Dyss had already backed off, expecting the tactic.

"City is under attack, the Viscount is the target, get him out," Dyss growled, into his communicator.

"Oh my goodness!" cried the secretary. "What do I do?"

"Follow your security protocols for…" he began.

"I'm sorry we don't have anything like that here, this was a peaceful place until you…" she argued.

"Forget it, let him die, see how you deal with it," he hissed, cutting her off. He eyed Kelvin, annoyed. "I hate pacifists."

"Captain Ogun," he called, trying someone else.

"Dyss," the Captain answered, instantly. "I have a team ready to go in and repel the attackers. They must have smuggled themselves past…"

"Never mind *them*, just get the Viscount out and keep him on your ship, he'll be safe there," Dyss instructed, unleashing another torrent of laser fire himself. His bolts ripped right through the wall, killing those taking cover behind it. Kelvin was eyeing his rifle.

"*No, she can't have one*!" Dyss grinned at the big robot. "I plan to join you and the Viscount as soon as possible."

"Yes," Ogun replied, cutting off.

More raced out in a foolish attempted to swarm through. They were cut down and burned by the joint fire of both Dyss and Kelvin. More charges were thrown and Dyss and Kelvin backed off a little more. Dyss felt so elated and excited it was all he could do not to whoop every time he brought one down. He'd forgotten how the adrenalin felt, and this reminded him of a time in his life when things had been much simpler. He never lost focus though; never let his emotions rule him. Instead he started to retaliate with a few buckshots of his own. Kelvin alternated between automatic laser fire and flamethrower. Between the two of them they probably seemed like a much larger force than they were to the mercenaries, simply because of the sheer firepower.

A cocktail of laser fire and flame became the baptism of pain for each new corridor gained by Clyde's ever decreasing force. This didn't bother Clyde, as he was only supposed to be a diversion. He knew there was no real chance they could ever get to the Viscount himself. Going after the landing craft, as Purella had wanted, was pointless as there were too many craft to take out. Preferably, he'd have brought in a greater force, but there had not been time, and this hadn't been planned.

"I thought you said they were pacifists?" demanded someone, in his ear.

"I did. I never said they weren't dangerous though," Clyde told him, nonchalantly. He nudged a woman next to him, and she turned to face him. "You're with me," he stated, an idea coming to him. She nodded, her mouth curving into a smile. They rushed back down the corridor they had just fought up.

***

The wave was colossal, a testament to the relentless strength of nature, and the cutterboat just managed to get over it in time before disappearing again behind another equally titanic wave. Instead of riding over it, this time the cutterboat sliced right through the wall of water. Satiah gritted her teeth and fought to stay at the controls as much as to use them. She swung left and right, snaking her way around the biggest waves as best she could. Purella, doing the same, was in hot pursuit. Another wave smashed into the side of Satiah's cutterboat, drenching her in warm salty water and nearly forcing her overboard. She returned to the controls just as another wave struck. She used the propellers at the end of the directional arms to give her some extra height. She rose above the next wave, feeling the spray as it just missed her. Down she went again, break necking it down its back like a tiny insect running across a huge beast's body.

Purella too was struggling. She swerved wildly, using the propellers to keep her away from the worst of the swells. Yet the ocean on Collgort-Elipsa was unlike that on any other planet. The currents were all colliding with one another constantly, due to the gravitational forces created by the cities in its sky. These waters were of different densities, and this in turn caused a never-ending rolling effect beneath the surface. This occurred as the water that was denser flowed under water of lesser density. The result was a rapids-style ocean with freak waves heading in all directions and hazardous maelstroms between them. These maelstroms, basically giant whirlpools, droned constantly as if with a distant but never ending sonic booming.

Purella was able to keep pace with Satiah only because she had someone to follow, rather than trying to figure out which way to go herself. She had given up hope of shooting at her, as she was literally unable to aim due to the rough and tumble of the water. Another upsurge clobbered the cutterboat, almost spinning Purella around completely. She adjusted the propellers to ensure she kept going, albeit backwards, straight after Satiah. The cutterboats crashed against one another and Satiah swung the directional arm around in a circular swing-like motion, spinning her own cutterboat around, and almost sweeping Purella off of her feet and into the swell. The propellers sparked as they tried to chew into the deck. Purella tried the same thing and the arms caught one another at the joint, making both cutterboats start to circle one another.

A laser bolt narrowly missed Purella and she threw herself to the floor, only to have the wind knocked out of her as the deck rose and she went down, effectively slamming into it. She rolled, finding cover behind some crates. Satiah, still holding on, eyed the directional arms, trying to find a way of detaching them. Another wall of water hit both ships, flattening her against the controls. Another influx, this time from the opposite direction, surged into her. As she reeled and spat out the water, she realised that if they didn't separate the ships they would both be smashed to pieces. A third swell rose and thundered into the ships with all the contemptuous subtlety of a heavyweight torpedo. Satiah could only look on in terror as it ploughed into her. Her feet left the floor and she let out a shriek as she crashed, back first into the rear directional arm.

Her head flicked back with the whiplash effect and almost knocked her out as she struck the metal hard. Desperate, she scrambled back over to the controls and tried in vain to unlock the two arms.

"*Come on!*" she hollered at it, over the hellish noise of enraged ocean. Maybe this hadn't been such a smart move after all. They all rose suddenly as one of the slightly smaller waves lifted them nearly ten meters. As the boats were moved the angle of the arms changed and there was space to move. Satiah yanked. Screeching as they came apart, the arms finally separated and both ships flew off, away from one another. Both women fought for control again. Satiah was quickly able to rise above the next few waves and then began to pick up speed as she followed the watery channel that formed as the breaker plunged. This normally only happened when the waves came to a shore, but here a similar effect occurred sometimes when the waves collided with one another.

Purella was following, although she was only just ahead of the channel's end, the swirls colliding mere seconds behind her. She aimed as carefully as she could and fired. The bolt screamed past the side of Satiah's head. She ducked instinctively but decided against evasive manoeuvres on the principle that doing anything other than going straight would result in disaster. She tried something craftier, lowering the rear directional arm so that the propeller blocked Purella's line of sight. Purella smiled grimly, knowing exactly why Satiah had been forced to do that. The channel was opening up ahead of them and Satiah pulled out from under the breaker, corkscrewing right and spinning around. It was Purella's turn to duck as Satiah fired two shots straight at her face. In the move, Satiah almost lost control and had to bank sharply to avoid tipping over completely.

Purella swung in close, dodging another upsurge, as both craft began to accelerate more quickly in the open, above the worst of the sea. Spray and foam still reached them along with droplets uncountable. Satiah's whole face was stinging from tiny pinpricks, not dissimilar to how hail would feel. She tried to see how far they had come. Not that far as it turned out, maybe a few kilometres. More laser fire came from Purella, as if to merely remind her that she was still there. Steeling herself, Satiah began to descend back down into the chaos of the waves. It was her best chance at losing or even killing Purella. The buffeting began again and the cutterboat rocked, jerked and shuddered beneath her. It took so much strength just to stand there and drive the thing! If she hadn't been soaked to the skin from the ocean itself, sweat would have achieved something similar by now. She'd given the others long enough now; it was time to end the madness. She braced herself, knowing if she did what she planned to do wrong, she'd be dead.

She decelerated abruptly, while raising the rear directional arm upwards and straight. Purella, not expecting the move and unable to slow down, crashed straight into her. The propeller sheared right through the front of Purella's cutterboat, opening up a huge gash that the water was quick to make use of. Purella, activating her distress call to Clyde, lobbed a grenade over onto the deck of Satiah's cutterboat, the principle being: if I go, I'm taking you with me. In the heat of the moment she'd actually forgotten all about Bert who would most likely be killed too. Satiah saw it land and in a last, death-defying move, she nose-dived off of the side and into the ocean. The blast was next, throwing up a fireball as an energy cell went up too. Purella wrestled with a survival pod, water swirling up to her knees as both boats went down rapidly.

***

Clyde and the woman blew the charge and the ceiling came down. They climbed up onto the next floor and were just in time to see Reed and Pat struggling with Bert out onto a landing platform. Clyde and the woman, unburdened by any deadweights, sprinted to catch up. They were just about to reach the doors when Clyde caught them.

"Sorry, you're out of time," he stated, rifle aimed at them. "Hand him over." Reed, thwarted, let the unconscious man slump to the floor. Pat, unwilling to give up, spun on them, trying to get her gun out. A stun bolt took her in the chest before she could even get it out of its holster. The woman then aimed directly at Reed, a stern gleam in her eyes.

"Don't do anything stupid," Clyde advised him, grunting as he picked Bert up and draped him across his shoulders.

"He's not worth saving," Reed replied, with feeling. Clyde eyed the little man levelly.

"Yeah, I think I agree with you there," he admitted. Reed tilted his head, evaluating Clyde properly.

"A mercenary who thinks is rare," Reed stated, watching him keenly.

"If you give her sugar and water when she wakes up, she should be fine after a few minutes,' Clyde told him, nodding to Pat. The woman still watched Reed as Clyde walked slowly away, then retreated with him too. Reed, sighing in disappointment, crouched and pulled Pat into his lap.

"Don't worry, it's not over yet," he assured her, as if comforting a crying child. He pulled out his communicator. Satiah was going to be furious but she had to know. He tried to call her but got nothing. Instead he called Dyss and explained what had happened.

"That tells us why they have stopped advancing," Dyss responded, bitterly. "Even with Kelvin to back me I think there are too many for us to get him back."

"They can't leave, the Federation destroyer would blow them out of the sky," Reed stated, with conviction. "Even *with* Bert onboard."

***

Safely in the pod and high in the air, out of the reach of all but the tallest of waves, Purella waited for rescue. She couldn't be sure if she'd got Satiah or not with the grenade, but there was no sign of her on the surface. No blood either, but surely no one could survive in that swirl for long. Bert too would be dead. She hated herself for killing him, but at the time it had been the only way she could think of to take out Satiah. Unavoidable collateral damage. Her communicator went off. It was Clyde.

"I need you to come get me…" she began, seriously.

"Satiah was a diversion… I've got the doctor back inside the freighter," Clyde told her. "What happened?"

"I don't know, she must have *switched* him out somehow…"

How Satiah had had time to pull something like that off, Purella couldn't imagine. It had to have been when she had been running to catch up, when she couldn't see what was going on through the cameras. Or she'd called someone to do it for her while she knew Purella was watching her. That meant Satiah might have known about Bavon.

"We can't come to get you as the Federation destroyer is effectively pinning us. We need to call in the *Dreadnaught*. I know it can't fight a destroyer singlehanded and hope to win, but it *can* distract it long enough for us to get away," Clyde stated. Purella sighed. She didn't want her ship to be damaged but she could see he was right. It was their best chance of escaping the planet unscathed.

"Do it," she agreed. "It would be silly to lose the prisoner a second time." Quint would murder her for sure if that happened.

"I'll get the ship to pick you up as it goes through and then you can take command and help us get Bert out?" Clyde suggested. A pain in her heart made her sigh. Why wouldn't Clyde join the cult too? It was such a waste of talent.

"Yes, good plan," she concurred, and meant it.

"Ten minutes," he warned her. She automatically began to count down in her head but her eyes still scanned the waves for any sign of Satiah. She seemed to have completely vanished.

***

The water was roaring in Satiah's ears and she managed to get her portable breathing mask into her mouth easily enough, but she wasn't rising back to the surface. The currents tore at her and pushed her around unceasingly. She was sinking quickly and soon she seemed free of the worst of the swirl. There were bubbles rising all around her. It took her a few moments to realise *why* she couldn't float. Methane bubbles were affecting the density of the water and thus made everything less buoyant. She frantically clawed, trying to swim back up but it was no use. She could feel the pressure gradually mounting on her ears.

Light from the surface was already starting to fade and the water had become noticeably cooler. She tried to activate her earpiece but it wasn't working. Fear welled up inside her. If she didn't do something the pressure of the water would crush her. Her ears were starting to hurt as they popped more and more. She flailed again but it was no use, this time she tried to get out of the bubbles by moving *along* rather than *up*, but they seemed to be everywhere she looked. She tried to see the cutterboats but they were coming down too, so there was no chance she could use her grapple-gun to drag herself back up. Now what? *Now* what?

She became aware of a high-pitched chirping noise. She wondered if it was her own skull starting to cave in or something equally as fatal. It was really starting to hurt now as the pressure continued to pile on. Then she realised it was the Obsenneth crystal, still in her pocket, making the noise. Was it being crushed too? Something grabbed her leg and she jumped in surprise. There were three of them, *creatures*, surrounding her. One had her legs and the other two grabbed her arms. She struggled against them, pulled one arm free and tried to get to the blade in her boot. They were strange creatures. They had *arms* and *tails* and were about nine feet long. They had no hair and their faces were pale and featureless. They had mouths and sharp teeth and their eyes were huge, oval and green.

She wriggled free and waved the blade defensively at them, her own bubbles from her breath blinding them to her. She began sinking again, and her ears crackled.

"Satiah," said Obsenneth, in her mind. "They are trying to help you. I called to them, *trust them*." Satiah could only shriek in pain as the pressure continued to mount. Again the hands grabbed her and this time she didn't resist. She felt the pressure reducing as she rose in the water. She opened her eyes. In front of her, two big green eyes regarded her solemnly. This one had long yellowy hair and seemed more female than the other two. Their powerful tails, or flukes, or whatever they were, seemed strong enough to keep them at the same depth. They were also gradually moving sidelong, presumably to escape the jet of methane bubbles.

"*What are you?*" Satiah managed, trying to ignore the pain in her head. The green eyes narrowed and the thing opened her mouth, displaying the same sharp teeth the other two had. A chirpy, bird like noise came from her.

"Yes, that's not helpful," Satiah replied, managing to get Obsenneth in her hand. Her skin exposed, the link was there. "Tell them I need to get back to the city. Did you see if Purella...?"

"They will not take you there," he said, uselessly.

"Can they understand me?" she asked, seriously. Her hand brushed against the arm of one of them and Satiah noticed its smooth and rubbery flesh with mild interest. "What are they?"

"No, they cannot understand you but they can understand me. They used to live in great underwater cities for as long as they can remember until the humans came here..." he was saying.

Satiah rolled her eyes, having heard stories like this before. *Oh great!* And what had those naughty humans done this time? And now, as a consequence of this insult, these creatures, righteously enraged, now intended to eat *her* or kill *her* in some way to exact their revenge? She was just glad that Ash wasn't around to hear this, he'd love it.

"...and destroyed all that with their gravitational cities, turning the oceans into... *this*. Since then they have only retained the ability to hunt and stay alive. Their culture is destroyed and they have lost much knowledge..."

"*I don't care about any of that!*" Satiah interrupted, irritated. "Are they going to kill me?"

"No. In exchange for saving your puny body, they want you to take the sky giants away," Obsenneth told her.

"*What?*" she shrieked, cross. "What's that supposed to mean?"

"I'll put that another way: you get the sky cities to leave this world and they will agree to save your life. Or else they will let you drop and die. It's up to you but I would like to point out that I need you alive, so I strongly suggest you think about it," Obsenneth said.

"*Hold on a second!*" she protested, levelly. "Let's just take this through in stages, *please!*" More chirping and the female grabbed Satiah's throat with a big muscular hand. She started to squeeze and Satiah tried ineffectively to free herself.

"She's asked you how such a weak creature could cause so much destruction," Obsenneth said. He sounded amused.

"Tell her to get off me or I'll break..." Satiah growled.

"*Satiah!*" warned Obsenneth.

"Tell her I'm not with them, tell her I'm not human, tell her anything, just..." Satiah hissed, trying to hold onto her breathing device. One of the males was trying to take it off of her. More chirping. The female released her and the male backed off. They were free of the bubbles now and all four of them just floated there in the twilight of the deep.

"Now," Satiah breathed, still staring at the female who *might* be in charge. "They want me to get those cities to move?"

"That is correct."

"If I don't: they will kill me?" she clarified.

"They will allow you to die, yes. I suppose that is essentially the same thing."

"What's to stop me from agreeing and then doing nothing?"

Satiah asked, expecting there to be more.

"They will curse you if you fail them."

"*Really?*" Satiah almost laughed. "*A curse?* You weren't joking when you said they had lost their knowledge, were you?" More chirping and the female came forward again. She put one fin/hand on Satiah's head and then removed it again.

"She is saying that she knows it is not your fault that this happened but they are dying and need help. You can help them, Satiah…"

"I don't know exactly how much of this you have been following, but I would like to remind you that there might be a battle about to kick off up there, and you *seriously* expect *me* to be able to get them all to leave?" she argued, levelly. "I have every sympathy for them, I really do, but collateral damage is *inevitable.*"

"So what's it going to be?"

"Yes, of course I will help them," she lied, instantly. She had to save herself; she had a mission to complete.

"Will you?" Obsenneth asked. Saying and doing were very different, after all.

"What do you think?" she demanded, angrily. "*I have a job to do.*"

"They could be *useful* to you, Satiah," Obsenneth stated, his tone one of patient persuasion. "Imagine having a whole species of lifeform alive *because of you*. Imagine how *grateful* they would be *to you* and therefore how useful they could later be." Satiah paused, knowing he was trying to manipulate her but not sure why.

"What is *your* interest in this *precisely?*" she asked, shadily.

"Your survival, *of course,*" he replied, expecting the question. "Without you, I have to start again." Yeah, *right*.

"Oh, so you're just *doing me a favour?*" she scoffed, sarcastically. *Tread carefully;* she cautioned herself in her mind, she really was just hanging there right above death.

"Only if you want to live."

Well, refusing would be tantamount to suicide so…

"Yes, tell her or them or whoever you're talking to, that I will get those cities moved but it will take some time," she stated, trying to buy herself some time. "Tell her that the humans *didn't know* what they had done. Tell her that they would *never* have wanted this to happen." Not too derisively, she hoped. More chirping. She knew that was a bit high-handed saying all that but it could be close to the truth. Besides, how useful would a bunch of overgrown fish be to her anyway?

"It is done, they will now help you *slowly* back to the surface," he said. Yes... it would be ironic after all this if she were to die from decompression sickness.

"Thank you for your assistance," Satiah replied, begrudgingly.

"It would be wasteful for a fascinating woman like you to be lost in such a way."

"You have a funny way of showing that you care," she retorted, not at all pleased by any of this.

***

The Viscount hurried onto the command deck of the Federation destroyer. Ogun was there and touched his hat to him, the formal mode of address on any battleship.

"How many are dead?" The Viscount asked, looking pale and sweaty. He wanted to know how many of his citizens had been hurt in the attack.

"Not possible to determine that as of yet, sir," Ogun replied, his tone professional.

"Sir!" called someone. "*Contact!*" Ogun turned to face the new enemy. A Dreadnaught, coming in fast, heading straight for them.

"Allegiance?" Ogun asked, straight faced.

"Unknown, sir," was the reply.

"Launch fighters, strategy seven," he ordered, calmly. "Hail them."

"No answer, sir!"

Dyss, Reed and Pat joined them.

"What's happening *now?*" Reed asked, flabbergasted.

"I think our friends down there have called in their backup..." Ogun replied, motioning to the screen with a dramatic wave of his hand.

"A freighter *is* departing on the opposite side of the city sir!" Ogun understood the diversionary tactic.

"Send orange squadron after it, they are *not* to destroy it, *cripple it only please*," he instructed.

"Sir."

"How can you know?" Pat asked, concerned that it might be evacuating civilians.

"It makes sense," Dyss stated. "Look at the timings of the movements."

"Sir, we have other signals coming in, destroyers. *Vinu destroyers* numbering *eight* are now in the outer exosphere. They are hailing us."

"Put them through," Ogun nodded, touching his hat. He stood still, his hands clasped behind his back as Captain Arnos appeared.

"Responding to the recent instruction to defend this world, what's the situation Captain?" Arnos asked, respectfully. Pat gasped in awe. It worked! *They had listened!*

"We are currently repelling another pirate attack, please array your ships in whatever formation suits your style best, Captain. We are expecting a Union response any time now and I don't need them breathing down my neck while I deal with this,' Ogun explained.

"Understood," Arnos stated, cutting off.

"Keep eyes on them, make sure they do what we have agreed," Ogun ordered, to his lieutenant. The man touched his hat and gave a sharp nod.

Ogun shot Dyss a cynical grin.

"I'd love to just be able to trust them *but…*" he said, not finishing the sentence meaningfully.

"We get it, smart moves." Dyss nodded, seeing what he was guarding against. If Arnos was lying it would give them time to react, should Arnos fail to obey Ogun's instructions. Flashes occurred as some of the flak from the Dreadnaught made it their way.

"They are making a fight of it, sir," someone shouted. Well, obviously!

"They are faster than they should be, the ship may have been modified!" someone else yelled.

"Tell everyone to keep their distance, go for the engines," Ogun shouted, over the confusion. Something made the ship jolt and Pat grabbed Reed in shock.

"Concentrate your fire," Ogun stated, the first signs of tension starting to appear on his face now.

***

Clyde winced as another explosion occurred. They were pelting through the sky, chased by maybe fifty fighters or some ridiculous number like that. The *Dreadnaught* was ahead, trying to provide something resembling covering fire. There were just too many fighters though.

"I'm getting ready to get out of this," Purella said, in his ear.

"You seen who else has turned up?" he asked, casually.

"Yes, that's why we *need* to get out of this," she stated, aware of the new arrivals. Twin laser bolts took out the last of his shields and he grinned as his grip tightened on the controls.

"Coming in on fire," he warned. A fighter zoomed past directly in front of him, only just avoiding collision. The tactic was to get him to swerve or change direction. Clyde didn't break, he just kept going.

He had a tremendous sense of being, holding onto those controls. Feeling the craft judder under the multiple impacts. A smile creased his face. It reminded him of the rides he'd been on when he had been a small child. The excitement, the high. He barrel rolled, as more and more firepower converged on his ever-depleting shields. The sounds he could hear were those bolts burning into the hull. The hangar was open and he screamed inside, his hull literally bursting into flames.

"*Everyone out!*" he shouted, commandingly. "Make sure the prisoner is out too!" He then got hold of Purella again as the ship was hosed down behind him. "*In and safe, time to go!*"

"Disengaging now," she replied, tense. He stripped to the waist, all heat and sweat as he breathed more slowly. He poured water over himself, still panting. Wow, what a dash!

The modified engines, the result of the mishmash of many of the latest additions, more than ten times faster than a regular dreadnaught, soon left their pursuers far behind.

***

Watching from the ocean surface, Satiah saw the *Dreadnaught* depart. A cutterboat was coming down towards her. She was held close to the surface by the reptiles. She still didn't know what they called themselves, she'd never bothered to ask. Kelvin was there, piloting it as well as anyone else ever could. She hauled herself in.

"Thank you, Kelvin," she smiled, seriously. Kelvin's eyes were not on her but were following her watery friends that quickly vanished into the depths. She watched too momentarily, feeling gratitude. So, *they* must have been those intermittent signals that the scanners had picked up each time they arrived on the planet.

She glanced up at the giant bulk of the floating city nearest to them, and then returned her gaze to the churning waters again. Despite how she had behaved, she did feel a bit sorry for them. Only a little bit! How could they have been so careless all those years ago? She knew people were always destructive and dangerous *and stupid* but… when you could see the hurt in those big green eyes… It just reminded everyone that our, that is to say *the human*, approach could be better. So… how could Satiah get them to move? She hoped that moving the cities wouldn't further destabilise their environment. When she looked up again she could see everything else that was going on. Fighters flying everywhere, destroyers higher up in the sky that weren't there before. A wave suddenly slammed into them and she almost fell in again.

"*Let's go!*" she yelled, not wanting another soaking.

"Bert has been taken prisoner again," Kelvin stated. She whirled on him. The cutterboat rose swiftly.

"How the hell did that happen?" she demanded, incredulous. It had been the whole point in drawing Purella away: to prevent that from happening.

"It seems that not all of those she brought with her were as easily convinced," he replied, in his normal way.

"Listen… *before we go back*… I would have died in that without the Obsenneth," she said, to Kelvin. He focussed on her. A wave buffeted them and she clutched a guard railing. Kelvin accelerated back towards the city, leaving the tempestuous seas far behind. "*It needs me* to complete its mission, therefore it intends no harm to come to me," she said, seriously.

"Until it no longer requires your help," Kelvin stated, levelly.

"*Until it no longer requires my help,*" she agreed, nodding slowly. She had to allow that much and she didn't know for sure that he was wrong.

"Where are the others?" she asked, changing the subject.

"On the Federation ship, there are many warships coming here," Kelvin explained. Satiah realised something. If ever there *was* a time to get the Viscount to remove his cities from this world, *this was it*. It was a masterful stroke of luck, in a way, that matters had come to a head at this time. Getting him to move could be much easier than she'd initially thought. And *next time* they picked a world, they had better make *sure* it really was uninhabited. She fleetingly wondered how many species had been made extinct by mankind's negligence. Someone had once said that humanity was a plague that killed everything it couldn't subjugate. Probably an immortal, someone like Ash, all self-righteous and... She decided not to think too much more about that, as her temper was stirring again. It sounded like the kind of cavalier thing that Ash would come out with. Yet, in this case, even Satiah had to admit they had a point.

Fighters were everywhere now and a few even formed an escort around *them*. Everyone was returning to the capital ship. Satiah confined her mind to the mission for a few moments. Without Bert, finding the cult's secret lair would be much more challenging, if not impossible. The Union would be moving soon, if they hadn't already, but now the lone Federation destroyer had the backing of the Vinu forces. Not enough to stop the Union, but maybe enough for them to think twice about starting a fight. What would the cult do when they found out, assuming they didn't already know, what had transpired here? How could she destroy them? *And where was that blasted gold?* She put her hand in her pocket, feeling the Obsenneth crystal there. All stone-like and innocent. And there was that too, she thought. She would have to sit down with Reed and Dyss now and think about how they would take on the rest of this.

***

Family reunions could be problematic. That could be said about almost anyone's. The Drass family were no exception. Darius had watched, interested, as they interacted. Nothing much to write home about. Ambassador Drass had wasted little time before starting an argument. The mother and a few others, though, actually took Milo's side and he was shouted down. Darius used this time to assemble some resources. Two brand new Covert-Class Phantom ships, supplies, extra power cores and anything else that he could think of that they might need. Satiah would appreciate that he'd not wasted his time on Earth. One additional thing he *had* observed while there, however, was the astonishing amount of activity in the military shipyards. No one would say what was going on, most likely because they didn't know, but everyone was pretty sure someone was going somewhere.

He had a fair idea of where: things must really be kicking off on Collgort-Elipsa. Cherry was busy signing delivery dockets. He returned to the ship and set the coordinates after performing a safety check. As he was sat there, looking out at the city in the view port, he spotted something. A Coalition destroyer. It was flying low, coming in to dock. He frowned at it. So *that* was why everyone had been so busy. The Coalition planned on sending part of their fleet there too. The Union would not like that either. The idea of the Federation and the Coalition fighting on the same side would really make them think again. He stroked his moustache thoughtfully, considering the political implications again. While it was not likely, it was still probable that this could go the cult's way and turn into a full-scale war. Unless they destroyed the cult first, of course…

He was fairly sure that full-scale war, excluding the cult obviously, was something that *everyone* hoped to avoid. He thought back to the scenario shortly before the Common Protectorate War. It had been similar. People angry at the economy, angry at the government, and of course, most damaging of all, angry at each other. It was difficult to remember it was not a cycle. It was *not* a pattern. A lot of people claimed that society and civilisation worked in cycles, history repeating itself etc, and that war was inevitable in order to create the balance. *The balance?* What was that supposed to mean? Some sort of fail-safe that God-like beings implemented to ensure man never challenged their power? Or was it just the rich enslaving the poor, using their own ideas against them as ever? As a Phantom agent,

Darius knew that the truth was unknowable simply because there was no real truth. While conspiracies were rife and some of them true, most were false. People were sheep, it was true, but that didn't mean they couldn't be dangerous.

It did make him angry when he heard people saying things that weren't true, and predicting cataclysms in the future that so many people seemed to fixate on. About their government, about their world or about their superpower. He knew it meant nothing, and that it was flawed even if it was sincere, but it still vexed him that he struggled to counter such obviously manipulative machinations. He remembered the first law of Phantom Squad. *You survive.* Above all else, that is what you do, even if it costs the mission. The election was coming soon and the chaos would begin again as those in power strove to prove that democracy existed. He wondered how *this mission* would affect that. It was an old established joke in Phantom Squad that *there was no such thing as democracy*. And while it did still amuse some… it did not amuse him. It would be time to leave soon. Never soon enough for him.

***

An uneasy standoff was now evident in the skies and the space all around Collgort-Elipsa.

Vinu and Shintu forces were evidently wary of each other but managed to divide the area so that they could control their own segments of it *without* infringing upon the other's regions. The Federation destroyer was acting as a neutral flagship for the defensive fleet. Reed looked at the computer to get a better idea of the precariousness of the state of affairs. The Viscount also watched, a stunned expression on his face. This was *his* world and *his* people, and now they had all these other tense guys patrolling everything. They were as likely to shoot each other as they were to defend the planet. Yet, nothing had gone wrong so far, so he kept his mouth firmly shut despite his own council jumping up and down in his ears all the time.

"Some ships did make a hasty escape too," Ogun was saying. "The majority seemed to be personalised transporters though."

"I do not blame them," murmured Reed, sombrely. Satiah thought one of those was probably *Amber* making a swift getaway, but she didn't say so. It was quite reasonable that she didn't want to meet Satiah in person in case Satiah got all patriotic and chose to kill her.

"I need to talk to the Viscount alone," Satiah announced, drawing in a breath.

Everyone except Reed moved a respectful distance away. She considered telling him to get lost too but then shrugged it off. So what if *he* overheard? He probably somehow knew what she was going to say anyway, the know-all!

"Viscount, I think it would be best for you to reassemble your cities and leave this world," she stated, seeing no other easy way of approaching the topic. To her astonishment he didn't immediately start arguing. "Your people are suffering here now and *it's not your fault*, but if you stay here for too long… that could be perceived as being your fault in later times."

"To be honest I had been thinking about it," he admitted, sadly.

"You could set up shop anywhere," she encouraged. "You don't even have to tell anyone where you're going. Not at first."

"And *where* would you suggest I go?" he asked, a rueful expression on his face. "*Coalition space?*" She almost rolled her eyes. Yes, *of course*, we're *trying* to save you and your pathetic citizens here!

"Wherever you want, just *not here*," she stated, letting that go. "Obviously you would have to never return."

"I would say that bringing all the cities together might be a smart move. It is easier to defend one than many," Reed agreed, subtly.

"It also makes us a bigger target," the Viscount argued, levelly. "What does Pat think about all this?"

"Not sure yet, but something tells me she would not be in favour of more people getting hurt," Reed answered, smoothly.

"It's for your own benefit," Satiah tried again. "There is no advantage to staying here now. Worst case could be that you're the ground zero for a whole new intergalactic war." That got his attention.

"You *really* think…?" he began, unsure how to take that.

"What I think *doesn't matter*. Staying here is an irresponsible thing to do, no matter *how* you look at it. *Get out now while you still can*," she stated, rudely. Reed winced. The Viscount, however, was too busy listening to her words to really notice her tone properly.

"I will give the order," he said, after a pause. "I must... I... Can you find us a world that *isn't* in Coalition space?" She shrugged.

"If that's what you want then yes, happy to help," she replied, her tone carefully neutral. The Viscount headed away to do what he had to do and she caught Reed gaping at her.

"You know, I didn't know you were *lying* about your talents in diplomacy," he grinned.

"I'm surprised, *I lie about a lot of things*," she reminded him.

"So why do you *really* want them to leave?" he asked, not taken in at all. "I'm guessing it had nothing to do with civilian deaths?"

"I have my reasons," she said, clinging to the mystery. She knew, were their positions reversed, *he* wouldn't just tell her either. Well, if he did he wouldn't make it easy. So he could simmer quietly, just as she normally had to!

She crossed her arms and leaned against the console with a grin.

"Well, don't look so smug, Satiah," he ordered, a little sharply. "I knew from the beginning that they would be forced to move. Indeed, from day one I was trying to persuade the Viscount to move."

"Move *allegiance*, not location," she corrected, amused.

"Perhaps, I never said *that*," he retorted.

"No, but it's what you wanted," she pointed out.

"Are you saying that you have wishes that *differ from* those of the Coalition?" he asked, grinning.

"No more than you do," she smiled, deviously. For a moment they just stared at one another, but as they were both such great performers, it was rather a waste of time.

"Yes," Reed allowed, at last looking away. "The Cult of Deimos. Do you have a plan?"

"I do," she replied, unable to resist blaming him a little. "Would have made things a lot easier had *you* not lost Bert."

"I will make up for it," he assured her, as if it was nothing at all to worry about.

"Besides, right now, *as you have his memories, you* might be all I need," she faced him again, her expression a little predatory. He gave a mock stagger away from her as if in horror.

"I gave you everything I had," he shrugged. "The bits we need are the bits we can't get at."

"True, but Kelvin and I *did* find the planet in question before we had to rush back here." He raised his eyebrows expectantly but she shook her head. He grunted in comprehension, knowing that if she had found anything she would have already told him. Then again, he'd not exactly expected a welcoming ceremony on the cult's behalf to be there.

"We did scans but nothing at all came up," she explained, thinking about it. "I imagine they have been there for decades and have easily remained hidden."

"I'm not even too sure of *how* to categorise them. The cult I mean. A *fraternal* organisation *with political interests?*" Reed sighed, still struggling with their bizarre ideology. "*Criminals* will have to do."

"Soon to be *dead* criminals?" she offered, grinning wickedly.

"I don't normally condone that sort of thing as you know, but in *their* case..." he trailed off.

"We all have our standards," she murmured, softly. "Now that we *know* they exist, they have already lost one of their main advantages."

"There's is some solace in that," he acknowledged, bleakly. Then he smiled. "It's interesting how Quint fits into this, isn't it?"

"You mean how he is *one of them* but doesn't *behave* like one of them?" Satiah offered, nodding. "I noticed that too."

He nodded. Saying that, they didn't have much to compare him against. Purella was his main instrument, though.

"Quint doesn't *think* like the others either. He was able to see straight through your little ruse with the missing battleship. He *only* uses people he can trust, and *even then* he never gives them *more* than they need to know. Makes you wonder *why* he needs the cult at all, other than for money."

"*That was actually Darius's idea, not mine.* I imagine that is probably the only reason," Reed said, nodding. She shook her head, going through it all.

"It's like he has contingencies in place for everything we might do. *A master planner...*" she said, her eyes narrowing. "He *knew* we would find a way of preventing the pirate attacks, therefore he engineers things so that it blows up in our faces. He does this by purposely destroying the Union ship. To do *that* he had to know which ship they were sending, when it was going... *everything.* The Cult must have considerable eyes to see all that."

"Worrying, isn't it?"

***

Purella slumped back into the chair, aboard *Dreadnaught*. They had had to run and she hated doing that, but they'd succeeded. Thanks to Clyde, Bert was once again their prisoner. And though she'd not managed to get Satiah's skull, at least she was dead. Even if she'd survived the grenade there was no way she'd have lived long in *those* waters. Clyde was sat in the chair next to her, and he was checking that no one was following them. It was unlikely, as they needed to stay to protect their precious city, but it wasn't out of the question. She allowed herself a malicious smile.

"With Satiah dead and the prisoner returned, Quint will be pleased," she stated.

"No rock though," he replied, as if it meant nothing without it. She frowned.

"True, but there will be no comeback from that. Satiah is dead, and it's not like even she knew what it was," she replied. Clyde thought back to the recording he'd listened to. Back when Satiah had been interrogating Kyle.

"*Neither do we,*" he replied, with more meaning than she could guess at.

She turned to face him, perceiving residual bitterness in his vibe.

"I don't want to fight you, Clyde," she said, softly. "*I really don't.*"

"Good for you," he remarked, uncaringly. "I just want this over with."

"Look, I'm *sure* I can..." Her communicator interrupted her. Clyde allowed a victorious smirk to cross his lips. She was turning into just another kind of servant for the powers that were. To make it worse, she didn't even realise it.

"Yes Quint," she said, glad of the chance to update him on her latest success.

"Kyle is dead," he told her, without waiting. "Corkscrew base is a wreck."

"What happened?" Purella asked, shooting Clyde a curious glance. He shrugged unhelpfully.

"I cannot say for sure, but this looks like Satiah's work if it wasn't the pirates themselves," he responded.

"...Should that matter? Surely we've moved beyond the need for pirates now?" she asked, grim.

"It matters, because it could mean that if it *was* Satiah..." he began.

"*Satiah is dead!*" Purella declared, over him. "I blew her up on Collgort-Elipsa right before we got away with Bert." There was a silence. She had expected some form of reward or at least a reluctant congratulation but got neither.

"...I did not expect that," he stated, honestly. "I considered her too skilful for you."

"Well, we all make mistakes," she replied, grit in her tone. Clyde, as ever listening in, was glad that Purella had not noticed his deception. He'd been ready to kill her there and then if he had to.

"Search your ship and make sure no one is on it that shouldn't be," he advised her. It had happened before, after all. "Then, once you're sure that you are clean, you may approach the cult."

"Thank you," she smiled, proudly.

"The Union fleet will arrive on Collgort-Elipsa soon, and when they do, either the Federation ship will withdraw or be destroyed. Are there any other forces there?" he asked, interested.

"Yes," she said, knowing this would displease him. "Too many for one Union force to handle. Several battle fleets are there. Vinu and Shintu." Quint went silent. "It might only take *one careless move* to kick off a fight among them though. They still distrust each other, no matter what the Viscount says. How could they not? After so many years of conflict."

"That *is* possible," he acknowledged. There was a silence, as all of them knew the chances of a battle breaking out were now significantly lower than they had been. This was all to the good in Clyde's mind. Making money was one thing, but creating all-out war for profits was not something he would just let happen.

"We will begin a full sweep of the ship," Purella stated, her posture lazy. "Then we will be on our way." She cut off before he could say anything else and she slowly turned to face Clyde.

"How did we *not know* Kyle was dead?" she demanded, confused. He shrugged. He'd deleted the record, that of Kyle's death, from the main computer although he'd kept a copy for himself.

"There has been no talk to listen to and the bugs revealed nothing," he replied. "If the base *was* destroyed it would explain *why* we're not getting anything." Purella thought about it and then decided to let it go. She was exhausted; besides, she didn't really care about the pirates. It's not like they were really needed anymore in any case.

"Sweep the ship," she ordered, standing slowly. "You find anyone that shouldn't be here, kill them." Clyde nodded and watched her go.

***

The door swished open abruptly and Bavon looked up.

"Can I...?" he began, as Satiah marched in. She shot him before he got any further in his greeting. The android, made to look like Bavon, exploded and fell from the chair, smoking and sparking. She raised an eyebrow, wondering where the real man was hiding. Had he *always* been an android?

"Bavon is still alive and we have to presume he is still on this planet somewhere," Satiah said, into her communicator.

"I will run a scan," Kelvin replied. She went around the desk and eyed the still sparking robot, disappointed. There had been a small argument about whether they should take him prisoner or not. Satiah had argued that he knew nothing that would help them, Quint would see to that. The man would only be an inconvenience and it was best that they just terminated him. Apparently Bavon had seen this coming... *He could have left days ago.*

Where would he go? Was he a member of the cult too? She began searching his desk, literally tearing it apart and sending everything to the floor. Dyss, who had just entered, got to work on the computer.

"There are no *passwords*," he smirked, in amazement.

"Don't you just love this planet?" she muttered, going through a bag aggressively. "They feel *so safe and secure* they don't even bother investing in some decent defence systems. *They had this coming.*" Dyss had to agree. She tipped it upside-down, scattering its contents all over the work station. A pistol, of very poor quality, several reams of Essps in note form, some clothing and some identity papers…

"*Seems silly to run without taking all this,*" she murmured, to herself.

"It also seems that Purella was able to see what we were doing from in here," Dyss stated, showing her the screen. She glanced at it, disinterestedly. It hardly mattered now. Then she stopped and thought about it.

"How far back do those records go and have any been erased?" she asked. He checked.

"Nothing has been removed as far as I can tell. I'm looking for Bavon now," he said, guessing what she was looking for. Satiah continued to rummage around, searching for anything else. Last of all she picked up the identity papers. There were two sets, one genuine and the other was a fake. A fake that had clearly been modelled on the correct set. The correct set *was* Bavon's and the other fake set was *almost* identical. He'd invented a new identity for himself. If he had already run, it made no sense to leave any of this behind.

"He has to still be here somewhere," Satiah stated, with certainty.

"*Got him,*" Dyss hissed, in triumph. She rushed to his side. There was Bavon all right, nearly thirty hours ago, slipping into…

"The disused infrastructure," she mused, a sly smile across her lips. Of course, where else would he be? Dyss brought up a diagram of the extensive layout and sighed.

"It will be a long manhunt," he muttered, trying to work out where to start.

"Flood it with gas," she suggested. "That should flush him out."

"And the citizens?" he asked, mordantly.

"Well, obviously evacuate *them* first!" she stated, irritably. "We don't know what else he may have stored in there or how long he's been preparing his little hidey-hole. He might have enough supplies to stay in there for months and…"

"*All right, all right!*" Dyss grinned, pulling out his communicator. "I'll talk to the Viscount."

No wonder Randal rated Satiah as his best agent. Or at least one of his best. She was very bossy though, Dyss couldn't help but note. Her communicator went off and Satiah answered.

"Yes," she said.

"Hi Satiah, it's me, Cherry! Darius and I are coming in to land in a few minutes, he told me to let you know," she informed.

"Great, I'll see you directly," she said, disconnecting. She turned to see Dyss staring at her.

"I heard that, did you speak to him about *you know what?*" Dyss asked, tense.

"I've been rather busy and have not got around to discussing *Jackdaw* with him," she responded, coolly. She leaned in close, studying his face for anything that resembled guilt. "*Don't worry though, I will.*" It was a wasted effort of course; Dyss was far too good at lying to show anything, even if there was something to show.

"This will be the first time that he and I…" Dyss trailed off, waving a hand at her by way of explanation.

"The first time that you have operated *together* since then," she smiled, simply. That did make sense. "Can I trust you not to try to kill one another?"

"You can trust *me*," he stated, his tone prickly. He was hinting that she was asking the wrong person, as she knew he would.

"Put it this way: if one of you dies in a way I find *suspicious*, *I will kill the other*," she stated, her pistol already in her hand. "Is that understood?"

"It is," he allowed, still uneasy about it. Hardly the reaction of a guilty man. Saying that: were they not all so good at playing these games?

"I shall tell Darius the same thing, naturally," she added, offering that to him as a tiny appeasement. "But who's to say you're not *both guilty* and will turn on me?"

He scoffed at that, but she didn't even smile. Her eyes were like laser beams. Brown gimlets of accusation and wary suspicion burning intensely into his.

"I think we both know that's not the case," he said, carefully.

"Be aware I have contingencies planned for it, if it is," she said, very deliberately. "The only thing those contingencies have in common with each other is that they will all be *fatal* for you both."

"You know, *I* am in charge…" he began, trying to wriggle out of this.

"*You forced me into this*," she hissed, rage in her face now. "Live with it or die because of it, the choice is yours. You know as well as I do, you can be as big a fish as you like in the cosmos out there… but in this room *with me*, I don't even see you as an equal. *You're just another killer.*"

He raised an eyebrow, wisely concealing how intimidated he really felt behind a regretful smile.

"You *can* trust me, Satiah," he stated, and meant it. That made her smile. It was a sad smile as if she really wanted to believe him but couldn't bring herself to.

"They all say that, don't they?" she reminded him, her tone melancholy.

"I'm never going to let anyone know about *him*," he assured her, guessing that *that* might also be playing on her mind. She might just decide to kill him anyway as he had blackmailed her, regardless of Darius.

"Consider this conversation a first and last warning of the consequences, should you be lying to me about that," she stated, unrelenting.

"*Reed* told me to do it," he reminded her, honestly.

"I know," she allowed, finally putting her pistol away. "That is why you're not already dead."

"Good to know," he smiled, smoothly. "The Viscount has approved your plan for the gas, by the way."

"Right, let's get this over with," she said, seriously. Dyss left the room, aware of how stressful that encounter had been, as his legs were almost tired from tensing up the whole time. Satiah eyed the cameras as the citizens, some on stretchers, were being evacuated. In the distance, she could see something coming through the clouds. It was another city. The Viscount must already be starting to reform the giant spacecraft that all the cities were still parts of. She wondered how long it would be before it was ready to leave. She slipped a small tracking device out of her pocket and under the desk. If it was discovered, she could blame it on Bavon, but she had to know where the city was going to go, and she wasn't sure she could trust the Viscount to tell her.

After that she grabbed the announcer.

"Administrator Bavon, it's Satiah, we know where you are. We're not going to come in and get you. You are of no use to us. We are going to gas the infrastructure as everyone else has been evacuated. If you wish to live, I suggest you come out unarmed. We will not shoot you if you surrender. Try anything else and you die, it's that simple," she stated, grimly. Her voice could be heard everywhere in the city so there was no question of him missing her threat. She saw Dyss standing next to the air pumping system. He raised a thumb, letting her know they were ready.

"Do it," she said, disconnecting.

***

Captain Alicia Knight strode onto the bridge of the destroyer. They were due to arrive at Collgort-Elipsa in less than a minute.

"Be ready for anything," she said, quietly. Until about nine hours ago, she had been happily patrolling a quiet backwater, contemplating the pros and cons of various methods of food storage. Then she'd been dispatched urgently, by fleet command, to Collgort-Elipsa in order to force a wayward Federation destroyer to go away. Apparently it had just destroyed a Union destroyer. How one destroyer could so utterly annihilate another without help was a mystery and implied that there was more to this than what fleet command knew. Or what fleet command *would say*. Her ship, Manta, was flagship of an eight-strong fleet made up of destroyers only. Her frigate she'd had to leave behind due to a shield oscillation problem.

Nevertheless, eight to one should be a reasonably unbeatable ratio, she had to presume. Assuming that they were right about there only being one... Dark skinned, with long blue hair, neatly tied to one side, her normal uniform was within the realms of neat... *just*. Her best was in her office back at the barracks.

"We're about to arrive, do you want a countdown?" asked the pilot.

"Not fussed," she sighed, briskly. "I don't suppose you could do a countdown to when we get to leave, could you?" A ten-second countdown began.

"Raise all shields upon arrival, battle stations assumed, I don't want them to get us when we're not ready," she stated, seriously. Several people shouted in response.

There it was, all big and blue, Collgort-Elipsa, getting larger and larger as they sped towards it. A series of alarms sounded and she looked around.

"What is it?" she demanded.

"Err... We have *multiple* readings Captain," someone said. "There are nearly thirty capital ships in orbit, plus seven support ships." Alicia hissed out a breath.

"Hold everything, we stay where we are, *no closer*," she ordered, thinking that fleet command had messed up again.

"They are trying to hail us," said one.

"Let me speak to them," she stated, clicking her fingers demandingly.

"...space. Identify yourselves now or you will be assumed to be hostile intruders..." a man was saying.

"My name is Captain Alicia Knight of the Nebula Union, Holder of the Blue Insignia, Warrior of the Realm and Chief Hawk of Brombarna," she stated, clearly. "Who are you?"

"Captain Arnos of the Wolf Fleet, Vinu navy, current command deputy of this allied-defensive force," he replied. "Listening into this signal is Captain Ogun of the Federation..." He began listing several officers of various ranks.

"*Get me fleet command and make sure all this is being recorded,*" Alicia ordered, waving at the officers behind her.

"We repeat, tell us your purpose here," Arnos concluded.

"Hold that thought," she replied, nonchalantly. "I just need to find out."

"Fleet command…" began a voice.

"*You idiots*!" she hissed, lividly. "Do you have any idea how close we just came to starting a war! We are outnumbered at over three to one! There is *only one* Federation ship here, the rest are all Vinu or Shintu!" There was a pause as presumably they went over everything she had just sent them.

"Formally ask them to surrender the Federation ship into our custody," the man replied.

"I can ask, but if *you* were them, *would you?*" she argued. "And when they refuse, which *I'm pretty sure they will*, what do I do then? Tell them I'm sorry for disturbing them and then hightail it out of here?" Silence. Come on, come on.

"Some of the ships are coming closer," warned an officer, behind her. She held up her hand for silence.

"Then tell them you wish to aid their protection of the planet," came the rather strange response. "Politically it's the only safe move we have left." He did have a point; in any case it was something that was unlikely to make things worse.

"Bit late for that now, isn't it?" she bit back, as she disconnected. She opened the channel up again. "Captain Ogun, I understand you recently engaged a destroyer in combat which you destroyed. I hereby respectfully ask for your surrender to us, the rest of the fleet can remain where they are," she offered, strongly. There was a pause.

"Captain Alicia," said a new voice, it was Reed. "We must *respectfully* decline. The Federation ship is performing an important role here and is not in a position to abandon its station for this or any other reason at the present time. Perhaps when this emergency has subsided you can try again." *Try again?* What did he think was going on here? A rehearsal? Alicia thought this was hilarious although she didn't show it.

"What emergency, please?" she managed.

"Our planet has been attacked and, in the absence of either Union or Coalition forces, others have stepped in to defend it," the Viscount answered. "The reason for this is twofold. First, neither you nor the Coalition could turn up without risking the wrath of the other which could lead to war. And second, without protection we were a sitting duck."

"I see," she smiled, tightly. "In that case I humbly present myself as additional protection for you, if that is permissible?" A silence began. A few looks were exchanged on the command deck around her but no one said anything and few even moved.

"It has been agreed," Reed said, in answer. "You may integrate but you will be split up and mismatched along with everyone else to ensure everyone can keep an eye on each other." *How comradely*, she thought cynically.

"I will begin immediately."

***

Sweat pouring down his face, Bavon sprinted for his life. As he raced around a corner, a blast hit the wall, narrowly missing him. He shrieked in fright and kept going. Satiah ran after him, trying to pick him off, gradually catching up. Deserted now, the city was moving towards the other segments in the air. She had to bring him down before he could escape into the one of the others. The gas was already being drained back out into the atmosphere. Knowing he was not going to outrun her, he slipped to the side when he was out of sight and crouched down. Hugging the wall as closely as he could he closed his eyes and waited. Satiah belted past, seeming to miss him. He stood, unable to believe his luck and turned to return the way they had run.

Dyss's fist floored Bavon instantly and he laid there, barely conscious, blood running down his lips and chin. Dyss whistled shrilly and Satiah came back, jogging lightly. She began to tie Bavon up capably, not caring how tightly the bonds dug into his skin. He should be glad they'd not just shot him. Between them, they escorted him back to the Federation ship where they had an *actual* detention area and proper guards to watch him.

"Questioning?" Ogun had queried. Satiah had shrugged.

"Unlikely, *I doubt he knows anything*. I'm sure the Viscount would like to have a bag to punch before this is over and it's not like *anyone else* is going to propugn him. Not now the cult have abandoned him," she replied, sourly. The Viscount may wish to punish the traitor himself, although he may choose to leave that to the Coalition. They returned to the bridge where the others were waiting.

"Darius is coming in to dock," Reed advised her, watching. It was a strange sight. All those cities, coming together to form a huge juggernaut in the sky. Satiah winced, wondering what it was doing to the oceans below. It had crossed her mind that before things got better for the creatures, they might become a good deal worse. Who knew how things would change for sure once the so-called *sky giants* were gone? In her peripheral vision, she observed Dyss turning to look at her.

"Tell him to wait in the hangar, I need to talk to him *alone*," she replied, making eye contact with Dyss meaningfully. He nodded slightly and looked away. She returned her gaze to Reed who was watching her closely.

"*Something else I don't know about?*" he enquired, grinning widely.

"How long will it take before it is ready to go?" she asked, pointing to the ship being assembled in front of them.

"I'm reliably informed that it should be ready in less than an hour," he answered, not looking away. "*Are you going to tell me?*"

"And it all *still works?*" she asked, her eyes narrowing under his scrutiny.

"I can't answer that, but it all seems to be going smoothly," he shrugged, as if it were obvious.

"I only ask as it's been on this world for practically a thousand years, a little *fluff* may have accumulated in the circuitry here and there in that time," she pointed out, stiffly.

"*Fluff?* Fine, I will check *after* I let Darius know that you want to talk to him," retorted Reed, as if she'd just asked him to sweep the back garden or something. She spun on her heel and made her way down to the hangar area. As she got there, she saw the two Covert-Class ships and couldn't help but smile. At last, something other than a battered freighter.

Darius and Cherry were waiting there for her as she got there.

"Dyss is on the bridge and I wanted a little conversation with you out of his earshot before we move on," she stated.

"I guessed as much," he replied, edgy. They moved away from Cherry who watched them casually.

"I've told him that I have plans for *every* eventuality with regard to both his *and* your loyalty to me," she said, seriously. She'd rehearsed this in her head, on the way to the hangar. She couldn't tell who, if either, were lying, and so planned to trust neither of them. "I just wanted to ask you to try and exercise as great a degree of caution towards Dyss as you can. I'm not saying trust him, I'm saying give him a chance."

"Have you talked to him about this?" he asked, directly.

"I went through his testimony and compared it to yours. I can see why Vourne dropped it, to be honest, it sounds so much like two sides of the same story until you add in your conjectures," she explained. "Clearly something went wrong and I'm sure it was by design, not an accident. But I don't know if... *How well did you know Vallin?*"

He eyed her sharply, understanding instantly where she was going with this, and what she thought might have happened.

"She *died*," he stated, a bit too defensively. "I hardly think *she* was behind the failure."

"*How well?*" she repeated, more softly.

"Well enough to know she *was* a loyal Phantom and wouldn't betray others," he replied, flatly.

"She knew how things were meant to go down, she was in a position to manipulate everything from the start, and she was the first person to accuse Dyss to his face..."

"That's *because he* was standing by the self-destruct..." he was quick to jump in.

"And maybe she didn't *expect* to find him there," she countered, meaningfully. "Because he shouldn't have been there; because he should already have been..."

"*She died!*" he spat, angrily.

"Did she?" Satiah asked, levelly. For a moment he just stared at her, the question catching him out completely. "You said yourself you didn't have time to check, which was *why* you felt guilty – which is only natural when you *lose someone you love*." She was digging her claws in now, figuratively speaking of course. For a moment, Darius's expression was blank, shocked. He didn't look confident, strong or casual like normal. He looked vulnerable. Then he rallied, realising what Satiah had done.

"She died," he stated, with finality. "Even if she survived the thing landing on her, she would have either been killed by the robots or when the ship exploded."

"There are other ways off of ships," she said, calmly. Dyss had theorised that Darius and Vallin might have been working together, but Satiah had settled on the idea that it had just been Vallin herself.

"No, *she wouldn't*," he stated, steadfastly. Of course Darius wouldn't easily believe that the person he had loved had planned to betray him. Not many ever did, especially when that person was talented at deception. But it would present another possibility to him that might allow him to put aside his suspicions of Dyss long enough for this mission to be over.

"*It's just a thought*," she said, backing off completely. "*It would explain why it's never gone anywhere*. As far as the rest of it goes, can I count on you not to *lose perspective*?" How was that for a sobering euphemism? It had the desired effect. He straightened.

"You can," he stated, the mask of normality completely returning to his countenance.

"Let's go then."

With Cherry in tow, they returned to the command deck. Satiah stole another glance at the spaceship that was still being brought together outside. Vast, modular in design, it reminded her vaguely of a giant, scaly, reptile's back. A mechanical leviathan emerging from the clouds instead of an ocean. Everyone formed a group to discuss what was going to be done next.

"Have you decided on a destination?" Satiah asked, nodding towards the craft. The Viscount nodded but said nothing. "Are you going to tell us what it is?" It was hard not to give a bitter smile with that question but it was precisely why she'd left a tracking device in Bavon's office. Even if he lied to them all, she would soon know the truth.

"So long as you all agree to tell no one until this business is over, certainly?" he countered. Everyone nodded. "Cenna 6."

"That's a *Federation* world!" Ogun was first to point out. "You can't go *there*."

"Why not? It's uninhabited, desolate *and* out of the way. I don't intend that we stay there. It is simply somewhere safer to be while we have a debate about our options," the Viscount said. Ogun didn't look happy, but didn't argue further.

"Won't you require any *additional* protection?" Dyss asked, eyeing him.

"*From what?*" the Viscount asked. "No one will know we're even there." Dyss shrugged.

"First we have to talk about what the Union will do when they realise that you're going to relocate," Satiah said, to the Viscount. "They will already be curious to see your cities combining into a ship, although right now they might think that you are doing it to make yourselves easier to protect."

"*If* they haven't already realised the real reason yet," Reed added, motioning toward the growing ship outside.

"He's right," Satiah stated, concurring with Reed. "First, they will most likely report the situation and request orders. We must ensure that they are unable to track you when you go."

"Quarkvert-bomb," Darius suggested, grimly.

"Very good," she nodded. "Do you have any?" That question she aimed at Ogun, who nodded slowly.

"I *do*, but if I use one, it *could* be interpreted as an attack," Ogun pointed out.

A Quarkvert-bomb was less of a weapon and more of an elaborate firework. Quarks are particles. Made up from hadrons, protons and neutrons, they are usually in possession of a certain electric charge. This charge can sometimes be released when the quark is destabilised or *subverted*. Add a material of equally explosive and dispersive quality, or a catalyst, and you have a device that, when detonated, could create a sizeable static discharge. This would effectively blind or confuse all but the most specialised sensor equipment for a few crucial seconds. It was like a very small and harmless electromagnetic pulse. These little beauties were not standard equipment, however, and Satiah would dearly like to know *how* it was that Ogun had them in the first place. At that moment though she had too much else to think about to bother to enquire.

"True," Dyss agreed thoughtful. "The best way to maintain innocence would be to have either the ship itself deploy them at the Viscount's direction, or, to have Darius or Satiah deploy them from the stealth craft we now have." With a commanding nod, Satiah delegated this task to Darius.

"Better use a cluster of them, just to be sure," Ogun suggested. Duds were always a danger. Darius was in accord.

"That still leaves us with a mishmash armada to deal with, even when the Viscount's ship is gone," Reed stated.

"Ogun can dismiss the Vinu and Shintu forces..." Satiah began.

"Telling them *what* exactly?" Ogun butted in. This was the part he was most concerned about. "And what about the Union ships? The second Arnos and the others go, I have no doubt that if they *don't* launch an attack, they will do whatever they can to trap me here."

"You could make it known that you have a *Coalition* delegate on board with you," Reed muttered, puffing out his chest.

"That might work," Satiah acknowledged, biting her lip. "I'm not sure it's enough though. What if they think or *pretend to think* that you're bluffing?"

"Arnos might not leave, even if I ask him to," Ogun reminded them. "He is aware of the political situation and strikes me as the kind of officer not to leave an ally in potential jeopardy. I'm not his lawful superior either, and with the Viscount gone, there will be no one here that outranks him."

"Once the city is gone there is nothing for him to protect," the Viscount pointed out. Satiah sighed.

"It may be worth including Arnos in some of our plans then," she said. "Just to avoid the possibility of him doing anything other than what we want him to."

"I should probably mention at this point that sometime soon a large Coalition fleet will turn up here," Reed said, wincing as everyone stared at him. "Well, how was I to know the Vinu and Shintu would believe the Viscount?"

"Get them to stop!" Satiah hissed, at him seriously.

"They may already have gone," Darius said, remembering what he'd seen when he'd been on Earth.

"Get them to turn around!" she amended, her tone the same.

"It wasn't me!" Reed explained, shrugging. "I advised they only send *one* ship."

"How many are they sending?" Dyss asked, inevitably.

"The Commandment Benefactor, Brenda, told them to send whatever they had to hand," Reed replied, awkwardly.

"When did this happen?" Satiah asked, trying to work out how long they had. If they were quick they might be able to get away with all this before they even arrived.

"I notified them when the Union ships arrived," Reed admitted.

"He *had* to," Pat said, leaping to his defence. Satiah knew that if she'd been there she may have considered doing that herself through Randal.

"...Fine, we have less than an hour," Satiah said, working it out. "Viscount, get moving!"

"You can't just...!"

"*Do it*, or you could be the star attraction in the biggest firefight since the Common Protectorate War!" she screamed over him. He ran off, Pat in tow.

"*No pressure!*" Reed bellowed, after them. Satiah shot him a glare but was unable to hold it and ended up grinning instead. That was one way to speed things along.

"The Union fleet may choose to remain here even if everyone else goes," Ogun said, seriously. "They may request fresh orders or something."

"We could give them a false set of coordinates for a supposed *rendezvous* with the city," Satiah suggested, thinking about it. "It will anger them but it cannot in any way be described as an act of war to *misinform* someone of their destination."

"I don't think they would believe it," Dyss replied.

"They don't have to believe it to go along with it," Darius said. Dyss shrugged.

"Try it."

"It doesn't matter *where* they go, so long as it's credible and they leave before our navy arrives," Reed said, eyeing likely destinations on a nearby screen. "It has to be seen as a place that would be a prospective, *preferably neutral*, location where the ship will be safe."

"Even if they remain I can't see them attacking the Coalition, not without provocation," Dyss said, thinking it over. "Whoever she is, Captain Alicia seems like someone who doesn't shoot unless she has to." Reed reflected how, despite the military being the ones who did the fighting, they were also the ones who seemed able to work together more quickly and readily than politicians. Even when they were on opposite sides. Politicians, even those apparently on the same side, often failed to work together so well. Had any other delegates or politicians been involved in this situation, Reed had no doubt that things would be far worse than they were.

***

Doctor Bertram Blake Cark is nearby. The cult wants him back. If you're interested... follow this signal. Clyde listened to what he'd set up as his lure. He'd recorded it himself. Satiah was certain to hear it; the obvious concern was that she would think it was a trick. He felt sure she'd come anyway though. He placed the beacon on the dark side of the pipe where it was out of sight. It would begin broadcasting as soon as he activated it. Purella was sure Satiah was dead, drowned or blown apart in the wild Frey that was the ocean of Collgort-Elipsa. Clyde was not so sure. It had been too easy for one thing, and for another Bavon had been captured. While he didn't know it was Satiah behind that, he felt it most likely was. Besides... *she had Obsenneth*. She had what the cult *really* wanted and even though he didn't know what it was, he was pretty sure he wanted to know.

***

Bert opened his eyes. The last thing he should have remembered was eating with Reed and Patricia. While that was something that he remembered… it was not the only thing. First there was that familiar ceiling, the ceiling of the makeshift cell he'd recently been cooped up in. And the rest was history. *His history.* The guilt, the shame, the fear! It welled up inside him like a flame, threatening to make him spontaneously combust right there. Tears began to rain down his face as he remembered his past and his whole body began to tremble. Those who had died, strangers, it mattered not what they were to him as they had died anyway. And his poor wife… As if summoned by the thought of her death, her killer rapped on the door.

"You are pathetic," Purella jeered, from outside. She had been waiting out there, watching him, and now he was awake, she'd decided that now was the time to twist the knife. She entered the cell slowly, her expression one of angry contempt.

"You had made it! You were on top of everyone and you let it slip through your fingers," she sneered, mockingly. "You even *deluded* yourself into thinking you could *just walk away*."

"…They will destroy you too!" he wailed, his whole body shaking with his sobs. "*They kill everyone!*" Her lips twisted in a grimace of hate.

"You before me," she stated, grabbing him by the back of his neck. He spasmed and contorted as the electricity from her glove flashed through him. She leered sadistically down at him as he howled, while convulsing uncontrollably.

"*You* nearly cost me everything," she hissed, in his ear. Even after she let go he continued to shudder and twitch.

"You killed the woman I loved…" he croaked, a gleam of pain in his eyes.

"I enjoyed that immensely too," she smiled, unfeeling. "Yet we both know that *had you never run away*, she would be alive today. So, if you think about it, *you took her from yourself.* Maybe you were trying to punish yourself in some warped way, maybe not. No one will care enough to find out."

"What happened to us?" he asked, bleakly. "What made us turn into *monsters?*" That question was heavily philosophical. Purella disliked philosophy but just to hurt him more she kept talking.

"Your weakness made you into what you are," she said, cruelly.

"She was only with you at all because of your money. If she ever told you she loved you for who you are, she lied. And, as you wanted to believe her, your gullibility won out."

It was spite. Mindless malice with no grounds in truth, even Bert knew that. Nevertheless, it hurt him. He'd loved her more than anything, and her loss robbed him of his sleep and self-tolerance. He'd had to forget, he'd had to erase it, or he would have lost his mind. It felt like the universe had arrived to even the score. A reckoning day for him. The soul remained a mysterious thing. It was almost like someone had purposely created it so that it could *feel* without thought. Emotions, even at an early stage when you are unaware of what emotions are, affect the core of what you are. Do they come from you or from somewhere else? Pain is inescapable. Something in him snapped.

With a bestial roar, he suddenly sprang at Purella. She wasn't expecting it: a mere second before, he had had no challenge in him. Her hand swept defensively, aiming for his neck. His teeth sank into her forearm as he bit down hard. She shrieked and punched him hard in the stomach, almost lifting him from the floor with her strength. He released her arm as he tried to breath. Another blow, another and another struck him as, enraged, Purella embarked on a savage beating. Bert couldn't fight anymore, that last lunge had been all he had and he crumpled almost instantly under the onslaught. Someone was shouting and two others rushing in, pulling her off of him. Had they not stepped in, she would have killed him there and then. Clyde had one arm and another man had the other. Purella almost turned on *them* in her rage, but managed to regain control of her equanimity.

"Are you two done?" Clyde demanded, grimly. "You need him alive, *remember*?" She examined her bleeding forearm, all Bert's teeth neatly marked in the red and white of her skin and blood. Clyde too stared at it. "We will get that treated," he stated. A faint weeping sound came from Bert and they all stared down at him.

"We're all dead..." he blubbered, quietly. "All of us... marked like victims of the pox." Purella looked like she was going to attack him again when Clyde interceded.

"*We're ready to move*," he stated, in her ear. "The ship is clean." Even if he had intended to ask her again to change her mind, which he had not, this was not the time. Neither was he going to lecture her on everything that was wrong with what she had just been doing. She'd had her chances and it was time to get out.

They left Bert where he was and Clyde took Purella to the medical room. The wound was healed in moments and she was looking pensive. He knew what she was thinking. She was thinking Bert might have a point. The cult did kill everyone, even their own. She might even be reconsidering her decision to join but it was too late now. Even the fact that they all knew the cult existed was enough to put them in danger. An arguably small one, as many openly said they believed the cult existed, but the luck of the draw was not something Clyde had faith in. Danger was danger when it came to his survival. He played to win… which was why he was now trying to play for both sides. While Purella was staring into space, something she was doing with increasing frequency these days, he checked that the beacon he'd planted earlier was still functioning.

***

The ship was complete. The Viscount looked on from the control room as people, trained but inexperienced, sat nervously at their stations. For over a thousand years the ship had been spread across the planet, acting as cities. While many were trained over those years to fly the ship, no one ever imagined they would need to. Darius was in position, his craft invisible to all. The Union ships were getting ready to depart to the coordinates Reed had provided them with. It was a plan that would ensure he and his people remained safe, but that would also *really annoy* the Union. He and his people needed to discuss and decide, once and for all, which superpower they would be in. Straddling the two was clearly impossible now. Amber had disappeared, giving further fuel to the secret belief that he'd had about her – that she had been in the employ of the Union somehow and had been planted on him. She'd done her best to be subtle, but as soon as Reed had arrived, she'd become more persistent with her *suggestions*.

He wished she'd stuck around long enough for him to tell her that it didn't matter to him who she worked for: he loved her anyway. A great sadness descended on him for a moment. He might never see her again, just as he might never see the planet again. It was unsettlingly cathartic and harsh at once. Too late now though; he had important things to do and he could show no weakness. Monumental things. Things that would contour the destiny of his people. Who hadn't heard that before? With all the best planning and prediction in existence, sometimes you had to just take a shot in the dark and hope for better options next time. Always assuming that there would be a next time...

***

Darius eyed the countdown on the screen beside him leisurely. When it reached zero, he was to remotely detonate the Quarkvert-bombs he'd just deployed. Cherry and Riff were behind him. They were listening to the 'chatter' of the fleets. At first it had all been very official but some personal stuff had started creeping through now that some mutual trust had been established. People asking after friends or relatives, that sort of thing. The Vinu-Shintu War, now suspended, had been raging a long time and Darius imagined there might not be that many tearful reunions. He was sure, however, that the CNC, Current News Corporation, would find one to cover and broadcast it everywhere with whatever negative spin they could think of. Now *that* would be a mission: to eliminate all the CNC editors. It was no less than they deserved.

The countdown hit zero and he activated. A blast of static discharge occurred, appearing as both a flash to the eyes and white noise to the ears. The ship, the whole society, disappeared into space. Almost immediately, as planned, Ogun jumped too, also vanishing. Arnos made his move within seconds after that and that left the Union fleet drifting there... alone. Well, alone, aside from two invisible craft that they did not know were there. One conveyed Darius, Cherry and Riff. The other held Satiah, Kelvin, Reed and Dyss. There was a minute or two where nothing at all happened. The Union ships began to assume a new formation but without any great hurry. They knew they'd been tricked; Alicia was probably trying to work out the best way to let her superiors know.

Satiah let out a breath and casually looked across at Reed who was watching the remaining ships, a sly grin on his lips. Dyss remained silent.

"You look *pleased*," she noted, to Reed. He turned to face her.

"You should be the happy one. You not only saved Milo Drass from an early matrimony, but you *stopped the war*!" he congratulated.

"*It's suspended, not over*," Dyss reminded, without conviction.

"You left out the cult," she stated, glowering at him. "And Dyss is right, peace, *long-lasting peace at any rate*, is not a guarantee here." Reed sighed.

"Well, *certainly not* with *that* attitude!" he protested, comically. She crossed her arms, her face becoming the definition of dissatisfaction. Reed cringed.

"I do have one or two thoughts on how to make the peace total *and* long-lasting," he said, at last giving up. "In any case, why are we still here? Shouldn't we be rushing off to reacquire Bert, or at least investigating... *where was it again?*"

"There is one last thing I need to do while I'm here," Satiah stated, eyeing the planet. She had to check on the creatures. First, to make sure they were still alive, and second, *to claim their reward...* whatever that might be. They had promised her nothing but her own life yet she was curious enough to see if, now they had what they wanted, they could be more generous.

"And what is that?" Dyss frowned, confused.

"It won't take long," she said, without actually answering the question. "Kelvin and I will handle it. You and Reed can join the others." Neither man moved. "*Okay...*" she smiled, playfully. She activated her communicator. "Darius, can you and the others join us here? I need to borrow your ship for a moment."

"On our way," he replied, instantly. Reed chuckled but Dyss didn't even smile.

"Nice to see that *someone* obeys orders," she remarked, a little tersely. It was a loaded remark, obviously. One that irritated Dyss still further, but with Reed there he couldn't say much. Reed, due to being annoying perceptive, guessed something was off and was itching to know what that might be. Both men also were intrigued by why she was so keen to return to the planet, now that there was, in theory, nothing to return to. Satiah wondered to herself: if ignorance was bliss *why* did they both look so disgruntled? She knew why, of course, and smiled benevolently at them, a mischievous gleam in her eyes. It made her feel good inside, knowing things that they didn't.

A few minutes later, she and Kelvin were descending down through the clouds. When they reached the ocean, the difference was instantly noticeable. Calm waters rippling gently in the strong breeze from horizon to horizon. Satiah couldn't help herself, she smiled.

"No more sky giants, eh?" she enquired, rhetorically. Kelvin, who knew everything that had happened to her, said nothing. He was telling her, *by saying nothing*, that he was still not happy about her and Obsenneth 'working together'. She began to change into a skin-tight diving suit, dark grey like all Phantom-made garbs. She replaced her boots, blade and belt over the top and wandered down the ramp. They were only a few inches above the surface, hovering there. She glanced over her shoulder at him.

"It will be okay," she assured, like a parent to child. Kelvin perceived it more like the other way around. A child ignorantly trying to reassure a knowing parent.

She attached a support cable to her belt so that, this time, she didn't need to rely on the creatures to drag her back up again. There was no sign of the methane bubbles, but while tempting fate was always part of her job, today she wasn't feeling particularly lucky. She tested her breathing device then dived in. She had weights on her belt to ensure she was able to retain depth and swam downward quickly. The water felt different to how it had last time. Cooler and clearer. Below her she was a huge dirt cloud. The whole seabed had most likely been pulled about during the exercise of bringing all the cities together and then moving them away as one. She looked around; her eyesight as good underwater as it was above, but could see no sign of anything living or dead.

It was quiet, just the usual underwater rumble. No chirps or squeaks at all. She pulled out the Obsenneth and removed her glove so that it would work.

"Time for you to play translator again," she ordered, as the usual orange glow appeared. "Call them to me." A voice, like that of an infant, began to speak. There were words but they sounded... odd. It made Satiah think of a possessed baby talking backwards at high speed. She eyed the crystal.

"That's *not* how they sounded before," she hissed, slightly unnerved by the ghostly tones.

"They have evolved since we last interacted," Obsenneth said, his own voice doing nothing to relieve her subconscious anxieties. "It is because of *you* that they now speak like this."

Me? What did I do? I only did what they told me to do! Then she remembered that they had touched her and began to see how this may have happened. "They're trying to emulate *me?*" she clarified, uneasily.

"It would seem so," he said. "I can't think why." She wasn't sure if that was meant to be an insult or not, but when the first creature came into view she began to see what he meant. Its pectoral fins had elongated into something closely resembling arms. At the end of each undefined limb, something akin to a hand was there. It had shrunk too, it was only a little larger than she was and its features had become an eerily precise facsimile of a human's features. Its hair, far longer and more voluptuous, was also exactly the same shade in colour as Satiah's.

"How flattering," she murmured. The creature stopped a few metres from her and made a noise. It sounded like what Satiah had said only faster and not every well pronounced. Satiah's eyes widened.

"Owwwwfatrinnn."

Satiah cautiously swam forward, her hand extended. The creature mirrored her exactly and their hands touched. Its flesh felt different too. It was still smooth and hard but warmer and... were those tiny nails on the back of each *finger?*

"Can you assimilate my language?" Satiah asked, aloud. The creature's green eyes, now much smaller and human like, blinked at her. The lips moved.

"Canasslamgag."

"It is learning quickly," Obsenneth encouraged. "The more you talk to it, exposing it to new words, the faster it will learn and the more like you it will become."

"Carriage. Gateway. Barstool. Monologue. Phosphorous. Test-tube. Sedative. Plinth," Satiah said, maintaining eye contact.

The creature repeated each word, each time sounding less baby-like and more fluent. Other creatures began gathering around, watching and leaning. Satiah finally got conclusive proof that it was getting there when it spoke a word she hadn't said. To be precise it said three words she had not said.

"You made them go," it said, its voice still high pitched but much more intelligible.

"I made them go," Satiah confirmed, clearly. "That is correct."

"We thank you, clothed animal," she said.

"*Human*," reminded Satiah, concealing her amusement. Another female swam forward.

"We have our gift for you in *thankfulnesslessness* for your actions," it said. Satiah had no idea what to expect seeing as they obviously didn't have money.

A large white *egg* was handed to her. Satiah hid her disappointment well.

"He will grow to protect you," assured the creature.

"*Lovely*," she said, graciously. *Let's hope he doesn't asphyxiate while defending me against people on land*, Satiah thought sarcastically. She would have to teach him to hold his breath for a *very* long time...

"He will acclimatise to atmosphere *you breathe*," it said, encouragingly. It touched Satiah's breathing mask softly. "You breathe the thin, cold... *air*."

"Well, that's going to be very useful," Satiah allowed, deciding she'd stayed too long already. Next, they might try to feed her or something and she wasn't hungry. "Maybe I'll come back one day and see how you are all getting on."

"We shall survive," it said, expressing determination in the form of a strained smile.

The rebuilding of *the Great Citadel*, whatever that was, was already underway apparently, not that Satiah cared. So much for appreciation! They'd given her, as a reward for saving all of them, *an egg*. To say she was unhappy would be a huge understatement but, if she was honest with herself, she'd known deep down not to expect much. An oath of unending loyalty would have been better. A new blade even... something she might have a use for. A baby... Well, she knew little of this strange lifeform so maybe it would surprise her. A lot about them had already done that, particularly their *evolutionary skills*. Satiah was no biologist, her strength was chemistry, but she understood enough to see the potential. A specimen that *no one knew* she had...

that she could do anything she liked with. Then she realised that, leaving aside all the ethics of that, she didn't have the time for any of that genetic business.

When she got back to the ship she gave the egg to Kelvin.

"Put it someplace warm," she ordered, unhelpfully. She hoped his advanced computer would be able to tell her exactly what it needed. And then there was the food it would need to eat and the growing rate... What the hell was she thinking about? She'd wasted enough time! It was time they snatched Bert back or, failing that, learn how to access the cult. The Union fleet, annoyingly, were still there when she reached orbit again.

"They are running computer probability checks of likely destinations," Darius theorised. "Standard procedure. It's only taking so long because there are so many destinations that are plausible." Satiah had initially thought the same: trouble was, if they didn't move, the Coalition fleet might do something about that when they arrived.

***

Alicia had not been at all surprised when the ship had left. She'd wondered why it was still there when she arrived. The departure of all other fleets was unforeseen and she'd wasted no time in reporting what had happened to her superiors. Thanks to some advanced techniques, tracing them directly was *impossible*, so she'd begun the lengthy process of logical deduction that would provide them with a list of probable destinations. It didn't take a genius to work out that this had all been the plan from the start. Even if the Federation and the Coalition were not working together, the Vinu and Shintu forces were. Everyone had heard the Viscount's speech by now, the one where he exposed an alleged conspiracy by persons unknown to engineer the whole war from the start. She had to admit it was plausible and certainly possibly; the trouble was, to her, it sounded like something out of a fictional story.

She'd recently discovered a long-running Union mission to get Collgort-Elipsa to join the Union and leave the Coalition. It was finding that out which solidified her suspicions that everyone was now working against the Union. Part of her couldn't blame them. Then again, she'd never really been into empire building. What was the point when you couldn't live long enough to really get it done, let alone enjoy it? She was aware that she was in a minority and that almost every politician alive entertained fantasies about total domination. Absolute power and all that nonsense. Ro Tammer had been a prime example of that sort. Alicia drummed her fingers on the console thoughtfully. Where had they all run away to? Her pilot had raised an interesting point as well. What had they been running *from*? Surely they couldn't have still been concerned about pirates? Not with a fleet *that size* in orbit. It was yet another mystery.

After the screaming match between her and command was over, they realised they had only one thing in common. Neither of them knew what to do next and she was starting to think that her initial feelings regarding this task had been on the button. It was a pointless waste of time. A *conference* was apparently taking place at the *highest level*; whichever level that was, to determine their next course of action. Alicia already had tried to bet four hundred Essps that 'going home' would *not* be their pronouncement. There had been no takers. In the meantime they were left floating there like a forgotten freighter awaiting permission to park in a shipyard for refuelling. She was seriously considering returning to her cabin for a nap when, at last, someone called them.

"Captain Alicia, this is Ambassador Hademan," a voice stated, formally. "We have had reports that a Coalition fleet is heading your way. Your new orders are as follows: withdraw to a safe distance from the planet, and observe the Coalition fleet should they arrive. If they approach you, you are to tell them that you are seeking pirate activity in the area and request their aid in doing so. Should they ask you to leave, play for time by telling them you have to get permission to abort your current assignment. Spin that out for as long as you can. The Coalition has obviously removed Collgort-Elipsa for a reason, and the government are very interested to know what that reason is. We currently believe the reason lies planetside somewhere, but we don't know for sure. That is what we want you to find out. We are sending an agent out to investigate also. Is that understood?"

"Sir," she nodded, deciding that scanning the planet again might be a good idea *before* anyone else arrived. After all, she was only looking for pirates, right?

"Pilot, perform a full scan of the planet," Alicia ordered. "Then I want you to plot us a patrol route that will give us the best coverage."

She wondered how long they had. The Ambassador had not said how long nor how they knew it was coming. Alicia knew to assume she had very little time, less than an hour, most likely.

"Should we not request backup?" asked another officer.

"No," she smiled, simply. "If they had wanted us to act as a mobile fortress, they would already have sent assistance. As politics go, this was more of a feint than a thrust." The man nodded. It had all been a lot of fuss over very little. The government cared about worlds changing allegiance, in case it began a trend, but the majority of those outside the government had more tolerance in regards to it.

***

"Do you think we should wait around and see what else they do?" Cherry asked, referring to the Union fleet.

"It might be an idea to await the arrival of the Coalition fleet just to ensure they don't start something," Reed mused.

"You still have the implant, why do we need Bert?" Dyss asked, interested. They were all in the control room of the Covert-Class ship. Satiah had quickly updated Rainbow and Randal on everything that had happened on her way there. Now they had to agree on the next step.

"We don't," Satiah shrugged, nonchalantly. "The only reason he became so important was that *they* wanted *him*. By hanging on to him we were delaying them. He is only one of many schemes they are running, though so I can see why you asked that. I was asking myself that question when I found out the truth about him. However, he has just become important again…" She trailed off and pressed a button on the console. Clyde's recorded message began playing. They all listened.

Doctor Bertram Blake Clark is nearby. The cult wants him back. If you're interested… follow this signal.

"I know that voice," Reed said, remembering. "He was the man who attacked the city while you were busy trying to distract Purella."

"The one who took Bert from you and Patricia?" Darius confirmed. He nodded. "A mercenary in Purella's employ."

"He struck me as pretty senior. He is probably the second in command," Reed elaborated.

"Then why is he offering to help us?" Dyss frowned, distrustfully.

"It's been transmitting for over an hour now," Satiah explained, ponderously. "The signal is pretty much constant and Kelvin plotted a course. He's going in circles. I think he's waiting for us."

"Sounds like a trap," Cherry said, thinking along the same lines Dyss had been.

"Some traps need live bait," Darius said, eyeing Satiah. She smiled knowingly.

"If you've *already decided*, what is the point in even discussing it?" Dyss asked, seeing the look.

"I thought she was going to give us a chance to back out once we all knew what she was planning to do?" Reed chanced, hopefully.

"Oh, you're not going anywhere, you started this, remember?" she sneered, playfully.

"Doesn't mean I'm selfish enough to want to end it too," he chuckled. She laughed.

"Actually I wanted to just make sure we were all on the same page and that I'd not overlooked anything," Satiah replied, a little smugly.

"You think we can snatch Bert back?" Dyss asked.

"That was not my plan," Satiah replied. "I was going to make contact with the guy, whoever he is, and play along a bit. See what he's after."

"Whilst...?" Reed asked, raising his eyebrows.

"...Whilst Dyss and Darius infiltrate the ship but remain in hiding until they reveal the entrance to the Hellion. They will have to go inside sometime. When we're inside we can call in backup," she smiled. "Do this right and we can wipe out the lot of them."

"The Union world... after what just happened, we cannot have Coalition troops coming in," Dyss stated, shaking his head. "I know it's out of the way and I know the odds of getting caught are low, but it only takes one..."

"I wasn't going to use Coalition troops for this. They are not good enough and, as you say, politically it would be risky," Satiah interrupted, in agreement. "*Division Sixteen, however,* have plenty of gung-ho veterans that are always eager to attack an enemy. *Real or imagined.*" Dyss nodded. He, like all the other Phantom leaders, had mixed feelings towards their Division Sixteen rivals, but no one ever denied their usefulness.

"I'd rather keep this unofficial," Dyss stated, seriously.

"I'm sure *you* would," she retorted, a bit of mockery in her tone. "You're in luck today though. Reed knows the right people to ask, *don't you Reed?*" She prodded Reed in the side and he squirmed.

"Well, *all right*, seeing as you asked *so nicely*," he smiled at her. "How big are we talking here?"

"Five hundred, at least," she replied, immediately. His eyes widened.

"What exactly do you have in mind, an all-out assault?" Darius asked, a little sceptical. "They will have contingencies for that…"

"No, if us four can get in, we can cause a distraction and keep them busy while the Division Sixteen guys come at them from another direction," Satiah answered.

"*Four?*" Reed asked, a little unnerved. He thought she meant that he too would take part in the action.

"Not *you*, I mean Kelvin," she told him, with a grin. "Not that I *didn't consider you*, of course, but your talents lie elsewhere."

"No need to get nasty," he muttered, slightly crestfallen.

"And if this is a trap?" Dyss asked, curious.

"We steal back the bait," she replied, as if it were obvious.

"If we can," Darius added.

"Well, it's either that or we wander around looking for the entrance to the Hellion in plain view of the cult," Satiah argued, seriously. "I know that some will say, *we're done here*. The war *is* over and Milo Drass *is* returned. The objectives, such as they were, can be ticked off. But I think everyone here is in agreement that we *have* to take out this cult. They are the reason the mission had to happen in the first place. *They started this.* We let them go, and they'll strike at us again. Maybe it will be years later, and maybe next time they will succeed. If there's *one thing* I know about *evil* like this: it's that it's endlessly patient. Guards are always dropped in the end, *we all know that*. They just wait for that to happen." Reed was astonished; he'd never heard her utter the word evil before. It wasn't that he thought she didn't have a conscience, as he knew she did, but the use of the word still somehow caught him unawares.

"Ideally I would prefer that we have another pilot. I can rig up a parallel control system easily enough," Satiah went on. "Reed, you'll have to do. All four of us won't be here. When we get inside the ship, you are to go to the cult's planet and remain concealed in orbit. The course is pre-set. I will call you when we arrive."

"As you say," he nodded.

"What do you want me to do?" Cherry asked, looking and feeling a bit helpless.

"Guard Reed with your life, he's *our* lifeline," Satiah replied, immediately. "He could be our only way off world, assuming we make it that far." She nodded.

"Suit up?" Darius asked, guessing her next command.

"Indeed," she nodded, and the three Phantoms went for the door. "Don't forget to call your *friend*, Reed," she reminded, over her shoulder.

***

Clyde had the *Dreadnaught* going in circles. The longer Purella took to get ready, the better. The beacon was still transmitting. He was starting to wonder if Satiah really was dead, as he'd expected her to be there already... assuming she wasn't hiding somewhere, of course. He couldn't move until Purella gave him the coordinates which, in his view, was the moment he would become an official target of the cult. Once he knew where they were, they would want him dead. He glanced at the scanners expectantly. Nothing. If Satiah was there she was impossible to see.

Purella was in her room, standing rigidly before the mirror. She was wearing her new cloak; the one Quint had sent her. She slowly slipped her black band away, allowing her golden hair freedom again. As a mercenary, or a bounty hunter, or *whatever she had been until this moment*... her life was over. She would soon be a member of the Cult of Deimos. A resurrection. She stared at herself in the mirror and waited for the exhilaration to come. The feelings of accomplishment and pride she had expected. They didn't come, only misery did. Why was she so sad? This was everything she had wanted. Everything she'd been shooting for since… since that day. The day the Phantoms had killed the rest.

Was that why she was sad? Because she'd not been able to add Satiah's skull to her collection? No, it wasn't even that. It was because of how Clyde was looking at her. That glint of revulsion in his eyes stung her. Quint had told her that joining the cult would mean sacrifice, *in more ways than one*, but she'd thought he'd meant… other things. She would miss Clyde, she could live with that but they were not even parting as friends. A tear left her eye and she brushed it away, furious with herself. *No, this was it!* It would not be long before things became good again. She would create her own scheme to bring down Phantom Squad once and for all and, with the cult's help, she would finally achieve that. A score settled at last. It would take years, she knew, but that didn't matter so long as it got done.

She ran through her inventory in her mind. Blade, gun, gloves and Bert. It was a shame about the gemstone. Yet another thing that Satiah had deprived her of! She moved outside and strode down the corridor towards the control room. She enjoyed the sensation of the cloak billowing a little in her wake. Clyde looked around as she reached him, eyeing her new costume with disdain.

"It clashes with the humanity in your eyes," he muttered, just loud enough for her to hear.

"These are the coordinates," she stated, flatly. She handed him a coil of readout which he took without a second glance. "Once we get there and Bert is safely returned… you can go."

"You're giving me this?" he frowned, talking about the *Dreadnaught*.

"You earned it, I think," she murmured, seriously. "In any case, I doubt I will be requiring it again."

"*Your home?*" he clarified, challenge in his tone.

"It's *not* a *home*, it's a bastardised battleship!" she snapped, levelly. He sneered.

"Call it what you want, it was the closest thing to freedom you ever owned," he replied, not backing down.

"I'm not getting into this!" she hissed, fighting to hold onto her temper. "It's my choice. Let it be. *I never lied to you about it!* Right from the start, I told you that *this* was what I *wanted*."

"And I told you it's...!" he shouted, suddenly on his feet. The communicator went off... as it had a habit of doing. They both stared at it for a moment, the atmosphere palpable. It was Quint. Who else was it going to be? His brother?

"I'm ready," she answered, summoning all her grit and confidence. She didn't want Quint to see this. He might see her feelings for Clyde as weakness and decide she was not worthy of cult membership. She knew *she* did. Feelings like compassion were always a weakness, and love was just another danger. She kept telling herself that love was just a cruel trick nature played to ensure reproduction took place. Yet wasn't it impossible to help how one felt?

"Good, not everyone will be here but half the cult is here to witness your arrival and your ceremony. You are the first female, after all," Quint explained, his voice the same as ever. She wondered briefly: *I may be the one who's joining, but weren't the others only interested in Bert really? Formerly one of their own, now a traitor, being burned alive?* She was sure, despite regular 'sacrifices' occurring, it would be rare that the victim was one of them. Someone they once trusted... perhaps 'trusted' was the wrong word. *Associated with* was perhaps more accurate. She kept all of that to herself, as anyone would.

"I appreciate how much you have staked in this," she replied, respectfully.

"Be prepared for thinly veiled prejudice," he advised, talking about those members still opposed to females being allowed to join. "You have proven yourself worthy to me, *that is all that counts*. Enough of the cult has agreed to this for it to be unstoppable. There are always a few who will be anxious to show their feelings regarding their loss though."

"That's democracy for you," she joked. Clyde smirked too, genuinely amused. Something that might have been a laugh came from Quint. A croaky, raspy sort of grunting sound, again like a computer imitation of what a real laugh was. It was unnerving. The smiles faded from both Purella and Clyde. It reminded them of the darker side of whom they were dealing with.

"Remember that today is *only* the inauguration. There will be much *more* to come for you. For us. How long will you be?" he asked.

"Couple of hours," she replied, after considering.

"I will see you when you arrive," he said, cutting off. Purella let out a breath and turned to see Clyde watching her closely. Their eyes remained connected for a few moments before he looked away.

***

Satiah flicked her hair out from the neck seal with practised ease and sealed the clasp. Next, she slid her equipment into her bag and finally pulled the helmet on. Air good, communications clear, equipment check and... she turned to face Kelvin.

"Power?" she asked, her voice sounding funny from inside the helmet.

"Maximum," he answered, in his usual monotone. This was likely their last chance to make sure they were good to go.

"That's what I want to hear," she nodded, grim. "Let's go." They all converged in a small room, a room that would soon be open to the mysterious darkness of space. An environment so inhospitable it made quicksand seem like a holiday destination. Reed would get as close as he could to the *Dreadnaught*, and they would leap out onto its hull. A strategy open to criticism because of a few flaws, but the plan Satiah felt would work best in this case. Someone wanted her there... someone was inviting her onto that ship. It would be rude to ignore them...

She made the ordinary hand gesture at Darius and Dyss. A horizontal hand wave, enquiring as to their state of readiness. Both responded with vertical chopping motions, indicating that all was as ready as it was ever going to be. They also did a brief communications check in order to make sure they could all hear one another. Next was another safety check along with the air, pressure and magnet checks. These checks were as mind numbingly boring as they were necessary. There was nothing more embarrassing than dying because of an equipment failure, yet it happened too often to discount. Finally, Reed was given the order to approach and radio silence began. Only once all three were aboard and safe would communications resume. She hoped Reed wouldn't come in too fast, or they would get splattered against the hull. Space debris was also a matter to consider, but the scans were clean. Just the normal background dust to be found. The computer would advise on speed and trajectory as always, but if the other ship suddenly slowed or accelerated, they could be in trouble pretty quickly. The grey ghost of the *Dreadnaught* could already be seen, coming in fast.

The walls slid away and suddenly they were weightlessly flying towards it. Four tiny things, too small for all but the most advanced equipment to detect, hurtling towards their target. The angle seemed as perfect as could be. They would slip in, and be able to run across the hull to slow down more easily. No one said a word. Satiah could only hear her own breathing in the form of tinny hisses and wheezes. It was easy to feel claustrophobic in those kinds of helmets, and again she was reminded of a recent experience she had gone through, one that made her tense her belly in case she had the urge to throw up. It was always a comforting thought to know that your skin was almost kissing the cold burn of frozen death, the ebullism and the other delightful symptoms of space exposure that vacuums typically presented. It was a lot to think about when you already can't breathe. Satiah focussed on the job in hand, no point in thinking about anything else. The hull was coming up now, and she braced herself. Her right boot found it first and she was careful not to kick away reflexively. She began taking long strides and lowered her hand to grab hold of anything she could.

She snagged a panel of armour and stopped abruptly, careful not to strain her arm. Kelvin was there beside her quickly, to ensure she was not going to float off anywhere. She glanced around. She could see Dyss but there was no sign of Darius. She was not concerned though, despite the obvious and unwanted complication she knew she had with them. He was most likely nearby, hidden by the body of the ship itself. Kelvin was already approaching an airlock, his red eyes seeing so much more than she could. Scanning, learning... watching. Was he still monitoring her? Of course he was, he was programmed by her to protect her... even from herself. Unless any had been installed since her last visit, Satiah knew the location of all four cameras on the ship and none of them covered the airlocks. Purella, or whoever, may have installed new ones since though. It was a possibility. Even a credible one. She carefully made her way over to join Kelvin, watching as their ship became smaller in the distance. On his third appendage Kelvin detached a digit and began to operate the manual override. They had to be quick; the ship could start moving at speed at any time. The airlock opened – the automatic controls would trigger no alarms as Kelvin had introduced a virus into the computer network. Hull detection systems would be offline for a few crucial minutes. How convenient.

Satiah entered the ship first and Kelvin sealed them inside. Air, heat and atmosphere flooded in. She opened the bag she had been carrying that contained her usual gear and clothes.

"Scan the surround," she told him, as she quickly redressed. He already was. She rolled up the suit efficiently and slid it into the bag. When it was inside she pulled on her customary black and dark purple flight jacket. The only purple parts could be seen as two long stripes that arched around the shoulders and down the back. It had once had chains and silver squares as decorations, but she'd long ago stripped it of those. It was thick, padded for protection and warmth, with plenty of pockets, some obvious and others well concealed. One was now the new home to her Obsenneth *friend*. Well, friend or enemy, she had it on her. So far it had taken pains to stay with her, but who knew when that could change?

"Clear," Kelvin told her. "Nearest occupant, twenty meters to the left." She slipped her pistol out of its holder and eyed the other device she had, her tracker. She was going to find the beacon and learn who was brave or stupid enough to want to get her attention.

She tapped her earpiece. "Who can talk?" she whispered.

"Me," Dyss said.

"Me," Darius said.

"Find places to hide, I'll tell you when it's time to come out," she instructed. "*Reed?* We're in and safe."

"For now, you mean?" he quipped, sounding relieved. He'd assumed all had gone well as chaos had remained trapped firmly in his own imagination, but nagging doubts always plagued him. "What do you want me to do?"

"Just follow the *Dreadnaught* and *stay* in stealth mode," she answered, softly. "They cannot find out that they're being followed.

We all know what to do if we are compromised. I'll let you know if I need you to do anything else. Have you heard anything back from Division Sixteen?"

"I've spoken with a few of them and they are thinking about it," he replied, ambiguously.

"*Thinking about it?*" she echoed, smiling grimly.

"Don't worry, they *will* respond, but I have no idea in what way."

"Please let me know when you know," she requested, trying to be patient. She'd learned some time ago that it was practically impossible to get Reed to do anything he didn't want to. Division Sixteen would have instant response units available, everyone had those, but the force they needed would be significantly greater than what was immediately to hand. She felt much more at ease this time. Last time she had been on her own, and had been grappling with many questions. Now she had a much clearer idea of what was going on and, as she had *Kelvin* with her, confidence was easy to maintain. Darius and Dyss were fine… so long as she could trust them not to kill one another. The search was fast, mainly because they had a good fix on the beacon, and also because the size of the ship and the small crew left a lot of space to wander around in. No patrols of guards. No cameras or alarms. It was ironic that pirates – thieves, in other words – put so little thought into their own security. They were almost on a par with Collgort-Elipsa's complacency. There were, she had no doubt, a few less of the pirates than there had been last time, thanks to Dyss and Kelvin.

There was nothing special about the corridor where they found it, concealed in the dark. As before, she noted the poorly maintained condition, and couldn't help but shake her head in disapproval. She cleaned everything she used meticulously and while she understood that there was not always an opportunity or even a need… it was hard for her to not keep everything in working order. Even things she never used. Satiah held the surprisingly clean-looking beacon in her hand and pondered the pros and cons of deactivating it. It only looked clean to her, as everything else around it was the polar opposite in terms of condition. In reality, it was just normal. A tiny blue light flashed every few seconds, but other than that it looked totally harmless. Kelvin scanned it to ensure it had no… *secrets*.

"It is an expensive model but it has no hidden treasures," he told her. "You were right, this was not an accident."

"Then how will whoever left it *know* that I have found it?" she pondered, confused. "There are no cameras, nothing in the device to give away that fact I've just found it, and no one watching."

"It could still be a trap," he cautioned. She glanced both ways along the corridor uncertainly, not exactly sure what she was expecting. Nothing… just the gentle thrum of the distant drive systems.

"If it is," she said, at last. "It's got *me* fooled." Why would someone risk probable death by letting her know *where* Bert was and then *not be there* to make sure she'd answered? Logic told her that something might have *prevented* them being there, a drawback of another kind. And again, if this *was* a trap, why was no one trying to kill her yet? Sometimes beings liked to play games… but to say that such an idea was reckless would be foolishly underestimating the consequences. Kelvin's metal hand was scrabbling around in the darkness where she'd found the beacon, seeking anything else that might be sequestered away there.

His hand clamped down on a communicator – he handed it to her and she gave him a triumphant look. It was scuffed, old and didn't seem to be working. She replaced the power unit with a spare of her own and it bleeped into life. Power, battery, signal… checking, checking. There was only *one* contact listed. Only one person to call?

"Thank you, Kelvin, *well found*," she said, activating it. It was answered almost immediately.

"Major Clyde," answered Clyde, casually. Satiah eyed the serial code on the communicator and said it out loud.

"One, one, six, nine, one, two," she said, clearly.

"Is that *Satiah*?" he asked, interested. She scowled. Too many people knew her name and she didn't like that!

"Is this *your* beacon?" Satiah countered, avoiding the question bluntly.

"I want to do a deal, do you like deals?" he asked, getting to the point. "I'm in my cabin, feel free to join me."

"How do I know this is not a trap?" she asked, feeling unsure. People did not normally take this approach. They either fought or flew... they rarely talked.

"I promise," he said, perceptibly smiling as he said it. She couldn't help but smile too... yes, what could he say that she would believe? Trust, the oldest and most dangerous of associates, was beckoning to her again. "It's not safe on this channel and in my cabin, we *won't* be disturbed. You can bring your metal friend too if you like but please... *no rough stuff*. I've just eaten."

"...Fine, *Clyde*," she stated, rudely. "Where is your cabin?"

"Are you still where you found the beacon?"

"I am." He gave her the directions anyone would need to find it. It was nearby... one could almost say expediently proximal. The real question was: was he actually there himself? Traps were a constant danger.

"Door's unlocked so you don't have to shoot or cut your way in. We should be moving in a few moments and therefore have some time to talk. I'm not sure what the delay is..." he trailed off. "You *can* trust me." She almost laughed out loud. Who hadn't said that to her?

"You can definitely trust *me* to *kill you first* if you're lying to me," she responded and cut him off. She eyed Kelvin.

"It's a forty-eight percent chance of betrayal," he stated, unhelpfully. She didn't know how she felt about this. It was all too easy and that was never a good sign. On the other hand, she *did* have backup.

"He's clever, I will be cautious. Let's go," she said, going for it.

***

It was a place that defied plausibility. A place that should never have existed. A place of terror. The Hellion was a thing, conceptually, that stood for everything any good person had to be against. Crimelord, a term often inappropriately applied, didn't even come close to describing who these people were. Who started this? Who founded it? Who built that place? The irony of all this was that, if they ever actually won and achieved domination, they would lose. Evil cannot coexist with anything for long... even itself. That is its great weakness – the ultimate argument of all being that evil can never triumph, because if it destroyed good, evil would lose its own identity. Without good there cannot be evil. Sure, this works in reverse too, thus ensuring the battle lasts forever... according to whose design? Maybe, if whoever was trying to create this balancing act thought through it further, they might see that they are as wrong as the forces they are trying to control? Always assuming they are in control...

Reed was in a dark reverie, locked in combat with an enemy he had faced before. It always wore a new face, always tried something different, but its stench remained the same. He was still thinking back to what he'd seen through Bert's eyes. The images didn't stalk him as such, as they were a product of someone else's mind, but it was the feelings that they created in him that wouldn't leave him. It was what they evoked. All those lives, innocent lives, taken by these... creatures. Creatures who dared to pretend to be civilised. Hate was always a trap, always so easy to work with. Hate is like a toy you can get out and play with. The more you play, the more you want to play, until one day it wouldn't be 'just a game' anymore. Reed was not weak enough to fall into that trap, but he knew something had to be done about this. Just knowing what *they had done* made him ashamed to be human. Ashamed to be sentient.

Conscience is much like a guide, a helpful tutor, watching over everything. Through it you should instinctively know what is right, and the opposite. Bad people do bad things for one reason only: because no one stopped them. These were the very worst people. They were the strongest embodiment of evil he'd encountered since... since the old days. This enemy would never stand and fight, it would always choose soft targets, as it was not brave enough to challenge the strong. In a way, it was pathetic. Bert was the same. Pathetic. Reed hadn't looked much further back into the man's memory. He hadn't looked into his life before he joined the cult. Now he was starting to wish he had, then perhaps he would understand better why Bert had done this, and wouldn't be so overpowered by loathing towards him. How he'd joined them and why? Why Bert might ever have thought it was a good idea? They say you couldn't learn from others' mistakes, only your own, but Reed didn't believe that. If you watched someone walk off the edge of a cliff and they died, you would quickly learn from that mistake. So... which cliff was he now standing on the edge of? What was the future?

People are frightened of things they cannot understand or cannot predict. Death and future events are scary for that reason. Many people have often stated that fearing what you cannot control is pointless. This is logically true but, as the old phrase goes, you cannot help how you feel. At least, not initially. And Reed was starting to fear the future again. Sometimes it was like a bright horizon, filled only with the dreamy promise of the best things that could happen. Now it seemed more like a gaping maw of death. He knew that it was both these things, and he also recognised that he was allowing this pointless speculation to distract him, but at that moment he had very little else to do. Never think too much... always a bad idea. He just had to follow the ship. He knew where it was supposed to be going, but there was no harm in making sure. He trusted Satiah to get the job done.

He tried to relax himself and move on mentally from his darker thoughts. They always tended to press in at awkward moments.

"Riff is asleep," Cherry said, entering casually. She'd found a rifle from somewhere, and was now patrolling the ship interior regularly... probably because she had nothing else to do. Reed didn't know if she was resentful at being left behind or not.

"Sleep is a gift," Reed smiled, meaningfully. "Why don't you have a small nap yourself? You make me feel guilty, watching you moving around while I sit here and cogitate on the infinite."

"It's okay," she smiled, awkwardly. "I know you have plans to make and things to calculate, but I..." She trailed off; clearly something other than inactivity was making her restless. Reed thought he knew what it was.

"You're worrying about what's going to happen, aren't you?" he asked, caringly. "I don't mean the assignment... I mean what happens to you *afterward*?"

Cherry looked like she was going to deny it but, for whatever reason, chose not to. She nodded, downcast.

"I... I just want to *belong* somewhere, and I don't know *where to go*," she admitted, trying to put what she was feeling into words. Reed listened patiently, in a way glad of the distraction.

"Since I met Satiah, everything has irrevocably changed for me..." She stopped and gave a snort of laughter. "Obviously, right?

Everyone knows there's no such thing as going back, I mean." Reed shrugged, maintaining the listening countenance. The concerned visage of someone who cared.

"I want to know *where I'm going*," she stated, finally saying it.

Reed raised his eyebrows as he nodded slowly and respectfully. It was tempting to ask a question to which there was no answer as a demonstration of how it was not that simple. A question like: *who really knows where they are going?* He knew, of course, that saying any such thing here would not help.

"Wise words are never hard to understand," he smiled, casually. "Looking back while going forward may seem unsafe but it's all we can really do. Nevertheless, the view isn't always so bad. I was warned once not to live in the past…" he smiled, remembering something from a long time ago.

"I was also cautioned not to dream constantly about potential futures," he went on, his smile growing. Cherry was concentrating hard on his words, seeking the answer she wanted. Or maybe just any answer, it was impossible even for her to know. We all look for what we want first: before we discover it's never really there. Even when we get what we want, we become disenchanted. How hard to please we are.

"You're saying not to worry about it. Not to plan or even think about it?" she clarified, confused.

"*That* would be impossible for anyone," he chuckled, gently. "My advice to you is to find something that you like and begin there. One way or the other, at least you might be happy. Things have a way of finding their place through time when pleasure is plentiful."

"Is happiness what we are all after?" she asked, seeming to keep pace with Reed's own thoughts.

"It's certainly part of it," he answered, seriously.

"What are the other parts?" she asked, intrigued.

"Made up only of factors from our own individual perceptions, in other words… There is no way any one person can know what anyone other than they themselves are after. And even if they *did* know: why ruin the mystery for everyone else?" he grinned. She giggled.

"You're a funny man."

"I've been called worse," he acknowledged. Haven't we all?

***

Alicia looked up as the alarms began to blare. She'd been expecting this but it was still a bit of mad rush of adrenalin when it happened. The Coalition fleet were here at last. She gaped as she realised the size of the force she was about to enter into complex dealings with. There were thirty-six destroyers, nineteen frigates and two dreadnaughts all converging on the planet. Even the most conservative people had to describe this build-up of force as substantial, surely? Perhaps high command circles were right that there was something very important to the Coalition that was still there.

"Get me those scan results!" she barked, rushing to see the battle computer's strategy. It would be retreat, of course, but it might tell her something that she may have overlooked. Like, more enemies coming in from another direction, with her luck.

"Captain, they're hailing us!" Well, of course they were! Leaving aside the fact that there was no one else, there was the obvious fact that they were in territory that they shouldn't be!

"Put them through," Alicia instructed, composing herself. A gruff-looking senior male appeared on the screen in front of her. A Fleet Admiral... *oh no*!

"This is Admiral Osckerr Snider of the Coalition Fleet," he stated, his tone official and hard. "Please stand by and allow us to board you." Alicia gaped at him. Board? Why would they...? "You are encroaching on Coalition territory, Captain," he went on. "It is procedure to ensure that you present no danger to either my ships or the planet itself."

"...I see," she agreed, hesitantly. What else could she do? They were too close for her to run now, and resistance was out of the question. He cut off and Alicia looked around at her stunned crew. They all stared at her, knowing what she knew. They were in trouble and their communications were being jammed.

***

"No one left alive, the place was a wreck," said the man. Quint turned to face him ominously.

"Any idea how it happened?" Quint asked, his voice never giving away anything. The man shrugged nervously.

"What evidence there is, suggests the fighting was widespread and seemed to happen mostly at the same time. I can only suggest that an argument turned violent. Visvenvar might have turned on Kyle in a bid to reclaim his position as leader, and it led to a fight to the death. On the other hand, it could just have been a fight of another kind that turned fatal," the man told him. Pirates were pirates. Indiscipline had been a problem that Kyle had frequently mentioned.

"You mentioned there were ships missing?" Quint questioned further. Survivors were still out there. They had to be.

"There were survivors indeed. You yourself encountered a freighter, didn't you?" he asked, curious. A suspicion crept into Quint's mind and he paused before answering. He had, at the time, assumed it was a pirate aboard that ship but...

"...I did," he allowed, leaving it at that.

"There was nothing obvious that might lead you to believe that it was the work of any single person or small group?"

"Nothing obvious no, the place was a wreck, and without anything from anyone or anything that saw it happen, I can't tell you what happened or who started what." This much was undoubtedly true.

Quint nodded and turned away to regard the stars once again. His walking stick clicked as he subtly activated it. In a split second, not more than an eye blink, it was a blade and he swung around, slashing open the throat of the man in a single move. The man collapsed, gagging and bleeding profusely. Quint regarded him solemnly.

"That is a shame," he said, his tenor still betraying nothing of the rage within. He'd had to die, of course, because not only had he failed, but he'd known too much anyway. With another slight touch, the blade slid back into position. Innocuous and elegant, from his youngest days, the sword had been his preferred weapon of choice. It made the kill more personal and it required greater skill to use than most guns. Now it was just his walking stick again. He should have been known as the man of many masks rather than simply Quint, as everything about him was a façade. A trick to conceal the truth. For his entire life he'd had to hide so much. Who he was. What he thought. What he wanted. All concealed behind mock constructions of all kinds. He watched as the man slowly died at his feet, in a growing pool of his own blood.

It was Satiah. It had to have been. Quint could guess how she'd done it. At present he didn't believe it had been her on the freighter, as it did not seem possible for her to have been on Collgort-Elipsa to fight Purella when she'd only just been orbiting Tweve a few hours previously. She could have got back directly from the base on Sunkiss in time though. Purella had said she was dead but she had lacked conviction. He had to assume that if Satiah didn't already know about the cult, she soon would, provided she was still alive. Surely there was no way for her to find the cult though? Purella didn't know where to go, and she had reclaimed Bert who couldn't tell her because of the memory implant he'd stupidly implanted in himself. All would be well and then they could continue their real work. Finding and completing that gemstone. Satiah still had that, he was certain. It was unlikely she would have willingly forsaken it… though he didn't know her. It was possible she wouldn't be interested in it at all, even if she knew what it was.

The Cult knew of the thing's existence and planned to claim the rest of it. They never knew though that he and Purella had found another piece of it. He'd never told them. With her in the cult with him, they could work together in secret to find the rest of it, and then they could use it themselves without even the cult knowing. It was still embryonic as plans went, and subject to plenty of alterations and adaptations, but it was a start. A way to power that no one else would even guess at. A way to never obey someone else's will again. A way to freedom through utter domination. A robot entered unobtrusively behind him. He'd heard it coming when it was still in the corridor outside.

"Clear *that* away," he instructed, to it. He pointed to the body at his feet. It obeyed without question… and it felt good.

***

The door opened and Satiah sprang in, pistol first, seeking targets. The room was dark, but light was coming from an open door beyond. It led to another room. The first room, the darkened one she was inside, was all functionality. Bed, table and crate, all very impersonal.

"In here!" called Clyde, from inside. Satiah smirked, seeing that he was taking no chances either. Kelvin went to follow her but she stopped him with a raised hand. Why did this feel like a test that she hadn't revised for? Oh wait, life always felt like that.

"Watch the door, I may need to get out in a hurry," she whispered, softly. "Record everything."

"Yes."

Satiah, satisfied, cautiously approached the next door. She stepped in swiftly, gun ready. Clyde, pistol aimed right at her, was sat at a table with a chair pulled out for her to sit opposite him.

This room, unlike the last, was like some kind of document repository. Diagrams, schematics, maps and all sorts of things littered every surface. Those that could not find a surface of their own had formed piles on the floor that rose almost up to her knees in places. There was just about room for the table and chairs. Clyde himself, despite his slouch, was plainly alert and ready for trouble. He was tall, and muscular in a way that showed even through his baggy combat clothing, and had thick white hair even though he hardly looked much older than she did. His deep blue eyes followed her every move with the attention of a trained killer.

"I hope you don't have issues about sitting and facing *away* from the only entrance, do you?" he quipped, grinning. She didn't answer.

"Your friend – Kelvin, is it? No doubt guarding the door in case I prove... *treacherous*?" Clyde asked, next. Evidently, he was not expecting her to answer. Satiah lowered her pistol and regarded him coolly, trying to make him out. Was he for real, or just a good actor? She decided it was safer to assume he really was *that confident*, because he'd earned his confidence the hard way. A highly dangerous individual... but that made perfect sense, looking at the company he kept.

"Well, let's put it this way. You're talking to your enemy. In doing so, you're technically betraying someone you know by doing that. *So what does that make you?*" she accused, shrewdly.

"Makes me a victim," was his quick replay. He lowered his gun too and leaned back in the chair. She remained where she was until he motioned for her to sit. She did carefully; the chair didn't look electrified, but it was hard to know for sure. For a few seconds they just stared at one another, neither saying a word.

"Surely as *a pirate*, you *have* victims. How does that make you one?" she asked, tartly.

"Well, aren't we all victims in one way or another? Victims of the system? Or do you consider yourself *a survivor*?" he asked, his tone prickly.

"And what system would that be?" she murmured, bleakly. He smiled.

"You have got some cojones," he stated, in respectful admiration. "But then, *as a Phantom agent*, that's only to be expected, right?" She didn't move or even react to that. She did wonder *how* he knew who she was, but she also knew he was negotiating and trying to get something he could use on her.

"Nice of you to say," she smiled, coldly. "Which system?"

"*Society*," he stated, with mischievous malice. He didn't really hate it, although it did irritate him from time to time. Not the idea or practises of a society – for him, it was more about the social side of it.

"*Aww*," she cooed, derisively. "Were you bullied as a child too?"

"Yes," he answered, honestly. "Now that I'm older and wiser though, I chose to see it as people identifying their own powerlessness and learning that they can get power over people by…"

"As fascinating as your childhood insights are, you called me here for a reason, get to it," she cut in, impatient. He grinned at her again.

"I understand I have someone you want?" he offered, still courteous in manner.

"What is Bert to you?" she asked, curious. Why would *he* choose to offer Bert to her? Why not the *lives of his accomplices* or even *the cult itself*?

"An embarrassment," he said, as if considering the question for the first time. "Truth is: to me, *he's no one at all* and I think that's true of you too, isn't it?"

"What do you mean by that?" she asked, interested.

"Clearly you're using him to get to someone or something else.

What I want to know *is:* how did you find out about him in the first place? My first thought was that we had an informer, but now *I'm not so sure...*" Clyde was saying.

Satiah realised how it must have looked when she first snatched Bert. She had been searching for Milo Drass at the time, and had incorrectly presumed that Bert was Milo until she'd actually seen him. Then she'd taken him on a spur of the moment decision, and naturally Purella would wonder *how* she'd known he was there. She chose to keep Clyde guessing.

"We have our means," she said, evasively. He chuckled.

"I'm figuring that he's still important to you *because* the cult want him. You know about the cult already, right?" Clyde asked, still grinning. How did he know all this? Still she acted unconcerned, she had to. In these situations, it was the best form of defence. Whatever he said or did: she couldn't let him know how it affected her.

"Why don't we just confine ourselves to discussing this deal *you* are after?" she suggested, grimly. It was a not so subtle reminder that he had been the one to make the first move. She didn't have to be there and he was wasting her time...

"I've never met a *real* Phantom before, that I know of. *I find you interesting*," he stated, seriously. "But if you *insist*... it depends what *you* want? Me? I just want to be left out of this. I want to live and I don't want to be molested in a court of law."

"Who are you?" she asked, thinking about it.

"Clyde, known also as Major Clyde, but it's a *strictly honorary* title. I was in the Coalition military once... made it to corporal but I had a bit of a falling out with an officer," he explained, keeping it vague. He could just be making all this up, but there was no way to know that.

"Over what?"

"A woman," he replied, shrugging.

"And he, this officer, engineered your removal?" she presumed.

"Well, long story short, I killed him and had to desert," he replied, admitting it. "He wasn't a beloved character in anyone's estimation, but prices have to be paid, don't they?"

"If you say so," she replied, noncommittal.

"You don't believe me?"

"Why should I? As sad stories go it's hardly *original*. Where's Bert?" she asked, again letting her exasperation show.

"How did *Kyle* die?" he asked, meeting her eyes with his. Again, she was instantly aware that he knew *still more* about what *she* had been doing. Either that or he was making some *very* accurate guesses.

"Who said he's dead?" she shrugged, maintaining eye contact. A trick *every* practised liar could perform.

"It was *you* actually," he stated, as if meant nothing to him. "What is *Obsenneth*?" She froze, caught out. How did he know about that? There had been no one else there that was conscious…

"You were not there, how could you know *who said what*?" she asked, her tone unsafe.

"I heard everything Satiah, *the whole interrogation*. My compliments. It was all going pretty well until that rock you stole from us *did something* to him…" he said, quickly.

"I accept your terms," she lied, promptly. "You can go free if you give me Bert. But I want *more* than that from you."

"Why does *that* not ring true?" he asked, leaning forward again. To show that she was not intimidated, she leaned forward too.

"Are you calling me a liar?" she asked, curious.

"What are we *really* talking about? What do you really want from me? It's not Bert at all, is it? You want to know more about Obsenneth, as I do. You know the cult wants it, but you don't know *why*, and Bert is only useful to you so long as he can lead *you* to *them*?" Clyde ventured, treading on dangerous ground. Okay, this guy was worrying her a bit now.

"You're only half right," she allowed, scowling at him. He was actually closer to seventy-five percent but she wasn't going to let him know that. "It's true I want to know more about the cult, but not because of any stolen rocks. I have my orders and I need to find the cult. Bert is my best chance at achieving that."

"I could take you to them if you're willing to hang around?" Clyde offered, artfully.

"I don't think so," she scoffed, as anyone would.

"All you have to do is hide somewhere here and you *will* find them. That's who Purella is going to see – to hand Bert to – as you have probably already guessed?"

"You know far too much," she stated, distrustfully.

"About *you* or about the cult?" he asked, with a half smile.

"All of this," she clarified, in a growl.

"So… *what?* You don't trust me?" he asked, trying not to sound too insincere.

"What you have me wondering about is this: what do *you get* by betraying everyone?" she mused, eyeing him closely.

"Aside from *my own life back*, you mean?" he asked, as if that something trivial. She nodded.

"*Purella is insane*," he stated, with a reluctant sigh. "She's always been unbalanced, and imbued with hatred against you. *Phantom agents are her worst enemies.* She even keeps skulls of the ones she's managed to kill, like some kind of trophy…"

"So what?" Satiah demanded, sourly. "Loads of people hate Phantom agents, because they are afraid of us, or because they blame us for something…"

"Yeah… Largely, that's probably true. But… Since she met *Quint*, it's been getting worse. She's increasingly distant and erratic," he detailed. "Plus, when she joins *them, which she will*, things might go south for us. For *me* in particular."

"Why *you* in particular?" she asked, highly intrigued by this. "And what do you know about Quint?" Clyde looked a little cornered for a moment. He'd made a mistake, mentioning Quint, and he knew it.

"She and I were lovers *once*," he confessed, seriously. Satiah regarded him coolly. She didn't know why that bothered her, but it did.

"And you think she will kill you because you know too much?" Satiah asked, grinning. "Assuming *I don't first?*"

"Nah, I don't think *you* want to kill me," Clyde replied, evaluating her again with his eyes. "I'm too unimportant, plus I am not a threat. I'm useful to you *alive*."

"What do you get, Clyde?" she sighed, unwilling to play on much longer.

"I get closure. I get to slip away... *plus I get you*," he said, cautious. She frowned at him.

"Me?"

"Well, you *and* Obsenneth," he replied, honestly. "You know what it is?"

"What if I do?" she asked, curious. He smiled.

"*So you don't?* That's fine, we can find out together," he suggested, as if he were suggesting they have a stroll down to an alehouse.

Would *you* trust this man? Satiah scowled, unsure what to make of him.

"I'm not even admitting I *have* Obsenneth," she stated, seriously.

"With respect, you have *already* admitted that you do," he smiled, with more passion now. "What you have is something that could bring *great power*. Enough power that the cult wants it. Quint wants it. Purella wants it. I... I'm happy to share it with you."

"You seriously expect me to just take *your word* for that?" she demanded, mordantly. "The word of a man who just sold out his own friends to me?" His eyes dropped and he slowly placed his pistol on the table, right in front of her and held up his hands.

"I don't know how else I can prove to you that I want to help you!" he hissed, at her. "I am a man of my word. I *honour* my promises..."

"You've promised me nothing yet," she argued, levelly.

"What would you *like* me to promise you?" he asked, more calmly.

"If I agree to allow you to help me with *this* situation... And you do not turn on me... And I let you live and let you go... Promise me that you will make yourself available to me *when* I need you," she requested, eyeing him. He leered at her, deliberately misunderstanding her words. She scowled. Typical man! "Or I could just *kill you now*, it's entirely up to you?" she said, crushing *that idea* instantly.

"...You want me to be one of your *informers*?" he confirmed, a little displeased.

"If you like," she replied, shrugging. "You have *many* pirate contacts. I daresay I might be able to use you from time to time. In the meantime... *if* you are a man of your word..." She trailed off.

"I'd hoped for better," he muttered, irritated. "I know it must be difficult for you to trust me, but..."

"No offence Clyde, but *they all say that. I* can always *use* informants. And maybe, if you also promise *never* to discuss Obsenneth with anyone other than me, *perhaps* I might let you help me," she allowed, thinking about it.

He smiled, a victorious smile. He had gambled on her not being able to learn much of the gemstone, mainly because he himself had tried to research it and had come up with nothing. If she was trustworthy too, they *could* work together and learn what Obsenneth actually was. Thinking ahead, the only real problem was likely to be *if* they succeeded... then betrayal would become a much greater possibility.

"Don't hurt yourself," he cautioned, as a joke. Her eyes narrowed but she permitted the hint of a smile to play at her lips.

"Speaking of getting hurt... It's time you told me *exactly* what is happening now," she told him. He nodded and lowered his hands. She slid his pistol across the table towards him and he replaced it in its holster.

"Now Purella has finally got Bert back from you, Quint has told her that she's basically in the cult now. *The first female member of the cult.* She's ecstatic because that's been what's she's after for years. We're going to take Bert to them where he will be executed as part of her *inauguration*," he explained, with contempt. Satiah picked up on his distaste.

"You don't like them, do you?" she enquired, a little amused.

"Hey, I love crime, don't get me wrong. I love stealing money, doing what I want and getting away with it but... *these guys*," replied Clyde, grinning mischievously. She gave him a sympathetic smile, as if he was telling her that he was mildly ill or something. His smile faded. "These guys are *not* just criminals... *they're sick.*"

"I *have* seen what they are capable of," she told him, in concurrence.

"What they stand for is just wrong," he stated, aware of the irony. "They want total domination of everyone. Frankly I've never been one for *that* idea. Sounds like too much work." She grinned at that.

"I see your point," she said, shrugging. "As far as I am concerned, they are *just* another enemy." She motioned to his communicator.

"Give me the details for *that* and be sure you keep it so that when this is over, I can contact you," she instructed.

"Deal," he nodded, more pleased now.

"Now, how long before we arrive?" she asked, inquisitively.

"Not sure, I've never been there before," he replied, honestly. "I doubt it is that far though. Purella will have been told by Quint where to go."

"Know anything about Quint?" she asked, seriously.

"No more than Kyle did," he replied, with a cunning smile. She smirked back at him.

"Like I said... *be discreet* for your own sake," she advised, sternly. "You may think it's clever to throw comments like that my way. *Let me remind you that it really isn't.*"

"Being your new informant, what benefits do *I* get?" he asked, teasingly. "Health insurance? Money?"

"You get to live," she smiled, coyly. "It may be several weeks before I call you so... be prepared for *a long wait*. I am exceptionally busy." He nodded, not satisfied but accepting.

"*That* I *can* believe." The ship suddenly shook and they stared at one another in joint accusation and then dawning comprehension.

***

Purella had still been deep in thought when the attack began. So distracted with the conflicting feelings inside her that she'd forgotten to take note of what was going on elsewhere. She wasn't exactly sure *when* the Federation destroyer had first appeared on the scanner, nor where it had come from. In Union space, it shouldn't have been there yet there it was, speeding towards them on an interception course. Without even attempting to hail her, it opened fire. Since escaping from Collgort-Elipsa, her ship's profile had probably been added to their ever-growing list of pirate targets. This destroyer, whatever it had been doing there, had recognised her and made its move. Where was Clyde? He was supposed to… The ship shook as some of the laser strikes found marks on the hull.

Clyde dashed into the control room, shouting orders and looking very angry. He knew, as not only had she been with him at the time but that she'd agreed to work with him, Satiah had not expected this attack. That told him that it was either rival pirates, or a Union attack force. Union attacks on pirates were rare, but they did happen. When he saw that it was a Federation ship, however, he was dumbstruck.

"What the hell are *they* doing here?" he demanded, to no one.

"Where were you?" Purella asked, still in shock. "You were supposed…"

"Trusting *you* to *watch where you're going*!" he spat back; with such vehemence it made her go quiet. The ship jolted and he swore.

"They've got us," he hissed, realising that this time there would be no easy escape. He ran a scan, anxious to find something. Anything that might help them.

"*There*!" she pointed at the screen. A nearby planet. A place where, if worst came to worst, they could ditch and await rescue. Another blast plunged them all into the deep red of emergency lighting. The computer reported three breaches in the hull and the loss of stern shields. One more hit and they could lose their engines. That was when the impossible happened. The destroyer stopped shooting and stopped following. It hung there in space like an angry guard dog watching an intruder escape over a fence. Purella and Clyde stared at it in silent astonishment. It had had them, they had been done for. Why had it stopped? Clyde recovered first. Why it had done what it did *mattered* but there was work to be done.

"Damage repair *now*!" he shouted. His voice would be heard all over the ship, and those he had rostered in would be starting to fix the hull.

Purella continued to stare at the destroyer as it became smaller and smaller.

"*Why did it stop?*" she asked, seriously. "Why?"

"I don't know," he replied, honestly. "I'm just glad it did."

"What was it even doing there?" she murmured, ponderously. Clyde regarded it again, trying to work that out. Its behaviour, appearing out of nothing and then holding off suddenly was odd. Maybe they were waiting to ambush a very specific ship and had mistaken the *Dreadnaught* for that ship? Unlikely. Were they guarding something secret and attacking anyone that got too close? This was Union space and just by being there, the Federation destroyer was trespassing. Unless it had permission to be there. A red flashing light informed him that the engines had been hit after all and fuel was leaking.

"We have fire on decks seven and eight!" shouted a woman.

"Hull breach two now sealed!" shouted a man.

"Any news on power?" Clyde, much calmer now, asked.

"Damage found, repairing now!" shouted someone else. Purella went for her communicator but was surprised when Clyde grabbed her wrist.

"I wouldn't tell Quint about this if that's what you're doing," he advised, grimly. "He might delay the whole thing." Purella paused, thinking it over. Since when was he so eager? Maybe he just wanted it to be over.

"Won't he wonder why we are late?" she asked, pointedly.

"He might," he replied, shrugging.

***

It had been a very close-run thing. Indeed, had Reed not been sitting there watching, it would have ended in disaster. The *Dreadnaught* was travelling swiftly along and Reed had been secretly stalking it as instructed when suddenly the scanners had revealed an unexpected complication. A Federation destroyer. It was moving in fast for an attack, Reed was sure. Most alarmingly of all, it seemed that the *Dreadnaught* was completely oblivious of its approach. Reed found that hard to understand but that didn't stop him for putting in an emergency call to Federation Fleet command.

"Admiral Wester, please," he requested, straightaway. "It's urgent! It's in regard to Federation destroyer activity in coordinate area 8096-7764! They must stop at once; they are *inadvertently* harming Coalition forces!"

"This is Admiral Wester," Wester answered. "That is Union space, and they are chasing a verified pirate target, can you elaborate."

"Three Phantom agents are aboard that ship as it is being used in an ongoing operation," Reed advised, swiftly. He winced as the *Dreadnaught* began to receive the pounding of the destroyer's onslaught. "Your ship needs to stop immediately!"

"One moment," Wester stated. He left the channel open so Reed could hear him issue the orders. One moment? That might be too long! It might only take one more shot to rip that ship in two! "Captain Clarrisa, *priority command*, disengage *immediately*!"

"Sir," she acknowledged. Almost instantly the destroyer stopped approaching, and stopped shooting. It loomed over its damaged victim, apparently indecisive.

"Let it go, I am aware it is on your wanted list, no error was made. I have been made aware it is serving a purpose regarding Coalition interests. The Coalition understand why you attacked and are not holding grudges," Wester explained.

"Admiral," she replied, crisply. Wester cut her off.

"It's done, now perhaps you wouldn't mind explaining further?" Reed's eyes widened in mild annoyance. However, anyone would want to know more, and Wester had raked up quite a list of favours to call in. It had been him, after all, that had ensured the Viscount's cities were protected in the first place. He had done this at Reed's personal invitation, casually disregarding the politics at the time.

"And would you mind explaining first what one of *your* ships is doing this far into *Union* territory?" he responded, chortling. "Are you not aware of the current political...?"

"More than aware, that's why I've sent instructions to my fleet, should the Captains deem sensible, to chase pirates even *into* Union territory," Wester replied, a little high handed. "We will not be bullied by the Nebula Union and their lax attitudes to criminals hiding in their space!" Reed noticed, with some amused irony, that he didn't sound completely dissimilar to Ro Tammer at that moment.

"Quite the crusader, aren't you?" Reed chuckled, calmly. "I have a great respect for your navy; until recently I was working with Captain Ogun. A very impressive example of Federation officer class, if you don't mind me pointing it out."

"...I'm sure *he* wouldn't mind," Wester remarked, clearly smiling. "*Please* excuse my lack of patience regarding the Union… they have been putting pressure on Raykur for days, because of that ship on Collgort-Elipsa. It's not right, given his *condition*."

"No, no, I quite understand. If it's any consolation, they have been giving us a hard time too," Reed said, cautiously. "Though it is only to be expected."

"So… Ambassador Reed… What's so *important* about *that* dreadnaught?" Wester asked, curious.

"Well, we're using *it* to lead us to something else. We don't quite know *what* yet, but it looks *peculiarly enthralling*," he answered, evasively. "It *is* related to pirate activity, to be sure, but we need to know more *before* we hit the doomsday button, as they say."

"I see," he replied, thoughtfully. "I hope we haven't just ruined it all for you."

"I don't know, I'm not sure yet, the ship is still *intact* but that's all I can tell you currently," Reed replied, honestly. "I can hardly blame any of you for the attack as you didn't know. I dare say we would all have done the same."

"*Fog of war*," Wester sighed, in agreement.

"Hoodwinks the best of us sometimes," Reed smiled, cordially. "I have detained you long enough, Admiral, I must get back to work."

"Understood," he replied, after the shortest of hesitations. Wester was interested in the operation. He hadn't had to say so to prove to Reed that he was. Relations between the Federation and the Coalition were better than they had been in years but it would be the easiest thing to ruin all that.

"If you're interested I will let you know the outcome," Reed offered, carefully. There was a lot he wouldn't be able to tell Wester but he owed the young man a lot. He had complied with both of Reed's, some would say odd, requests, and he'd done so without complaining.

"Thank you, Ambassador, I would appreciate that," he smiled. They disconnected and Reed sighed in relief. Talk about dancing with death: you couldn't stop until death stopped *or*... it stopped you.

Next, he called Satiah to explain what had happened. She had mixed feelings.

"I hope there are no more lurking nearby. You might not be quick enough next time. I don't know the extent of the damage, but we lost local lighting at one point," she told him.

"You're still drifting so I'm guessing the engines were hit," Reed said, considering. "How are the others?"

"Fine, no injuries," she replied.

"And have you made contact with whoever it is yet?" he asked, interested.

"I have. It *seems* he's sincere in his desire to aid us, though I will remain vigilant," she answered, cryptically. "It also seems that he fears the cult's retribution. *Plausible but possibly not true.* So far he's not done anything to give me reason to believe he will switch sides again."

Satiah was sat in the very chair Clyde had been. The attack seemed to have taken *everyone* by surprise. Had Reed not been there, she was pretty sure they would be dead. Even if they had somehow survived the explosion, the mission would have been delayed at best, possibly even aborted. As it was... they had got away with it. While Clyde played his part, that part being the one where he acted like he had not betrayed anyone, Satiah touched base with Randal.

"How are you doing?" Randal asked, rapidly. "I see you dragged Dyss out of his office, we can see the path he took through the cobwebs."

"Things became too hectic for just two of me to deal with," she replied, seriously. "I've got nothing on your gold, by the way. Any news?"

"*Nothing...* No one seems to know where it went," Randal stated, more irritated now than angry. "We don't know, the pirates don't know and no one else is putting their hand up."

"Well, now that the company know their own employees were in on it, I don't think they're in any position to criticise us," she smirked.

"How are things… you know, between you and them?" he asked, intently. She paused, considering her response with equal intensity.

"Provided I don't leave them alone together for too long, I think they'll cope," she replied, at last. "Got to go, will keep you updated."

Her next call was to Rainbow.

"Hey, are you all right? I heard about that run-in you had with the PAI agent, Randal was *furious*," he began, animatedly. Oh yes, Nerva, the Primary Agency of Investigation operative who'd attempted to kill her on Sunkiss.

"It was nothing," she replied, anxious to move on to what she really wanted to talk about.

"*Nothing!*" he exclaimed, scoffing with hushed laughter. "There might even be an enquiry!"

"To be honest, if there is one, it's been a long time coming," she stated, careless. She knew she was not the only agent to have had troubles with rival operatives. Technically they were supposed to be on the same side, even if they weren't working as a team. So much for that.

"Anything I need to know about Tweve?" she asked, pointedly.

"The masked constellation?" he quipped. He knew where she meant but, as he had discovered, there were actually four planets with that name.

"We will get to Quint in a moment," she muttered.

"As you know, it used to be part of the Confederacy until the war, now, since the Treaty of Dreda, it's been under the Union umbrella," he listed, sounding bored. "Archaeologically, the world holds some interest, mainly due to a lost civilisation rumoured to have once colonised the cosmos millions of years ago."

"Like the Rallith?" she asked, interested. There was a stunned silence.

"How do *you* know about *them*?" he asked, in shock.

"They are mentioned in the Venelka files," she smiled, unable to stop herself sounding a little smug. "Is that all?" She knew he would be wondering what else she knew, and he knew she knew that, and it could go on for a while.

"No, it is *not* all," he replied, trying to sound superior. "Until *recently* the planet was a popular tourist destination because of the solar winds causing natural light displays of great beauty in the thermosphere. This would happen only at the places of higher altitude, most likely the poles. They are called auroras. Whatever, they *were* very popular and there were also tours of the ruins on the surface of the planet too."

"*Recently?* You mean ten years ago or so?" she guessed, eloquently.

"Got it in one," he said, without missing a beat. "The place was closed down, *allegedly to be reopened*... only it never did."

"Probably when the cult moved in," she said, seriously. Rainbow agreed. "I am surprised. Shutting it down might have attracted *more* attention than allowing it to continue. I would have used it as cover."

"I get the impression they value their privacy *highly*."

"There is no such thing." He made a noise of begrudging agreement.

"*Quint?*" she asked, softly. "Do you have anything?" Rainbow sighed, and her heart sank.

"Sorry, Satiah, I got nothing. Guy is as grey as a ghost. I was thinking, he wears a mask, right? And he's hiding in the *masked* constellation?" Rainbow theorised. "Do you think he's trying to tell us something?"

"He has concerns about his own complexion?" she offered, giggling. "Rainbow, I think you're in danger of wandering down *Conspiracy Avenue* again."

"You do know that's a *real place*, don't you?" he grunted. She raised her eyebrows a little. Okay, that was scary, should she believe it?

Quint remained an enigma. A masked mystery that cast everything around him into menacingly beckoning shadows. He was starting to remind her a little of Vourne. Vourne never wore a mask, but he did have a habit of trying to influence everything he could as secretly as he could. He would use trusted intermediaries... *like her*... to do his dirty work for him. Quint had used Kyle like that... and Purella, apparently. Clyde had all but confirmed that. Purella wanted in, with regard to the cult, and Quint was facilitating *that* while using her for his own schemes. One of his schemes concerned Obsenneth too... She felt in her pocket, her hand gloved, for the rock. It was there. Innocently playing the part of an *innocent* stone that was merely a solid aggregate of some *equally innocent* mineraloids. Quint had been trying to perpetuate one war and possibly attempting to start another. And to think it had been pure luck that she'd stumbled onto this...

"Satiah?"

"No, I do not," she smiled, ruefully. The real question was: were Quint's plans his own or the cult's? Well, in a way that didn't matter, as her response would be the same whichever was the case. Stop them.

"I'll keep looking, of course, but I'm starting to go over the same ground, running out of places to look," he went on.

"Maybe – when I find out for myself I'll let you know," she smiled. "Assuming I'm still able."

"Take care," he said, seriously. He disconnected and she eyed Kelvin, who was standing by the door. No one had disturbed them, despite the recent attack. The fuss was dying down now too. Everything was gradually returning to the calm it had been before.

"Clyde is returning," Kelvin informed, in warning. "He is alone." Good timing.

Clyde entered, looking stressed.

"We just got attacked by a Federation destroyer," he explained. "Damage is mostly repairs. We got seriously lucky. They had us right where they wanted but for some reason they let us limp off." He wanted her to ask him why they had not continued the attack so that he could then accuse her of somehow orchestrating it.

"I didn't realise we were in Federation space," she remarked, playing dumb.

"We're not," he stated, the hint of accusation still in his tone. She eyed him, allowing her indignation to well up.

"I hope you're not inferring that *I* had anything to do with it?" she ventured, coldly. "Blowing myself up would seem a rather stupid idea."

"I agree, it's just weird that you turn up and then this happens within a few minutes," Clyde replied, more calmly.

"Your beacon could have attracted it," she suggested, with a shrug. He had deactivated it the moment that she had contacted him, of course but it was possible. Clyde, realising that if she *did* know anything she wasn't going to *say* anything, let the matter drop.

"Regardless, we will be on the move again shortly," he told her.

"Hopefully they will not think anything of your lateness," she replied, thoughtfully. "I know I would."

"I'm sure Purella can smooth things over; besides, this time *the truth* should serve well enough as an explanation," he replied, grimly.

"*For once*," she replied, the flicker of a smile on her face. That made him smile too.

"You're okay hiding in here? You don't want anything?" he offered, having trouble deciding what to say. She frowned at him, in confusion.

"*What did you have in mind?*" she asked, warily.

"I don't know, some water or something? *No poison, obviously*," he added quickly, at the end.

"The only thing I require from you is for you to *not* give me away," she reminded, stiffly. "Nothing else."

"No harm in being friendly," he smiled, amused by her reaction.

"There is *always* harm in being friendly," she stated, sourly.

"*Come on*! We're partners now, *right?*" he asked, pleasantly. Loaded questions were always being fired at her these days, and it did not seem very fair.

"I haven't decided yet," she replied, pushing her hair behind her ear.

"Well, *while you're making your mind up*, how is me asking after your comfort a problem?" he asked, that grin back again.

"...If you need something to do, go and... polish your boots or something," she instructed, dryly.

"Okay, I know when I'm not wanted," he said, making eye contact. She held his gaze; her brown eyes part contest and part incitement.

Clyde gave another grin as he backed slowly away and the door sealed. Satiah remained where she was for a moment, entertaining a few ideas in her imagination that she knew she shouldn't. There was a beat of silence as she realised Kelvin was watching her closely. For a moment she thought he was going to state she was going insane again.

"Your pupils were dilating…" Kelvin began.

"Shut *up*," she said, sighing and rolling her eyes. She returned her attention to some of the files that she had been reading on Clyde's desk.

"You adjusted your hair…" he stared again, trying another way to make his point. She did not want to listen though.

"I *said* shut up," she growled, irritated.

"You're becoming unnecessarily defensive…" he noted.

"Come here and say that," she replied, exasperated. "I'm not sure what you're *trying* to accomplish by telling me these apparent observations of yours, but I would like you to *stop right there*."

PART FIVE

Justified Means

Birdcalls were all that the bracing gusts conveyed that morning. Trilling warbles and quavers that, when recorded and sold, were often used to promote relaxation and escapism to those under stress. Ambassador Hademan was awaiting a call of another kind. A call that had taken longer than expected to arrive. So, as he often did, he left his quiet office for the picturesque landscape he was fortunate enough to have nearby. Light woodland and hedgerows stood as outposts in open fields where the grass was up to knee height in places. He sat down on an antiquated bench that he occasionally had lunch on, in the early afternoon, and enjoyed the view. The breeze whipped his curly grey hair about, but his piercing blue eyes remained unmoved. He turned briefly to regard the ancient looking building some distance behind him. His office.

Once a primitive fortress of stone, the designer, clearly an admirer of the bygone, had preserved most of the outer shell while rebuilding it. Inside everything was pristine and modern looking. Hademan and the architect obviously had something in common, at least in regard to aesthetics. His office, though surrounded by the ultramodern, was customised. Oak panelling, a wooden desk and all manner of antiques decorated his workspace. He liked it for two reasons. First, it was different, unique and unmistakable. A way perhaps of reminding himself that he could make his mark if he wanted to. Second, because of its look it always caught visitors off guard. It would distract them; make them easier for him to deal with. Wouldn't it be fantastic if it were as easy to make the universe look and be how you wanted? The people in it to think the thoughts you wanted them to… that way everything would be under control!

His communicator went off softly. He didn't like loud alert tones, they disturbed the peace. It occurred to him momentarily that the communicator must be one of the rudest devices ever invented. It would be the equivalent of someone approaching you and making a loud and annoying noise in your ear until you chose to talk to him or her. They did have and serve a purpose though. It was his receptionist, not the call he had been expecting.

"Yes?" he answered, making the effort to be patient. His receptionist was efficient, obedient and, best of all, discreet. It was very hard to find people like that.

"He's here in person, master," she said, coldly. He grunted. That explained the lateness of the call. He'd chosen to come and talk to Hademan himself.

"I will be back directly," Hademan smiled, as he stood. He began to amble back to the office. "Offer him a drink, you know his favourite?"

"It is the same as yours master, *Imanare*," she replied, her tone unchanging. Just the name of the drink made him want to taste one.

"Better make that two," he replied, picking up his pace. He entered via the back way and took the stairs (he never trusted elevators) to his office. He entered just as the main door opened. His receptionist, Lacey was her name, led the way in. Another older man followed. He, like Hademan, was well dressed and formal looking. He was almost completely bald but for a stubborn silvery fringe of hair that circled around the back of his head and over his ears. His brown eyes regarded Lacey's hips as she moved ahead of him, more watchfully than lustfully. Probably checking her for the tell-tale signs of a concealed weapon. She *was* armed, of course. One of her other duties was acting as bodyguard to Hademan. He looked up casually and smiled at Hademan.

"I hope you'll forgive the intrusion?" he asked, as she took his coat.

"Intrusion from a friend is almost always forgivable. Drink?" Hademan replied, sitting down. He chose not to sit behind his desk but instead occupied the chair next to the one his old friend was going for. Magnus, or Legislator Magnus, was his name and he was an advisor to the Premier. The Premier, head of the government, effectively ruled the Nebular Union. Lacey poured two large glasses of the dark, pungent liquid and handed them one each. She was careful to hand Magnus his personalised glass. An antique style of mug, with dimples throughout the glass and a handle also made of glass.

"You know," Magnus began, staring into the beverage with pleasure. "This is what coming here is really about." Hademan smiled, knowing that he was joking but could forgive him even if he wasn't. Lacey straightened; hands clasped behind her and awaited another instruction. Hademan glanced at the time. She had three hours left to kill before the end of her shift but he was feeling generous that day.

"I'll see you *tomorrow* Lacey," he said, meaningfully. She glanced at him to be sure she'd understood correctly before quirking a smile.

"Very good, master," she replied, marching out. She closed the door behind her with just enough emphasis to let him know that the building was empty. There was nothing usual in that, these days. She, however, took security very seriously... another reason why he employed her. For a little while the two men sat in silence, enjoying the drinks and remembering *other times*.

"Is there something wrong?" Hademan asked, at last. Magnus's presence told him that something was out of place. High position, a love of *Imanare* and age was not the only things that the two men had in common. They both were the current High Priests of the Cult of Deimos. *The leaders.*

"I'm to be there for the Ceremony of Distance and the initiation of Sister Purella," Magnus said, calmly. "The Bishops are chosen and all is ready. I just wanted to ask you if she met with your approval?"

Hademan nodded slowly, he'd been half expecting this. Magnus had left it late in the day to ask, but it was not *too late*, Hademan supposed.

"I have been reassured by two of the current Bishops that she is ideal," he replied, cautiously. "I have never investigated or met her myself, but I'm told she has proven both her loyalty to us and her ability. You are worried about those with prejudice?"

"A little, though we shall see what happens," he replied.

"I heard that you increased the size of the fleet that went to Collgort-Elipsa?" he then enquired, changing topics.

"Escalation," Hademan replied, shrugging. "Two eyes for one and all that."

"We have lost contact with that fleet. It seems Quint was right about how the Coalition would react," Magnus stated. That got Hademan's attention. He chose to hold back the obvious questions like when, how and what happened.

"*The man in the white mask*," he murmured, instead.

"I was against *his* initiation," Magnus chuckled, remembering. "I cannot deny that he has proved himself since, though I confess… I still neither like nor trust him."

"Just like all the others then," Hademan couldn't resist smiling. That brought a smile to Magnus's face again.

"*This is true, this is very true*," he said, chuckling. "I wanted to ask what you think best… about the fleet?"

"If things have already gone so far it shouldn't require any further pushing from us," Hademan acknowledged. "We just need to know what has happened to that fleet, and so does everyone else."

"And what of the Federation?"

"That *was* an unfortunate complication," Hademan admitted, with a slight groan. Through insightful manipulation, Hademan and Magnus between them had managed to remain the leaders of the cult for the best part of thirty years.

That had not been achieved with ease, and it was a constant struggle to remain in charge. Mostly everyone in the cult was overly ambitious, mistrustful, arrogant and greedy. The camaraderie of the cult was very real among some members, and very fake among others. There had been more than a few attempts to oust Hademan and Magnus, sometimes as individuals and once as a pair, but they had managed to come out on top every time. There had been so many schemes, so much money and so much plotting over the years that all this seemed normal to them. This *was* the closest they had come to orchestrating an all-out intergalactic war, however.

"Ensure the Premier receives only what information we want him to, obviously, and do everything you can to make sure that he thinks it's his own idea," Hademan went on. "The government will try to prevent an outbreak of war, but we have the numbers to paralyse them. Keep them tied up with bureaucracy and protocol. The public will be in uproar and the Premier will think he has no choice but to retaliate."

"Agreed," Magnus nodded, considering. "Have we made any progress on that gemstone yet?"

"No... all quiet as the grave. I have found someone who might be able to help and he's agreed to assist once we've negotiated a fee," Hademan frowned. "Perhaps when the war is over?"

"It may have to be. What have you told him about it?" Magnus enquired, interested.

"Only what we agreed, why?"

Magnus shrugged and eyed the repository on Hademan's desk. Hademan followed his gaze, got up and opened it. Inside the orange gemstone remained... as it had for years.

"Just checking," Magnus chuckled.

"Well, *without the other pieces*, it is useless," Hademan reminded him. That had been on the note they had found with the gemstone... all those years ago. They believed it.

No one knew who had written the note, why they had, or what had happened to break up the stone in the first place. Yet it was rumoured to be, when complete, a thing of great power. The note itself sounded more like some kind of archaic prophecy than it did an instruction manual, but the idea was there.

Separate they now are, the five with senses of their own. Above all else they desire to return. To come back and be one again as once they were. Cut apart by those who failed to see,

now they wander the stars seeking one another. When back together they are brought, an ancient power shall become naught. A battle that should have been long ago, now will be fought. A new and greater power will rise and those who helped share the prize. Find. Connect. Understand.

Both men liked things with power, and liked to have that power for themselves. This stone was no exception to their way of thinking. Over their years of friendship, they had moved up into the circles of the most powerful individuals in the Union. They had earned the ability to manipulate the cosmos. The Cult had helped them at first, particularly in the early days, and now they were in the best positions to repay it. Taking it to levels higher that it had reached for a long time. And this rock, Hademan was certain, would help them too. When they found the other parts of it.

Hademan sat down again and offered the bottle to Magnus. Magnus pretended that he wasn't interested in more and then grinned.

"Why not?" They had another. They indulged in memories and in-jokes as any old friends would. To see them there, no one would suspect the truth. They looked so normal. Finally, Magnus stood to leave.

"I will move straight to the Hellion and I'll catch up with you in a few days," Magnus promised. They shook hands and then hugged.

"Take care," Hademan said, like always.

"You too."

***

Amber knew she had talents but this was a new one. Seduction was one of her best abilities, but another new one that she'd just discovered was... playing dead. She'd known it was a risk, Satiah had warned her. She'd taken some precautions and they had paid off. She had gone to report to her superior as normal. Everything had gone well until she'd hit the doomsday button and mentioned *the Cult of Deimos*...

"*What?*" Gower had asked, eyeing her sharply. Too sharply to be *unknowing*, she knew. Her heart sank, appreciating that Satiah had been quite correct. They had people *everywhere*. Amber had to keep playing of course, keep following her plan; her very survival depended on it and much else…

"Apparently, this whole war has been orchestrated by some group called the Cult of Deimos," Amber repeated, playing along. "At least, that is what the Coalition agents were saying."

"And you… *believe this*?" he asked, slowly. She swallowed, knowing what to expect and what to do. She sighed and moved over to the window. Presenting her back to him… making herself an easy target. The device was prepared.

"I do," she replied, as if it was hard for her to say. "There is too much plausibility and truth in it for me to ignore it. That's *why* I thought it best to report it to *you*. But *be careful* who you trust with this, sir, we don't know how far this goes."

"Very true, *you* don't," he had replied, coldly.

That had been when he'd shot her. In the back, the place traitors often choose. She had gasped and fallen dramatically to the floor. No last words, no dying hand grasps… she had just lain there, motionless as a corpse. Gower had hissed, she assumed in anger, and then he'd made a call to someone. It was in a language she didn't understand, but the meaning was palpable. He was a member of the cult too, and was reporting that they may have been compromised. She remained where she was, despite the discomfort. It was only when she heard him moving towards the door and she knew his back would be turned on her that she had acted again. Rolling over onto her back, she aimed and put a bolt between his shoulder blades, returning the favour. Gower slumped to the floor with an animal-like groan. Taking no chances, she'd taken the time to deploy a cold-blooded shot to the head. Then she had fled the building.

It was now time for her to find another job.

She had considered simply maintaining the pretence of death and going into hiding, but his betrayal had hurt her too much for her to ignore. She'd trusted him once! Trusted him with her life and her secrets. She might as well have trusted her enemies! He'd reported her death, she hoped, to the cult. That might give her a few days' grace, and she knew how to disappear. The question was: should she? Or should she stay and fight for her Union? She was sure she could persuade the Viscount to have her back, but she didn't know where he was. Besides, the idea of revenge greatly tempted her. She had been used by the cult as a tool as much as the government... always assuming they were not one and the same thing. This was too big for her to fight alone and she knew it. She could always defect, of course...

***

Was this a court martial or not? Captain Alicia knew that she and her crew had certain rights under the Common-Protectorate-Conventions, and so far no one had been harmed. Nevertheless, the fact that she was now sitting before three high-ranking officers, with an apparent adjutant to her side, made her imagine that she was on trial for something. As interrogations went, though, it couldn't have been less official or scripted. She'd been offered 'the basics', meaning she'd been provided with anything she desired, within reason. She'd opted for a snack, when she was nervous she had to eat – it was that simple.

"Captain Alicia," she was asked directly, her other titles forgone for expediency. "I have to formally ask you to explain this intrusion on Coalition territory. Please be aware that this is being listened to by others who are not here. Please explain?"

"Pirate activity drew us into this area," she said, evasively. Technically it was true, but everyone knew it was not the whole story. "I was going to ask for assistance to track them but I didn't have time before my arrest."

"You are *not* under arrest," the officer next to her said, as if that were obvious. "You're just helping us with our enquiries." He said it with such conviction that it made her wonder if he really believed that. Well, whatever the case, arguing was not a smart idea.

"*Oh good*," she smiled, without meaning it. "There is some tell of pirate attacks on Collgort-Elipsa too, and I wondered if they were connected."

"That is being looked into," was the instant response from the Vice Admiral.

"The Viscount did send out a formal request for protection," she pointed out. Granted, it had not been intended for the Union, but he'd not specified that it wasn't either.

"Yes, that request was to us," he replied. Again, arguing would achieve nothing.

"And now you are here, I can offer you my assistance in tracking down any attackers," she offered, pointlessly.

"Tracking down *the city itself* might be a better idea," he replied, a tinge of amusement creeping into his voice.

"Imagine *that*, heading out and *forgetting* to let *anyone* know your destination," murmured someone, dryly.

"Yeah, it's like they didn't want to be found or something."

"Well Captain, it's clear that whatever pirate activity that was here has ceased. Therefore, there is no reason for you to remain. We thank you for your swift response regarding the protection request," the Vice said, firmly. So… that was how it was going to be. All handshakes, faint praise and a 'please shut the door on your way out' vibe.

"No problem, I'd be happy to stay and lend *any* assistance…" she began, guessing that they would refuse any such offer. He raised his hand, a knowing smile on his face. She sighed and grinned back. Everyone had fulfilled any obligations here. Everyone was being very deliberately nice to one another. She rose, saluted and then went for the door. The Vice followed her out for a less official chat.

"I think we are of one mind here, Captain," he stated, walking beside her. "We follow orders, but no one wants war. Now the city is gone, there is no point in *anyone* coming here. Makes you wonder why they didn't move it away sooner."

"Yes," she concurred, thinking about it. "I'd put money on someone somewhere being very angry at how peacefully we handled this."

"It was a set up. I have recorded evidence that the destruction of your warship was *not* as a result of Federation action. It exploded of its own accord immediately after it arrived," he explained.

"*I* believe you, but the administration never will," she replied, sadly. "I looked at the timings and thought it rather quick to have had a battle."

"Twenty-three seconds," he nodded, grim. "*My sympathies*. It's clear that an unseen player is behind all this and while we may never know who, at least we did not fall for it."

"It points to someone *within* the Union," she said, with conviction. She shook her head, dismayed. "Someone with access to the ship and information on its movements."

"It does," he replied, thinking about it. "How are you going to explain your return to your superiors?"

"Given the political climate I really don't think blaming it on you is a good idea," she joked. "I tell you what. I'll orchestrate a *maintenance problem*, or as you may know it, a structural failure. Then I will have to withdraw the whole fleet as, one ship down, it will not be strong enough to repel you."

"They *might* see through that," he replied, shrugging.

"Possibly. Frankly, my relationship with fleet command has never been that fantastic, *I'm sure I'll live*," she stated, thinking about it. "Now the city has gone, *to be honest*, the *only* people my departure should unduly upset will be the warmongers."

"I doubt they would be silly enough to give themselves away. Apparently, *after what the Viscount said*, there have been a lot of... *unexplained incidents* within the Union."

"...Like what?" she asked, stopping in her tracks. He shrugged.

"Suicides, people going missing, some sort of greenmailing scandal, *I don't really know* – I left in rather a hurry," was his reply. Alicia's heart was pounding, fear in her eyes.

"Scratch that. Is there *any* chance my fleet *could* stay here?" she asked, seriously.

***

The preparations were on schedule. In his habitual red uniform, Bishop Mickorsi oversaw the process. His tall frame and gaunt, verging on cadaverous, features defined his spine-chilling countenance. The longer than average nails on his skeletal hands, yellowy in tinge, slowly peeled the wet skin off of the fruit he was eating. Outside of the cult, he was a Chief Examiner of the Nebula Union Constabulary, and had risen to the rank of Bishop within the cult due to one or two major cover-ups he had facilitated. Notably the Hapshin-Massacre, some nineteen years ago. Another initiation, he'd seen so many and indeed remembered his own with a vague fondness. Tonight, however, marked a precedent, a new direction perhaps; after all, there was always a first time. The first female member.

As Bishop, he had access to the cult's history and while he knew it was true that there had never been any female members, he also knew that one of those who had *founded the order*, thousands of years ago, had been female. In any case, as a result of this change, he wondered if this would lead to any alteration in the ritualistic elegance of the cult. The High Priests would decide on that but it did make him wonder. He'd heard the whispers of a few members not so enamoured by the idea of female membership. They were in a minority, but it could lead to a potential schism in the future. He'd highlighted this as a concern of his own, of course, and that was all he had to do. It still troubled him though, and that was when he saw something else that bothered him... Quint.

Quint was just standing there, as if he was rooted to the spot. The bustle of the others went on all around him, but Quint remained where he was as if unaware of them. He was the one who'd pushed for this Purella to join them. Mickorsi had at first believed that perhaps they were lovers. Now he was not so sure. He approached Quint and nodded to him.

"How soon before she arrives?" he asked. "I understand she is bringing the sacrifice with her?"

"She is," Quint replied, his voice as hard to read as ever. "She is less than an hour away but I've told her that she may have to wait."

"I will make preparations to deactivate the TS," Mickorsi stated.

The TS, *or Temporal Shift Device*, was a part of the Hellion's defence system. Specifically, it was the main part. The Hellion, under the ruins, existed at the end of a tunnel. The tunnel always appeared blocked off while the TS was functioning. This was because the block, made up of earth, rock and other debris, was made corporeal by the TS. The block had once existed in the past before it had been cleared during the construction of the Hellion, yet the TS brought the blockage forward in time to seal the tunnel and cut off the Hellion below from any unwanted visitors. It was impassable because, though it *was* physically *there*, it couldn't be influenced by anything physical without time distortion occurring. To touch it would be to cross a barrier in time, unprotected, and thus would kill anything alive or damage/destroy that which was not. It was a formidable obstacle.

It could very simply be deactivated and reactivated from within the Hellion. Only the High Priests could deactivate it from outside the Hellion. There was also the side-effect of scan interference, which was another advantage of this system: when active, it was impossible to scan the area and get a clear reading.

"Is there any news of the Union fleet?" Quint asked. Mickorsi sighed. He'd had no updates.

"If there is, I have yet to hear it," he answered, casually. "Magnus will know."

"There is a chance they may have been destroyed. If the Coalition moved in and the fleet refused to back down, it's possible," Quint went on.

"Assuming the Coalition *sent* a fleet. The Federation may have sent their own," Mickorsi pointed out. "Arguably, now the city is removed, there is less reason for *anyone* to fight *anyone*. There is nothing to defend and no one to impress."

"It's not over until it's over," Quint stated, stubborn. Mickorsi was not used to Quint displaying his feelings like that. Clearly something had angered the man. Assuming, of course, that he *was* a man. Who knew what face hid behind that pale white mask? Mickorsi knew that Quint had some sort of grudge against the Coalition, but he'd never delved further into it. Quint had been enthusiastic working on the High Priest's plan to start a war over Collgort-Elipsa. Mickorsi was pragmatic by nature and, if something failed, then it failed. It didn't have to be the exclusive matter that every later decision was based around. In this case, so there might not be a war? So what? There were plenty of other ways to make money and, if it was revenge he wanted, well, there were other ways to get that too. He saw no reason in promoting animosity between Quint and himself though, so he temporised.

"Very true, brother," he answered, tactfully. With that, he left to turn off the TS. As he moved past it, he glanced up at the statue of Banshincubus, focussing briefly on the narrow openings of its eyes.

He didn't know why, but he felt like they could actually see him. He reached a console, hidden in the wall and activated it with his hand print. White lights flickered on, illuminating him completely for a moment. Then he deactivated the TS. The way was open, and soon the brethren would be there in their hundreds to witness the initiation. The merriment would be a long one, he supposed, as initiations were rare these days.

***

The damage was repaired and they were underway once again. The mystery as to how they had been allowed to escape remained but, due to the relief of being alive, most people were happy to let it remain a mystery. Federation destroyers were not known for their leniency, especially when it came to pirates. Purella had retreated to her room, leaving everything on autopilot. This was it, no turning back and all that nonsense. She fell into her old fantasies, imagining what the ceremony would be like. She was now in the stages of dreaming bigger, thinking ahead to a time when she would rule the cult herself. This was what the years of hard work had been about. She glanced at the skulls of the enemies she had vanquished and smiled. She would make them all pay! She would engineer their downfall!

Clyde felt mildly absurd as he knocked on the door *to his own office*. The door opened and Kelvin regarded him mechanically.

"What is it *now*, Clyde?" Satiah asked, from behind Kelvin. Clyde huffed theatrically.

"Can I come in?" Clyde asked, sarcastically.

"Of course," she replied. Kelvin moved aside and Clyde entered. Satiah was still sat at his desk, where he'd last seen her.

"I wanted to know… what's going to happen?" Clyde admitted, seriously. "When we get there."

"*Doesn't everyone?*" she quipped, softly. Then her eyes rose to regard him properly. She smiled grimly in the dim light. "I can't answer that but *probably* a big fight. That's what usually happens, am I wrong?"

"What about *Bert?* Will you try to save him or just use him?" Clyde asked, crossing his arms. She did her best to pay no attention to his appealing muscle tone.

"Why are you *so* interested?" she countered, suspiciously. "I thought we had decided everything and, so long as we agreed to get in touch later about you know what and... you get to leave this without any stains... *Why?*"

"I know *you and him*," Clyde began, nodding to Kelvin. "You're pretty formidable. But I don't think you can do this *alone*."

"*Perhaps*," she allowed, without further explanation. He tilted his head to the side, evaluating her countenance intently. "Depends what *doing this* entails, surely?" He ignored the question.

"Always assuming... you *are* alone?" he guessed, astutely.

"I don't like working with others. *Others can let you down rather badly*, if you know what I mean," she evaded, adeptly. Clyde had just betrayed Purella, so he could hardly claim he was loyal enough for her to trust.

"Well, that's true," he smirked, knowing she was hiding something. "I was going to ask if you might need backup?"

"From *you?*" she asked, feigning incredulousness.

"I'll take that as a *no thank you*," he responded coolly.

"*Please* don't take what I say the wrong way," she said, smoothly. "*It's a simple no*. The *thank you part* is you reading too much into it." He smiled grimly.

"The mercenaries on board this ship don't work for Purella, *they work for me*," he stated, flatly. "Why? *I'm* the one who pays them. If you get into difficulties: that might be worth remembering."

"So you're not all going to be joining Purella in the Hellion then?" she asked, with exaggerated politeness.

"No, members only, we're not members ergo we can't go in," he reminded her. "This is also why I strongly suspect she intends to kill us. If not her, then the cult instead. Because we know *where* they are and *what* they are. Putting it bluntly: we're liabilities."

Satiah could understand the motivation that he was voicing. Her problem was figuring out if it was candid or not. Going in with her, in her mind, would make it so much easier for him to betray her. Sometimes the closer the enemy was, the harder he was to see. Granted, he'd had good opportunities to turn on her already and he had not done so. But there could be a very good reason for the delay in said hypothetical treachery, convenience being just one of those potential reasons. Whatever the reason, assuming there was one, it was impossible for her to know it yet. If he *was* sincere then she had no reason to worry. He should surely be able to figure all that out himself though, so he *shouldn't* be taking her obvious distrust of him so personally.

"My advice to you is: be ready to get away fast *or* defend yourselves," she replied, emotionlessly. "You must know *why* I'm not taking a risk and going in with you either beside or behind me?"

"You need all the help you can get and you know it," he stated, while trying not to laugh. Then he became more serious again. "I have a vested interest in your survival, *remember?*"

That was true and she'd not tried to hide it. She leaned back in the chair, ponderously.

"Say *I let you join me…* What would be the benefits?" she asked, mulling it over.

"To me or to you?" he asked, interested.

"The possibility of *both* must exist, surely?" she jested, carefully. Then she realised something. "You want to kill her, don't you? *Purella, I mean?*"

"It's got nothing to do with her, *this is all about you*," he replied, aware of the cliché. "I am aware that if I go in with you, she and I might meet. But I promise you *I won't hesitate.*" She raised her eyebrows.

"I thought you said you loved her?" She had asked that with an undertone of mockery.

"*Once, yes,* but that has changed. Like I said, I'm pretty sure *even if* she doesn't try to kill me *herself*, she will have no qualms about allowing one of her *new friends* to try instead." Satiah nodded, that was reasonable.

"Quint is *my* target, not Purella. Quint is the one who seems to be most directly behind everything," she told him, observing his reaction closely. He'd not revealed much of the man in the white mask, but that didn't mean he knew as little as he claimed.

"Kyle *and* us," Clyde nodded, following her reasoning.

"And Bavon," she reminded him.

"Well, this won't come as *any surprise to you* but I don't like him *either*," Clyde said, seriously. "I already told you about that time he heard me whisper to Purella, and there's no way he should have been able to hear that. And it's largely *because of him* that Purella has changed." Clyde had shared his thoughts on the benefits *that mask* seemed to bestow on its wearer. It reminded Satiah of the voice too. The creepy mechanical monotone he always used. A sort of not-quite-human note rang true about it. She also recalled that time she'd been talking to Dyss and for a moment he sounded a bit similar. At the time she'd put it down to a bad signal, some distortion maybe, now... No, it couldn't be Dyss. That made no sense!

Everyone seemed so sure that Quint was a man, but no one had ever once seen his face. Costumes could be padded to make even the shapeliest of females to look more masculine. She'd done it herself enough times to know that much. Celestine had sounded very similar in that message to Milo... She'd discounted it at the time as it was not an *identical* voice, but it was possible... Yet there was another possibility too... One that, *if it was true*, would explain a lot that went wrong a decade earlier.

"Actually yes, you did tell me that," she allowed, finally answering him. "And you maintain you *still* have no clues as to his identity?"

"I *would* have told you," he said, in such an earnest way it was hard not to believe him. Unfortunately, Satiah had seen and heard *many* brilliant liars in her time, Vourne being up there with the best of them.

"Why don't we compromise?" she suggested, deciding to at least try and fit him in. He pulled a sceptical face which she chose to ignore. "You and *you alone* leave this ship and put *someone you trust* in charge. You *don't* try to get into the Hellion, but you remain out there in case I need help, should I have to run?" He thought about it. He didn't have to be on the ship when and if Purella called him. He could just *say* that he was.

"And if you *don't make it* out...?" he left the question unfinished.

"Feel free to come after me if you like, but my advice to you would be to run as if something very nasty was chasing you," she shrugged, as if it couldn't have mattered to anyone.

"I think I'll come and get you," he grinned, playfully. "Like I said, *I need you.*" She scowled.

"Fine, do what you like, it's your funeral."

***

The lights danced across the sky in just the kind of way that showed why it had once been a popular tourist destination: Planet Twelve. The *Dreadnaught* burst into view before slowing and starting a more leisurely approach. Clyde, at the controls, glanced uneasily over at Purella.

"Here we are," he murmured, sounding so extraordinarily casual. The kind of tone that inferred they had just arrived back at their homestead after an incredibly long flight.

"No last attempts to change my mind or remind me how *there is no going back?*" she enquired, an undercurrent of ridicule in her tone. He grunted to the negative and looked away.

"Do we call them or will they call us?" he questioned, instead. Satiah had placed a device on Clyde's collar, so she could hear everything that went on around him.

Purella frowned.

"I'm not sure – *Quint...*" she began, and her communicator interrupted her as usual. Clyde smiled forlornly. "I'm here." Clyde couldn't hear Quint but he felt sure Quint would hear him if he said anything, so he remained silent.

"I understand," Purella said, formally. "I will be there soon." She cut him off. "Prepare the shuttle."

"The one in *hangar two?*" Clyde asked, letting *Satiah* know which one was being prepared, and which one she had to sneak onto in order to follow them down to the planet.

"Yes," she replied, confused by the clarification. They only had two and the other one wasn't going anywhere any time soon.

"Will you be requiring Bert?" he asked, to delay her further.

"*Of course!*" she frowned, irritated.

"And you're *really* intent on going through with this?" he asked, pretending to get to his real point. She sighed, as she had expected this. Expected and... not come up with anything to counter it.

"*Clyde...*" she began, emotionally.

"We could still run now, *no one here would blame you*," he suggested, as if *he* really wanted it that way. Which, of course, he didn't anymore. Instead of biting his head off, like he had predicted she would, she only smiled sensitively.

"It will be okay," she promised, with a surprisingly delicate voice. "Thank you for... being here. I couldn't have done all this without you and I won't..." Her voice cracked. "*...I won't forget you.*" She was plainly in a bit of a state, and he'd not seen this level of emotion from her *ever* before. Worried that he might actually succeed in persuading her to change her mind after all, ironically enough when he *didn't* want to, he quickly changed tactics.

"I'll take you down," he stated, brusquely. He wasn't enjoying this manipulation any more than she was. He *had* once loved her, and it was always a bad idea to pick at old wounds.

"Will you...?" she stopped herself. Then she leaned on the console, bracing herself with her fists. She stared at the floor and swore under her breath a few times. After a few more moments she regained control. She straightened and pulled her new cloak more tightly around her.

"Let's go," she growled, containing her emotions like an unstable reactor core. Clyde, as he always used to, walked beside her. He hoped Satiah had had enough time to sneak aboard the craft. Purella's hand found his and held onto it. He let her. As they got into the hangar, the mercenary who'd helped Clyde capture Bert back on Collgort-Elipsa was standing by the ramp of the shuttle. Purella, upon seeing the other woman standing there, let go of his hand.

"Prisoner in?" Clyde asked the woman. She nodded.

"Sir?" Yana replied, with a question in her voice. She wanted to go with them. Clyde thought about refusing to let her accompany them. Satiah had insisted that he go alone but then, if the cult *did* turn on him, he might need her help.

"Sure," he nodded, and Yana fell in behind them. Purella glanced over her shoulder at the other woman but didn't object. They quickly reached the control room, Clyde kept a sharp look out for Satiah.

There was no sign of her. He knew enough about her skills to not be surprised, but it would be good if she could tell him somehow if she *was* actually there or not. She'd not gone into her tactics, certainly not in any detail, for what she intended to do upon arrival with him. He sat in the pilot's seat and began powering up the ship.

"Stay in orbit, *like I said*," he reminded the man in the control room. Those three words spoke volumes to the crew he was leaving behind. They were ready to react to the worst. He only hoped it wouldn't come to that. If they were betrayed, regardless of anything Satiah might do, he intended that the crew on the Dreadnaught got away. He didn't know how the cult would strike if they chose to, but he knew they could.

"Will do, sir," was their response.

***

"Let's hope they don't scan us," Dyss said. Satiah, Kelvin, Darius and Dyss were in a small spares room, towards the rear of the shuttle.

"They will, but with that other mercenary, they will be one over the expected number already. They will put it down to an accompanying party to guard the prisoner," Satiah reasoned.

"You *hope*," Dyss stated.

"Look, they can't shoot us down, not with Bert *and* Purella on board," Satiah growled, irritated. "Trust me, everything will be just fine. It's when we get inside that I will be worried."

"Are we going to save Bert or not?" Darius asked, guardedly. He was aware that the cult was intending to sacrifice Bert.

"Your call, Dyss," Satiah smiled, glad to give him that decision.

Dyss shrugged.

"If it's easy then do it, if not, lose no sleep over it," he responded, careless. "He has outlived his usefulness to all parties concerned in this one."

"*Almost*, yes," she corrected. "His last role to play is his own death, as far *as the cult is concerned*. He will be an example to any of their members who are *wavering*, shall we say."

"What about our reinforcements?" Dyss asked, in a curious tone. Satiah hadn't actually spoken with Reed again.

"On the way," she replied, seriously. "I'm not sure exactly what will come to help us but I'm reliably informed that they will be there."

"They *who?*" Dyss persisted, reasonably.

"Division Sixteen," she repeated, guessing what kind of a reaction that would get.

"You must know more than that by now…?" Dyss began, enraged. The door opened, making him fall silent. Satiah couldn't help but snigger at Dyss having to contain himself as the mercenary entered. Yana dumped a crate heavily on the floor before spinning on her heel and leaving the room again without noticing she was being watched by four others. Darius let out a breath in relief.

"No one else could respond in time," Satiah whispered, quickly. "Don't worry about it, we *can* trust them."

"*Trust them to do what?*" muttered Dyss, sarcastically.

"*Whatever I need them to do!*" she hissed back, irritably. It was Darius's turn to snicker quietly to himself. There was noticeable movement of the ship and the engines began making a slightly different sound. They were in the upper atmosphere, less than a minute to go.

The three agents and Kelvin remained silent as the craft levelled off and began a swift descent. Satiah ran through her mental inventory a fourth time. Pistol, blade, mines, Obsenneth, charges and rifle. She fought against the temptation to check the rifle yet again. Randal had tried to call her but hadn't left a message. She guessed that that meant he'd just wanted an update and that nothing urgent needed to be debated. Engines powering down. A judder occurred as the landing was completed.

"On me," she whispered, loudly. She slipped through the door and the others filed out silently after her.

***

Clyde marched out onto the rocky ground and surveyed the scene in front of him. Ruins stretched as far as the eye could see in all directions. High above, the lights sustained their never-ending show that few beings took the time to watch. A cold wind blew, whistling spookily through some of the derelict structures nearby. He turned to regard Purella.

"Lovely place," he remarked, sardonically.

"You may either remain here with the ship, or return to the *Dreadnaught*," she replied, emotionlessly. She pulled the hood over her head and began to walk away slowly. "It's up to you from now on," she called, over her shoulder. Clyde didn't reply and turned to regard the other woman. She was staring right at him, a question in her eyes. Behind her, still aboard the shuttle, he thought he saw a movement. He knew what he had to do.

He gave Yana an inviting smile that would look quite chilling to some. She smiled back, approached and rose onto her toes to kiss him. He wrapped his arms around her, pulling her in, kissing her lips hard. She did the same, as she'd been in love with him for months. He had no real feelings for her, but she'd been a pleasant distraction from Purella. He'd told her that he didn't love her but she'd only kept coming back for more, perhaps hoping to make him love her through sheer persistence.

He opened one eye, still locked in the passionate embrace, just catching a glimpse of robed figures hurrying away in the direction Purella had gone in. In the back of his mind, he wondered if his way of distracting the only guard might have provoked jealousy in Satiah. He hoped so. Once he was sure they were gone he ended the kiss by smoothly pulling her hair to make her look up. She stared up at him, her eyes wide with lust, breathing hard.

"Why don't we take this inside?" he growled, seductively. Well, what else was he going to do while he waited?

***

Purella continued on about forty paces ahead or so. She'd never looked back, but Satiah was ready to slip into cover the second she did. Clyde had been able to distract the mercenary long enough for them all to slip past without having to kill anyone. She caught herself wondering why he'd not just knocked her out and then buried that train of thought. Stop! Focus!

"I wonder *why* she chose to land so far away from the entrance," Darius pondered, thinking it might tell them something about the defences of the Hellion.

"Just be glad she did. It wouldn't have been so easy to sneak out of the ship were we in the middle of a landing area," Dyss replied.

"Two life signs," Kelvin warned. They froze and turned in the direction he gave to look. Other cult members making their way towards the Hellion, most likely.

"Good," Satiah growled. This was what she had been hoping for. "I'll keep following Purella; you two get their cloaks and render them unconscious." Darius and Dyss departed quickly and quietly. "And if you bump into anyone else, get me one too."

"What colour?" joked Darius, grimly.

She didn't answer, just continued to stalk Purella. Kelvin was now directly behind her. She didn't need to tell him to keep scanning. There was a tunnel coming up, and Purella was going straight for it. That had to be the way in. Purella, completely unaware of that anyone was coming after her, approached the entrance. She did stop and turn, but Satiah and Kelvin had been ready and slipped into the shadows.

Purella could see nothing, she had a lot on her mind and she imagined the cult was probably following her. No one else could be there, surely? She continued to watch for a few seconds, eyeing the route she had taken. There was no one in sight, but still she felt that someone was watching her. The cold wind blew, making its eerie whiny noise again. Her cloak flapped. Shrugging the feelings off as paranoia, she continued on, whilst listening for any accompaniment of unknown footsteps. There was the cave ahead, as she had been told, and a movement from within the darkness made her halt once again.

"Identify yourself," growled a voice from the darkness of the entrance. Slowly Purella raised her hand, showing off a silver and green seal Quint had provided her with.

"Pass, Purella," he replied. She smiled, a little relieved, and entered the tunnel beyond. Satiah, who'd witnessed the exchange, halted while she tried to work out the best way to proceed. There were a few options. Rushing in, guns blazing was not one of them – certainly not one she felt had any chance of success. Sneaking in would have been her preferred option, but that seemed like an impossibility. It may be possible to tunnel in but there was not time for that.

"Darius," she whispered, clearly. "Did you find anything on the bodies? A pass or something?"

"Each of them were holding these seal things, we figured they were important so we took those too."

"They must be a way of displaying to the guard that you are a member," Satiah replied, seriously. "Well found."

"Three more approaching," Kelvin warned. According to Bert's memory, the cult had around five thousand members, it was fortunate that they only ever seemed to arrive in ones and twos.

"Great, I'm about to get my own membership," Satiah said, a determined smile on her lips. "I will be ready to move in soon." She and Kelvin scrambled up a steep incline, careful not to dislodge any stones and she lay flat atop it to await the people.

They walked in single file as they came... unknowing. With precision shooting, although at that distance anyone could have done it, Satiah brought them down in less than a second. She scrambled back down.

"Get rid of that one," she ordered, pointing. She wrestled the cloak off of the closest one and hurriedly put it on. She found the seal and then turned to regard Kelvin. He had rather unsuccessfully pulled a cloak over himself to help disguise the fact that he was... well, actually, it didn't help at all. Satiah coughed to disguise a sudden attack of the giggles. To watch one of the most efficient killing machines struggling against a reluctant cloak was, to her at least, highly amusing.

She forced herself to concentrate and began to drag the last body out of sight. It would have to do until they were close enough to kill the sentry. Kelvin did his best to make himself smaller and less... angular. The constant twilight and plethora of ruined structures made sneaking around incredibly easy. There were also many convenient recesses for otherwise inconvenient bodies. She then returned and adjusted his costume in an effort to aid the impression that he might be a normal living being.

After a few minutes of waiting to regroup, they all approached the entry tunnel together. Satiah glanced up at the sky, marvelling at the complexity and richness of the patterns of the lights. It made sense that the one aspect of the world that was beautiful would make it incredibly so... looking at the rest of the place, she imagined it would be quite depressing. Even with the lights, the ruins gave the whole world a haunted feeling, as if the eyes of long dead creatures were watching you from the shadows. Waiting for the right moment of unwariness to strike. They trudged on, listening as the odd bit of stone clattered away from their feet. *What a lovely place.*

"Identify yourselves," the guard called, to them. All four of them held up the seals, as they had seen others do. There was a silence, a long enough one to make Satiah think they could be in trouble.

"Pass," he said at last, sounding bored. They did, moving into the darkness of the tunnel, doing their best to behave normally. Satiah supposed that the odds of anyone other than members finding this place were so low that the guard probably wondered why he bothered. Membership, most likely, was the only reason anyone had to be there. They entered the tunnel, having taken the decision to leave the guard alive. The tunnel was completely dark and only Kelvin could see.

"Two thousand seven hundred and twenty-eight life signs ahead," he warned. Satiah's heart began to beat a little faster. Apprehension, intrigue and insecurity plagued the back of her mind. She was aware briefly of that moment when her heartbeat and her footsteps seemed to be almost musical in their timing. Boom-boom-crunch, boom-boom-crunch. That was when she began to hear the first sounds from beyond. The chanting. It was an eerie sound, only made worse by the echoic qualities of the tunnel. A high-pitched shriek of a tone was almost constantly wavering in the background, while bestial barks and growls cried out over the top. Sometimes together, sometimes as individuals, their *song*, for want of a better term, was apparently never-ending. There may have been words, but if there were, Satiah couldn't make them out. Besides, part of her didn't really wish to know what they were saying. It was, in short, an unpleasant cacophony. Ritualistic, sinister and foreboding all at once.

There was a pale light ahead that they were all heading towards, how encouraging was that? Satiah realised they were passing over a narrow channel of blackness, an opening beneath them where the singing was coming from. She peered down as the chanting became noticeably louder, betraying the gap in the rock. She could see the flickering flames of torches and what could have been a mass of cloaked figures about ten metres below... it was hard to see. If she'd had more time she'd have used her specs but it was little more than a fleeting glance as she continued to follow the subway. The light was getting brighter and larger as they got closer. Darius could see that it was a marker and that an entrance, presumably to a cave, was close by.

He was right. Beyond was a large cavern, full of cloaked figures. These were beings talking to one another as if before a performance. There was food and drink and a general ambience of quiet merriment. Expectation. Satiah looked all around, careful not to expose her face too much, trying to take everything in. It would be very difficult to pick Purella out of the crowd, unless she'd removed her hood. While mostly everyone wore black, there were at least four in red and one, curiously enough, was in white. According to Bert's memories, those in red were the bishops, and the one in white could only be Quint. If Purella was anywhere... surely she would be with Quint.

"You three stay together and *no fighting*. I'm going for a wander, should I get into difficulties, feel free to step in," Satiah ordered.

"Acknowledged," Dyss replied, in her ear.

"No problem," Darius replied. Kelvin remained silent.

She slipped her specs on, determined to at least get as many members' faces down on record. Carefully she made her way towards Quint. She flashed quick glances around, catching the odd face here and there. Frighteningly, she'd already spotted two people that she recognised. They were politicians. One was from the Nebula Union and, more worryingly, the other was from the *Coalition*. She knew that what she uncovered here was a potential game-changer. While Phantom agents were technically allowed to do whatever they deemed necessary to achieve their mission, killing politicians, *particularly those on your own side*, was *discouraged*. Given that she planned to attack this place with a considerable force, it was unlikely he would survive. Would she pay for it if he died? In this case, she judged she was likely to be excused on the grounds that he was clearly a member of the cult and it would most likely not be her to pull the trigger. *Whatever*, he was on her data now so she couldn't claim that she didn't know he was there.

She got within earshot of Quint, and the smaller cloaked figure with him was indeed Purella. She listened in.

"...War has been avoided," Quint finished, his voice sounding as strange as usual. Satiah was careful not to look over and or stare at them, it might give her away. Instead, she pretended to regard the selection of food that was available. She remembered hearing him talking to the pirates back when she'd listened in before. Oddly, even though she could now physically see him, she felt she'd learnt nothing. The lack of features on the white mask he was wearing was also deceptive, making it harder to work out which way he was facing. Like a portrait whose eyes followed her as she moved, his face seemed to be facing her. She concentrated, pushing her uncertainty away.

"Tensions are still high," Purella said, lightly. "It would not take much to ignite them fully."

"Agreed, but it seems that the High Priests may have other ideas," Quint replied. "To me, they appear to have more interest in solidifying their current power base than they do in expansion."

"I have heard that there have been *events* recently...?" She trailed off.

"Yes, a few key opponents have been removed; however, we have suffered a few unexpected losses. Caution is paramount. I know you do not wish to revisit this subject, but there is the chance that, before she died, Satiah may have tipped the Union government off about the cult."

Satiah raised an eyebrow. She had indeed done that via Amber, but what was more intriguing was the fact that even Quint seemed to believe that she was dead. This was a good sign, as it was an indicator that she'd not been detected yet. She'd been concerned that Clyde might change his mind about helping her. It seemed he was as good as his word... *so far.*

"Rumours *are* ever present," Purella dismissed, a little overconfident.

"True," Quint allowed. "Though it might make you think again when you consider that one of our casualties was Bishop Gower." Purella's eyes widened.

"Wasn't he our most influential ally in the SRB?" she asked, though she already knew the answer.

"He was," Quint replied, giving no clues as to what he was feeling or thinking. Purella knew that this was a bad sign. If a government agency, one they did not have under their sway, knew of them and had actually killed him...

"*That's why* you think Satiah told them," she noted, gravely.

"It's a theory, but the bishop believes it to be a coincidence."

"Clumsy of him," she smiled, the ambition gleaming in her eyes. Quint didn't react at all. Satiah listened hard. He turned, facing Satiah's direction. She kept perusing, acting normally without revealing her face. Purella seemed to realise he was doing something other than thinking.

"What?" she asked, curious. Quint turned back to face her with that occasional abruptness he had sometimes.

"It's nothing," he replied. "Do not move too fast, Purella. Tonight is a celebration, I suggest you enjoy it. Ambition is a dangerous quality in this place. People will approach you, to make friends with you. They do this only to learn your weaknesses. Be prepared for anything, and stay evasive."

"...Fine," she agreed, a little irritated. Satiah was relieved; she'd been worried that Quint had somehow clocked her. Clyde had warned her about Quint's impressive senses, how he could hear things no one should be able to hear normally. He might be able to see things too...

"It's taken us *a long time* to get this far, it would be a shame to waste the effort," Quint concluded.

"I know," she replied. It was a fight for Purella not to remind him *who* was doing the most of it. Quint, despite his flaws, had delivered so she felt she should remain allied to him. It was only because of him that she was even there! She wondered how often he would remind her of that in the future. The red figure of Bishop Mickorsi joined them, a calculating smile on his face.

"Quint," he smiled, tilting his head to the man in the white mask. Quint said nothing. Mickorsi turned his attention to Purella.

"And you, *my dear*, are what all this fuss is about? Purella, is it not?" he enquired, all escargatoire charm and charisma.

"What fuss?" she asked, without smiling. She was too on edge for flirting with anyone.

"I am Bishop Mickorsi. You will be the first female to become one of us," Mickorsi smiled, taking her discomfort in stride. "It is I who will be leading the ceremony today, though I will probably be joined by one of the High Priests. I am honoured to meet you." There was a lot of pride in his tone but the question in it still lingered too. Like a moth circling around a flame. Who was going to get burned?

Quint still said nothing and seemed to stare back into the crowd again, as he had before. She couldn't see what he was staring at, if anything. Perhaps he was just looking around casually, though she knew by now that Quint never did anything casually. Purella fumbled for a good response, suitable and yet slippery.

"And I *you*, Bishop," she managed, wondering what Quint was doing. They shook hands, and she had to fight against the urge to electrocute him. She did not like him, she decided. Too slimy.

"I will leave you to prepare yourself," he said, backing away and returning to the throng. The moment he was out of earshot, Quint abruptly turned to face her again.

"Don't trust *him*," Quint told her, as if she hadn't already figured not to.

"I don't intend to," she remarked, unable to keep the disgust from her tone. "Upset you, did he?"

"He plans to," he replied, but said no more. She raised an eyebrow. Did the infighting *never* end? She had hoped that the cult might be above that kind of thing. It seemed endemic. When she rose to High Priest, she would end it.

"And you plan to stop him?" she couldn't resist asking.

"That will not be necessary," he replied, the master of mystery.

"And that is *because*...?" she wanted to know.

"Because you will do it for me," he stated, with such certainty that she was taken aback. "I will be back later, call me if you need me, I have to..." He trailed off and looked into the crowd again. She frowned, trying to see what he was looking at again. "I have to take care of something."

He walked away, without waiting for her to reply. He didn't go in the direction he had been staring in, nor did he go for the tunnel and the way out. Instead he went into another passageway, leading deeper into the catacombs. Purella watched as one of the many cloaked figures separated from the crowd, and paced after him. Another informer, she guessed, and returned her attention to the others around her.

Satiah had found everything she had heard rather irritating. It asked as many questions as it answered. All she'd got out of it was the Bishop's name, and the fact that the High Priest *might* be there. Quint had been staring in her direction, and at one point she was convinced that he was onto her. Then he'd ended the conversation and gone away. Curiosity gripped her. Where was he going at such a crucial point? Okay, nothing had started yet, but surely it was all to begin soon?

She decided to follow him. Padding out after him, she hoped Purella wouldn't think anything of it. Quint was a fast walker and she had to keep introducing one or two quicker paces of her own, just to keep up. Too late, she suddenly thought of something. She didn't know the layout of the tunnels. If this was a trap she might not be able to find her way back out. Even if it wasn't a trap, she could still get hopelessly lost. Choosing to take that chance she continued. They passed a few other figures in the catacombs but mostly it was empty. Quint suddenly halted, right in the middle of the passageway. She did the same and held her breath. Was he listening for her? Awaiting the giveaway footstep? The treacherous shuffle of clothing? The tell-tale gasps of badly-suppressed breathing...

He waited there for nearly twenty seconds before moving on. He *had* to know! She glanced over her shoulder – no one there. She began to follow again, concerned that she might lose sight of him. He entered a door to the right of the tunnel and she carefully followed, maybe seven seconds later. The room was well lit, an area designed for living. Bed, kitchen and other facilities were in plain sight. More importantly, Quint wasn't. He'd gone. She turned; pistol ready, to see if he was standing on either side of the doorway. No one. She moved to face the room again. Where did he go? She'd certainly seen him enter and he'd hardly had time to do anything clever. He could be crouching behind one of those seats...

She didn't know that the *ceiling* was a hologram or that, above her, Quint was watching every move she made. Quietly he edged along a metal beam above her as she moved further into the room. When she was in the right place he activated the door. The door closed and Satiah spun to cover it, expecting an attack. Something slammed into the back of her head and she went down with a groan. Her pistol clattered out of her grasp and she tried to climb onto her feet again, disorientated. Unbalanced and dazed from the blow, she stumbled forwards immediately back onto her hands and knees. Quint, now standing behind and over her, brought his stick down again, this time knocking her out completely. Using his stick again, he rolled her onto her back and delicately pushed her hood back to reveal her face.

"*Satiah*," he said, aloud. "I should have known." So much for Purella's word.

***

Legislator Magnus, wearing his blue cloak, returned to the control room of his ship. They were approaching Tweve.

"A few hours to go," the pilot told him.

"Good, good," he acknowledged, casually. He settled into a comfortable chair with a weary sigh and lit a long-style-smoky. Mickorsi should be ready by now, but there was never any harm in delaying things. A message arrived for him and he read it slowly. The good feeling he had, had begun to ebb away. Two more members had been killed within a Union security force. That brought the total up to eighteen. More than usual was to be expected as they made this grab for power, but no one had anticipated this many losses. At even their worst-case scenario, only six had been predicted.

There had been other failures too. Targets missed. Enemies still alive that shouldn't have been. Once all this was over, he was going to have to clear all this up. The possibility that something had gone badly wrong occurred to him, and he began to suspect that somehow, someone who shouldn't have, may have learned that the cult did indeed exist. Even if they had, they couldn't have caused all this just because they had had some idea of the plans. He scrolled through a report of Mickorsi's from a few days earlier. It was a summary of one of the projects that Quint was managing. A picture of Satiah, the one of her escaping Purella's ship with Bert, appeared on the screen in front of him. Phantom Agent Satiah, he read. Further on in the report, she had been reported as believed dead. He sent the details back to Hademan, to warn him that if anything had gone wrong, it was likely that she was responsible.

***

Reed tried Satiah for the fourth time and still didn't get an answer. He knew she was awaiting his call and was rather worried that she wasn't answering. In the end he gave up and tried Dyss who *did* answer.

"Where's Satiah?" Reed asked, seriously.

"No idea, she's been gone about half an hour," Dyss said, in a similar tone. "*Why?*"

"I can't get hold of her and I needed to tell her that the reinforcements have arrived. I'll patch them through to you," Reed answered. At last, Dyss thought, hoping they would be strong enough to take care of the cult.

"Hi, this is Captain Berry of Division Sixteen, we're cloaked and in orbit of Tweve, what do you need?" he asked, to the point. Dyss raised his eyebrows. He'd expected them to be within a few hours of the planet, not already sitting up there!

"This is Phantom Leader Dyss, conversing with you on Phantom Satiah's behalf, what do you have?"

"Eight hundred elite troops, and four hundred support soldiers," he answered. Dyss was impressed; there was no way anyone else could have responded so fast with such numbers. Not without clearance, anyway.

"One moment, we will let you know when to move in. Reed has a layout for you, there are defences we need to disable before you can start," Dyss replied, being practical.

"Good, we will move on your order," he stated. Dyss eyed Darius.

"We need to disable the scanners and the ground defence systems," Dyss ordered. By *we* he meant *you*. Darius picked up on that instantly.

"*Satiah?*" Darius asked, being difficult.

"No, *me*," Dyss growled, knowing what he was getting at. Darius didn't move.

"We have to assume something might have happened to her, we have to assume that we take it from here," Dyss stated, his voice hard. He hoped Darius would remember where they were, even if he couldn't forget his grudge.

"She is in charge," Darius stated, obstinate.

"*She is not here*, Darius," Dyss stated, frostily.

"Funny how history repeats itself," Darius replied, his own tone tense. He was talking about both Operation Jackdaw, and Satiah's tendency to vanish at awkward moments.

"Division Sixteen are here, ready to move in. They can't move in *until* the defences are down," Dyss spelt out. "I'm only following *her* plan, Darius, and I trust you to follow her orders even if you won't follow mine." There was an anxious silence.

"Leave it with me," Darius said, moving off. "I'll let you know when they are down." Dyss watched him go, wondering if he would try to get hold of Satiah for confirmation of the order... which was just what *he* was trying to do. He knew though that if *Reed* couldn't get through to her then that had to mean... He looked around suddenly realising that he was alone. Not only had Darius gone, but Kelvin too had slipped away without him noticing.

***

Premier Jakirk held onto his partner's hand as the building shook again from another explosion. Emma was on the verge of tears, she'd only come in to deliver his breakfast like normal, and then suddenly the whole city had collapsed into anarchy. Soldiers stood around in confusion while their officers argued about insane orders, and in some cases even killed one another. This assault on his compound though was not so hard to understand. Someone was trying to kill him. The only reason they'd not succeeded was because of a last-minute tip-off. A tip off from the SRB. Some kind of plot had been uncovered and, at the last minute, two teams of agents had moved in with the express purpose of moving the Premier of the Nebula Union to a safe and undisclosed location. They had been about to go through with this when three more teams arrived and started attacking them.

Jakirk, Premier of the Union and its leader, was now seriously paranoid about who was trying to save him and who was trying to kill him.

"Okay, leave it to me! Just hold them off as long as you can!" shouted a woman. Jakirk and Emma, his lover, stared at one another, uncertainty and panic in their eyes. Amber, drenched in sweat staggered into the room, looking for them. She rolled her eyes and pulled the desk away to reveal them crouching there.

"Premier, sir!" she hissed, saluting. "First Lady! You have to come with me, right now!" She grabbed their hands and began to pull.

"Will someone please explain…!?" he began, knowing the protocol. Thing was, Amber was a stranger to him and his most trusted bodyguard had been dead nearly an hour now.

"No time!" she yelled, pulling him along behind her. For a second she wondered what exactly he thought needed explaining – it all seemed rather clear to her. Another explosion and screams. The building shook and they all ducked instinctively. Instead of leading them to the designated exits, Amber was taking them down to the levels beneath the city.

"This is not the right way!" he reminded her.

"Sir, they *know* your evacuation plans, they *know* what you will do when threatened!" she shouted, persuasively.

"Who is they?" Emma demanded, levelly.

"That is a question for later, right now I have to get you to safety and I think I can do that!" Amber insisted. This wasn't her style at all. She was not a warrior or even a woman of action, she was meant to be a honey-spinner, but her duty was easy to understand.

She blasted open the door leading into the maintenance area. She'd only studied the layout briefly and she hoped that she remembered it correctly. The main problem she had was that that the floors all had the same layout, so it was next to impossible to tell which one you were on. Coughing from all the dust, they hurried through a disused record storing facility before darting out into the back of a factory. Next, she led them through a seemingly never-ending series of assembly lines and checkpoints before reaching a vehicle parking area. They emerged into the open just in time to see a missile strike the building opposite. A lone ship was there and, shouting encouragement over her shoulder at them, Amber led them aboard. In moments they were taking off, and heading towards space. They were seen, but crucially they were not recognised and were able to slip away from their enemies' clutches.

As soon as she'd made the jump, she hurried back to the passenger area where Jakirk and Emma were waiting.

"Any injuries?" she asked, still breathless. Fit as she was, this was a bit beyond what she was used to. They shook their heads, too out of breath to answer properly.

"Will you explain what is happening?" Jakirk asked, at last. She sat down opposite him, weariness in her eyes.

"It all began a few days ago and... *basically*, there is this thing called *the Cult of Deimos*. And it wants to *kill you*. The main problem for you, is working out who is loyal to you and who *isn't*. This cult has members *everywhere*, or at least it seems to. Am I making *any* sense?" she asked, feeling that she was not being at all helpful. Emma was nodding, fully listening.

"Well... you're making more sense than anyone else has today," Jakirk muttered. "Where are we going?"

"I... I'm not sure. I have to get you somewhere safe and I intend to do that, but after that I don't know," she admitted, seeing no reason in hiding it. This was not what she did. "I... I need to make a call," she stated, standing up again rather shakily. "Please wait here."

She made use of the facilities, and dressed herself up a little before returning to the control room. She took a deep breath... this would be awkward. She put in the code, one she had memorised a while ago... and waited. It was about eight seconds in when she began to drum her fingers on the console from agitation. Part of her didn't even expect him to answer, and so she was mildly startled when the Viscount's face appeared on the screen in front of her. He looked tired and unhappy, not too dissimilar to how she probably looked, she thought idly.

"Amber," he said, his voice almost but not quite polite. "I had not expected to hear from you... *ever*." The last word was loaded with all his emotions, accusations and mood. She lowered her head for a moment, seeking the right words.

"How are you?" she managed. *How are you?* Who did she think she was talking to? Before he could answer she jumped in again, trying to repair at least that little bit of damage. "I mean, *I'm sorry*," she said, quickly. "I'm sorry I lied to you and I'm sorry all this happened." He remained silent when she was finished, as if waiting for more. "We have to be sorry for so much in life, a lot of it not *really* our fault. Sorry for the dead, sorry for the sick, sorry for the dying... we shouldn't be *sorry* for any of that. But *this*... What I've done to you... *I am really sorry for*." She wasn't entirely sure where that had all come from, but she was on a bit of a roll. "I'm sorry out of choice because it was my choice that hurt you."

That rant seemed to have defused the first set of explosive remarks that he might have said. He waited a little longer and only when he was sure that she was done did he answer.

"I'm reliably informed you're not a model at all and that, in fact, you work for the Union, is that true?" he asked, quietly. She sighed, here it comes, the painful part.

"Yes, I was an operative for the Nebular Union security branch SRB. My purpose was to seduce you into joining them. I failed."

"So when you told me you loved me...?" he trailed off.

"I lied," she replied, trying her best not to sound cold. "I had to." He looked away from her briefly, his expression flickering in and out of various looks. He was fighting to hide his feelings but she knew him too well for it to work.

"So... *why* are you calling me now?" he asked, taut.

"I need your help," she admitted, honestly. He let out something that could have either been a laugh or a sob, it was impossible to tell.

"If you don't agree, I *will* understand," she said, cautiously. Then she switched on the charm again. "But if you help me now you will show that you're a much better person than I am. And you will remind me of why I *almost* fell in love with you." It was a risk. Saying that might provoke anger, it certainly would in someone older and more experienced. But she gambled on him believing what he wanted to believe.

"Do you...?" he stopped, before trying again. "Are you coming back?"

"Only if you let me," she stated, firmly. "My circumstances have altered rather significantly in the last few hours. I need somewhere to hide where no one else will find me. I have the Premier of the Union and his partner Emma with me, we have been forced to flee."

His expression changed completely to one of shock.

"*What?* Are you okay?" he asked, immediately. Ah yes, his overprotectiveness. She'd forgotten about that.

"You can see *I'm fine*," she smiled, softly. "Please listen! I don't want to make you do anything you don't want to." By saying that, she was aware she was manipulating him again, ironically enough by trying not to. He was too compassionate for a politician, that man.

"Of course, we are hiding too," he smiled, his grin seeming to make him look even younger somehow. "I suppose we could *all hide together*, but we're not allowed to talk to anyone." There was a beat of silence. She smiled herself and raised an eyebrow.

"So… why are you talking to *me?*" she asked, already knowing the answer.

***

"Well… *not really*," the Vice Admiral stated, confused. "You think you could be a target?"

"I have no idea," Alicia admitted, still scared. "I knew nothing about any of this until you mentioned it just now."

"You have a fleet! You can go anywhere within your own territory," he suggested. "Why not pretend you're chasing real pirates to make it *look like* you're trying to fit in with us?" That was reasonable.

"Well, it's a better idea than any I've come up with," she remarked, seriously.

"Okay then – oh, before you go, can you just fill out this form about how well you were treated as a prisoner of the Coalition navy?"

"What?"

***

Hademan couldn't believe what he was hearing. The Premier escaped! The SRB team killed! Everything seemed to be collapsing into chaos. He sent out a hold signal to all remaining agents. There was no point in reinforcing the failure. A message from Magnus arrived and he glanced through it. It seemed a lone Phantom operative had somehow caused all this. It seemed hard to believe, but then all it would take would be one mistake from someone else and everyone would believe it. Yes... hold off now and wait seemed to be the best strategy. After a few months, when the calamity had subsided, they would regroup and begin again. It had happened many times before and would continue to happen in the future.

***

Satiah opened her eyes groggily. Her head hurt and she was having trouble working out where she was. It was dark... too dark to see anything well, anyway. She was on her back, her hands tied above her head and her feet tied down. Whatever she was laying on crackled, clicked and bent when she moved. It felt like wood. And what was that smell? Was that oil? There was a noise too... a snuffling noise. She was not alone.

"*Who's there?*" she whispered, seriously. A sob. Then a bright light dazzled her as it came on. She closed her eyes, grimacing. There was white figure in the corner who had been watching them.

"I had been *concerned* that you survived your near drowning," Quint said. "There is normally a queue for the sacrifice, but you have priority. We shall see if fire succeeds where water failed."

So... she was on a pyre. That would explain the wood and oil. She heard him moving, he was going to leave! That was... unusual. Normally people would ask questions or inflict pain, usually both. They didn't just stroll off, in any case.

"Quint," she groaned, trying to look at him properly. "Don't you have any questions for me to refuse to answer?" He paused, and then approached her. He stopped right by her side, his white mask making it impossible for her to learn anything.

"Your name is Satiah, you're a Phantom agent. You probably didn't come alone? In any case, I'm *assuming* you did not. You're here either to rescue *him*..." he pointed a gloved hand and she looked across to see Bert lying next to her, his face red and swollen, "...or to destroy the cult. Either way, *you have failed*. So *that* is why I have no questions for you to refuse to answer... because I already know all the answers."

"Then... can *you* answer one of *my* questions? It's no problem for you if I'm to die anyway," she asked, interested. He didn't answer but didn't go anywhere. "*Who are you?*" she asked, genuinely wanting to know. She had an idea now. The more Quint spoke, the things that were said... it pointed to a familiar mind-set. A conversant way of thinking and acting that Satiah herself had. The manner of a Phantom agent. Quint turned and headed for the door again but once more hesitated before leaving.

"It's your final sacrifice and it would be a terrible way to die. Without knowing *who it was* that caught you," Quint remarked. There was a short silence before Quint just left, the door closed, and Satiah was once again plunged into darkness. Frustrated, Satiah tried to get free but the knots were unyielding. It was her own fault; she'd *known* it might be a trap!

"*Bert!*" she hissed, as she struggled. "Bert, you have to help me..."

"No, it's no use, we're going to die," he snuffled, uselessly. If only she could kick him...

"Since when did *that* matter?" she growled back. "*Come on*, we can get out of this..."

"I deserve this, I deserve it..." he murmured, again and again. The man was conquered, there was no fight left in him at all.

"Bert, *if you don't help I'll kill you myself*, come on!" she retorted, irascibly. Nothing at all this time, and she swore as she struggled more frantically. Then she stopped, forcing herself to think more calmly. Her hands were at the wrong angles to try most escapology routines. And... bizarrely... it was like whoever had tied her *knew exactly* what they were doing. She tried again and then relaxed. Where was Kelvin? Looking for her most likely... *Obsenneth*. She tried to roll onto her side to land on top of the rock to somehow get it to work, but she knew without her skin it would most likely do nothing. Quint may even have taken it from... no, there it was, she could feel in there through the material. Interesting... everything else was gone.

"How can *I* help? I'm tied down *as well*," Bert asked, seriously.

"Can you reach me at all?" she asked, trying to shimmy in his direction. His hands were suddenly on her face. "Watch it!" she growled, angry.

"Sorry, I can't see..." he began. She arched her back.

"Jacket pocket!" she ordered. A few minutes passed as each strained and struggled to get the rock out from her pocket. She fell back in relief at last as he got it.

"Now what?" he asked, in bewilderment.

"Get it close to my hand as you can!" she instructed. She heard it land next to her head. "Nice," she muttered, sarcastic. She nuzzled it, trying to push it further up towards her bound hands with her nose.

"Are you trying to talk to *me*?" Obsenneth asked, glowing orange. She pressed her nose to it again.

"Easy with the *glowing, someone could be watching*: can you help with these ropes?" she asked, urgently. "If you don't I'll be killed, presumably burned alive and we both know that's not going to help *you*."

"For a Phantom agent, you're not very good, are you?" Obsenneth asked, mockingly.

"You help me or I *will* let Kelvin crush you," she threatened. Suddenly the stone was no longer on her nose but in her hand. Matter transition or telekinesis? She didn't much care at that moment so long as it assisted *her*.

"I cannot free you from your bonds, Satiah," Obsenneth told her. "But I *can* help. When the next person comes in, I can *compel* them to release you."

"What if there is *more than one of them*?" she demanded, unhappy at the recommended solution.

"What are you doing?" Bert asked, unable to hear any of this.

"*Not a lot*," she grunted, trying yet again to free herself. She made up something about trying to use the stone to cut through the rope. She remembered the knife in her boot and tried to see if it was still there. It was. So, Quint wasn't that clever then.

"New plan," she said, to Obsenneth. "The blade in my boot, can you do anything with that?"

"Why didn't you mention that before?" he asked, and she felt something moving in her boot.

"I'd thought you would already know about it, seeing as how you can read my mind," she retorted.

"You told me to stop..."

"Just get on with it!" she snapped, increasingly angry.

She felt the jolt and suddenly her legs were free. The blade flew past her and she could feel it sawing through the rope easily. Her hands were free in seconds and she sat up.

"Would you like me to...?" Obsenneth began. She replaced the rock in her pocket, severing her mental connection to it. She grabbed her blade and began cutting through the bonds that held Bert down.

"Now, are you going to grow some balls and help me?" she demanded, through her teeth.

"How did you...? Help you do what?" he asked, fearfully.

"*End this*," she replied, as if it were obvious. "Did you hear what Quint said when he was talking to me about *why* I was here?"

"Yes," Bert replied.

"Well, I'm not here to save *you*," she growled, levelly. "But that doesn't mean you can't be useful to me... One last sacrifice is what he said so... *that's what he's going to get*."

***

Quint eyed the collection of items he'd found on Satiah. An earpiece that he couldn't get to work, advanced visual equipment he was sure would be known only by its model number, her pistol and... *no gemstone*. Its absence was not so much a surprise as an annoyance. He'd actually been delighted that she was still alive, even if she *had* infiltrated the Hellion. It meant he might get another chance at finding that gemstone. He'd awaited her awakening with the singular purpose of finding its location, but had quickly changed his mind. Not only was it highly unlikely she would ever tell him, but he didn't want her to understand what she had found, or even to know that he was interested in it. Most importantly, he wanted no one in the cult to overhear the interrogation. She didn't have it on her, so that meant that either she'd sequestered it away somewhere, or she had discarded it. Then there was the other issue... had she come alone?

He was pretty sure he knew *how* she had made it down. She'd once again slipped through Purella's clutches, which was easy enough, at least to someone of Satiah's ability. He'd told her he knew why she was there but as she wasn't working alone... *who else had slipped in?* And... should *he* report it? Since the beginning he'd been trying to undermine the High Priests with the goal of eventually replacing them. While reporting her capture would no doubt improve his reputation in their eyes, if one of the High Priests were to be killed... it *could* be a golden opportunity for him. And he couldn't be blamed for this if it all went wrong, he had the ideal scapegoat. *Purella*. It was on *her* ship that Satiah had obviously arrived there. Quint was certain that Satiah would escape and execute whatever plan she had unless he stopped her. If he did nothing, and *through her actions* the High Priest and many Bishops were to die, then the way would be open for him.

All of this was why he'd left all her equipment, in plain sight, within a few metres from where she was locked up. He was sure she would escape with or without help, and just to make things extra easy for her... why not let her have what she needed. Just in case, he'd slipped a small explosive inside her pistol which he could detonate anytime he liked – just in case she somehow caught up with him. If she didn't escape, she and Bert would be burned alive and no one would ever know. If she did, he could be *far* closer to achieving his goal – within a few hours instead of a few years. He wondered briefly if it would be unlucky if he placed a bet on it or not.

***

"The code is seven, four, nine, eight," the man admitted, in a pleading tone. Darius had him pinned against the wall, one hand on his throat and the other holding a gun to his head.

"And *why* should I believe *that?*" Darius asked, ice cool and in control.

"I swear!" wept the man. "*I swear!*"

"Don't, it's a bad habit," Darius growled, and pistol-whipped him into unconsciousness. He then turned to face the controls and pulled the seat away from them. He quickly found the main defence computer and used the code to disarm all systems. Everything went from green to red, and yellow digits began to descend from one hundred percent marks into lower figures.

***

Bert watched as Satiah manhandled the body of their guard onto the pyre and began to tie him down. He was still alive, of course. He had to be... so everyone heard the scream when the fire began. She noticed her gear neatly placed there... as if *for her to find*. After checking for traps, she replaced her earpiece, her specs, her grapple gun and... *her pistol*. As she slid it into the holster, she paused, and pulled it again, only replace it a second time. She then repeated the motion twice, a frown on her face.

"Something wrong?" Bert asked, watching her.

"No," she lied, instinctively. There *was*... it was ever so slightly *heavier* than it had been before. Someone had tampered with it. Quint, most likely, she reasoned. This meant Quint *wanted* her to escape... *Why?* Kelvin entered behind her and she spun before relaxing.

"*Where have you been?*" she growled, rhetorically. "Bert! You know how this works," she went on. "I need you to guide Kelvin and me. Take that cloak and use it to hide who you are." She was taken back in memory to that soldier she had shot to prevent her from being burned, and was not amused by the irony. This guy, though, was a member of the cult, so she was sure he had it coming. Another call in her ear, the third in as many seconds.

"Your head injuries are minor," Kelvin stated. She scowled at him, like she didn't already know that! Luckily the situation was giving plenty of distractions to help take her mind off the pain.

"You will have to tell me *when* it is time to burn him!" she hissed, making sure she had Bert's attention.

"*What?*" she hissed as she answered the call, infuriated.

"*Oh dear,*" came Reed's voice. "Someone's in a bad mood, aren't they?"

"Someone just got smacked in the head and, unless you want the same, I suggest you get to the point," she retorted, rolling the body over to make sure the gag was still in position. It was not time to remove it yet, but if he awoke and started shouting, it could ruin everything.

"Our friends are here, awaiting your call to move in," he explained, quickly.

"Good, I'll call you back," she said.

"Dyss?"

"Satiah?"

"Update me, I hear Division Sixteen have arrived," she said, briskly.

"Darius is taking care of the automatic defences. I'll put you through to Captain Berry," he replied, efficiently.

"Hi Satiah, where do you want us?" Berry asked.

"Start moving in now. Concentrate on taking out their escape craft *before* you move onto the Hellion itself. We need to kill as many of them as possible. Wait for the final okay from me *before* drawing first blood," she instructed, seriously.

This would have to be timed well.

"Will do," he replied.

"Darius?" she asked, knowing he would understand what she wanted to hear.

"System is down, I don't know how long it can be down before anyone notices," he responded, quickly. "Do you need support?"

"Good, stay there in case anyone should try to reactivate it," she commanded, thinking ahead. It would be a shame is after going to all the trouble of turning everything off, someone just wandered in and switched it all back on again.

"I've changed the codes and sabotaged the manual override," he said, having already thought of that. "They would have a hard job." He was right, but she still didn't want him too close to Dyss. Not without her being there to break up the infighting.

"Okay, *all of you*, this is what's going to happen…" she began, taking a deep breath.

***

Mickorsi and Magnus shared the stage as the brethren gathered for the Ritual of Distance. Purella was also on the stage, her hood removed, revealing her face to all. She stood slightly to one side of the others, where she had been told to stand: the place where Quint himself had stood ten years before. As always, the other members took their places, unaware of the contrasts they were. Like coins: one side for the real them, and one for the others. Did they think this *was* the real them, or simply another act to hide their real eyes from reality? Outside they would be normal beings to the eyes of all, but in here *they were the brethren*. They were the cult and they dreamed of domination.

Mickorsi gestured for Magnus to go first, Magnus did the same. The pair shared a brief laugh at the point when they both tried to move forward and then Magnus began. The silence fell as everyone watched, listened and waited.

"As at all times, my brethren, we *honour* the occasion with the *Ritual of Distance...* Where we distance ourselves from *all* worldly concerns with this gesture. We draw *our line of fire* to set us apart from that *accepted yet malign corruption*. No serpent that still slithers may enter... *We* embody *the only* alternative path, the path where the light and the dark are one... And so with these sacred words *the ancient one stirs...* He hears us, my brethren, *he hears our call!*"

Kelvin and Bert eyed the struggling guard as he tried ineffectively to free himself from the pyres. They awaited the line. The next line. The signal for the guards to ignite the pyres.

"With the shedding of our false selves... *we cross that distance!*" Magnus bellowed. Bert gave the signal. Kelvin and Bert dropped their torches and the roaring flames began...along with the screams. Bert looked down and watched the nearest guard endure what was to have been his fate. It didn't matter what it was for, murder was always wrong he reasoned. Politics didn't matter, feelings didn't matter, it was all wrong, all of it. He considered jumping on to burn with him, but he lacked the courage which, he began to realise, had been his problem all along. He'd been with the cult because society had frightened him, and he had been *too scared* to stop bad things from happening... and now, even though he was working *against them*, he had progressed to actually *doing* those same bad things himself.

"*Now!*" screamed Satiah, as she emerged from the top of the statue, a position overlooking the entire place. She just opened up with the rifle, first sweeping the stage, and then the crowd. Mickorsi stood no chance, taking the worst of the first blasts. He was sent flying off the edge of the stage from the kinetic force of the bolts. Magnus was winged and fell out of sight with a shout. Purella, the only one to react in time, ducked and ran forward so that the body of the statue prevented Satiah from getting her. For a few seconds she just couldn't believe it. She'd been *so sure*... She glanced up just in time to see Quint watching her from a doorway. *He knew*. He knew she had failed and now she would have no future here. Not after this. How had she found them here? *How?* A fierce rage grew inside her. Even if she had to die in the process, she was going to *kill* Satiah for this!

The whole place shook as some kind of missile impacted on the surface far above them. Satiah ignored it and kept firing at the entrance tunnel, cutting down anyone who tried to escape that way. Dyss, who'd still been within the crowd at the start, took cover from the mayhem as he fired into it. The crowd, unsure of where to run or who was shooting at who, was trying to scatter, but there didn't seem anywhere safe to run to except further into the Hellion. Dyss saw the pale form of Quint retreat further into the catacombs before he could take a shot. Why was he not trying for the exit? According to all the data they had, there was only one way in or out. So why would Quint not take it? Kelvin emerged, his metallic bulk now finally revealed from the cloak as he rose to his full seven feet height, and unleashed fire on anyone unlucky enough to be in the way.

Unobserved, Purella began to climb up the side of the statue after acquiring one of the many ceremonial swords that were used to decorate it. Satiah continued aiming, brought down another and another. Mostly everyone had fled into the catacombs now, and more shooting occurred as the guards at the entrance encountered the first of the Division Sixteen men. An instinct, from deep inside, otherwise known as her infamous sixth sense, told her to turn. She did, just in time to avoid instant death. Purella, eyes mad with rage, swung the sword at Satiah. The blow ripped the rifle from Satiah's grasp and sent her stumbling back. She rolled with a scream, down the side of the statue and onto the metal grille just a metre above the fire. The grille bent under her from the force of the fall and she pushed off the hot metal to see where Purella was. Purella was coming after her.

Knowing that Quint had done something to her pistol, Satiah had to find another weapon and quick. She seized another of the ritualistic blades from the side of the statue and was just in time to parry the blow from Purella. She staggered back as Purella had put all her strength and weight into the thrust. The fire continued to burn under them, making them cough from the smoke they were inhaling as they slashed and swung at one another. Metal clanged sharply alongside the sound of laser gunfire. Satiah also took note of Purella being gloved too... *she remembered those gloves.* Did Purella know about what Quint had done to her pistol? Could she be bluffed into surrendering? Purella recklessly charged, a form of wrathful gleam still in her eyes. Satiah sidestepped and attempted a backslash as the other woman went past. Purella had expected it and forward rolled so that Satiah's blade swished harmlessly through the air above her.

Satiah had been trained in the arts of fencing, though it had been nearly twenty years since she'd last used swords. Purella, who'd never really been trained in anything, had learned how to fight with pretty much anything she had, relying on her instincts and reactions to give her the edge where her technology failed her. Back and forth they went for a few minutes, the smoke from the sacrificial fires blinding them intermittently, and choking them constantly. Satiah came in close, flicking her blade straight up at Purella's face. Purella arched her back, narrowly missing it and pushed it away with her own blade. Satiah's boot found her stomach and she stumbled back, coughing and winded. She fell back onto one knee, trying to breathe. Satiah didn't follow her.

As Purella rose to face Satiah again, she halted. Satiah had a pistol trained on her.

"*Drop it!*" she ordered, coldly.

"Why? You'll kill me anyway," Purella countered, levelly. "That's what you *people* do. That's *all Phantoms* do." The vehemence in the word *Phantom* was not lost on Satiah. Purella was the last survivor of the Varn-Utto, deservedly or not, she had good reason to hate Satiah, current scenario notwithstanding.

"It's a chance you'll have to take," Satiah countered, hoping that her own pistol didn't blow up in her face if she had to use it.

"I *watched* my friends die as your operatives cut them down," Purella stated, taking a step towards her. *Friends?* Ha, like she knew what *they* were. Satiah held her ground; if she took even *one step back* Purella would *know* she was bluffing. "You're no different from us! You choose to become slaves to governments, we only wanted freedom." Freedom to what? Freedom to kill? To enslave? To hurt others? *Yeah... some freedom. Yeah... we all hate the government, so what?*

Satiah also took a step forward of her own, as she would were her pistol safe to use.

"Either let it go, or I shoot it from your hand," Satiah growled, determinedly. The flames beneath them were dying out now that the wood, oil and bodies had been burnt out. Shooting could be heard from above as Division Sixteen piled in to attack. Purella seemed to be genuinely going through her options. All the rage was put aside as she considered her circumstances and the things she left behind. She had no chance with Quint or the cult now, and she'd burned her bridges with Clyde. She was... *alone*. That idea didn't scare her as much as depress her.

"Even if I don't kill you right now, *they will*. If you want to live, you're going to need my help," Satiah offered, persuasively. "And..." This was it, the real gamble, time to put her new theory to the test. "I *probably* should tell you something. Something that will highlight a new perspective for you." Purella took a slow, uncertain step back.

"Always assuming I would take *you* on your word," she replied, tentatively. She tightened her grip on her sword, mentally preparing herself for a trick.

"You hate Phantoms more than anything because of what they did to your friends? Then how come you have been working for one *recently?*" Satiah asked, crisply. "You know that Quint used to be *one of us*, right?" Purella smirked, shaking her head.

"Do better next time," she argued. Then she frowned, wondering *why* Satiah had not just shot her. Why was she playing for time suddenly? Did she think she needed Purella alive for something?

"Prove it," Purella challenged, staying where she was. As she had thought Purella would, Satiah did not advance further. She used the time to see if any other weapons were within reach.

"How else do you think he... *or she...* knew exactly who *I* was?" Satiah asked, smugly.

"That's not proof, that's conjecture," Purella argued, tilting her head to the side. Despite her best effort, doubt was growing in her mind. "*She?*"

"Oh yes, she's fooled everyone. *You*, me, *the cult...*" Satiah trailed off, as if thinking about it for the first time. "She's been playing all of us."

Purella hated herself for even listening to this, but part of her was starting to wonder. Those times when Quint had been incommunicado. His/her secretive tendencies, never telling people what he or she was really up to. His/her ability to accurately predict the enemy's actions and strategies, seemingly at will. She already knew he/she was hiding that business about the gemstone from the cult and that he/she…. *This was insane*! And yet, *because it was so crazy* was the reason why Purella *was* listening. Surely if Satiah were lying, she'd be more plausible? Another look into Satiah's face and eyes gave her no clues. Purella smirked again, trying to hide her indeterminacy.

"You're trying to trick me, *it won't work by the way…* just like *your pistol doesn't work*," Purella smiled, secretly gambling that she was right about the gun.

Satiah thought about maintaining the pretence but Purella didn't give her time. She sprang forward again, preparing a wild slash to eviscerate Satiah. Satiah simply dropped the pistol and backed away, trying to lure Purella out from behind the back of the statue and into the tunnel beyond. Here they would be more evenly matched and, as they were both new to these tunnels, neither would have the advantage of knowing the layout.

"Stand and fight! *Coward*!" screeched Purella, frustrated by Satiah's evasions.

"Not likely," scoffed Satiah, pushing a crate over between them so that Purella had to jump over it to follow. They entered a tunnel, luckily deserted. Purella lunged and Satiah blocked adeptly. Wary of Purella's gloved hands, Satiah knew she had to keep her distance.

Nevertheless, when Purella got careless and leaned in too far, Satiah raked her nails across the other woman's face. Purella hissed in pain and reflexively touched the four gashes on her cheek after she'd backed away a little. The blood, wet and warm, was clearly visible, even on her glove. Purella forced herself to calm down. She'd nearly beaten Satiah once before, except that *now* Satiah knew what her gloves could do, so she had altered her strategy. She was waiting for

Purella to make a mistake and then she would move in. Purella stopped attacking and smiled defiantly, she too would change her tactics.

"If you want me, you'll have to come get me!" Purella stated, almost in triumph. Then she turned and ran. Satiah watched her go, disconcerted. Did she chase or didn't she? Purella was not important, Quint was her target now, yet if Purella were to get away it would not be a good thing. Could Purella get past Division Sixteen?

And if she *was* planning on *escape*, she seemed to be going the wrong way. It was possible that she had another way out – though, if she *was* new to this place, it seemed doubtful. If she got away she would only be a problem that would return later, Satiah decided. She took off after her, pumping her arms, forcing herself to go as fast as she could. She was gaining on the other woman. Satiah thought about simply hurling her sword into Purella as they ran. *Knives* Satiah could throw very well... a sword, on the other hand, required greater strength and she wasn't sure she could do that whilst running at full speed.

***

They had moved on. Everything seemed to have gone quiet. After playing dead for he wasn't sure how long, Magnus sat up and looked around. The statue was burning now; dead cult members littered the ground around him. He had worked out what must have happened. Somehow, someone had infiltrated the cult. It was a constant risk. Purella seemed the most likely suspect which was why he discounted her. She was too obvious. Whoever had done this could have been in the cult for years. The enemy had come in fast and hard. They had been prepared, the defences had failed them... it all pointed to considerable inside involvement. He knew though that at that moment, escape was what he had to be thinking about. Reprisals could wait: *indeed, they would have to.* He wondered if Hademan even knew this was happening. Distant laser fire occurred.

Everyone had been hounded into the tunnels, where there was no hope of escape. Their perfectly secret lair had become a rat trap with no way out. They would rebuild, they would start again, the cult would survive this and it would make those who had caused this pay dearly. He stood and began to creep along, slowly making his way up to the entrance tunnel. To him, it was a cynical wonder that there didn't seem to be anyone guarding it. He came out into the ruins after stepping over the bodies there. He crouched as two fighters shot by overhead; he stood again, squinting as he tried to make out who they were. Whoever they were, they seemed to be Shintu fighters, but he saw through that straight away as the mockery it was meant to be. *You did it as these guys, so that's who we're doing it as.*

He turned and was struck by a bolt to the head. He hit the floor, dead before he reached it, eyes still open. There was a flash of light in the distance as the sights of the sniper reflected the lights in the sky. More fighters flew past overhead and fired their missiles, literally into the ground. They were trying to blast their way into the Hellion. All this was visible as Clyde and Yana watched on the scanner.

"Did you *know* this was going to happen?" she asked, not angry, just curious. He shrugged.

"This kind of thing is *always* on the cards," he replied, sighing. "Which bit? That guy being picked off, or the attack in general?"

"*All of this*. I ask only because they don't seem to have shot at *us* yet," she smiled, knowingly. Again, he played it cool.

"Maybe we're just not on their list," he smirked, as if it hardly mattered. They watched from the safety of the ship as the fires in the ruins, highlighted by the lights in the sky, provided what some might call a *dreamy* milieu. She put her arms around him carefully.

"Remind me never to make an enemy out of you," she simpered, in his ear.

***

Deep within the Hellion, the caves and passages gave way to a vast open area full of treasures and mysteries without number. The mountains of crates, some of which had been there for thousands of years, could be navigated by walkways crisscrossing above them, or alleys that contained them in large squares. The remaining members of the cult, still battling the Division Sixteen troopers, had been forced to make their final stand here, amongst the loot they had hidden over the years. The fighting was now intermittent as it switched from all out fighting to eye-blink incidents of sudden death. A terminal game of hide and seek in which, surely, there could be no outright winner. Quint hurried through this obstacle course of demise and mayhem. He knew Satiah would come after him and that there were certainly others. He didn't need to reach the surface to escape. He had a backup plan.

Concealed amongst the crates was a secret transmat pad. When activated it would teleport whoever was on it to another location entirely. A place among the ruins above where a ship was waiting. He knew exactly where the pad was and how to activate it. Unfortunately, since he'd installed it, nearly five years ago, a lot of other crates had been stacked over where he had concealed it. Angrily, he began to push everything else aside, trying to get to his lifeline. He had planned for Satiah to escape, in the sense that he'd thought through the consequences that best suited him. He'd not considered the possibility that not only had she not been alone but that she'd invited a whole army along for the ride. He began to realise that the cult, whoever ended up in charge after all that, had just been mauled. Badly mauled.

At last, he uncovered the edge of what he was looking for. A noise, a footstep, from not far away, made him dive behind the crates for cover. Dyss opened up his weapon on a walkway overlooking where he had been, shattering crates and sending sparks everywhere.

"Give it up, Quint!" barked Dyss, unleashing another volley. Taking a chance, Quint broke cover and dived onto the transmat, vanishing instantly. Dyss leapt down from the walkway, rolling to prevent injury as he landed and then jumped through the transmat himself. Quint materialised in among the ruins and sprinted forwards. The ship was not far, maybe five hundred metres ahead. Dyss appeared a few seconds later, just in time to see Quint slip behind a rock and continue running. His path to the ship had good cover and at that speed Dyss wasn't sure he could shoot him down.

The strongest instinct was to chase but, with all his years of experience, Dyss didn't bother and looked to *where* Quint thought he running to. He saw the ship, poorly concealed under a ruined structure and smirked as he raised his communicator to his lips.

"Reed, put me though to Berry," he requested, calmly. Quint was running fast but Dyss knew he had enough time.

"Berry!" Berry called, immediately.

"I need an airstrike, coordinates, about four hundred meters…" he paused, to look for an indicator of direction. He spotted a moon.

"...*West* of me."

"On its way," Berry advised. "Keep your signal going, it will use it to home in on."

"Will do," Dyss sighed, wondering if Quint would make it to the ship before...

A roaring noise began and, as if sensing what was about to occur, Quint changed direction and dived for cover. He vanished in the explosion as multiple strikes converged on the ship. It went up with a blast that sent out a wave of concussive force and sent up a filthy mushroom cloud. After the sounds had died away and the dust settled, Dyss listened.

"Ta," he said, in low voice. "Keep your pilot circling the area, please. I might need him."

"Will do, he's got your communicator details," Berry replied, cutting off. Cautiously, Dyss began to approach the area he'd last seen Quint. Some of the ruins had collapsed because of the explosion. Careful not to make himself a target, Dyss peered out from cover. The ruins stretched out before him and he sighed. Quint could be *anywhere* in there!

"Satiah, this is Dyss," Dyss said. "Quint's not in the Hellion, he's out here somewhere. I'm going to need help to bring him down."

"Okay, stay where you are," Satiah replied. "Hold on a second..." Rapid gunfire sounded in his ear, followed by silence. "...Sorry about that. Darius and I will join you shortly."

"Good, good," he said, disconnecting. He frowned as he continued to look around. There was nowhere else for Quint to go, now he'd taken out the ship, except... the ship Purella had arrived in! Judging by the speed of the air response, they couldn't be that far from the Hellion. He glanced around and could see smoke in the distance, blackening the horizon, adding a new aspect to the lights in the sky.

"Satiah, you might want to warn your *friend* that Quint could be heading his way," Dyss advised.

"Okay," was the breathless response. She was in so much of a hurry that she didn't even bother to remind him that they were not friends.

***

Satiah was in a dark place. Literally, not philosophically. She would have preferred the latter. She knew Purella was in there with her... *somewhere*. She made the call to Clyde.

"Need help after all?" he answered, sounding relaxed.

"You might. Quint could be running in your direction, it would be a smart idea to put some distance between you and the ground. You will not be shot down, they all have orders to ignore you," Satiah whispered, peering between crates. A darker shadow moved across the gap on the other side. Purella.

"Will do, thanks for the update," he said, casually. "Are you sure...?" She cut him off; she didn't need any distractions now.

A shuffle. She tensed, expecting an attack. All the crates abruptly surged forward, not directly at her but closer. She leapt upwards, grabbing a chain and ignoring the pinches as the links bit into the flesh of her fingers. The crates slid underneath her and Purella leapt out from cover, brandishing a chain of her own. Satiah let go and tried to dive out of the way. She cried out as the chain slammed into her back like a metal whip, stinging and numbing together and sending her flying. She rolled, as Purella continued to chase. The chain sparked as it struck the metal floor right where Satiah had been. Next came a sideways stroke which Satiah only avoided by ducking. She leapt to the side, using a support beam to intercept the chain. The chain hit the beam, wrapping around it as it struck, as if unstoppably attracted to it. Before Satiah could do anything, Purella was flying right at her.

Satiah grabbed her wrists and fell backward, pulling Purella down with her. She planted her feet in Purella's chest as they went down and rolled whilst kicking out, flipping Purella over onto her back heavily. Satiah seized the chain but instead of using it as Purella had, she hurled it right at her. She was worried that if she used it like Purella had and Purella caught it, she could electrocute her through the chain. It took Purella in the backs of her legs and she went down with a scream. Satiah paused, trying to work out how to finish this. She had to help Dyss and Darius. It wasn't that she doubted that they could take Quint without her, but she was worried they might end up fighting one another instead. Purella rose slowly, gripping the chain and wrapping it around her fist deliberately as she too went through potential-next-moves in her mind. There was a silence as each awaited the other to make the first move.

What little light there was flickered out briefly after another distant missile found a mark. Purella attacked. Satiah too moved forward as she knew Purella would expect her to move back. The chain did hit her but she was close enough for it to be the end nearest Purella. She open-palmed forward into Purella's chest, then tried a knuckle-plunge aimed at her sternum. She met only Purella's arm as the other woman tried to turn away. Satiah put in a kick. She certainly hit Purella, but she couldn't see where. A blow caught her on the side of the head and she staggered to the side. There was a clatter as the chain hit the floor, presumably after Purella had dropped it. Suddenly Purella and Satiah were in a pile on the floor, unable to see anything with any clarity. Blows were exchanged; sparks flew as Purella missed Satiah and zapped the floor instead.

Purella turned, trying to put some distance between them, then felt Satiah's fist crash into the side of her knee. She cried out, the leg momentarily losing all feeling, and rolled away. Sensing the weakness, Satiah pursued her, going for her injured leg again. The second blow, somehow more painful despite the pins and needles, floored Purella. Snarling, her hand found the chain and swung around. Satiah cried out as it caught her across the head. She slumped back against a wall, stunned by the blow. Purella continued to wave the chain around frantically and somewhat pointlessly as she couldn't see her enemy. Satiah, aware her head was bleeding, crawled away a short distance but stopped when she collided uncomfortably with something else.

Purella heard the noise and guessed what must have happened. She tried to stand, but her leg was still too unsteady, even as feeling returned.

"Still alive?" Purella jeered, hoping Satiah would answer. "I bet that must have hurt, huh?" Satiah rolled her eyes. "I have killed Phantoms before, *you're nothing special.*"

If that were true, she wouldn't be telling me, Satiah reasoned. She felt about for something… anything she could use as a weapon.

"*Come on!*" Purella shrieked, nervous. "Prove you're not the coward they were! Maybe you'll get lucky and not just be another skull in my collection!" Satiah slowly rose to her feet, using the wall to lean on. She slowly slipped her blade from her boot and gripped it strongly. Purella had now stooped to calling her all the names she could think of in order to provoke a response.

Satiah hurled her blade in the direction Purella's voice was coming from. It sliced into her arm and Purella screamed in pain as Satiah slammed into her. The chain was dropped again as Satiah grabbed her around the throat and launched Purella backwards with all her might. Purella stumbled back, trying and failing to get a grip on Satiah. She tripped over something and smashed through glass before collapsing onto her back. Shrieking from the multiple glass wounds and the blade in her arm, Purella ripped the blade out of her skin. Some of her own blood splashed onto the glass below her, adding a crimson tinge to the multiple reflections.

Satiah found what she needed running along the wall, held in place by a few bolts. She wrenched it free of the wall and pulled away the protective cover. Next she waited, ready for the final move, ignoring her pain and staying focussed, listening as the glass slivers fell from Purella as she stood. Purpose – reaction. Purella threw the blade ahead of her as she advanced; hoping Satiah was still close by where she had been before. She wasn't. There was nothing subtle about Purella's new assault. She was nearly at her limit and she couldn't take much more punishment with serious injury. She guessed Satiah was in a similar condition, although she couldn't be sure of that, so one last all-out attack seemed to have a good chance of succeeding.

As Purella charged recklessly through the remains of the glass doorway, Satiah touched her chest with the live cable she'd uncovered. Electricity doesn't move through you, the electrons in your body do all the moving. Your body essentially takes on the role of a resistor in a circuit with no reward other than painful but swift death. Satiah hoped that none of that was lost on Purella in her final moment. Purella let out one last howl as the flash occurred and smoke issued from her cooked flesh. All her muscles spasmed, sending her flying backwards onto the ground. Dead in a second, if Satiah had blinked she might have missed it, it was that fast. Satiah replaced the cable on the wall and turned to try to make out where Purella was. She was back on the glass, laying on her side, dead, her face registering the shock in more ways than one.

"*You don't deserve an epitaph,*" Satiah growled, as she moved away.

***

"She sounded busy," Clyde remarked, in a way he thought wasn't loaded. Yana was watching him intently, starting to realise that she had yet another rival for his affections. The ship rose nearly twenty metres into the air. He activated all the lights so that they were easily visible. Then he couldn't help but scan the surround. He didn't like to admit it, but he was worried about Quint finding him. Purella might have been blinded by her own plans, but Quint would be sure to realise the truth about how Satiah had got there.

"*That* wasn't Purella," Yana stated, seriously. He glanced over at her. She was talking about Satiah, though she didn't know it.

"No, I... I don't think we'll be seeing Purella again," he replied, softly. Yana smiled, she'd never liked Purella.

"Who was it?" she asked. He was looking at her again in that way he did when he began to see *why* she was asking.

"Don't get jealous, Yana," he warned, his tone becoming one of sadness. "I'm pretty sure you don't need to worry about her."

"I'm not jealous," she lied, a little too quickly. "I just wondered who she was. This woman you now seem to *be taking orders from?*" He smirked, knowing she was trying to manipulate him by bruising his ego. He didn't like taking orders from anyone, but he'd long ago accepted them as a necessary evil.

"She's a potential business associate; you know how *they* work, right?" he assured, with too much conviction.

"You like dangerous women, don't you?" she smiled, interested.

"Only so long as they are not dangerous to *me*," he chuckled.

***

"*Fantastic*, he could be *anywhere!*" Darius complained, not unreasonably.

"Granted," Dyss replied, trying to contain his irritation. "Whatever, we are to await Satiah before we move after him."

"I see," Darius sighed, a little bitter. He knew why she'd ordered that, but it irked him anyway. Quint could get away! The High Priest was dead, as were the bishops and mostly everyone else. Only Quint and Purella remained at liberty. The sound of vehicles approaching made both men turn. Captain Berry, with Satiah holding onto him, arrived on a short-range transporter. Kelvin was on another, and two or three other Division Sixteen troops arrived. Satiah, looking a little worse for wear, leapt off Berry's transporter and jogged lightly over to them. Kelvin and Berry followed.

"Down there?" she asked, nodding to the ruins.

"So *Dyss* tells me," Darius responded, overdoing the innocent tone just to rile the other man. Dyss didn't rise to it. Satiah sighed, also letting it go without comment.

"Anything, Kelvin?" she asked, putting on her specs. She scanned, he scanned and the others just looked.

"I am detecting nothing alive," Kelvin stated. One of Satiah's lenses identified a footprint in the wet mud some hundred metres ahead.

"Well, he may not be there *now* but *someone was* fairly recently," she murmured, zooming in.

"The area *is* surrounded," Berry stated, eyeing the craft in the distance still circling the area.

"How big is this area?" Dyss asked, levelly.

"Just over two square kilometres," Berry answered.

Well, it could be worse, Satiah supposed. "Was he armed?" she asked. Dyss shrugged. It might be considered by some to be a silly question, but she was more interested in what *kind of weapon he had* rather than if he had one or not. Now, the real question, did she tell Dyss and Darius who she thought Quint really was? She thought about it. She couldn't prove it yet, so… perhaps it was better to wait until they had a body to confirm her suspicions first *before* she blurted anything she might regret.

"Okay, this is how we do this," she said, ponderously. "Kelvin and I will take the middle. Darius? You're on my right and Dyss?"

"Left," he correctly fathomed, rolling his eyes.

"Stay in constant contact, let me know the second you think you have him," she said, careful not to say *her*. All three of them pulled out their weapons. Satiah had procured a rifle from Berry, seeing as she'd had to ditch her pistol earlier.

"Purella?" Darius asked, seeing the blood on Satiah's forehead.

"Aye," she sighed, gruffly. After Kelvin's healing and painkilling injections she was feeling much better. Purella had been tough, there was no doubting that, but *Quint*...

"Let's go," she said. Splitting up, about ten metres separating each of the three, they slowly climbed down and into the ruins. Soon they lost sight of one another as they cautiously began to explore the carcasses of architecture in search of the man *or woman* in the white mask. It was quiet, even the fighter still circling the area seemed weirdly subdued.

"Nothing?" Satiah whispered, to Kelvin.

"It is possible that he is shielded from detection," Kelvin reminded her.

"I know," she replied, in acknowledgment. She removed her specs and stood still for a moment, using what might once have been a pillar to support herself and to hide behind.

What would *she* do if it were her in Quint's place? Her compatriots dead or captured, her way out destroyed... being hunted by her old friends/new enemies?

It was entirely possible that he had yet another way out; perhaps someone else would come and get him. She had told Reed and Berry to watch out for any incoming ships. Anything else unusual that they could think of... Where was he?! And why couldn't they detect him? Satiah edged out from her position, carefully looking for any sign of movement. A flash from the sights of a gun, the roll of a stone dislodged by a clumsy step or anything... there was nothing. On she went, with Kelvin close behind. The lights continued their play high overhead as if intentionally trying to make her job more challenging. She edged forward again, aware that she could be presenting herself as a target from more than one direction.

"Anything?" she whispered.

"Not a sign," Dyss replied. Silence.

"*Darius?*" she asked, instantly concerned at the lack of response.

"…No…" he said, at last. "Sorry, I thought I heard something. Just my own imagination, I think."

"Okay," she said, understanding. She glanced over her shoulder at Kelvin. He made a sign, one that meant nothing had changed. She moved on and peered down into a… oh no, a cave! Its gaping maw seemed to smile at her as if to say: I could lead anywhere.

"I've got a cave entrance here," she told everyone, quickly. She knew it was her decision whether she searched it or not. She knew she had to as, arguably, Quint shouldn't be able to get out of this any other way. She hoped it was the *only* cave.

"What's it to be, Satiah?" Dyss asked, a hint of contest in his tone. He knew her dilemma; even a child could guess it. Would the mind games never end? She smiled, no, of course they wouldn't.

"Kelvin will watch the entrance, you two keep going, same instructions stand. *I'm going in*," she stated, not feeling half as brave as she sounded. Kelvin's metal hand landed on her shoulder and her brown eyes met his red ones. She knew what he was saying.

"You know I'm not a fan of suicide," she grinned, as she put her specs onto night vision mode. She began to half climb and half skid down the steep cave shaft. She had a torch on the end of her rifle and one in her pocket, but they might give her away, assuming she could still be given away. She wouldn't have been surprised if Quint was watching the entrance… *if* he was down there.

Down and down went the shaft, too far for her to see the bottom. It was not as steep as before, maybe a fifty-degree angle downwards. And of course, the same in reverse if she had to run back up. She swallowed, sweat inching down her face. The cave was warm too, which made it worse. She was already starting to feel thirsty, but she convinced herself it was more psychosomatic than an actual bodily requirement. The entrance was now a tiny speck of light behind her, the darkness once again all around her. Somehow it never lost its creepy touch. Like invisible fingertips caressing her skin in a needy, sinister way. She shrugged it all away, forcing it into the back of her mind. Fear wouldn't help her. Cold reasoning and rational thought would. After a few more minutes she reached the end of the shaft.

It opened out into a vast cavern, though this cavern was natural and had all those lovely extras that nature sometimes provided –

stalactites, stalagmites and weird, faded paintings on the walls. Beasts? Demons? *The locals?* Satiah couldn't make out what they were meant to be. She carefully slid between two stalagmites, almost as tall as she was. She didn't see the lake until she almost fell into it. So clear was the water, she could see the crystals far down in its depths, gleaming enticingly at her. She didn't need to touch it to know that the water would be ice cold. Swallowing, she did yet another circle of the cavern, anxious that Quint might somehow get behind her.

The voice in her ear almost made her jump in fright; her hand went for her non-existent pistol.

"Still nothing," Darius said, his voice low. "I've reached the troops on the other side."

"Thanks," she murmured, hoping her voice wouldn't carry too far. Then she froze and spun to face a large rock that she could have sworn wasn't there a moment before.

"It's a negative from me too," Dyss added, obviously disappointed but not impatient.

"Go over the ground *again*," she ordered, through her teeth. She was still staring at the rock. "We keep going until he is found."

"Right." She crept closer to the rock, cautiously. With a nervousness that made her curse herself, she poked it with her rifle barrel. No, just a rock.

A movement in the corner of her eye made her leap aside, just in time to avoid another boulder that was thrown down at her from above. She landed on her back with shriek, the boulder rolling into the lake with a splash, and fired at Quint as he turned to flee into a passage above her.

"*He's here!*" she screamed, managing to stop herself wasting more ammunition. After the long silence, the noise was most welcoming.

"*Both of you, down here now! Kelvin,* move in to the main shaft!" She was running now, almost falling several times as the ground was very uneven and rocks were everywhere. How could Satiah get up to that level? The fact that Quint had tried to kill her in such a way hinted that he had no other weapon, but it was not a guarantee.

"Kelvin, scan the cave system, tell me if there are any other ways out," she ordered, panting. She scrambled up a wall and hauled herself into a shaft that led to… somewhere else. She crouched there, catching her breath and trying to work out what Quint might try next. Clearly he'd had plenty of time to flee further, but he had waited to try and kill her. A silence had descended again, this one more intense and daunting still. She followed the tunnel along, once she'd got her breath back. It was almost a dead end, save for a hole that led down at the end. She climbed down cautiously, as some of the rocks were proving slippery. She emerged into another cave beyond.

A bloodcurdling, growling clamour made her freeze in her tracks. A reptile, all teeth, talons and scales, came rushing out at her from a side passage. It was big, almost twice her size and didn't look particularly friendly. She reacted instantly and fired two shots into its face, while getting ready to dodge. It crashed to the ground, skidding to a halt and sending small stones scattering everywhere, dead. She remained where she was, expecting more. She slowly rotated where she stood, rifle ready. And this planet had been a tourist destination once! Well, obviously there hadn't been that many cave tours… certainly none that had returned, anyway. She moved forward again, wondering why it had not attacked Quint. Did this mean she'd gone the right way? She walked through something sticky and casually pulled the web strands from her face. Any giant arachnids, perhaps? And why not? She could hear something… the sound of running water on rocks. She moved on, following the deceptively tranquil sounds.

***

"…So that's why I'm leaving," Amber finished, sombrely. The Premier and his spouse just sat there, stupefied. "I want to live, and live comfortably. At least for a while," Amber went on. They were back in the passenger area of the ship they'd fled on.

"And you're *sure* you can trust the Viscount not to betray us?" the Premier asked, again. Well, the question he'd asked before required the same answer, but had been phrased differently. His partner shot him a censorious glare.

"*Leave her be*," she requested, softly. "Can't you see she's out of her depth here… just like *us*?" He pulled a face and shook his head.

"I'm sorry, I…"

"You're a *politician*," Amber reminded him, coldly. "Yesterday's local champion, today's figure of power, and tomorrow's criminal." Even Emma looked shocked, as well she might, at that, but neither of them argued the point. It was often the case that people who were responsible for so much, caused problems that only they could cause. It was ironic that in some cases they were the only ones who failed to realise what they had done. The only people who tended to be incorruptible, when it came to power, were those that never wanted it. Consequently, everyone who got into power was corruptible, as those who didn't want it rarely chased it. Some more than others certainly, and while these flaws were understandable, that didn't make them acceptable. Saints have pasts, and sinners have futures, what can you do other than live with it, and of course *yourself*?

"You could say that none of this is your fault, namely *one person cannot control or know everything at once*, and it's a reasonable point – *yet*... I'm having a lot of trouble believing it lately, *after what I've discovered*," Amber admitted. "That is why I'm leaving."

"Because you can't trust anyone? *Even your own side?*" Emma clarified, empathically. For years she had felt that way with everyone her partner worked with, but she'd put it down to her own insecurity.

"There are no sides, not really. There's only *your own side*," Amber stated, feeling sad. "I don't know what's going to happen. Perhaps we stopped the bad guys today, whoever they are, perhaps we didn't. Either way, I want out."

"Well, we still should thank you for saving us," Emma said.

"Just *don't* do it officially, the fewer things my name is on, the better," Amber stated, seriously.

"What are we going to do?" Emma asked, at last the despair making itself known in her tone. "Have you been usurped?"

"I don't think so," Jakirk smiled, convincingly. Amber knew though that he had to be feeling the pinch. "I just don't know who to call."

"I know at least two people who can and will help you, but they will have the same problem as you," Amber warned. "This Cult of Deimos is everywhere. Some four hundred suspects are dead, along with tens of our own..." She stopped herself momentarily. "...*Your own* security forces. There will be more, but they will have gone to ground. I suspect that other forces have attacked recently too, so they will have had a beating, that's for sure."

"Can you tell us who you think is on our side?" Jakirk asked, hope in his eyes.

"Maybe later," Amber said, as a light started flashing. "*We're nearly there.*" She left them where they were, and returned to the control room, just as a planet was looming up. She activated the communications unit and identified herself.

"Landing area seven, the Viscount is waiting for you," said a woman, in response. Amber couldn't help but smile. She'd been fairly sure he'd forgiven her, but part of her had been concerned that she'd simply read too much into what he had said. The planet was barren and probably only a temporary hiding place for Collgort-Elipsa, but it was certainly not where she imagined they would go. A Federation world. The huge spaceship that had once been all those cities was in orbit, and she quickly found it, coming in for a casual landing. An artificial atmosphere was being generated so they could all survive the brief walk from the ship. A figure was standing there, awaiting them. Well, several figures, but Amber was only really interested in one of them. The Viscount. The rest sort of blended into the background for her. She let the others go first, taking the time to make sure her hair was suitable and then timidly walked down the ramp.

She stopped, and stared at him for a few seconds. He stared back. She began a slow approach, wary. He too began to advance towards her. They stopped less than a metre apart.

"Hi," she said, awkwardly.

"Have you done something with your hair?" he asked, a grin appearing suddenly.

"How would you know?" she couldn't resist biting back.

"Drat, that was a gamble," he admitted, seriously. "I'm glad you came back. How long will you be staying?"

"*Who knows?*" she muttered, bleakly. Then she smiled up at him. "*A while.*"

"Well, that's good to know," he said, carefully putting his arm around her. He steered her toward the entrance. "I know that this is more complicated now but… how do you feel?"

"Right now? *Famished.*"

***

"Plot a course for our previous patrolling area," Alicia stated, quietly. She'd tried to get hold of Fleet Command but no one was answering, so she and her officers had spent the last half an hour reviewing the ever-constant CNC bulletins. Some people called it news; she called it experiments in vindictive sensationalism and scaremongering. There was a lot of confusion, and the way they reported it gave the impression of utter chaos, but it boiled down to two inescapable realities. The Premier was missing, presumed evacuated, although there was no confirmation of that, and an attempted takeover had been made by organisation/individuals unknown. So, in the absence of further orders, Alicia had chosen to play dumb and return to her previous assignment. She didn't know what was going to happen but she hoped that, whichever side proved victorious, they would not blame her for retreating. In a way, it was ridiculous to do anything else. The Coalition officers had been exceedingly generous and she wasn't about to abuse that generosity.

She looked up to see a young officer watching her.

"Yes?" she asked, wondering what fresh madness this would be.

"Do you think he's dead?" he asked. He was talking about the Premier. There had been some speculation about this possibility already, but she had learned the hard way never to rush into suppositions.

"There is a chance that he could be," she stated, reservedly.

"If he is… what do you think will happen?" he asked, uneasy. She realised he was more uneasy about antagonising her than he was about the political situation. She smiled reassuringly.

"Then we will elect another to take his place, I fancy," she said, stating the obvious. He had actually only just been elected for his second term, so the timing could have been better. "At least, that's what happened *every other time* one has died or come to the end of his term."

That hadn't been what he had asked and they both knew it, but what went unsaid was the only answer. No one knew. He nodded and saluted before leaving her in peace. She glanced out at the oceanic world that had once been Collgort-Elipsa and now spun unnamed. She no longer really cared where they had hidden. It was no longer her problem, not with all this other stuff going on.

"Captain, there are some strange signatures coming from the planet," warned an officer nearby. "Power signatures. As if someone under the ocean just started several huge energy generators at once."

"*Not our concern anymore*," she smiled, impartial. "Let's get out of here."

***

It was a dead end. Reed had heard that the expression originated from prehistoric times, back when routes within fortresses would be cut off, trapping enemies in dead ends or loops, to prevent them from escaping or continuing the attack. Nevertheless, regardless of the phrase's origin, he could think of none better to describe the caves Satiah and the others were pursuing Quint within. It bothered him that someone as apparently smart as Quint would choose such a place to hide in. Maybe he hadn't *known* that there was no other way out, and he *had* tried to escape via a hidden ship *first*, but still… It nagged at the back of his mind like part of a dream one could not quite recall. Everyone had landed now and Kelvin was by the entrance. Dyss and Darius had gone in after Satiah… as she had gone in after Quint. Reed, Captain Berry and a few hundred troops had surrounded the entrance.

***

She had been right about the water, it was freezing. Only up to her knees but ice cold, it was current-less and clear as the crystals she'd already seen. Satiah waded through it carefully. Twice now she had fallen and, thanks only to the strength of her protective clothing, she'd sustained only bumps and bruises. Nevertheless, as any who regularly traverse caves would know, there were hidden hazards everywhere. The air, cooler now, was stale and smelly. That told her they were getting to the deeper areas where air didn't move so much and… the system would end close by. She was starting to tire now too, and she could only hope that Quint was struggling like she was. A loud crash came from ahead of her and she stopped, seeking a target.

The noise echoed everywhere, making its precise source hard to pinpoint. It eventually faded to nothing, replaced again by the usual noises one hears in a cave. The occasional droplet of water landing on water. A sort of hollow murmuring that might or might not be a distant voice. There were two tunnels she could see, both, by all appearances, seemed to be heading the same way. She edged forward, deciding to take the left one first. In the darkness she missed the tripwire completely and, so lightly was it strung, she didn't even feel it until it was too late. The blade, about the size of her finger, silver in colour, shot out from a tiny hole in the wall and into her leg. She gasped in agony as she felt it embed itself in her thigh muscle. She remained standing, tears in her eyes and concentrated on just staying quiet. Quint could be listening from somewhere. It was a flesh wound, a bad one but still *only* a flesh wound. She had been lucky. An inch further and it would have severed her femoral artery and she'd have bled out in four minutes, give or take.

Still holding in any potential noise, she yanked the blade out of her skin and gingerly moved her leg. The bleeding was not bad but it could become bad soon. It hurt to put weight on it and to move it. Slowly she crouched, glad of the specs that gave her vision. Doing this in complete darkness would not have been so easy, putting it mildly. She raised her leg, elevating the injury, spat on it a few times in an effort to keep it clean and removed her jacket. She ripped some of her tunic away and efficiently fashioned a crude but effective gauze bandage. She tightly wrapped and tied it around the injury. She sat like that for a minute or two, leg still elevated, wondering *why* Quint hadn't attacked yet. She was certain that, despite her effort, he *must* have heard something. That *was* always assuming that it had been Quint who had *set* the trap...

A noise from behind her made her tense. She rose, feeling the thigh on her good leg burn as it did all the work. She lowered her leg and once again tested it. The pain was still there, obviously, but it faded a lot once she'd injected herself with one of her painkillers. The bleeding was contained, it would do. Then she peered back the way she had come. It could be Darius and Dyss. Or it could be Quint.

"*Where are you?*" she whispered, trying and failing to stop her voice from shaking.

"On our way," came Dyss's unhelpful reply, in her ear.

"Watch out for traps," she counselled, inwardly wishing she could have had such a forewarning. She limped carefully forward, expecting an ambush to be somewhere ahead.

The pitch darkness still dug its talons into the fear centre of her mind. The idea of being trapped down there forever, cut off from light by a rock fall or just by becoming lost, was festering there. Using techniques from Phantom training, decades before, she suppressed it.

"Kelvin," she called, quietly. "Where am I now, in relation to the end of this place?" Kelvin's answer was hard to hear, the depth was starting to make itself known.

"About four thousand and ninety metres," he answered. That seemed like an immeasurable distance at that moment for her.

"Ok," she said, moving on.

The tunnel was descending again, getting steeper. Strange fronds of some kind of plant life dangled down from the roof. They were long and sickly yellow in colour. Moisture droplets made their journey down from the room, along them and onto the ground with the evocative dripping sound everyone knew. Taking no chances, Satiah didn't allow any of the plants to touch her. They didn't look poisonous, but there is little in life more deceptive than looks. As she went forward, on her hands and knees, for a second wondering how many languages she could curse this place in, she spotted something ahead. Uneven ground, twenty-two languages actually. Granted, in these caves, *everywhere* was uneven, but not like this. She could see shapes protruding from the floor, barely a few millimetres in height but they were there. It was like tiles or something. Something of manufacture and not of nature. Another trap! Being cautious, she threw a stone at them. Nothing.

She approached and stood, once she was clear of the vegetation. Her leg was still throbbing dully but she ignored it. She stared down at the squares before her. They began and ended in a long channel in the middle of the ground. Unsure if what she was doing wasn't a massive overreaction to a bit of harmless floor decoration, she edged around the side rather than stepping directly on any of them. Then she was in the cavern beyond. There were carvings in the rocks, piles of rusted metal that long ago might have been *something*. Dust was everywhere. Then a voice rang out, a familiar computerised voice.

"You took your time, Satiah," Quint said, from somewhere.

"Thousands of years before this planet was found by the Union, it was home to a species of insect that created these caves and lived on the surface. According to some studies, they died out because of plague. Others claim they were wiped out by a rival clan from another world, hence the destruction up there. This cavern was their Queen's cell or sanctum... the place where the queen bred and multiplied. You did well to get past their traps... though I see you were not entirely unscathed." Again, as with the noises, it was hard to tell where it came from. Satiah presumed that Quint could see her, as why else would he begin speaking?

"What do you want?" she asked, playing for time. *Come on, Darius*!

"Any chance I could be allowed to leave and be forgotten?"

"No," she stated, honestly. Saying anything else wouldn't be believable anyway. Without warning, a bright light burned into existence, illuminating the whole cavern and dazzling Satiah. She cried out, and ducked to the side to try and avoid the attack she knew had to be coming. Something hard and long struck her wounded leg, a precision strike. She screamed and collapsed. A boot caught her in the side, rolling her back-first against a boulder. She threw out an arm to try to block whatever was coming next. Quint seized her arm, pulled her up and threw her across the cavern. She landed hard but rolled back onto her feet trying to breathe. The kick to her ribs had winded her. Then, Quint was standing just a few metres from her, white mask, white robes and all. Slowly the masked figure stepped onto her specs; they'd been knocked from her face during the fight, crushing them underfoot.

She'd dropped the rifle too, and she realised what Quint would do as he did it. He turned out the light, plunging the whole place back into silent darkness. Satiah limped backwards slowly, blindly until she reached the wall.

"Over here," mocked Quint, from somewhere to her left. She backed away to her right and Quint started laughing.

"Not so brave when you cannot see your enemy, are you?" Quint asked. Satiah didn't answer. She crouched suddenly and produced the blade from her boot. A noise from behind her made her roll forward. She crashed into a rock painfully. More laughter. She had to control herself and stood again, wincing as her leg hurt. She couldn't see, and he was using her hearing against her. She suddenly felt hands on her back, pushing her roughly forward. She stumbled forward uncontrollably. Tripping on something unseen, she went down and hit the floor with a cry.

"I can hear your heartbeat getting faster and faster, as death gets closer and closer to you," Quint went on. This time it sounded like he was to the left of Satiah. Satiah knew she was being toyed with, but the longer the game went on, the closer help got... or so she hoped. Trusting her instinct, she suddenly lashed out to her right with her blade. She connected with something and Quint uttered a noise of surprise and pain.

"I don't need my eyes to kill you!" Satiah snarled, through her teeth. Something slammed into her and her face struck the wall so hard she was almost seeing stars. She landed on her back with a groan, spat out blood and did not get up again. She tried but she was too dazed to synchronise her limbs properly.

The light came on again. Quint was standing over her, walking stick in hand. Knowing she couldn't fight, Satiah tried talking instead.

"Why did you leave?" she gasped, seriously. The question seemed to have no effect, but as Quint did nothing she guessed she was getting somewhere.

"Was it because of Jackdaw?" she chanced, pushing her luck. Quint stepped closer.

"What do you know about Operation Jackdaw, Satiah?" Quint asked. She'd guessed right! *Now what?* Where did that get her *exactly*?

"I know you betrayed your friends and the one you loved," she went on, her hand finding a stone suitable to throw.

"The one I *loved*?" echoed Quint, as if seeking clarification.

"Well, *claimed* to love," she corrected, allowing bitterness into her voice.

There was a long silence. Quint seemed to be thinking.

"*Why did you do it?*" she asked, again.

"...Don't *you* ever get tired of *obeying orders?*" Quint asked, the voice becoming softer. "Orders you know would sound so much better coming from yourself? Don't you ever wonder why? Not why they are asking, but why they are asking *you*. *Why you*?" Okay, she was sensing there might be a little problem with authority here, she understood that.

"From time to time," she admitted. Who didn't? "Their motives *or* the fact that they are using you to get a job done is hardly something to complain about though. It's why money was invented, isn't it?"

"No doubt you see it as something to aspire to?" Quint asked, condescension obvious. "If you *know* who I am… why did you ask me who I was before when I captured you?"

"*Then* I wasn't sure," she said, getting ready to throw the stone.

"Who I am doesn't matter to the dead," Quint stated, drawing his sword from the stick and aiming the blade at her throat. She was about to throw when Quint looked up and behind her. Slowly Quint began to back away and Satiah became aware of two dark figures advancing towards them. Dyss and Darius moved in, each with a pistol trained on Quint. Satiah's relief was palpable but she didn't show it, she just slowly rose to her feet.

"*Better late than never*," she muttered, just loud enough for the two men to hear. Quint too heard the words. Slowly as the two men removed their hoods, Quint recognised them.

"How did *you* survive?" Quint demanded of Darius. "Only *Dyss* was to live!" he stated, once again displaying Phantom-like quick-thinking.

Darius spun on Dyss, pistol aimed. Dyss made no move against *him* though, reluctant to leave Quint unguarded. Satiah was the only one to realise exactly *why* Quint had said that. It was his best chance of escaping if he could get Darius and Dyss to turn on one another. It was an easy thing to do if you knew how. Only Satiah recognised the danger in time to do something about it.

"*No!*" Satiah screamed, pushing Darius's gun down towards the floor. There was a crash as Quint threw the sword at Dyss, who dodged adeptly.

Darius was not to be so easily fended off, however, and a backhanded blow sent Satiah to the ground onto her side, blood trickling down from her nose. None of them *saw* exactly what happened next, as the light went out again and it always took precious seconds for even the most advanced technology to adjust. Two shots were fired. One hit rock, the other hit Dyss in the shoulder and he went down with a grunt. Dyss had fired the first at Quint and missed. Darius had fired the second. Darius was pushed out of the way before he could fire again as Quint made a dash for the exit. Quint had almost got away when Satiah's blade, hurled at a target she couldn't see, slammed into the back of his leg. Quint went down, the sound of computerised pain odd to hear.

Darius tried to stand but was flattened by Satiah, who anticipated where he would be and what he would try to do.

"Stand down! *I order you to stand down!*" she screamed, in his face.

"Did you not hear…!" he began, livid. Various arm locks were exchanged with Satiah eventually pinning him.

"Every word! And I don't care, *obey my orders!*" she screamed, just as angry. Finally, he stopped struggling and breathed out acceptance of the instruction. She stood and turned to help Dyss, only to receive her own blade in her chest. Quint had torn it out of the wound and returned the gesture. Perhaps it was aimed at Darius and she'd got in the way, nevertheless it was hard not to take being stabbed personally. She stood there for a moment as if in astonishment, conscious of how deep it had gone.

"*Darius!*" she growled, falling to her knees. "Darius… I'm down… I'm down…" Darius aimed three shots as Quint limped down the tunnel, away from them. Satiah fell back and lay still, trying to stay calm. Dyss rose, clutching his shoulder and wincing in pain. Satiah felt Darius crouching next to her but she couldn't see *anything* in the blackness.

"You're okay, we've got you, *we've got you,*" he assured her.

"Kelvin!" she called, using her earpiece. "Code one, *code one…!*" She was struggling to stay conscious, hypovolemic shock was attacking her. She needed oxygen and she needed to control her blood loss fast. *She needed Kelvin.*

"What happened?" Dyss growled, disorientated. His body armour had taken the worst of the blast, but pain radiated all across his arm and back. There was a silence, and Satiah wanted to scream at the pair of them, but scarcely had the energy to croak.

"Quint *knew* about Jackdaw... She set Dyss up to take the fall for it ten years ago... *but Darius got away too*," Satiah uttered, with difficulty. She could sense Darius about to deny that explanation and tried to forestall him. "It's the truth. *Vallin tricked you both.*"

"I don't believe you," Darius replied, grimly. "*Why* would she do that? How could she do that?" Both were questions Satiah couldn't answer, but Quint's behaviour had seemed to prove her theory correct.

"*She died*," Dyss argued, ironically echoing Darius's words.

"She's as alive as *you* are," Satiah argued, leaning more heavily back into Darius's hands.

"She wouldn't! *I knew her!* She wouldn't ever betray any of us!" Darius stubbornly insisted.

Dyss remained silent. Evidently he was more easily convinced than Darius. He'd never been in love with Vallin, which probably helped. Then there was the fact that it had been partly *because* of his suspicions *of Darius and Vallin* that Satiah had come up with her theory... The theory that Quint was really Vallin in disguise. Dyss had been thinking along similar lines for many years but as soon as Quint mentioned Jackdaw, Dyss had seen through the trick. That was why *he hadn't* turned on Darius. He had realised that if it *was* Vallin, as Satiah was arguing, *she* had already tried to kill Darius *before*. Back when that mysterious explosion had occurred when they had been trying to arrest him. Vallin had been faking her own death, he was sure of it. So there was no way they could be working together *now*, if ever. Darius though had thought that as Quint seemed to know Dyss and had said the word Jackdaw, it confirmed some of what he had suspected. If Satiah hadn't been there, Dyss realised, both he and Darius would now likely be dead.

"Get after her!" Satiah ordered, weakly.

"No," Dyss stated, firmly. "I think we will stay with you until Kelvin gets here. Then... *Darius and I* will take it from then on." Darius eyed him speculatively. The vibe of unfinished business was so strong that Satiah felt she could almost taste it.

"It seems I was mistaken, Darius... *Sorry* doesn't seem *enough* really, does it?" Dyss stated, very unapologetically. A crashing sound was approaching. It could only be Kelvin, smashing his way through any obstacle. It was hard to hamper something when it couldn't feel pain.

"Do you think *she*...?" Darius almost choked on the word, at last starting to concur. "Do you think she's heading back for the entrance?"

"No idea. She's trapped wherever she goes and, *thanks to Satiah*, she is now wounded," Dyss stated, patting Satiah's shoulder. She winced, as it hurt her.

"*Don't thank me yet*, it will only make her more reckless and dangerous," Satiah whispered, only just hanging on to the waking world.

Red eyes betrayed the big robot's arrival as he sprinted through the tunnel.

"You two go," she instructed falteringly, again. "You've given her ample enough lead." Dyss activated the light that Quint, or rather Vallin, had been using to disorientate Satiah with.

"We *can* wait, like he said, there's no easy way out," Darius suggested. He was starting to feel a bit guilty for clobbering Satiah in the nose earlier. Luckily, in the dark, he'd only hit Dyss once when he'd shot him, again thanks to Satiah's intervention.

"Just get out," she snapped with the last of her strength, irritated. The men took off running down the tunnel as Kelvin crouched beside his mistress. Painkillers came first along with metabolised oxygen and she sighed as the familiar yet welcoming numbness spread across her body. Then came the other standard defending drugs that would protect her from infections and any contamination from Quint's blood.

Finally, after healing the flesh wound on her leg into invisibility, Kelvin turned his attention to the blade. Wisely, Satiah hadn't pulled it out and had remained as still as she could. The fingers on the end of his appendages produced smaller blades of their own. They cut through her tunic around the wound. She lay still, almost serene. It was nothing she hadn't been through before. One of his hands spread across her belly, to surround the blade, the other began to ease the blade out. She hissed in mild discomfort but the painkillers were very effective. The hand across her belly was using precision energy shield technology on an almost microscopic level preventing *any* blood loss. Then, with her body mapped out in his computer mind, every last hair and nerve ending, the reconstruction began.

The organ damage was repaired quickly; the wounds closed up delicately and then completely healed in minutes. Finally, her skin sealed up, the scar fading and fading into nothing. Like it was never there. She sat up grinning, a little lightheaded from blood loss. The fluid and white cells would be back in about a day, but the red cells would have taken longer without the artificial stimulants Kelvin had provided her with.

"Thank you, Kelvin," she said, mildly mischievously. He handed her blade back to her, handle first.

"Remember this is for *your enemies*," he stated. She giggled as she rose to her feet, the muscles in her abdomen aching as she laughed. She cleaned the blade on her jacket before replacing it in her boot.

"I will try to remember that," she said, accepting what Kelvin regarded as humour without complaint.

"Obsenneth failed to save you *that time*," Kelvin noted. Her shoulders slumped.

"You just *can't* let it go, can you?" she groaned. "You know, if I *had* died down there, I *might* have been spared another round of this argument."

"It's how you programmed me."

"Oh, so it's *my* fault now, is it?"

"Blame was not suggested."

"Well, it was *received anyway*!" There was a short silence and then she remembered what Quint had done to her specs. "*Great*! Now I can't see a flaming thing!"

"You're going after them?" Kelvin asked.

"Of course," Satiah said. Then she smiled, thinking about what Cherry might once had said. "*They're men*. They'll never get this done without help."

***

Limping, Quint scrambled along the tunnel. It was time to cut all losses and pull out. At one point, Satiah seemed to guess who he was somehow, but when she'd continued, it became apparent to him that she was mistaken. He wasn't sure how, but she was. His identity was still unknown then, so escape was still his best option. There was no chance of him taking on all those troops up there waiting, he would have to evade them, by hook or by crook. A shot ricocheted off of the tunnel wall not far from him.

"If you surrender, you will be taken in alive!" Dyss bellowed, from behind him. It was a sincere offer, but Darius knew Quint wouldn't take it. Quint didn't answer, just picked up his pace as best he could.

"You won't get off this planet alive any other way!" Darius shouted.

Quint scrambled over a ridge and cried out as he fell into the icy depths of the lake. Still able to breathe from his mask, Quint sank like a stone. He could still see and negotiated his way through the knife-like crystals at the bottom easily. Dyss and Darius dived in after him; he could hear the sounds they made as they hit the water. He spotted a tunnel leading deeper and Quint, knowing it was the only way for him, swam down it. He'd never known it was there before, and he hoped it would not end in nothing. He released the cloak that was holding him back and continued to swim swiftly forward. Dyss and Darius swam strongly after him, slowly catching up.

***

"But *you're all right?*" Reed asked, yet again.

"You can see that I'm just dandy!" Satiah retorted, downing water and then pouring some over her head to cool down. "They're still down there, but I had to come back up to get a set of goggles. Quint smashed mine."

"Well, while you're here, *about that Dreadnaught*. Do you want *anything* done about it?" Reed asked. There was a brief silence while she tried to remember what he was talking about.

"Oh, *that Dreadnaught*," she said, seriously. "It's full of pirates and mercs, but it's relatively unimportant. You might as well let it go. I'll talk to the new captain later about the laws he has to abide by now."

"Randal's been trying to get hold of you..." Reed began, as she stood up again.

"Yes, I know *it's bad*, but I can't help it if some of the members of the cult were Coalition! He should know that actually it's a good thing that they're dead and gone. If the cult has people in the Coalition, it makes sense that they also have agents in the Federation too. Tell him it might be worth warning Wester about them…" she ranted, as Kelvin handed her a pistol. It was another of her personalised guns, to replace the one she ditched in the Hellion. Identical in every single way to the last. She much preferred it to any rifle, even though she wasn't sure why.

"No, will you just *listen* for a second!" he pleaded, seriously.

"That's rich coming from *you*," she muttered, remembering that not so long ago she'd said something similar to him.

"*He's found the gold!*" Reed yelled, earnestly. That stopped her. She faced him properly again. "I don't know any of the details, he just told me to pass that on." *How* had Randal managed that?

"*Just as well*," she said, waving it off casually. "I might never have got around to looking."

"Now, you *will* be careful this time," he requested, eyeing her tattered clothes. "I don't need to be a doctor to know what you must have sustained down there…"

"*I was careful last time*," she responded, unhelpfully. Then she frowned. "*Where's Bert?*"

"We don't know," he shrugged. "Does it matter?"

"I don't know," she replied, thinking about it. "While you were in his head before, you didn't happen to find any other chips, did you?"

"Of course not!" Reed sighed. "*Why?*"

"Just an idea," she grinned, her eyes gleaming mischievously. "I thought Quint might somehow be able to control him in some way. Maybe help in an escape attempt."

"I *highly* doubt that," Reed replied, disbelievingly.

"The mind is, when everything is said and done, the most dangerous weapon of all, isn't it?" she wisecracked, starting to skid down the cave entrance again. Reed shivered and watched as Kelvin followed her down.

"Now we're up here, any idea on where they all went?" Satiah asked, adjusting the goggles.

"They are deep, but they are no longer in the same area of the caves," Kelvin responded. "They appear to be underwater currently."

"*Of course they are,*" she groaned, not looking forward to swimming through that icy water. "Let me know if that changes."

***

Pat scampered down the corridor and pressed the buzzer on the Viscount's door.

"Sir, we have something urgent to talk about!" she called, concerned. The door opened and he appeared.

"What is it?" he asked.

"Two Federation destroyers have turned up and want to talk to you," she informed. He rolled his eyes.

"This is starting to get tedious," he hissed, pacing along swiftly. They entered the main control room where a Federation Captain was on the main screen, patiently waiting.

"I am the Viscount," the Viscount told him. "I am aware that we are trespassing, but we do not intend to remain here…"

"I think I should stop you there," said the man.

"I'm here on the authority of President Raykur. He had told me to formally allow you to take possession of this world, should you wish to remain here. He is aware, as I am now, of your situation," the Captain said.

"*Ah…*" the Viscount was amazed. He'd not expected acceptance to be so easy.

"The world is worthless to us, according to the government so… there is no objection from us should you wish to remain," the Captain went on.

"The people have yet to decide," the Viscount smiled. "Thank you for informing me of this."

"Duty," the Captain stated, by way of explanation. "Should you wish to join the Federation, you need only call us?" The Viscount smiled again, ah yes, he was not surprised by *that* invitation.

"I will let you know."

***

"No one knows what's happening," Clyde laughed, as he spoke with those still in orbit. Yana rolled her eyes. It had been nearly eight hours since they had arrived now. "Let me have a chat with some people down here." He cut off and called Satiah.

"What?" came a breathless voice. Yana paid close attention while trying not to look as if she was.

"It's me. Can we go now?" he asked, seriously. "The crew of the *Dreadnaught* are getting twitchy."

"Of course you can go, I never understood why *you* stayed so long," she replied, with too much conviction.

"Curiosity," he smiled, unruffled.

"While you're gone, waiting for me to call you, I want your word that you will start trying your hand at forms of moneymaking that aren't illegal," she said.

He raised his eyebrows and thumbed at the console to Yana as if saying: can you believe she asked *us* that? Yana shrugged, trying to look nonchalant.

"We will do our best to stay away from trouble," he stated. "Provided you keep your promise and call me about you know what." Yana frowned.

"Fine," Satiah agreed, sounding preoccupied.

"Any luck with Quint yet?" he couldn't resist asking.

"We have him trapped and wounded, it is only a matter of time," she replied, as if he were a journalist of something.

"Good," he said, leaving it at that. He hoped she was right. "And Purella?" Yana eyed him tensely.

"She's dead," Satiah responded, coldly. "I gave her a chance to surrender but... well, you know how it goes. Bother you, does it?"

"It would have once," he allowed.

"I'm sorry – if it's any consolation I would have preferred her to surrender too," she replied, smirking in memory.

"No, no," he said, knowing what she meant. "Take care with Quint... *I need you*."

"By *me*, you mean *what I have*," she corrected, being difficult. He smiled, her feistiness inciting both respect and amusement in him.

"Whatever you want to believe," he said, ignoring Yana's scowls.

"Just go," Satiah said, cutting off. He was sure she'd smiled when she'd said that. He turned to face the glowering Yana, a casual expression on his face.

"See, nothing going on there at all," he stated, unable to stop himself from being funny. "Let's get back to the *Dreadnaught* and out of here."

***

Satiah entered the first cavern once again. It was as bleak as it had been before, but then she'd hardly been expecting it to be happy she was back.

"They are coming closer," Kelvin warned, referring to the chase.

"Quint knows his way around, and he will *know* this is the only way out. With Dyss and Darius after him, he will try to run. *He will have to pass us here…*" she reasoned, thinking about it. She would wait in ambush, much as Quint had for her before. She adjusted her pistol to stun. If she wanted to take anyone alive, it would be Quint. She crouched behind a rock, able to see the entrance plainly without anyone being able to see her from anywhere in the cavern. Kelvin moved to crouch beside her. His red eyes flickered out, ensuring that nothing would give them away. She smiled, anticipating the moment.

Less than fifty metres away, the underwater fight raged. Dyss caught Quint's leg and tried to drag him back. Quint had allowed himself to be pulled back and then pushed Dyss away with both his legs. Darius had then grabbed his arm and attempted a throat job. Quint allowed his armour to take the blow and pushed Darius away too. He swam on, increasingly desperate. He reached the shallows and erupted from the water as he waded to get out. He was back in the cavern that the entrance tunnel brought people into. He would have to find a way of bringing the place down and burying Dyss and Darius alive. Darius too emerged, further back. Quint managed to get behind the rocks before any shots were fired.

He sprinted for the tunnel, the only way out, ignoring his injury as best he could. Then, from a completely unexpected direction a blast hit him. He turned, barely conscious, trying to see… *who it was*. Satiah fired again, this time rendering Quint unconscious. The splashing continued as Darius reached the shallows and Dyss surfaced.

"*Hold!*" she called, to make sure Dyss and Darius didn't shoot her by accident. Hands up in the air, she slowly stepped out from cover. "He's down." She and Kelvin moved in, as did Dyss and Darius. They all stood over Quint, a silence enveloping them for several seconds.

"Dead?" Darius asked, gruffly.

"Stunned," she told them. "Who wants to get that mask off of…?" She left it at that. Dyss turned to Darius.

"Go on then," Dyss said, grimly. Darius rolled the body over and Kelvin activated all his lights, illuminating everything fairly well.

Side by side, Dyss and Satiah stood; arms crossed, looking down as Darius gradually removed the mask. Satiah couldn't believe the face she saw. A mass of curly blonde hair and a beard of the same colour covered the face of… a stranger. A man. Most definitely not Vallin. Then who…?

"*Alarris*," Darius gasped, as surprised as she was. Satiah knew the name, she remembered it from… *Jackdaw*. Alarris had been one of the other Phantoms on that mission. He, like the others, had been presumed dead. Darius was looking at her now, an angry gleam in his eyes. She had been wrong, Vallin had been just an innocent victim.

"…Sorry," she shrugged, as if the revelation was nothing to her. "I incorrectly assumed it was the second in command who had betrayed you because she accused Dyss of the same thing. I should have believed you about Vallin." The apology was meant but it lacked a certain conviction, partly because she still felt that as she had been unwillingly dragged into this from the start, and therefore owed nothing to either of them. Dyss just stood there listening. He, unlike Satiah and Darius, had been out of the loop and had never made the connection between Jackdaw and Blacklight at all until Quint had said the word.

"I… don't know what to say," Darius replied, bleakly. "I can't blame either of you for any of it." They stared down at Alarris, melancholy making mutes of them all for a while.

"Neither can I," Dyss replied.

"How did he get off the ship?" Darius asked, thinking back to that day. The few seconds to spare before the explosion.

"You'll have to ask him that," Satiah replied, coolly. Dyss sighed and leaned against the rock.

"*Ten years,*" he mused, not out of bitterness but sadness.

"Do you want to do it *here* or somewhere more suitable?" Satiah asked, talking about the inevitable interrogation. Both men stiffened as if only just remembering what they had to do.

"We'll take him back," Darius stated, sourly. "We owe it to Vallin and the others to nail him for this."

"When he wakes up, he's probably going to want to know who brought him down… don't tell him," Satiah smiled. When he had left her to die, he'd not told her who he was so this was a tiny pinch of payback. He'd probably work it out though, simply because of the fact that she'd done as he had. She knelt and injected a powerful sedative into Alarris.

"You've got twelve hours," she sighed. Kelvin picked Alarris up and began to move up the tunnel.

Dyss and Darius followed sombrely. Satiah was left alone, staring down at the discarded helmet that Alarris had worn. She gave it a kick, sending it rolling away and into the water of the lake. *You break my glasses? Fine, I'll drown your helmet!* Then she began to follow the others up the tunnel, glad that it was over. Well, almost over. She hurried to catch them up, coming up behind Dyss like an avenging angel. She knew it had been Reed's idea, but she felt she needed to once again remind him of their status, now she had more than a little leverage. She had not only saved his life, but she had sorted out his problem with Darius. She had to make him know that if he ever tried to blackmail her again… death would be his only response.

"You know… If Darius *had* shot you, it would have made my life much easier," Satiah said, in Dyss's ear. He faced her, astounded.

"I thought we had established that I had no intention of *ever* using that information again," Dyss said, coldly.

"We *agreed* nothing," she stated, her eyes angry. "After what has been discovered, I would appreciate it if you would leave me alone in future. Now that you have no excuse to distrust Darius, you can use *him.* I'm *Randal's,* all right?"

"Message received," he replied, grimly.

"If I hear or even suspect that you've told *anyone* about..." she began, levelly.

"*Satiah*... Whatever you want is fine by me. You saved my life down there, regardless of your motives for doing so. And you finally solved the most damaging mystery of my life... *Trust me*," he assured her, "I would never do anything against you willingly."

The next few hours passed quickly as everyone departed. Two thousand nine hundred and eighty-nine of the cult had been killed. Division sixteen had lost forty-one troops. Charges were set and the Hellion was destroyed in a series of controlled explosions.

"The secondary charge is always the one that does the most damage," someone remarked.

The act of destruction changed the whole landscape into something resembling a small valley. Satiah returned to her ship and collapsed into the pilot's chair. Sleep was begging her to close her eyes but she still had work to do. She had to transcribe a brief and discreet mission report.

***

During the checks that Kelvin did for his mistress's constant safety and peace of mind, he had scanned the Covert-Class ship she was currently using. An unusual reading had brought him into a storage area where Satiah had ordered him to keep the egg that she had been rewarded with. It was getting warmer, and he could detect movement from within. Repeated scans of said egg helped him formulate an image of what remained within. Compared with images of the creature he had seen her with, this creature had much more in common with human anatomy than it did with theirs. Satiah had explained that their evolutionary capacity was that of rapid cellular reconstruction levels. As a result, it was impossible for him to calculate how much longer it would be before it hatched. One thing was clear already about the lungs though... it could breathe in both water and air.

***

Watching the lights in the skies as she artfully compiled her report, Satiah quietly concentrated. This had to be done right, and by *right* she meant *cleanly*. Kelvin waited behind her to provide details she might not be able to recall. They had just completed the Rosenhan-

Ring test on her and, much to her relief, she *was* still very much *compos mentis*. Then Reed had come to see her and she began to wonder again. How sane could *anyone* be, working like this?

"I can see you're okay, but I'm sorry about your wounds," he stated, awkwardly. She knew why he was really there, of course. Dyss had most likely had a word with him about Carl. That, or he'd decided to talk to her about it of his own accord.

"Quint will be sorry too when he wakes up," she replied, with a cold smile. Reed sat down next to her.

"I'm sorry about dragging you into this Satiah, I really am. I hope you won't hold it against me," he smiled, hopefully.

"If you promise never to be so silly again, I might just let you get away with it," she said, a playful tone to her voice.

"I promise never to use Carl against you again," he stated, very exactly. "And thank you for your help. I'm not sure I would have been able to end that war without you."

"*Reed...* next time... if you *really* need my help, just ask me," she stated, making eye contact. "I *promise* not to just say no without a good reason."

"Yes, but we both know that you're very good at thinking up reasons," he joked.

"I'm very good at a lot of things... that's why you want me," she said, seriously. He pulled a dismayed face. "Want me *to help you*," she clarified, grinning.

"I want you because I know I can trust you," he stated, honestly. "Well, trust you to be yourself, if that explains it."

"You trust me to do the nasty stuff you won't or can't do?" she asked, smiling.

"*Sadly*, sometimes things call for ruthlessness I can't always provide," he admitted, his eyes soulful.

"It's not a bad thing," she said, unsure why she was telling him that. "Your compassion is... refreshing for me... *sometimes*." He chuckled.

"We're making a bit of a mess of this conversation, aren't we?" he chortled.

"*So what's new?*" she jested, in agreement. They stared out at the lights in the sky together for a moment.

"Do you want me to help with your report?" he offered. She shook her head.

"Not this time," she told him. He gave her an uncertain look.

"You're *not* going to tell *the truth*, are you?" he asked, as if such a thing was an appalling act of brutality. And for those who couldn't take the truth because they found it *too offensive*, it probably was. She giggled quietly.

"It's fine, just go home and never talk to me again," she smiled, good-humouredly. The second he was out of the room she began the report...

(LR) OPERATION BLACKLIGHT (LR) REPORT: Dated at end. Designation (TS). Top Secret. Status COMPLETE. Satiah reports... Milo's ship, Elven Star, found drifting at coordinates: 8433-1118. See reference file one. Upon discovery of recent messages on Milo's communicator, signal traced to Poro 8, specifically Permyon, a Vinupisha stronghold. See reference file two. After a second infiltration, Milo Drass was located and returned to Earth. See Phantom Darius's report. Objective one complete.

Initial intelligence, including staged attacks on Collgort-Elipsa and current political theory, are in reference pack 1. Significant indications led me to investigate local pirate activity. There were obvious signs that the attacking forces lacked the appropriate level of military discipline in regard to formational flying and precision bombing. Symbols were also faked. Military equipment fitting description of attackers found in pirate cargo holds.

Sources repeatedly pointed to an authority and organising figure Quint who was operative on behalf of the Cult of Deimos. It became clear that he was supervising both Purella and her activities, along with Bavon who worked as an informer, and Kyle's actions. Money and power would appear to be the main motivations behind all these forces.

Pirates proved to be behind the attacks on Collgort-Elipsa. Federation protection obtained under the command of Captain Ogun. Nebula Union reacted to intrusion of Federation but their ship was destroyed on Quint's orders. This was to heighten tension and provoke war. Upon its destruction the Union responded by sending a greater force to either make the Federation retreat, or destroy them. I'm reliably informed that under no circumstances were any shots to be fired with regard to the destroyed ship. No such restriction was placed on the second.

Pirates traced to secret base on Comet Sunkiss, Corkscrew base, see reference file three. Infiltration taken in roughly 12 hour window. Interrogation confirmed Quint's links to Cult of Deimos. PAI agent Nerva encountered and, with regret, killed. He shot first. Upon discovery of pirate manipulation, the Viscount was successfully able to negotiate a ceasefire, effectively ending the Vinu-Shintu War. It is my understanding that intensive negotiations have begun with a view to maintaining the peace.

Collgort-Elipsa moved to prevent anything untoward happening to its inhabitants. Its location reported to be Cenna 6, a Federation World, see reference pack two. Coalition force was sent to former world and it held a Nebula Union fleet for some hours before all forces departed. No shots fired. Investigation into pirate activity used as official reason for presence of fleet on Coalition territory. Objective two complete.

Prisoner acquired, Doctor Bertram Blake Clark, see reference file four. Information gathered eventually led me to planet Tweve. See reference file four for details of planet. Decision to attack the Cult taken. Division Sixteen provided the force used. See reference pack three and Captain Berry's report. Quint revealed as moniker of former Phantom Agent Alarris. Alarris incorrectly presumed dead ten years previously at conclusion of Operation Jackdaw.

All casualties listed on reference file five & Captain Berry's report. The cult was not destroyed, only about half of it according to available data. These individuals remain unidentified. Future cult plans and locations unknown. Their threat is substantial and needs to be addressed with all due expediency. It seems from available data that they have a strong influence within the Nebula Union, but their influence in the Coalition and Federation is weaker.

To summarise: Milo Drass found alive and returned to family. Vinu-Shintu conflict ended. Collgort-Elipsa moved. Cult of Deimos identified. Operation Jackdaw resolved. Purella deceased. Nerva deceased. Kyle deceased. Bavon incarcerated. Alarris incarcerated. Bertram Clark unaccounted for. Clyde unaccounted for. Phantom Darius recommended for distinction, reason given: he suffered ten years of wrongful mistrust without complaint. His loyalty needs to be rewarded or you might have another Alarris on your hands. Dated. Report ends.

She hadn't bothered to check Darius or Dyss's reports to see if they tallied with hers or each other's. She felt sure that they would. As always, there was so much that went unsaid. She'd not declared anything about Obsenneth, for obvious reasons. This meant that she'd also had to miss out everything about those strange creatures in the ocean. She'd remained vague about Kyle's death. Clyde, too, she'd scarcely mentioned, allowing him to slip under the radar. She'd decided that it would be best to leave out her early blunders and keep things referring to Jackdaw down to a minimum. The dangers that the cult presented *had* to be highlighted. *Phantom Command needed to take notice of that threat.* There was also the mystery of Bert's vanishing act to think about: no one knew where he had gone. The last time she'd seen him, he'd been in the Hellion, helping her fake the sacrifices.

And *Alarris*... She wondered who would have the delightful task of interrogating him. She had no interest in conducting it herself, and she knew that Dyss and Darius would be too conflicted to be chosen. Then again, so might *any* Phantom agent. Traitors were rarely spoken of, for obvious reasons. While some might even argue there was no point in interrogating him, there *was* the chance he could reveal more cult members, if nothing else. She suspected that they would either never mention him again *officially*, or they would concoct a brilliant tale of him dying heroically for the mission. She had thought about writing her own version of the truth, or as she saw it: a completely fictional account of his death, and submitting it to Phantom command as a *suggestion*. Then she'd decided not to, on the principle that if they liked it they might want her to do it again.

She'd left out any mention of Colonel Celestine, on Darius's behalf, to prevent any potential danger to her career. The same went for the necklace Milo had given her. He had taken it back with him to his family, but she knew never to include anything she didn't have to. Randal preferred blunt transparency. Amber too, couldn't be revealed, though the information she'd provided was. She'd also kept Vallin's name out of it. No sense in muddying the waters. Sometimes it really seemed like these mission reports were not worth doing. She imagined *every* Phantom doing this with *every* report... It was quite amusing, actually. Finally she thought forward to the debrief. Technically, Dyss would normally be the one to go through her mission report, as he had assigned it to her, but as he had become physically involved to a degree, that would mean that someone else would have to review it. That someone was Randal. For once, Satiah was pleased about that.

Agent Nerva was a problem too, but Randal already knew everything important about that. The PAI needed to learn to share intelligence... then again, she knew that Phantom command was no better. That was the problem about not trusting anyone. You occasionally got in each other's way... sometimes with fatal consequences. But betrayal could have those same consequences too, and Satiah had been the better agent and she had lived – so, she supposed, in a way it was just another risk she had to stand against. But next time: what if *she* died? Friendly fire she'd always found to be a rather silly term. Nothing about any fire is friendly, particularly when it's coming from your own *friends*.

She lay on the bed, on her way back to Earth, jacket under the bed with Obsenneth in its pocket. Exhaustion had caught her again, and she was not troubled by bad dreams. Reed had hitched a lift with her, claiming *matters of great urgency* were the reason he had to get back to Earth as soon as he could. Well, *that,* and something about an expired expenses form. Everyone else had gone their separate ways, if only for as long as things allowed. Cherry had asked Darius to take her back to Earth and he'd reluctantly agreed. Dyss and Berry had remained behind for a few hours to search for Bert. In her pleasant dreams, Satiah imagined being rewarded with a whole year's holiday for having to do someone else's mission. That was how she knew it was only a dream... they said yes.

***

Wide awake and wary, Satiah waited in Randal's office as he went through her report. As usual, there were no clues from his facial expression, no occasional noises as to what he was thinking... *or suspecting*. She battled valiantly against the temptation to fidget. His eyes rose to regard her at least once and then returned without comment to the written word. She hated it when he did that, it made her think that he could see into her mind and that he could learn the truth. She still had the shadow of the Vourne conspiracy in her mind, and that was a constant reminder of how careful she had to be. No one could ever know... She concentrated on keeping her breathing nice and even, losing herself in the simple rhythm.

"There *is* one thing *I don't comprehend*: why you took the mission in the first place. You could have refused and *for once* had every right to do so. Why didn't you?" Randal stated, eyeing her deviously. She came back to reality, her answer prepared.

"The idea of allowing *such a pointless war* to continue compelled me to try to *help*," she said, very believably. "They do say that war is the worst crime of all, don't they?" She didn't overdo it, but she came close by trying such a schmaltzy tactic. "Besides, *I* don't understand how *you* managed to find that gold, so that makes us even," she added, with a shrewd smile. He raised an eyebrow and started to laugh. He didn't believe her for a moment, as he was more than aware of her lack of empathy, but he chose to leave it be. He knew that she had her secrets, but who didn't?

"Yes... you wouldn't believe what happened," he said, wryly.

"If you don't tell me I can't agree or disagree with that."

"As you know, you left it in the capable hands of your fellow operatives, while you reported to Phantom Leader Dyss. They made their way back here but were intercepted by, *would you believe*, a medical *containment* force," he told her. She rolled her eyes in dawning understanding.

"A plague was thought to have broken out on a nearby world and all vessels within a certain area had to be quarantined. All communications were jammed and there was no way for them to do anything or go anywhere until they were released. This only happened a short while ago, *their release* I mean. So you can imagine my astonishment when they finally called me to explain exactly what had happened." She could indeed. "After that, they delivered the gold and I passed it back to its rightful owners... *whenever they choose to collect it.*"

It was actually quite funny. All the confusion that situation had led to, because of something completely unrelated occurring somewhere equally unrelated. She remembered subjecting Kyle and Clyde to questions regarding that gold, and being frustrated by their uninformative answers. She'd thought they were being evasive at the time. Now it was clear there was no way they could have known what had happened. That happened so often. A bit of evidence misinterpreted to cause all sorts of problems. She'd done it often enough herself.

"You did notice the bit where I reported the threat that the cult represents, didn't you? Or are *you* a member as well?" she joked, casually.

"Yes... *yes, I did*," he replied, gravely. "I will naturally see that it goes through the proper channels. My biggest worry isn't that we have been infiltrated by them, but that the government will not take it seriously. They'll probably just sigh, roll their eyes, and with *exaggerated* patience remind me that that is what good vetting is *for.*" Satiah had to concur with him on that. Well, she'd done her bit.

"Have you heard anything from the PAI about Agent Nerva?" she asked, curious.

"Only the official jargon I always get when I talk to them, they are probably still trying to figure out *who he was*," he joked, cynically. "I will let you know if I hear anything. I wouldn't let it worry you." It wouldn't.

"Well, if that's all sir, I have things to do," she stated, getting up.

"Oh come on, don't rush off, you might at least stay for a drink!" he protested, mildly irritated.

"You *have* approved my week of recuperation," she stated, eyeing him. He sighed. "I wanted to start as soon as possible."

"Might I at least know *where* you are going for the week in case I need you for anything?" he asked, already knowing the answer.

"You have my communicator's details," she smiled, crisply.

"*Satiah*... Why all this leave *all of a sudden*? Don't get me wrong, as I know there was a time fairly recently where you hadn't taken any for years, but..."

"I have come to value my life outside of this," she stated, elusively. "Don't worry, *I'm not staying away forever.*"

"Good, I have a mission ready for you; your week away is a well-timed one, if nothing else. You will *love* this one," he assured her. Just him telling her that she was going to *love it*, worried her. She let it go though as she was *rather eager* to get going.

"Goodnight, sir."

***

Birdcalls were not all that the bracing gusts conveyed this time. Lacey was like a statue, silently standing and listening. Hademan was sitting on his bench, no food this time, staring bleakly into the middle distance.

"...There were *no* survivors," concluded the man. A cult acolyte, Farrow had not been present at the Hellion when whatever happened, happened. It had been thorough. No technical data remained and the place had been levelled systematically and efficiently. The wind caused his black cloak to flutter and sway. Lacey looked at Hademan, wondering briefly if he was in shock. This had all seemingly come from nowhere.

"No word from Magnus?" Hademan asked, a lull-like quality to the softness of his voice. Much like the uneasy peace before the tempest. He knew, as he had always known, that things could go wrong. The line they had chosen to follow could always be cut, but over the years complacency had crept in. A comfort zone had been formed. And now he had paid the price for not playing things as close as he once had. He had lost his only true friend...

"Nothing," Farrow growled. Hademan looked down at the ground for a moment before standing and walking a few paces away slowly.

"It seems that Satiah was responsible. *Somehow* she infiltrated the Hellion, called in reinforcements *and killed everyone*," Farrow went on. "The place is barely recognisable."

Hademan eyed the tiny computer screen he was holding, the picture of Satiah rescuing Bert from Purella's ship was displayed there. The one Quint had identified her from. He zoomed in on her face and eyes, assigning them to his memory, before deactivating.

"Thank you, Farrow, that will be all," Hademan said. "You will join the others in hiding and await the new coded signal as discussed. Expect it within the month. I have changed all of the regular channels as a matter of protocol. She may have had time to acquire all sorts of information about us. As a result, we will remain quiet for a time; you're all up to date with the revised covers." Farrow nodded and departed. Lacey moved over to put her hand on Hademan's shoulder.

"I'm sorry for your loss," she said, and meant it. She had liked Magnus too. "...Your next visitors are here."

"Magnus was an old friend ... he knew the risks," Hademan replied, calmly. He smiled and patted her hand softly in thanks. "That doesn't mean, however, that he will be un-avenged."

They returned to his office and he sat at his desk while Lacey brought the first of his visitors up to see him. For a few minutes he was alone and he stared at Magnus's glass, now never to be used again, over by the drinks cabinet. His countenance darkened with the rage within ever so slightly. He knew even the drink would no longer taste the same to him, not now, thanks to this memory. The cult had been hit hard and he knew he had to repair the damage. There was only one thing that he could think of which would give him the power to do that in his lifetime. His eyes rested finally on the casket on his desk. There was a knock at the door.

"Yes," he stated.

Lacey entered with a tall, thin man following her. His face was tanned, rugged and he had a well-kept black beard. He was dressed in a dark blue overcoat, resembling a trench coat in all but a high black leather collar. Its shimmering texture made Hademan think of velvet. His brown boots were high too, and unpolished. They were worn but clearly comfortable and reliable to the man. His name was Jamal.

Lacey nodded to Hademan.

"Jamal, from the Professional Problem Solvers Association," she said, her eyes gleaming.

The gleam was one of amusement, as all three of them knew such a name was both inaccurate and misleading.

"Please be seated," Hademan said. Jamal sat down, a serious expression on his face.

"What can I do for you, Ambassador?" Jamal asked, his accent thick and fluid. Hademan produced a blue cube. It was a large capacity data storage device but it was mostly empty.

"I need you to find something for me," Hademan stated. He handed the cube to Lacey who, in turn, handed it to Jamal. "The details are on there. It's all the information I have. Your fee will be paid in full upon the success of your search. I have paid twenty-five percent already as agreed. Should you need additional funding to aid your search then, provided you can justify it, you can have it."

"As you say, Ambassador," Jamal concurred, staring at the blue cube. He rose to his feet. "I will begin at once." He nodded to Hademan, then to Lacey who scowled back at him. He left the room.

"Are the trackers on his ship activated?" Hademan asked, darkly.

"Every one of them," she answered.

"And is Denep in position?" he asked, going through his mental list. Denep, another acolyte of the cult, had been assigned a mission by Hademan himself earlier. To work with Jamal.

"Yes," she replied, stone faced.

"Perfect. I wouldn't want Jamal to *find* the other stones, only to decide to keep them from me, or to escape with them," Hademan stated, sombrely. She nodded.

"Now, bring the Highwayman in, please." She nodded and soon returned with another man. This one was taller still, and had a completely different air. An air of danger. Zarris was dressed in an all-black bodysuit and had two pistols, one on each side, openly displayed for all to see. Each was silver, long barrelled and polished well. So well, in fact, that they cleanly mirrored everything on their reflective surfaces. It was as if the room had become colder with his presence. Zarris smiled the smile of a predator as he regarded Hademan and Lacey. Neither smiled back but he kept smiling, uncaring.

"Please be seated," Hademan said, again.

"If it's all the same to you," Zarris growled, "I prefer to remain standing."

"*You will* address the ambassador with the *correct* formality…!" Lacey began, insulted. Hademan raised a hand to caution her, but Zarris spoke before he could.

"My respect for him is of equal proportion to his respect for me," Zarris smiled, calmly. "I address anyone how *I* like to. I'm not paid to be *nice*."

"*It's fine, Lacey*," Hademan told her, making eye contact with her. She fell silent at once. "As Zarris says, he's not paid to be nice."

"Speaking of pay…?" Zarris implied, more grimly.

"I agree, money is not an issue," Hademan stated, grit in his tone. Zarris picked up on it and eyed him, curious.

"First I want to ask you something. Is this target *personal* or not?" Zarris enquired, crossing his arms.

"It is," Hademan replied, careful to mask his real feelings. Zarris let out a dark chuckle.

"Good, always the most fun," he responded, genuinely pleased. "Who and where?" Hademan hit a button and the screen behind him displayed the picture of Satiah. Zarris eyed the picture, his eyes all evaluation.

"An operative of some kind?" he guessed, immediately.

"Apparently one of the best… *just like you*," Lacey smiled, cynically. Zarris ignored the jibe and continued to stare at Satiah's image.

"Her name is Satiah and she is a Phantom agent," Hademan informed. Zarris's eyes narrowed. "Is that a problem?"

"Phantoms are tough," Zarris stated, shrugging. "I admit I would normally prefer easier targets, but the job is the job. Where is she?"

"That will be for you to find out," Hademan replied, seriously.

"She could be anywhere."

"...Very well. So you want her alive *if possible*?" Zarris asked, knowing that that alone would make his job much harder.

"Yes," he replied, starting to daydream. "She must be made to *pay* for what she has done."

"I see," Zarris replied, unemotionally. He did not ask what she had done. Not only did he like people to know how little interest he had in their motives, but he knew how disconcerting it was when he didn't ask the obvious questions.

"Do you work alone?" Hademan asked, interested.

"Sometimes," he replied, vaguely.

Soso was Zarris's squire and had been for over twenty years. They always worked together, with Soso acting as his pilot and support in all things. Zarris had never mentioned him by name before and saw no purpose in telling Hademan about him now.

"Should you require help, I can provide some," Hademan told him.

"That could be very useful," Zarris replied, noncommittally. He didn't trust anyone else's men; he'd learned that lesson too many times. "Do you have any additional information about her?"

"No, I'm sorry," Hademan replied, without meaning it. Zarris smiled sadly.

"*Well, it would have made it all too easy, wouldn't it?*" he growled, being grimly rhetorical.

"...You may go," Hademan told him. Without a word Zarris spun on his heel and left, his boots echoing loudly on the floor. Hademan sat back in his chair, suddenly feeling very tired.

***

Carl looked up as the ship came in to land. He stood and approached the glass barrier, expectant. It was hard for him to describe exactly how Satiah coming back to see him again made him feel. Part of him had never believed it would happen. He found her utterly terrifying but sort of irresistible too. A tricky combination. A call came in and he hurriedly put the device in his ear. She was still the only one who ever called him. Her voice was rich and posh sounding, so massively different to her personality. It sounded to him as much demanding, as it was enticing. And when she looked at him... those eyes defied description for him.

"You're early," stated Satiah, in his ear. He was. He had terrible timekeeping skills but her coming back was something he *really* didn't want to miss for obvious reasons. He had rehearsed his reply, so that he didn't freeze and didn't make himself seem stupid.

"So are you," he protested, doing his best to play it cool. "I know what you're like and I didn't think you would appreciate lateness."

"Depends on your excuses," she teased. He could see her strolling down the ramp out of her ship, carrying a bag across her back.

"*How long can you stay?*" he asked, unable to stop himself.

"Maybe a week," she said, lightly. "Assuming you can keep me that long?" He smiled.

"I'll do my best. I've been trying those exercises you suggested," he replied.

"*Trying?*" she echoed, as the door opened. He opened the glass door for her as she reached it. She seemed scarily the same as he remembered. He was sure he'd remembered wrong. He knew what she did for a living, the terrible things that she could do. And yet he couldn't resist her. She disconnected her earpiece and placed the bag on the floor at her feet. For a second or two they just stared at one another. Her expression became impishly thundery.

"Did you say *trying?*" she asked, imperiously. He nodded hastily, trying to find the words but he'd suddenly forgotten them. She put her hands on her hips as she studied him, looking for weaknesses. She looked so severe.

"Well, I..." he blathered, still unprepared for this.

"*Enough!*" she snapped, grabbing his collar and pulling him closer. "I would like to believe you have done nothing more than fantasise about me since the moment I was gone... *Right?*"

"I..." he began, awkwardly.

"*Awww...*" she giggled, pulling him into a hug. "I should stop scaring you so much, it can't be good for you. *I have missed you.*" Her heat and scent were intoxicating to him. She felt the Obsenneth gemstone being pressed against her but she ignored it. It was time to forget all that for a while.

"I'm in love with you," he blurted, in her ear.

"Of course you are," she smiled, gently biting his ear lobe. "Well, I'm not going to apologise for that. I can't control your heart... although I *can* make it beat faster." It was hard not to lose each other and become trapped in eye contact. Memories, dreams, feelings that journeyed from birth to death and then back again were experienced by them both. Oddly she somehow couldn't tell him that she loved him in return, for some reason. And this was in spite of recently being on the point of openly declaring it to him and having to stop herself. Fortunately he didn't seem to notice.

"Satiah..." he managed, at last, "I *really* missed you too." She didn't answer that instantly, she just stared at him, her eyes losing focus. More memories flooded her. She had missed him too, so much so that it had almost led to tears at one point. There was a fear there too, but she pushed that away for another time.

"Take me to your home," she requested, with a mischievous smile.

"But... you already know where it is," he pointed out.

"Do you think you could carry me there?" she grinned.

"Are you okay?" he gasped, concerned.

"Of course! I just can't be bothered to walk," she smiled, kissing him again.

"You're so... You're so good you're bad," he stated, struggling for words.

"What do you think you mean by that?" she mewed, as if she was talking to a simpleton. "Are you going to carry me home or not?"

"I could but then that would be *all* I could do," he laughed. She laughed too.

"If you carry the bag for me I *suppose* I could walk," she said, in a long-suffering voice.

"It's a deal," he agreed, excitedly grabbing it. It was heavier than it looked and he almost staggered. She grinned at him.

"You okay with that?" she asked, being annoying.

"It's fine," he grunted, going red with the effort. "What's in it?"
"No idea, it's not even mine; I just wanted to see you exercising."

THE END

Printed in Great Britain
by Amazon